# THE PATIENT

*Michael Palmer*

arrow books

# ABOUT THE AUTHOR

Michael Palmer is the international bestselling author of eleven novels, including, most recently, *The Society*. His novels have been translated into twenty-six languages and have been adapted for film and television. He trained in internal medicine at Boston City and Massachusetts General Hospitals, spent twenty years as a full-time practitioner of internal and emergency medicine, and is now involved in the treatment of alcoholism and chemical dependence. He lives in Massachusetts.

# THE
# PATIENT

---

# SIDE
# EFFECTS

## Michael Palmer

arrow books

This edition published by Arrow Books in 2005

Arrow Books
The Random House Group Limited
20 Vauxhall Bridge Road, London SW1V 2SA

Random House Australia (Pty) Limited
20 Alfred Street, Milsons Point, Sydney
New South Wales 2061, Australia

Random House New Zealand Limited
18 Poland Road, Glenfield
Auckland 10, New Zealand

Random House (Pty) Limited
Endulini, 5a Jubilee Road, Parktown 2193, South Africa

The Random House Group Limited Reg. No. 954009

www.randomhouse.co.uk
www.michaelpalmerbooks.com

A CIP catalogue record for this book
is available from the British Library

Papers used by Random House are natural, recyclable products made from wood grown in sustainable forests. The manufacturing processes conform to the environmental regulations of the country of origin

ISBN 0 09 190736 5

Printed and bound in Great Britain by
Cox & Wyman Ltd, Reading, Berkshire

*For Beverly Lewis*

# Acknowledgments

The many, often lonely and uncertain hours spent here in front of my Mac have been much more bearable because of my friends and family. This page is one of the ways I get to express my appreciation to them.

At the Jane Rotrosen Agency, Jane Berkey, Don Cleary, Stephanie Tade, and Annelise Robey have made writing easier for me in many ways.

At Bantam Dell, Beverly Lewis, Christine Brooks, Irwyn Applebaum, Nita Taublib, Susan Corcoran, and Barb Berg have done the same.

Sam Dworkis, Mimi Santini-Ritt, Sarah Elizabeth Hull, Dee Jae Jenkins, Matt Palmer, and Beverly Tricco have been invaluable as critical readers.

My deepest gratitude to Holly Isbister, Pamela Kelly, and the rest of the crew in the Brigham and Women's Hospital magnetic resonance operating room for your hospitality, professionalism, and skill.

When blocks seemed insurmountable and another rewrite too daunting, Luke, Daniel, Matt, and Bekica have helped to keep everything in perspective, along with many friends of Bill W.

And finally, thanks beyond measure to my friends Linda Grey, who brought her genius as an editor to the final rewrites of this book, and Eben Alexander III, M.D., whose remarkable gifts as a physician, surgeon, and scientist made the whole project possible. Whenever I needed neurosurgical facts or techniques, Eben was always there. Any errors or oversights are mine, and are doubtless due to my neglecting to review them with him.

MSP

# THE PATIENT

# Prologue

Sylvan Mays, M.D., stood by the vast window of his fifth-floor office and gazed out at the countryside, where late afternoon shadows were lengthening across the Iowa River. At fifty, he had just gone over ten million in net worth and was one of the few physicians who had actually seen his income increase since the advent of managed care. The decision to remain in Iowa had certainly been the right one. For sure, he had his detractors. Success always brought those. He was too entrepreneurial, some said – a big fish in a small pond, too intent on building himself into a neurosurgical version of DeBakey or Menninger.

*What's so wrong with that?* he wondered. DeBakey and Menninger were world renowned and respected, doing good on a global scale. What was so wrong with wanting to emulate them?

The gleaming seven-story Mays Institute for Neurological Surgery had put Iowa City on the map and brought millions of dollars in research and industrial development grants to the university. Now, his robotics team was closing in on a real prize – the first microrobot to be approved by the FDA for use in neurosurgery. A preliminary application had already been submitted. Six months, maybe less, and the few remaining bugs in the system would be worked out. As it was, he was revered for cranking through more brain tumor cases than anyone else in the country. Now, with several researchers on the robotics project, and Sylvan Mays' name on every scientific article the group generated, he was gaining recognition as a top researcher as well.

He checked his watch. Five minutes or so before Frederick Wilson was due. As with his previous appointment, Wilson had insisted on being the very last patient of the day. At first, Mays had been put off by his prospective patient's demands. But what a find he'd turned out to be! Wilson was eccentric as could be, yet ready to reward handsomely anyone who did him good service. A quarter of a million in cash just for evaluating his case. Four times that when the surgery was completed, plus a healthy donation to the Institute. Wilson was the patient of a surgeon's dreams, except that his tumor was bad – as bad as any so-called benign tumor could be. A slow-growing subfrontal meningioma with some extension, steadily compressing normal brain tissue. Progressive neurologic difficulty had begun. Now, the only choices Wilson had were surgery or a stuttering, inexorable death.

Mays was sure he would be able to get to the tumor, but not without doing some damage – maybe a lot of damage. Then there was the actual dissection. He had probably excised more tumors like this one than almost any other surgeon in the world; if he couldn't do it, it was doubtful anyone could. But even for him, the dissection would be chancy. Wilson had come to him impressively well informed, and had asked specifically about the robotics system. Rather than risk losing him to some other surgeon, Mays had chosen to tell him that employing the robot in the OR was possible, but not definite. *By no means definite.* Hadn't those been his exact words? The exaggeration had been necessary initially. Now, it was time to back off.

The trick, as with all cases like this, was to hang crepe – to stress the dangers inherent in the surgery and lower the patient's expectations to the point where even a marginally successful operation would be welcomed as the work of a genius. The man had seemed reasonably easygoing and understanding enough at their first meeting, yet he was sharp, too. That much was certain.

But so was Sylvan Mays. Until Mays had the chance to study the MRIs, he had refused to talk in anything but generalities. Today, though, they would have to get down to business – to go over the specific anatomical challenges and potential surgical stumbling blocks inherent in

4

Wilson's case. First, it would be necessary to dispel Wilson's belief that the only way to reach his tumor was by means of a robot.

Mays wandered over to what he thought of as his wall of fame – dozens of photos and testimonials from world leaders and other celebrities. 'Neurosurgeon to the Stars,' one publication had dubbed him. 'Brain Tumor? Head for the Cornfields,' another had headlined. 'Is This Heaven? . . . No, It's Iowa – Unless You Need a Neurosurgeon.'

'It damn well *is* heaven,' Mays said out loud.

He paced to his desk and hit the intercom.

'Yes, Syl?'

Sandy had used his first name. The waiting room had to be empty.

'Mr. Wilson arrive yet?' he asked, just in case.

'Not yet. There's no one here at all at the moment. No one at all. . . . Hint, hint.'

As always, Sandy Alter's flirting over the intercom immediately turned Mays on. At thirty-one, she was a hell of a gal Friday, with an aerobics instructor's body and a wicked imagination in bed. And even more exciting, after almost a year, she didn't want anything from him other than a night or two a week, enough cocaine to elevate their lovemaking from great to sublime, and no talk about his wife or kids. Could life get any better?

'I wish we could do it right now,' he said. 'Tonight can't come soon enough for me.'

'Me either.'

The stiffness inside Mays' slacks intensified. At that moment, through the intercom, he heard the outside office door open and close.

'Mr. Wilson,' Sandy said. 'Nice to see you again.'

The intercom was switched off, then on again, and she announced Wilson's arrival.

Mays positioned himself behind his desk, on which lay Wilson's file, took a deep, calming breath, and asked Sandy to send him in.

*Okay, Sylvan,* he thought. *It's showtime.*

Frederick Wilson limped into the office, a cane in his

right hand and an elegant black leather briefcase in his left. He set the briefcase down, shook Mays' hand enthusiastically, and lowered himself into one of the two mahogany chairs on the patient's side of the desk. He was dressed as he had been on his first visit to the office – dark suit, conservative tie, white shirt. His thick gray hair was brushed straight back, and his beard and mustache – equally gray – were neatly trimmed. His intelligent dark eyes were partially veiled by heavy-rimmed spectacles with lightly tinted glass.

As so often happened, Mays found himself seeing his patient with Superman-like X-ray vision, staring beyond Wilson's face, eyes, and skull at the fleshy tumor that was infiltrating and displacing his brain. *Poor bastard.*

'You've verified the deposit?' Wilson asked in a modest accent that Mays had decided was probably German or Russian.

'Barclays Bank, Grand Cayman. In my name. Yes. Yes, I have.'

'There will be no tax problems that way . . . for either of us.'

Eccentric. Mysterious. Clearly a man of wealth and breeding, yet with no health insurance. Electronic cash transfers only. When the time came, Wilson would speak to Bob Black, the hospital administrator, and transfer funds for his impatient treatment. But first, Mays had had to pass muster in an interview that lasted most of an hour. His background . . . his training . . . his family. . . his interests outside of medicine . . his specific experience with the kind of tumor Wilson had . . . and finally, the status of his robotics research. Mays knew he had acquitted himself well, and was not in the least surprised when Wilson had called the next day to inform him about the money deposited in Grand Cayman and to formally accept him as his surgeon.

'So,' Wilson said now, 'I have offered money for a service and you have agreed to provide it. I have given you a down payment for that service and you have accepted. We have set a fee to you and to this institute when the service is rendered that will total well in excess of a million dollars, tax free. It seems, then, we have entered into a business arrangement.'

'I . . . I guess I never thought about what I do that way before, but yes, I suppose we have.'

'Excellent. Let's talk about expectations, then.'

'Yes. I think at this point that's quite appropriate.'

Mays straightened himself in his chair, cleared his throat, and met Wilson's gaze with an expression that he hoped was sufficiently grim. Now was the time to begin to paint the picture of guarded pessimism. But before the surgeon could say another word, Wilson began speaking.

"Given the benign nature of my tumor, and the magnificent qualifications, experience, and skill you have described, I expect nothing less than a complete cure. I expect to be speaking as well as I am now, to be walking without a limp, and to have full use of my senses and my intellect.'

'But –'

'I also expect to have no evidence of residual tumor on a postoperative MRI study.'

'But –'

'Is that clear?'

Mays felt a sudden chill.

'I . . . I expect an excellent result, of course, but I can't make those sorts of promises. No surgeon can.'

'You've told me you are the best in the world at this sort of surgery. You told me your robotic system was capable of bypassing the usual route from my skull to the tumor.'

'I said it was *potentially* capable of that, yes. But I also said our robotics project was still in the experimental stage.'

'And you accepted my money without hesitation.'

'Yes, but –'

'Then I expect full satisfaction.'

'I understand. However –'

'Dr. Mays. Close your mouth, please, and listen carefully. I have not paid you a quarter of a million dollars to debate this point. I expect you to perform the way you

7

have promised me you can. To guarantee that I get your best work, my people are currently observing your wife and daughter. When the day of my surgery arrives, they will be entertaining your family at a place of my choosing until I am safely out of danger, and your radiologist as well as one of my choosing has reviewed my MRI films. When I know that I am safe, unharmed, and free of tumor, your wife and daughter will be returned to you. They will be treated well, I promise you that.'

Mays felt as if he were being strangled. There was nothing in Wilson's manner or expression that suggested flexibility. The man must be insane.

'I . . . I can't agree to this,' he finally managed. 'No surgeon can.'

'Our arrangement has been established. I have the right to expect complete satisfaction. I have the right to recourse if you fail.'

'You're not buying a used car from me, Mr. Wilson. This is neurosurgery.'

'Precisely why I have sought out the very best, which you assure me you are. The terms are nonnegotiable, Dr. Mays.'

The shirt beneath Mays' armpits was soaked. He felt as if his bowels might let loose at any moment.

'I refuse,' he managed, with forced bluster. 'I refuse to be bullied and threatened, and I refuse to operate on you under these circumstances. Go find yourself another surgeon. There are plenty of them as qualified as I am.'

'That is not what you told me at our first meeting.'

'All right, all right, there are only a few. But that makes no difference. I will not operate.'

'Dr. Mays, I am very disappointed in you.'

'I don't give a damn that you're disappointed, Wilson. I won't be pushed like this. Be reasonable, man. This is brain surgery we're talking about. Nothing is certain in brain surgery. Christ, man, nothing is certain anyplace.'

Wilson sighed.

'That is where you are wrong, Doctor. One thing is very certain.'

He calmly opened his briefcase and extracted a heavy pistol with a long silencer on it. Without waiting for another word, he aimed from his chest and fired.

Mays saw the muzzle flash, and actually heard the spit of the shot. But he would never appreciate the perfect placement of the bullet hole, exactly equidistant between the bridge of his nose and his hairline. An expression of amazement froze on his face, and his head jerked backward, then slowly drifted forward until it slammed onto the desk.

Frederick Wilson took his file and every piece of paper with any reference to him, and placed them all in his briefcase. Then he carefully wiped the arms of his chair. He stopped by the door to ensure that he had overlooked nothing, then stepped out into the reception area. The receptionist smiled up at him.

'Well, that didn't take long,' she said. 'Did Dr. Mays want to see you in the office again?'

'No,' Wilson replied, without the hint of an accent. 'He didn't say a word about that.'

He removed the silenced pistol from behind his briefcase and, from ten feet away, firing almost nonchalantly from his hip, put a shot in precisely the same spot on Sandy's forehead as he had on Mays'. Then he placed all potentially incriminating files and papers in his case, hooked his cane over a chair, and, without any sign of a limp, strolled back into Mays' office. He was upset by the disappointing session with the surgeon, although not with his decision to terminate the relationship. The man was a pompous ass. A few thousand to the bank manager in Cayman would transfer the quarter million back into his account. And that would be that for his dealings with Sylvan Mays.

After a final check to ensure he had removed all trace of his ever having been at the Institute, he retrieved his cane, reacquired his limp, locked the outer office door behind him, and hobbled off down the hall.

# Chapter 1

They were nearly three hours into the operation and not one cell of the cancer had yet been removed. But by neurosurgical standards, three hours was still well within the feeling-out period – especially for a procedure involving experimental equipment. And despite huge progress recently, ARTIE most certainly remained experimental.

'Let's try another set of images with enhancement of the tumor, please.'

To a physician, all growths, benign and malignant, were tumors, although the term 'cancer' was generally reserved for malignancies – those tumors capable of spreading to distant organs. This particular cancer, a glioblastoma, was among the most virulent of all brain tumors.

Staring straight ahead at the eight-inch monitor screen that was suspended from the ceiling to her eye level, Jessie Copeland set her gloved hands down on the patient's draped scalp, which was fixed by heavy screws to an immobile titanium frame. The physical contact wasn't technically necessary. From here on, ARTIE would be doing the actual surgery. But there was still something reassuring about it.

'You playing gypsy fortune-teller?' Emily DelGreco asked from across the table.

'I just want to make certain the guy hasn't slipped out from under the sheets, gotten up, and run away while I'm trying to decide whether or not our little robot pal is in position to begin removing this tumor. For some reason ARTIE's movements forward and left feel sluggish to me – not as responsive to the controls as I think he should be.'

'Easy does it, Jess,' Emily said. 'We always expect more from our kids than they can ever deliver – just ask mine. The sensors I'm watching, plus my monitor screen, say you and ARTIE are doing fine. If you start feeling rushed, just say "Berenberg".'

Emily, a nurse practitioner, had been on the neurosurgical service at the Eastern Massachusetts Medical Center for several years before Jessie started her residency. The two of them, close in age if not in temperament, had hit it off immediately, and over the intervening eight years had become fast friends. Now that Jessie was on the junior faculty, Emily had moved into the tiny office next to hers and worked almost exclusively with her and her patients. Neither of them would ever forget Stanley Berenberg, one of the first brain tumor cases the two of them had done together. His operation had taken twenty-two hours. They did the delicate resection together without relief. But every minute they spent on the case proved worth it. Berenberg was now enjoying an active retirement, playing golf and carving birds, one of which – a beautifully rendered red-tailed hawk – held sway on the mantel in Jessie's apartment.

'Berenberg . . . Berenberg . . . Berenberg,' Jessie repeated mantralike. 'Thanks for the pep talk, Em. I think ARTIE's just about ready to start melting this tumor.'

Jessie had decided to apply to medical school five years after her graduation from MIT with a combined degree in biology and mechanical engineering. She had spent those five years working in research and development for Globotech, one of the hottest R and D companies around.

'I didn't mind making those toys,' she had told neurosurgical chief Carl Gilbride at her residency interview, 'but I really wanted to play with them afterwards.'

Under Gilbride's leadership, the Eastern Mass Medical Center's neurosurgical program, once the subject of scorn in academic circles, was a residency on the rise, drawing high-ranking applicants from the best medical schools in the country. Jessie, who was comfortably in the middle of the pack at Boston University's med school, had applied to

EMMC strictly as a long shot. She was astonished when, following the interview, Gilbride had accepted her on the spot. There was, however, one proviso. She had to agree to spend a significant amount of time in his lab, resurrecting work on an intraoperative robot that a now-departed researcher there had abandoned.

Working in Gilbride's lab throughout her residency while carrying a full clinical load, Jessie had learned that her boss's true forte was self-promotion, but she had been elated to spearhead the development of ARTIE-Assisted Robotic Tissue Incision and Extraction. The apparatus was an exciting fusion of biomechanics and radiology.

Now, after some preliminary animal work, she and ARTIE were finally in the OR.

Over the past few years, Jessie had viewed countless video images produced by the intraoperative MRI system. What she was studying now was the continuous, three-dimensional reconstruction of the brain beneath the intact skull of the patient – images that could be rotated in any direction using a track-ball system bolted to the floor beside her foot. The on-screen presentations of the MRI data were undergoing constant improvement by the extraordinary genius geeks in Hans Pfeffer's computer lab. And Jessie could not help but marvel at the pictures they were producing. The malignant tumor and other significant structures in the brain could be demarcated electronically and colorized to any extent the surgeon wished.

Jessie had always been a game player – a fierce competitor in sports, as well as in Nintendo, poker, billiards, and especially bridge. She was something of a legend around the hospital for the Game Boy that she carried in her lab coat pocket. She used it whenever the hours and tension of her job threatened to overwhelm her – usually to play the dynamic geometric puzzle Tetris. It was easy to understand why the MRI-OR setup excited her so. Operating in this milieu, especially at the controls of ARTIE, was like playing the ultimate video game.

MRI – magnetic resonance imaging – had progressed

significantly since its introduction in the early 1980s. But the technique had taken a quantum leap when White Memorial Hospital, the most prestigious of the Boston teaching hospitals, had designed and built an operating room around the massive MRI magnet. The key to developing the unique OR was the division of the seven-foot-high superconducting magnet into two opposing heads – 'tori,' the manufacturer had chosen to call them, a torus being the geometric term for any structure shaped like a doughnut. The tori were joined electronically by under-floor cables, and separated by a gap of just over two feet. It was in this narrow space that the surgeon and one assistant worked. The patient was guided into position on a padded sled that ran along a track through a circular opening in one of the magnets. Jessie understood nearly every aspect of the apparatus, but that knowledge never kept her from marveling at it.

'Let's do it,' she said, crouching a bit to peer under the video screen and make brief eye contact with her friend. 'Everyone ready?'

The scrub and circulating nurses acknowledged that they were, as did the radiology imaging fellow and the team working the console outside the OR. Through the glass viewing window, Jessie could see radiologist Hans Pfeffer-Ichabod Crane with a stethoscope in one pocket, a calculator in the other, and an IQ that had to be off the charts. The imaging system was as much his baby as ARTIE was hers. He had been watching, motionless, for every minute of the three hours. Now, as their eyes met, he simply nodded.

'Come on, ARTIE,' Emily said. 'Do that thing that you do.'

The flexible robotic surgeon, three-quarters of an inch long and a third of that in width, was packed with microelectronics and gears. The guidance console by Jessie's right hand was connected by microcable to six pods – tiny sets of pincers – three to a side. The pods enabled ARTIE to move along – and, where necessary, even through – the brain with minimal damage to the

13

structures it passed. In addition to the guidance cable, ARTIE carried two other fine tubes, one capable of delivering ultrasonic waves powerful enough to liquefy tumor cells, and the other, a hollow suction catheter, designed to remove debris or to implant slivers of radioactive isotopes. Not counting the tubes and cable, the remarkable little robot weighed less than two ounces.

Jessie stretched some of the tension from her neck and began the meticulous process of liquefying and removing the large glioblastoma. She had inserted ARTIE up through the patient's nose and into the cranial cavity, and then guided it to the diseased tissue. The tumor would have been virtually inoperable by conventional methods because of the normal brain tissue that would have been destroyed in the process of simply reaching the spot. ARTIE had made it with only minimal damage to healthy brain. Test one, passed with honors.

'He's working perfectly, Jess,' Emily said. 'Just don't let him forget for a moment that's *brain* he's sucking on.'

'To do that I'll have to change his program. I have him thinking he's operating on kidney. I thought he'd be less nervous that way.'

The two women communicated with each other directly, while overhead cameras recorded the operation. They spoke over their shoulders to the nurses and technician, and by microphone to the team managing the console. Although neither of them was large, gowned as they were, surgeon and assistant virtually filled the spaces between the huge MRI tori. As long as neither of them keyed the microphone, by keeping their voices low they could conduct a conversation in virtual privacy. But at the moment, there was no need to speak. It was time to begin the actual operation. For a silent, motionless minute, they shared the appreciation that for the next three to ten hours, a narrow, twenty-six-inch space would he their world.

Bit by bit, Jessie began the dissection of the cancer, dissolving the cells with ultrasound and removing the resulting debris. As the procedure progressed, Emily monitored the various parameters within ARTIE and occasionally broke the viselike tension with small talk about the latest examples of Carl Gilbride's florid egomania, about her two teenage sons, or about Jessie's life – especially her mother, Paulette, whose shameless determination to do something about her forty-one-year-old daughter's single status was a cartoon that never failed to amuse them. From here on, Emily was the supporting player, but she handled her role well. The two of them had spent so many hours together in the operating room that they functioned essentially as one. But today a third player had been added – a tiny robot that might, with time, revolutionize neurosurgery.

An hour passed with little conversation. To Jessie, it seemed like a minute. Every microscopic movement of the robot had to be visualized in three dimensions: anterior, posterior, right, left, up, down, and every diagonal in between. She asked the console tech for *Scheherazade*, one of a dozen or so CDs she had on file to be played while she operated. The slow, hypnotic music instantly softened the hollow, tiled silence. The electronically enhanced tumor as displayed on the monitor was crimson – a deadly hydra, its many tentacles probing deep into the dark blue of normal brain. ARTIE, the defender of the realm, was bright yellow. Delicately, deftly, Jessie directed its snout and the ultrasonic sword it wielded, Bit by bit the crimson receded. Bit by bit the blue expanded – swollen but intact brain, filling the void where the tumor had been liquefied, then aspirated. Another hour passed. Dave Brubeck replaced Rimsky-Korsakov on the sound system. Two of the eight tentacles and a portion of the cancer's body were now gone.

Still, to Jessie, ARTIE's responsiveness in one particular maneuver seemed slightly sluggish.

'Em, is there anything the matter?' she asked. 'I still feel out of sync some of the time. There's a choppiness when I try to back ARTIE up. Have you checked each of the pods?'

'I will. . . . I don't see anything striking, although numbers five and six are spinning a bit more rapidly than the others. I'm not sure, but I would think that's just because they're moving through liquefied tumor and aren't actually connecting with solid tissue.'

'Maybe. I'm telling you, Em, we've still got a lot to learn about this little fella.'

Jessie suddenly stopped humming along to Brubeck's 'Take Five.' Something was definitely wrong with ARTIE.

'Em, check the pods again, please,' she said with unmistakable concern.

When she called for ARTIE to move right, forward and posterior, the robot gave a sharp jab to the left.

'The problem's in five and six,' Emily replied. 'RPMs are staying up. They're not shutting off.'

'Jessie, you're drifting posterior and left,' Hans called in over the intercom, his English perfect although his Dutch accent remained pronounced. 'A millimeter. . . more now. . . . You are closing in on brain stem.'

Disaster. Jessie battled the controls, but she could see that ARTIE wasn't responding the way it had been. From beneath her hair guard, sweat beaded across her forehead. Several drops fell onto her glasses.

'Wipe, please, John,' she said, turning her head briefly so the circulating nurse could dry her with a cloth sponge. 'My glasses, too.'

The image on the screen was devastating. A rim of blue had begun to appear between one of the crimson tentacles and the robot. ARTIE was veering away from the cancer and through normal brain tissue toward the densely packed neurons of the brain stem, where even a millimeter of tissue destruction, properly placed, could be lethal.

'Jess, you were right,' Emily said. 'Things just went haywire on the panel here. Five and six are continuing to spin. And now four is acting strange. It's like ARTIE's had a stroke or something.'

'Damn,' Jessie muttered, tapping rapidly at the key that should have reversed the malfunction.

Communication between the panel and ARTIE had somehow been disrupted. An overheat someplace? A computer glitch? Jessie cursed herself for not delaying the procedure until Skip Porter returned from having his painfully abscessed molar taken care of. A wizard with electronics, Skip was her lab technician and knew ARTIE at least as intimately as she did. But the truth was, with the robot buried deep in the brain, all the knowledge in the world wasn't going to salvage the operation.

The blue rim expanded.

'You're well into brain stem now, Jessie,' Hans reported.

Unspoken was the estimate of the neurologic damage that had already been done. Jessie could feel the deflation of her team's energy and enthusiasm. There had been such high hopes for this day, ARTIE's first under actual OR conditions. Somebody switched off the stereo.

Now there was only dense silence.

Jessie stepped back, clear of the tori, and looked over to Hans Pfeffer, shaking her head sadly. Then she moved back to her spot by the table. It would take an hour or more to back ARTIE out, if they could do it at all.

Across from her, the expression in Emily's eyes, framed by her hair cover and mask, was grim.

'Thank you, everyone,' Jessie said suddenly. 'You all did a great job. ARTIE's close. Really close. But I guess he's not quite there yet.'

She shut off the power to the robot, then took a scalpel and sliced through the control cord.

'Hans, thank you,' she said. 'I'll retrieve ARTIE at autopsy, and then we'll give him an autopsy of his own.'

'Sorry, Jess,' Emily murmured.

Jessie pushed the monitor screen up toward the ceiling and pulled down her mask.

'Me, too,' she said.

She hated losing. God, how she hated losing. But at least this defeat hadn't affected a living patient.

She pulled the drapes free and loosened the screws from the cadaver. Pete Roslanski had had a miserable six months before his glioblastoma took him. The tumor had already done irreversible damage when it was diagnosed. Surgery was out of the question. ARTIE, which even now had yet to be approved by the hospital's human experimentation panel, could not have been used in any event. It had been a wonderful gesture on Pete's and his family's part to allow his body to be operated on this way.

'It's a step at a time,' Emily said. 'And today was a big one for ARTIE. He's almost there, Jess. Just keep doing what you've been doing, and you're both going to succeed. Just be grateful no one's pushing you.'

'Yeah,' Jessie said flatly. 'I am grateful for that.'

# Chapter 2

Alex Bishop picked up the staccato tapping of Craft's cane half a minute before he actually spotted the man approaching from his left. Still, he remained motionless, as he had been for most of an hour, pressed against the base of a tree, with a clear view of all the accesses to the F.D.R. Memorial. Mel Craft, now the deputy assistant head of the directorate of CIA operations, had promised he would come alone, and given their history, he had every reason to keep his word. But Craft was the ultimate Company man, and Bishop was nothing if not cautious. Surviving seventeen years as an operative in some of the diciest spots on earth was a testament to that.

It was six in the morning. Pale sunlight filtered through a broken sky and sparked off the wind-whipped chop on the Potomac. It had been nine months since Bishop had last been in D.C. By and large he couldn't stand the place, but he considered the area around the river to be as beautiful as anything any other city had to offer. Two runners and a bicyclist passed the blind man, each unable to keep from glancing back curiously at him. No threat there. Bishop made a final visual sweep of the area and left his concealment, moving stealthily across the thick grass toward Craft. He was still five yards away when the deputy turned toward him.

'It's okay, Alex,' he said in his heavy Mississippi drawl. 'I'm alone.'

'There's a bench twenty yards to your left. I'll meet you there.'

'Jesus, Alex, if you can't trust me, you are in a pretty damn sorry state.'

'You're right about that,' Bishop murmured.

He watched until Craft was seated, then turned his back to the river and made a wide, wary arc before settling down at the far end of the bench, three feet away from his onetime partner. At forty-five, Craft was two years older than Bishop. But the torture that had ended his fieldwork, plus the twenty-five inactivity pounds he had put on since then, had added a decade to his looks.

'I can smell your gun,' Craft said. 'What is it, under a newspaper?'

'The *Post*.'

'I'd like to tell you to put it away, that you don't have anything to be so paranoid about.'

'But I do, right?'

'Alex, you were supposed to report in a month ago to begin your new assignment training the incoming class at the farm.'

'I can't. Things are finally starting to break.'

'The powers that be already consider you a liability. And you know as well as I do that's a very unhealthy thing to be considered, even if you're not.'

'Mel, one of the powers that be is *you*. You've got to stall things for me.'

Craft removed his mirrored sunglasses and rubbed at the scarred craters where his eyes once had been.

'I can't control some of the people you've upset by going AWOL,' he said.

'You've got to, Mel. Malloche is in trouble. He's got a brain tumor of some sort.'

'How do you know?'

'I found out about the tumor from a source in France. The entire staff of an MRI lab in Strasbourg was wiped out, each with a single center shot to the forehead. That shot is the only thing Malloche has ever done with any consistency.'

'So?'

'So, a week ago the bastard surfaced here in the U.S. – in *Iowa* of all places.'

'How do you know? You've never even seen the guy.

20

Almost five years chasing after him, and you've never even seen his goddamn face.'

Bishop ignored the jab.

'A neurosurgeon named Sylvan Mays and his secretary were killed in his office. Center forehead shot. One apiece.'

'I still don't see –'

'Mays was one of the top neurosurgeons in the world. He's developing a kind of robot that can reach tumors that were considered inoperable.'

'So why did Malloche kill him?'

'I figure Mays didn't know who he was dealing with, and made some promises to Malloche that he couldn't keep.'

Craft shook his head.

'Alex, there's a pretty large contingent on Capitol Hill and even some people at Langley who don't even believe Claude Malloche exists.'

'You know better.'

'What I know is that it's over, my friend. The agency gave you three years, then four, then five. Now they want you home. I'm sorry you didn't get him, Alex. But now you've got to accept that it's over.'

Bishop slid a foot closer, tightly gripping the .45. Even blind and ten years out of the field, Mel Craft had more killing skills than most operatives.

'You thought it was over for you in El Salvador, too,' Bishop said.

Craft took a deep breath, then exhaled slowly. After fifteen hours of unspeakable torture at the hands of a right-wing death squad, he had been sightless, hopeless, and praying for death. Then the commotion had begun. A minute or so later, Alex Bishop was untying him, having killed all seven of Craft's captors – three with his bare hands. El Salvador was Bishop's trump card, and he had just played it.

'Okay,' Craft said finally. 'What do you want?'

'Malloche is headed for a hospital in Boston.'

'How do you know?'

'There are only three other places in the country that are doing the same sort of research as Mays. This surgeon in

Boston is the one people tell me is farthest along. If I can find that information out, Malloche knows it, too. I'm willing to bet he's headed there right now.'

'I'll do what I can, but I can't promise anything. They want you real bad, Alex. In the fold or in a box.'

'I need some time, Mel. I need a cover to get me inside, and I need a contact at the local FBI. And all of it's got to be done real quick and real quiet. Malloche always seems to know who to pay off.'

'And who to *knock* off. You really think this is it?'

'If it isn't, I promise you, I'm done.'

'If I can't convince Stebbins and his internal affairs thugs to back off, you may be done anyhow.'

'That's my problem. Will you at least try?'

'If I do, I don't want to hear any of that "remember El Salvador" shit again. Agreed?'

'Agreed.'

'If it had been you tied to that chair, I would have tried the same harebrained one-man attack you did.'

'I believe you would have.'

'But this is no time to be harebrained, Alex. You've been part of this organization long enough to know how berserk internal affairs can get about someone they feel is a loose cannon. And operating inside this country definitely makes you one of those.'

'By the time they find me, it'll be over.'

'Don't underestimate them.'

'I won't, Mel. I've stayed alive this long by not underestimating anyone. But if they come after me, they'd better send someone who wants to get me as much as I want Malloche. And I don't think that person exists.'

'I'll do what I can. Just watch your back.'

# Chapter 3

'. . . "You may lose the vision in one or both of your eyes." '

'As long as it's only one or both.'

'Okay, then. Initial here. . . . "You may lose the use of one or both of your arms." '

'Arms? I mean, really. What do I need arms for, anyhow? Show me *one* unhappy amoeba. I can scratch my back on a tree like the bears and eat pie like those guys in the county fair. Mmmmmm.'

'Initial. . . . "You may lose the use of one or both of your legs." '

'Jessie, please.'

'Sara, hospital policy says I have to read this neurosurgery op permit to you out loud, and you know what a policy nerd I am. So stop giving me a hard time and let me finish.'

'Giving *you* a hard time? It's *my* damn brain tumor.'

'Touché.'

Jessie set her clipboard aside and sat down on the edge of Sara Devereau's bed. Sara, an elementary school teacher with three kids, was only thirty-nine. She was facing a third operation on an astrocytoma that had been maddeningly tenacious. Her first procedure, done five years ago by Carl Gubride, might or might not have been adequate. Jessie had her opinion, but with only the op note and X rays to go by, she knew it wasn't fair to judge . . . even him.

She had assisted him on Sara's second operation, nearly two years ago. When he announced he had finished the case, Jessie felt certain he had not been aggressive enough. But what could she do? At the time, she was chief resident. He was chief of the department.

Following the second procedure, she had gone out of

23

her way to get to know Sara. Their contacts outside the hospital weren't frequent, but they did manage a lunch or a late-afternoon drink from time to time, and twice Jessie had been invited to Sara's home. The woman had taught her more about courage, more about taking life as it came, about adjusting to calamity, than any other patient she had ever had.

As she and Sara grew closer, Jessie had tried to understand – to place herself in Gilbride's shoes that day; to forgive. But she could never free her memory of the overwhelming apprehension and helplessness she had felt the moment he suddenly stepped back from the table and announced that he had completed the reoperation on Sara, and had gotten as much tumor out of her brain as was necessary to effect a long-term favorable outcome. He had then stripped off his gloves and gown in the theatrical way that was his trademark and hurried from the OR to catch a plane to speak at an international conference, leaving Jessie to replace the skull flap and close the scalp incision over a cancer that she strongly feared had been inadequately excised.

Sara's 'long-term favorable outcome' had lasted just twenty-two months.

A few weeks before, with the sudden development of headaches and thickened speech, Damocles' sword had finally fallen. The news from the MRI was grim. The surgery Sara was facing this time had a chance of being curative, but only a slim one. Her response to the devastating report was typical – whatever had to be done, should be done. She and her family would deal with it and make the best of it. If the cancer could possibly be overcome, she was determined to be the one to do it. As long as she was aware and moving about, she had precisely the same gift as did everyone else in the world – this day.

But she had insisted that this time Jessie perform the operation. And Gilbride, clumsily masking his relief, had turned over the reins.

Jessie and Sara were in room 748, one of ten private rooms on the neurosurgical floor, which occupied the seventh of eight stories of the Surgical Tower. Over the five years since its grand opening, the forty-five rooms and offices on Surgical Seven had been more of a home to Jessie than her Back Bay apartment.

It was nearing four in the afternoon. Jessie had just arrived on Surgical Seven for patient rounds, following an hour in pathology during which she had helped extract ARTIE from the late Pete Roslanski's head. Tech Skip Porter, his jaw swollen like a plum from his dental encounter, had taken the tiny robot to their lab for a painstaking, under-microscope dissection. Jessie suspected that it wouldn't be long before they had some answers. Upset though she was over ARTIE's failure to complete the operation, she was pleased with the way it had performed in the early going, and totally relieved that she had gone with a trial run on a cadaver. From the early work guiding the robot through watermelons, to testing on pigs, then finally primates, she and Carl Gilbride had improved their technique just as she and Skip had improved ARTIE's. Now, as soon as Skip had made a diagnosis, they would consider gearing up ARTIE-2 for another cadaver trial. Then, who knew? Maybe Gilbride would be ready to make a presentation to the human experimentation committee.

For the moment, though, ARTIE had to be Skip's problem. Sara Devereau was just the first of twenty-two patients on the two file cards Emily had prepared for afternoon rounds. Jessie, locking in a commitment that would force her to leave the hospital before eleven for the first time this week, had agreed to meet her friend Eileen at a duplicate bridge game at seven forty-five. But Sara was also a friend, and the only one of the twenty-two who was pre-op for tomorrow. If there was any rushing to be done, it would not be in room 748. If Jessie couldn't make it to the Cavendish Club, Eileen could always drag her husband, Kenny, away from his computer for the evening to play with her.

Emily's extensive training, years of experience, and superb clinical judgment made it easy for Jessie to delegate responsibility to her. After sending her off to see the first few patients, she closed the door and returned to her spot on the edge of Sara's bed. In a little more than twelve hours, their lives would be joined in a mortal struggle against a virulent, resilient cancer, that was eating away at Sara's ability to move and think. There were things that needed to be said between them.

'Tomorrow's going to be tough,' Jessie began.

Sara's eyes held none of their usual playfulness.

'I'm running out of steam, Jess.'

'I know you are. I would have cracked long ago. You've been a titan. Everyone around here has gotten stronger from watching the way you've handled things – especially me. Sara, you and I both know I'm not God. But I promise you I'm going to do everything in my power to make this third one the charm.'

'I never questioned that, but it's good to hear anyhow. You know, it's funny. I'm ready – at least as ready as I'm ever going to be – for the surgery. But I keep having this weird, unanswerable question running through my head. How am I ever going to know that I didn't wake up from the anesthesia? Isn't that silly?'

'No. It's hardly silly. It's the ultimate question in every surgical patient's mind. They just don't always express it as eloquently as you did. But in your case, at least, the question's not unanswerable.'

'It's not?'

Jessie shook her head.

'No. Because you're not going to be under. Sar, I went over the MRIs again. This damn thing is very close to a lot of important centers. Speech, motor, facial movements. I need you awake if I'm going to push this dissection to the limit. You'll get a local and some sedation, but no general except in the very beginning. In exchange, I give you my word that I won't sing during the operation.'

Sara mulled over the offer.

'No singing, huh? . . . Okay, it's a deal.'

'We'll use continuous MRI monitoring of the procedure.'

'But not that little robot you told me about?'

Again Jessie shook her head.

'I don't think he'd improve matters. This will be your third operation. There's a sort of scar-tissue superhighway right down to the tumor. I can get there through the scar without causing any problems. Getting enough of the tumor so that your body's natural defenses can take care of the rest – that's the test. But I was always pretty good at taking tests.'

Sara reached out and took Jessie's hand.

'My chances this time?'

Jessie pondered the question with solemnity.

'That depends,' she said finally. 'Have you been giving generously when the plate's been passed around?'

'Of course.'

'In that case, I think we're in good shape. I'm a pretty experienced surgeon, and God only knows you're a damned experienced patient. Together with the power of your offerings to the church, I don't see how we can miss.'

'What if I said I never give anything when that plate comes around?'

Jessie squeezed her hand and smiled.

'I'd still tell you we were okay . . . because *I* give – every chance I get. You can't be too careful in this neurosurgical business, you know.'

Surgical seven, like the floors below it, was a broad circle, serviced by a bank of four elevators and one stairway. The nurses' station and supply rooms occupied most of a central core, along with the kitchen, conference room, and two examining rooms. Near the elevators was the six-bed neurosurgical ICU. Around the core, with views ranging from neighborhood rooftops to urban vistas, were thirty patients' rooms, with a total capacity of fifty. The circular hallway between the core and the rooms was known – especially by the nurses – as the Track.

In addition to the elevators and main stairway, a narrow auxiliary staircase joined Surgical Seven with Surgical Eight, which housed the neurosurgical operating rooms and recovery room. Because of shielding requirements and the massive weight of the superconducting magnet, the MRI operating room was in the subbasement, hewn into the surrounding rock.

The offices of the neurosurgical faculty, including Jessie's, were spaced along a broad corridor that extended west from the elevators and connected Surgical Seven with the main hospital. The corridor, lined with black, spoke-back Harvard chairs, also doubled as the waiting area for outpatients.

Suddenly bleary, Jessie promised Emily she'd be back to finish rounds in twenty minutes or so and headed to her office. What the tension-filled hours with ARTIE in the OR had started, the session with Sara Devereau seemed to have finished off. She badly needed time alone.

*'Contrary to what you might have been led to believe, gender does matter in our business. The two most powerful influences – one positive, one negative – that will define you as a physician will both be that you're a woman.'*

The words were Narda Woolard's, a med school professor of surgery, and a role model for Jessie from the day they met. Rather than trying to convince female med students to ignore issues of gender when competing with men for university appointments and other positions, Woolard ran a seminar on how to capitalize on them.

*'The deep sensitivity and empathy intrinsic to most women will make you that much better a physician regardless of the specialty you choose. But those same qualities will make medicine harder on you than on most men . . . especially if you choose a specialty like oncology, or critical care, or certain branches of surgery, where a fair percentage of your patients are going to suffer and die in spite of everything you can do for them.'*

Jessie's office was a lilliputian, one-window cubicle, made to feel even smaller by dark cherry paneling. A desk, two chairs, a locked filing cabinet for patient records and journal articles, and a set of shoulder-to-ceiling bookshelves on one wall all but filled the room, although she had managed to personalize the space with a couple of small watercolors, some framed photos from her rafting trip down the Colorado, and a planter.

Narda Woolard's words were echoing in Jessie's head as she sank into her chair. She did five uninspired minutes of Tetris and set a timer for fifteen minutes. Then she put her feet up on the desk, leaned back, and closed her eyes. Usually even fifteen minutes was long enough for her to drift off, enter some sort of REM sleep, and awaken rejuvenated. This time, her thoughts refused to slow. Early on in her internship, a cynical resident, already in advanced burnout, first exposed her to what he called Fox's Immutable Laws of Medicine: *Good guys get cancer. Trash survives.* Who Fox was, the resident never explained. But Jessie had seen the laws hold too many times ever to ignore them. And Sara Devereau was an exceedingly good guy.

Could Sara have been cured by a properly aggressive initial operation? Jessie had wondered this many times. Had Carl Gilbride even given the case much thought? How would he have felt if he had been to Sara's house? Met her husband? Her kids? Would he have spent an extra hour or two at the operating table? Gone after those few extra tumor cells? Fat chance. Throughout her experience with the man, Jessie had never heard him admit to so much as a shortcoming, let alone an actual mistake – and there had been many over the years. . . .

*What difference does it make now, anyway?* Tomorrow morning Sara would have her last shot at a surgical miracle. The envelope was going to have to be pushed and pushed some more. Walking, sight, arm use, speech . . . there was no telling what would have to be risked – even sacrificed – in the interest of getting all the tumor. And there was no predicting what was going to be left of Sara after the operation was done.

*Go to hell, Fox, whoever you are!*

'Jess?'

Emily had opened the office door and was peering in. Jessie realized that she'd been out cold, tilted back in her chair, orbiting Neptune. Her timer, which she had apparently shut off, was clutched tightly in her lap. Forty-five minutes had passed.

'Whoa,' she said, shaking the cobwebs loose, brushing some wisps of hair away from her eyes, and fumbling for her glasses on the desk. 'I don't think we're in Kansas anymore, Toto.'

'You okay?'

'Let's just say I needed the rest.'

'I'm glad you got some. Ready to finish rounds?'

'I am.'

'It shouldn't take too long. Oh, before I forget, there was a call for you at the nurses' station just a little while ago from Dr. Mark Naehring.'

'The shrink?'

'Exactly. Remember that show he put on at grand rounds?'

'Who could forget it? That poor woman.'

Naehring was a psychopharmacologist. In front of an amphitheater filled with two hundred or so physicians and other practitioners, he had used a combination of drugs to rapidly and very effectively hypnotize a middle-aged woman with profound emotional illness. He then extracted, for the first time, a terrifyingly vivid description of childhood sexual abuse at the hands of her father and his brother, at times both at once. Naehring then used more medication and posthypnotic suggestion to remove all memory of his patient having shared anything. He would introduce her revelations gradually in their therapy sessions, making use of a video where needed.

'Hopefully, the breakthrough helped her in the long run,' Emily said.

'Do you have any idea what he wanted?'

'I do. He's heard about the functional MRIs we're doing to map patients' brains while they're awake during surgery, and he wondered if he could come into the OR sometime and watch you do it. He believes some of the drug combinations he's been using might be useful in keeping patients sedated but completely responsive.'

'Interesting. Did you invite him to observe Sara's operation?'

'I did. He'll be at a conference all day tomorrow. He said to please call him next time.'

'Terrific. Hey, maybe he can use some of those meds on me,' Jessie said. 'He can probe me to find out how I could have turned out the way I have with a mother who spent years grooming me to be the perfect happy homemaker for some lucky guy.'

'What a failure she's been. Imagine having to live with your daughter growing up to be one of the finest neurosurgeons around.'

'Okay, okay, you can have that raise. Now, how's our service doing?'

'Not bad, actually. I've seen everyone but Dave Scolari.'

'Any problems with the others?'

'Let's see. Mrs. Kinchley wants to change rooms because Mrs. Weiss snores. Mr. Emspak wants to pull the shunt out of his head and go home because he has tickets to the ball game this weekend. Mrs. Davidoff is in her sixth day without a bowel movement. She won't let us discharge her until she has one. I told the nurses that whoever gets her emptied out wins dinner for two at the Top of the Hub.'

'Courtesy of her HMO. Anything else?'

'Dr. Gilbride's patient, Larry Kelleher, has a fever. I couldn't find much, so I ordered blood cultures and the usual tests.'

'Carl's patient with a post-op fever? Not possible!'

'I know. I know. I couldn't believe it myself.'

They were still trading digs at their department chief when they entered room 717. New England Patriots linebacker Dave Scolari looked up at them impassively. He was a beautiful man – twenty-six years old, six foot three, with a 250-pound body that could have been chiseled from granite. He was also paralyzed from the neck down as the result of a fluke helmet-to-helmet hit. Surgery had stabilized his cervical fracture, and he had gotten back some movement in his hands, but the outlook for major recovery was guarded. Scolari, a fearless warrior on the field, had all but given up.

'Something funny?' he asked.

Jessie apologized, silently cursing herself and Emily for not regaining their composure before going in to see a patient – especially Dave. One of her coverage partners had done the surgery on Dave's neck, then had gone on safari, so over the intervening weeks, she had spent a fair amount of time with him. Initially, he had responded to her, teasing her about looking too young to be a neurosurgeon, even calling her Doogie Howser. But as the reality of his situation and his prognosis hit home, his enthusiasm began to wane. Now, though he tried being civil and went through the motions with his therapists, it was obvious to everyone that the spark was gone.

'More cards,' she said, gesturing to the walls, which were virtually covered. 'I'll bet most of them are from beautiful women.'

'I haven't looked. The nurses hang them up.'

Jessie took one down and studied the photo of a woman who had to be a professional model.

'Maybe you should read them. This one gives her phone number.'

She showed Dave the photo, but got little reaction.

'Nice looking,' was all he said.

Jessie conducted a quick but thorough exam. His grip seemed marginally less feeble than it had been.

'Dave, I think there's improvement here. I really do.'

'Come on, Dr. Copeland. There's been no change. You know that as well as I do.'

'No, Dave, you *don't* know that as well as I do. I love playing games, but not this kind. If I say you're improving, you're improving. You've got to stop this. The more negative you are, the less you'll benefit from the therapy you're getting, and the less your body will respond to any of those X-factors that go into the medical miracles we're always hearing about. I'm sorry to sound so sharp. I hope you know that I'll do anything I possibly can to help you. But you've got to help yourself.'

Scolari looked away.

'Sure,' he said. 'Anything you say.'

Jessie wondered how she would respond to having life as she knew it end with the ghastly suddenness his had. No more neurosurgery, no more walks, no more volleyball at the Y, maybe no more dressing herself, or even feeding herself. Did she have what it would take to retool? She knew there was no way she, or anyone else, could really answer that question until they were where Dave Scolari was now. She set her hand on his shoulder. The muscle tone was gone, and she knew that atrophy had already begun. But some bulk was still there.

'You just do your best,' she said, clearing a rasp from her voice. 'Whatever hand you're dealt, fair or not, is going to be your hand. Just try to do your best, Dave, and chances are some good things will happen. Say, listen. I've got an idea. Do you think you could handle having a quadriplegic friend of mine come and visit you? His name's Luis Velasco, and he's quite an incredible person. . . . Dave?'

'Whatever.'

'I'll take that as a yes. I'll call Luis tonight. Hang in there, pal.'

Jessie followed Emily out of the room.

'Let's intensify his therapy,' she said. 'Make sure they're doing enough electrostimulation.'

'You really think he's getting stuff back?'

'I'm sure of it. Not a breakthrough, but definitely something. Dave's just too depressed right now to accept the change and work with it. That's understandable, too. When your idea of activity is knocking someone's block off on a football field, a little flicker of a couple of fingers just doesn't cut it. We can't let up on him, though. Any guy who thinks I look too young to be a neurosurgeon is definitely worth saving.'

Emily took Scolari's chart off a rolling rack and wrote orders for the intensified therapy. Then she and Jessie headed for room 710, a double that, for the past few days, had been occupied by only one patient – thirteen-year-old

33

Tamika Bing. Before they reached the room, Jessie stopped and flipped through the girl's chart.

Seven days had passed since Jessie performed the excision of a glioblastoma infiltrating deep on the left side of Tamika's brain. The operation had gone as well as she could have hoped, given the nature of the problem. Tamika's motor function, a major concern, had been completely preserved. But the teen's ability to connect with words appeared to have been lost. With that realization had come a devastating depression and an inertia even more disabling than Dave Scolari's. Only the threat of tubes down her nose had gotten her to eat anything. And getting her to leave her room and take a walk was out of the question.

Friends, family, nurses, social workers, psychiatrists, Jessie – no one had made a dent.

'What am I going to see in there?' Jessie asked now.

'Guess,' Emily replied.

'Any ideas?'

'The shrink wants to start her on an antidepressant.'

'Ugh. As if having her brain messed with surgically isn't enough. Well, I guess we don't have another option. Has she used the laptop her mother brought in?'

'Nope. Her mom says she was on it all the time at home, and even took it to school. Apparently it was her prized possession. She won't touch it.'

'Poor baby.'

Tamika's half of the room was as cheerful as the nurses and her mother could possibly make it, filled with cards, letters, pictures, stuffed animals, candy, magazines, and a portable CD player with headphones. In the middle of the comfortable clutter, propped in bed at almost ninety degrees, the girl sat, her wide, dark eyes staring straight ahead at nothing in particular.

*Fox's laws.*

'Hi, Tamik,' Jessie said. 'How're you doing?'

The two of them had gotten along well – very well – right up until the surgery. Since then, the teen hadn't acknowledged her at all. This moment was no different.

'I see you haven't opened the CD I brought you,' she said, holding up the rap album she had picked out for the girl. 'Want me to put it on?'

Nothing.

'Come on, Tamika. At least write me something – anything. Type it if you want.'

Jessie centered the portable computer on the Formica tray table across Tamika's lap.

Nothing.

She looked to Emily for guidance, but the nurse only shrugged. A quick exam, a final try to get some sort of response from their patient, and they turned to go. Carl Gilbride was standing in the doorway, watching them.

The neurosurgical chief was, as always, impeccably dressed and groomed – tan suit, silk tie, wing tips, gold Rolex, starched and pressed lab coat, perfectly straight name tag – *Carl W Gilbride, Jr., M.D.; Chief of Neurosurgery*. His wavy brown salon-cut hair and his round, rimless glasses helped produce an image that reminded Jessie of an SS interrogator in a grade B war movie.

'Carl, hi,' she said lightly. 'I thought you were going to be off lecturing for the day.'

He stood motionless in the doorway, glaring at her.

'What in the hell did I just hear about you doing a case with ARTIE in the operating room?' he said, giving no indication he cared about the girl in the bed behind her. 'Just who the fuck do you think you are?'

# Chapter 4

'Carl, please. Take a deep breath and try to stop snarling at me like I just shot a white rhino. I didn't hurt anyone or do anything wrong. At least I don't think I did. Pete Roslanski was dead. A *cadaver*! He and his family wanted his body to serve some purpose beyond fertilizing the north forty of some cemetery. You were away. I couldn't have asked your permission even if I wanted to.'

Jessie and Gilbride confronted each other across the table in one of the examining rooms on Surgical Seven. She had managed to curtail his tirade in Tamika Bing's room before it got any more abusive, and to lead him down the hall. The teenager, who had surely overheard what was said, had reacted not at all. She merely lay there as she always did, propped up in whatever position the nurses had chosen for her, staring straight ahead at nothing.

Gilbride's fury had only marginally receded. He still looked like a bullfrog being squeezed tightly from below. Over the years Jessie had served in his residency and worked in his lab, he had lost his temper with her any number of times. Enduring his explosions went with the territory. And in truth, she really wasn't treated much differently from any of the others who were on his B list. His A list consisted of those who never expressed a viewpoint or treatment approach different from his. And that sort of obsequiousness she was simply incapable of displaying – or even faking, as most of those who *were* on the A list did.

She suspected that merely having two X chromosomes would have also been enough to disqualify her from the A's. She had been the first – and to this point the last –

female resident Gilbride had taken into his program, and the only woman on the neurosurgical faculty. It took just a few months of her residency – and of his snide, offensive, at times near-illegal asides – for her to understand how desperately the man must have needed her technical expertise in his robotics lab to have accepted her. There was even a rumor that he had once let slip his belief that she would wash out of the program before a year was out, and end up working full-time on his research.

But on the plus side, she wasn't playing the résumé-and-wait game every year in a field dominated by XYs, and she had a damn good job in a hospital that had risen to near the top of neurosurgery programs. She had friends like Emily and Hans Pfeffer, almost universal respect from her colleagues at EMMC, and at last count was the busiest surgeon in the department, next to the bullfrog himself. And finally, she had ARTIE, which, although technically Gilbride's, was a child she was determined to see into adulthood.

In the interest of continuing her work, she could handle whatever Gilbride dished out, as long as he didn't demand she compromise her beliefs too much. But the scene in Tamika's room had represented a clear-cut escalation in the tension between them. Gilbride had never chastised her in front of a patient before, let alone so harshly.

She took pains to maintain eye contact with the man and focused on two objectives: first, to defuse his anger before he said something irreparable, and then, to try to find out exactly why he was so steamed over what she had done. The clock over Gilbride's left shoulder read almost six-thirty. Her chances of making it to the Cavendish Club in time for the bridge game were almost as remote as the chances of her playing well now even if she did.

'Carl, I'm sorry,' she began, not completely certain for what she was apologizing.

'You should be. What right did you have to tie up an entire operating room team, plus the radiologists, without clearing it with me?'

'Bill Wellman had canceled his OR case. The team was

just waiting around for their next case, and Pete Roslan –'

'Dammit, Copeland, I'm not done talking. Why is it you always have the bullshit ready before anyone even has a shovel?'

'Sorry.'

'You know, I carry a beeper just like you do. You could have paged me.'

Jessie could have enumerated the many times Gilbride had gone ballistic because she or one of the other B-listers *had* paged him for something less than a nuclear spill on Surgical Seven. Instead, she muttered another apology. This fire was simply going to have to burn itself out.

'You've done good work in the lab,' he went on. 'I have no complaints about that. But I think you tend to forget that *I* had started developing ARTIE before *you* ever came on board here. Those grants that pay for you, Skip, and all that equipment are *my* grants. The patents on ARTIE have *my* name on them. You aren't his adopted mother, you're his nursemaid and his tutor. If you forget that fact, you'll be history around here. I promise you that.'

Jessie sighed.

'Exactly what did I do that upset you so?' she asked.

'You brought our research out into the open, that's what you did. How many people were there today?'

'I still don't –'

'How many?'

'I don't know. Ten or eleven.'

'Jesus. I'm surprised you didn't insist on having someone from anesthesia there, too.'

Jessie came perilously close to admitting that, in fact, a friend from that department had stopped by, and would have returned had the procedure not been terminated so abruptly. But why was Gilbride so upset about the number of observers? The chief didn't wait for her to ask.

'Copeland, operating with ARTIE prematurely may have jeopardized the whole project – on more than one level. There's a race going on here – a race that ultimately could be worth hundreds of millions of dollars, to say nothing of a place in medical history. It's damn serious business – serious enough that the police came to see me last week to question me about where I was when that fatuous womanizing Sylvan Mays got himself killed; serious enough that Terwilliger and his group at Baylor are bad-mouthing us and our work every chance they get, and may have cost us grants I've applied for from the NIH and the MacIntosh foundation. I was expecting to hear from both of them weeks ago, and there hasn't been a word. Then there's that son of a bitch at Stanford. His robotics work may or may not be as far along as ARTIE. The way that he holds his cards so close to the vest, it's hard to tell. They may actually be ready to go with patients. I don't know. But I do know that they are in direct competition with us for every cent in grant money we get for this project. If word gets out that you had a major failure in the operating room, there's no telling what the fallout will be.'

'But –'

'There's more, dammit. Just shut up and let me finish. I've already submitted our application to the human experimentation panel here at the hospital. When word gets out that ARTIE ate away half of this poor stiff's brain stem, what do you think they're going to do?'

'It was a minor technical problem. I'm almost sure of it.'

'Really? And suppose it was operator error? You've had more screwups in the animal lab than I have – many more.

*Yes, because I was trying to do much more complicated maneuvers than you've ever risked,* Jessie wanted to shout.

'I suppose operator error is always possible,' she said instead, her fists balled at her sides. 'But I think I was on top of things. Whatever it turns out to be – even if it's that I have more practicing to do – it's got to be better to know about it now than when we're operating on a live patient.'

'That is beside the point. I didn't bring you into my lab to end up second to that bozo from Houston or any of the others. If Terwilliger scoops us on this because we had to go back to the drawing board, there's going to be hell to pay.'

'I'm almost certain the problem is mechanical and will be easily correctable. Skip is working on it now.'

'I know. I just came from there. He works for me, remember?'

*How could I possibly forget? How could anyone forget that we all do?*

'Look, Carl, I'm sorry. From now on I won't even change a lightbulb in ARTIE without clearing it with you.'

'See to it that you don't. Now, I want a detailed op note and Skip's report on my desk by morning.'

'But –'

'I don't care if you have to type it yourself. I want it.'

Without waiting for a response, Gilbride stalked off.

Jessie checked the time and pictured Eileen excitedly pulling out the convention card the two of them used, then heading off to the bridge club, which was a good half hour from her house. It was too late now for her to talk her husband into playing. With any luck, there wouldn't be some inept loner hanging around the club waiting for a partner, and Eileen could play with the director. Jessie used Information to get the number of the Cavendish.

'Ray, Jessie Copeland here. . . . Yeah, I know, I know. I miss seeing everyone there, too. Actually, I was planning on playing with Eileen tonight, but I'm not going to be able to make it. Do you think you could play with her? . . . Ralph Pomm? The guy with the horrible toupee? Ray, he's kind of tough to play with. Can't you match him up with someone else? . . . I see. Okay. Tell Eileen I'm sorry, and that I'll call her tomorrow.'

*Ralph Pomm* – self-centered, loudly opinionated, and pedantic. Everything she and Eileen hated in a partner.

*Well, Eileen,* Jessie thought as she headed back toward her office, *at least he's not Carl Gilbride.*

# Chapter 5

Jessie's day of reckoning with Sara Devereau began at five in the morning with fifteen minutes of stretching and two dozen push-ups, followed by a cup of decaf and half a melon, a quick shower, and finally two games of Pin Bot – the full-sized pinball machine that occupied a significant portion of her living room. It was clear from the pile of covers on the floor by her bed that her sleep had been fitful, although as usual, she had no clear recollection of any dream. If a nightmare was responsible for the bedding pileup, she was reasonably certain that a bug-eyed bullfrog had played a leading role.

As always on a day when she was scheduled to operate, Jessie felt keyed up – excited and on edge. She was the starting pitcher in a World Series game, but with no hope of being taken out for a reliever no matter how hard she was being hit. Facing a day as the principal in the neurosurgical operating room was a rush few would ever experience. And Jessie loved the feeling.

One of the fringe benefits of being a surgeon was not having to build up a wardrobe of business clothes. Scrubs and a lab coat were always as fashionable in the hospital as they were functional. Jessie dressed in sneakers, khakis, a button-down shirt, and a blue cardigan, and spent a minute in front of the bathroom mirror, applying a bit of lip gloss and some mascara. Her shoulder-length hair was still mostly chestnut brown, but each day, it seemed, there were a few more gray strands. Monique, the Newbury Street stylist she saw every couple of months, had started pushing for a cosmetic response.

*Maybe someday*, she thought, fixing her hair back with a

turquoise clip. *Right now you've got a little neurosurgery to do.*

She trotted down three flights and exited her building by the basement door. A year or so ago she had won a lottery among the tenants in all of the apartments that allowed her to pay through the nose for one of the parking spaces behind their building. On days like this one – rainy and raw – the absurd tariff seemed almost worth it. Swede, her five-year-old Saab, had begun to nickel-and-dime her, and was especially cranky in rainy-and-raw. Still, out of loyalty, she was totally devoted to the machine. Today Swede turned over on the first try – a good omen.

Traffic to the hospital was so light that Jessie made the drive to parking lot E in fifteen minutes. Her assignment to E – an eight-minute walk to the hospital – easily counterbalanced her success in the apartment building lottery. Monthly petitions to the parking office to move to one of the garages had yet to be dignified with a response. As she hurried, jacket over head, to the hospital, she reminded herself for the hundredth time to get an umbrella.

By the time Jessie arrived on Surgical Seven, Sara was floating through a drug-induced haze. Her husband, Barry, and their three children were at her bedside.

'Hey, I was beginning to think you weren't going to show up,' Sara said thickly.

'Wouldn't miss it for the world,' Jessie replied. 'At last the chance to look into that goofy brain of yours and find out what really makes Sara Devereau tick.'

'Tell me something. How come I got all that pre-op medication and I'm still scared to death?'

Jessie grinned and took her friend's hand.

'Beats me,' she said. 'I guess you're just chicken. Listen, Sara, we're going to do it this time. If it's humanly possible to beat this thing, we're going to be fearless, and we're going to do it.'

Jessie knew that the pep talk was as much for her own benefit as her patient's, and she suspected Sara knew it as well.

'Fearless,' Sara said. 'I trust you, coach.'

'What can we expect?' Barry asked.

Jessie knew better than to measure her response too much. Sara's kids were not naive. They had been through this twice before.

'The tumor is right alongside some vital neurologic structures,' she began, 'including the nerve packages that control Sara's right visual field, right arm, and right leg. But we've got to be especially careful operating around what's called Wernicke's area. That's the center that controls speech and language.'

'Mom could lose her ability to speak?' the oldest child, Diana, asked.

'Yes. I certainly hope not, but that's a possibility. And maybe even to *understand* speech.'

Jessie could see nine-year-old Jared's eyes begin to well up. She moved aside so that the boy could take her place beside his mother. *Enough*, she decided. The rest would be between her and Sara.

'There is one thing you all need to know,' Jessie added. 'Even if this operation is the total success I hope it will be, we might not know the results for a while – days, even weeks, afterward. Brain tissue has been pushed aside by the tumor. Once the tumor is gone, normal tissue will fall back to where it used to be. But there is always swelling of the brain cells when there is any manipulation or injury, and there might be a period after the operation when things don't work right. Please don't get discouraged if that happens. After the first twenty-four to forty-eight hours, things should improve tremendously. Now, if you don't have any other questions, I'm going to go and get ready.'

She hugged Barry and shook the children's hands, whispering to each to be brave. Telling them not to worry would have been foolish.

Jessie made quick rounds on her patients, then spent twenty minutes studying Sara's MRIs and reviewing her operative plan. The tumor was in a temporo-parietal location, just above the ear on the left side, just adjacent to the nerves of Wernicke's area. Speaking . . . understanding spoken and written words . . . reading . . . writing. The biggest danger of the operation would be failing to get out enough tumor to effect a cure. But the risk of having Sara Devereau living out her life in a hell devoid of expressive and receptive language was not far behind. Loss of a limb or a visual field was one thing. Permanent loss of the ability to communicate or to be communicated with was something else again.

Knowing too much and fearing that she didn't know enough, Jessie followed her pre-op ritual, walking slowly and deliberately down the eight flights to the subbasement. Then she paused briefly before a pair of glass doors before stepping into the world of MRI-assisted surgery.

By the time Jessie emerged from the dressing room after changing into fresh scrubs and her OR Keds, Emily was in the prep area, shaving Sara bald with a disposable, double-edged safety razor. Thousands of hours and hundreds of thousands of dollars had gone into making anesthesia and surgical equipment insensitive to the MRI's massive magnets, which, themselves, were never turned off except in the event of some mechanical disaster. Once into the OR, even the most insignificant metal object would be snatched across to the housing – a missile with deadly potential. Ultimately, it had been less expensive to build a small prep area than it would have been to develop and manufacture non-ferromagnetic razors.

On the wall of the prep area was a blown-up photo of a janitor, smiling broadly as he pushed an industrial-sized floor buffer along. A red circle and slash had been painted over the picture, which was actually posed for and taken by the residents after an EMMC maintenance worker had missed the multitude of warning signs and cheerfully buffed his way into the MRI operating room. The huge buffer, ripped from his hands and sucked chest-high across ten feet of air, slammed against one of the tori with destructive force. Shutting down the semiconductors to remove the buffer had cost tens of thousands of dollars and closed the operating room for weeks.

'How're things going?' Jessie asked.

'Excellent pre-op meds,' Emily said. 'She's just passing the second star to the right. Sara, I think you'll love this new hairdo.'

'Hey, what works for Michael Jordan works for me,' Sara replied dreamily. 'Your scalpel sharp, Doc?'

'We're all set,' Jessie said. 'The plan is to put you to sleep until we finish the noisy parts.'

'I never did like listening to my skull being drilled.'

'When you wake up, you'll be on your side with your head fixed in a frame.'

'I remember.'

'You'll have an airway in your throat, but we'll take it out when we need you to talk. You'll also have on the pair of special goggles I showed you. The goggles will project words or pictures. I may ask you to describe some things you see with one or two words, or else just to think about them. While you're doing that, we're going to be making a map of the parts of your brain that are working at that moment. It's called a functional MRI.'

'Functional MRI,' Sara echoed.

'Jessie,' Emily cut in, 'I hate to spoil this highly informative session, but I think she's probably too squashy to get much out of it. You have already gone over all this, yes?'

'Yes. I'm just . . . I don't know. . . trying to be thorough.'

'That's fine. Listen, we're going to do great.'

'Yeah,' Jessie replied, with less enthusiasm than she had intended.

'I mean it.'

'Thanks. I know. Anesthesia here?'

'Yup. Byron Wong.'

'Radiology?'

'Everyone's here. And I'm ready. You can do this, Jess.'

'Yeah,' Sara muttered, as if from down a long tunnel. 'You can do this.'

'I only wish I didn't have to,' Jessie said. 'See you inside.'

As she turned and headed for the sinks to begin a

lengthy scrub, Jessie was thinking about the cocktail party catch phrase she had heard so many times . . . *I mean, it isn't exactly brain surgery.*

Bulky in her surgical gown, Jessie stepped into the narrow world between the MRI tori just as anesthesiologist Byron Wong and the circulating nurse slid Sara through the opening in the magnet to her left.

'We'll keep her out with propofol and midazolam,' Wong said, 'but not too deep. It'll take just a minute or two to wake her up when you're ready. She'll be uncomfortable being on her side for I don't know how many hours, but thanks to the midazolam, when we're all done, she won't remember how miserable she was.'

'If a tree falls in the forest, and there's no one around to hear it . . .' Jessie said, bolting Sara's head into the frame that would hold it motionless throughout the surgery.

'Pardon?'

'Nothing, nothing,' Jessie said, setting the crosshairs of three lasers so that they would intersect at the center of where she visualized the tumor to be, targeting things for the MRI. 'I was just wondering how much someone is suffering if they have complete amnesia for the time when the suffering happened.'

'You're very deep,' Emily said.

'I know that. I know I am.'

The mindless banter between the two friends would continue on and off throughout the operation. Emily had developed a sixth sense as to when Jessie needed the connection, and when she simply had to be left alone with her thoughts and the awesome responsibility of her job. Because of the teaching hospital's demand that the residents assist on as many cases as possible, there was constant pressure on Jessie to use them. And, remembering her own residency, generally she did. But for the most difficult cases, she still always stood her ground and insisted on Emily. If she was the World Series pitcher, Emily DelGreco, wise and experienced, was her favorite catcher and lucky rabbit's foot rolled into one.

After a thorough antiseptic prep, they spread out sterile drapes especially designed for the narrow work space between the tori. Then she and Emily adjusted their MRI screens. It was time. Jessie closed her eyes for several seconds and cleared her mind with a few deep breaths, until one word dominated her thoughts: *steady.*

'Ready, Byron?' she asked, her eyes still closed.

'All set.'

'Holly?'

'Ready to go,' the tech at the outside console said through the speakers.

'Ted?'

'Viva Las Vegas,' the radiologist replied. Jessie opened her eyes slowly.

'Suction up,' she said. 'Scalpel, please.'

Working with practiced quickness, Jessie made a question-mark incision just over Sara's left ear, then worked the scalp away and began freeing up the temporalis muscle – the broad muscle that closes the jaw. All the while, she was concentrating on locating the upper branch of the facial nerve and the vessels arising off the temporal artery. Cutting through any of those structures would have permanent consequences.

'Nice job,' Emily whispered as she helped move the temporalis aside. 'Real nice.'

Jessie called for the bone drill and made a series of large holes that she then connected with a smaller bit.

'Carpentry's done,' she said as Emily wrapped the bony segment in wet gauze and passed it back to the scrub nurse. Jessie then ran her fingers over the thick membrane covering Sara's brain. 'The dura's pretty badly scarred down,' she reported.

'You mean Gilbrided down,' Emily whispered.

'Shhhh,' Jessie said, her eyes smiling above her mask. 'Let me be sure my microphone's off before you say anything about our esteemed leader.'

With each progressive layer, the surgery became more demanding. Damaging the veins in the dura, some of which were bound in scar tissue from the two prior operations, could easily cause a stroke.

'When you're hot, you're hot,' Emily said, suturing back the membrane after a perfect dissection. 'What do you think Paulette would say if she saw how her little girl spends her days?'

Jessie ran her fingertips over the folds of Sara's cerebral cortex.

'We're going to do a rapid imaging sequence with contrast,' she said. 'Have the IV gadolinium ready.' She shut off her microphone. 'My mother's more interested in how I spend my *nights*. Or should I say how I *don't* spend my nights. She thinks I never date.'

'I guess that means she's not wrong *all* the time.'

'Hey, watch it. I date, and you know it.'

'Example?'

'That lawyer from Toronto. The one I met when I went to Cancun. I even flew up to Canada for a couple of weekends with him. Remember?'

'Jess, I hate to tell you this, but that was almost two years ago.'

'I've been busy. Gadolinium in, please. Besides, all he talked about was how much opportunity there would be for me in Canada. When I suggested *he* might like Boston, I thought he was going to have a seizure. Look, look, there it is, Em. Great pictures, Ted. Perfect. Just think of all those chemists who called gadolinium a useless rare earth element. Surely someone should have known that a hundred years later we were going to invent magnetic resonance imaging and it would he the perfect contrast material. That just goes to show you – never discount anything. Byron, ten minutes and I'm going to want her to start waking up. Em, you get her goggles on while I expose this beast. Holly, how about something mellow – maybe that Irish harp CD. We're going to get this sucker. We're going to get every bit of it.'

Mapping by MRI was the key. Mapping tumor. Mapping functioning brain. Superimposing the two. Melting one with ultrasound. Leaving the other intact.

Speed was also important. Although brain swelling was generally well controlled during surgery, it was always a concern. The more the swelling, the more the blurring between thinking tissue and tumor. Jessie hummed along with the harp as she worked, melting obvious tumor with the ultrasonic selector as Emily helped suction out the resultant debris. Soon, the obvious tumor was markedly depleted. The general anesthesia had been turned off. Sara Devereau, her brain widely exposed, was awake.

*Now we see who's a warrior*, Jessie said to herself.

'Sara, it's me. Everything's going great. Can you hear me?'

'I can,' Sara replied hoarsely.

'Remember, you're in that frame. You can't move.'

'Can't . . . move.'

'Open your eyes, please, and think about what you're seeing. Don't say anything unless I ask you to. Just think it.'

Functional magnetic resonance – another miracle – was based on detecting the chemical change in hemoglobin where thinking brain was using extra energy and drawing extra oxygen from the blood. Jessie had been around for much of the development of the technique, but it still astonished her. *Amazing*, she thought as she worked. . . . *Amazing . . . amazing . . . amazing. . . . And the geek shall inherit the earth. . . . That's it, sweet baby . . . just keep thinking . . . just keep thinking.*

Jessie watched the map of Sara's functional gray matter develop on the monitor screen. Moments later, the radiologist superimposed the tumor on it. Then, as quickly as possible, Jessie began melting cancer cells once more, all the while getting closer and closer to thinking brain.

'What do you see, Sar? Tell me what the guy's doing?'

'Ski-ing.'

'And now?'

'Run-ning.'

'She's starting to swell,' Jessie whispered. 'Jesus, is she swelling. Byron, please give her fifty of mannitol.'

'Fifty going in.'

'What do you see, Sar? Talk to me. Talk to me.'

'M . . . ma . . .'

Jessie felt her aggressive approach to the resection begin to blunt. 'Em, there's too much swelling. Everything's shifting, getting distorted. Byron, give her some steroids. Make it ten of Decadron.'

'Ten in.'

'Easy, Jess. You can only do what you can do,' Emily said.

'Sara, what do you see? Sara? Em, suck here. Right here.'

*God, I'm too deep. I know I am.*

Jessie was far less emotional in the operating room than she was in the rest of her world. But even at her coolest, she was not the ice cube some surgeons were. With the reality of a partial or complete loss of communication for her patient on the line, Jessie knew she was tightening up like a heated bowstring. The sudden swelling and the intertwining of normal and abnormal cells had made further surgery impractical, if not impossible. Maybe she had gotten enough already, she reasoned. Maybe Sara's own immune system could take care of whatever was left behind.

*I don't think I can go any further.*

'Sara, it's Jess. Tell me what you see. . . . Say something. . . . Anything. . . . Come on, baby, say something.'

The best Sara could muster was a guttural groan.

'Em, I don't know,' Jessie said. 'I'm right there. I'm right at speech pathways. Maybe in them already. It's like the tumor's just melted into brain.'

'You want to stop?'

'I . . . I don't know.'

This was it – the moment she had prayed would never come. She had allowed herself to hope for an operation that was perfectly clean – everything crystal clear and well defined. No overwhelming scarring, no dangerous swelling, no wrenching decisions. She surveyed the edema distorting Sara's brain. If anything, it had gotten a little worse. *Too soon*, she told herself. It was still too soon to tell if the mannitol and Decadron would reduce the swelling.

But as things stood, there was still some definition of structure – not much, but some. If she waited for the treatment to work and instead the swelling worsened, the chances of avoiding critical speech areas, and probably other structures as well, would be even slimmer than they already were. The bowstring tightened.

The only safe thing to do, she decided, was to stop.

Before she could voice that decision to Emily, the door to the OR pushed open and a man strode in wearing scrubs and a mask, but no covering over his rippling brown hair nor his spit-polished wing tips. . . . Gilbride.

'Jessie, where's Skip Porter?' he asked with not so much as an acknowledgment that there was brain surgery going on, let alone on a former patient of his.

*Jerk.*

'Skip? He had some emergency oral surgery yesterday. I think he went to have it checked before coming in today. He usually only works afternoons on Mondays anyway.'

'Well, I need him. The president of Cybermed was at the meeting this morning. He's in my office right now and he wants a look at ARTIE.'

Jessie looked down into Sara's incision. The swelling was no better, but thank God, no worse.

'The prototype from yesterday has been taken apart,' she said through clenched teeth. 'ARTIE-Two should be around.'

'Well, it isn't. I looked all over the lab and I can't find it. Cybermed has the clout to make ARTIE number one in the area of intraoperative robotics. And here I can't even produce the damn thing.'

Beneath her mask, Jessie calmed herself with a lengthy exhale.

'Did you look in the cabinet over the central sink? That's where we always keep both ARTIEs locked up.'

'No, I . . . The cabinet with the combination lock?'

'Exactly. You had us set the combination for your birthday, remember?'

'Oh . . . yes. It's been a while since I . . . since I needed to do any work in that lab. I'll go check. Carry on.'

Gilbride turned and was gone. Just like that. Not a word about Sara Devereau. Jessie wondered how much of the conversation Sara had heard, and whether it registered that the surgeon who had done her first two operations had breezed in and out without even acknowledging that she was on the table.

Jessie felt the bowstring relax. Her shoulders sagged comfortably. The tightness in her jaw vanished. Gilbride had just saved her from making a decision she would have regretted for the rest of her life. There was still tumor in Sara's brain – too much tumor for Jessie to believe her body could fight for long.

*Fearless.*

In the heat of the moment, with her friend on the table, swelling distorting the anatomy, and faced with a tumor among the most difficult she had encountered, Jessie had lost her objectivity. She had forgotten her promise to her friend and to herself.

*Fearless.*

'Ted, I want a new set of images of this sucker,' she heard herself say. 'Everybody, this is the captain speaking. I want you all to just hunker down and let your honeys know you might be late for dinner. We're going to be at this for a few more hours.'

# Chapter 6

Boston's fleet center was a near sellout. Pacing about the carpeted VIP room, Marci Sheprow could hear the crowd, like the white noise of the ocean. Both were sounds familiar to her. She had spent the first nine of her eighteen years living at home with her parents on Cape Cod. The next eight she had lived, essentially, in a Houston gymnasium, training with several dozen other gymnastics hopefuls. But unlike the others, Marci had made it to the pinnacle of her sport. Two Olympic golds and a bronze. She was back living on the Cape now, more often than before, anyway. And when the time came, maybe after college, she planned to take a piece of the millions she had already banked and buy a place near her parents.

She had no intention of competing in the Olympics again, but every time she said that, her coach and parents just smiled. They knew as well as she did that there was little about competitive gymnastics she didn't love. And now she was riding a wave of incredible popularity, especially in New England.

'Hey, babe, what gives?'

Shasheen Standon, Marci's closest friend on the U.S. team, was eating a pear, and offered a bite.

'No, thanks. My stomach's a little queasy, and I've got a little bit of a headache.'

'It must be a virus. It sure can't be nerves. You ain't got none of those.'

'Come on. You of all people know that's just b.s.'

Marci was famous on the team and in the press for her calm, almost blissful demeanor when she performed. She was approachable, though – not like those Russian and

Romanian ice maidens. Still, her routines were described in the *New York Times* as 'breathtakingly daring.' 'The whole package,' another writer gushed.

'You know,' Shasheen said, 'now that you mention it, you don't look that great. Remember, this is only an exhibition. Maybe you should pack it in tonight. Let us second stringers have center stage;'

Marci punched her friend lightly on the arm.

'A team gold and an individual silver on the uneven bars. Some second stringer you are. I may cut back on my routine, but I can't back out. I'm local. Do you have any idea how many family and friends I have out there? You stayed at my house last night. You know.'

'That was a pretty wild scene, that's for sure, especially that Uncle Jerry of yours. Well, just go easy. Leave out some of the crazy Sheprow moves.'

'Maybe. Maybe I will.'

Marci bent over and effortlessly touched the carpet with her palms. At five foot five she was on the tall side for a gymnast, but she was remarkably lithe and the strongest girl on the team. She was also 100 percent athlete, totally in tune with her body. And tonight, she simply didn't feel right. She went up on her toes and snapped her hands across her body, then up toward the ceiling. To the casual observer, she would have looked lightning quick. But she knew that she was unnaturally aware of her right leg when she flexed at the ankle, and that her right arm felt slightly sluggish as well. They had been on tour for more than a month, with shows sometimes three nights in a row. Maybe she was just wearing down.

Across the room, Shasheen was entertaining several of the girls and coaches with one of her stories. Marci smiled. *Talk about loose.*

'Five minutes,' the promoter called into the room. 'Five minutes, everyone. Marci, that deal with the governor's going to happen at intermission. I told his people you felt uncomfortable being singled out, but they reminded me that you're the only one on the team from Massachusetts, and that the small print in our contract says we have to cooperate with this sort of thing. It's just a plaque of some kind. Your folks'll love it.'

'Viva Sheprow,' Shasheen cheered with her typical sly edge.

The others laughed and applauded. At one time or another, everyone on the team had had differences with the others, but by and large they had stuck together pretty well. Marci bowed to the group and nodded to the promoter that she was okay about the plaque. She pulled on her warm-up jacket and tried, unsuccessfully, to shake the strange leaden feeling from her right arm. Finally she zipped up and followed the others out to the arena.

As Marci had anticipated, there were few empty seats in the house – probably the biggest crowd they had drawn on the entire tour. Through the playing of the national anthem and the introduction of the team, Marci tested her muscles – fingers, hands, arms, shoulders, neck, legs. *Better*, she thought. Everything felt better. She went up on her toes again. No real problem. Well, maybe a little weirdness.

*What in the hell is going on?*

She was scheduled to perform on the balance beam and uneven bars, as well as the vault. Then she and two others were to do a series of synchronized tumbling passes. Maybe she could beg off that.

'You okay, Marse?' Shasheen asked.

'Huh? Oh, yeah. I'm okay, I guess.'

'What did you say?'

'I said I'm okay.'

'Marci, you're not speaking right.'

'I'm okay.'

Her words sounded fine now. This was like the flu, she thought, or some kind of sugar thing. She typically wouldn't eat for hours before a competition, and even though this was only an exhibition, she should never have had a frappe and sandwich. The loudspeaker announcer called the eight of them to their places. Shasheen was starting on the uneven bars. Marci would be vaulting.

'Knock 'em dead,' Shasheen said, giving her a thumbs-up as she headed across the arena.

'Yeah,' Marci whispered to no one. 'You, too.'

She followed a teammate toward the head of the runway leading to the vault horse. Her individual gold medal was on the balance beam, but of all the events, vault was the most natural and automatic for her. Again, her right arm and leg seemed heavy. She felt confused and, for the first time, frightened.

Knock 'em dead.

Marci watched her teammate do an adequate vault, then heard her own name reverberate through the vast arena.

*Mom, something's wrong with me. What should I do?*

Marci looked to her left, where her parents, sister, relatives, and friends took up most of three rows. Barbara Sheprow, with her flaming red hair and the white suit she had bought for the occasion, beamed at her and pumped both fists in the air.

*Mama?*

Marci suddenly became aware that the entire Fleet Center had become eerily silent. Everyone was watching her . . . waiting. She hadn't even begun going through the mental prep to vault.

She turned toward the runway, shaking her hand and contracting the muscles in her arm. If she waited any longer, there was no telling what she would feel like.

*You can do it. There are no judges. Just do a decent vault. Nothing special. Go for it.*

The silence in the arena was replaced by a nervous buzz. It had to be now.

Marci rose on her toes and began her sprint toward the horse, arms pumping. She knew her speed was down, but it was too late now. She could pull it off. Even feeling lousy, she could pull it off.

A step before the take-off ramp, her right leg seemed to disappear. When she planted it, there was almost nothing there. She was airborne, but not nearly high enough to complete a vault. Panicked, she reached out reflexively for the horse, but her right arm failed her completely. She did an awkward, clumsy turn in the air and fell heavily on the horse. Air exploded from her lungs. She toppled forward helplessly. Her consciousness began to fade. The last sound Marci heard before blacking out was the cracking of bone in her wrist.

# Chapter 7

'Jessie, Del Murphy here. Are you free to meet me in the ER?'

It was just after nine when Jessie answered the page from Murphy, the neurologist on call. She was taking a short break in her office, but for much of the past five hours she had been in the neurosurgical ICU. Sara Devereau had shown no signs of regaining consciousness following what had turned into a ten-hour battle to remove enough tumor from her brain to give her a chance at a cure. Jessie had a dreadful sensation that her friend was not going to awaken with intact neurologic function if, in fact, she woke up at all.

'I can be down in just a few minutes,' she said. 'What do you have?'

'I have Marci Sheprow.'

'The gymnast?'

'She blacked out during an exhibition at the Fleet Center tonight, fell, and broke her wrist. The fracture's been set and casted by Bill Shea. But he didn't like her story of passing out, and called me. I've gone over her. She's stable, but she's got some neurologic findings, and I just got a look at her MRI.'

'I don't like the sound of that.'

'Probably not as bad as it could have been. Come on down.'

Jessie splashed some cold water on her face and made another quick stop in the unit. Sara, her eyes taped shut, was hooked to a ventilator by a clear polystyrene tube that ran up her nose, down the back of her throat, and between her vocal cords. In addition, the usual array of catheters, monitor cables, and other tubes were connected to her.

'She looks so peaceful,' Barry Devereau said.

'She is, in a way. Certainly, she's in no pain.'

'But there's a battle going on.'

'There's a battle going on, all right,' Jessie echoed flatly. 'I don't expect there to be any change tonight, Barry.'

'I'm going to stay just the same. I have someone with the kids.'

'The nurses'll take good care of you. I'm backing up the residents and covering for all private cases tonight. I take calls from home, but at night I can get back here in no time at all.'

'I don't know how you do it.'

Jessie rubbed at the fatigue stinging her eyes.

'It's not all that hard,' she said, 'as long as you don't look in the mirror.'

'No, I will not have a resident touching my daughter, and that's final. I want this . . . this Dr. Copeland down here now.'

Jessie stood outside the doorway to room 6 in the ER, vainly searching for a way to avoid having to deal with Marci Sheprow's mother. Del Murphy had warned her about the woman as they were reviewing the MRIs. Aggressive, entitled, smart, protective, and very suspicious.

'Not frightened?' Jessie had asked.

'Not that I can tell. At least not that she lets on.'

Del had correctly read the MRIs as showing a very localized, well-defined tumor – almost certainly a low-grade meningioma – pressing between the inner skull and Marci's brain on the left side, directly over the areas controlling movement of the right arm and leg. If there was such a thing as good news for someone with a brain tumor, this diagnosis and location was it.

Jessie made a futile attempt to smooth some of the wrinkles from her lab coat and scrubs, and cursed herself for not thinking to replace them before coming down. Then she noticed that she still had on the pink canvas Keds she had worn in the operating room. *Lord*. One look at those and Barbara Sheprow would probably be on the phone, calling an ambulance to spirit her daughter across town to White Memorial.

'Oh, well,' she breathed, and stepped into the room.

She introduced herself first to Marci, then to her mother. The Olympic gold medalist, an icon well known in virtually every country in the world, looked frail and very young. But the spark in her green eyes belied that impression. Barbara Sheprow glanced over at Del Murphy uncomfortably.

'I . . . I expected a . . . what I mean is, Dr. Murphy didn't say you were . . .'

'A woman?'

'That, yes, and so young.'

'I'm afraid I can't do much about the woman part,' Jessie said, 'but, I can be very reassuring about not being too young.'

'I didn't even know there *were* women neurosurgeons,' Marci's mother said, pushing.

A dozen flip remarks crossed Jessie's mind, but stopped short of her tongue.

'There aren't too many of us, Mrs. Sheprow, but there are some. And as you might suspect, we've all had to be twice as good to make it to where we are. As I hope Dr. Murphy will affirm, I'm a very well trained and experienced neurosurgeon.'

'I appreciate the reassurance,' Barbara said, sounding not at all reassured. 'I had Marci brought here because Bob McGillvary, our doctor down on the Cape, knew Dr. Shea, the orthopedist who fixed her wrist, and Bob referred us to him. I . . . I never dreamed we'd be needing a neurosurgeon.'

'Well, at this point, I'm not certain what you need. But I do know that to do my job right, I need to hear in Marci's own words what happened tonight.'

Barbara Sheprow looked over at her daughter. Jessie could almost hear the woman weighing her options. This was the mother of an Olympic champion, Jessie reminded herself – a woman used to dictating to others, not to being dictated to herself. Finally, Barbara stepped aside and motioned for Jessie to go ahead.

Del Murphy mumbled something about seeing a consult and returning in a little while, and left the room, perhaps sensing that as long as he was there, Barbara Sheprow would be directing her clinical concerns to him. Under Barbara's watchful eye, Jessie's history-taking and neurologic exam lasted half an hour. During that time, she could sense a pleasant rapport developing between herself and Marci, who was brighter and more philosophical than she had anticipated. The MRIs and current neurologic findings suggested that surgery did not have to be done on an emergency basis. But the nature of Marci's sudden weakness and loss of consciousness shouted a clear warning. There was no question an operation was in her near future.

Finally, Jessie had all the information she needed. Marci's father and younger sister were brought in from the waiting room.

'This is Dr. Jessie Copeland, Paul,' Barbara said to her husband. 'She's on call for the neurosurgical department. It's her job to evaluate Marci and give us her opinion as to what's happened.'

*Not exactly a vote of confidence*, Jessie thought.

She slid the MRI films into the two view boxes and described to Marci's father what she had found.

'When would you be doing this procedure?' Paul Sheprow ventured when Jessie had finished her explanation.

Jessie could see the man's wife stiffen.

'Now, Paul,' Barbara admonished, 'no has said anything about *who* would be doing Marci's surgery, let alone *when*, or even *whether*.'

'But I thought – '

'Please, dear. Dr. Copeland, is this the best hospital for Marci to be having this surgery?'

'It is certainly *one* of the best. We have a great deal of significant research going on, and we do a lot of brain tumor surgery.'

'We?'

'The department, I mean.'

'And where do you rate in that department?'

'Mother!' Marci exclaimed. 'Give her a break.'

'I will not. This isn't exactly deciding who is going to do your nails.'

'If I've got to have an operation, I think she'll do fine.'

'I'll tell you what, Marci. When it's your child's head someone wants to operate on, I'll let you decide whether they should or not, and who should do it.'

'Look,' Jessie said, 'there are forty or fifty neurosurgeons in Boston. Any one of them would be happy to give you a second opinion, and also a second choice. I want you to be totally confident in me or whoever does this surgery. Having this kind of operation is frightening enough without your having doubts about the surgeon.'

'If you did the procedure, when would you do it?' Barbara asked, not acknowledging Jessie's words of reassurance.

'This is a benign tumor in that it doesn't spread to other sites in the body,' Jessie replied. 'And as I pointed out, it appears to be the kind of meningioma that is the easiest for us to remove. But the skull is a closed container, and there is pressure building up. The episode tonight was a pretty strident warning.'

'So you're saving soon.'

'Two days, three. I wouldn't wait much longer than a week.'

'And are there other treatment possibilities? Radiation? Chemo?'

Jessie shook her head.

'Barb, Dr. Copeland sounds pretty confident in herself,' Paul ventured.

Barbara Sheprow never had the opportunity to tell her husband to keep his thoughts to himself. For at that moment, lacking only a flourish of trumpets, Carl Gilbride swept into the room followed by two residents. He was as impeccably dressed as Jessie was rumpled, and he exuded stature and confidence.

'Mrs. Sheprow, Mr. Sheprow, Marci, I'm Dr. Gilbride, the chief of neurosurgery here at EMMC,' he said, shaking hands with the parents, while cutting Barbara off from Jessie like a champion wrangler. 'I had just stopped by the hospital to check on a post-op patient, and heard you were here.'

*What post-op patient?* Jessie wanted to scream. A news flash on TV; a call from the orthopedist or from someone else – those were possibilities. But not a nine o'clock drop-in to check on a post-op. *Give me a break!*

The passing of the surgical baton took just five minutes. If only Gilbride were as masterful in the OR as he was in situations such as this one, Jessie thought, Sara Devereau might never have needed two re-operations.

'Dr. Copeland is one of our finest young surgeons,' Gilbride said after his cursory exam and glance at the MRI. 'I assume it was her opinion that an operation is necessary on this meningioma, and fairly soon.'

*Finest young surgeons.* Jessie swallowed back a jet of bile. Gilbride was only six or seven years older than she was, if that.

'We'd be pleased to have the chief of neurosurgery handle this,' Barbara said, carefully avoiding eye contact with her.

Jessie could see Gilbride's chest puff like a pigeon's.

'Well,' he said, 'I'm certain that for someone who has brought such glory to us all, we can free up an OR whenever we need one. There is some danger in waiting, and it's been my experience that people are much happier just getting this sort of thing over with.'

'I agree with you there,' Barbara said.

'Good. My recommendation is the day after tomorrow. I'm scheduled to present a lecture at the Midwest neurosurgical meeting in Chicago that day, but the topic is research that Dr. Copeland has been assisting me on. I'm sure you won t mind standing in for me there, Jessie, yes?'

'Well, actually, I have Sara Devereau in the ICU right now and –'

'You can fly out tomorrow, give the talk at eleven the

next morning, and be back by evening. The department will fly you there and you can take my room at the Hilton. The staff here'll be happy to cover your patients for the short time you'll be gone. After all, we are a team.'

Jessie was already inching back toward the door. For sheer gall, stealing a patient this way fell short of some of Gilbride's past showstoppers, but it was right up there. She wondered if the uncomfortable heat in her cheeks was translating into anything people could see.

'That will be fine,' she said. 'Marci, good luck with all this. Dr. Gilbride is a very good surgeon. You'll be back on the balance beam before you know it.'

The girl clearly looked embarrassed, but said nothing. It was as if she had seen her mother in action too many times to bother.

'Thank you, Jessie,' Gilbride said, oblivious to the silent exchange. 'Alice, in my office, will have the carousel of slides and your tickets ready for you first thing in the morning.'

The best Jessie could manage was a tight-lipped nod.

'Thanks,' she said. 'Good luck.'

Feeling perilously close to tears, she hurried out of the ER and back up to Surgical Seven. She rarely tried to contain herself if she felt like crying, even in public. But dammit, she vowed, there was no way Carl Gilbride was going to be the cause.

At ten there was, as always, still more to do, but Jessie decided that a fifteen-hour nonstop workday was enough. Gilbride's obnoxious performance in the ER hadn't broken her spirit, but it had surely left a dent. She felt totally stressed. Her back and neck ached, and she was frantic for a protracted soak in the tub.

The hospital was located not far from some of the toughest neighborhoods in the city. There was a shuttle that ferried employees to the various parking lots, but at night it only ran at the time of shift change, between ten forty-five and midnight. Jessie was in no mood to wait forty-five minutes. She had made the walk by herself any number of nights without incident, trusting her instincts, her New Balance cross-trainers, and the cylinder of Mace in her purse.

She made a quick, final sweep through Surgical Seven, wrote some orders, and changed back into her civvies by the OR. Then she headed to the main lobby.

Carefully avoiding eye contact with any of the gaggle of reporters waiting for news of Marci Sheprow, she signed out with the operator and left the hospital. The night was moonless – dark and cool, with fine, wind-whipped mist. On evenings like this one, Swede was not at its most reliable. For Christmas, Jessie planned to get it a complete physical with a new battery and whatever else was recommended by the specialist. If it let her down tonight and didn't start, she decided, that checkup was going to come much sooner, and would include a colonoscopy.

For whatever reason – maybe the heavy darkness, she thought – Jessie kept checking over her shoulder as she walked briskly to parking lot E. At one point, she actually thought she heard footsteps. The mist was building toward a steady rain. By the time she crossed the gravel to her car, she was running. She fumbled with her keys, then unlocked the door and slid behind the wheel. Relieved, she quickly locked the doors, then sat there, panting. Finally, she slipped the key into the ignition and turned it. Nothing. Just an impotent click.

'Oh, Swede,' she groaned, staring out at the dimly lit parking lot.

The rain was increasing. Around her, the windows began to fog. She opened hers a crack, then tried the wipers, which worked, and the headlights, which did also. *Not a dead battery.* She turned off both and tried the ignition again. Nothing. Suddenly, a sharp rapping on the passenger window startled her and seemed to stop her heart for several beats.

'Y-Yes?' she managed.

'Open the window, please,' a man's voice said. 'Security.'

Jessie leaned over and smeared a circle in the

condensation with the side of her hand. All she could make out was a blurred face. She opened the window an inch.

'Identification,' she said.

The man, rainwater dripping off the hood of his poncho, quickly held up a hospital ID. Grateful, Jessie didn't bother reading the name. She opened the window another few inches.

'My car's dead,' she said. 'The battery seems okay, but nothing happens when I turn the key.'

'Can you pop the hood, please?'

Jessie did as he asked and felt the car dip from his weight as he bent over the engine. The beam from his flashlight intermittently swung up from under the hood and dispersed across the fogged windshield. Jessie opened her window as far as she could without getting soaked.

'Do you need any help?' she called out.

'I don't think so. A wire's come off the ignition. I've just about got it back on. There. Try it now.'

Jessie turned the key and Swede rumbled to life.

'Bless you,' she murmured.

The guard appeared at the driver's-side window. His face was largely hidden by his poncho, but what Jessie could see looked pleasant enough.

'You're all set, ma'am,' he said. 'I was just heading back to the hospital when you came running by. I'm glad I decided to wait.'

'Well, I sure am, too, I can tell you that. Do you have a car here?'

'No, I was walking.'

'Well, get in. I'll drive you back.'

'I'm soaked. I don't want to get your –'

'Come on, get in. This car doesn't care, and neither do I.'

Jessie leaned over and opened the passenger-side door.

'Thanks,' the guard said, sliding in.

'That's my line,' Jessie said.

The man, about her age, was tall and broad shouldered. He had deep-set, dark eyes and the sort of rugged looks that women into Hollywood hunks might not have found attractive, but that she had always liked.

'It got nasty in a hurry out there,' he said, pushing his hood back from his closely cut, light brown hair.

'I'm very grateful to you for sticking around. Did I look that helpless?'

'Hardly. I'm new on the job, and to tell you the truth, after a career in the Marines, it's a bit boring. A woman running through the rain at this hour definitely caught my attention. I appreciate the ride back.'

'It's my pleasure. I'm Jessie Copeland, one of the doctors at the old place.'

She extended her hand. The guard's thick fingers enfolded it.

'Well, I'm pleased to meet you, Dr. Copeland,' he said, noting that Jessie was better looking than her photo in the hospital directory. 'My name's Bishop. Alex Bishop.'

# Chapter 8

Not surprisingly, Carl Gilbride's 'room' at the Chicago Hilton was a suite. It had been hard for Jessie to leave Sara in the care of one of the other neurosurgeons, but there had been absolutely no improvement in her level of consciousness or neurologic function. And Jessie strongly believed there wouldn't be any over the day she would be away. The symptoms and clinical course of cerebral edema – brain swelling – were impossible to predict with any confidence. Some post-op patients were alert within a few hours despite significantly increased intracranial pressure and documented swelling on their MRIs, while others, with much less edema, awoke only after being out for days, weeks, or even months.

It was midafternoon when Jessie had called Barry Devereau with the lack-of-progress report. Then she had changed for the trip in the on-call room. Marci Sheprow's impending surgery, scheduled for first thing in the morning, was, of course, the talk of the hospital. Coming down the Track earlier in the day, Jessie had seen Barbara Sheprow approaching and had actually ducked into a patient's room rather than open the curtain on what was certain to be a strained, even embarrassing, interaction with the woman. She also felt some relief each time she walked past the gymnast's room and the door was closed. She knew she was allowing herself to become a player in Gilbride's theater of the absurd, but she was also able to acknowledge that she was only human. By the time she had picked up Gilbride's slides from his secretary and taken a cab to the airport, she was ready to get away from Eastern Mass Medical Center – even if it was only for a day.

On the flight to Chicago, she had resolved to try harder to accept the fact that nothing she could ever do would change her department chief one iota. That grand decision did little to boost her spirits.

One thing that did give her a lift was her brief contact with Alex Bishop, the hospital guard who had reconnected the wire in Swede's ignition and kept a miserable evening from becoming even worse. Bishop was a former medic in the Marines, and was in the process of applying to Northeastern's physician's assistant program. He seemed incredibly intense, but he also had a droll, self-deprecating humor that appealed to her as much as his looks.

After stepping out of her car, he had said, 'Well, see you around.'

She had nearly replied, 'When?'

Jessie set aside the notes she had made for her presentation, opened the closet, and took out the two suits she had brought to Chicago – one a conservative charcoal gray befitting the stand-in for Carl Gilbride, and the other a butter yellow number with a short straight skirt and cropped jacket. It was no contest. The yellow outfit made her feel feminine and yes, maybe even powerful. And who knew, perhaps some guy who was neither married nor lethally self-absorbed would be in the audience. Emily was right. It had been too long. It was time to get her nose out of people's cranial cavities and look around.

She wandered out to the sitting room of her suite and called the neurosurgical ICU at Eastern Mass Medical. As she had anticipated, Sara's condition was unchanged. Jessie had known better than to expect any improvement, and yet she had held her breath, waiting for the terse report.

Gilbride's presentation, as it turned out, was scheduled for one in the afternoon, not eleven in the morning as he had told her. She could have gone down to the lecture hall to listen to some of the other talks. Instead, she decided on a nap. First, though, she took a twelve-dollar mason jar of cashews from the in-room minibar and washed some of them down with a few swallows from a three-dollar can of diet Coke. God only knew, she had earned the indulgence. With any luck, sometime in the future the expenses for her trip would float across Gilbride's desk, and there they'd be – fifteen bucks' worth of cashews and Coke. She opened a five-dollar Toblerone bar for good measure, and set it aside after one small bite.

*I'm a vindictive enemy, Gilbride*, she thought as she checked off the three items on the minibar tally sheet. *Take that! And that!*

The phone rang with the wake-up call she had requested, anticipating that the strain of the past two days and whatever Freudian factors were at work might have her napping through her presentation. She arranged for a delayed checkout and gathered her things for the talk, which Gilbride had modestly titled 'Robotics and Intraoperative MRI: A Marriage for the Ages.' Finally, after one last survey in the mirror, she headed down ten flights to the Northeast Salon.

*Gilbride and Copeland*, she was thinking. *A Marriage for the Ages.*

Jessie was infinitely more comfortable teaching a small group of residents or students than she ever would be standing up before a crowd. She was grateful that most of this talk was commentary on slides, with the house lights down. Except for the clearing of throats and an occasional cough from among the 150 or so attendees, she felt alone much of the time, lecturing in a cocoon of darkness. Carl Gilbride, a master at such presentations, had interspersed his charts and photographs with a number of cartoons, some of which were unabashedly sexist. Jessie had weeded out the most offensive ones, and then appalled herself by leaving in two of the borderlines, just to show the almost-all-XY audience that she could be one of the boys.

She had been allotted forty-five minutes and was pleased and relieved to realize that, with seven minutes left, she was done. She turned on the house lights from the lectern and asked for questions. Three microphones had been placed along the center aisle. Immediately one surgeon was up at each one – a good sign that the entire crowd hadn't drifted into dreamland. The first two questions were softballs – simple clarifications she could easily handle. Both men – neither of whom looked like potential spice for her personal life – complimented her on an excellent presentation and fascinating research. *So far, so good,* she thought as the two physicians were quickly replaced at their microphones.

The third questioner was a tall black neurosurgeon from California named Litton, a researcher in one of the programs developing a competitor for ARTIE. In their brief encounters with each other, Jessie had found him to be impressively intelligent and absolutely humorless. He had arrived fifteen minutes late, during one of the brief lights-on periods of her talk. She sensed trouble even before Litton began speaking.

'Dr. Copeland, Ron Litton, Stanford University, here. I want to congratulate you on an excellent presentation of fascinating research into the field of intraoperative robotics. But there is one thing troubling me.'

'Yes?'

'You said that to this point you've done some work with your ARTIE on animals and cadavers.'

'That's right.'

'And that you and your department head, Dr. Gilbride, had begun making preparations to submit a proposal for approval by your hospital's committee on human experimentation.'

'That's exactly what I said, yes.'

'Then I would suggest that perhaps you and your chief of neurosurgery should get on the same page. I was several minutes late arriving for your presentation because I was glued to the television in my room. CNN, to be precise.'

'Dr. Litton, I don't understand what that has to do with our submitting a human experimentation protocol.'

'Dr. Copeland, I certainly hope you have approval from that committee already. Because according to the news and the interview with Dr. Gilbride that I just watched, earlier today he used your friend ARTIE to excise and successfully remove a tumor from the brain of the Olympic gold medal gymnast Marci Sheprow.'

# Chapter 9

'Dr. Gilbride, would you say that from what you've seen of Marci Sheprow so far, your surgical robot has scored a perfect ten?'

Gilbride, looking earnest and professorial, met the cameras covering his press conference warmly.

'Nothing in neurosurgery can be taken for granted, Charlie,' he said, tenting his fingers, 'but at the moment, Miss Sheprow is looking very good, and we're expecting a rapid recovery. The trauma associated with traditional surgery was certainly diminished through the use of our intraoperative robotics.'

*Come on, Carl, have you no shame?*

Jessie sat slumped in stunned silence on the couch in her suite, watching her boss perform for the cameras and at least two dozen microphones bunched on the table before him. To his left, propped on an easel, was an artist's graphic rendering of Marci Sheprow's head, the location of her meningioma, and the path followed by ARTIE. It was as if Gilbride were General Schwarzkopf and Marci's brain Iraq. It appalled Jessie, but did not at all surprise her, that he had commissioned the artwork *before* he did the surgery.

'Dr. Gilbride, Pat Jackson, Associated Press. Could you give us some idea of the future of robotics in neuro-surgery?'

'In *all* of surgery, Pat. Advances in medicine are coming so fast. People forget that CT scans weren't in general use until twenty years ago, and MRIs just over half that. Ultrasound's been around since World War Two, but with nothing like the sophistication we have today. Now there's fiber optics, which has made all of the various scopes possible, and looming on the horizon is robotics. The potential is limitless, and I've told the researchers in my department that it's full speed ahead in this area.'

*Jerk.*

Jessie wondered about her future at EMMC. Had Gilbride left her any option but resignation? He had lied to her about getting ready to apply for authorization from the human experimentation panel. The five-member panel was largely made up of his cronies. Clearly he had already gotten approval from them for a clinical trial with ARTIE, and was just waiting for the perfect case.

And then there was the matter of Marci Sheprow's tumor. It wasn't much of an exaggeration to suggest that a reasonably competent neurosurgeon could have successfully removed her meningioma with a Black & Decker drill, a teaspoon, and a Swiss Army knife. This was hardly the sort of case for which ARTIE was being developed. But Only the few who were present when Jessie was working on Pete Roslanski's tumor knew how much damage ARTIE-2 could have done to Marci's brain had it malfunctioned the way ARTIE-1 had. No wonder Gilbride had gone haywire about her cadaver trial. He was already primed and waiting for the right moment to make history. The technical problem she had encountered, however remediable, would create a major glitch in his plans should word filter back to the human experimentation panel. Enter Marci Sheprow – a morsel just too tasty to pass up.

The news conference was continuing, but Jessie had seen and heard all she cared to. She left her suit and underwear where they fell on the bedroom floor and stood in a steaming shower for twenty minutes, washing herself over and over, as if she could somehow scrub away the contamination from her association with the man.

She dried her hair, then pulled on jeans and a crewneck sweater and packed up her things for the flight home. It would be fairly late by the time she returned to the hospital and it was doubtful she'd have to be dressed up to face the press. Even if someone did manage to connect her to

ARTIE, so what. She was just the robot's nursemaid. Gilbride was its press agent.

She started out of the room, then returned to the minibar and added a three-dollar bag of M&M's to her purse.

*Take that!*

The phalanx of satellite broadcasting vans parked in front of the hospital was the first giveaway that Jessie had seriously underestimated the media's devotion to Marci Sheprow, and their fascination with the technology that had saved her life. There were security guards everyplace she looked, and clusters of news and camera people in the main lobby and hallway. As she showed her ID to a guard, several reporters began calling out questions to her on the off chance that she had something – anything – to do with Marci. Others began shuffling toward her like extras in a zombie picture.

Jessie hurried up to the OR dressing room on Surgical Eight and changed into scrubs and a lab coat. Then, full of nervous tension, she raced down to Surgical Seven.

Marci was still in the NICU. Jessie had planned to stop in and see her after she had checked on Sara, but Barbara Sheprow caught her eye as she passed and motioned her in.

'How was your talk?' Barbara whispered, conscious of her sleeping daughter.

'It went fine. I'm so pleased with what I've heard about Marci's operation.'

The gymnast was off all life support, and looked to be breathing comfortably.

'She's opened her eyes several times, and has even spoken. But mostly she's been sleeping.'

'That's certainly normal.'

'Dr. Copeland, I hope there're no hard feelings about my decision to go with Dr. Gilbride on this.'

'This isn't a contest, Mrs. Sheprow. It's your child's life. You've got to be as comfortable as possible with her surgeon. I wouldn't want to be that surgeon if you weren't.'

Without waiting for further conversation, she brushed

some hair from Marci's forehead, studied her perfect, unlined face, and said a silent prayer of thanks that nothing had gone wrong during Gilbride's grandstand play. Then she left. Barbara was obviously ecstatic with the decision she had made in choosing Gilbride. Jessie hoped she would never know how shamelessly her daughter had been used.

Sara remained on assisted ventilation, but the covering neurosurgeon's notes stated that she had begun gagging a bit on the breathing tube – a slightly hopeful sign. He had also reported a flicker of movement on Sara's left side. *Flicker of movement.* A brilliant, vibrant teacher and mother of three, and that was what her world had been reduced to. *At the moment.* Jessie reminded herself. *At the moment.* But she also knew that every passing hour with minimal or no progress, each passing day, made a recovery without major deficits less likely.

Jessie did a brief neurologic exam, which revealed no reflexes, poor muscle tone, and nothing approaching even the flicker her covering doctor had described. This was not just a battle, this was Sara's Armageddon.

Looking down at her friend, she wondered how Barry and the kids would react to the news that she had decided to resign from the staff. What about Tamika Bing and Dave Scolari and Mrs. Kinchley and her other patients? What about Skip Porter, and Hans, and all those who had helped breathe life into ARTIE? If only Gilbride had stayed on his side of the line. Minimal, unavoidable contact she could have handled. Now, she was being forced to make a choice that would only hurt people – most prominently, she reflected sadly, herself. She wrote a few perfunctory orders on Sara and headed, downcast, toward the ward, intending to make quick rounds on her patients before heading home. The unit charge nurse called to her before she reached the doors.

'Jessie, hi,' the nurse said, handing over an envelope with Jessie's name printed on it. 'Dr. Gilbride said you would probably be in here tonight. He left this for you.'

More than curious, Jessie thanked the nurse and hurried

to her office with the envelope before opening it.

MEMO
From: Carl W. Gilbride, M.D.; Chief, Department of
 Neurosurgery
To: Roland Tuten, M.D.; Chairman, Professional
 Standing, Credentials, and Promotions
 Committee
Re: Jessie D. Copeland, M.D.; Instructor in
 Neurosurgery

Dear Dr. Tuten:
I am writing to inform you of my intention to
recommend Dr. Jessie D. Copeland for a promotion
from clinical instructor to Assistant Professor of
Neurosurgery, effective as soon as I receive approval
from your committee. Dr. Copeland has served this
department and Eastern Massachusetts Medical
Center with distinction, and has been especially
instrumental in the development of our program in
intraoperative robotics. It is my intention to reward
her for these efforts with this upgrade in her academic
rank.

*Assistant professor* – a serious step toward tenure; a
significant raise in pay. Jessie stared down at the memo.
She had believed herself to be two years away from a
promotion, maybe three – if she got one at all. She also
knew that she would be leapfrogging several members –
*XY members* – of the department. She wasn't a militant
feminist, but she couldn't deny her satisfaction at the
idea.
 'I wanted to wait to speak with you until you had read
that.'
 Carl Gilbride, looking no less fresh than he had during
his press conference hours ago, stood in her doorway.
Jessie held up the memo.
 'In the outside world they throw people in jail for
accepting a payoff like this,' she said.

Gilbride slipped inside the office and closed the door behind him.

'Call it what you wish,' he said. 'Either way, you've earned it. I knew you'd be upset by what happened today.'

'I'm worse than upset, Carl. I'm horrified and furious, and . . . and mortified. ARTIE wasn't ready for something like this, and you know it.'

'That's not what Skip Porter told me. He said that . . . that little problem you had the other day was purely mechanical – a broken wire, not any design or computer flaw. Besides, when is a new technique or drug ever *really* ready? At some point, clinical scientists have just got to take the bull by the horns and do it.'

Jessie shook her head slowly.

'Spare me, please,' she said.

'Jessie, I appreciate all you've done with ARTIE. But I also don't think *you* appreciate some of the realities of financing a research-oriented neurosurgical department.'

'Carl, you placed that girl in danger for no reason.'

'If there was any trouble with ARTIE, I was set to open her up and go after her tumor that way. And don't say the device was used for no reason. Look at these.'

Gilbride withdrew a large, stuffed manila envelope from his briefcase and passed it over. It contained dozens of congratulatory e-mails, phone messages, faxes, and even several telegrams. Patients from countries around the world were already contacting Gilbride, asking him to take a crack with ARTIE at their 'inoperable' tumors.

'Please, I was hopeless until now,' one fax read. 'I have nothing to lose. Please help me.'

'Congratulations,' Jessie said, hoping her tone reflected her lack of sincerity.

'Two of those faxes and one of those telegrams are from agencies that could or do help fund our research,' Gilbride said, reaching across the desk to separate them from the others. 'Here.'

The telegram was from the medical director of Durbin Surgicals. Jessie knew that a good portion of the work on ARTIE had been done with their help through a grant that was in Gilbride's name, but for which she had written the application.

Dear Carl. We at Durbin are proud that research done in part under one of our career development awards has made such an impressive impact. Congratulations to you, Dr. Copeland, and the rest of your staff. I suspect when you apply for a renewal you will find smooth sailing.

'And look. Look at this one. It's from the executive director of the MacIntosh Foundation in Los Angeles. You've heard of them?'
'Of course.'

Dear Dr. Gilbride,
Congratulations on your successful use of intra-operative robotics in the case of Marci Sheprow. As you know, the MacIntosh Foundation is committed in part to the furtherance of medical science as it directly impacts the public. I know you have been anxiously awaiting our response to your recent grant application to our agency. We are impressed with what you have accomplished, and will be evaluating your research for one of our Class 1 awards, which, as you may know, has a minimum value of three million dollars. I will be contacting you directly should we require any further information, or should our grant awards committee reach a decision on your application.
Sincerely,
Eastman Tolliver
Executive Director

'Three million,' Jessie said, genuinely impressed.
'Just the beginning. Because of this case, we're going to be right up there with the elite programs in the country. My guess is that by the time this week is over, we'll be getting more referrals and doing more tumor cases than any other program around. We're also going to have

79

tremendous clout when it comes to competing with places like Stanford and Baylor for money – especially with Iowa no longer in the picture.'

'Carl, I appreciate all you're saying. But I just can't forgive you for lying to me about not having the human experimentation approval.'

'I didn't. The day after Marci presented to you in the ER I pushed through the approval. Not before.'

Jessie eyed him suspiciously.

'You can provide me proof of that?'

'If you want it. Jessie, I understand you're angry. People get angry with me all the time. It's part of running a department and pushing it toward the top of the heap. But I don't want the department to lose you. That's what this promotion is all about. Now, what do you say?'

By claiming that he had not lied regarding the HE panel's approval, Gilbride had opened the door just a sliver for Jessie to remain at the hospital. It was really all she wanted.

'My guess is it's going to be pretty crazy here tomorrow,' she said, her voice neutral.

'I think you could say that.'

His smug expression said he knew he had won. Jessie thought about demanding written proof of the date the HE committee had approved ARTIE. But she knew Gilbride well enough to suspect he could produce such a document even if it belied the truth. And why should she hurt herself, Sara, and her other patients over this, anyhow? she thought. Better to try to do things on her terms – to take the promotion and begin making some discreet inquiries to other neurosurgery departments in the city and around the country.

'I'll do what I can to help you out,' she said.

'Spoken like a true team player,' Gilbride replied.

# Chapter 10

Alex Bishop had taken a furnished studio in a clapboard tenement a mile from the hospital. It was midnight, and his shift at the hospital had just ended. On the way back to his room, he stopped at a convenience store for some Diet Pepsi, a dozen Almond Joy candy bars, and several packs of nicotine gum. His last cigarette had closely followed his decision to hunt down Malloche. Until the man was behind bars or dead, no more smokes. That was the deal he had made with himself, and it had been a bear of a promise to keep. Periodic nicotine gum or patches helped keep the craving under reasonable control, but nothing had touched his substitute addiction to Almond Joys, which was now up to five or six bars a day. Each morning he did a hundred push-ups and four times that many sit-ups as penance.

The tenement was in a fairly tough neighborhood. Bishop headed there half hoping some punks might try to shake him down. He was going through one of those periods when he simply craved action. But he knew this just wasn't the time. He needed to show whatever restraint was necessary to keep from calling attention to himself.

Everything was coming together.

The robot-assisted operation on Marci Sheprow had eliminated what lingering doubt he had regarding Claude

Malloche's choice of a surgeon. The Mist, as some called the elusive, genius killer, was either on his way to Eastern Mass Medical Center, or he was already there. And Carl Gilbride was to be his surgeon. It hadn't been easy to gather information discreetly on Gilbride, but gradually a picture of the man was beginning to emerge. And thanks to the ignition wire he had loosened on Jessie Copeland's car, before too much longer, the pieces of the Gilbride puzzle that were missing would be filled in by her.

What Bishop knew so far was that Carl Gilbride was an empire builder, much like Sylvan Mays had been. He had a humble background, and had begun living above his means as soon as he could. Now, he was an autocrat, forging a department that was already considered among the best in the country. Socially, he and his wife were tight with Boston's upper crust. Mrs. Gilbride was on the board of the symphony.

Did Gilbride seem like someone Claude Malloche could buy? Based on the information Bishop had gleaned so far, the answer was unequivocally yes. If the price was right, would he do the surgery even if he knew who Malloche was? That question remained to be answered.

Getting close to Jessie Copeland was going to help fill in the gaps and also make it easy for him to get a fix on the neurosurgical patients on Surgical Seven and in the outpatient department. Through his offhand inquiries, he had heard nothing but good things about her, and he felt fairly certain from some of what had been said that she was not that tight with Gilbride. In that respect, she was just what the doctor ordered. His initial impression was that she seemed too nice and too feminine to be earning a living cutting into people's brains. But he had known a number of nice, exceedingly feminine women in the agency who were quite capable of blowing a person's brains to bits if the job required it.

It would all have been so much easier if only he had gotten one dependable look at Malloche, just one. But the Mist never did business personally, and when he did come into the open to any extent, he used disguises and very often, substitutes. This time, though, he was nearing the end of the line.

Bishop's studio was on the third floor of the rickety four-floor walk-up. He hadn't slept much since coming to Boston, but still, he was pleased to note, his legs had some spring. He reached his apartment door and had his key in hand when he stopped. The two hairs he had set in place between the door and the jamb were gone. They might have fallen or been blown free, but there was no breeze at this level. His .45 was inside the room, wrapped in a towel beneath a corner of the mattress. There was no way he could have brought it in to work. Running away now would ruin any chance he had to get Malloche. If someone had been in his apartment, or was there now, dealing with the situation immediately was his only option. And the fire escape was his only chance.

Bishop crept softly up to the fourth floor, then up the narrow flight to the roof. Totally under control, with the arm strength of a gymnast, he swung himself over the roof's edge, lowered himself onto the wrought-iron fire escape by the fourth floor, and inched down a flight. The curtains to the west window of his apartment were drawn, but he could just make out furniture shapes through a narrow opening between them. The lights were off, but there was some illumination from the south-facing window just over the pullout that was his bed. From what he could see, the place looked empty.

For five minutes, ten, he remained crouched on the landing, motionless, peering in. Then suddenly he saw movement just to the left of the door. A man, solidly built, arose and went into the john for a minute or so, then returned to his spot. Bishop couldn't be positive, but it appeared the intruder was carrying a gun loosely in his right hand. He continued observing between the curtains until he felt certain the man was alone. A gun in trained hands versus surprise. Under most circumstances, Bishop knew, he would take his chances with his reflexes and the gun. This time, he had no choice. He might well end up cut to shreds before he reached his target, but the windowpanes were small and the wood framing them was old. Besides, this wouldn't be the first time he had gone through a window – in either direction.

He took an Almond Joy from the plastic bag, opened the wrapper, and took a bite, careful as he always was to get the right mix of coconut, chocolate, and almond. What remained of the bar he held on to as he stepped up on the railing of the fire escape. He flipped it against the window lightly enough to produce a sound but preserve some ambiguity. Then he reached up and grasped one of the stairs leading to the fourth floor.

The intruder warily approached the window. Bishop didn't wait for him to open the curtains. A feet-first entry would have been safer, but infinitely less effective. Instead, Bishop pulled his uniform jacket over his head and dove straight in. Wood and glass exploded into the room. His head hit the man in the midchest like a medicine ball, while his hand latched onto his wrist. He hyperflexed the joint and the gun clattered free even before the two of them had hit the floor. A sharp elbow to the jaw, followed by a powerful backhand to the opposite cheek, and it was over. Five seconds – maybe six.

Bishop rolled over the pieces of wood and shards of glass and had the muzzle of the man's Smith & Wesson .38 jammed up under his chin before his cobwebs had cleared. The intruder was beefy enough – taller than Bishop by a couple of inches, and a good twenty to twenty-five pounds heavier. But he was just a kid.

'Scoot toward the door!' Bishop snapped. 'I don't want to kill you, but I will if you give me any trouble.'

When he could reach the switch, he flipped on the overhead light. *Kid, indeed!* The man looked like a collegiate football player. Twenty-six, tops. He was bleeding from the corner of his mouth and from a fairly decent gash on his forehead that was going to require some stitches. To his credit, or perhaps his discredit, he didn't seem that frightened. Bishop straightened up and moved several feet away.

'Stay flat on your back, legs together, arms out,' he said.

'Just like a snow angel. Okay, who sent you?'

'Internal affairs. I wasn't supposed to hurt you, just talk to you.'

'Thank goodness for that. And what were you supposed to say?'

'That this is your last chance to come back to the farm.'

'How did you know where to find me?'

'They told me you were here at the hospital. I spotted you yesterday and followed you here. Can I get up now?'

'No. If all you were supposed to do was talk to me, you could have done it there.'

He took his cell phone and dialed a number in Alexandria, Virginia. Clearly, Mel Craft had been sleeping.

'Mel, it's me, Alex. Internal affairs sent someone after me.'

'Damn. Where is he now? How badly is he hurt?'

'He's on the floor of my apartment. Nothing that a few stitches won't take care of. Christ, Mel, he looks like he's seventeen.'

'I'm twenty-eight.'

'Shut up! Mel, how did they find me?'

'How do you think? I.A. knows we were partners and what you did for me. Hell, everyone knows. The bastards must have had my phone tapped when I made those calls to Boston for you. I never told them a thing. I didn't have to. Alex, I told you in D.C. If they want you, sooner or later they'll get you.'

'Not with this kind of punk, they won't. Mel, talk to them. Tell them I let Dennis the Menace here off with nothing more than a scolding. Tell them I need to be left alone for two weeks.'

'I'll tell them, Alex, but I can't make any guarantees. And Karen and I are leaving first thing in the morning for ten days in Brazil. I'll do what I can before I go.'

'Right now.'

'Okay, right now. Alex, the last five years have changed you – hardened you in ways that no one who knows you thinks are good. You'd be much better off if you'd just let the whole thing drop.'

'Five hundred people, Mel. That's how many that bastard or his men have killed. Five hundred. Probably more.'

'Says you, Alex. Let it go.'

'Tell them to give me my two weeks, or promise them for me that the next twenty-something they send after me will be shipped back to them in a bag.'

'I'll do what I can. I'm glad you took it easy on the kid.'

'I think he is, too. Have a good vacation, Mel.'

# Chapter 11

Chaos.

Two days had passed since the successful surgery on Marci Sheprow – two days of reporters and faxes, telegrams and news briefings and CNN broadcasts. For Jessie, all Carl Gilbride's triumph had meant was more work. Since her return from Chicago, she had, to all intents, been covering her practice and his.

The bright spot for her was the embryonic connection that had developed with Alex Bishop. Yesterday, a chance meeting in the cafeteria had led to a half-hour 'date' for coffee later that evening. As she had sensed during their ride back through the rain from lot E, there was much more to the man than one might have expected. He was two years older than she was and well past a marriage that had produced no children. While in the Marines, he had finished college with a degree in philosophy and had seen action in the Gulf. He liked the same sort of movies she did and seemed to be better read, although since she left for medical school thirteen years ago, most people were. And to top matters off, his looks were even more appealing to her than they had been that first night. As things were left, they would try to meet in the cafeteria again tonight, same time, same seats.

Although she hadn't gotten home from the hospital until almost 1 A.M., Jessie had set her alarm for five o'clock and headed back in. With the exception of two new cases – an elective aneurysm resection for tomorrow, and a pre-op to be done on a tenacious glioblastoma – her service was pretty much as it had been. Tamika Bing was still in her near-catatonic state despite the best efforts of psychiatrists and physical, occupational, and speech therapists. Mrs. Kinchley and Mrs. Weiss were complaining in private about each other to the staff, then each denying she had ever said any such thing when the matter was brought up to the pair of them.

Of all Jessie's patients, only Dave Scolari seemed changed. His eyes were noticeably brighter, and he smiled warmly as she came into his room.

'Hey, Doc, how goes it?'

'It goes. I stopped by last night, but you were asleep. I see you've been getting more mail.'

She motioned at the cards and letters that were open on his tray table – an interest she hadn't seen from him before.

'My mom handles them for me. We've started answering some, too. I just tell her what to say and she writes it down.'

Jessie felt her heart leap. She had seen enough medical miracles to know that faith and attitude were prime ingredients.

'That's great, Dave. I'm glad you're doing that,' she said. 'So will a lot of people be when they get your reply.'

'There's something else I have to show you,' he said, looking like a kid who had just brought home an unexpected A.

His jaws tightened into the grimace of extreme effort, and his eyes narrowed with strain. Then suddenly, shakily, his right arm came off the bed. At the same time, his fingers moved. It was subtle reeds in a gentle breeze. But in neurology, movement of any kind meant intact nerve conduction pathways.

'I can do the other side a little, too,' Dave said.

Jessie took his hand in hers, then hugged him.

'Oh, Dave. This is the best,' she said, wondering if he fully appreciated the mammoth implications of his minute movements. 'This is just the best.'

'That friend of yours, Luis, keeps coming by to see me. He's quite a guy.'

'Oh, he is that,' Jessie said. Luis was an artist and Boys Club coach who had taken his life in many wonderful directions since the tragic auto accident that had paralyzed him.

'After he left, I just decided I was going to do this. I tried for hours. Then, last night, all of a sudden, I could. I haven't told anyone yet. I wanted you to be the first.'

'It's a tremendous step forward, Dave. Just wonderful. Now you've got a heck of a lot of work to do.'

'I'm ready,' Scolari said.

Jessie sailed through the rest of her rounds. When she arrived back at her office, just after eight, a plump, dowdy-looking woman in her fifties was seated outside in one of the waiting area chairs. It took several seconds before Jessie realized it was Alice Twitchell, one of Gilbride's office staff. 'Quiet,' 'competent,' 'colorless,' 'proper' were the words she had always brought to Jessie's mind.

'Hi,' Alice said somewhat sheepishly. 'I guess I'm on loan to you from Dr. Gilbride.'

*Now what?*

Jessie unlocked her door and motioned the woman inside.

'You're on *loan* to me?'

'Dr. Gilbride said that for a while, you were going to help him out screening referrals and handling some of the calls.'

'He told you that?'

'He did. In fact, here are some messages and memos to get you started.'

Alice handed over a stack of papers.

'I don't believe this,' Jessie couldn't keep herself from saying. 'I just don't believe this. Exactly where are you supposed to work?'

Alice shifted uncomfortably, but held her place.

'Dr. Lacy's on vacation for two weeks,' she said. 'For now, I'm to be across the hall in his office. The phone people will be here in just a few minutes to add a line to your phone and hook me up with you. Dr. Copeland, I can see you're upset. I'm sorry. This wasn't my idea.'

'I know, Alice. I know. It's just that I was already working twenty-six-hour days. I don't know what more he expects me to do.'

But Jessie did know precisely what Gilbride expected

her to do – everything that got in the way of his next press conference or television appearance. She could go to him, ask why she was getting the secretary and the extra work, and why not one of the other surgeons, but there was no reason to bother. Gilbride would have some disparaging remark about each of the others' ability to get organized and get things done, sandwiched around some smarmy praise for her. No, he would say, Jessie was the logical choice – the *only* choice to keep the place moving while he was doing what had to be done. He would be sure to mention teamwork a dozen or so times, and dress it up with reminders of her intimate knowledge of ARTIE, as well as of her impending accelerated promotion. Gilbride was a total jerk, but he was also a damn sly one. Jessie glanced at the first memo.

'Here, Alice,' she said, resigned, 'write a letter to these people thanking them for the donation to the department that they dropped off in Marci's name, and also for their note. Assure them that the money will go directly to neurosurgical research.'

'Thank you, Doctor,' Alice said.

Chaos.

The referral calls started at nine and continued unabated for the rest of the day. Pennsylvania, Utah, Canada, London. Private doctors, individuals, even other neurosurgeons. Several frantic patients simply showed up at the hospital, begging for Gilbride's evaluation. Almost all of them had significant disease. Apparently, Gilbride had also given Jessie's name to the hospital public relations people. Reporters for a number of lesser-light publications and broadcasting stations were being patched up to her for comment.

Midway through the day, Gilbride called. By that time, Jessie's clinic appointment book was filled for weeks, and she had actually begun to book some of those patients in to her surgical schedule before seeing them in order to hold the OR time, anticipating that she would agree with their referring physician that surgery was necessary.

'So, Jessie,' Gilbride said cheerfully, 'I'm down here at Channel Four, getting set for their call-in show. How goes it?'

'How do you *think* it goes, Carl?'

'I spoke to Alice. She says you're doing fine, and that the cases are rolling in.'

'Oh, they're rolling in, all right. We're very busy. But then again, we were busy before all this started. Carl, these people want you, not me.'

'But Alice says you've been scheduling them for yourself.'

'Some of them. Some just hang up when I tell them you're not available.'

'I hope none of those hang-ups were HCs.'

'HCs?'

'Highly connecteds. You know, senators, big businessmen, celebrities, foreign diplomats – the kind of people who can pump prestige into a program like ours just by walking through the doors.'

Jessie felt nauseated and had to remind herself for the thousandth time that nothing she could ever say or do was going to change Carl Gilbride.

'You mean like Marci,' she said.

'Precisely. Those are the ones who need to be referred directly to me. Teamwork.'

'Yeah, sure, teamwork.'

Gilbride simply steamrolled over her sarcasm.

'What about that guy from the MacIntosh Foundation?' he asked. 'Any word from him?'

'Not yet.'

'Well, let me know as soon as you hear anything about that.'

'Three million. I remember. Carl, I can do this for a little while, but not indefinitely.'

'I assure you, once Marci's out of the hospital, all this will begin to die down.'

'I certainly hope so.'

'Remember, HCs should be referred to my office right away. Alice is doing her best to work them into my schedule as quickly as possible.'

'HCs to CG,' Jessie said acidly. 'I just noted it down.'

Following the agency attempt to ambush him in his apartment, Alex stopped going anywhere unarmed – opting for his .38 revolver holstered beneath his left pant leg. It was ten o'clock, and as he had done the evening before, he had left his assigned area to wander through Surgical Seven, taking note of any new patients and targeting any male between thirty and fifty-five for further investigation and observation. This time, though, he had a guide. Jessie Copeland had met him in the cafeteria for the second evening in a row, but they had been together for less than ten minutes when she was called back to the floor to check on a patient. Unaware that he had already been there several times, she had invited him to come along to get a first-hand look at where she worked and what she did.

While she was in with her patient, Bishop wandered down the hall a few doors, glancing into the rooms. The hospital computer had already told him that there were currently forty-four patients on the neurosurgical service – only seven of them possibles. After a brief check, he was fairly certain that none of them was Malloche. Still, he managed to obtain fingerprints from the rooms of five of the men to send to Paris. Interpol had two sets of prints on file they felt might be Malloche's. With Malloche it was always *might be*.

Jessie came out of room 713 and hurried down to him. She wasn't exactly a knockout, he was thinking, but she was certainly good looking in a bookish sort of way, even when she was harried and overtired, which seemed to be most of the time. It bothered Bishop to have lied to her about himself, but in truth, not that much. In his job, the ability to lie seamlessly was a survival skill – one he had perfected over years of practice. When he had his man, he would set things straight with her. Meanwhile, he had no intention of trusting her or anyone else any more than he had to.

It made things easier that she seemed attracted to him.

The more they talked, the more he learned about Gilbride and the rest of the service. Perhaps under other circumstances, he would have been open to exploring the possibilities between the two of them. But this wasn't other circumstances. He had bet the ranch on nothing more than a hunch, and he had less than two weeks to amend five years of failure. If he was wrong about Malloche coming to EMMC, or if the Mist eluded him in some way, not even a surgeon like Jessie Copeland would be able to put Humpty together again.

'Hi,' she said. 'Sorry to take so long.'

'No problem.'

'Actually, there is. The guy I just went over needs a spinal tap, and he's got so much arthritis in his spine that the resident just can't get the needle into the right space.'

'So you're going to do it?'

'I'm going to try. From the time I was a medical student, no matter what happened in the hospital, I could always look over my shoulder and know there was someone with more experience watching out for me. Now that I'm the attending surgeon, when I look over my shoulder, no one's there.'

'I think I'd faint.'

'I doubt it. You don't look like a fainter. Besides, I don't think you made it through the Marines by passing out.'

'Actually, you're right. I hold it all in and then get sick later when no one's around. Listen, you just go ahead and tap that guy's spine. I'd better get back on my loop or I'll get sacked before I even get my first paycheck.'

'It was great talking with you again, even if it was just for a little while. You're kind of funny. I like that in a security guard.'

Bishop sensed she wanted plans to be made for them to see each other again, but she had already gone more than halfway in that regard.

'So what do you think?' he asked. 'Would you like to try and get together outside the hospital sometime?'

'Wait. You mean there's an "outside the hospital"?'

'I can prove it.'

'Then let's. The night after tomorrow is a definite possibility for me.'

'Oops, I'm on the schedule. How about the night after that?'

'Um, I'm on call.'

'Lunch. Lunch tomorrow,' he said.

'Maybe. Just call first. Gilbride's celebrity has come at a price, only I'm the one who's paying it. This dating stuff is easy, huh?'

'Don't worry. Not much that's worthwhile is.'

Bishop left the neurosurgical floor and headed down the long corridor past Jessie's office and the others. There was something about her that unsettled him. Maybe it was her unassuming confidence, maybe her eyes and the way she smiled at him. In spite of himself, he knew he was wondering what it would feel like to hold her. His love life over the five years he had been after Malloche had consisted of nothing more intense than scattered one-night stands, some with professionals. That was the way he wanted it. Not once over that time had he become emotionally entangled with a woman. Jessie Copeland was one to beware of.

Distracted, he hurried around the corner, and nearly collided with an elderly, stoop-shouldered janitor who was mopping the floor outside Carl Gilbride's office.

'Oh, excuse me,' he muttered, barely looking at the man as he passed.

'Have a good night, Officer,' the old man said.

Claude Malloche, his hair and fake mustache snow white, continued his mopping until he was certain the security guard was gone. Then he pulled a device from his pocket, opened the door to Gilbride's suite in less than fifteen seconds, and dragged his mop and bucket inside. Quickly, he crossed the receptionist's office, entered Gilbride's, and closed the door behind him. The high-powered light and camera he took from his pocket were espionage quality. He spread out all the papers on Gilbride's desk and rapidly photographed each one. Next he turned to the file cabinet.

Twenty minutes and three rolls of film later, Malloche was back in the hallway, humming the melody of a French folk tune as he nonchalantly worked his way toward the exit.

# Chapter 12

It seemed hardly possible to Jessie, but over the next few days, life for her at the hospital became even more hectic and exhausting. In addition to her thirteen inpatients, she was covering Gilbride's large service as well, while the chief continued to stump for publicity, new patients, and grant money like a manic politician. More than once, Jessie had to rein in her anger by remembering that harboring resentment was like drinking poison and then waiting for the other guy to die.

In the office, the calls, referrals, inquiries, letters, donations, and requests for interviews, personal appearances, and patient appointments made life a whirlwind, second-to-second affair. Even Gilbride's unflappable secretary Alice Twitchell seemed to be fraying at the edges.

Then there were Jessie's inpatients. She visited Sara in the NICU three or four times a day. Although Sara remained comatose, she *was* breathing on her own and showing other very soft signs that the coma was getting lighter. Not exactly startling improvement, but certainly no setback either. Jessie had resigned herself to being encouraged by anything even slightly positive. But she also knew her objectivity in Sara's case had flown south. It was wrenching to see the expressions on Barry's and the kids' faces as they tried to come to grips with the reality that this might be all they got back of their wife and mother.

Dave Scolari was a different story. He was moving both arms fairly easily now, and even showing some action in his legs. Jessie's quadriplegic patient, Luis Velasco, had become something of a fixture in Dave's room – a cheerleader who saw in the linebacker the chance for a level of recovery that he, himself, would never be able to achieve.

After more than a week, Elsa Davidoff had finally managed a bowel movement and had been shipped off to a rehab center. Jessie wondered what the insurance utilization review people would say when they got a look at the reason for six additional hospital days. Actually, she didn't care whether the UR people approved or not. If nothing else, she was striking a blow for pre-managed-care kindness and patients' rights by honoring the elderly woman's demand that she not be sent out to rehab until her colon had proven it could function.

Marci Sheprow was out of the NICU and, in fact, only a day or two from being out of the hospital altogether. Her family and Gilbride held twice-daily press conferences in the hospital auditorium, and late this afternoon, Marci herself would be wheeled down to participate for the first time.

Jessie had tried to take advantage of the gymnast's celebrity by wheeling her into Tamika Bing's room. Marci was charming and patient, but her visit evoked nothing from the mute teenager. Tamika, her laptop still open but untouched on her tray table, looked as if she knew who her visitor was, but she reacted no more than that. Soon, the utilization folks would be nipping at the department's heels about her hospitalization, and plans would have to be made for her discharge. Jessie was pulling out all the stops to keep her as an inpatient because the therapists and psychiatrist were still hopeful and still pushing. She knew there was no way she would get approval to cover an in-hospital stay at a rehab center, and it was certain Tamika's mother, who was holding down a factory job, wouldn't be able to take her for daily outpatient therapy.

Alex Bishop continued to be a pleasurable island in the madness. Although they had yet to manage any extended time together outside the hospital, they had walked around the neighborhood for half an hour last night, and he had visited her on Surgical Seven a number of times. He continued to be a source of little surprises, including a

97

better than passing knowledge of opera and, once she had given him instructions and turned over her Game Boy, a deft hand at Tetris. With her demanding on-call schedule, and his assignment to the evening shift, she feared they might be doomed to an unending in-hospital courtship. The drastic initial measure she opted for was to meet him tomorrow at noon in the North End – Little Italy – for lunch and two hours of strolling the shops and uninterrupted conversation. If the neurosurgical service managed to survive when she was tied up in emergency surgery, it could manage while she was tied up in veal scallopini.

Jessie's aneurysm case, which she had done in the regular neurosurgical OR, had gone beautifully, but in the MRI-OR, the post-Marci deluge of patients had intensified an already existing problem – no available time. Marci's three-and-a-half-hour case notwithstanding, the usual MRI-guided operation took anywhere from five to seven hours. Adding prep and clean-up time, that meant each of the two specially trained teams could do one case a day. A third team could be assembled from parts of the other two when absolutely necessary, but to try to do more than two cases a day was to ask for burnout and shaky judgment from the staff.

Already, the MRI-OR schedule was booked solid for more than three weeks. A number of those cases were appropriate for ARTIE, although Jessie was still uncertain whether she or the robot were ready. Patients with brain tumors were being reassured, as much as Jessie and Emily could justify that waiting around at home for a few weeks would not lessen their chances of a successful operation . . . unless, of course, there was a sudden complication like bleeding into the tumor or rapid pressure buildup from the unanticipated obstruction of spinal fluid flow.

Although Jessie did most of the preliminary patient evaluations, a number of the MRI cases were going to be Gilbride's – all of them high visibility. Some of the new patients Gilbride dashed by and met on the fly, while the more important ones he would see in an evening office session. The lowest-level HCs he would not meet in person until they had been checked into the hospital the morning of their operation. Jessie knew that at this pace, with all Gilbride's distractions and his marginal surgical skills, disaster was just a cut away.

It was six in the evening when the intensity of the day finally began to ebb. There were enough patients for Jessie still to see, and enough paperwork to catch up on, to keep her in the hospital until ten, but the way things had been going since *the* operation, home by ten-thirty was tantamount to a vacation day. Her first stop would be the NICU to check on her post-op aneurysm patient, and also on Sara. Not surprisingly, though, before she could leave her office, the phone was ringing again. Also, not surprisingly, the caller was her department chief with more work for her.

'Jessie, hi,' he began. 'Sorry to be calling you so late about this, but I'm in the middle of taping *Talk of the City* for Channel Five, and I didn't check in for messages until a few minutes ago.'

'That's okay,' Jessie replied dully. 'What do you need?'

'Do you remember me reading you a cable from a guy named Tolliver at the MacIntosh Foundation?'

'Yes, I remember. It's hard to forget three million dollars.'

'Well, I just got word that he's coming to check out our setup personally.'

'That's terrific,' Jessie responded with little enthusiasm. She sensed what was coming next.

'There's just one problem. I've been invited to do a phone interview on the *Imus in the Morning* radio show at nine tomorrow, then I'm meeting with the hospital administration to discuss some extra lab space for the department. So I've arranged to have Tolliver contact you when he arrives at the hospital. Just show him around and be your usual charming self. Whatever he wants to see or do is fine.'

'But –'

'Take him out somewhere for lunch if I'm not back.

Maybe that Sandpiper place. Just turn in your expenses to Alice and the department'll take care of reimbursing you. She's a real peach, isn't she? Listen, the producer's waving at me for something. I've got to go. Keep up the good work, Jess. Three million will buy a helluva lot of research.'

Before Jessie could insert a word, she was listening to a dial tone.

'All bleeding eventually stops,' she muttered, picturing Alex Bishop marching off into the sunset with a plate of veal scallopini. 'All bleeding eventually stops.'

Jessie's post-op aneurysm patient, a thirty-eight-year-old, high-powered businessman named Gary Garrison, was awake and lucid.

'Any stock tips?' she asked.

'McNeil. They make Tylenol. If this headache of mine doesn't let up soon, I'm going to push their stock up all by myself.'

Jessie had him describe the pain and location. Then she checked his neurologic status and used an ophthalmoscope to examine the arteries, veins, and optic nerves on the back surface of his retinas, searching for the changes that warned of brain swelling.

'Not serious,' she proclaimed, finally. 'Between your initial hemorrhage and what I did in getting that artery clipped, the structures in your skull have had quite a bit of trauma. They're allowed to hurt. One more day, I suspect, and you'll start to feel much better. Feel like leaving the unit?'

'Not really.'

'Good enough. That's all I have to hear. I'll explain things to your HMO in a way they'll understand.'

'You're the best, Doc.'

Jessie wrote out some orders and passed them to one of the nurses. Then she headed into Sara's room. A candy striper stood at the bedside, massaging cream into Sara's hands. The volunteer, whom Jessie had never seen on Surgical Seven before, was a waif-like brunette, maybe in her late teens, with wide, dark eyes and close-cropped hair.

'Hi,' said Jessie, startling the girl, who was engrossed in

her work. 'I'm Dr. Copeland.'

'Oh . . . hi. I'm Lisa. I just started here.'

'Welcome to Oz. It looks like you've caught on quickly. I'm sure Sara appreciates the hand massage.'

'Thank you. I did a lot of volunteer work in hospitals when I was in high school. Now, I'm taking a semester off from college, but I wanted to do something that mattered while I was figuring out what comes next.'

'I thought you looked a little old to be a candy striper.'

'My mother says I'm a little old to be taking time off from college,' the girl said, grinning.

'Hey, I'm a neurosurgeon, and I *still* don't know what I want to do when I grow up. Have you thought about medicine?'

Lisa blushed.

'I . . . I don't do very well in the sciences,' she said. 'I'm considering working with kids – probably because I think I'm destined to always look like one. Do you want me to leave?'

'No. Of course not. I want you to keep at it. Sara Devereau is very important to me. And I believe that things like hand massages play a significant role in a patient's recovery. I'll be back a little later. Thanks for what you're doing here.'

'Thanks for talking with me,' Lisa said. 'Most of the doctors I've dealt with seem too stressed to stop and talk to anyone.'

# Chapter 13

Late the next morning, Eastman Tolliver, the three-million-dollar man, arrived at Eastern Mass Medical on schedule. Jessie had returned to the hospital at six feeling irritable and frustrated. Instead of spending a few relaxing hours away from the hospital with the first man in whom she had been interested in a couple of years, she would be baby-sitting a foundation bureaucrat.

Gradually, though, as it usually did, her practice lifted her spirits. Her patients were all improving, or at least were no worse. Sara, though still unconscious, continued to show signs that her coma was becoming lighter. Shortly after rounds, Jessie successfully revised a spinal fluid drainage shunt in a long-term tumor patient – a nice procedure when it went well, simple and life-saving. And finally, Marci Sheprow had gone home, and with her went the stress of avoiding eye contact with her mother. The fallout from her surgery would go on indefinitely, but at least that chapter was closed.

Jessie had expected the worst from her job as escort to Tolliver. In fact, their time together proved a most pleasant surprise. He was distinguished looking, with dark, intelligent eyes, hair graying at the temples, sharply cut features, and perhaps ten pounds of excess weight. In addition, he was charming, urbane, and intelligent, and best of all, a seasoned bridge player.

Over crab Louis at the Sandpiper, they talked about the game, about his six years as executive director of the MacIntosh foundation, and of course about ARTIE and Carl Gilbride. In what seemed like only minutes, an hour and a half had flashed by. During that time, Jessie had used her cell phone to answer a half dozen pages, the last few dealing with the burgeoning group in her waiting area.

'It's really enjoyable talking with you,' she said, 'but I'm afraid that if I don't show up at my office soon, the patients waiting for me are going to unionize. What time this afternoon will you be meeting Carl?'

Tolliver absently twisted his thin gold wedding band and looked at her strangely.

'I assumed you knew,' he said.

'Knew what?'

'I spoke with Dr. Gilbride by phone this morning shortly after I arrived at the hospital. Apparently last night he was invited to be on the *Today* show tomorrow morning. He's leaving directly from his commitment at the medical center and flying down to New York to meet with the producers. He'll be back at noon, right after the show. Meanwhile, you were right there to wine and dine me as he promised, and as you have done most charmingly.'

'I . . . I'm really sorry I didn't know,' she said. 'And did he say I would be your hostess until he gets back?'

Tolliver's expression suggested he was used to the conflicts and spur-of-the-moment schedule changes that accompanied dealings with highly successful people.

'He did say something like that,' he replied, 'yes.'

'Eastman, I'm a little embarrassed. I would have loved to have spent the afternoon and evening with you, showed you some of the city, or even played some bridge. But I'm on in-house call tonight.'

'Actually, as I told Dr. Gilbride, I have no problem starting the formal part of my visit tomorrow, because I really could use a bit of rest and relaxation. Maybe I'll stop back this evening and follow you around. But most likely I'll see you in the morning after I watch Dr. Gilbride on television.'

'Either way would be fine.'

Jessie said the words sensing that she wasn't being perfectly honest. She really did prefer he stay at his hotel tonight rather than come back to the hospital to follow her around. Alex's shift would be starting at three.

'Are you sure you'll be all right?' she asked. 'For obvious

reasons, I can't have you in to see patients. But you can wait in the lab with our robotics technician until I'm done. After that I'll be happy to show you around the hospital.'

'I promise you I am very resourceful. Besides, I came to the hospital straight from the airport. I'd like to check in at the bed-and-breakfast where I'll be staying.'

'Not a hotel?'

'Wherever possible, I prefer to have the foundation's funds go toward medical research. Besides, this place comes highly recommended by our travel people. I have been promised that it is warm and charmingly decorated.'

'Where is it?'

Tolliver referred to a sheet in his jacket pocket.

'Hereford Street. They said it was walking distance from the hospital.'

'Only if you really love to walk. It's in the Back Bay, not far from where I live. With luggage, I'd suggest a cab; without luggage, good shoes.'

'A cab it will be. I have been told that this B-and-B has a small but well-equipped exercise room. I think I shall avail myself of it this afternoon. Looking fifty in the eye is powerful motivation.'

'Exercise . . . exercise. I vaguely remember once knowing what that was. I'm jealous.'

They walked the three blocks back to the hospital.

'Well, thank you,' Tolliver said after retrieving his bag from Jessie's office. 'I believe I'm going to enjoy my days here. And I hope Carl Gilbride knows what a jewel he has in you.'

'Oh, he tells me all the time,' Jessie replied.

When Jessie had finally finished seeing the last of her patients, Alice Twitchell brought in yet another stack of messages, hospital charts, and other Carl Gilbride-generated flotsam.

Jessie flipped through the pile.

'Lord,' she said. 'There's a couple of hours' worth of work right here. Well, at least I'm through with the outpatients.'

Alice grinned at her sheepishly.

'I'm afraid I have to tell you that there is one more patient for you to see. He and his wife have been here for almost two hours. His name is Rolf Hermann. He's a count or something from Germany, and he has a brain tumor. Apparently his wife spoke with Dr. Gilbride by phone. Now they're camped outside his office, and she's insisting that they're not moving until they see him. Dr. Copeland, he's staying over in New York tonight.'

'I know. Goodness, a German count. Talk about your HCs.'

'Pardon?'

'Nothing. Nothing. Listen, you go ahead and get a TV moved up to your office so we can watch the boss tomorrow morning. I'll go talk to the Count.'

'He's an impressive man. And his wife is very beautiful.'

'Thanks for the info. Dr. Gilbride didn't say anything at all about this fellow to you?'

'No. As you know, he's been forgetting to mention a lot of things lately.'

*Kill!*

'Well, take the rest of the day off as soon as you can, Alice,' Jessie said sweetly. 'I'll see you in the morning.'

While Jessie and the other surgeons in the department used the Harvard chairs lining the corridor as their waiting area, Gilbride had an anteroom of his own – a walnut-paneled, leather-furnished space across from his equally elegant office. The Count and his wife looked born to be in rooms as richly appointed. Seated across from them were two men and a woman in their late twenties, each of them trim, athletic, and dressed expensively. They were presented by Hermann's wife as the Count's sons and daughter – not her children, Jessie noted, but his. None of them stood to greet her.

Rolf Hermann, powerfully built, could have been forty but, judging by his children's ages, was at least ten years older than that. He was square-jawed and craggy, with thick, jet black hair, pomaded straight back. He shook hands with Jessie and greeted her in heavily accented

English. His wife, who introduced herself as Countess Orlis Hermann, was stunning. In her early forties, perhaps even younger, she had a high fashion model's bearing and figure. Her fine porcelain face was perfectly offset by straight sun-blond hair, artistically cut just above her shoulders. Her beige suit almost certainly owed its existence to some exclusive designer. From the first moment of their meeting, the Countess's pale blue eyes remained fixed on Jessie's like a magnet, leaving no doubt in Jessie that this was a woman accustomed to having life go her way.

'Well,' Jessie began, clearing her throat, 'it's very nice to meet you both. I'm . . . an assistant professor of neurosurgery here at Eastern Mass Medical.'

'That's very nice,' Orlis said in fluent English, much less accented than her husband's, 'but we came to see Dr. Gilbride. I'm afraid an assistant *anything* just won't do.'

Rolf stopped her with a raised hand and spoke to her forcefully in German. Orlis calmed visibly.

'I'm sorry,' Jessie said, 'but Dr. Gilbride is in New York until tomorrow afternoon.'

'But that's impossible,' Orlis said. 'He said we should come today.' She held up an envelope of X rays. 'My husband has a tumor in his head. Dr. Gilbride said he would remove it.'

Jessie could tell from the Count's expression that he was taking in every word.

'In that case,' she said, 'I'm certain he will. But until tomorrow, he's two hundred miles away.'

'This is just not acceptable.'

Clearly the calming effect of the Count's words had already worn off.

'Countess Hermann,' Jessie said, 'for the past week Dr. Gilbride has been extremely busy. For the same reason you heard of him all the way across the Atlantic, so have others from all over the world, many of them very seriously ill. I have been helping with the initial evaluation and scheduling of most of these new patients. I will be happy to do the same for your husband. But not here in the waiting room.'

This time, Rolf Hermann leaned over and spoke softly into his wife's ear. He squeezed her hand, completely enveloping it in his massive paw.

Orlis's lips tightened. Finally, she nodded and passed the X rays over.

'Where do you want us to go?' she asked.

'My office can hold the three of us,' Jessie replied. 'Your family would best wait here, or else in the chairs in the hallway just outside my office.'

Orlis gave the orders in German, and the Count's children nodded.

'They will come to your office,' she said. 'They and their father are very close. They are very concerned about him.'

Jessie led the entourage down the hall. Rolf Hermann walked rigidly upright with determined strides, although there was, Jessie noted, the slightest hitch in his right leg. She left the younger Hermanns in the corridor and motioned the couple to the two chairs by her desk. Orlis evaluated the space disdainfully, hut finally took her seat.

'My husband understands English perfectly,' she said, 'and he can speak it, although not as well as I. For that reason he has asked me to tell you his story.'

'That's fine, as long as you know, Count, to speak up at any time. This is no school exam or contest here. It is your health. I promise you will not be graded on your English.'

For the first time, the Count's smile held genuine warmth.

'Thank you very much,' he said carefully. 'Orlis, please.'

'Two and a half months ago,' she began, 'my husband had a fit – a shaking all over during which he soiled himself and became unconscious. What do you call that?'

'A seizure.'

'He had a seizure. We took him to our doctor; and he ordered those X rays.'

Jessie placed two of the MRI films onto the fluorescent view boxes on the wall to her right. The dense tumor, almost certainly a rather large subfrontal meningioma, glowed obscenely amid the much darker normal brain tissue. The location was dangerous, and the shape of the tumor suggested that it was the type of meningioma that was poorly contained, with extensions infiltrating the brain tissue surrounding it. An ARTIE tumor if ever there was one.

'The tumor is right here,' Jessie said, pointing it out.

'Yes, we know. Our doctor referred us to a brain surgeon, but he gave us no confidence that he could remove my husband's tumor without causing a good deal of damage. Our doctor then suggested we search for a surgeon in London or in the United States. We were in the process of doing that, and already had Dr. Gilbride's name on a very short list of candidates, when he performed his miraculous operation on that young gymnast.'

'I see. Well, I'm sure Dr. Gilbride can help you. But you must know that surgery such as this is risky. Parts of the tumor are situated right alongside normal brain tissue. The dissection is extremely difficult. There may well be residual neurologic deficits.'

'We would prefer to speak with Dr. Gilbride about that.'

Jessie felt overwhelming gratitude that the Count would not be her patient.

'Very well,' she said. 'He should be back sometime tomorrow afternoon. You can come back then.'

'Excuse me, Dr. Copeland, but we have traveled a long way, and we have no intention of leaving this hospital.'

'But –'

'My husband has had two seizures. If he has another, I want him here. We intend to pay in cash, so we will have no problem with your insurance or your health care system. I will be happy to leave enough money with your hospital administrator in advance to cover all the expenses of our stay, including my husband's surgery.'

'Mrs. Hermann, I don't know if we can do this.'

''Then I suggest you speak to the director of your hospital. I will be happy to speak to him as well.'

'I guess I'd better do that.'

Jessie went down the hall to Alice Twitchell's temporary office, and was rather easily able to reach Richard Marcus, the hospital president. A few minutes later, she was back in

108

her office. Marcus had confirmed what she already knew – running a hospital was all about money.

'The president of the hospital will be happy to meet with you in his office. We have a private room available on Surgical Seven, the neurosurgical floor.'

'Actually, we will need two. The Count's children plan to stay near him as long as he is in the hospital. I assure you they will make it their business to be in nobody's way. We will pay whatever rate you charge.'

Jessie knew better than to argue, and it was clear from the way the Count held his arms tightly folded across his chest that he had no intention of intervening again.

'Countess,' Jessie said, 'if Dr. Marcus says it's okay, and we have the room, you get the room.'

'And private nurses.'

'We have agencies that can provide you with that. The head nurse on Surgical Seven will know how it's done. Anything else?'

'Yes. I wish to know when my husband's surgery will be performed.'

'Now *that* I absolutely cannot tell you. For one thing, that's Dr. Gilbride's decision. For another, our MRI-assisted neurosurgical suite is booked solid. It may be some time before your husband can be fitted into the schedule.'

Countess Orlis Hermann's smile was patronizing in the extreme. 'We shall see about that,' she said.


It was after seven when Jessie caught up with Alex in the cafeteria. He and another security guard were sitting together. She was about to head back to the floor when he spotted her and waved her to join them. Wanting not to seem too eager, she grabbed a salad, some chips, and a decaf, and stopped to say a few words to a resident she barely knew. By the time she ambled over to Alex's table, the other guard had left.

'I was going to call you to meet for dinner,' he said, 'but some guy went berserk in the ER, and Eldon and I had to deal with him. Then Eldon insisted we take our dinner break together.'

'Why did he leave?'

Alex's grin reminded her of Clint Eastwood's.

'I guess he left because I asked him to,' he said.

'Oh,' Jessie managed, hoping she looked more composed at that moment than she was feeling. 'Well . . . how's your day?'

'Actually, they've scheduled two too many guards on this shift, so it's been pretty light. They offered me the chance to go home.'

'And you didn't take it?'

'The choice was an empty apartment and a Mel Gibson video versus the chance to get together with you, *and* get paid for it.'

'Oh,' she said again. 'I like that you say what's on your mind.'

'That may be why I've never won any popularity contests. How's your day been?'

Jessie's beeper went off before she could answer. She glanced at the display.

'It's the ER,' she said. 'Hold that last question.'

In less than a minute she was back.

'Trouble?' Alex asked.

'Big-time. An eight-year-old boy's being brought into the ER by ambulance right now with a gunshot wound to the head.'

# Chapter 14

From the moment the call came from the rescue squad that they were on the way in with eight-year-old Jackie Terrell, the clock began ticking. Jessie and Alex left the cafeteria and raced to the ER.

'Mind if I come and watch you work if my supervisor okays it?' Alex asked.

'If it's okay with him, it's okay with me, so long as you don't expect any attention.'

'I'll go call him.'

Jessie had already instructed the ER nurse to mobilize the OR, CT scan people, and blood bank, and to locate the neurosurgical resident on call.

The twin dragons they would be battling for the child's life were tissue damage and blood loss. Either could be lethal. The rescue squad had reported heavy bleeding, typical of a gunshot wound to the organ in the body with the richest blood supply. As usual, the paramedics and emergency medical technicians had done their jobs well. Two IV lines were in, plasma volume expanders were running, and pressure was being applied to the obvious bleeding points. But to Jessie, the most important piece of information they had radioed in was that although the boy was unconscious, there had been some definite purposeful movement on his left side. In neurosurgery, movement meant hope. And hope demanded speed.

Throughout Jessie's training, there was an unofficial competition among the residents to see who could get a head trauma patient with an open skull fracture or gunshot wound through labs and CT and into the OR the fastest.

Anything over ten minutes from ER door to OR table was automatically disqualified from consideration.

The ER was bedlam on two fronts, neither of which had anything to do with Jackie Terrell. A full cardiac arrest was being worked on in the major medical room, and in one of the trauma rooms, the surgical residents were dealing with a stabbing victim. Jessie knew that what she needed most right now was an experienced nurse who knew her way around head trauma and around EMMC. What she got instead was a new grad named Larry Millei, eager to please but very green.

'Please page Emily DelGreco and get her down here right away' was Jessie's first order.

The neurosurgical resident on duty, Steven Santee, was in the ER when she arrived, preparing a stretcher for their case in one of the available trauma rooms. He wasn't the sharpest of his group of residents, and certainly was not the one she would have chosen to assist her on this case, but he was a damn hard worker.

'Don't bother, Steve,' she said. 'We're going right from the door to CT. Just keep bugging the lab. I want ten units of O-negative blood in the OR when we arrive. We'll use them until we get the kid cross-matched. It'll be your job to draw blood on him unless the rescue people did it when they started his lines.'

'They're two minutes out,' Larry Miller called down the hall. 'Emily said she'll meet you in the OR and will have everything ready when you get there. Anesthesia's on the way there, too. So are the nursing supervisor, a scrub nurse, and a circulating nurse. Do you want me to come with you?'

'With Emily meeting us, we may be okay. But then again, I may need another pair of hands.'

'Will I do?'

Jessie hadn't noticed that Alex had come into the ER. Now, she sized up the situation.

'You don't mind being a gofer for blood and instruments?'

'Hardly. You sure it's okay for me to help in the OR?'

112

'Hey, I'm the surgeon. It's okay if I say so. And you won't faint on me?'

'We already discussed that, remember?'

'Well, then, stick around. As soon as the kid gets here, we're going to CT. You be the motor for his stretcher. Steve and I will do the evaluation. Emily will make sure the OR's got everything we need, and do what she can with the lab.'

Santee, Larry Miller, Emily, and now Alex. A ragtag medical army if ever there was one – especially poised to battle such potent foes. But at least, as far as Jessie knew, there were no expanding egos on the team. Each of them would do whatever she needed – no questions asked, no improvising.

Jessie felt energized, but she had dealt with enough gunshots to be frightened as well.

'They're on the drive,' Larry Miller called out.

'Steve,' Jessie said, 'take a minute and get what history you can from the rescue squad, especially the caliber of that bullet. Alex, Larry, we get the stretcher and go. I want this kid in the OR within eight minutes.'

At that instant, the doors to the ER glided open and the battle began in earnest.

'Drive-by shooting,' an EMT said breathlessly, handing over their paperwork. 'We assume it was a handgun. The poor kid was just in the wrong place at the wrong time.'

'Thanks,' Jessie called out, as Alex took over at the rear of the litter. 'You can pick up your stretcher at CT. Just have someone follow us.'

There was a CT scanner that served the ER alone. In fifteen seconds, Jackie Robinson Terrell was on the table. Jessie's heart ached as she looked down at the naked child, spattered all over with his own blood. His body was as perfect as most eight-year-olds' – not an ounce of excess fat, muscles just beginning to become defined. His smooth, chocolate skin was unscarred. But the pressure dressing on his head was soaked through with crimson.

The entry wound, just behind the child's left ear, was in a bad spot, but it could have been even worse. An inch to the right, and it would have shattered the torcular – the bony ridge at the base of the skull that protected the confluence of the straight and sagittal sinuses, the largest blood-filled cavities in the brain. Had the torcular been hit that way, Jackie Terrell would still be on the sidewalk, covered from head to toe with a sheet, lying in a pool of his own blood. Now, at least, he had a chance.

'Poor little guy,' Jessie murmured as she checked his pupils for size and responsiveness to light. 'Poor baby. Larry, could you please go back to the ER and see where this child's parents are. If you find them in the next minute, bring them here. Otherwise, explain what's happening and bring them to the Surgical Eight waiting room. Then go save us an elevator in the Surgical Tower.' She turned to Lydia Stewart, the radiologist. 'Stew, give me just five cuts through the hemispheres and two through the posterior fossa, please. As soon as you're done, we're out of here, so please hurry.'

'What do you think?' Alex asked.

Jessie shook her head.

'I don't know. His pupils are still mid-sized. That's a good sign. But he's got no corneal reflex, and he's losing blood fast. He was probably just playing out there – maybe thinking about what he wanted for his birthday . . .'

She shook her head as if clearing it, then reached over and took two lead aprons from the wall, handing one to Alex.

'Is this necessary?' he asked.

'That depends on whether or not you think your gene pool is worth protecting. Listen, when we get to the OR, I want you to put on scrubs and stay on hand. We really are short-staffed and I may need you to run errands.'

Jessie held Jackie Terrell's little hand as the CT scanner whirred. Moments later, the radiologist called out that the views were on the screen. The pictures were grim. Fracture lines everywhere, a massive collection of clotting blood, and definite brain destruction. It was as if an egg had been dropped onto concrete from ten feet, but had somehow stayed together.

'We're out of here,' she said, motioning Alex to help her lift the boy onto a gurney.

They hurried through the hospital to the bank of elevators in the Surgical Tower. Larry Miller was there, holding the doors of one car open. Standing back a ways were a dozen or so curious onlookers, anxious to check out the emergency before going about their business. The three of them squeezed into the elevator with the gurney. For eight floors, Jessie's arm was pressed tightly against Alex's. As the doors parted, he briefly squeezed her hand.

'Good luck,' he said.

'This way, quickly,' she replied, racing to the front of the stretcher. 'The men's dressing room is right over there. Cap, mask, shoe covers, and scrubs.'

Jessie checked the time as she and Larry Miller exploded into OR-2 with Jackie Terrell. Almost nine minutes. Not a prizewinner, but good enough. Emily was there, scrubbed, gowned, and ready to begin prepping the child's scalp. The anesthesiologist, Byron Wong, stood by his instruments, set to slip in a breathing tube and connect his other highly sophisticated monitoring equipment. Ten units of uncrossmatched O-negative blood were arranged on a tray by his station. With almost no antibodies to the proteins in type A or type B blood, nor to the Rh factor protein, O-negative blood could be treated to absorb most of what antibodies *were* there, and then used for emergency transfusions until properly cross-matched blood could be obtained. Not optimum, but then nothing about this case was close to that.

As Jessie and Wong were transferring the child from the stretcher to the OR table, he suddenly cried out and flailed with his left hand, actually hitting Wong on the shoulder.

'Jesus,' Jessie said, 'he's moving. We've got a chance.'

Steve Santee poked his head in.

'Dr. Copeland, Jackie's mother is in the family room. His father is a bus driver. They're trying to locate him now.'

*Excuse me, Mr. Terrell, but we wonder if you could drive on over to Eastern Mass Medical. Your eight-year-old son has been shot in the head. . . .*

115

The notion made Jessie cringe.

'Get scrubbed, Steve,' she said. 'Emily, after he's intubated, get two units running. I want him left ear up. Do a quick prep, then stay next to me. Steve'll work across from us. I'm going to say a word to the boy's mom and then scrub. I want to make the incision in two minutes. Three tops.'

'You've got it,' Emily said.

Charlene Terrell, an expansive woman with a gentle face, was wringing her hands. An older woman, who introduced herself as a family friend, sat with an arm around her.

'We're going to operate in just a minute,' Jessie said after brief introductions. 'Jackie's been hurt very badly.'

'He's a wonderful boy,' Charlene sobbed. 'Please save him. He's our only child.'

'I'll do my best.'

'Thank you, Doctor. Oh, thank you so much.'

'One thing. Is he left- or right-handed?'

'Jackie? Oh, he's right-handed. You should see him throw a ball. He's only in third grade, but he already can play with the middle-school kids.'

'Thank you, Mrs. Terrell.'

*Grim.*

Jessie hurried to the prep room. At this point she had neither the time nor the inclination to go into any of the gunshot-wound details with her patient's mother. Until the operation was completed, there was nothing she could say that wouldn't make a very bad situation worse. Right-handed meant that most of the vital speech and movement centers were on the left side, precisely around the bullet's path. Tamika Bing's situation, only with right-sided motor deficits as well.

As she scrubbed, her concentration was almost exclusively on the child and on the surgical approach she was going to take. Almost. One corner of her mind was dominated by a spinning tangle of images – Alex Bishop, Carl Gilbride, Marci Sheprow, Sara Devereau, Tamika Bing, Eastman Tolliver, Orlis Hermann, and the Count, tossing about along with multiple reminders to herself that she wasn't the one who had pulled the trigger and shot the eight-year-old. Nor was she God. She was simply the one who was on call, and who was doing her best to save the child.

'You ready?'

Alex had come up from behind and was standing a few feet away.

'Ready as I'll ever be,' she replied. 'You can stand behind me to either side. There's a riser you can step up on to give you a better angle.'

'I'm praying for the kid,' Alex said.

Jessie's eyes locked on his.

'You keep on doing that,' she said. 'I never refuse help.'

The approach Jessie had settled on was pretty standard – a wide scalp flap around the entry wound, drill away as much bone as necessary, and then go for the large collection of congealing blood that the CT scan had located just above and behind Jackie's ear. Retrieving the bullet and working around the other fracture fragments would come later in the case. The child was anesthetized now, so there would be no more movement, no cries. But the team was driven by what they had seen.

*Quick but careful*, Jessie said over and over to herself. *Quick but careful.*

'He's losing a lot of blood,' Emily said. 'The rescue squad brought tubes in, so the lab has had a head start with the cross-match.'

'When do you think we'll have the blood?'

'Five minutes, no more.'

'Hang a couple more units of O-negative, Byron. Alex, could you please call the blood bank and find out how much longer?'

'Right away.'

Emily elbowed her friend.

'Nice helper,' she whispered.

Jessie glanced up at Steve Santee, who was engrossed in sectioning the persistent bleeding.

117

'Behave,' she shot hack, her voice shielded by the sound of the aspirator. 'That's it, Steve. Suck right here. We're doing fine.'

'They'll be ready in the blood bank in a minute,' Alex said, returning to his riser.

'Maddy,' Jessie said to the circulating nurse, 'this is Alex Bishop from security. He's also soon to be a physician's assistant student at Northeastern. Would you please take him with you to the blood bank and bring us back eight units.'

*Quick but careful.*

Around the bullet hole, the child's skull was like broken pottery. Jessie removed most of the shards and much of the clot, while Emily and Steve continued aspirating blood, keeping her field clean. The bullet had stopped short of crossing the midline, but had damaged a good deal of brain before it did.

*Jackie? Oh, he's right-handed. You should see him throw a ball.*

Alex and the circulator returned with the blood, and he again took his place on the riser.

Jessie forced herself to remember some of the miracles she had seen since entering neurosurgery – the patients who should have died, hut instead ended up living quite functional and rewarding lives. Meticulously, she picked off the bleeders, cauterizing them by running electric current through her bipolar forceps. Bit by painstaking bit, the ooze lessened. And as it did, the extent of the damage became clearer.

'Just keep up with blood loss, Byron,' Jessie said. 'It's still hard to predict, but I will say that I've seen worse.'

'You're doing an incredible job,' Emily said. 'Alex, I hope you have a good view of this, because you're never going to see a gunshot case handled better.'

This time Jessie threw the elbow. She knew Emily was saying things just to keep her from getting too tense, but she was beginning to regret having confessed her newly evolving connection with the man.

'Quit it!' she whispered.

'A little advertising never hurt,' Emily whispered back.

The bullet had entered at a slightly upward angle, shattered the inner table of the skull, and ricocheted to a halt just to the left of the midline. Jessie recovered it with ease, then began cleaning away tissue that was clearly damaged beyond healing.

*Maybe Jackie Robinson Terrell will throw again*, she was thinking at the moment the anesthesiologist said, 'Everything all right? I'm getting a drop in pressure.'

'I don't see –'

Jessie never finished the sentence. A sudden, continuous gush of dark, venous blood welled into the surgical field from beneath the posterior skull. Jessie's heart rate rocketed.

'The occiput *was* fractured!' she cried out. 'The torcular's torn.' The bone fragments over the network of vital blood vessels had been held together so tightly by the bleeding and swelling around them that the CT scan hadn't shown the fracture lines. 'Byron, pump in every ounce of blood you have and send for more! Steve, let's get the boy facedown immediately!'

'But the sterile field –'

'To hell with the sterile field! This child's going out!'

'I need him supine if I'm going to be of any help in keeping his pressure up,' the anesthesiologist said.

'Byron, he's got to be prone! If I can't get at this bleeding, nothing you do matters. Scalpel, please. Scalpel, dammit!'

Frantically, with no attempt at continued sterility, Jessie cut away the posterior portion of Jackie Terrell's scalp. The bone over the torcular was split down the middle, and blood was pouring out from the sinuses beneath it.

'Suck here, Steve! Em, you, too! Byron, we need more blood! Oh, Jesus!'

'The Doppler monitor on his chest is recording something,' Wong said. 'I think it's air in his heart.'

Jessie continued packing the bleeding area, but it was like trying to sandbag a waterfall.

'Pressure?' she asked.

'Forty. Jessie, there's definitely air being sucked into his circulatory system. His heart's filling with it.'

'Blood! We need volume!' Jessie ordered, unwilling yet to believe what she was hearing. 'Put the table in Trendelenburg position. Adjust it until he's not bleeding out or sucking in air!'

'Pressure zero,' Wong reported. 'The air embolism is huge now. Heart rate is dropping. . . . Flat line. We've got flat line.'

Jessie fought a few minutes more. Then she stared down at the blood, which continued to well up over her gloves but was now slightly frothy from the air that had been sucked through the damaged sinuses into the child's circulatory system.

'That's it,' she heard her voice say from a million miles away. 'There's no sense in continuing anymore.'

For a full minute, no one in the operating room moved. Then Jessie shook her head.

'I'm sorry, everyone,' she said hoarsely. 'I'm really sorry Each of you did a great job.'

Alone in her office, Jessie stared out her single window at a pair of swallows that had settled on her ledge. It had been hell telling Charlene Terrell that her son had died on the operating table. Hell trying to explain to her that what ultimately killed her child couldn't have been anticipated and couldn't have been fixed.

One of the things Jessie had come to accept as a neurosurgeon was that many of her patients would never he perfectly, or even reasonably, intact after their surgery. All that was available to those cases and their families was to move the goal markers of their lives – the expectations – and to start over from wherever they could. But this – the inhuman senselessness of Jackie Terrell's injury, the sudden, unforseeable catastrophe in the OR – this was more pain than she ever wanted from her specialty. Gilbride, Tamika Bing, then Sara, and now this. Maybe it was time to consider moving to the lab for a while. Or maybe it was time simply to realize that she didn't have the steel plating necessary to make it as a neurosurgeon. Lost in her thoughts, Jessie barely heard the gentle knock on her door.

'Yes, come in,' she said after clearing her throat.

Alex Bishop slipped in and closed the door behind him. 'Hi.'

'Hi, yourself.'

'I thought maybe you could use a little cheering up.'

'A little cheering up might elevate me to miserable.'

Except for Emily, there was no one in Jessie's world that she would want visiting her at this moment. Yet Alex Bishop, with his wonderful, troubled eyes, and his gentle voice, was a welcome sight.

'Your nurse told me there was no way anyone could have predicted that cracked bone when it didn't show on the CT scan,' he said. 'She told me you had saved that kid's life, but when you removed the clot you also released the pressure that was holding the pieces together, and the crack opened up.'

'I guess.'

'It was awful for all of us to go through. It must be ten times as hard for you.'

'Thanks for understanding that. I'll never get used to this sort of thing.'

'I hope you don't.'

She put her hands on his, then stood and let him hold her for a time.

'I'm glad you came up here,' she said.

# Chapter 15

Jessie spent a restless night in one of the tiny on-call rooms, rebreathing lungfuls of stale air and answering just enough phone calls to keep from reaching any deep, renewing sleep. She awoke for the last time at six, vaguely aware that she had been dreaming of Jackie Terrell racing through a brilliant, sunlit day over a carpet of emerald grass, chasing an endless succession of fly balls.

Throughout the evening, reporters had paged her to ask about the boy. They all were referred to the hospital's public relations people, who read or faxed them a statement she had helped to prepare. Undoubtedly, Eastern Mass Medical Center would be on the front pages for the second time in a week. This time, it was doubtful the item would stimulate any three-million-dollar grants.

Jessie showered, pulled on a fresh set of scrubs, and tried a brief meditation. Still, as she headed over to the cafeteria for her usual in-house fare – sesame bagel with sliced tomato and cream cheese, coffee, and a banana – she felt unprepared for another frenetic round of post-Sheprow neurosurgical clinic. The four physicians she joined in the doctors' dining room were engaged in what had become the standard, almost exclusive, mealtime conversation at the hospital – a can-you-top-this of managed care horror stories and jokes.

Generally, Jessie's zeal to make rounds on her patients and get her day going kept her from spending more than fifteen or twenty minutes with the breakfast crew. Today, although the stories and humor were as stale as the air in the on-call room, she couldn't pull herself away. She even tried out a joke she had recently heard about the managed care executive who died and went to heaven, only to find out God had limited him to a three-day stay. The polite reaction from the others told her they had already heard it.

Finally, at seven-fifteen, she paged Emily and met her on Surgical Seven for rounds. Their patients were reasonably stable. As Jessie anticipated, Gary Garrison's headaches had begun to abate. He was still frightened of a rebleed from his aneurysm, though, and jumped at her offer of one last day in the ICU. Dave Scolari's hands and arms were making remarkable progress, and his legs were showing encouraging strength as well. A miracle. They were heading out of Dave's room when Emily mentioned Jackie Terrell for the first time.

'Did you see the *Globe* this morning?' she asked.

'Nope.'

'They wrote about the heroic efforts of the doctors at Eastern Mass Medical.'

Jessie knew her friend well enough to leap ahead some steps.

'I'm okay about it, Em,' she said. 'Honest, I am. I'm not blaming myself for something even the radiologist couldn't see. It's just so damn sad, that's all.'

Emily put her arm around Jessie's shoulder.

'I know, pal. I know it is. I went home last night and demanded that my kids turn off the tube and snuggle up with me on the couch for half an hour.'

'Good move. They're great guys.'

'Speaking of guys . . .'

Jessie smiled coyly and shrugged.

'Dunno,' she said.

'You do, too. I can see it all over your face. Did he come to see you after the case?'

'Maybe.'

'Ohmagosh, you really are bit, and it sounds like he might be, too. I think that's great.'

'We'll see. Look, I'm sorry for being in such a testy mood this morning. Gulbride's off being famous again, so I'm facing another crazy day in outpatient. It's like he opened this dam of referrals and then just swam away.'

They turned in to the next patient's room, a tumor case of Gilbride's. Jessie was surprised to see Lisa Brandon, the candy striper who had been with Sara, seated at the bedside.

'Evening shift one day, day shift another,' Jessie said. 'Are you going for some sort of volunteer-of-the-year award?'

Lisa shifted uncomfortably.

'I hope it's all right that I'm here again. Actually, there isn't much for me to do at home, and I really like helping the patients.'

'In that case we're lucky to have you. Work all three shifts if you want. Why not? I do.'

Jessie introduced Lisa to Emily as a leader in the don't-know-what-to-do-when-I-grow-up club, and Emily proclaimed herself a founding mother of the organization.

'Cute kid,' Emily said after they had left the room.

'She's no kid. She's in her early twenties.'

'Have you looked at the birth date on your driver's license lately, honey? She's a kid.'

It was mid-afternoon. Jessie was in Carl Gilbride's office waiting for Eastman Tolliver to join the two of them for what would essentially be catch-up rounds for Gilbride on his patients. He had returned from New York City a short while ago in triumph – a full ten minutes on the *Today* show, followed by an interview with the *Times*, a hastily called grand rounds presentation at Columbia Presbyterian, and a lunch meeting with a robotics manufacturer interested in cutting some sort of deal for ARTIE. Now, after finally telling his secretary to hold all calls, he was shamelessly pumping Jessie for any information that would give him an edge in his quest for a three-million-dollar grant.

'So what do you make of this guy?' he asked.

'Carl, I only spent an hour or so with him yesterday. He's pleasant, and very interested in our program. That's all I can say. I expected he might come in for rounds this morning – I invited him – but he called and said he'd wait until you got back.'

'Did he seem angry I wasn't here?'

'Not really – at least not as far as I could tell. He seems very, I don't know, Californian. Sort of laid-back.'

'Surely he must understand that I would never have left him hanging except that this was all very important stuff.'

'Critical. How many times does a body ever get invited to be on the *Today* show?'

'Exactly. So, what's his background? What are his interests?'

'He hasn't been at the MacIntosh Foundation all that long – six years, I think he said. Before that he was a college professor of some sort.'

'He's bright, then?'

*Bright enough to see through you, I fear.*

'Yes, that was my impression.'

'Mine, too,' Gubride said. 'I think we should –'

Gilbride was interrupted by his secretary buzzing in with the announcement that Tolliver had arrived. The foundation director strode into the office and greeted them both with vigor.

'Dr. Copeland, I'm terribly sorry to hear of that child's death,' he said.

'Thank you,' Jessie replied, noting that her department chief hadn't mentioned a word about the case.

'I was in your cafeteria and heard some people talking about what a heroic job you did by even getting the boy to the operating room.'

Jessie sighed.

'The whole thing is very tragic.'

*Tragic.* The word seemed to galvanize Gilbride into action. It was as if he couldn't stand to let any negative connotation hang in the air.

'So, Eastman,' he said, clearing his throat for a transition, 'what do you think of what you've seen so far?'

Tolliver's expression flickered annoyance at Gilbride's inappropriate lack of subtlety. Jessie was as certain she saw the reaction as she was that her chief hadn't.

'So far, so good,' he said. 'But I'm still anxious to learn more about ARTIE, and to watch him in action.'

'Well, I can't say that I blame you,' Gilbride said. 'I believe we are seeing the future of neurosurgery – perhaps even of all surgery – in our little robot.'

'Have you experienced any problems with the device?'

'Some mechanical glitches, but nothing major.' – Unseen by either man, Jessie rolled her eyes. – 'Even though we're doing cases now with ARTIE,' Gilbride went on, 'We're still working with him in the lab. The search for perfection isn't just the motto of our research unit, it's the rule. We see the next generation of the device being even smaller, more maneuverable, and more powerful than the one we're using. I believe it's no exaggeration to say that at some point, not that far down the road, the surgeon interface between the robot and the MRI may be eliminated altogether. The device could simply be inserted beneath the patient's skull and turned loose, as it were.'

'Sounds like something straight out of science fiction,' Tolliver said.

'So were Jules Verne's submarine and rocket to the moon,' Gilbride responded, now clearly on a roll. 'MRI-assisted surgery is merely in its infancy. The future is limitless.'

Jessie felt her gut knot. Just a short while ago, a mechanical malfunction had caused ARTIE to rip into the normal brain tissue of her cadaver-subject. Still, she knew better than to so much as mist on Gilbride's three-million-dollar parade – at least not until she was ready to start searching for a new position. If Gilbride wanted to compare himself as visionary with Jules Verne, so be it.

'Well,' Tolliver said, 'you certainly make a good case for your invention. However, before I return to California, I would hope to see this ARTIE perform an actual operation. Is that possible?'

Gilbride's bluff had been called. Not surprisingly to Jessie, Eastman Tolliver had no intention of buying a pig in a poke. If the MacIntosh Foundation was going to lay heavy money on a device, he wanted to see it in action. Jessie knew what was coming next.

'So, Jessie,' Gilbride said, turning to her, 'you have my

OR schedule. Are there any cases appropriate for ARTIE?'

*No, Carl. As a matter of fact, at this stage of the game, there are no cases anywhere that are appropriate for ARTIE.*

'Actually, Emily has the OR schedule. We'll be meeting her in the ICU. You can decide for yourself once you've gone over it and met your new patients.'

'And I shall.' Once again Carl cleared his throat, signaling he was about to transition. 'So, then, shall we make our way to the ICU?'

Rounds began smoothly enough, with Gilbride at his bombastic best, leading an entourage that included Jessie, Emily, two other nurses, two medical students, two residents, and the foundation director on a leisurely patient-by-patient tour – first of the unit, then of the rest of the floor.

By and large, Gilbride's patients were docile and seemed happy to have their surgeon back and grateful he had stopped in to see them. There were, however, three of the sharper ones who made snide or angry remarks about his lack of involvement in their cases. Jessie wasn't certain whether the cynicism was ignored by Gilbride or simply went over his head. But the jab of one elderly patient, Clara Gittleson, clearly hit home.

'Dr. Gilbride,' she said crisply, 'I have to tell you that I never knew how little attention you were paying to me until Dr. Copeland and Emily started coming around.'

Gilbride mumbled something that might have been an apology. A nerve twitched at the corner of his mouth. He asked Jessie a number of questions about the woman's post-op mental status. Finally, he suggested that a psych consult might be in order to deal with what was obviously a combination of depression and reaction to post-op medications. Jessie glanced over at Tolliver, who seemed unaffected by the exchange but remained steadily focused on Gilbride.

As they headed for the next room – Rolf Hermann's – Jessie lagged back and subtly motioned for Emily to join her.

'Have you been in to see Orlis yet?' she whispered.

'Dragon Lady? Oh, yes. I stopped by a few hours ago while I was checking to make sure everything was in place for the emperor's return. She wanted to see me about as much as she wants to see a zit on that perfect face of hers.' Emily adopted a passable German accent and added, 'I vish only to speak viz Ducktor Geelbride.'

'Well, Orlis, be careful what you wish for. You just might get it.'

'I can hardly wait.'

'Dr. Copeland,' Gilbride called out from outside the door, 'would you mind terribly continuing on rounds with us?'

Jessie hurried up to the group, presenting the next patient as she arrived.

'Count Rolf Hermann is a fifty-three-year-old married German man, the father of three, who was perfectly healthy until he experienced the first of two seizures about six weeks ago. Evaluation in Europe led to these MRIs.'

Jessie knew better than to upstage Gilbride by identifying the tumor or giving any clinical opinions. Instead, she merely nodded to Emily, who took Hermann's MRIs off a stainless steel rolling cart and slid them onto two of the view boxes inset in the wall across from his room. Gilbride's thoughtful pacing back and forth in front of the films was clearly for the benefit of Tolliver and perhaps the medical students, because all of the others could have made the correct diagnosis from a passing train.

'Well,' he said finally, 'it appears what we have here is a large subfrontal meningioma, wouldn't you say, Dr. Copeland?'

'I would, yes, sir.'

'Well, what do you think of this tumor as appropriate for our intraoperative MRI with robotic assist?'

Jessie knew that if any case was ideal for ARTIE, this one was. But she still had serious reservations.

'I think ARTIE would be one way of getting at it,' she said, choosing her words carefully.

'Excellent. We're in agreement, then. Mr. Tolliver,

here's your case. Dr. Copeland, is there anything else you think I should know about this fellow?'

'Not really.'

'Well, then, let's go meet the man.'

'He speaks some English,' Jessie said, 'and understands it completely, but his wife does most of the talking.'

The room, which was large for a single, was packed even before the arrival of the medical entourage, with Orlis, her husband, and his three grown children sharing space with a considerably overweight private-duty nurse. Jessie introduced Gilbride, feeling as if she were passing off the baton in a barefoot relay race across hot coals.

'Well, it's a pleasure indeed to meet you,' Gilbride said. 'However, before we conduct our business, I must ask your children and nurse to wait in the hall. We are a teaching hospital, and after I bring everyone in who is making rounds with me today, I'm afraid this room will get a bit crowded.'

'You will not be bringing everyone in,' Orlis responded. 'Count Hermann will not take part in any medical circus.'

'Ka-boom!' Jessie whispered to Emily.

The initial test of wills between Gilbride and the Countess lasted through several exchanges before the Count intervened and brokered a compromise. Jessie and Emily would stay, along with Hermann's older son, Derrick, a man with watchful eyes, strongly built like his father, but with little resemblance beyond that. Tolliver, who observed the conflict and resolution from the doorway, smiled understandingly and motioned that he would be waiting in the hallway.

'Now, then,' Orlis said, immediately seizing the initiative, 'exactly what is the procedure you intend to do on my husband, and when will it be done?'

'I will answer each of your questions in due time, dear lady. But not until I have had the chance to examine my patient.' He turned from her and continued speaking with a deliberateness that bordered on patronizing. 'Count Hermann, I am pleased to make your acquaintance. I look forward to the successful treatment of your problem.'

'I wish that will be so,' the Count said.

Orlis, her expression stony, stood aside as Gilbride did a more painstaking and meticulous neurologic examination than Jessie had ever seen him perform.

*Spare me*, was all she could think. It was comforting and amusing to know that a few feet away, Emily was thinking the same thing.

'An excellent exam,' Gubride said finally, putting his reflex hammer and the tuning fork used to test vibratory sense back into his lab coat pocket. 'Excellent. Count Hermann, your neurologic exam is surprisingly good. Your tumor is rather slow-growing and nonmalignant, which means it does not spread to distant parts of the brain, or to other organs. However, it is taking up increasing amounts of space, and has begun compressing normal brain tissue. You will need surgery to remove it.'

The Countess inserted herself between the two men, making no attempt to hide her impatience to hear something she did not already know.

'Do you intend to use the same device you used successfully on that young gymnast?'

Almost in spite of himself, Gilbride glanced at Jessie. She looked away.

'Well, yes,' he said. 'I suspect we will do this operation in the MRI operating room, and we probably will use our robotic assistant.'

'We don't want probably,' Orlis said sharply. 'My husband came here because you said you had something to offer that other neurosurgeons did not. I want everything necessary to be done for him. He is a very special man and helps a great number of people.'

Gilbride rose to meet the challenge.

'I appreciate your anxiety, Madame,' he replied, 'but I feel I must remind you that I am the surgeon. If I think robotic assist will help us remove your husband's tumor, that is what we will use. And if not, well then, we shall not. I hope that is clear?'

Orlis looked to the Count, who nodded his agreement. Then she thrust back.

130

'When will the operation be done?' she asked.

Gilbride turned to Emily.

'You have the OR schedule?'

Emily, clearly unwilling to be anyplace but on the sidelines of this battle, handed the notebook over to Jessie.

'We're limiting ourselves to the MRI operating room?' Jessie asked.

'Precisely,' Gilbride replied.

'Okay. The room is maxed out for three weeks. We have two cases a day booked every day, including Saturdays.'

'But I have promised Mr. Tolliver I would be doing an ARTIE case that he could observe. We need to fit Count Hermann into the schedule by the end of the week.'

Jessie sighed.

'Tomorrow Dr. Wilbourne from Infants and Children's has his case scheduled first thing in the morning. In the afternoon is the re-op on Terence Gilligan. He's in the unit right now and not doing well. He really needs to have his surgery done as quickly as possible. The day after tomorrow, your patient, Lindsay Pearlman, is first. She's quite symptomatic, and I think there would be a serious risk in delaying her. After her is that man you're going to do with the surgical team from China. They're all flying in tomorrow. Thursday I'm doing Ben Rasheed in the morning. He's been postponed twice, and he really has to be done soon or something disastrous is going to happen. It might be possible to push the Thursday afternoon case into next week. That's your re-op on the Hopkins boy.'

'What are you trying to say?' Orlis demanded.

'In my opinion,' Jessie went on, 'the best we could do – the very best without endangering patients who are much more unstable than Count Hermann – would be three days from now in the afternoon slot.'

'That is ridiculous and unacceptable,' Orlis snapped.

'Orlis,' the Count said, holding up a calming hand.

The Countess took a deep breath and exhaled slowly,

'Dr. Gilbride,' she said, nearly shaking, 'my husband has had two seizures already. I want this surgery done tomorrow or Wednesday at the very latest.'

'Jessie,' Gilbride said, 'I would rather not keep Eastman here any longer than necessary.'

Jessie shrugged.

'These cases are really in critical shape,' she said. 'I would hate to delay any of them any more than they already have been, and I don't think you want to tell the Chinese they're being bumped.'

Gilbride studied his fingers, clearly weighing the political and malpractice implications of putting off a case and having some sort of catastrophe befall the patient.

'Thursday afternoon it is,' he pronounced finally.

Orlis's porcelain face reddened.

'This is unacceptable,' she said again.

Gilbride seemed to enjoy having the upper hand. Clearly this was one HC who had pushed him too hard.

'Furthermore,' he said, 'I would suggest that you and your family check into a hotel until Thursday morning.'

'We are paying in cash, Dr. Gilbride. We have Dr. Marcus's permission to occupy our rooms, and we will not be leaving.'

'Suit yourself, Countess.'

'Dr. Gilbride, I want you to know that we are not accustomed to this sort of treatment.'

'Mrs. Hermann, I assure you there are a number of other neurosurgeons in the city.'

Without waiting for a response, Gilbride swung around and led Emily and Jessie from the room. Eastman Tolliver was waiting just outside the door, where he couldn't have helped but hear everything that had transpired. Jessie tried unsuccessfully to read anything into his expression. Removing Rolf Hermann's tumor by any method was hardly going to be a stroll in the park. And although confidence was as essential a quality in a surgeon as a steady hand, the line between self-assuredness and hubris was a fine one. Jessie wondered now if Gilbride's determination to impress Eastman Tolliver had just pushed him across it.

# Chapter 16

Jessie had just finished dinner with Alex in the cafeteria when she was paged to an in-house number.

'This is Dr. Copeland, returning a page.'

'Ah, yes, Jessie. Eastman Tolliver here. I hope I'm not interrupting you.'

Jessie looked over at Alex, who had cleaned their table and was now pointing at his watch and motioning that he was leaving. 'See you later,' he mouthed.

'No,' she said to Tolliver. 'You're not interrupting anything.'

'I wonder if at some point this evening we might talk for a bit,' Tolliver said.

'Is there a problem?'

'No, nothing like that. I just had some questions that I felt you might better be able to answer than Dr. Gilbride.'

*I'd really rather not get involved in this grant business any more than I already have been. . . . Nothing personal, but I think you should direct any questions you have to Carl. . . . I am absolutely beat, and I had hoped to make it an early night tonight . . .*

In the few seconds it took her to answer, Jessie rejected half a dozen responses that were each more accurate than the one she ended up giving.

'Of course. Where are you now?'

'In the library going over your – I mean Dr. Gilbride's – grant application, and boning up on my neurosurgery.'

'I can be done by nine. Will that be too late?'

'Nine will be fine.'

'Tell you what. Meet me in the lobby. You can escort me

133

to my car, and I'll drive you to your place. We can talk on the way.'

Over the next hour Jessie returned eleven phone calls – seven of them for Gilbride. There appeared to be no letup in the frenzy he had created with his gold medal operation. It was actually five after nine by the time she had changed out of her scrubs and made it to the lobby. Eastman Tolliver was there, dressed conservatively in a lightweight tan suit, button-down white shirt, and muted tie. Perhaps sensing that she had had a long day, he wasted no time on small talk.

'So,' he said as they descended the stairs from the main entrance, 'Dr. Gilbride has told me that he has a case scheduled Thursday afternoon in which he will probably be using your robotic assistant. I am planning on returning to California shortly after I observe that operation. I was hoping that before I leave, we two might talk a little business.'

'Business?'

'Yes. I would appreciate it very much if you could tell me about your recent misadventure with ARTIE.'

Jessie looked over at him, stunned.

'Misadventure?'

Tolliver's dark, intelligent eyes sparked.

'I didn't come all the way to Boston just to be charmed by your department chief,' he said, 'although I have been positively disposed toward him thus far. I came to learn about your work and to gather the information necessary to make what will amount to a four-million-dollar decision.'

'Not three?'

'Probably not. And please, don't feel you are breaking any confidences. Dr. Gilbride has encouraged me to speak with whomever I wish.'

Jessie couldn't help but be impressed with the man's thoroughness. Pleading ignorance at this point hardly seemed appropriate.

'Well, I don't know for certain what you mean by misadventure,' she said, 'but I assume you're talking about the procedure I did on a cadaver not too long ago.'

'Precisely.'

'ARTIE was functioning perfectly, but a microcable snapped, and I lost control of him. It was that simple.'

'Could that happen again?'

'I would hope not, but speaking as a former engineer, I can tell you that with something mechanical anything can happen.'

'But the design of these cables is as good as it can be?'

'If a thing is man-made it can be improved upon,' Jessie replied, 'but for the moment, I would say yes, the guidance system on ARTIE is as good as we can make it.'

'Did you participate in the decision to use the device on Marci Sheprow?'

Again, Jessie stared over at him.

'Eastman, I seldom get too nervous performing brain surgery,' she said, 'but the possibility that I might say something that will cost my department a four-million-dollar research grant is another matter altogether. Perhaps we should discuss all this with Carl.'

'I'm sorry. Jessie, yours is not the only program in intraoperative robotics that has applied to us for financial assistance. To make the fairest decision, these are the sorts of things I need to know – the reason I came all the way across the country to evaluate your program firsthand.'

Jessie thought for a time, then shrugged.

'No,' she said simply. 'Carl made the decision to use ARTIE on Marci Sheprow without consulting with me. Nor did he have to. It's his department, his lab, and his invention.'

'But you're the principal researcher, yes?'

'I think you know the answer to that.'

'I believe I do. And I want you to trust that your response will be kept strictly confidential.'

'I have a degree in mechanical engineering.'

'I am aware of that.'

'Well, I was hired as a resident with the understanding that I would spend some time in the lab working on ARTIE. So I guess you could say I was the principal researcher on the project. But believe me, Dr. Gilbride has been on top of things every step of the way.'

'I have no doubt that he has. The operation Dr. Gilbride was referring to, it will be Count Hermann, yes?'

'Yes, it will. I suppose you heard that when you were in the hall.'

'It was difficult *not* to. In fact, after I overheard the exchange between Dr. Gilbride and the Countess, I made a point of stopping by later to speak with the Hermanns.'

'The Countess actually talked to you?'

'I found both of them quite easy to converse with.'

'She's pretty angry at us.'

'Perhaps. But I believe she is simply frightened for her husband. It seems to me that she loves him very much. Tell me, Jessie, in your opinion, is the decision to use ARTIE on Count Hermann the correct one, or is this just being done on my account?'

Jessie looked over at him, but said nothing.

'Please,' he implored. 'It's very important that I know how you feel about this.'

Jessie felt her mouth go dry. Tolliver was extremely intuitive, and clearly had been asking questions around the hospital. She wondered if he sensed that she didn't believe ARTIE was ready to be used on anyone – or, more to the point, that anyone, including her, was competent enough with the device at this juncture to use it on a difficult patient. Even assuming that ARTIE had no further mechanical problems, the ability to see a tumor in three dimensions and to guide the robotic unerringly through normal brain tissue would come only with time. For sure, she felt her skills improving with practice, but she still wasn't confident enough to lay one of her patient's lives on the line.

She knew she was going to have to lie to Tolliver, risk costing her department a four-million-dollar grant, or pick her words with the care of a soldier on land-mine detail.

'I believe the technical problems I encountered have been dealt with,' she said. 'I also believe that ARTIE has a great deal to offer to patients whose tumors are difficult to reach.'

'In the right hands.'

Jessie unlocked Swede's door for Tolliver and waited to reply until she had pulled out of the lot.

'Dr. Gilbride is a skilled surgeon with a great deal of confidence in himself,' she said finally. 'That confidence is job one in our specialty. Without it, a neurosurgeon might just as well pack it in.'

Jessie could feel Tolliver studying her, deciding whether to push the matter any further.

'Thank you, Jessie,' he said at last. 'I am most grateful for your candor. You have my word that any other questions I have I'll ask Dr. Gilbride.'

In his mind, forty-eight-year-old Terence Gilligan had never lost a fight. He had been beaten in the ring a number of times and, on occasion, pummeled. But he had never really lost because he had never broken. Even when his knees refused to straighten, he had never given up. The British had beaten on him, too. He was one of the Rowdies – an arm of the IRA in east Belfast that was noted for its toughness. They had rousted him, hauled him in to the station house, and slapped him around for hours. But they always came away empty. And gradually, they came to know not to bother with Gilligan.

This brain tumor thing was no different, he thought now. Those rotten cells would come to know the same as the Brits – don't bother with Gilligan.

He had been through so much in his life, it was hard to believe he was lying in a bed in the intensive care unit of a hospital in Massachusetts, with tubes stuck in almost every bloody opening in his body. But that was the way things were. First the girl from South Boston, visiting her ancestral home, then the flight from Ireland to be with her, and finally the merging of his life with hers, her family, and the rest of the Americans.

Gilligan coughed against the huge tube that passed down his throat, connecting his lungs to a breathing machine. Forty years of fags had done his breathing in. Now it seemed like forty years since he had last smoked one. With the friggin' tube down, he hadn't been able to speak to anyone for days, neither. Did they even know he could hear them? Understand them – at least some of the time? Did they even know how uncomfortable he was? Or that he was aware of tomorrow's trip back into the operating room to try and clean out the brain tumor that had regrown, it seemed, in just a few months?

*Shit, what lousy luck. If the bullets don't get you, the cancer will.*

Gilligan shifted his weight, trying to find a comfortable position. He could barely move with all the bloody tubes, to say nothing of the straps around his fists and ankles that kept him from getting at them.

'Mr. Gilligan, hold still now. It won't do you any good to pull out your breathing tube.'

Gilligan blinked, trying to focus through the dim light on the woman, who was backlit from the outside hallway. She spoke with a heavy accent, though not one he immediately recognized. He waved at her with one hand as best he could.

*Pain medicine. If you can't run some bloody fag smoke down this tube, at least give me some more pain medicine so I don't have to think about it.*

'I'm from anesthesia, Mr. Gilligan,' the woman said gently. 'I'm here to give you some medicine to help you sleep before your surgery tomorrow.'

*Well, it's about friggin' time.*

The woman came closer. She was wearing a long white coat, a mask, and something covering her hair. From what he could see, her eyes looked nice enough, and her voice, not much more than a whisper, was soothing. She had a syringe full of the sleeping medicine in her hand.

'Just hold still, now, Mr. Gilligan,' she said. 'You'll be feeling better in just a short while.'

She slipped the needle into the IV tubing and emptied the syringe.

*Bless you, Sister. Bless you.*

'Sweet dreams.'

Almost before he realized it, the woman was gone. Still

there, though, was her perfume. Odd, Gilligan thought. Of all the many nurses and woman doctors who had cared for him, none had worn any perfume that he could remember. He forced himself down into his pillow and waited.

*How long did she say it was going to take to work? How long has it been?*

Suddenly, a strange, unsettling emptiness filled his chest and throat – the sensation of his heart flip-flopping.

'Somebody go in and check on Gilly,' he heard one of the nurses say 'He's starting to have runs of extra beats. They look ventricular.'

*Extra beats. Now what in the hell does that –?*

'Quick, Becky, Gilly's fibrillating!'

The extra beats in Gilligan's chest exploded into a terrifying vacuum, and he knew, well before he lost consciousness, that his heart had stopped beating.

'Code ninety-nine, room seven! Call it in!'

*Hurry girls, hurry!*

'Get the cart. Molly, call Dr. Dakar!'

'Code ninety-nine, Surgical Seven ICU! . . . Code ninety-nine, Surgical Seven ICU! . .

*Hurry! . . . Fix me! . . . I'm dying!*

'He's still in fib.'

'Give me three hundred joules. Get ready to defibrillate!'

*Oh, God, please . . .*

'Three hundred!'

*Oh, God . . .*

'Okay. Ready, everyone . . . Clear! . . .'

# Chapter 17

There was a pall over Surgical Seven when Jessie arrived at work. Terry Gilligan, something of a mascot on the neurosurgical service because of his dense brogue and infectious wit, was dead. His cardiac arrest had occurred during the early-morning hours and was intractable to the heroic efforts first of the nurses, then of the entire code team. He had been on assisted ventilation because of a seizure and borderline pulmonary reserve, and his tumor was a bad one. But no one had come close to giving up on him.

On a morning that had begun so badly, Jessie was relieved that at last Carl had opted to stay around and see patients. With only her own work to attend to, her day gradually smoothed out. But nothing prepared her for what she found waiting when her afternoon clinic was over – waiting in room 6 of the neurosurgical ICU. When she arrived, the ubiquitous candy striper, Lisa Brandon, was rubbing lotion into Sara Devereau's feet.

'Well, hi,' Jessie said. 'Here you are again.'

'Here I am,' Lisa said cheerily.

'You know, everyone on the service is pulling for you not to figure out what you want to do with your life, Lisa. You're far too valuable as a volunteer here.'

Lisa brushed aside some slips of dark hair.

'That's very kind of you to say, even if it isn't true.'

'Ah, but it is. You're doing a great job with the patients – this one in particular.'

'Thank you. Well, I think we have a surprise for you here.'

*We?* Jessie looked quickly at Sara. Reasonably peaceful,

but deeply comatose. Still, something about Lisa's proud expression made her pulse jump a notch.

'Luckily, I'm one of the few neurosurgeons in the world who likes surprises,' she said.

'Okay, then,' Lisa replied, 'here goes.' She raised her voice. 'Sara, it's Lisa. Dr. Copeland's here. Can you open your eyes?'

For two fearfully empty seconds there was nothing. Then, suddenly, Sara's eyelids fluttered and opened.

'Oh, God!' Jessie exclaimed, grasping her friend's hand. 'Oh, God. Sara, it's me, Jessie. Can you hear me?'

Sara's nod, though slight, was unequivocal.

'She started responding to me about an hour ago,' Lisa said. 'I almost called you, but then I asked the nurses when you were expected, and they said you'd be up soon.'

Jessie barely heard the woman. Tears welling, she was stroking Sara's forehead and looking into eyes that were clearly looking back at her.

*Conjugate gaze intact . . . pupils midposition, reactive,* her surgeon's mind automatically recorded. She reached over and grasped Sara's other hand as she had at least once every day since the surgery.

'Sara, can you squeeze my hands?' she asked.

The pressure, faint but definite, and equal on both sides, broke the dam. Jessie made no effort to wipe aside her tears.

'Oh, Devereau,' she said, 'where in the hell have you been?'

Sara's lips struggled to form a word. Over and over again they opened and closed. Finally, there was the faintest wisp of a sound.

'J . . . Jessie,' she said. Jessie turned to Lisa.

'Did you tell the nurses?' she asked.

'No. I thought you might want to.'

'Well, you're right. I do want to.' She crossed to the door. 'Hey everyone, room six. On the double. Our patient has something she wants to say!'

Because of Terry Gilligan's death, the entire MRI-OR

schedule was moved up. Tomorrow's morning case would now be Gilbride's operation with the team of Chinese neurosurgeons. In the afternoon, Jessie would operate on Ben Rasheed, a fifty-year-old black laborer and father of four, who presented with severe weakness in his left arm and leg, and was found by Jessie to have a rather large tumor on the right side of his brain – almost certainly an astrocytoma. The sooner the tumor could be removed and graded for malignancy, the sooner appropriate post-op therapy could be instituted – most likely radiation.

With a potentially difficult case tomorrow, followed in the evening by her first real date with Alex, Jessie decided to head home at eight – for her a quite reasonable hour. After reviewing Rasheed's films again, and making some notes regarding the surgical approach she would use, she took the shuttle to lot E and drove to the Back Bay.

She straightened up her apartment, defrosted some lasagna she had made a month or so ago, and ate it between shots in one of her higher-scoring games of Pin Bot. It had been two years since she scraped together every bit of cash she had and bought the one-bedroom condo. Generally, she felt the apartment served her needs quite well, although her feelings about it often mirrored what was transpiring in the rest of her life. Tonight, with Sara awake, Alex looking like he might be the start of something good, and an exciting OR case in the afternoon, the place felt perfect.

At ten o'clock, when her beeper went off, she had just brewed a cup of Earl Grey, run a steaming tub, lit several scented candles, and set out her favorite huge bath sheet. The callback message on the LED was from the evening shift nursing supervisor on Surgical Seven. Being paged by the extremely capable nurse when she wasn't on call was unusual, Jessie thought – unusual enough not to ignore.

'Dr. Copeland, I'm really sorry to call you like this,' the woman said, 'but Dr. Sanjay is up here from anesthesia. Apparently there's some problem with Ben Rasheed.'

'What kind of problem? I just went over him this morning.'

'Oh, it's nothing medical. Dr. Sanjay says Ben told him he wasn't having surgery tomorrow. Wait a minute – here he is.'

Jessie steeled herself for what she knew was going to be a struggle – understanding Sanjay, who spoke perfectly good English, but so rapidly and with such a dense Indian accent that he was always hard to follow.

'Your patient, Mr. Rasheed, tells me he is not going to have his operation tomorrow afternoon. Instead, he is going to have it in two days' time. According to your patient, someone named Hermann will be taking his place.'

Jessie covered her eyes with her hand. What in the hell had the Countess done now? Borne by her years of making decisions as a surgeon, she ticked off her possible courses of action in seconds, discarding each as impractical, given the circumstances, the hour, and the personalities involved. Finally, only one option remained.

'I'll be there in twenty minutes,' she said. 'Go ahead about your business. I'll page you after I've had the chance to speak with Mr. Rasheed.'

At ten-thirty in the evening, the ride to EMMC took just fifteen minutes. The best part about coming to the hospital at such an hour was that there would be parking spaces in the central underground lot. Throughout the ride, Jessie tried to find some explanation for Ben Rasheed's sudden refusal to be operated on tomorrow other than that he had sold his OR time to Count Hermann. But no other rationale made sense.

As she turned in to Longwell Street, which ran along the back of the hospital, she peered up at the Surgical Tower. From this side, her office was visible seven stories up. Suddenly, she pulled the Saab over and stopped. There was a light on in her office. Moments later, the silhouette of a figure passed behind the sheer white curtain. *Housekeeping?* Hard to believe at this hour, she decided.

She hurried into a parking spot and raced through the basement to the Surgical Tower elevator. She stepped from the car on seven, hesitated, and then used a nearby house phone to call security, hoping that Alex was around. Instead, her call was answered in two minutes by the guard whom she had seen in the cafeteria with him, a bear of a man named Eldon Ellroy.

The corridor outside the offices was on evening-light status, with every other fixture dark. There was no light coming from beneath any of the doors, including hers. Gently, silently, Ellroy tried the knob. Locked. Then Jessie inserted the key, turned it, pushed the door open, and stepped back into the corridor. Nothing. Ellroy reached around the jamb and switched on the light. The tiny office was empty. He motioned her inside, and she confirmed that there was nothing out of place. Ellroy reassured her kindly that ever since the hospital started cutting back on electricity, security had been getting many more calls such as hers. Then he left.

Jessie stood in the silence, still tensed. The papers on her desk and in her drawers seemed in order, but she couldn't shake the feeling that someone had been there. Finally, she marginally convinced herself that the light and silhouette she had seen were in one of the orthopedists' offices on Surgical Six. Turning off the light and carefully locking the door behind her, she headed to the ward and Ben Rasheed's room.

Rasheed's ebony face, set off by a clean-shaven scalp, was thick-featured, deeply lined, and, to Jessie, handsome. His outsized, heavily callused hands could easily have palmed a basketball. He had a spirit that made him one of Jessie's favorites, and loved to tell stories about his life as a bodyguard, chauffeur, and construction worker, and to drop the names of the famous people with whom he had, at one time or another, crossed paths.

Rasheed's half of the double room was adorned with photos of his wife and children. As soon as he saw Jessie at the doorway, he playfully ducked beneath the sheets. She pulled up a chair and waited. Rasheed stayed where he was.

'I ain't comm' out until you say you're not mad at me,' he announced.

'Ben, I *am* mad at you. You can't do this.'

144

Slowly, tortoiselike, Rasheed emerged. His expression was deadly serious.

'Doc, I *got* to,' he said.

Jessie took a calming breath.

'Okay, okay. Start from the beginning.'

'A few hours ago, this woman come to see me. She spoke like, I don't know, like a Nazi in a war movie.'

'I know who she is.'

'Okay. Well, she says that her husband's very sick and needs an operation bad, but that he can't get no time in the operatin' room for two days. She says that if I change places with him, an' let him have my time, I could have his.'

'How much money did she offer you?'

'I . . . I promised I wouldn't say.'

Jessie was about to demand to know, but then realized there was no need. Ben Rasheed was anything but dumb. He knew what was at stake for himself. If he was making this decision, the money had to be enough for him.

'Ben, this is potentially a very dangerous thing for you to do,' she said. 'You've already had some major symptoms. With this type of tumor, things can come apart very quickly. That's one of the reasons we've put you in the hospital to wait for your operation.'

'I know that. But I also know you won't let nothin' bad happen to me.'

'Ben, that's a little naive. The longer we wait, the more chance something bad *will* happen. And if it does, I can't make any guarantees.'

'But you said that about the operation, too, Doc. No guarantees. I know this tumor in my head might kill me whether I wait an extra day or I don't. I got four kids, a wife, an' a mortgage, an' I got nothin' in the bank an' no life insurance. For what this lady's gonna pay me, I'm willin' to roll the dice. Christ, for that kind of money, if she wanted my kidney, I'd hand it over. I know you're angry with me, Doc. I'm sorry 'bout that. But a man's gotta do what a man's gotta do.'

Jessie knew that were their roles reversed, she would have made the same choice.

'Okay, I'm not angry with you, Ben,' she said. 'One thing, though. You don't have to tell me the amount, just tell me the terms.'

'Some now, more after the guy's operation.'

'I want you to get it all up front. Mrs. Hermann has cash. I'm certain of it.'

'You gonna talk to her about that?'

'You bet I am,' Jessie said.

The exchange with Orlis Hermann was brief and to the point.

'I don't know how much you offered Ben Rasheed, Mrs. Hermann,' Jessie said, 'but I want it paid in full before the Count's operation tomorrow.'

'Or what?' Orlis asked.

The two women faced off across the dimly lit hospital room, with Rolf Hermann and one of his sons looking on. Jessie refused to blink.

'Or I'll do whatever is necessary to get your husband taken off the MRI-OR schedule and pushed back to his original slot.'

'I have already spoken with Dr. Gilbride about the change in schedule. He wants to do this operation as quickly as possible.'

'I don't care,' Jessie replied. 'I believe he also wants to keep me on his staff.'

Orlis studied her resolve, then said simply, 'Mr. Rasheed will have his money tomorrow morning.'

'One more thing. If I hear of you interacting with any of my patients again without my permission, I'll move heaven and earth to have you and your family shipped to another hospital. Is that clear?'

'Get out,' Orlis Hermann said. 'Get out of here this instant.'

Jessie stormed from the room, left word with Sanjay, the anesthesiologist, that his afternoon case had changed, and hurried down to her car. She was determined that Orlis Hermann wasn't going to ruin what had been a wonderful day. With any luck, the water in the tub would just take a little heating up. She was at the parking attendant's booth when she realized that her purse was still on the chair in her office.

'Sorry, but you can't leave your car there,' the sleepy attendant told her when she tried to park it off to one side.

Weary of conflicts, Jessie turned around and eventually pulled into the slot she had just left. She took the elevator back to Surgical Seven, inserted the key in her office lock, and opened the door. As she was reaching for the light switch, a strong hand snatched her wrist and jerked her inside. At the same instant, the man's other hand clamped tightly across her mouth.

# Chapter 18

Even before she heard his voice, Jessie knew it was Alex.

'Jessie, it's me,' he whispered. 'I'm going to let go. Just promise me you won't scream. . . . Do you promise?'

She nodded. His grip lessened and finally released altogether. Jessie turned, rubbing her mouth, and glared at him through what light the filmy curtains permitted. She felt as if she had been gored.

'I knew you were too good,' she said.

'I'm sorry.'

'Can I turn the light on?'

'How about the one on your desk?'

Jessie switched it on and moved quickly to her own chair before he could stop her or object.

'That was you in here a while ago, too, wasn't it?' she said.

'By sheer chance I looked out the window just as you pulled over to the side of the street. I wasn't sure, but I thought it was you.'

Jessie forced her lips tightly together until she was certain she could speak without crying or screaming. Absurdly, she flashed on the tub in her apartment, and the tea, and the candles. Alex just sat there, arms folded, waiting. At least there was nothing smug in his expression, she thought. At least there was no half-assed, knee-jerk attempt at fabricating some lame explanation for why he had twice broken in to her office.

'Well,' she managed finally, 'you haven't killed me, so I assume I'm going to get some sort of tale to convince me you're not just a low-life snoop or thief or pervert – something like that you're an undercover cop working on a case?'

His smile was uncomfortable.

'Actually, I'm CIA.'

'Uh-huh.'

'Well, sort of CIA.'

'Sort of.'

'We get paid by the CIA, but we function pretty independently. I should say functioned. We've been broken up and those of us who are still alive have been sort of decommissioned.'

'We?'

'An antiterrorist group, I guess you'd call us.'

'Does your "group" have a name like SPECTRE or SMERSH?'

'No. No name.'

'ID?'

'No.'

'A phone number?'

'Not really. There's a guy in Langley who'd probably vouch for me, but he's on vacation.'

'On vacation. . . . Alex, what were you doing in my office?'

'I'll tell you, but I need you to promise you'll give me the benefit of the doubt.'

'Benefit of the doubt? Until I hear a reasonable explanation for what you just did, I'm not promising to give you the benefit of anything.'

He studied her for a time, then sighed.

'I was getting ready to go through your patient records,' he said.

'Of course. You broke into my office to go through my patient records. What else? I should have guessed that right away. How foolish of me.' Jessie felt herself coming unraveled.

'I wish you wouldn't do this,' he said.

'What I'm going to *do* in about ten seconds is call the police.'

'If that's what you think you have to do, I won't stop you.'

'Is this some sort of bluff? You think if you tell me it's okay to call the police, I won't?'

'No. No bluff. Listen, if I go out to get something from my locker, will you wait here for me?'

'Are you going to bolt?'

'No.'

'Look at me! Are you going to take off?'

'Jessie, that's the last thing I'm going to do. Will you wait here? There are lives at stake.'

'My, my, such high drama. Go ahead. I'll wait. But before you go, I want to tell you that I'm feeling a little used by you, for whatever silly reason. And I hate that feeling. So whatever it is you're going to go and get from your locker had better be good, or else don't bother.'

Bishop stood slowly and, never taking his eyes from her, backed out of the office. Jessie sat there, staring unseeingly at the elegant paperweight Emily had given her last Christmas, feeling too stunned and disappointed to move. She knew there was nothing Alex could tell her that would erase the hurt. She thought about just leaving – going home to bed. If she stayed and Alex didn't come back, she'd be relieved. If he did return, she'd probably not believe anything he told her anyway. So why not just go?

*Shit!*

Employee lockers were in the subbasement. Jessie timed out five minutes, and was about to head home when Bishop returned carrying a large manila envelope. He looked relieved to see her still there.

He sat down, cradling the envelope in his lap. 'What I told you before is the truth. For years I've worked undercover for a branch of the CIA. Mostly I've been in Europe.'

'Go on,' she said, interested in his story, but disinclined to believe it.

'Have you ever heard of Claude Malloche?'

'No.'

'That's not surprising. Not many people have. In fact, in some places he's called the Mist or some equivalent, suggesting that he really doesn't exist. But he does. He kills for a living. A prime minister or a plane full of tourists, Malloche really doesn't care as long as the price is right. He's French by birth, but he comes and goes – Germany, the Balkans, Russia. He has places all over. I have reason to believe that he or those who work for him have killed more than five hundred people, if you count the jetliner explosion over Athens five years ago, and the one over the Canary Islands two years ago.'

'I thought Arab terrorists were blamed for that Athens one,' Jessie said, upset with herself for participating in his tall tale.

'The money was Arab, and one of their splinter groups claimed responsibility, just like the Algerian separatists took credit for the Canary Islands disaster. But Malloche blew up both planes for those groups. I'm certain of it.'

'And why are you so certain?'

'Because, for five years now, tracking down Claude Malloche is all I've done.'

'Pardon me for stating the obvious,' Jessie said, 'but it would appear you're not very good at your job.'

Bishop sighed.

'Unfortunately, there are a few important people in Washington who agree with that assessment,' he said. 'In fact, they're the same ones who aren't even convinced there is a Claude Malloche. They think he's a figment of the CIA's imagination, used to explain every assassination or bombing we're unable to solve.'

'Like Santa Claus gets credit for Christmas presents.'

'Jessie, you have every right to be furious with me. But please, just hear me out.'

'Go ahead.'

'Malloche is like the bull's-eye at the center of a target. Surrounding him is a small organization I have heard called the Dark – maybe ten or twelve men and women who are suicidally loyal to him. They are the only ones who ever have contact with him – and live. And around that group is another ring of supporters, much more diffuse and less informed, and then another ring. So far the network has proven impossible to penetrate very deeply. We've lost several people trying. Those at the center have no political agenda other than money. Malloche himself is ruthless, brilliant, incredibly careful, and absolutely without regard for human life – *other* humans' lives, that is.'

'And you've been chasing him.'

'At the moment, I'm all that's left of a unit that once was six. Four of the others have disappeared, and are presumed dead. One is teaching recruits. I can't get more men or more money to keep after Malloche.'

'Because people in Washington don't think he exists.'

Bishop looked as if he were about to speak, then nodded instead.

'Do they know *you* exist?' Jessie asked.

'They've demanded that I stop what I've been doing and return to Virginia to join my former partner and become an instructor for new recruits to the agency. I'm overdue to report by almost a month now. They've already sent a man here to bring me back or kill me.'

'And did you kill him?'

'I could have, but I didn't. Next time they send someone, I will probably have to.'

'That's great to hear. There really isn't a phone number I could call to verify all this?'

'Not really.'

'How do you get paid?'

'I don't think I do anymore. But when I did, it was a rather complicated, convoluted process.'

'Of course. Forget I asked. You have a photo of this Malloche?'

'Maybe. Maybe dozens. He doesn't look the same in any two of them.'

'Fingerprints?'

Bishop shook his head. 'Maybe,' he said again.

'Okay, no definite photos, no definite fingerprints, no definite proof he exists. No pay stubs to prove *you* exist. What has all this got to do with me and my patients?'

Bishop extracted some eight-by-ten-inch photographs from the envelope, hesitated, then handed several of them over.

'These are pretty gruesome,' he said, 'but after watching you in the OR with that child, I know you can handle it.'

The photos were of corpses – one man and two women in white coats, another woman, quite young, in street clothes – taken in a medical clinic of some sort. Each of them had been shot in the center of the forehead, right above the bridge of the nose.

'Explain.'

'These photos were taken about three months ago by the police in an MRI clinic in Strasbourg, France, right on the border with Germany The shot placement is a trademark of Malloche's. It's the only thing I've ever found him to do with any consistency. Look.'

He passed over several more photos of various victims. Each had been shot in virtually the same place.

'Two months ago,' Bishop went on, 'I was able to question a man in one of those outer rings I spoke about, but one not that far from the center. It's a break I've worked years for. The guy had been picked up by the police in Madrid in connection with a political killing there. They had him on video from a surveillance camera. He offered to cut a deal in exchange for being allowed to disappear. One of the arresting officers had known me for years, and when he found out what the killer was bringing to the table, he contacted me immediately. Basically, what the guy said was that Malloche has a brain tumor and that he's looking for a doctor to operate.

'I began sending out alerts to the FBI in this country, and the equivalent agencies throughout Europe, although I always knew he'd surface in the U.S. or, a remote possibility, in Italy or the U.K.'

'Why those places?'

'You tell me.'

'The finest neurosurgeons, the best equipment.'

'With the U.S. head and shoulders above the others.' He extracted another set of photographs from the envelope and continued. 'Three and a half weeks ago, a prominent neurosurgeon in Iowa was shot to death in his office, along with his secretary.'

'Sylvan Mays. He was involved in the same sort of robotics research we are.'

'Exactly. Did you know him?'

'I've heard him speak at some conferences, but we'd never really met. I think Carl Gilbride knew him pretty well.'

'From what you do know of this Dr. Mays, do you think he's the sort who might have come to Claude Malloche's attention?'

'Perhaps. If Malloche really exists.'

'Do these help convince you? I got them from the Iowa City police. The one sprawled out on the floor is Sylvan Mays. The one at her desk is his receptionist.'

'Same bullet holes.'

'Malloche has a thing about witnesses. Mays' wife says he had been talking about coming into a lot of money but he wouldn't say how, and there's no extra money in any of his bank accounts. I have a feeling Mays had already agreed to do Malloche's surgery, and then something went wrong. Malloche decided he didn't trust him, or Mays tried to back out for some reason.'

'Bad idea, it would seem. Okay Alex, I've seen enough.'

'You believe me?'

'Hell no. And if this Claude Malloche really does exist, I have no reason to believe you're not him.'

'Jesus. Jessie, I'm telling you the truth. I'm certain Malloche has learned all he can about robotic surgery and Marci Sheprow's operation, and has decided to have Carl Gilbride perform his surgery.'

'Then why not go to Carl?'

'I've checked around. I get the sense that Gilbride would be willing to cut almost any corner – or any deal – depending on what was in it for him. I don't know if I can trust him. I don't have time to check on whether or not he has made any major deposits over the last couple of weeks either, so I've just got to go with my gut. And my gut says Malloche is here or he's gonna be here real soon. Five years, Jessie. Five years and this is the best shot I've had at the bastard – maybe the last shot.'

'Well, good luck, and good night.'

Jessie stood to go.

'Please, wait, Jessie. I told you that our unit had lost four men.'

'Yes.'

'Well, two of them were killed when an informant we trusted sold us out and we were ambushed by Malloche's people. One of those men who was killed was my older brother, Andy. I was wounded. He was dragging me to cover when he was shot by a long-range sniper right here.' Bishop pointed to the spot just above the bridge of his nose. 'His killer fired from nearly half a mile away Malloche is one of the very few people on earth who could have made that shot.'

'If that's really true,' Jessie said, 'I'm sorry. I honestly am. Now, I'm going home.'

'Wait! Dammit, Jessie, please. I need your help. This is my last chance. I'm not going to give up and go teach at their secret agent school, and the agency is going to keep after me. If I kill one of their men, they'll just send someone better.'

'I think you should give up.'

'With Mays dead, this seems like the obvious place for Malloche to go – specially after Gilbride got all that publicity for operating on that gymnast. So far, though, I haven't been able to figure out whether or not Malloche is here. Since I arrived, I've been lifting prints off glasses and other things from every new male patient who's come onto the neurosurgical service. I've sent them to Interpol, and today I brought them to D.C. in hopes of matching them to any of the two or three dozen maybes I've gotten on Malloche over the years.'

'And?'

'Nothing. I've got to know more about each of the patients. And when we determine which one Malloche is, I may need help capturing him. There are just too many doubters. I need him alive. But even dead, I have a chance to identify him.'

'What do you mean?'

'The witness in Spain, the one who told me about Malloche's brain tumor?'

'Yes?'

'His name is Cardoza. He claims he's seen Malloche – several times. He looked at all the photos I showed him, but refused to say whether any of them was or wasn't Malloche. He wanted to cut a deal for passage for him and his family out of Spain, and enough money to set them up wherever they went.'

'Why didn't you make the deal?'

'How could I trust him? He was still in prison. He could have pointed out anyone.'

'But now you trust him?'

'I do. Apparently Malloche found out Cardoza had been speaking with us. A few weeks ago, his apartment was blown up. As I said, he was locked up, but his wife and kid weren't so lucky. The police in Madrid have him someplace safe for now, and they're moving him around. But Malloche has money to burn, so it's only a matter of time before someone on the force takes a bite and sells Cardoza out. They offered to take him out of the country for the time being, but he refused. He wants Malloche dead.'

'What about the photos, then?'

'A dozen or so nos, one maybe. That's the best he could do. The maybe is so blurred that it could be anyone. As soon as I have a suspect, Cardoza'll be flown over.'

'This is just crazy. You're working this case all by yourself?'

'I have a little help from the local FBI. Not much, but a little.'

'So who killed Cardoza's wife and child?'

'What?'

'If this Malloche is as good as you say at killing, it's a little hard to believe he hasn't killed Cardoza as well. And if this whole phantasmagorical story of yours is true, it would seem you had quite a bit to gain from blowing up that family in Madrid yourself.'

Bishop's look held genuine admiration.

'You know,' he said, 'the truth is, if I had thought of doing it, I very possibly might have. But I didn't.'

'Killing an innocent woman and a child?' Jessie said. 'How noble.'

'I told you I didn't do it,' Bishop replied, 'but I also told you how much getting Malloche means – how many lives his capture or death will save.

'Well, either way, I don't see how I could possibly be of any –' Jessie felt a sudden chill. She took several deep breaths through her nose, trying to maintain some composure. 'Alex, or whatever your name is, tell me something. That car trouble you saved me from, was that rigged?'

There was the briefest hesitation, during which Jessie was certain Bishop was mulling over whether or not to lie.

'I . . . Jessie, I was desperate to learn about Gilbride,' he said. 'I needed to get inside the neurosurgical service quickly. From what I could tell, he wasn't someone I could trust. You were. I had to get close to you.'

'Jesus.'

'I'm sorry. I really am. Jessie, I admit the way I met you and some of what I told you about myself was contrived, but none of what I've told you tonight has been. I'm sorry I had to lie, but I need your help. I'm *begging* you to help.'

'Get out!'

Bishop stood.

'Jessie –'

Jessie leaped around the edge of the desk and punched him viciously on the side of his face. Then she pushed the photos at him. He clutched them clumsily against his chest and backed into the hall.

'Alex?' she said less stridently.

He took a step back into the doorway.

'Yes?'

She moved forward and slapped him, raising a crimson, palm-shaped welt on his cheek.

'I'll think about it,' she said.

She slammed the door in his face.

# Chapter 19

Midnight . . . twelve-thirty . . . one. Lying in her darkened bedroom, Jessie watched the time pass on the lighted dial of her clock radio. One-thirty . . . two. She remembered a vial of sleeping pills in her medicine cabinet from some bygone era in her life. Although she hadn't taken any in years, and they were probably expired, she seriously considered trying one or two. Finally, she picked up the novel she had been inching through at a page or two a night, and padded out to the living room couch. She was wearing her usual sleeping garb – an extra-large T-shirt, this one from Earth Day. Nothing more.

She was furious at Alex's deception, but even more, she was angry at herself for buying into it. Fairy tales were tales – it was as simple as that. And expectations, as often as not, led to pain.

*Keep your expectations in check, tend to business, and good things will come*, she told herself. Alex Bishop was nothing more than a pothole in the road of her life.

She set the book aside and tried some warm milk. Nothing was going to calm her thoughts. Gratefully, Ben Rasheed's selling his OR time had left her with a relatively light day ahead. If she had to endure a night without sleep, so be it. She had the proven constitution to work thirty-six hours with little or no rest, although her body inevitably paid the price when she did.

*Was Alex telling the truth?* she asked herself.

The photos were impressive, but they could just as easily belong to the killer as to the CIA. The sicker the man, the slicker the lies. Who said that? Maybe no one. Maybe the line was all hers. The slicker the man, the sicker the lies.

Two-thirty.

Jessie queued up a ball in Pin Bot and lost it between the flippers after just five seconds or so – a catastrophe that could have been avoided by a right-hand nudge that was usually routine for her. This simply wasn't going to be her night for anything. She opened the novel again, read a few sentences, and then set it aside. The questions kept rumbling through her mind like tanks.

How could Alex be so certain Malloche was headed to Carl for his surgery? Was he really the dogged CIA pursuer making an expert guess based on five years of tracking down his prey, or was he one of Malloche's people, or even Malloche himself, in the process of making up his mind about who would cut on him? If Malloche was Mr. Thorough, as Alex claimed, it only made sense that he would check up on Gilbride and the whole neurosurgical service at EMMC before letting Carl drill open his head. And what more reliable, efficient way to do that than to start up a romance with one of the surgeons in his department?

*Why in the hell couldn't it all have been real?*

She rubbed at the exhaustion stinging her eyes as she again confronted the most troubling question of all: What if Alex was telling the truth? What if he *was* so set on capturing this Malloche that he would use her as he had? And even if she ever did come to trust what he was saying, could she possibly agree to help him? What about the patient/physician confidentiality she so treasured? Did it not extend to Gilbride's patients – even to one who might be a killer?

The telephone startled her so that she sloshed some of the warm milk onto her thigh.

'Hello?'

'Jessie, it's Alex. Please don't hang up.'

About to do just that, Jessie kept the receiver to her ear.

'What do you want?' she asked.

'I need to talk to you.

'No!'

'Jessie, please. Everything I told you in your office was true. Deceiving you the way I have was stupid and cruel. I'm sorry I did it. I'm under tremendous pressure, and in the world I come from almost nothing matters more than getting the job done. But it was still a dumb mistake.'

'Okay, you've apologized. Good night.'

'Wait!'

'Dammit, Alex, you've hurt me. I don't want anything more to do with you. Now –'

'Listen, Jessie. Malloche is in your hospital right now. I'm almost certain of it. If I'm right, there's a good chance people are going to be killed – maybe me, maybe you, maybe even some of your patients.'

Jessie sensed herself freeze at the last possibility. She felt certain Alex knew that she would. *Damn him!*

'Where are you?' she asked finally.

'I . . . I'm right outside. I've been here for a couple of hours, thinking. I had decided to leave and not try to speak with you until the morning, but then your light went on.'

'So you knew where I lived and which one was my apartment. Why am I not surprised?'

'Jessie, I'm going to get Malloche no matter what. But it would be a hell of a lot easier and maybe a lot safer for everyone with your help.'

Jessie chewed anxiously on her lip, wishing she was anyplace else.

'Ring the bell. I'll buzz you in,' she heard herself say.

Her condo was on the third floor. There was a security camera mounted downstairs in the outer foyer. Channel Two. She switched on the TV and flipped to the channel. Alex, wearing a light windbreaker, entered the outside door and looked up at the camera as if he knew she would be watching.

The doorbell sounded. She went to her bedroom and pulled on a pair of sweatpants and a hooded sweatshirt. She then stood by the intercom box, reminding herself that, Malloche or CIA, the man she was about to allow into her apartment at two-thirty in the morning was a professional killer. The bell sounded again, and she buzzed him in. Then she opened her door and watched him trudge up to the top of the wide, carpeted stairway that had once graced a sea captain's mansion.

'Thanks for seeing me,' he said.

Fatigue etched his face.

She motioned him to an easy chair and took a place on the end of the sofa farthest from him.

*The sicker the man, the slicker the lie*, she reminded herself.

'What do you want from me?' she asked.

Bishop leaned forward.

'I'm almost certain Rolf Hermann is Claude Malloche,' he said. 'In fact, I've contacted the people in Madrid. They're in the process of sending Jorge Cardoza over here right now. There are many factors in favor of Hermann being Malloche, and not many against it. That wife of his is what made me suspicious of him in the first place. Although I've never seen her, I've been told that Malloche has a remarkably beautiful wife – a former recruit of his from Austria. Her name's Arlette. Not Orlis.'

'The Countess seems pretty cold, all right,' Jessie said, 'but Rolf actually seems like quite a nice man, and he barely speaks English.'

Alex laughed disdainfully.

'My bet is he can speak it and half a dozen other languages without an accent. I've got people in Europe trying to see if there even is a Count Rolf Hermann, but that could take time.'

'You don't have a lot of that, I'm afraid. Hermann's being operated on tomorrow afternoon – hell, it's *this* afternoon now.'

Bishop looked startled.

'I thought he was on the schedule for Thursday.'

'His wife paid off one of my patients to switch. Dr. Gilbride is operating on him as the second case later today.'

'If I tip my hand and make a move on Hermann before Cardoza gets here to identify him, and I'm wrong, I'll most likely have ruined everything. Malloche will hear about it.

I don't know how, but he will. He'll go someplace else, and I'll lose what is probably my last chance.'

'But you think it's Hermann.'

'Right age, right build, right wife, right timing, European. Yes, I think it's him. And those so-called children of his. They're bogus. I'd bet on it. If he's operated on today, when will he be ready to leave the hospital?'

'Assuming there are no unusual problems from the surgery, it could be anywhere from five to seven days. But this is a tough tumor. Given its location' – *and the flaws in Carl's surgical technique*, she wanted to add, but didn't – 'there is the significant possibility, even with our robot helping with the operation, that there will be damage to some intervening structures. If that happens, he could be in the hospital much longer.'

Jessie suddenly realized that she had just crossed the line and disclosed information on a patient. If she allowed Alex to hang around her, it wouldn't be the last time. She was either in, or she was out.

'In that case,' Alex was saying, 'I'm not going to do anything that will interfere with the surgery. If I'm right about Hermann being Malloche, and if there is a God, the man will end up permanently paralyzed from his eyebrows to his toes – totally aware, but immobile forever. The perfect justice.'

'Your justice, maybe,' Jessie said. 'I'd like you to go now.'

'But –'

'You've apologized to me, you've said your piece, you've asked me to help you. Now I'd like you to leave me alone. I told you in my office I would think about getting involved. At the moment, I'm disinclined even to speak to you anymore. If that feeling changes, you'll hear from me.'

Their eyes met, and Jessie quickly looked away. She couldn't stop remembering the hour after Jackie Terrell's death – Alex's touch, how much his caring and insight into how she was feeling had meant to her. Well, he wasn't going to get to her again. Intellectually, she was becoming inclined to believe what he was telling her. But she was not ready to forgive the lies.

Alex stood and seemed for a moment as if he had something else to say. Then he simply shook his head in frustration.

'Thanks for listening,' he said as he left.

# Chapter 20

There was an electric tension surrounding the MRI operating room as one by one the players began to assemble for the robot-assisted tumor extraction on Count Rolf Hermann. Jessie stood outside the room, watching the silent, slow-motion ballet through the heavy glass observation window, and wondering if the broad-shouldered man being ministered to by the anesthesiologist was, as Alex had claimed, the ruthless, remorseless killer of hundreds.

To her right, Hans Pfeffer and the console tech were checking and rechecking their instruments. Jessie pictured the action a floor above them where, in the cluttered, space-age computer center, half a dozen geek geniuses were preparing their remarkable machines to process the imaging data sent to them by the massive MRI. Their focus throughout this operation would be not on the patient, but on the tumor and the normal structures surrounding it. In addition to Pfeffer, a Dutchman, there were scientists from Germany and Sweden, Russia and Israel and the U.S. And for the next four or five hours, the life of a man they had never laid eyes on would be in their hands.

It was well within her rights for her to watch the surgery, but Jessie still felt obligated to get Carl's permission. Although she had spent significantly more hours than he had working ARTIE through any number of test matrices and animal models, as well as the ill-fated effort on Pete Roslanski, she felt like the understudy, asking the star if she could watch from the wings. For a few seconds, it seemed that Gilbride might actually refuse her request – surprising, given that he relished an audience for his performances.

'Well, Jessie, I certainly don't mind you hanging around during the procedure,' he said, finally, 'but with Eastman Tolliver on a riser behind me, and Skip Porter in the OR as well to keep an eye on ARTIE, I think it might be a bit crowded in the room. How about you watch the proceedings outside on the screen in the console area.'

'Actually, that's what I was planning on doing,' she replied.

'Fine, then. I've gone over ARTIE most thoroughly with Skip, and both of them appear to be in perfect working order.'

He chuckled at what was, for him, a raucous joke.

'That's great.'

'The tumor is sitting pretty for a transsphenoid approach – up the nose and in.'

'Up the nose and in,' Jessie parroted, trying to sound more enthusiastic than sarcastic.

Hermann's meningioma was, indeed, the ideal tumor in the ideal location for ARTIE. But Jessie remained unconvinced that Gilbride – or even she herself, for that matter – was fluid enough, and comfortable enough with guiding the apparatus, to risk using it on a patient – even one who might be a remorseless killer.

It was nearly two in the afternoon of a day that had started clear and sunny, but had clouded over by noon. Jessie estimated she had slept at most for an hour and a half, just before dawn. For once, she was glad she was not the one operating.

Skip Porter entered the console area from the scrub room, waved a dripping hand at Jessie, and backed into the operating room to be toweled off, gowned, and gloved by the scrub nurse. He was tall, gangly, and refreshingly free of ambition, with bleached blond hair and a ragged goatee that reminded Jessie of Shaggy in *Scooby Doo*. He also had a commitment to perfection in his work, and a practical understanding of electromechanics that rivaled any Jessie had encountered at MIT. If Skip was nervous about his second case with ARTIE and Gilbride, he hid it well. His report to Jessie on the Marci Sheprow surgery was that both robot and surgeon had performed admirably, and that the tumor dissection, however straightforward, had been flawless. But he knew, as did Jessie, that Rolf Hermann's complex meningioma presented an infinitely greater challenge.

ARTIE-2 was sterilized and covered on a steel tray. Porter would check it out one final time as he attached it to the port next to the guidance panel where Gilbride would be working.

There were seven in the OR now: the scrub and circulating nurses, anesthesiologist Pramod Sanjay, a med student rotating through Sanjay's service, a neurosurgical resident from Ghana named Danl Toomei, who would be Gilbride's assistant, Skip, and of course, the patient. Next to arrive was Eastman Tolliver, looking fit and trim in his sky blue scrubs. His eyes smiled at Jessie from above his mask as he came over to shake her hand before entering the OR.

'I must say, this is all very exciting,' he said.

'Yes, it is,' she replied, 'although I'm not sure Count Hermann would share our enthusiasm.'

She nodded at the scene through the window, where the anesthesiologist was sliding Rolf Hermann through the central opening of the MRI and into position between the huge tori, where his head could be bolted to the circular immobilization frame.

'Quite a remarkable scene,' Tolliver said. 'Most impressive.'

*Carl would be pleased to hear you say that,* Jessie thought.
. 'I've been down here dozens and dozens of times as observer and surgeon, and it still amazes me,' she said. 'To someone who hasn't seen it before, it must be like landing on another planet.'

'Perfectly put. I'm very excited. Well, I guess I'd better get in there.'

'You'll have the best view looking over Carl's right shoulder. That way you can watch the patient, the control panel for ARTIE, Dr. Gilbride's hands, and the MRI screen.'

'Excellent. That's where I'll set up, then.' He looked

through the observation window and added, 'I'm going to say a prayer for that poor man.'

*And I'll say one for Carl.*

'In the OR, prayer is always a good idea.'

Tolliver lingered for a few more seconds and then entered the operating room.

Eight in. Moments later, with the arrival of a translator, there were nine. One to go. The crowd around the console outside the OR had swelled as well. Danl Toomei's back was about all anyone could see through the observation window, so most were clustered near the twin screens – one projecting the surgical field from an overhead camera, and the other displaying a duplicate of the images being transmitted to Gilbride and his assistant from the computer center.

*Surgical theater at its best,* Jessie thought. *Hog heaven for Carl Gilbride.*

Moments before Gilbride made his appearance, Jessie's attention was drawn through the crowd to the safe area – the area thirty feet or so from the OR door, beyond which scrubs did not have to be worn. Alex Bishop was there in his hospital security uniform, leaning casually against a thick, concrete-covered support pillar. There was nothing casual, though, in his eyes or in the set of the muscles of his face. He was alternating between scanning the observers and peering as best as he could manage through the window into the OR.

His gaze connected with hers, and he nodded briefly She returned the gesture and then shrugged her bewilderment at the whole deal.

*Where's the truth, Alex?* she wondered. *Where's the truth?*

For a time the images of bodies arranged in a grotesque tableau, with bullet holes in their foreheads, occupied her thoughts. Her unpleasant reverie ended abruptly when, hands up, palms in, dramatically banging the scrub room door into the wall as he backed through it, Carl Gilbride crossed before the multitude and entered the OR.

*Let the games begin,* Jessie thought as Gilbride was

quickly gowned and gloved. Having seen his often rushed and awkward technique in the OR, Jessie realized that ARTIE, with its meticulous, microscopic abilities, might well represent an improvement.

She scanned the two monitor screens. The operative field was prepped and ready. The color-enhanced image of Hermann's brain tumor, displayed by the crew upstairs, had excellent resolution. At the moment, normal brain tissue was navy blue, and the meningioma canary yellow. Blood vessels, appropriately, were crimson. On the other side of the observation window, all the principals were in position. Although Gilbride was largely screened from her by the resident, Jessie could see Eastman Tolliver on an eight-inch riser, watching intently from over Carl's right shoulder.

A four-million-dollar grant . . . Claude Malloche . . . Count Rolf Hermann . . . Alex Bishop . . . so much was riding on the next few hours.

'Ready, Dr. Sanjay?' Gilbride asked.

'No problems,' the anesthesiologist said.

'Dr. Toomei?'

'Ready, sir.'

'Mrs. Duncan?'

'All set,' the scrub nurse replied.

'Dr. Pfeffer?'

'At your command, sir,' the radiologist called out.

'Well, then, scalpel and periosteal elevator, please.'

The approach to getting ARTIE into place was straight-forward. With the Count fully asleep, a probe would be inserted through a small incision up one nostril, and a half-inch hole would be drilled through the skull where the bone was thinnest. A fine guide wire would be fed in through the opening, and ARTIE would then be sent in along the wire, and directed to the anterior edge of the meningioma. If all went well, most of the two hours or more that would have been spent simply reaching the tumor by traditional methods would have been saved, to say nothing of the elimination of much of the damage to intervening structures.

*Go, ARTIE!* Jessie cheered. *Go!*

The insertion went perfectly, and was accompanied by murmurs of amazement from those in the crowd, when Gilbride announced he was in position and ready to begin the dissection. Jessie had to admit grudgingly that the neurosurgical chief was handling the controls of their invention quite expertly.

The ultrasound liquefaction and removal of Hermann's tumor began uneventfully. Gilbride, working with appropriate care, seemed firmly in control. In spite of herself, every few minutes, Jessie's attention drifted away from the screens and over to where Alex was watching. From time to time, he was gone, no doubt going through the motions of his security job. But mostly he was there, up against his pillar, watching.

'Okay, Dr. Sanjay,' Gilbride said. 'I think it is appropriate now to awaken our patient for some functional MRI mapping.'

Jessie studied the tumor image on the screen. About a third of the meningioma had been removed – the most accessible part. There was still a good deal that could have been melted away before Hermann's cooperation was needed. It was almost as if Gilbride was stalling doing whatever he could to delay an attack on the portion of the tumor that was most intimately adjacent to normal brain.

It took a while for the anesthesia to lessen. During that time, Gilbride continued to pick away at what remained of the bulkiest portion of the tumor. Jessie was watching the monitor nonstop now. She was certain no one else appreciated it yet, but several times, Gilbride had started ARTIE off in the wrong direction, then quickly reversed. He seemed to be having trouble with the spatial relationships between the views of the tumor and the movement of the robot. To Jessie, ARTIE was essentially a video-game race car, able to move in any direction, but with controls that were in a fixed position. So when ARTIE was moving in one direction, a right-hand move on the control panel meant a right turn. Rut in the opposite direction, a right turn meant going left on the controls, and in between, there were literally an infinite number of permutations. To a video-game junkie like Jessie, the moves were second nature. Rut she could see that as the field of surgery grew smaller and smaller, Gilbride was having more and more trouble maneuvering.

Twice he turned off the audio and called Skip Porter over for a whispered exchange. Both times, apparently assured by Skip that the robot was functioning properly, Gilbride returned to the surgery.

'Count Hermann,' he said now, 'lift your right hand a bit if you can hear me.'

The translator; a nurse who had translated on occasion for some of Jessie's patients, spoke from behind Gilbride, just to Eastman Tolliver's left. Despite his adequate comprehension of spoken English, it had been the Count's decision to have commands relayed to him in German. If Alex was right about the man's facility with languages, Jessie was thinking, the request was part of the charade. Through the overhead camera, Hermann's chest, where his hands rested beneath the drapes, was visible. Immediately after Carl's order was translated, the Count responded with the requested movement.

The operation proceeded for another twenty minutes. Jessie wished the overhead camera was focused on ARTIE's control panel rather than the essentially static operative field. That view, along with the MRI, would have told her a great deal. Again and again now as the dissection became more difficult, she saw Gilbride miss once, even twice, before directing the robot along the proper course. The errors were minuscule hitches – like the feints of a prizefighter before striking in the other direction. Rut they were errors nonetheless. She was certain of it.

As ARTIE ate more and more into the tumor, closer to normal brain, Gilbride was clearly having more and more difficulty controlling its movement. At one point, where fibers of normal brain had to have been damaged by an errant thrust, Hans Pfeffer looked over, caught Jessie's eve, and shook his head grimly.

Alex, perhaps reading her expression and intensified concentration, managed to connect with her long enough to mouth the words, *What's happening?* Her response was a shrug.

Gilbride placed the LED goggles on his patient and requested a functional magnetic resonance sequence, the brain mapping alternating with more dissection. Twice, Hermann seemed unable to follow commands. Both times, ARTIE was slightly off course. This was no mechanical failure. The technique, at this level, was simply beyond Gilbride's ability. At one point Jessie thought he might back the robot out – admit he could go no further and simply opt for a full, open craniotomy. But Gilbride persisted. She wondered if it was getting to the point where he was pitting Rolf Hermann's brain against a four-million-dollar grant.

Another muted conversation with Skip. Another helpless gesture by the research technician.

*ARTIE is functioning fine,* Jessie could almost hear him whispering.

Hans Pfeffer made his way over to her and pulled her aside.

'Do something!' he whispered.

It was the most animated she had ever seen the laconic Dutchman.

'You have a suggestion?'

'There's the microphone. Tell him to stop. The robot's just not ready for this.'

*Oh, ARTIE's ready, all right*, she wanted to reply. *Ready and able.*

'Hans,' she whispered back, 'Carl is chief of this department, and one of the most powerful men in this hospital. He controls my job, and I would bet a good portion of your research funds as well. Nobody would survive busting in on him in the middle of a case with an audience like this. Nobody.'

There were concerned murmurs in the crowd now as first the other radiologist then the two neurosurgeons observing the case picked up on what was happening.

'Get in there!' Hans whispered. 'Jessie, get in there before –'

Pfeffer stopped in midsentence. He and Jessie stared at the screen where a faint gray puff had just appeared, right at the snout and just to the left of ARTIE, clearly outside the boundary of the tumor. The smudge was tiny but unmistakable, and it was definitely expanding. A deep arterial hemorrhage – the neurosurgical equivalent of a nuclear explosion. Guided off course by Carl, one of ARTIE's pincers had torn an artery. Seconds later, Gilbride's strained voice came over the intercom.

'Dr. Copeland, are you still out there?'

Jessie ran to the microphone over the console.

'I'm here.'

'You see what's going on. ARTIE's malfunctioning. Could you come in here, please?'

On the screen, the hemorrhage was continuing to grow. Count Rolf Hermann had begun writhing as the pain caused by rapidly building pressure deep within his brain overcame the twilight anesthesia that had been used for his functional MRI.

'Pramod,' Jessie ordered to the anesthesiologist, 'put him to sleep and drop his pressure. Give him forty of Lasix and a hundred of mannitol *stat*. Carl, I'll be right in.'

The crowd parted as Jessie made a quick check to be certain she was wearing no metal, pulled on a hair covering and mask, and hurried into the OR. The scrub nurse was waiting with gloves and a gown. Danl Toomei stepped back from his spot between the tori across from Gilbride to allow her in. As she moved into his place, she looked over at Gilbride. What she could see of his face was blanched, but there was no way to read his eyes. Above and behind Gilbride's right shoulder; looming like a surgical specter, seemingly transfixed by the scene, was Eastman Tolliver.

'Enhance the hemorrhage, please,' Jessie said.

'Roger that,' one of Pfeffer's people in the lab upstairs replied.

In seconds, on her screen and Gilbride's, the blood leaking into Hermann's brain was transformed into a crimson grid. Almost certainly, the torn vessel was a branch of the left anterior cerebral artery.

Gilbride cut off the sound. He leaned forward so that no one but Jessie – not the scrub nurse, not even Tolliver – could hear what he was saying.

'It . . . the robot just broke down,' he whispered. 'I couldn't control it.'

'I know,' Jessie responded.

'That hemorrhage is huge already. Pressure's building. What should we do?'

'Fry it,' Jessie said simply. 'Do you mind if we switch sides so I can get at ARTIE's guidance console?'

Gilbride hesitated. It required no telepathy to know why. His patient's life versus the humiliation of giving up the principal surgeon's spot in front of a large audience – for most not a difficult call, but for Carl, gut-wrenching. Jessie was about to remind him that he could always blame the disaster on a mechanical defect, when he apparently reminded himself.

'Come on over,' he said.

Jessie took her position at the control panel and switched on the microphone.

'Hey, guys,' she called to the crew upstairs, 'see if you can get me some sort of enhancement of the left anterior circulation and a leaking artery just branching off it. I'm going to try and swing ARTIE around and cauterize the tear.'

'We copy,' came the heavily accented voice of Israeli programming wizard Manny Geller.

The neodymium-YAG laser – YAG for yttrium aluminum garnet – was a relatively recent addition to ARTIE, giving it the power to cauterize along with its existing abilities to melt tissue with ultrasound and to suction debris and fluid through a fairly large tube. This would be the first time Jessie had used the laser on human tissue. But there was no time to open up Rolf Hermann's skull and go after the bleeder directly.

The image beamed down from the computer lab was exactly what Jessie wanted.

'There it is,' she said. 'See?'

The leaking vessel was microns from ARTIE. The trick would be to back the robot up and turn it slightly. Slowly, but with unerring control, Jessie completed the maneuver.

'Okay, cross your fingers. Ready, aim . . . fire.'

She depressed the button controlling the laser beam. The blood surrounding the leak instantly boiled. Immediately, the expanding hemorrhage stopped. For one minute, two, they stood there in silence, watching the screens.

'Jessie,' Hans Pfeffer called in, 'the bleeding's stopped and the repair seems to be holding. Well done. Well done.'

Someone standing near Pfeffer began clapping, then several more joined in, the sound reverberating through the speakers in the OR. Moments later, the OR staff in the room was applauding as well – all except the man standing across from her.

'Nicely done, Doctor,' Gilbride said, loud enough for all to hear. 'I'm afraid it's back to the drawing board for our friend ARTIE.'

'Before we bring ARTIE out, I want to try and aspirate as much of the hemorrhage as we can.'

'Please do. After Count Hermann wakes up, we'll have to discuss removing the rest of the meningioma sometime in the future.'

Jessie stared at her boss, but said nothing. She had seen enough miracles, including the one in NICU 6 right now, to know that anything was possible. But the truth was, Rolf Hermann, or Claude Malloche, or whoever the man lying there was, had about as much chance of waking up from this tragedy as she did of winning the lottery.

# Chapter 21

Knowing the space-age efficiency of the hospital grapevine, Jessie was certain that word of the fiasco in the MRI-OR had spread throughout the hospital by the time Rolf Hermann was transferred to the NICU on Surgical Seven. His condition was listed with the switchboard operator as critical, but that really did not tell the whole story. The Count's pupils were dilated and unreactive to light or any other stimulus. The Rabinski sign – an upward movement of the great toe when the sole of the foot is stimulated – was present bilaterally, signifying that there was essentially a functional disconnection of the brain from the rest of the body.

Carl Gilbride was distracted and irritable, and several times snapped at the nurses as his patient was being transferred to the unit bed. For brief moments, Jessie actually felt some sympathy for the man. But in the main, she was disgusted with him and not a little embarrassed for the department. The combination of his hubris, greed, and inflated opinion of his surgical skills had led him to a series of decisions that would ultimately cost a life and, in all likelihood, a four-million-dollar grant as well. Now he had insisted that Jessie accompany him into the family room to speak with Orlis Hermann and the Count's sons and daughter. Orlis was waiting for them in the family room along with her stepdaughter and one of her stepsons. Jessie mused on where Hermann's other son might be at so critical a time, then took a seat behind Gilbride. As she surveyed the family, she wondered if Rolf Hermann's beautiful wife could really be, as Alex claimed, an assassin and hardened mercenary, and if the grown offspring, sitting there statuelike, could be nothing more than bodyguards, chosen from Claude Malloche's elite inner circle. If these people were capable of murdering Sylvan Mays, who hadn't even performed an operation on Malloche, how would they treat the ones who had botched it?

*Tone it down, Carl,* she was thinking. *Tell them it's bad, but for God's sake, don't tell them it's hopeless.*

'Well,' Gilbride said, tenting his fingers in a blatantly pensive pose. 'I'm afraid the news isn't good. Things started off well enough, and we had a good deal of the tumor removed, but then we ran into some . . . problems.'

'Problems?' Orlis said stonily.

'Mrs. Hermann' – Gilbride paused as if searching for words – 'during the operation, your husband had a fairly large hemorrhage into his brain.'

'A hemorrhage? From what?'

'I can't say for certain. Sometimes, during major surgery, arteries just . . . rupture. In this case, with the Count's tumor situated so deep in his brain, it's possible that an artery might have been nicked and bled.'

Orlis quickly translated in German for the Count's offspring. The son asked a question, which she answered. Jessie tried to get a read on the group, but failed completely. If they were all killers, then they were damn fine actors as well. If they weren't killers, then Alex was either dead wrong, or a deadly sham himself.

'What can we expect now?' Orlis asked.

*Please,* Jessie pleaded silently. *Please tell them there's hope.*

If Gilbride handled things right, at least there might be time for Alex to make a move before anyone got hurt.

The neurosurgical chief shook his head grimly. His expression was tight and severe. Jessie had seen the look before. The man was preparing to paint the bleakest picture possible in hopes that any improvement would make him look good. It was exactly what she had been praying he would not do.

'Well,' he said, tenting his fingers again and looking

down at them, 'the hemorrhage was quite extensive. Dr. Copeland and I were able to use our intraoperative robot to cauterize the vessel and stop the bleeding, but I'm afraid by that time a good deal of damage had been done. I –'

'Dr. Gilbride,' Orlis said, her blue-white eyes impaling him, 'would you please stop mumbling and stalling and tell us if my husband is going to survive this.'

*No!* Jessie's thoughts screamed. *Don't react!*

'Mrs. Hermann,' Gilbride replied, clearly frayed, 'I know you're upset, but I do not appreciate being spoken to like that.'

'I brought you a man who was completely intact, and you hand me back a . . . a vegetable. What do you expect, praise?'

Jessie couldn't remember the last time she had seen Gilbride so uncomfortable. He stood and faced Orlis, his arms folded across his chest, his cheeks flushed.

'Mrs. Hermann, you and Count Hermann read all the possible outcomes of his operation and attested in writing to your acceptance of them. Now, we'll continue doing everything we can for him. When there is any news to report, we'll find you. In the meantime, beginning tomorrow afternoon, for the forty-eight hours I'm in New York, Dr. Copeland will be covering my service.'

'New York!' Orlis exclaimed, almost in unison with Jessie.

'I'm due to sit on a panel at a very important conference tomorrow afternoon at NYU,' Gilbride said with far too much pride in his voice.

*For God's sake, Carl, can't you hide that outrageous ego for once? Our lives could depend on it.*

'Dr. Gilbride,' Orlis said with chilling calm, 'I promise you that if you leave Boston with my husband in this condition, you will regret it.'

Jessie expected a combative response from her chief. Instead, Gilbride just stood there, transfixed by the woman.

'We'll talk about it in the morning,' he said finally, in a strained, unnatural voice.

Without so much as a glance at Jessie, he turned and hurried from the room.

Jessie forced herself to remain still – not simply to leap up and follow him.

'He's very upset,' she managed to say.

'You'd best speak with him, Doctor Copeland,' Orlis replied with her same frightening calm. 'Tell him I meant what I said. I don't want him leaving this hospital for any reason other than to go home and rest. If he deserts my husband, he will regret it.'

*Regret as in Sylvan Mays?* Jessie wondered. 'I'll tell him,' she said.


'Raise your right hand. No, Devereau, your *other* right hand. Are you ragging on me?'

'Just . . . want see . . . if you were pay . . . attention,' Sara said thickly.

With great effort, she raised her right arm off the bed and issued a clumsy but unmistakable thumbs up. Jessie answered her in kind.

*Progress, progress, progress*, she chanted to herself. All that ever mattered in neurosurgical post-ops was progress. And progress Sara most certainly was making.

Shaken by the exchange with Orlis, Jessie forced herself to focus through the neuro check on her patient. Orlis . . . Alex . . . Gilbride . . . Malloche. In the kind of acute-care medicine she practiced, distraction was often the touchstone to disaster. She was beginning to feel smothered. She badly needed to talk to *someone* about what was happening. Emily DelGreco was the only candidate.

Jessie wrote down the order to keep Sara in the NICU, although clinically she no longer needed it. The nurses on the floor were quite good, but the ones in the unit were special, with a bulldog determination to do whatever was necessary for their patients' recovery. Until utilization review began making a fuss, or the bed became needed for someone else, or Sara jumped up and demanded a transfer herself, she would remain right where she was.

178

By the time Jessie had finished writing, Sara was asleep, exhausted. Jessie brushed her cheek gently, then headed to the phone at the nurses' station.

Emily had begged off work for the day. There was a show at her younger son's school. Jessie hoped she could reach her at home. It would be a huge relief to share the burden Alex had placed on her.

Emily's oldest, Ted, answered.

'Mom's not here, Jessie. She went out an hour or so ago. I thought she was with you.'

'Why would you think that?'

'She got a phone call, then she said she had to go to the hospital for a while.'

'Did she say who called her?'

'Nope. I just assumed it was you.'

Jessie shifted nervously. The DelGrecos lived in Brookline, just a short way from Eastern Mass Medical. If she had left an hour ago, she would be here by now.

'Your dad home?'

'Nope. He almost never gets home before seven.'

'When he does, would you ask him to page me at the hospital?'

'Sure.'

'And if you hear from Mom, tell her the same thing.'

'Okay. Is something the matter?'

'No, no. Just some stuff going on with one of the patients that I want to check with her about. This place is so huge that your mom's probably in another part of the hospital right now. I'll have her paged.'

'You still have that pinball machine in your apartment?'

'Of course. You'll have to come over sometime soon and play. As I recall, you came close to my record last time.'

'Hardly close. But I'd like another try. That was fun.'

'Take care, Ted.'

Jessie set the receiver down and immediately paged Emily. Fifteen minutes went by without a return call. Jessie was hunched over Sara's chart, writing a progress note, when Alex Bishop startled her from behind.

'Hey, Doc,' he said softly.

'Jesus, don't sneak up on me like that! Clear your throat or something.'

'Sorry.' He looked about to ensure no one was listening. 'Can I talk to you?'

'Alex, I still don't know if I feel comfortable saying anything to you about our patients.'

'You don't believe what I've told you?'

'I . . . don't know what to believe.'

He passed over a piece of paper.

'Here's a phone number in Virginia. Ask for a man named Benson, Harold Benson. He's head of internal affairs at the agency. They're the ones who are after me. He knows me and what I've been doing these past five years. If you tell him the situation and ask him nicely, he might say who I am.'

'It won't prove anything. These phone things can be set up.'

'Okay, then, Doctor,' he said, his eyes narrowed and hard, 'play it any way you want. I said I was sorry for not starting with the truth. I can't do any more than that. With or without your help, I'm going to bring Claude Malloche down. If people get hurt in the process, it'll be on your head as much as mine.'

He turned and started down the hall.

'Wait,' Jessie called out, stopping him. 'What do you want to know?'

Alex walked slowly back. The intensity in his eyes was still there, but not the unsettling hardness.

'Thank you,' he whispered. 'What's the situation?'

'Your friend Hermann, or Malloche, is in room two on a vent,' she said, feeling relief at having made a decision.

'So I saw. Is he going to wake up?' Jessie shook her head.

'Stranger things have happened,' she said. 'But in my opinion, if he wakes up, look for a star in the east.'

'How long can he go on like this?'

'I couldn't say. Hours? Weeks? I've been surprised both ways.'

'But he's not going to wake up.'

'He had a hell of a hemorrhage. There's been pretty massive brain damage. That's all I can say.'

180

'Okay. As far as I know, Jorge Cardoza will be on his way here from Madrid tomorrow. If Hermann is still on the respirator, we'll have to find a way to get Cardoza into the hospital without having him run into the wife.'

'If it comes to that, I'll see what I can do to help. Right now, Orlis is in a pretty foul mood.'

'Her name's Arlette, remember?'

'Orlis, Arlette – whoever she is, she just threatened Dr. Gilbride.'

'She did what?'

'He said he was flying to New York tomorrow to be on some sort of panel, and that I'd be in charge of the Count while he was gone. She told him he'd regret it if he did. Carl was pretty shaken up.'

'Good. That could save his life. Maybe it's time to tell him what's going on – who he's dealing with.'

'And you're certain who that is?'

'Virtually. Interpol hasn't been able to come up with any match for the fingerprints I sent them. But that's not surprising. They have a few dozen sets on file from assassinations that are believed to be Malloche's work, including those murders at that MRI clinic in France. But it's possible not a single one belongs to him.'

'Or they could all be Malloche if he's more than one person.'

'Nice theory. But he's only one person all right. That guy right in there. How did Gilbride screw up so badly in the operation?'

'He shouldn't have read his press clippings after the Marci Sheprow surgery. That's how.'

'If Malloche dies, I want his body.'

'If Malloche dies, I want protection for Carl and me.'

'I'll find a way. Meanwhile, we're going to stay on the job.'

'We?'

'I told you I had a little help.'

'But –'

'That's all I can say.' He scribbled a phone number on a piece of progress note paper. 'This is an answering service here in Boston. They have instructions on how to contact me if necessary. If anything happens to Hermann, just call and tell them. We'll wait it out until Cardoza arrives. Meanwhile, if Malloche dies, I'll be going after his body, his wife, and those three junior killers. Once we get a positive ID from Cardoza and then get Arlette Malloche and her so-called stepchildren into custody, we'll learn what we need to know.'

'You scare me, Alex.'

'Sometimes, even after all these years, I scare myself. Jessie, I know how difficult it was to decide to help me. Thank you for trusting me.'

'I don't,' she said.


Jessie watched as he made his way down the corridor, pausing just long enough to glimpse into room 2 as he passed. *Five years.* Almost as long as it had taken her to complete her neurosurgical residency. It was a hell of a long time to chase an obsession – especially with so little success. Now, with no firm proof that the patient in 2 was Malloche, and with the man so near death, it was possible Alex's quest would end not with a bang, but with the whimper of lingering uncertainty.

Jessie checked the time – nearly twenty minutes since her page to Emily had been sent. She wondered if Emily's beeper could possibly be malfunctioning or might simply have been turned off. At that instant her own pager sounded. The display gave Alice Twitchell's name and extension.

'Oh, Dr. Copeland, I'm so glad you answered so quickly,' Carl's meticulous assistant said. 'I'm in Dr. Gilbride's office with Mr. Tolliver. He's having a severe headache – a migraine. He told me to page you and not to bother trying to find Dr. Gilbride. Could you possibly come down and have a look at him?'

'I'll be right over,' Jessie said. 'Alice, do you by any chance know where Emily DelGreco might be?'

'Gee, no, Dr. Copeland,' the woman said apologetically. 'I have no idea.'

# Chapter 22

When Jessie arrived, Eastman Tolliver, wearing gray slacks and a navy blue blazer, was supine on the Moroccan leather sofa in Carl's waiting room, a pillow under his knees, his feet hanging several inches over the armrest. He held the crook of his elbow pressed tightly across his eyes, and was actually trembling with discomfort. There was a wastebasket strategically placed on the rug beside him. Alice Mitchell was trying to move his arm enough to get a damp washcloth onto his forehead.

'Eastman, it's me,' Jessie said, kneeling at his side. 'Can you hear me all right?'

Tolliver nodded.

'It's beginning to let up,' he said hoarsely. 'I've had these before.'

His speech sounded just a little bit thick.

'How long has it been this time?'

'Fifteen or twenty minutes,' Alice said. 'Dr. Gilbride was supposed to meet Mr. Tolliver forty-five minutes ago, but he called to say he'd be late.'

'We had some business to attend to in the unit,' Jessie said.

She gently removed Eastman's arm from across his face.

'You look a little peaked, my friend,' she said, beginning her neurological evaluation with the observation that the skin fold on the right side of his mouth was marginally less pronounced than that on the left. 'Could you open your eyes? . . . Good. Now, follow my finger if you can.'

*Pupils midposition, reactive . . . Slight weakness in lateral gaze, right eye . . . Possible slight droop, right lid . . .*

'Eastman, could you show me your teeth, as if you were

183

smiling?' *Possible facial weakness, right* . . . 'Please stick out your tongue. Good. Now, squeeze my hands.' *No obvious upper extremity weakness.*

'It's letting up,' Tolliver said.

'Good. Eastman, when's the last time you saw a doctor for these headaches?'

'I don't know. A couple of years, maybe. He said they were migraine headaches.'

'Do you take medicine?'

'Over-the-counter sometimes. That's all.'

Jessie walked over to where Alice Twitchell stood watching.

'Alice, please call the ER and have them send a surgical resident, a gurney, and a nurse up here, *stat*,' she said. 'Then call radiology and tell them I'm going to need an MRBI tonight.'

'Yes, Doctor.'

Alice scurried away.

The color had begun to return to Tolliver's face, and his eyes no longer seemed glazed over. The abnormal neurological findings were persisting, but while they were potentially a harbinger of serious pathology, like an aneurysm or a tumor, they were also consistent with certain variations of migraine. Fortunately, Jessie knew that with the technology at her disposal, it wasn't necessary to guess – or to wait very long.

'Eastman, how is it now?'

'Quite a bit better.'

'Good. I've noticed some things in the rather incomplete exam I just did that concern me. I think you should have a few blood tests and an MRI.'

'Are you sure I need all that?'

'I'm very sure. Your symptoms and my findings are quite possibly all due to migraine headaches, but I can't be positive. It may be fine for you to travel back to California, but not before we see your MRI. Have you had one before?'

'No, I haven't,' Tolliver said, still lying motionless enough so that Jessie knew his pain was persisting.

'Okay,' she said, 'just take it easy. The stretcher will be here before long. Don't try to sit up.'

'You're the boss.'

Carl Gilbride cleared his throat to announce his presence in the doorway.

'What's going on here?'

'Oh, hi, Carl. Mr. Tolliver's having a headache. Twenty or twenty-five minutes now, pretty severe. He has a history of migraines.'

Gilbride approached the sofa.

'Eastman, how are you feeling?'

'Not perfect, but improved, thank you.'

'Well, that's excellent news. Excellent. I've made dinner reservations for us at the Four Seasons. But you can feel free to rest a bit more for now. We have plenty of time. The chef there is the best in the city.'

'Um, Carl, could I speak with you for a moment?' Jessie asked.

'Certainly, what is it?'

'In your office.'

'Oh, nonsense,' Tolliver cut in. 'Carl, Dr. Copeland has had a chance to examine me. She is concerned enough to want me to have an MRI and some blood tests.'

'For a migraine?'

'Carl,' Jessie said, 'Eastman had a slight right facial droop, a little bit of thickness of his speech, and maybe some eye signs as well.'

Without excusing himself, Gilbride inserted himself between her and Tolliver, and peered down at the man's face.

'Follow my finger, Eastman,' he ordered, repeating some of the maneuvers Jessie had already done. 'I don't see anything,' he pronounced.

Not, I don't see anything *now*, Jessie noted. The implication in his words and tone was that there was nothing the matter – that the observations that had so concerned her were inconsequential. Jessie steeled herself for a confrontation. Whether or not the signs were still present was immaterial. They *had* been there, and many serious neurological conditions had waxing and waning findings at some stage. Her patience with her department chief had just about run out. Tolliver saved her from a potentially destructive blowup.

'Look, Carl,' he said. 'I like a good meal as much as the next fellow, but I also want to be certain this headache is a plain old migraine. It hurt like the devil.'

'Very well, then,' Gilbride replied in a voice that already had some pout in it, 'I'll call down and see if we can get a CT scan.'

'Carl ,' Jessie said, 'I've got a team from the ER on their way up here right now to bring Eastman down for some bloodwork and an MRI.'

Unseen by their patient, Gilbride glowered at her.

'That's fine,' he said icily. 'More than I would have done for what seems like a garden-variety migraine, but if Eastman doesn't mind missing dinner, we'll do it. I'll take over from here and walk him down.'

'Actually, Carl,' Tolliver said, 'I'd prefer it if Dr. Copeland continued as my doctor.'

'But –'

'I know it upsets you, but I am the patient. And at the moment, if it is all right with Dr. Copeland, she is my choice.'

Was Tolliver's unequivocal insistence on her some sort of comment on the bungled surgery? Jessie suspected so. Whatever the reason, she felt nothing but delight.

'I'll be more than happy to honor your request, Eastman,' she said, carefully avoiding eye contact with her chief.

At that moment, both Jessie's and Gilbride's beepers went off almost simultaneously. Then the phone across the hall in Gilbride's office began ringing.

'It's the unit,' Jessie said.

'Mine, too.'

Alice Twitchell came racing over breathlessly.

'Dr. Gilbride,' she said, 'Count Hermann has had a cardiac arrest. They're working on him now, but they want you over there. Dr. Copeland, the people from the ER are on the way up.'

'Thank you,' Jessie replied.

'Oh, that's just awful news about Count Hermann,' said Tolliver. 'Simply awful.'

Gilbride looked almost apoplectic. Jessie imagined that there was no place on earth he would less like to be than supervising the resuscitation on his recent surgical calamity.

'Jessie, I'd appreciate it if you would honor Eastman's request and function as his primary physician,' he said, through nearly clenched teeth. 'Meanwhile, I'd best hurry on over to the NICU.'

'I'll be up to help as soon as I can. Carl, have you seen Emily around?'

'DelGreco?'

'Yes.'

'Not today I haven't.'

'Thanks,' she said, but he had already hurried off.

Moments later the elevator arrived, and the team from the ER emerged.

Jessie introduced Tolliver to the resident and nurse.

'Eastman, you're in good hands for now,' she said. 'While they're getting your tests done, I'm going to run over to the unit and see if I can help Dr. Gilbride. I'll see you downstairs in just a little while.'

'I have the utmost confidence in you,' Tolliver said. 'Let's hope this is nothing serious.'

'Let's hope that, indeed,' Jessie replied.

But as she aided Eastman onto the stretcher and helped wheel him over to the elevator, every bit of instinct and intuition she posessed was telling her otherwise.

# Chapter 23

Philanthropic director comes to evaluate neurosurgical program and ends up needing an emergency MR. . . . Patient he watched be operated on has catastrophic result, then has cardiac arrest.

*What else could possibly go wrong?* Jessie wondered as she hurried down the corridor of the office wing and through the doorway to the Surgical Tower. As a medical student, and even as a resident, she had always been excited by the frenetic action and drama of a full code 99. Now, while she accepted them as an essential part of the hospital, codes no longer held any allure. Their outcomes were, more often than not, preordained. Patients could frequently be hauled through the initial crisis, but unless the underlying problem was dealt with, and quickly, it was just a matter of time before their next code 99.

Catherine Purcell, the evening nursing supervisor and a longterm veteran of the hospital wars, was standing just outside the doorway to room 2.

'Hey, Catherine,' Jessie said, 'how goes it in there?'

'I think the Grim Reaper is well ahead. The patient was sort of stable, then suddenly he lost his pressure and went into V. fib. Now even that rhythm is degenerating. Thank God Joe Milano from cardiology is running the code.'

'Is Dr. Gilbride in there?'

'Oh yes, he certainly is. What's with him, Jess?'

'What do you mean?'

'He stopped by the unit an hour or so ago to check on Count Hermann. Two of my nurses were talking and one of them laughed. Gilbride thought they were laughing at him, even though both of them claim he wasn't even the

188

topic of conversation. He called me and is threatening to have the nurse who laughed disciplined or even kicked out of the ICU.'

'Which nurse?'

'Laura Pearson.'

'Jeez. These nurses can be harsh at times, but of all of them, she'd be the least likely to say anything unpleasant about anyone. Carl's just a wreck over this calamity, I think – hypersensitive for a while. He'll get over it.'

'He'd better. I have a black belt in defending my nurses. Does the Count have any chance brainwise?'

'Not much. I'd better get in there and see if I can lend a hand.'

'If you have a chance, speak to Gilbride about Laura.'

'Will do. Catherine, have you by any chance seen Emily?'

'DelGreco? No. But I've only been wandering around the wards for a couple of hours. If I do see her, I'll tell her to give you a page.'

'Thanks.'

There was the usual code 99 crush of bodies in room 2 of the neurosurgical ICU – nurses, med techs, a respiratory tech, an anesthesiologist, and several house officers, with a couple of medical students thrown in just to increase the critical mass. And of course, there was Carl, still in his spotless, starched lab coat, standing just close enough to the action to act as if he were in charge, while deferring – at least Jessie *hoped* he was – to the medical resident and to cardiology fellow Joe Milano, each of whom was far better equipped to handle a code than any staff person.

Rolf Hermann had been detached from the respirator. A respiratory tech was squeezing a breathing bag to ventilate him through his endotracheal tube. The bedsheets had been thrown aside. Hermann's naked body looked vulnerable, although the man was over six feet tall and quite sturdily built. In addition to the breathing tube, he had a monitoring/blood-drawing line in the radial artery at one wrist, an infusion line in a vein higher up in his arm, a tube through his nose and down into his stomach, connected to suction, and a catheter draining his bladder into a plastic bag that hung below the bed. There were cables connecting the EKG leads on his chest to the monitor, and others snaking up from an oximeter on one of his fingers and a port on the arterial line. Viewed this way, he looked like anything but the deadly, merciless killer of hundreds who had been the object of Alex Bishop's obsession for five years. But illness and injury were great equalizers, and count or killer, there he was.

Jessie worked her way through the crowd to Carl's side.

'How's it going?' she asked.

Gilbride kept his eyes fixed on the action. He looked frazzled and irritated.

'What in the hell did you say to Tolliver that turned him against me?' he said out of the side of his mouth. 'Joe, have you given him any IV bicarb?' he called over to the cardiology fellow.

'We don't use it anymore,' the fellow called back.

'I knew that. I just thought this might be an exception. I think we should shock him again, yes?'

'After we give him some more epi, Dr. Gilbride.'

'Right. Give him the epi, then shock.'

'Carl,' Jessie said, 'I didn't say anything at all to him except what you know – that he needs an MRI.'

'Four million dollars,' Gilbride said, pausing theatrically between each word. 'That's what that man holds in his hand. Get ready to shock, everyone. Go ahead, Joe.'

'We're shocking. Everyone clear! Now!'

There was a muffled pop from the paddles that the cardiologist held pressed against Hermann's left chest, and four hundred joules of electricity were sent streaking through the Count's body. His arms flapped off the bed, then fell back down heavily. His legs flared out, then relaxed. Five seconds passed with no response. Then the cardiograph pattern on the monitor showed one beat . . . then nothing . . . then suddenly another. . . and another.

'I'll be damned,' Jessie said, marveling at the quickness and skill of her younger colleagues, and trying to remember that once, not that long ago, she was as good at all this as they were now.

Helped by a heavy dose of cardiac medications, Rolf Hermann's heartbeat rapidly stabilized, and his blood pressure rose from zero to sixty to ninety. His blood oxygen content rose as well. The patient was a save . . . at least for the moment.

'Do you think he arrested because of increased intracranial pressure?' Jessie asked.

'Maybe,' Gilbride replied, still looking straight ahead. 'I'll give him some more diuretic and up his steroids. If Porter hadn't mistuned that damn robot of his, none of this would be happening.'

Jessie was about to leap to Skip's defense, but decided against it. Gilbride was on a knife's edge as it was. This was not the moment.

Hermann's pressure and pulse were holding steady. One by one, the room began emptying out. This round, at least, had gone to the caregivers. But Jessie knew that the Reaper was, if nothing else, patient. Barring a miracle inside the Count's skull, another round wasn't far off.

'Do you think we could talk for a couple of minutes?' she asked.

'I've got to go speak to the Dragon Lady about her husband's latest crisis. You know, if you hadn't admitted these people to my service without waiting for my approval, none of this would be happening.'

Jessie refused to be provoked.

'What I have to say won't take but a few minutes,' she said. 'It has to do with the Count and his wife.'

'I've got to go speak with Hermann's family. Then I'm going to go down and check on Tolliver. After we confirm that his MRI is negative, there's still time for me to get him to the Four Seasons and maybe smooth things over. I can't believe he was in the OR for this fiasco.'

*Neither can I*, Jessie thought.

'Carl,' she said firmly, 'I want a few minutes with you. Right now. It's very important.'

Startled by her tone, Gilbride looked directly at her for

the first time. Still, he appeared distracted and unfocused.

'I'll . . . um . . . meet you in the conference room in just a minute,' he said. 'I need to see what the cardiologist wants to do here.'

Jessie went directly to the nurses' station and had most of Emily's home number dialed when she set the receiver down. If Em had checked in or returned home, her son Ted would have told her to call Jessie. He was that kind of kid. One more hour, she decided. If there was no word from her by then, it would be time to panic.

The small conference room was located just to one end of the unit. Jessie waited there only a minute or two before Gilbride arrived. He had the look of a treed animal. To the outside world, he was still the king of robotic surgery, in demand at hospital conferences and on talk shows. But his immediate universe was coming unraveled. He perceived himself, not without justification, to be the brunt of cruel jokes throughout the hospital. He was in the process of having a very highly connected post-op patient die of surgical complications. And perhaps worst of all, the man holding the purse strings of a four-million-dollar grant had all but issued a vote of no confidence in him by choosing to be cared for by one of his junior faculty.

'So,' he said brusquely, 'what do you want?'

'I . . . I want to talk to you about Orlis and Rolf Hermann,' Jessie said, wondering how she was going to pull this one off.

'Go on.'

'This may be hard for me to explain, and hard for you to accept, Carl, but I have reason to believe that Hermann may not be a count at all, and that both he and his wife may in fact be quite dangerous.'

Gilbride's anger gave way to absolute incredulity. Jessie could read his thoughts.

*Now what kind of goddamn trouble are you trying to cause me? Haven't you done enough?*

'I don't understand,' he said.

Jessie tried as best she could to explain about Alex Bishop and his theories. She could tell by Gilbride's expression and body language that he was simply not equipped for another assault on his academic fiefdom – especially one with no objective proof whatsoever.

'This is insane,' he said when she had finished. 'You think these are the people responsible for Sylvan Mays' murder?'

'It's quite possible.'

'And this man – this Bishop – he's masquerading as a hospital guard but he's actually CIA?'

'That's what he says, yes.'

'But he hasn't given you any concrete proof of that?'

'He gave me a phone number of someone in Virginia that he said might vouch for him.'

'But you haven't called?'

Jessie felt as if she were being cross-examined by a hostile attorney. She felt herself pulling in.

'No,' she said. 'I couldn't see the point.'

'So what do you want me to do about all this?'

'I want you to be careful, Carl. Especially with things going so poorly for Hermann. I don't want to cross Orlis in any way until Bishop has the chance to sort out what's going on. And that includes your not going to New York tomorrow. I'll help you talk to her right now about what's going on with her husband. But let's not do anything to rile her.'

'She doesn't frighten me one bit,' Gilbride said, clearly at the end of his tether. 'And I don't know who this Bishop is. But before I disrupt my service and go accusing anyone of anything, I want to see some proof. Until then, I'm still the chief of this department, and I'll make any decisions that need making regarding our patients. Now, I would like you to accompany me into the family room to update Countess Hermann on this latest development.'

Jessie followed Gilbride into the room, where Orlis Hermann was waiting, this time with all three of the Count's offspring. The session lasted less than ten minutes, and was even more unpleasant than the last one, with Gilbride stumbling through yet another blame-anyone-but-himself explanation of another tragic Rolf Hermann outcome. The woman almost certain to be Hermann's widow before too much longer received the news of her husband's cardiac arrest stoically, but her chilling gaze, locked every moment on Gilbride, made Jessie shudder.

'You will do everything you possibly can to save my husband's life,' was all Orlis said when he had finished.

Then she nodded toward her stepsons and stepdaughter, and the four of them stood in unison and marched out the door. The last of them had just left when Jessie's beeper went off, directing her to an extension she didn't recognize.

'Em,' she said out loud, hurrying over to the phone.

Her call was answered instead by the radiologist on duty. Jessie listened intently, then turned slowly to Gilbride.

'That was Don Harkness in radiology,' she said. 'He wants to review the findings on Eastman Tolliver's films with us.'

*I guess it's not a migraine*, she wanted to add, but didn't.

In strained silence, the two of them took the elevator down to the basement and crossed through the tunnel to the MRI unit in the emergency ward. Don Harkness, a veteran radiologist, greeted them and then motioned toward the view box and Tolliver's films.

'Well, I'll be . . . ,' Jessie murmured.

Gilbride and Jessie looked at each other in amazement. The tumor in Eastman Tolliver's head was slightly smaller than Rolf Hermann's, and a bit more to the left of center – not an identical twin, but certainly fraternal.

''The man's got problems,' Harkness said. 'A subfrontal meningioma, I should think. Big 'un, too. Now, that's one you don't see every day.'

# Chapter 24

Although she wasn't on call, Jessie had chosen to spend the night in the hospital. Her closest friend had vanished. No note, no call, no signs of personal trouble, no hints of emotional instability, no evidence of an abduction – just a phone call to Emily at home . . . then she was gone. Jessie had been too worried to go home.

It was not yet six-thirty in the morning when she awoke in one of the windowless on-call cubicles, momentarily disoriented in the pitch darkness, her mouth desert dry, her lungs burning from four hours of inhaling stale air. She switched on the bedside lamp and was grateful to see the cup of water she had left on the scarred table beside it. Wetting her fingertips, she rubbed some water on her eyelids, then drank the rest and sank back onto the pillow. Dreamlike, the highly charged events of the previous night drifted into focus.

Eastman Tolliver had taken the unfortunate news of his MRI results about as Jessie had expected – a dismayed, softly uttered curse, followed by an attempt at a brave smile, and finally a resigned declaration that he would do whatever it took to beat the tumor. These were, Jessie knew, only baby steps in the process of coming to grips with the nearly unfathomable diagnosis of a brain tumor. The heavy work would take place over the few days remaining before surgery. And while the depth of the success of that work was unpredictable from patient to patient, it often had a major bearing on the outcome of the treatment.

'Maybe it's all the time I've been spending around the patients here,' Tolliver said, 'but while they were wheeling me down here, I had this feeling it was going to be . . .'

His voice drifted away, and for a brief while, he stared up at the ceiling. He then stated his decision to stay in Boston and have his surgery performed at EMMC. Gilbride made several hardly subtle efforts to insert himself as the physician of record, but Tolliver would have none of it.

'I've made up my mind, Carl,' he said. 'I know what happened to poor Count Hermann could have happened with any surgeon, but I've watched Dr. Copeland in the operating room, and I've spoken with her patients, and I have chosen Dr. Copeland to do it. It's as simple as that. It says a good deal about you that you have a surgeon of her caliber on your staff.'

'Whatever you say,' Gilbride managed, barely unclenching his jaws.

'However, when I do go into the operating room,' Tolliver went on, 'I'd like to know that you'll be there as a consultant.'

'Of course.'

Jessie suggested an immediate admission to the neurosurgical service, and promised to schedule Tolliver's operation as soon as possible. Tolliver convinced her instead to allow him to return to his room to gather some things and to call his wife, Kathleen. She would then fly in from California as soon as she could arrange for someone to take her place in caring for her mother, who was incapacitated by Alzheimer's disease. However, Tolliver was quick to add, setting a time for surgery should not be predicated on his wife's arrival. He wanted it done as quickly as possible.

'Just get this thing out of my head,' he said.

Two hours after his release from the emergency room, Eastman Tolliver had returned to EMMC and was admitted as a patient to Surgical Seven.

Meanwhile, Jessie had left the hospital and driven over to the modest two-story house Emily shared with her husband, Ed, and their two sons. Jessie felt that Ed, a software engineer at a firm in Cambridge, responded to the crisis less emotionally and more analytically than Emily would have done had he been the one to have disappeared. But there was no misinterpreting his anxiousness. At Jessie's urging, he called the Brookline police and an hour later an officer did stop by more out of courtesy than concern. The man had clearly encountered too many of these situations to get worked up about this one at this point.

'It's almost always some sort of misunderstanding,' he said, in a clumsy and totally ineffective attempt to calm everyone. 'A meeting or an appointment that Mrs. DelGreco's certain she told you about, but didn't – something like that.'

Jessie rolled her eyes. Emily was as meticulously organized as anyone she knew, and considerate to a fault.

The policeman then pulled Ed and Jessie away from the boys and asked them about the possibility that Emily was seeing someone else.

'I suppose anything's possible,' Ed replied clinically.

'Nonsense!' Jessie exclaimed. 'Emily tells me when a *movie star* is attractive to her. If she was involved with someone else I guarantee you I'd know about it. I suspect it's police procedure to wait a certain amount of time before considering a person actually missing, but in this case you shouldn't waste time waiting, Officer. Emily is an incredibly responsible woman. She would never disappear like this without telling anyone – unless she didn't have the chance.'

The policeman had responded with patronizing reassurance that they would do whatever was necessary as soon as it was clear Emily had been missing at least twenty-four hours.

Jessie finished the last of the water from the bedside table, and forced herself to use the narrow, molded-plastic shower.

*What in the hell happened to Emily?*

The question overrode all her other thoughts. She searched with little success for an explanation that worked with all she knew of the woman. Finally, she began ticking through a list of scenarios that didn't jibe with what she knew. Maybe there *was* another man. Ed DelGreco was a decent-looking guy, and certainly bright, but he was dry as toast. It wasn't an impossible stretch to believe that Em could have left Ed and run off with someone. But it was inconceivable that she could have done it to her boys. No, something bad had happened to her. Jessie felt almost certain of it.

Was it possible that Emily's disappearance had something to do with the Count and Orlis Hermann? Had she seen or heard something she shouldn't have? Jessie pondered those questions for a time, then toweled off, pulled on a fresh set of scrubs, and fished out the number Alex had given her.

'Four-two-six-nine-four-four-four,' a woman's sterile voice said.

'Alex Bishop, please.'

'You may leave a message.'

'Can you get it to him?'

'You may leave a message.'

'Okay, okay, Ask Mr. Bishop to page Dr. Copeland, please.' Jessie hesitated, then added, 'Tell him it's important.'

*Em, where in the hell are you?*

Jessie joined the breakfast bunch in the cafeteria, but found it impossible this day to tolerate their humor. Making rounds on Surgical Seven was the only thing she felt she could handle. With the exception of Ben Rasheed, who would remain a ticking bomb until his surgery later that day, her service – nine patients right now – was in excellent shape. Making rounds on the group would have to be a boost to her spirits, and starting early would give her some extra time to talk with each of them.

As always since Sara's surgery, Jessie started her rounds in NICU room 6. Although it was only seven-thirty, she was not that surprised to find Lisa Brandon at work, using lotion to massage Sara's back.

'So, how's my patient?'

'Just . . . good,' Sara said.

Lisa helped her onto her back and cranked up the bed.

'I'm going to see if the nurses have anything for me to do,' she said. 'See you later, Dr. Copeland.'

'Thank you, Lisa.'

Sara's neurologic exam showed signs, albeit not striking ones, of continuing improvement in many areas. Voluntary movement present in all extremities with some decent leg strength. . . . Cognition good. . . . Speech somewhat disjointed but largely discernible. . . . All twelve pairs of cranial nerves intact. Clearly, Sara was nearing the edge of the woods. She was certainly ready to be moved out of the unit and, barring a major complication, could be in a rehab facility within a week.

One friend a virtual miracle, one friend missing. . . . *Patrons with heart conditions should refrain from taking this ride.*

The two women talked for a time, although Jessie carried most of the conversation. They spoke about the weather and movies, Sara's kids and Jessie's personal life, and even what it was like to be operated on while awake. And finally, Sara drifted into an exhausted sleep. Jessie pushed herself up from the edge of the bed and was heading out of the room when she noticed a thin volume on the bedside table, folded open, with a passage circled in pencil. It was Shakespeare's *Richard III*. The marked passage was probably one Barry Devereau had read to his wife – perhaps many times.

*True hope is swift, and flies with swallow's wings;*
*Kings it makes gods, and meaner creatures kings.*

'Hang in there, Sara,' Jessie whispered. She headed into the hall – way, then added, 'Em, you hang in there, too.'

'Dr. Copeland, there's trouble in two,' a nurse called out.

Jessie hurried to Rolf Hermann's bedside. His daughter was asleep in the guest chair, a pillow bunched beneath her head. A cardiac pacemaker wire, inserted after the code 99, had been added to Hermann's array of tubes and monitor cables. It was a temporary wire, inserted through a blind stick into the subdavian vein beneath the Count's right collarbone and threaded down until it made contact with the inner lining of his heart. The pacer control box to which the wire was connected was taped to his upper arm.

Pacemaker, IV, breathing tube, mechanical ventilation, catheter, feeding tube, eyes taped shut. Rolf Hermann or Claude Malloche – whoever he was – was more dead than alive. The code 99 had been a success, but the underlying cause of his cardiac degeneration, which was most likely a disruption of the nerve pathways from the brain regulating his heart rhythm, remained unchanged. And now, another grave situation was developing. His blood pressure, as displayed on the monitor screen from the cannula in his radial artery, was 75/30 . . . and dropping.

A normal heartbeat pattern on the monitor with a falling blood pressure. Cardiac pump failure – the sort of circulatory collapse that not even a pacemaker could help. Roif Hermann was on the barge, as the residents often put it – on the barge and about to cross the river of no return.

'Hang a dopamine infusion, please,' Jessie said to the nurse. 'Then call the cardiology fellow, the neurosurgical resident, and Dr. Gilbride.'

Hermann's daughter woke up with a start, and appeared lost and alarmed. She was in her early to mid-twenties, lithe, with short, straight brown hair and an aquiline nose that dominated her face. Jessie patted her shoulder to calm her, then led her out into the hall and turned her over to one of the nurses, with instructions to go find Orlis and to bring the whole group to the family room. Rolf Hermann's heartbeat hadn't stopped yet, but it was going to.

Jessie sighed and turned to the unit secretary. There was no sense in just sitting around waiting for the inevitable.

'Code ninety-nine, NICU two,' she said. 'Please call it in.'

200

# Chapter 25

After the medical nightmare Count Rolf Hermann had been through, his death would be almost anticlimactic. With his ventilator-driven respirations, the cardiac meds, and the pacemaker, he was essentially being continuously resuscitated. He could go on indefinitely this way so long as his heart continued to circulate blood with enough force to perfuse his organs. But the drop in blood pressure was a signal that his pump was failing. Speeding up his heart rate with the pacemaker might help for a while, Jessie thought – long enough at least for the room to fill up once again with the usual crush of combatants and onlookers. But the ultimate negative outcome was approaching rapidly.

The cardiology fellow, Joe Milano, was still on call, and in fact had been on his way up to check on Hermann and his pacemaker when the code 99 was broadcast. He rushed into the room, checked the monitor screen, then slid into place beside Jessie.

'I had the pacer set to take over if he dropped below seventy,' he said. 'Now he's pacing at one-twenty.'

'His pressure had dropped to seventy-five,' Jessie replied. 'We've hung some dopamine, and since there's no fluid in his chest that I can hear, we're pushing fluid to increase his circulating volume. But I thought that increasing his rate with the pacemaker might drive up his pressure some.'

'And look, it has,' Milano said, gesturing to the pressure readout of 79. 'That was a heck of a good move – specially for a neurosurgeon.'

'I was a doctor once, remember? Any other ideas?'

Milano checked the clear plastic urine collector hanging from the bed frame.

'There's not much pee. Has this been emptied recently?'

'Three hours ago,' a nurse responded. 'There wasn't much output then either.'

'We can push the pressors and start pumping on his chest,' Milano said. 'If we do that, we're sort of committed to a balloon pump assist as well. As usual, it's hard to know where to draw the line.'

'The family wants everything possible done,' Jessie said.

'Is it worth trying to put a shunt into his head? It's almost certain the fallout from his cerebral hemorrhage is causing this, along with some underlying cardiac disease.'

'There's no evidence for an acute obstruction of the outflow of spinal fluid from his brain. That would be the only neurosurgical condition we might be able to remediate in the OR. His problem is massive brain swelling, not acute hydrocephalus. A shunt wouldn't help.'

'And his brain swelling's not going away?'

Jessie shook her head. 'No,' she said, glancing over at the doorway and wondering when Gilbride might appear. 'It doesn't look like it.'

'In that case it seems like we're swimming against the tide regardless of what we do.'

'Pressure's down to seventy again,' the nurse said.

Her tone was a none-too-subtle request that one of the physicians in charge make a decision whether to plow ahead with meds and chest compressions or stand back and let Hermann's pressure keep on dropping.

'It's too bad,' Milano said softly. 'The guy comes all the way over here from Germany to have his operation, and ends up like this.'

'Sixty-five,' the nurse said.

'I don't know ' Jessie said. 'My head is telling me we'd better pull out all the stops. My heart says that doing that is a cruel and expensive exercise in futility.'

She looked past the crowd to the hallway again. Carl Gilbride wasn't there, but Alex Bishop was, dressed in his brown security force uniform. He caught her eye and asked the obvious question with a gesture. She replied with a barely perceptible shake of her head. At that moment, Gilbride strode past Alex and into the room. Despite having left the hospital at ten last night for what Jessie assumed was a decent night's sleep, and despite his spotless lab coat and designer shirt, he looked haggard and edgy.

'What's going on here?' he demanded.

'Pump's failing,' Milano said.

'So, get it going.'

Gilbride looked reproachfully at Jessie.

'How long have you been here?' he demanded.

'Ten minutes or so.'

''And you're not doing anything?'

'We were just discussing whether it was appropriate and fair to send for a balloon assist pump.'

'Milano, get him through this,' Gilbride ordered. 'I don't care what you have to do.' He turned to Jessie. 'Because of you, I've canceled appearing on a panel in New York City that was very important to me. And now I get here and find you just standing around.'

'Begin compressions,' Milano said to the medical resident, the resignation in his voice making it clear the order was against his better judgment. 'Someone please call down to the CCU and have the intra-aortic balloon pump brought up here. Might as well call the cardiac surg people as well to help with the insertion.'

'I'll call them,' Jessie said quickly, anxious to get out of the room.

She was furious at Gilbride's public rebuke, but she was also a bit sheepish that she hadn't been as aggressive as he was being. Still, dead was dead. And the most exhaustive, expensive interventions in the world weren't going to bring back Rolf Hermann's brain or, for that matter, his heart.

She hurried past Alex with just a brief nod that he should follow. Then she stopped at the ward secretary's desk, called the coronary care unit, and asked to have a nurse wheel up the balloon pump. The apparatus, a long balloon that was inserted into the abdominal aorta through an artery in the groin and inflated with each heartbeat, could raise the blood pressure in some cases of pump failure. Next Jessie put in a page for the cardiac surgery team. Finally, she walked down the hall to a small alcove opposite the only empty room in the NICU, and motioned to Alex that the coast was clear.

'Is he going to make it?' he asked at once.

'Define *make* it,' Jessie replied. 'Joe Milano, the cardiologist, is damn good, but I don't think anyone's *that* good. Do you know that I called you early this morning?'

'I do, yes. I'm sorry. They just reached me with the message.'

'What were you doing?'

'I was off getting a hearse.'

'A hearse?'

'A hearse, the black dress suit, the subdued tie, the works – all courtesy of the greedy folks at Bowker and Hammersmith Funeral Parlor. They have even offered their cooler to stash Hermann's body in until Jorge Cardoza gets here.'

'Very clever. When will he be arriving?'

'This afternoon. His plane lands at three. Is Hermann still going to be among the living by then?'

'Define *living*. I was ready to call it quits on the resuscitation before Carl got here. But he canceled an appearance in New York because of the Count, and now he's determined the guy's going to survive this.'

'It'll be dangerous bringing Cardoza into the hospital. There's a chance one or another of Hermann's so-called family knows him.'

'Well, speaking as a betting woman, my money's on your not having to.'

'Will you help me get Hermann out of the hospital? I know where the morgue is, but I don't know much about the protocol.'

'Jesus, Alex. I'm still not even certain who you *are*, and you want me to risk my career by stealing a body from my own hospital?'

'Forget I asked.'

'I'll do it. I'll do it. But listen. You've got to help me, too. I'm very frightened about my nurse practitioner, Emily.'

'What do you mean?'

'She's disappeared. According to her son, yesterday evening she got a phone call, then said she was going to the hospital. He assumed it was me calling, but it wasn't. She hasn't been heard from since, and I'm very worried.'

'Has her family called the police?'

'Yes, but they won't do anything until she's been missing at least twenty-four hours.'

'Missing, huh. That is a little worrisome. She's never done anything like this before?'

'Never. That's why I called you. I want to make a deal. If I help you with Hermann, I want you to get your FBI friends involved right away in finding Emily.'

'I don't know if –'

'No deal, no body. And I mean it. I want them on the case today no matter what the Brookline police say.'

'I'll do my best.'

'Look at me, Alex. Right here in my eyes. . . . Dammit, I wish I could tell when you're lying.'

The nurse from the coronary care unit raced by, pushing the orange-crate-sized intra-aortic balloon pump ahead of her.

'Go ahead back in there,' Alex said. 'I won't be far away.'

'Why don't you use the time right now to keep your end of the bargain and call your FBI friends? Emily DelGreco. Her number's listed in the Brookline directory under Edward DelGreco.'

'Okay. Okay. You're like a frigging pit bull.'

'There's a side of me that pit bulls run away from. You came dangerously close to bringing it out once. For both our sakes, don't do it again.'

She hurried away without waiting for a response, and rejoined the throng in room 2.

The blood pressure readout on the monitor showed 50 now. Rolf Hermann's skin was gray, mottled with deep violet. His eyelids were taped closed. A respiratory tech was using a breathing bag to supply him with 100 percent oxygen. By any definition, the Count was far more dead than alive. Still, the team, driven by a frantic Carl Gilbride, pushed on. The resident continued pumping on Hermann's chest while Joe Milano gave med orders to the nurses. And now a cardiac surgical resident was on the scene as well, preparing Hermann's groin for the insertion of the intra-aortic balloon, and calling out his supply needs without checking to see if anyone was listening. It was a medical circus maximus, and at the center stood Carl Gilbride, no more effective than Nero might have been while watching Rome burn around him.

Jessie was torn between diving in to relieve the exhausted resident who was doing the chest compressions, and simply skulking off to a quiet corner of the hospital until the madness was over. Finally, she decided on a compromise, and moved to a spot next to Gilbride. There was a particular favor she wanted to offer him when it was appropriate to do so.

'Any change?' she asked.

'You might have started all this sooner,' Gilbride said, never turning away from the action.

'I'm sorry,' she replied, unwilling to take the bait and start up an argument about the definition of futility.

'It doesn't look good.'

The pressure was down to 45 – poor even for artificial external cardiac compressions.

'That chest pumper's running down,' Jessie said. 'I think I'll take over.'

'Nonsense. You're an assistant professor. Pumping is a resident's job.'

He called out and caught the attention of the neurosurgical resident. Then he pointed at Hermann's chest and pantomimed the order that the man take over the cardiac compressions. To Jessie, it was as if Nero was now demanding that a bucket of water be tossed on the conflagration. The personnel transfer took place on the bed without missing a beat, but the pressure readout remained essentially unchanged. Five more minutes passed. Fifteen people – residents, students, nurses, technicians, faculty – had been tied up for the better part of an hour now. Thousands of dollars in equipment, medications, and lab tests had been expended.

'Balloon's in and functioning well,' the cardiac surgery resident announced.

'Stop pumping, please,' Joe Milano requested.

The room was suddenly silent save for the beeping of the monitor, the puffs of the Ambu breathing bag, and the soft thump of the intra-aortic balloon assist. Every eye was fixed on the monitor. For a time, maybe a minute, maybe two, the blood pressure reading stayed at 50. Then slowly, like the orbit of a dying satellite, it began to deteriorate. Down to 47 ... 42 ... 40. Seconds after the pressure hit 40, Rolf Hermann flat-lined. No one moved. The silence in the room continued as everyone on the resuscitation team waited for Carl Gilbride to decide whether or not it was over.

There was nothing from him. Not a word.

Finally, Joe Milano spoke up.

'Dr. Gilbride, I appreciate how much you want this guy to make it. But I'm not sure what else we can do.'

'This all should have been started sooner,' Gilbride said.

He turned and stalked from the room.

*Jerk.*

'That's it. Thank you, everyone,' Jessie blurted, hurrying after Gilbride, and catching up with him at the nurses' station.

'Sorry,' she said, wanting to throttle the man.

'Where're his wife and the others?'

'Waiting in the family room.'

'Well, I suppose I'd best get this over with.'

'Be careful. Remember what I told you about her.'

'What you told me is nonsense. Killers! Fake security guards! I just want to get this whole business over with. I never should have canceled my appearance in New York. Never. And now Mrs. Levin has developed a headache and a fever on the day she was supposed to be discharged. As soon as I finish with the Countess, I'm going to have to perform a spinal tap on her.'

'Would you like me to do it?'

'I think you've done enough for one day.'

'How about Orlis? Do you want me in there with you when you speak to her?'

'I think I can handle that myself as well.'

'Okay,' Jessie said. She crossed her fingers for luck and went for the brass ring. 'How about the death certificate? Can I fill that out for you?'

Gilbride mulled the request over, then finally said, 'I suppose so. As long as you make sure the cause of death is listed as cardiac, because that's what it was.'

'Cardiac arrest, due to arteriosclerotic heart disease, with meningioma as a coincidentally existing condition. How does that sound?'

'It sounds like the way it should be. Now, if you'll excuse me, I have a great deal to do.'

'So do I,' Jessie murmured as he walked away.

# Chapter 26

It took nearly twenty minutes for the nurses to clean up room 2. They removed all the tubes and lines from Rolf Hermann's body and untaped his eyelids. Jessie offered to help, but was shooed away. Instead, she sat behind the counter of the nurses' station filling out the death certificate – the one piece of paperwork that would be necessary to remove the Count's body from the hospital.

Please print in black pen only.

> **Cause of Death: Cardiac Arrest**
> **DUE TO: Cardiogenic Shock**
> **DUE TO: Arteriosclerotic Cardiovascular Disease**
> **Co-existing Condition: Subfrontal Meningioma**

A few properly placed words and *poof*, Gilbride's wish had been granted. A surgical calamity would go into the books as a coronary. And unless the family demanded the certificate, no one would be the wiser. Difficult though Orlis was, Jessie did not think that idea would occur to her. Deservedly or not, Gilbride was off the hook.

*The pen is mightier than the scalpel.*

Jessie smiled at the thought as she block printed in the final pieces of demographic data. She looked up just as Orlis Hermann and Rolf's daughter came down the hall and entered his room. A minute or so later, they emerged and approached her.

'So,' Orlis said with chilling matter-of-factness, 'my husband is dead.'

'We're all very sorry,' Jessie replied, standing.

'Your Dr. Gilbride didn't seem all that remorseful when he spoke to us just now.'

'I assure you, he was. He kept everyone in there doing the resuscitation long after most doctors would have stopped.'

'What do we do now?'

'If you were local, I would say all you needed to do was call a funeral home. Coming from another country, I'm not sure. If you don't mind waiting in your room out there on the floor, I'll speak to the nursing supervisor. She knows all the rules. I assume you're planning to take the Count back to Germany.'

'We are.'

'I'm sure that complicates things somewhat, but I think the first step is still calling a funeral home. There's paperwork that needs to be done here as well. Dr. Gilbride has quite a caseload, so I've offered to do it for him. But there may be some delay – a few hours, perhaps.'

Jessie was rambling deliberately, hoping that Orlis would agree to stay around the hospital, as Alex needed her to.

'I don't mind,' Orlis said. 'I need to get my husband's things together anyway.'

'Will the Count's sons be in to see him?'

'No. They are off on business right now. They should be back shortly, but there is no need to keep Count Hermann's body up here until they arrive. Although they were very close to their father, they are not sentimental in that way.'

'Fine. I'll take care of everything, and I'll be in to see you as soon as I have information.'

'Do that. . . . Dr. Copeland?'

'Yes.'

'Your chief killed my husband. You do know that.'

A knot of tension materialized in Jessie's chest. Whether or not Alex was right about Orlis Hermann being Arlette Malloche, the woman *was* absolutely chilling. Jessie chose her words carefully. She had no desire to defend Carl Gilbride, but this was hardly the situation in which to allow principle and emotion to get in the way of common sense. Even if Orlis Hermann was nothing more than the Count's distraught wife, she was still a potential litigant against Gilbride, EMMC, and probably Jessie as well. If she was, as Alex believed, a murderer capable of extreme vengeance, then there was no reason to provide her with any more justification for violence than she already had.

'What I know, Mrs. Hermann,' she said, 'is that your husband had a large brain tumor that was unfortunately situated in a spot that was technically very difficult to reach. The more difficult the location of such a tumor, the more likely there will be complications. We really are sorry.'

'Tell me something honestly, Dr. Copeland. Would this have happened if you had done the surgery?'

The question caught Jessie by surprise. In all her dealings with Orlis Hermann, she never once felt the woman had the least interest in what she could or could not do in the operating room. A myriad of responses to the question flashed through her head – none of them truthful.

'I hope you will understand that I cannot possibly answer that question,' she said finally. 'I've had my share of surgical triumphs just as Dr. Gilbride has, but I've had some surgical tragedies as well.'

For a few moments, Orlis Hermann stood there silently, her eyes locked on Jessie's. Then, almost imperceptibly she nodded.

'We will be waiting in our room for word from you,' she said.

She took her stepdaughter by the arm and led her away. Moments later, Alex appeared at Jessie's side.

'What'd she say?'

'She'll be waiting to hear from me about what to do with the body.'

'Time frame?'

'I told her it could be a few hours before I have any information.'

'Great. Nice going. If worse comes to worst, the body will just be missing, and she'll have to wait around until it's found.'

211

'Unless that makes her suspicious and she takes off.'

'I have that possibility covered, I think. She's being watched.'

Jessie looked at him queerly.

'Watched by whom?' she asked.

'I'll tell you soon.'

'Oh, I just love secrets,' she said with unbridled sarcasm.

'I gave my word.'

'As long as *I* can count on your word, too. You know, Alex, as hard a woman as Orlis is, and as many awful things as you think she and her husband have done, I believe she's feeling a deep and genuine hurt over what's happened to him. And you know what? So am I.'

'In that case, maybe I should bring out those photographs again,' Alex replied. 'I have no sympathy for that woman or her husband. I only hope he somehow knew he was dying when that artery started bleeding into his brain. I can't tell you what a joy it will be, to be the one shoving Claude Malloche's body into a hearse.'

'Vengeance is mine, sayeth the Bishop.'

'Amen.'

'Pardon me for saying it, but would your brother have endorsed this five-year vendetta of yours?'

'My brother's dead. The choices I've made are mine. But the answer to your question is yes. We were both recruited by the agency right after college. We both knew what we were getting into. We both felt like patriots serving our country, and we both hated our country's enemies. If Malloche had any credo at all, it was an absolute loathing for America and Americans. If he had killed me, Andy would have hunted him to the ends of the earth.'

Jessie sighed.

'In that case, we should get moving.'

'Do you have a plan?' he asked.

'Yes, but it's complicated, so pay attention.'

'Ready.'

'Okay. First, I give you this paper. Second, you change into your undertaker suit. You got this so far?'

'Go on.'

'Next, you come and haul off the body.'

'That's it?'

'I checked. It's essentially self-serve. You stop at the pathology department desk, show them the death certificate, and sign a log. After that, no one cares. It's yet another example of the cardinal rule of moving about a hospital: If you look like you know what you're doing, as far as anyone is concerned, you know what you're doing.'

'I've noticed that, playing hospital guard.'

'People's first option is always the one that isn't going to cause them any extra work. I'm going to put that principle to the test right now.'

'How?'

'Just to make sure everything's in place when you make your appearance as Digger O'Dell, the friendly undertaker, I'm going to tell the nurses I need a break from this floor and from Carl, and offer to spare someone the job of accompanying the security guard when he wheels the body down to the morgue. I don't think it would be wise for you to play the guard *and* Digger, but if you hurry I'll still be down there waiting when you drive up in your hearse.'

Alex looked about to ensure no one was watching, then took her hand in his and held it for several seconds.

'I'll meet you in the morgue,' he said.

He had disappeared around the corner before Jessie realized that she hadn't even thought about pulling away from him.

Jessie assisted two nurses in transferring Rolf Hermann's body to a gurney. Then she and the guard, a paunchy man named Seth, who seemed to pale at the sight of the Count's corpse, headed off for the morgue. *Five hundred murders.* It was hard enough for her to accept that any man could be responsible for such horror, let alone that it was the one lying beneath the sheet. Cunning, thorough, brilliant, paranoid, meticulous. Those were just some of the adjectives Alex had used to describe Claude Malloche. Now, it seemed, the monster's headstone might read:

*'Here lies a man who made only one mistake in life. He chose the wrong surgeon.'*

The morgue was in the basement of the main hospital. It consisted of an unlocked room, adjacent to the autopsy suite, with twelve stainless steel refrigerated boxes built into the wall for body storage. Formaldehyde fumes hung heavy in the air. There was no one around, so Jessie left Seth waiting with the gurney and walked through the autopsy room and across a corridor to the pathology office, where an indifferent secretary slid a black loose-leaf notebook across her desk to log the body in.

'I think the funeral home is on its way over,' Jessie said, paving the way for Alex's imminent arrival.

The woman mumbled, 'Yeah, okay.'

*No problem here,* Jessie was thinking.

She returned to the morgue, where Seth had posted himself in the hallway outside the door.

*No problem here either.*

'Listen,' Jessie said, 'I just spoke to the funeral parlor, and they're sending someone over right away. Why don't you go on back to work. I'll stay here until they arrive.

'You sure?'

'It's fine. I'm sure.'

Jessie watched until the grateful guard had headed down the passageway to the elevators. Then she reentered the morgue and lifted the sheet from Rolf Hermann's gray mottled face. Gradually the stagnant blood in his capillaries would be drawn by gravity into the dependent tissues, and his complexion would assume the pallor of death. From her first encounter with a dead body in anatomy corpses had not particularly affected her – even the ones whose demise was grisly. Hermann was no exception. Perhaps it was the ability to detach that had made her so successful as a surgical student, then later as a resident. Whatever the reason, looking down at the body now only made her wonder about Claude Malloche – and about the man who had hunted him for so long.

*Five years*, she was thinking. Alex Bishop had given up

214

five years of his life for this. Hermann's eyes were open a slit. Jessie peered at them, wondering about all they had seen during their life, and what had driven the man behind them.

'Jessie?'

The woman's voice, from behind her, brought her heart rocketing to her throat. She whirled, pulling the sheet back into place over Hermann's face in the same motion. Nursing supervisor Catherine Purcell stood, arms folded, just inside the door.

'Oh, hi,' Jessie managed. 'You startled me.'

'I can see that. Sorry. Is there a problem?'

'No, not really. I was just wondering about the guy. I did his admission workup for Carl, but I never really got to talk with him. Because of the language barrier and his wife's bossiness, almost everything went through her.'

Jessie's mind was racing. Alex would be here anytime. Catherine Purcell was one of the sharpest people in the hospital, and his looks were striking. It was reasonable to think she might recognize him.

'The nurses in the unit told me you had walked the Count down here,' Catherine said.

'They were busy and I just wanted to get off the floor for a while. Weren't you on last evening?'

'Betty Hollister's got the flu. I told her I'd cover. You need help loading him into the cooler?'

'No . . . ah . . . the funeral home called the floor before we left and said they'd be right over. I didn't see any sense in moving him around any more than necessary. Have you heard something about Emily? Is that why you're here?'

She worked her way toward the door.

'No. I heard she's still missing. I have no idea what could have happened.'

'I'm really worried.'

'In that case, I'm worried, too. But I came down to find you because I'm worried about someone else – Carl. I think he's losing it.'

'You mean like going crazy?'

'I mean exactly that.'

'Catherine, could we maybe leave here to talk about it? The fumes are starting to make me queasy. The funeral guy knows to stop at the path office. I left the death certificate there.'

'Certainly.'

*Nicely done*, Jessie was thinking to herself as they reached the bank of elevators. The doors parted and Catherine stepped into the car at the moment the doors to the next car opened and Alex emerged, dressed in an ill-fitting black suit and pushing a narrow stretcher. There was only a moment for their eyes to meet, but in that moment, Alex saw inside the elevator, assessed the situation, and looked down.

'He's in the morgue,' Jessie said. 'The pathology office has the certificate.'

'Thank you,' Alex said.

'I could swear I've seen that man someplace before,' Catherine commented as the elevator doors glided shut.

Jessie's pulse leveled off at two hundred or so and began to slow.

'I imagine this isn't his first trip here,' she said hopefully.

'No, I suppose not.'

'About Carl?'

'Oh, yes. You remember I told you last night how he was absolutely certain Laura Pearson and another nurse were laughing at him, and threatened to have her fired?'

'Yes.'

'Well, now he's up on Surgical Seven, shrieking at the nurses because there are none of the special spinal tap sets on the floor that he insists on using.'

'Oh, yes. The famous Gilbride kit.'

Jessie tried to stay focused on Catherine and their conversation, but she kept picturing Alex, alone in the morgue, loading the body of his nemesis onto a borrowed stretcher for the trip to a hearse. *Five years.*

'Special spinal needle, special pressure monitor, special clamps, special drapes, special disinfectant,' Catherine was saying. 'Everyone else uses the standard, disposable kits, but Carl insists on his wacky setup.'

'I know. He insists that the residents use it, too, but unless he's watching they never do. It's become sort of a joke passed on from class to class. It's just one of those power things, Catherine. Carl demands the kits simply because he can.'

'Well, now he's up there berating anyone and everyone because there aren't any.'

'He's stressed. This Count Hermann thing has turned his world upside down. Surely central supply must have some of his sets made up and sterilized.'

'One, thank God. They're sending it up now. But Jessie, you've got to do something to calm the man down before we have a mass walkout on our hands. Or before I slip twenty of Valium into his butt. He's always been hard on people, but never this abusive. It's really appalling.'

'I'll do what I can.'

They heard Gilbride ranting the moment the doors opened on Surgical Seven.

'You know how much time I've wasted up here, waiting for this? I could have seen half a dozen patients in my office! From now on, I want at least two Gilbride kits on this floor at all times, is that clear?'

Clutching the sterile, towel-covered tray that held his precious spinal tap set, Gilbride was still railing at one of the nurses as Jessie approached.

'Carl?'

He whirled to face her.

'I don't want to hear anything from you either, Doctor,' he snarled. 'This is my service, and I'll run it my way. Now, if you'll excuse me.'

He was muttering unintelligibly as he turned away. Just behind him, Jessie could see the candy striper, Lisa Brandon, emerging from Sara's new room. She was looking back over her shoulder into the room, saying something about getting more lotion. To Jessie, watching the catastrophe develop, the collision seemed to take place in slow motion. Gilbride took two rapid steps backward and was turning when he slammed into Lisa, driving her back a few feet and almost knocking her down. The

Gilbride kit – the only one in the hospital – went clattering to the floor.

For two or three stunned, silent seconds, Gilbride could only stare down at the broken tubes and contaminated instruments. Then he transferred his gaze to Lisa.

'God damn it!' he bellowed. 'Who the hell are you?'

Without waiting for a response, he reached down and snatched Lisa's laminated ID from where it was clipped to her jacket pocket. He studied the picture, then looked at the woman, then looked back at the ID.

'I . . . I'm sorry,' Lisa stammered. 'I really am. It was an ac –'

'What in the hell kind of an ID is this?'

'What do you mean?' Lisa asked.

Jessie took a step closer. To her left, Orlis Hermann and one of her sons were standing by the door to their room, taking in the scene.

'I mean this thing is fake. The ID number doesn't start with a V like all volunteers' numbers do, and you can't possibly have gotten this just three weeks ago, because if you did, you'd still be in orientation, and not up here putting your hands on my patients and smashing into me. Now, who in the hell are you?'

He nearly shrieked the words.

'Dr. Gilbride, if we could just speak in private,' Lisa said, urgently but quite calmly and with surprising authority.

'Nonsense! I want security called. I want you out of here right now.'

'Dr. Gilbride, please, I –'

Gilbride turned to the unit secretary.

'Get security up here right now,' he bellowed. 'In fact, tell them to call the police.'

Jessie kept her eyes on Lisa Brandon, who appeared furious and somewhat uncertain as to what to do, but not at all intimidated.

'Dr. Gilbride, quiet down,' she said firmly. 'I *am* the police. FBI.'

She handed him a leather case with a badge. Then, just

as quickly she took a step forward, produced a pistol that had been concealed above her boot, and leveled it expertly at Orlis.

'Don't move, Mrs. Hermann,' she said. 'Or should I say Madame Malloche.'

Orlis just looked at her, her lips pursed in a strange half-smile.

'Madame Malloche will do just fine, dear,' she said. 'Arlette Malloche.'

There was a momentary silence, which was broken by the soft, distinctive spit of a silenced revolver. A dark hole materialized in the center of Lisa Brandon's forehead, just above the bridge of her nose.

'Oh, God!' Jessie cried, rushing toward her as the FBI agent lurched backward and fell heavily to the floor.

'Don't move and don't bother checking her,' a man said. 'I couldn't possibly miss at this range.'

Jessie's head swung toward the voice. Standing in the doorway of his room, the silenced pistol in his hand still smoking, was Eastman Tolliver.

# Chapter 27

The moment Lisa Brandon's body hit the tiled floor, Arlette Malloche and her team of three 'stepchildren' were in action. Armed with semiautomatic weapons, moving with speed and skill, they fanned through Surgical Seven as if perfectly prepared for the situation.

The woman who had posed as Hermann's daughter dashed from room to room, disconnecting the phones and throwing them into the hallway. The younger of her 'brothers' hauled a suitcase from their room and raced out toward the doors connecting the tower portion of Surgical Seven with the main hospital. The second man, who seemed to Jessie to be the leader of the three, emerged from their room with a tool kit, and headed toward the elevators. Meanwhile, Arlette, her weapon at the ready, assisted Claude Malloche as he directed the shift nurses, Jessie, Gilbride, and Catherine Purcell to move over to the nurses' station.

Physically Claude Malloche still looked like Eastman Tolliver, but there the similarity to the man he had portrayed ended. His facial expressions, the set of his jaw, his posture, demeanor, and even his English were completely changed. The kindness and patience in his eyes were gone, replaced by the kinetic alertness of a tiger.

'Down, right now!' he ordered to Jessie and the others. 'Sit on the floor against that counter.'

Four nurses, two aides, a lab tech, and Jessie did as they were ordered. As she slid to the floor, not far from Lisa's body, Jessie realized that thirteen-year-old Tamika Bing – the girl so traumatized by her loss of speech that she had been virtually catatonic since awakening from anesthesia –

had witnessed the killing. The girl remained motionless, propped up in bed as usual, staring straight ahead. But Jessie could tell she was riveted on the scene evolving outside her room. She wondered what the grand total of Malloche's victims would be if all the witnesses like Tamika Bing and relatives like Alex Bishop were counted as well.

It was that notion that made Jessie suddenly appreciate how clearly she was thinking – how calm she was, given their situation and the unspeakable violence she had just witnessed. Perhaps her clarity reflected the realization that she, of all of the captives, was in no danger – at least not for the time being. Malloche did have a brain tumor, and he had chosen her to be his surgeon. She was safe. But soon, very soon she suspected, demands were going to be made of her. When that time came, she had to be ready with a few demands of her own.

'What in the hell is going on here?'

Carl Gilbride had not taken his place with the others. Instead, he had stepped forward, hands on hips, to confront Malloche.

'Let's see,' Malloche said with syrupy sarcasm. 'To the best of my recollection, the woman lying over there identified herself as an FBI agent, pulled a pistol from her leg holster, and ordered my wife not to move. Then I shot her. I do not believe a medical degree is required to determine that she is dead.'

Jessie was in position to see Carl's expression – a strange mix of defiance and utter befuddlement.

'You're not Eastman Tolliver,' he said, clearly unable to put the pieces together.

'Brilliant deduction, Dr. Gilbride. If you must know, I borrowed Eastman Tolliver from among the correspondences I found in your office. His secretary in California was kind enough to inform me he was out of the country for several weeks. Now, I'm telling you one last time to get down on the floor with the others.'

'Carl, please do as he says,' Jessie urged softly.

'I . . . I will do no such thing,' Gilbride blustered. 'I

221

simply will not tolerate someone coming onto *my* service, in *my* hospital, and pushing people around and shooting them. We have patients to care for here.'

Moving like a striking snake, Malloche whipped the barrel of his pistol across Gilbride's cheek. The neurosurgical chief lurched backward, clutching his already hemorrhaging wound, and dropped heavily to his backside just a foot or so from Jessie.

'That wasn't necessary!' Jessie snapped at Malloche.

She grabbed a box of tissues from the counter above her and pried Gilbride's hand away from his cheek. The gash was only about an inch and a half long, but deep – just below the cheekbone, and almost through to his mouth. It would be no problem to sew, but even sutured by a crackerjack plastic surgeon, the resulting scar would be a reminder every time Carl looked in the mirror – provided he survived long enough to do that. She placed a wad of tissue on the wound and set Gilbride's hand against it with the whispered instruction to press hard.

'Oh, it *was* necessary, and it *was* deserved,' Malloche replied. 'I hope you can all see that your health, your pain, your very survival mean nothing to me. Nor do your precious egos. So keep quiet unless you are asked to speak, and do as we say, and you have every reason to expect that you will not end up either like our FBI friend over there, or even like our esteemed neurosurgical chief.' He stepped forward and looked down at Carl with disdain. 'Dr. Gilbride, you are a hollow, fatuous ass of a man. It was you who was responsible for Rolf Hermann's death, not any mechanical failure of your robot. That device functioned perfectly, but you didn't. Your arrogance, greed, and surgical incompetence killed that man as surely as if you had put a gun to his head and pulled the trigger. I want you to hear that. I want them to hear it.' He gestured to the group huddled on the floor and continued the sweep of his arm to include the rest of Surgical Seven.

'Excuse me,' Jessie said calmly, 'but could you please tell us exactly who Rolf Hermann was?'

Malloche's expression was smug.

'He was a count, actually, although a rather penniless one. He was delivered to me by the neurologist – I should say the *late* neurologist – whom I went to see in consultation. I asked about patients whose tumors were similar to mine. Count Hermann was beginning to develop neurologic weakness. I still had no signs except for my seizures. Hermann was told by the man, as was I, that his tumor was virtually inoperable. If we did insist on surgery and could find a neurosurgeon who would attempt it, there was a very high, if not certain, risk of serious neurological impairment.'

'So the Count was a stalking horse for you – a test case.'

'I am nothing, dear Doctor, if not careful,' Malloche replied. 'I assured Rolf that whatever happened here in America, his family would be well cared for. That was far more than his so-called doctors in Germany were able to offer. At worst, he knew his wife and children were provided for, and he would get the services of one of the finest neurosurgeons in America. At best, he would have a cure from his brain tumor, and financial security for the rest of his life. Not a bad deal, if I do say so. Not a bad deal for me either, considering the outcome of poor Rolf's operation.'

Ten minutes passed, then twenty. No one moved. The buzz of patient calls for assistance echoed down the hallway, but went unanswered. One by one, the three young killers returned, each whispering a report that clearly pleased Malloche. The five terrorists huddled, while Arlette continued to keep her weapon aimed at the group on the floor – specifically at Carl Gilbride. Finally, Malloche turned and spoke to the captives.

'The doors onto Surgical Seven have been sealed and wired with enough explosives to blow the top off of this building.' He nodded toward the younger of the two men. 'Armand, here, was personally trained by me, so I can assure you he has done an expert job. And Derrick, over there, has seen to it that only one of the elevators will stop at this floor, and then only when I wish it to.' The other man, broad shouldered and Aryan, with a blond crew cut, did a half-bow for the captives. 'And finally, you should meet Grace, who left a girls' finishing school right here in Boston to seek adventure in Europe, and found it with our merry band. She has disconnected all the phones, except the one here in the conference room. No one, but no one, will make contact with the outside unless I allow it. Is that clear? . . . Dr. Gilbride?'

'C–Clear,' he managed.

'Dr. Copeland?'

'I want that poor woman's body moved into the back room, where the patients can't see it,' Jessie said.

Malloche's expression remained unchanged, except for his eyes, which narrowed as he studied her. She had no doubt he understood the significance of her demand. The battle of their wills had begun.

'Derrick,' he said finally, in English, 'would you please do as Dr. Copeland requests.'

'Very well,' Derrick replied, his English heavily accented.

'There,' Malloche said. 'I've shown my good faith. Now, I think you and I must speak in private. The rest of you will be allowed one by one to get a chair to place right here. Armand will accompany you. From now on, no one will leave this spot unaccompanied whether it is to go to the bathroom or to see one of the patients. Dr. Copeland?'

He motioned her toward the small conference room to the left of the nurses' station.

'Before we speak,' Jessie said, 'I want to go in and talk to the child who has witnessed all this.'

'Another demand. My, my. Very well, then. Grace?'

Grace, her gun hanging at the ready from its shoulder strap, walked Jessie into Tamika Bing's room and stood by the doorway, a respectful distance away. Jessie pulled a chair over to the bedside and sat.

'Tamika, I'm sorry for what you have just seen. I know it was awful for you,' she whispered. Not surprisingly, the girl continued staring straight ahead. 'Some very bad people have taken over up here. One of them needs an operation just like you had. After the operation is done, they'll leave. Meanwhile, I don't think anyone is going to be allowed up here, including your mother. Do you understand? ... Tamika?' Jessie stood, then bent down and kissed the girl on the side of her forehead. 'Hang in there,' she whispered.

By the time Jessie emerged from Tamika's room, each of the staff was seated on a chair in front of the counter, and one of the nurses had pulled a chair over for Carl and was helping him into it. Humiliated and physically beaten, his authority stripped away, he seemed to have aged twenty years in just an hour.

'Carl,' Jessie said softly, 'I'll sew that cut up as soon as I can. Meanwhile just stay right here and keep pressure on it.'

Gilbride nodded vacantly.

'So,' Malloche said to her, 'I have honored two of your requests. Now we should talk.'

He unscrewed the silencer, slipped it into his pocket, and holstered his gun. Then he followed her into the conference room and motioned her to a seat across from him.

'Sit, please, Doctor,' he said. 'We have some business to discuss.'

'Your tumor.'

'I would like you to take it out as soon as possible.'

'If I refuse?'

Malloche gauged her resolve, then retrieved a phone, plugged it in, and dialed a local number.

'Put her on,' he said.

Malloche passed the receiver over.

Jessie listened to a few seconds of silence, then a tentative 'Hello?'

*Emily!*

'Em, it's me. Oh, God, are you okay?'

'He hasn't hurt me, but he won't tell me anything. What's going on?' Malloche took the phone away before Jessie could reply.

'She's safe for the moment,' he said, setting the receiver down. 'But I will not hesitate to order her killed if you fail to cooperate. I believe you are a very capable surgeon with a special piece of equipment. I want this tumor out of my head.'

'ARTIE's not ready for this.'

'I believe it is. I want the surgery done by you, with MRI guidance and robotic assistance, tomorrow.'

'I need time to check the system. We'll have to get your lab work done, and you need to be examined by an internist and an anesthesiologist. I also need to speak to people about adjusting the schedule. . . . I'm not in charge of the OR.'

'Tomorrow.'

'If there're problems with the operation, do I end up like poor Sylvan Mays?'

Malloche looked genuinely impressed.

'I assume our FBI friend had you looking for me?'

'She had me on the alert, yes. She didn't want anyone else to know who she was.' Jessie forced herself to back up the lie with a steady gaze. 'Later, when I thought Rolf Hermann was you, I tried to tell Carl, but he didn't believe a word of what I said.'

'Good old Carl.'

'So, answer my question. Do I have any assurances you'll let me live?'

'If you do your job and do it well, you have nothing to fear. You also have my promise of what will happen if you refuse to do this operation. As to what will happen if there are complications, I cannot say. My family is very devoted to me.'

'The day after tomorrow,' Jessie said. 'You'll be seriously affecting your chances if we have to do this as a semiemergency.'

Malloche weighed the demand.

'You're going to cause a large number of people great inconvenience,' he said. 'Tomorrow afternoon.'

'Only if everything is ready. And one more thing.'

'Yes?'

'I want Emily DelGreco to assist me in the OR.'

'I can't allow that. Carl Gilbride will assist you.'

'Please. Carl's incompetent. You said so yourself. And

right now, he's a doddering wreck. Emily's the very best I have ever worked with. Keep her away and you only hurt yourself.'

Again, Malloche took time before replying.

'You win again,' he said. 'But I promise you, if there is a problem with any phase of this procedure – any problem at all – not one patient or staff member on Surgical Seven will leave this hospital alive. Is that clear?'

Jessie took a deep breath.

'Clear,' she said.

She had gotten Emily back and had given Alex added time to act, once he discovered Hermann was not Malloche. That was the best she could do.

'Could you tell me one thing?' she asked.

'Perhaps.'

'How are you going to keep an entire hospital floor sealed off without a massive response from the outside?'

For the first time since their discussion began, Claude Malloche smiled.

'It's a bit like bridge,' he said. 'As long as you play as if the cards most dangerous to you are in the hand of the opponent who is positioned to do you the most harm, you will generally be a step ahead.' He slid the phone across to her. 'Call Richard Marcus and tell him it is essential that he meet us just outside the pathology office in ten minutes.'

'But what if he –'

'Just call him!'

Jessie snatched up the phone and was patched through to the hospital CEO's office immediately. Malloche watched and listened intently until she set the receiver down.

'Ten minutes,' she said.

# Chapter 28

Richard Marcus, rotund, balding, and not much taller than Jessie, had been the CEO of Eastern Mass Medical Center for six years. A physician with an MBA, he was a decent and intelligent man whom Jessie had always liked and respected. Under his guidance, the hospital had evolved from mediocrity to a place of rising prestige and public confidence. His main failing had always seemed to Jessie to be that he would rather listen to himself than to others. But unlike with Carl Gilbride, who suffered from the same malady, persistence usually succeeded in getting Marcus's attention.

Marcus was waiting outside the pathology office when the elevator doors opened and Jessie emerged with Malloche and Derrick. Both of her companions, she knew, carried weapons – Malloche's concealed beneath his sports coat, and Derrick's beneath a black windbreaker with an elastic waist. Marcus had met with Eastman Tolliver previously and recognized him immediately.

'Mr. Tolliver,' he said heartily, 'good to see you again.'

Malloche simply grinned and took Marcus's proffered hand. Marcus looked as if he expected an introduction to Derrick, but when none was forthcoming, he extended his hand and introduced himself. The terrorist held his grip as briefly as possible and said nothing. Nonplussed, Marcus turned to Jessie inquiringly.

'Richard,' she said, 'I think we should go down the hallway, to where we can talk.'

Marcus scanned from one to another of the three and then did as she had requested.

'So, what's this all about?' he asked.

Malloche nodded that Jessie could do the honors.

'Well, Richard,' she said, 'it's all about that this man is not Eastman Tolliver.'

'But –'

'His name is Claude Malloche. Have you heard of him?'

'No, I haven't, but –'

'Mr. Malloche kills people for a living, Richard. And right now he and his people are holding all the patients and staff on Surgical Seven hostage. The doors to the neurosurgical ward are closed off and wired with explosives. The elevators can't be taken to the floor unless Mr. Malloche brings one there. The reason for all this is that Malloche has a brain tumor that he wants me to operate on. Apparently the FBI knew he was sick, and after all the publicity over Marci Sheprow, they thought he might be coming here. They had an agent on Surgical Seven working undercover as a volunteer. Malloche just shot her to death. Until he has recovered successfully from his surgery, he intends to keep everyone up there prisoner.'

The color had drained from Richard Marcus's face. He pulled a handkerchief from his pocket and dabbed at the sheen of sweat that had materialized across his forehead and upper lip.

'I . . . I don't believe this,' he managed.

'Believe it, Dr. Marcus,' Malloche said. 'It is very important that you believe it. I had hoped to have my surgery and return to my home without incident. Fortunately, we were prepared for other possibilities. But we need your help.'

'My help?'

'Would you please take us over to the microbiology laboratory.'

Marcus hesitated.

'Richard, please,' Jessie said. 'They're both armed. Just do as he says. Malloche, please don't hurt anyone.'

The killer looked at her placidly and gestured Marcus toward the lab. They stopped outside the door – heavy oak with a rubber seal around it. A pane of glass filled the upper half, with MICROBIOLOGY stenciled across it in gold. The room beyond the door was largely Corian counters, sophisticated glassware, stainless steel refrigeration units, and incubators. Two men and two women in lab coats were busily working with agar culture dishes, viral tissue culture bottles, and microscopes.

Jessie knew one of the four, Rachel Sheridan, fairly well from a ski trip to New Hampshire and some other hospital-sponsored social activities. Rachel, divorced with a school-aged daughter, was athletic, fun-loving, and popular. Sound from the room was somewhat muffled by the door and seal, but Jessie could still make out that one of the men – she thought his name might be Ron – was asking for help identifying the microorganism beneath his scope. Music, maybe Mozart, was playing in the background.

Viewed this way Jessie almost felt as if she were watching the four technicians on television. *Almost.* A dreadful apprehension was building in her gut. Malloche looked chillingly calm, almost dreamy. His lips bowed in a half-smile, and he nodded to Derrick, who extracted a small transmitter from his jacket pocket and pulled up the antenna.

*'NO!'*

Before Jessie could even scream the word, Derrick depressed a button on the face of the transmitter. From inside the room, they heard a muffled pop and the sound of breaking glass. A small puff of grayish smoke billowed up from beneath a counter. The technicians spun toward the noise. Jessie cried out and lunged for the door, but Malloche grabbed her lab coat and scrub shirt firmly at the neck and pulled her back.

'Opening that door at this moment would be a foolish mistake,' he said.

'Oh, God,' Jessie murmured.

Beyond the glass, a hideous dance of death had already begun. Rachel Sheridan, standing closest to the gas, lurched backward as if she'd been kicked in the chest by a mule. At almost the same instant, she began retching violently, setting the counter awash in vomit and splattering two of the others. Her head had twisted abnormally to one side. Her face, frighteningly contorted, had turned the color of gentian violet.

Seconds later, two of the others were staggering about as well, vomiting uncontrollably with projectile force, and sending glasswork, incubators, and stacks of culture dishes crashing to the floor as they thrashed about. The grotesque discoloration of their faces and almost inhuman torsion of their necks mimicked Rachel's. The three of them were collapsing to the floor when the fourth, perhaps having held her breath, began to twitch and clutch at her belly. As she stumbled to one side, she looked through the glass and saw the group standing there, transfixed. With overwhelming panic distorting her face, she stretched an unsteady, clawed hand in their direction.

*Help me!* came her silent scream. *Help me.*

Then she, too, began retching.

In less than two nightmarish minutes it was over. The four technicians, grotesquely discolored, soaked in vomit, lay dead on the floor, limbs splayed, faces violet, necks twisted almost ninety degrees to one side.

Richard Marcus turned away and braced himself against a wall. Jessie, who had been standing shoulder to shoulder with him, also looked away.

'You monster,' she said, her back still to Malloche. 'You fucking monster!'

She whirled and threw a closed-fisted punch at his face. Malloche caught her fist as calmly as if it were a tennis ball she had lobbed to him, and squeezed it just hard enough to warn against any repeat.

'Easy, now,' he said. 'We don't want anything happening to that hand of yours. Perhaps we'd better head back up to Surgical Seven before someone has the misfortune to come along and see us. With the ventilating hoods in that room, the gas should be dissipated in just a minute or two. Come along.'

Jessie supported Richard Marcus, who was ghastly pale and perspiring heavily. Once in the elevator, she lowered him to the floor. Gradually, his color began to return. Derrick made a call on a two-way radio, and they headed upward. Somewhere between the third and fourth floors, Malloche threw the emergency switch, stopping the car.

'I'm sorry if our little demonstration upset you both. But I need your complete cooperation as well as your confidence that my threats are not idle ones. Dr. Marcus, do you hear me?'

'I . . . I hear you.'

'Then look at me, please. You have a very important role to play in all of this, and you have precious little time to prepare.'

Marcus struggled to his feet.

'Bastard,' he muttered.

'There, that's much better,' Malloche said. 'The gas whose power you just witnessed is called soman. You may have heard of it as GD, currently the most virulent neurotoxin known to man – far more potent than sarin. Some friends of ours in Baghdad have made a generous supply available to us. But I assure you that, depending on placement, population density, and the prevailing wind, a generous supply of soman is not needed to cause a massive amount of damage. We have placed radio-detonated vials, much larger than the one whose effects you just witnessed, in well-camouflaged spots in heavily trafficked areas throughout the city If anything should happen to prevent my surgery, or if I should not wake up promptly after leaving the operating room, not only will all those on Surgical Seven pay the price, but a significant proportion of the city as well. Is that clear? . . . Dr. Marcus?'

'Oh, God. Yes, it's clear, it's clear.'

'I will be cured of this tumor in my head, and I will make it safely out of the hospital. Is that clear, Dr. Copeland?'

Jessie sighed.

'Clear,' she said.

'Okay. I'm glad we're on the same page. Now, Dr. Marcus, you have about two days to keep the public at bay, maybe three, depending on my recovery time. In the process of so doing, you will save the lives of a great many people. First, I want you to empty the pathology department and seal it off. Then announce to the media that there has been a biological disaster here at the hospital – a deadly viral exposure of some as yet unknown sort, requiring that the microbiology lab and the neurosurgical service on Surgical Seven be sealed off. Inform the public that the rest of the hospital is perfectly safe, but as a precaution it is being closed to all but essential personnel. All other hospital employees should be told to stay away until the crisis has passed. Go to minimal staffing. Double or triple all pay for those who come in. Discharge as many patients as possible at once. Chain off all entryways except through the main lobby. Divert all emergencies to other hospitals. Clear?'

'Yes, but –'

'Then you are to do whatever is necessary to muddle efforts to get to the bottom of the problem. If one agency wants to investigate, tell them another already is. Create as much confusion and dissension as you can. Whatever you need to do to buy time you must do. Derrick, here, or one of my other people, will be with you at all times seeing to it that you perform the way I know you're capable of. Another of my people will be out in the city, connected to us by radio, and never far from the vials of soman. Please do not do anything that will force me to conduct another, more extensive demonstration of its virulence.'

'I – I'll try my best,' Marcus replied.

Malloche threw the switch and returned Marcus and Derrick to the basement. Then he took Jessie back up to Surgical Seven.

'Dr. Copeland, I have decided that my surgery will take place tomorrow afternoon no matter what. Offer whatever assurances and financial inducements necessary to assemble the essential operating room personnel. Fail in this regard, and I promise you a quite sizable group of people will suddenly be on intimate terms with soman.'

'I don't see how –'

'Dr. Copeland, my patience is thin, and my demands are not up for debate. Now mobilize whomever you have to and get this goddamn tumor out of my brain.'

# Chapter 29

Over the seventeen years since the CIA had recruited him, Alex Bishop had become used to dealing with informants. Most were no less criminal than those on whom they were informing. Jorge Cardoza was no different. A scarred, rodent-faced little man, he had made it up the ranks in Claude Malloche's organization simply because he was quite proficient at the one skill Malloche demanded – killing.

As Alex inched back from the airport into Boston through the Sumner Tunnel, he assessed the man who he knew was responsible for the deaths of many. Cardoza, dressed in worn jeans and a stained polo shirt, sat slumped in the passenger seat, head pressed against the side window, staring out at the exhaust-stained concrete and tile. He had traded information on Malloche for his own freedom and had paid dearly for that decision. Now, with his wife and child dead, and a hefty price on his head throughout Malloche's organization, information was all that was keeping him from being thrown to the wolves. With no money and no support whatsoever as far as Alex could tell, he was attempting to start his life over again in Uruguay – the one place outside of Europe where he had relatives.

'You promise I can have my money and my plane tickets out of here as soon as I have done what you want?' Cardoza asked in Spanish.

'You identify this body and I will keep my side of the bargain,' Alex replied, his Castilian Spanish fluent and with little accent.

'What if the man you have is not Malloche?'

'Then I will have made a very serious misjudgment, and you will still be free to go.'

'With the money.'

'Yes.'

'And the tickets.'

'Yes. But I am certain the man I have *is* Malloche.'

Alex used his cell phone to call the FBI answering service that was functioning essentially as his office. No word from Jessie, no word from Lisa Brandon. Both were good signs. Arlette Malloche was still at Eastern Mass Medical, apparently willing to accept as necessary the delays in allowing her to claim her husband's body. It would not be long now. Once Malloche was positively identified, he was sure the Boston FBI would cooperate fully and move in on Arlette and her people.

'It has been hard on me,' Cardoza said.

'I know, I know.'

*Ratting on your cohorts often is.*

'Malloche has forced me to do this.'

'Yes, he has.'

'You are a good man, Bishop.'

'That means a lot coming from you, Jorge.'

The Bowker and Hammersmith Funeral Parlor, in the city's Dorchester section, was straight out of *The Twilight Zone* – weathered sign, gray, peeling clapboard siding, front steps that creaked and groaned on the way up to a porch that couldn't possibly have supported an oak casket and full complement of pallbearers.

'I need a funeral parlor that will rent me a hearse and store a body, and not ask any questions,' Alex had asked his FBI contact.

Bowker and Hammersmith's number was given to him without hesitation.

Alex pulled the rental car into the driveway on the side and motioned Cardoza to bring along his luggage – a single black nylon gym bag, small enough to carry onto the plane. They entered the funeral parlor through a service door and went directly to the basement room that held the refrigerated walk-in storage unit.

The man Alex had dealt with at the funeral home had identified himself as Richard Jones. He had gladly taken five hundred dollars, along with another thousand that would be returned when the hearse was. Now, as Jones put it, he was out of the loop and would be gone until the body had been identified and someone from the coroner's office had come by to pick it up.

Alex flipped on the light and directed Cardoza to wait while he went to get Malloche.

*This is it*, he was thinking. *Five years.*

He wheeled out the body and pulled the sheet down to the nipples. The lips had pulled back in a gaping, toothy rictus so that it looked as if Malloche were grinning at him. Unsettling.

Jorge Cardoza approached the corpse cautiously, then bent over and studied the face.

'You have my money and my ticket?' he asked.

'Right here.' Alex patted his pocket.

'And I get them no matter what?'

'No matter what.' Alex felt suddenly cold. There was no reason for Cardoza to be stalling like this unless –

'It's not him.'

'What?'

'I don't know who this is, but it is not Claude Malloche.'

Alex braced himself on the stretcher and stared down at the corpse.

'Could he have had plastic surgery?'

'I saw him just three or four months ago,' Cardoza replied. 'There is no resemblance.'

Alex grabbed the man by his shirt and pulled him up onto his tiptoes.

'Look at me, Jorge! Look me in the eyes and say this isn't Malloche!'

'Bishop, I want the man to be dead as much as you do. He killed my wife and child, and he wants to kill me! But this is not Malloche.'

Slowly, Alex released his grip.

'I don't believe this,' he said. 'I . . . I was so certain. What about Arlette? Have you ever seen her?'

Cardoza shook his head.

'I only know that she is said to be a very beautiful woman,' he said. 'Now, please. . . .'

Bishop replaced the sheet, wheeled Rolf Hermann's body back into the refrigerator, and closed the door. There was no sense trying to keep Cardoza around to identify a man who might already be back in Europe after having been operated on at some other medical center. He had lost, and that was that. With luck, Malloche would die from his goddamn tumor. But it was doubtful Alex Bishop would ever hear about it.

Numbly, he walked the Spaniard back to the car, gave him his tickets and money, and dropped him off at a T station.

# Chapter 30

Through late afternoon and into the evening the moans of Surgical Seven patients begging for services or explanations was constant. The beepers of Carl, Jessie, nursing supervisor Catherine Purcell, and the lab tech were sounding so persistently that Malloche finally had them confiscated and turned off. Worsening the situation, Malloche's headache had returned with force, causing him to be increasingly irritable and uncommunicative. Finally, he ordered some painkiller from one of the nurses and returned to his bed.

Arlette readily took over, controlling the siege with even more dispassion than had her husband. Nurses were sent to aid patients only one at a time, and never unaccompanied. One guard was constantly watching the staff seated along the nurses' station counter, while another was positioned by the doors and elevator, wiring more explosives in place. Arlette herself spent much of the time at the doorway to her room, watching as news reports of the biological disaster at Eastern Mass Medical Center unfolded on television. At other times, she patrolled the corridors, her semiautomatic slung at loose readiness over her shoulder.

Carl Gilbride was still in near shock. Except for the thirty minutes it took Jessie to guide him to the treatment room and sew up the gash in his face, he sat slumped in his chair, showing no particular interest in his surroundings, at times even dozing off. At five, his patient Lena Levin lapsed into a coma from the bacterial infection that was building rapidly where he had recently removed her tumor. Jessie was allowed to examine her and then confronted Arlette.

'She needs to have a spinal tap and be moved into the unit,' she said.

'The unit is closed. The patients and the staff have all been moved in here.'

'I want to call an infectious disease consult to discuss her therapy and order some antibiotics.'

'No calls. Use what medicine you already have here.'

At that moment, one of the nurses came racing up to Arlette in a panic, with Grace a few steps behind.

'I need to call home,' she said breathlessly.

'No calls,' Arlette responded.

'It's my son. He has a seizure problem and he needs medicine I give him, that my sitter doesn't know about.'

'I said no calls and I mean it. We let you, and everyone will have a reason to need a phone. We have more important things to attend to.'

'Please,' Jessie said.

Arlette shot her a withering look and demanded, with a jerk of the muzzle of her machine gun, that the nurse get back to her seat. After the woman had settled down, Arlette motioned Jessie over to a spot away from the others.

'My husband's headache is worsening,' she said.

'I'm not surprised.'

'I want his surgery done first thing in the morning, not tomorrow afternoon.'

'A pediatric neurosurgeon has the OR booked. There's a very sick child who needs his tumor out.'

'Get the case postponed.'

'I can try, but I want you to let that nurse call home.'

'What I'll do instead,' Arlette said, 'is to kill her.'

Jessie sized up the threat and realized that Arlette wasn't bluffing. She saw beyond the woman to where Tamika Bing lay propped up in bed as usual, watching and listening.

'I'll do what I can,' Jessie said.

Calling from the treatment room, with Arlette monitoring, she succeeded in convincing the surgeon that with the burgeoning crisis in the hospital, it was prudent to forget about using the MRI operating room at all, and instead arrange to do his case at the Hospital for Infants and Children. Then, with Armand following her, she went to check in on some of the patients, beginning with Sara. Her friend was lying on her back, eyes closed. She looked peaceful enough, but her breathing seemed slightly rapid.

'Hi, pal,' Jessie said '. . . . Sara?'

She had expected a quick response. Instead, Sara remained as she was. Anxious, Jessie took her by the shoulders and rousted her gently. Sara's eyes blinked open, and she forced a smile. But she seemed to be having trouble focusing.

'Hey . . . ,' was all she managed to say.

'You okay?'

'I . . . okay.'

'Sara?'

Sara's reply was slow in coming – too slow, Jessie thought. She did a rapid neuro check, including a careful examination through her ophthalmoscope. Everything seemed okay . . . everything except the patient. Gradually, Sara became more able to answer questions appropriately, but she still appeared marginally less aware and more sluggish than she had been. Jessie mentally scrolled through half a dozen diagnostic possibilities, including medication toxicity and simple exhaustion. But the one diagnosis that worried her most was a slow pressure buildup from a blockage to the flow of spinal fluid in and around the brain. The obstruction, if there was one, was most likely caused by scar tissue, a blood clot, or local tissue swelling. And if it became a total blockade, it would result in acute hydrocephalus – a true neurosurgical emergency. But right now, without access to the scanners in radiology, Jessie could do nothing but watch her closely.

*Damn you*, she thought as Armand followed her around to Tamika Bing's room. *Damn you all.*

The thirteen-year-old appeared as she always did – stiff and motionless, gazing out at the spot in the hall where, just a few hours ago, a woman had been shot to death. Jessie wondered if there was anything at all she could say to the child that would blunt the impact of having witnessed such brutality. She pulled up a chair.

'Hi, Tamika,' she said. 'Here I am, back again. . . . Everyone is very upset about what happened to that poor woman. She worked for the FBI, and she was trying to help us all when she was shot. . . . When this is all over, I'm going to find her family and tell them how brave she was. . . . Tamika? . . . Please look at me, baby. I want so much to know how you are feeling and to help in any way I can.'

Suddenly, almost imperceptibly, Tamika Bing's hands moved from where they were folded in her lap up to the edge of her tray table. Her eyes remained fixed straight ahead, her posture rigid. Aside from chewing food that was placed in her mouth, it was the most purposeful movement Jessie had seen her make since the surgery. Again the girl's hands moved. Now her fingertips were touching the edge of her laptop. The computer was always open and ready on her tray table, but as far as Jessie or Tamika's mother knew, it had never been used.

Jessie risked a peek at Armand, who stood at attention by the doorway, peering over to check on them from time to time, but without much interest. Mostly his focus was out in the hall. Tamika's fingers were now on the keyboard. Jessie shifted her chair just enough to be able to read the screen. The girl struck the keys softly, with the economical movements of a skilled typist.

Give me a phone connection and I can get outside, she wrote.

Stunned, Jessie stared first at the screen, then at Tamika. The girl continued looking straight ahead. But Jessie noticed the corners of her mouth were drawn up ever so slightly.

*Fooled you*, the expression was saying.

*Bless you, child.*

'So, dear,' Jessie said with clarity, careful to avoid any change in tone that might alert Armand. 'It's so nice that

you're practicing your typing again. Let me see what else
you can do.'

```
My friend Ricky checks his e-mail
all the time. I can get a message to
him.
```

Jessie's pulse was racing. The phone cable lay on the
floor, still connected to the wall. She checked the back of
the laptop to establish where the modem port was. With
luck, lots of luck, they might have a connection to Alex – a
connection Arlette and her crew would know nothing
about.

'Yes, of course,' Jessie said. 'I can get that for you,
Tamika. I'll be back in just a little while with that medicine
you need. Meanwhile, you just rest. You're doing terrific.
Absolutely terrific.'

With Armand not far behind, Jessie went to the nurses'
station and retrieved the red loose-leaf notebook that was
Tamika Ring's chart. Now, both Armand and Arlette were
watching her, but neither of them seemed particularly
interested as she opened the record and began writing a
message to Alex on a progress note sheet. She said a silent
prayer of thanks that she had jotted the number of his
answering service in her pocket-sized clinical notebook.
The book, hers since medical school, was tattered and
swollen to the point where an elastic band was required to
hold it closed. It was packed with normal lab values,
medication doses, diagnostic tables, and other reference
cards. For a decade now, when she was in the hospital and
not in the OR or showering, the little black book was never
out of her possession. Her message completed, she wrote
Alex's answering service number at the top of the progress
report sheet, then slowly slid the paper free from the
binder rings. Moments later, the weeping of the distraught
nurse diverted Arlette and Armand long enough for her to
fold the sheet and drop it into her pocket. Their response
also gave her an idea.

Broad-shouldered linebacker Dave Scolari was up in a

chair by his bed, wrapped in a blanket, his head immobilized inside his steel cervical halo. He was still unable to bear enough weight to walk, but the therapists had fitted him for braces and were glowing about his future prospects. Quadriplegic less than two weeks ago, he now had excellent movement and strength in his arms, and improving coordination in his hands. As Jessie anticipated, Armand took his post by the door. She took her stethoscope from her lab coat, placed it around her neck, and positioned herself so that she could converse with Scolari without being easily overheard.

'What in the hell is going on here, Doc?' Scolari asked. 'Who took my phone? I've been ringing the call button like crazy. Nobody answers. Who in the hell is he?'

'That's Armand. Armand, this is Dave.'

The killer looked over at them disdainfully and locked his hand on the stock of his weapon.

'Armand and some others have taken over Surgical Seven and sealed us off from the rest of the hospital,' Jessie went on. 'They plan to be here for a couple of days.'

'Did they hurt you?' Dave asked.

'No. They've killed five people so far and are threatening everyone else, but I'm immune. They want me to operate on their leader.'

'Enough!' Armand barked in heavily accented English. 'Finish what you have to do and move on.'

Jessie set her stethoscope in her ears, but kept the earpieces pressed just outside her auditory canal opening.

'I need a diversion, Dave,' she whispered as she pretended to examine him, her back to Armand. 'Something loud that will bring all these people running in here.'

'I'll try.'

'It's got to be convincing.'

'I understand.'

'In ten minutes. Do it at exactly five past.'

'Got it,' Dave said, looking up at the wall clock.

Armand was moving toward them when she pocketed her stethoscope and stepped back.

'You're coming along fine, Dave,' she said. 'That little wheeze in your chest is nothing to worry about.'

The clock ticking, she led Armand back to the room next to Tamika Bing's. With a minute to go, she reentered Tamika's room and again fixed her stethoscope in place. At precisely five after the hour, there was a loud crash from Scolari's room, followed by eerie, animal-like, bellowing cries of pain. Another crash. Armand turned and raced toward the sound. A moment later, Arlette hurried past the door without looking in.

Jessie quickly tucked the note she had written under Tamika's thigh, then picked up the phone cord and ran it under the tray table before inserting the connector into the back of the laptop. Finally, she pulled the sheet over the cord, covering as much of it as possible. She had just set a towel on the tray table to shield the rest of the cord when Armand reappeared at the door.

'Come quick,' he commanded.

Jessie kissed Tamika on the cheek.

'Remember to dial nine first for an outside line,' she whispered.

I knew that! the girl typed.

Dave Scolari was thrashing about in what was probably his attempt at feigning a seizure. He had somehow managed to knock over his sturdy bedside table and his tray table. Saliva was bubbling from his mouth, mixing with blood from where he had actually bitten through his lip. Jessie was relieved to see that the cervical halo was intact.

'He's having a seizure,' she said. 'I need medicine to stop it. Tell the nurses to bring me a syringe with ten of Valium in it.'

Arlette hesitated, then nodded to Armand that he could carry out the order. A minute later, he handed Jessie a loaded syringe. She jammed the needle just beneath Dave's thigh, and injected his robe with tranquilizer. Then she bent over and put her lips by his ear.

'You did good, Dave,' she whispered. 'You did real good.'

# Chapter 31

Corrigan's tavern was a dark, musty corner saloon not far from the Bowker and Hammersmith Funeral Parlor. Alex sat on a stool at one end of the bar, working on a tumbler of scotch – the second of what he planned to be a series of twenty or so. The evening crowd was drifting in, and the level of smoke in the place was actually starting to get to him.

*Well, so be it*, he thought. The deal he had made with himself about no cigarettes until Malloche was dead or in prison never mentioned secondhand smoke. And if the shit gave him lung cancer, so what. He had blown everything that mattered to him, and blown it all big-time. Along the way, he had called in enough markers from the agency, the FBI, and certain politicians to finish forever any chance of ever getting more help in catching Malloche. Then there were all the ways he had lied to Jessie, and the risks he had convinced her to take in helping him with Hermann's body. And for what? Now, he had no place to go and no one who cared. After this fiasco, it was likely that even the people at the academy would want nothing to do with him.

There was also the slight matter of the body he had stolen from the hospital – another gem. He had called and left a message for Richard Jones at the funeral parlor to contact Orlis Hermann on Surgical Seven. That was the best he could do at the moment.

*What difference does it make anyhow?*

Alex sipped at his scotch and tried to remember the last time he had been certifiably, gut-tearing, bury-me-before-you-wake-me drunk. It wasn't anything he was especially looking forward to, but then again, what was? Okay, he acknowledged, Jessie Copeland would have been something to look forward to. Every single day. He cared about her – more than for any woman he could remember. He cringed at the thought of calling her with the details of the monumental failure of his life. She had just begun to trust him. Now, she'd never believe anything he ever had to say.

What did he have to show for his forty-three years on earth? A one-room flat in Paris that he could barely afford, a future at the agency that he could probably measure in weeks, and a résumé that was one prolonged blank spot. His bank accounts were woefully thin, and his connections to friends and family had long ago been sacrificed on the altar of destroying Claude Malloche. What more could a good-looking, brilliant woman like Jessie Copeland possibly want in a man?

He drained the last of the scotch and was about to order a third when he caught a fragment of conversation from a man standing behind him. Actually, what he overheard were three words: Eastern Mass Medical. He spun around on his stool.

'What about Eastern Mass Medical?' he asked a group of four.

'Where the fuck have *you* been all afternoon?' a lumberjack-sized construction worker, his speech beginning to thicken, roared at him.

The others laughed. Alex blew past them, grabbed the larger man by his shirt, and hoisted him up on to his tiptoes. This is what he *really* needed at this moment, he was thinking. A huge wise-ass to bring down to size, not a self-destructive bender. The bender could come after.

'I asked you a question,' he said.

The giant stumbled back, brushing Alex's hand aside in the same motion. The talk throughout the tavern abruptly ceased with anticipation. For several seconds, no one around them moved or spoke. There was the scraping of chairs as others in the place stood to watch. Then the man, perhaps sensing from Alex's expression and stance that he was some sort of psycho, put his hands up, palms out.

246

'Hey, pal, easy does it,' he said. 'Cool your jets. This is a friendly place. If you don't like the way we do things here, go somewhere else.'

'I asked you about the hospital.'

'Okay, okay. They had some kinda outbreak there. A virus, I guess. I don't know for sure. A bunch of people are dead, though. I do know that much.'

'The hospital's closed down,' someone else chimed in.

'It was four,' another offered. 'Four people are dead.'

With the crisis in the bar over as quickly as it had begun, the patrons now seemed to be talking all at once about the developments at EMMC. Alex pushed a twenty toward the bartender, found a relatively quiet corner, and called the hospital. He got a recorded message saying that all hospital lines were tied up, that the hospital was temporarily closed to new patients, and that all emergencies should be taken to Eastern Mass Medical's associate institution, White Memorial, or to one of the other Boston hospitals.

A previous page to Jessie had gone unanswered. Now, he tried her again. The recorded electronic hospital page operator answered, and promised his message had been sent.

Four people dead. The hospital sealed up. Alex dialed his answering service.

'Oh, yes, Mr. Bishop,' the FBI operator said. 'We were about to try to reach you. A call just came in for you a few minutes ago. Someone named Ricky Barnett.'

'Never heard of him.'

'It was very strange. He sounded like a little boy, and he was very shy. He said that he had a message for you from a friend of his.'

'A friend? Who?'

'He didn't say except that she was in the hospital.'

```
Call Alex Bishop at 4269444. Message
from Jessie. Tolliver is Malloche.
Lisa dead. Five of them have wired
Surgical 7 to explode. Soman gas
hidden all over Boston. Will be
```

      released if there is any trouble for
      Malloche. Four killed in lab as a
      demonstration. Be careful.

Alex sped toward EMMC with Ricky Barnett's e-mail message propped against the steering wheel.

*Tolliver is Malloche.*

Bishop felt a dreadful spasm in his gut at the news. Not only had he completely missed his target, but because of his incompetence, agent Lisa Brandon was dead, and Jessie – and it appeared many others – was in serious danger. The irony was almost more than he could bear. Claude Malloche was right there on Surgical Seven, all right. But he was most certainly not there for the taking.

Thirteen-year-old Ricky Barnett told him that he had formed a secret computer club with Tamika Bing and two other kids. The e-mail message from Tamika, which Alex had the boy spell out for him letter by letter as he transcribed it onto a blank bar tab, had been sent from the hospital earlier in the afternoon, but wasn't retrieved until Ricky came home. Alex had him send a message back to Tamika, telling Jessie he understood and would do what he could. Now, he was trying to learn about soman. He was about a mile from the hospital when his cell phone rang.

'Agent Bishop?'

'That's right.'

'Abdul Fareed, here. I'm a toxicologist at Georgetown. I do some contract work for the agency. They said you wanted information on soman.'

'I do.'

'If you're dealing with soman, you've got trouble. It's also called GD. It's an inhaled neurotoxin – the most powerful stuff of its kind. Works three or four times as fast as sarin, the gas those fanatics used in the Tokyo subway. Respiratory and central nervous system collapse all at once. One hundred percent fatal from a single decent breath.'

'Any antidote?'

'The only antidote I know of, carbamate physostigmine, is almost as toxic as the gas, and has to be taken *before* exposure. I've got a call in to a friend of mine in Jerusalem who is one of the world's experts on neurotoxic gases. If she has anything to add to what I've said, I'll call you.'

'Okay. If I don't answer, call my service and insist on speaking to someone from the agency or the FBI. Tell them all you know.'

'One other piece of information I can pass on is that the half-life of soman is pretty short. If you're at ground zero, and there's decent ventilation, and you can hold your breath for two or three minutes, you've got a chance.'

'Thanks, that's very reassuring.'

Alex hung up and dialed a number in Virginia.

'Seven-eight-two-eight,' a woman answered. 'May I help you?'

'This is Alex Bishop calling back.'

'Oh, yes, sir.'

'Were you able to get any of the information I wanted?'

'Yes, sir. Eastman Tolliver is the executive director of the MacIntosh Foundation in Valencia, California. They fund research projects, mostly in the medical field. Mr. Tolliver has been on a trip to China for over two weeks. He's not expected back for another ten days. That's all we have right now. Is there anything else we can do?'

'No, no thank you.'

Police had cordoned off the area a block away from the hospital. Filling the streets outside the blockade were mobile broadcasting vans and enough police cruisers to suggest that the rest of the city might be ripe for the picking. From what he could tell, no one seemed anxious to get any closer to EMMC than they were. With no CIA ID, it took fifteen minutes and two phone calls before Alex was waved past the wooden barriers.

He pulled onto a side street just across from the main hospital entrance and waited. Ten minutes later, an unmarked, windowless van pulled up behind him. He waited until the lights had been cut, then scanned the area for anyone who might be watching them. Finally, he gathered up his security guard uniform from the back seat, left the rental, and approached the van on the driver's side.

The two FBI agents inside introduced themselves as Stan Moyer and Vicki Holcroft. Moyer was a slightly built, balding man in his forties, whose heavy-lidded eyes and wire-rims made him look more like a classics professor than a Fed. Vicki was young, though not as young as Lisa Brandon. Her blond hair was pulled back in a ponytail, and her features, while undeniably pretty, were also sharp and businesslike.

'Back door's open,' Stan said. He waited until Alex was inside, then asked, 'Is it true that Lisa's dead?'

'I believe so.'

'She was a terrific kid.'

'I know.'

The van was equipped with three TV monitors, several telephones, and banks of instruments on both sides. Alex freed up a chair from its tie-down straps and scanned the consoles. Then he brought the two agents up to date on what he knew. Vicki worked her way into the back and took a seat beside him.

'I'm glad we were around,' she said. 'Stan and I helped design this van. There are others who can handle most of this equipment, but not like us.'

'The problem spot is the seventh floor of the Surgical Tower, right over there.'

Vicki peered at the tower through the front windshield and shook her head.

'Too high to pick up anything through our parabolics. We've got fiber-optic cameras, though, and some pretty awesome little microphones. If we can slip them up through the floor, or down through the ceiling, we should be able to see and hear a heck of a lot. Stanley's a master at doing it if you can get him up there.'

'I don't know. Maybe. They've got about forty hostages up there right now, and a million hostages out here. That gas could be hidden anywhere.'

'And what's your connection on the floor?'

'Believe it or not, it's a thirteen-year-old kid named Tamika Bing, with a laptop. She's a patient on Surgical Seven. Somehow she's been able to get an e-mail message out to a friend of hers named Ricky Barnett. He called me.'

Vicki brightened.

'How much into computers are they, do you know?' she asked.

'I can find out by calling the kid in Roxbury. He and Tamika formed some kind of computer club. I know that much.'

'That sounds promising. We'll call and ask him if Tamika has an ICQ number.'

'ICQ?'

'It's an instant messaging system. If she's got one, I can download the ICQ software from our office in just a few minutes so that we can hold a give-and-take conversation with her from right here.'

'Here's the boy's number,' Alex said. 'He's waiting to hear from us. I need to change back into my security guard uniform so I can get into the hospital. Vicki, if you haven't had a cardiogram lately, you may want to look the other way.'

The woman smiled, picked up the phone, and turned her back to him.

'What are you going to do once you're in there?' Stan asked.

'I'm not sure. First, maybe, I'll try to speak with someone in maintenance, or else the hospital CEO, to see if I can get blueprints of the place.'

'The CEO is otherwise occupied,' Stan said. 'He's supposed to be holding a press conference right now. No, wait, it's not as late as I thought. It should start in a minute or two.'

He clambered into the back, electronically raised a satellite dish that had been concealed in the van's roof, and switched on one of the monitors. All the local channels were getting pictures from the same single feed – an unadorned podium in the main foyer of the hospital, fitted with several microphones. For a time, there was only a technician, readying some cables. Then, a drawn and clearly troubled Richard Marcus approached the podium. Behind him stood a scientist in a lab coat, and a man from security.

'I am Dr. Richard Marcus. For more than six years I have been the CEO of the Eastern Massachusetts Medical Center. My specialties are internal medicine and, ironically, infectious disease. I am here to give you all a briefing on the situation in our microbiology lab and on Surgical Seven, our neurosurgery floor. To this moment, there have been five deaths, four in the lab and one on Surgical Seven. We strongly believe the deaths are due to a very rapidly acting microorganism – most likely some sort of virus, which causes a brain infection called encephalitis, characterized by massive brain swelling and in most cases, rapid death. There is evidence of several more cases still evolving on Surgical Seven, so we have shut the floor down, and effectively sealed off the hospital as well. We currently have a team of microbiologists at work. That is all the information I can share with you at this time. However, we will bring you updates every hour on the hour, and immediately if there are any major developments. Hopefully, next hour there will be some telephone hookups here at this podium so reporters can phone in questions. Meanwhile, I beg your patience as we try our best to contain this outbreak. Thank you.'

Marcus left the podium without calling on the scientist to speak.

'Impressive man,' Stan said. 'Maybe there is no gas. Maybe it is a virus.'

'Highly doubtful,' Alex replied.

'Why?' Vicki asked.'

'Well, for one thing, that security guard standing behind Marcus was one of Malloche's men.

# Chapter 32

From the windows of Surgical Seven, Jessie could see the phalanx of news vehicles and police cruisers lined up along the streets a block away from the hospital, like strobe-lit spokes on a wheel. It was after eleven. The surgery on Claude Malloche was less than seven hours away.

Scrub nurse . . . circulating nurse . . . console technician . . . Hans Pfeffer and one of his computer people . . . Skip Porter . . . Jessie decided to involve only a skeleton crew in the operation. One by one, she had contacted the team to notify each that the case they would be working on first thing in the morning was a matter of great urgency, and could only be done with MRI assistance. She guaranteed them a sizable bonus and assured them that there was no danger from exposure to Eastman Tolliver, who was in the ICU, isolated from the rest of the patients on Surgical Seven. Of the group, only the scrub nurse balked at the idea of coming in. Jessie actually resorted to having Richard Marcus call to assure the man that he would be placing himself in no danger. Finally, the team was set. Only Emily was missing, hut Arlette had promised that she would be brought to the floor sometime during the night.

Jessie didn't even bother to point out the obvious that the way they were doing things, both surgeon and assistant would be operating with major sleep deprivation. Except for delaying the case so they could rest, which was simply not going to happen, there was nothing anyone could do about it.

Determined to have as few people as possible involved with Malloche, Jessie elected to forego the standard pre-op medical clearance and instead had Malloche's man Derrick help her wheel him down for a chest X ray and EKG, which she then had the appropriate on-call residents review.

Next came choosing an anesthesiologist. Jessie was pleased that Michelle Booker was available and willing to do the case. Booker, a descendant of slaves and the daughter of an uneducated single mother in Alabama, had finished first in her class at Tuskegee Institute, then first again at Harvard Med. She was already a full professor in her department, though she was only Jessie's age. She was also intuitive enough, Jessie believed, to pick up on some of what was going on without asking too many questions. Jessie felt bad at having to involve anyone in such a potentially perilous situation, let alone someone as essential to the medical community as Michelle. But a great many lives hinged on Malloche's surviving his surgery. The pre-op anesthesia evaluation was conducted in the recovery room on Surgical Eight.

'So, Mr. Tolliver,' Michelle said after she had completed her history and physical, 'our plan is to put you to sleep initially so that the tiny robot can be worked into place. Then we will wake you for most of the remainder of the procedure so that Dr. Copeland can monitor your neurologic function while she resects your tumor. Do you have any questions regarding that or any other aspect of tomorrow's procedure?'

'No,' Malloche said. 'You've explained things well. Several days ago I was in the operating room, observing the robot at work on a case. I know what to expect.'

'That's excellent. Still, I'm told that the sensation of being awake during one's own brain surgery almost defies description. I plan to keep you sedated as much as possible, even though you won't actually be asleep.'

'You're the doctor,' Malloche said.

'Correction,' Michelle said. 'I'm the anesthesiologist. That woman over there by the window is The Doctor, capital T, capital D. And you couldn't do any better. Jess, do you have anything to add to what I've said? . . . Jessie?
. . .'

254

Jessie was gazing out the window at nothing in particular. Booker's description of the procedure had sent an idea flashing through her mind – something important, she was almost certain. But the notion had vanished before she could get a fix on it.

Now, an hour later, back on Surgical Seven, Jessie was still struggling to reconnect with the thought. Something Michelle Booker had said to Malloche had triggered an idea . . . something . . .

With Grace dogging her step for step, Jessie wandered around the Track, carefully pausing at each patient's doorway. Although she tried to show interest in all of them, only two of the patients really concerned her at this moment: Sara Devereau, who continued to seem just a bit more sluggish than she had been, and Tamika Bing.

Tamika had made contact with Alex, and in fact was on-line continuously now with someone named Vicki. Jessie had risked going into her room twice during the evening and managed to come out each time with a message from Alex. The first, which she had read right off the screen, said simply:

```
I am with you. Please be careful.
When is Malloche's operation? A.
```

The second was more detailed.

```
We are working on penetrating the
hospital. Understand that Orlis
Hermann is Arlette Malloche and that
there are three plus her and Malloche
on Surgical Seven. Any more? Probable
contact point will be the MRI-OR. Any
idea where the soman might be hidden?
Tamika, good job. Jessie, hang in. Be
careful. We're going to win. A.
```

With her captor standing so close, Jessie felt reluctant to speak to Tamika of anything but how she was doing. She did risk another pass with her stethoscope and some whispered words of encouragement. Then she remembered that all Malloche's people she knew of were accounted for when she spoke by phone to Emily.

'Tamika, you're doing great,' she whispered. 'Tell Vicki there is at least one more of Malloche's men outside the hospital.'

While Jessie continued listening to her chest, Tamika silently typed out the message. Moments later, Jessie was walking the halls again, frantically trying to reconnect with the thought that had eluded her on Surgical Eight. As she passed Claude Malloche's room, she paused. Through the semidarkness, she could see the monster, asleep on his back, the sheet over his chest rising and falling with each easy breath. Jessie had never encountered anyone so depraved.

Aside from his wife and perhaps his cadre of trusted followers, there was no one in the hospital – hell, probably in the world – whose life meant anything to Malloche except as it served him. To assure a successful operation and subsequent escape, he would think nothing of killing every person on Surgical Seven, or possibly even hundreds more on the streets of the city. It was easy now for her to understand Alex's hatred of the man and the obsession with bringing him down. If only there were some way she could enter Malloche's room, crouch down by his bed, and make some sort of subliminal suggestion that he –

The thought was never completed. It yielded instead to the evanescent idea that had been tormenting her so. This time, though, the notion stuck in her mind like a well-thrown dart, and quickly grew in clarity. Afraid that something in her expression might betray her to the young terrorist Grace, Jessie turned from Malloche's room and headed, as nonchalantly as she could manage, down the hallway. Her heart was racing. The logistics of her plan would be tricky, but there was a possibility, however remote, that it might work. And with so many lives at stake, she had to try. The first step might actually be the most dangerous. She had to chance going back into Tamika

Bing's room with one more message for Alex.

With Grace several paces behind, Jessie followed the Track back to the nurses' station and slid Sara's record from its holder. As before, she block-printed the message for Alex on a progress note sheet and waited until Grace's attention was momentarily diverted before tearing the paper free from the binder rings and folding it in her pocket. Now, all she needed was some excuse to reenter Tamika's room. Absently, she put her hand in her lab coat pocket. Her Game Boy was there. Sharing it with the girl wasn't the strongest motivation for a return visit, but it was at least something. She pulled it out and approached Grace, yawning.

'Well, I think I'm going to turn in down the hall there,' she said.

'Good idea,' the woman replied coolly. 'You need to be at your best tomorrow.'

'Before I do, though, I want to stop in seven-ten again just for a minute.'

'What for? You were just there.'

'The kid in there had a brain tumor taken out by me. The cancer had eaten away her speech center, and now she can only communicate by her computer. She has no games on it and she's getting very bored. I promised her a go at my Game Boy.'

'You stay here. I'll bring it into her.'

'I . . . I need to show her how to work it. It won't take but a couple of minutes.'

For an interminable few seconds, Grace mulled over the request. Then she shrugged.

'Okay. But make it quick. You need to get some rest.'

Jessie reentered Tamika's room. The girl, still propped in bed, was dozing.

'See her in the morning,' Grace whispered.

The sound was enough. Tamika awoke and instantly tapped on her tray table to get Jessie's attention.

No new messages, she typed.

Jessie shielded her from Grace and passed the progress sheet over.

**FIND DR. MARK NAEHRING. URGENT HE MEET ME IN MRI-OR AT 6 A.M. BRING MAGICAL MEDS HE DEMONSTRATED AT RECENT GRAND ROUNDS. MATTER OF LIFE OR DEATH. JESSIE**

'So, Tamika,' she said in a strong voice, 'here's that Game Boy I promised you. Let me show you how to run it. This switch right here . . .'

While Jessie droned on, Tamika glanced down at the note and quickly typed it. Then, as Jessie handed over the electronic toy, she retrieved the paper and stuffed it deep into her lab coat pocket.

'Just what in the hell is going on here?' Arlette Malloche stormed into the room.

As Jessie leaped back from the bed, she noted that Tamika had instantly broken off contact with Vicki.

*Good baby!* she cheered. *Send the message later.*

'Everything's fine,' Grace said.

'Is it? It seems like the doctor's been in here all night.'

'Just twice before this. She's been in several rooms that much. This time, she was just dropping off a toy.'

'Well, she's finished going into any patient's room until Claude's surgery is done. Dr. Copeland, a room has been prepared for you. Get to bed at once.'

'I want to see Sara Devereau,' Jessie said. 'She may be in some trouble.'

'I said you're going to bed, and that's it.'

Suddenly, Arlette's eyes widened. Jessie followed her line of sight to the telephone cord snaking from the wall outlet up under the bed-sheet. Muttering a curse, Arlette pushed the tray table back from the bed. The cord straightened, then pulled the computer off the tray table and onto Tamika's lap. Furious, Arlette slapped Tamika across the face, then, in almost the same motion, slapped Jessie as well.

'What is going on here?' she demanded. 'Who connected this?'

Tamika, who never even flinched at being hit, tapped on the computer to bring Arlette around to see the screen. She typed

```
I DID IT. I WANTED TO E-MAIL MY
BOYFRIEND.
```

'She's mute from her tumor surgery,' Jessie tried to explain. 'The computer is the only way she can communicate with –'

'Shut up!' Arlette snarled. 'Grace, did she send any e-mails while Dr. Copeland was here?'

'None,' Grace said, clearly frightened.

'You checked?'

'Yes . . . yes, I checked everything she did.'

'For your sake, I hope that's true.'

She snatched up the laptop, tore it away from the phone line, and lifted it above her head.

'Please don't,' Jessie said. 'It's her only –'

Arlette slammed the computer on the floor. The cover flew off, the casing split, and the screen shattered.

'Get to bed,' she said. 'Now!'

# Chapter 33

The ventilation system to the surgical tower was a series of aluminum tubes about the size of the opening in an MRI machine. Arms extended, Alex inched his way through the maze, using raised toeholds to move up from the entry port on Surgical Five. He wore a miner's helmet with a spotlight above the brim and carried a blueprint of the system in one hand. In the other he clutched a tape measure with which he was keeping track of his progress and location. Strapped to his back was a small knapsack containing a slender video camera and a transmitter, as well as metal shears, drills, bits, and other tools for boring. His pistol was jammed into a shoulder holster tucked beneath one arm.

The circular shape of the Surgical Seven hallway made positioning the camera and microphone a problem. The ceiling over the nurses' station was the ideal location, but it was unlikely he could get the setup in place there without one of Malloche's people hearing him or noticing the tip of the fiber-optic camera. He had instead chosen a location just around the bend from the nurses' station as the spot least likely to be detected and most likely to help monitor the situation on the floor. Now, to the best of his calculations, he was there.

He had always had difficulty being in tight quarters. Now, he had been negotiating the two-foot tube for over an hour. Each heartbeat seemed to echo through the cramped space. He was drenched in sweat and finding it hard to breathe. For increasing stretches of time, all he could think about was standing up. But there was no room to stand, and no place to go but forward.

He extended the tape measure and once again checked his position on the blueprint. As best as he could figure, he was twenty feet from the center of the nurses' station. Off to both sides of him, narrow ducts snaked away to the patients' rooms and core service area. The ducts helped to relieve some of the dreadful feeling of being unable to straighten up or even turn over, but the anxiety was still there every second. He worked the backpack off his shoulders and removed the metal shears and powerful drill. Two drill holes in the aluminum and he would be able to cut an opening large enough for him to work on a panel of the drop ceiling.

*Easy does it,* he urged. He could do it and get out. He just had to stay calm.

It took a while, but finally the eight-inch-square opening in the ventilation pipe was complete. Alex shut off his headlamp for a time and lay in the darkness, regaining his breath and his composure. Silence was crucial now – absolute quiet and skill in handling the drill. Slowly, carefully, he set the bit in place and squeezed the trigger on the housing. The pressboard of the ceiling panel gradually gave way as flakes of the material spun off.

*Slowly . . . slowly.*

Almost directly below where he was working, Jessie walked along the corridor toward the room that had been designated by Arlette as her sleeping quarters. Behind her followed the ever-present Grace, accompanied by Arlette herself. Suddenly, just as Jessie was precisely beneath the place where Alex was working, no more than a few feet from him, his drill bit caught on something in the ceiling panel. Before Alex could adjust and react, the drill housing spun out of his hand and dropped onto the panel with a thud that might as well have been the impact of a wrecking ball. The panel gave way at one end. Instantly, weapon ready, Grace leaped up and pulled the entire piece down. Alex, exposed above the opening in the aluminum, was fumbling for his weapon. But Arlette and Grace were way ahead of him.

'No!' Jessie screamed as they opened fire. 'Noooo!'

Several shots caught Alex flush in the face, while a dozen or more slammed through the aluminum and into his body. A thick, heavy rain of blood fell from the ceiling, splattering on the floor and pocking Jessie's white lab coat with crimson. Alex's face, a red mask of death, pressed grotesquely through the opening in the aluminum.

'Oh God,' Jessie moaned. 'Oh God ... Oh God ... Oh –'

*'Jessie?'*

Gentle hands pressed down on her shoulders.

'Jess, wake up.'

Soft, reassuring whisper ... warm breath on her ear.

The horror of the nightmare began to fade, and with it the almost painful rigidity in Jessie's body. She was facedown, clutching her pillow in a near death grip, jaws clenched. Her scrubs were damp with perspiration. Slowly, she turned and blinked herself awake. Emily looked down at her, her face shadowed with concern.

'You must have been having a real bad one,' she said.

Jessie sat up, still trying to shake off the startlingly vivid dream. Then she threw her arms around her friend.

'Oh, Em. I'm so glad you're here. I was worried to death about you. Are you okay?'

'Nothing that a week in the Caribbean won't take care of.'

Jessie managed to stand. Leaning in the doorway, dressed in scrubs, his gun over his shoulder, was Derrick.

'What time is it?' Jessie asked, still less than fully awake.

'Five-thirty.'

'The OR. We're due in the OR at six.'

'I know. There's still time for you to shower and change. I brought a clean set of scrubs for you.'

'Have you had any sleep?'

'I'm okay. I understand from Mrs. Hermann that I'll be assisting you and ARTIE in the OR.'

'She's not Mrs. Hermann. Her name's Arlette Malloche. Eastman Tolliver is actually her husband, Claude. They kill people for money.'

'The guy who had me tied up never said anything about

who he worked for,' Emily replied, 'but I'm not surprised. My, my. I guess this means Carl won't be getting that big grant.'

Jessie grinned momentarily.

'Guess not,' she said. Her expression darkened. 'Lisa Brandon, the candy striper who was so kind to Sara, was actually an FBI undercover agent. Carl got her killed by losing his temper and forcing her to disclose who she was. Since then he's come damn close to getting himself killed as well.'

'He's bunked in the room next to yours and –'

'Sara!' Jessie exclaimed.

'What?'

'Sara – I've got to get in to see her. Arlette wouldn't let me last night. She was starting to seem, I don't know, sort of sluggish.'

'Jess, she's been sluggish since she woke up.'

'I know, but she seemed more so to me.'

'Okay, I'll go check on her. You shower. Here are the scrubs.'

Jessie took the clothes and turned to Derrick.

'Can my nurse, here, go to check the woman in seven thirty-seven?'

'If Arlette says it's okay.'

Derrick radioed down the hall, and in a minute, Grace appeared at the door.

'Tell her I'll be down as soon as I've changed,' Jessie said.

As Derrick followed Emily down the hall, Jessie checked the ceiling, half expecting to see it stained with Alex's blood. How much prophecy was there in her dream? She also wondered if Tamika had managed to send the message about Mark Naehring before her laptop was destroyed. If so, they had a chance. If not, there was really nothing else she could think of to do. She would just have to perform the best surgery she could and pray that ARTIE functioned to its potential, and that Malloche recovered and made it out of the country without any more killing. Deep inside, though, she knew that praying for no more killing was wishful thinking. Claude and Arlette Malloche were animals – animals with their teeth on the throat of the hospital and, indeed, of the city.

Grace closed the door to the hallway and stood by the open bathroom doorway while Jessie undressed and stepped into the shower. Hot water, soap, and shampoo did good things for her flagging morale. Alex and Emily were still alive, and even Carl had survived. Tamika Bing had broken through her horrible depression, and had helped put a long-shot plan in motion. Jessie closed her eyes for a time and let the hot water beat against her face. She was toweling off when Emily came bursting into the room.

'Jess, come quick,' she said, breathlessly. 'It's Sara. She's in big trouble. I think she may be going out.'

Jessie grabbed her glasses, pulled on the fresh scrubs, and bolted past Grace and down the hall. Sara indeed was *in extremis*. She lay motionless in bed, unconscious and unresponsive to voice or touch. Her respirations were labored. Her pupils were dilated and barely reactive to light – a sign that there was massive brain swelling, which was pressing a portion of her brain stem up against a bony ridge on the floor of her skull.

'Acute hydrocephalus,' Jessie said. 'I'd bet the ranch on it.'

Something – possibly a small clot or piece of scar tissue – was obstructing the flow and drainage of Sara's spinal fluid. The fluid, which was formed in the choroid plexus organ in the brain, was now blocked from flowing throughout the central nervous system and down around the spinal cord. But production of fluid by the plexus was continuing, and the resulting buildup of pressure within the rigid containment of her skull was about to become lethal. Jessie cursed herself for not being more aggressive last night when she had sensed that something in her friend's condition might be changing.

'I'll call the OR,' Emily said. 'The team should all be in by now.'

'You'll do no such thing!'

Arlette Malloche barged into the room and confronted Jessie.

'This woman must have an immediate drainage procedure to relieve the pressure that's building up in her brain,' Jessie said. 'She needs to be brought to the OR right now.'

'The only person who will be brought to any OR right now is my husband,' Arlette said.

Jessie was about to beg for her friend's life, hut she stopped abruptly. To people like Arlette Malloche and her husband, begging was nothing but a sign of weakness – certainly nothing to be respected. Instead, Jessie confronted the woman with all the hatred, all the fire, that had been building inside her.

'Arlette,' she said, 'I'm drawing the line here. Claude's operation can wait until I perform the drainage procedure on this woman. I swear that if you allow her to die, there is no way I will operate on your husband, no matter what you do to me.'

Arlette gave her the haughty look of an Olympian goddess confronted by the demands of a mere mortal. Then she calmly took her weapon from her shoulder and forced the barrel of it between Sara's teeth and deep into her throat. Sara's reaction to the violent insult was a faint, impotent gag and some involuntary movement of her arms.

'My husband is due to head down to the operating room in fifteen minutes,' Arlette said. 'If you are not there with him, I will begin killing one person on this floor every minute until you are, beginning with this woman right here. Do you understand?'

Jessie and Emily exchanged looks.

*Is it worth calling her bluff?* they asked one another. *Right here – right now, simply refuse to operate on the man.*

Jessie was well aware of the answer. The price of that hollow victory was hardly one she was willing to pay. She cared about the lives of others, and Arlette knew that as well as she did, just as she knew that Arlette cared not at all. The clash of wills, at this moment at least, on this battleground, was no contest.

'I understand,' Jessie said quickly. 'Now please, take that out of Sara's mouth.'

'Fifteen minutes,' Arlette said, withdrawing the muzzle. 'Don't test me on this.'

She turned toward the door.

'Wait!' Jessie cried. 'There is something I can try right here.'

Arlette made a regal turn and assessed the faces around her. It was as if she saw the chance to become something of a benevolent despot in the eyes of the staff and her people. There was everything for her to gain by relenting here and nothing to lose.

'You have ten minutes,' she said. 'At five of six, I want you out of here, accompanying my husband to the operating room.'

'One thing.'

'Yes?'

'Your people took a piece of equipment from me that I need right now – a twist drill. It looks like a big screwdriver with a black handle and a drill bit at the other end.'

'It looked like a dagger to us.'

'I'll need some other equipment, too.'

Arlette nodded to Grace, who motioned Jessie out of the room and followed her off down the hall.

'Don't do anything stupid,' Arlette called after them.

By the time Jessie returned with her twist drill, a scissors, a prep razor, a hemostat, and a Silastic catheter, three minutes of her ten had elapsed. Even worse, one of Sara's pupils had become larger than the other and no longer constricted in response to the beam from Jessie's penlight. The lethal brain-stem herniation and compression was happening. Perhaps sensing that death was in the offing, Arlette had chosen to remain in the room to monitor the procedure.

'I should have made this diagnosis last night,' Jessie muttered as she and Emily shaved away some fine new hair from the top of Sara's scalp, an inch back from her front hairline, and just to the right side of the midline. 'I could have taken her to the OR and done this right. Now it's too late. It . . . it was just crazy here last night. I should have taken a stand then.'

'Just do what you can do, Jess,' Emily said. 'We both know she still has a chance.'

They pulled Sara down in the bed. Jessie gloved, then climbed up on the mattress, beside Sara's head. Next she squirted some russet-colored Betadine antiseptic on the spot and on her drill, and began manually twisting a hole into Sara's skull. There were less than five minutes left. The procedure did not go quickly. The twist drill was as much standard equipment to a neurosurgeon as a stethoscope was to an internist. But it was used infrequently and only in the most dire emergencies. Jessie began to wonder if she had the arm strength to complete the procedure.

Across the room, Arlette, positioning herself so that Jessie could hardly miss the movement, brought her weapon off her shoulder, and cradled it in front of her.

'Two minutes,' she said.

'Hand me that catheter and a hemostat, Em, please. I'm through the dural membrane.'

Jessie snapped one end of the catheter into the hemostat, tunneled for an inch beneath Sara's scalp, and pushed it through the skin to the outside. Then she grasped the other end and worked it through the hole she had just made in the skull and dura, and down toward the ventricle chamber, where the mounting pressure was greatest.

'One more minute and you're done here,' Arlette said. 'And I mean it. I gave you your chance.'

'Go for it, Jess,' Emily said.

Jessie gripped the catheter and with a twisting motion forced it into the ventricle. Instantly, spinal fluid under high pressure shot through the catheter, actually hitting Emily on the sleeve.

'Yes!' she exclaimed. 'Oh, yes!'

Quickly, Emily fixed the catheter to a drainage system.

'Time's up!' Arlette announced. 'Let's go, Doctor.'

'I can't leave her yet,' Jessie implored.

Arlette readied her weapon and strode to the bedside, clearly ready to finish Sara off.

267

'I'll stay with her,' Emily said quickly.

Arlette glared at her.

'You'll do nothing of the sort. I want you both out of here and on your way to the operating room.'

Her voice was strident now. Jessie was certain that at any moment she would simply raise her weapon to Sara's head and blow it apart. But the drainage catheter hadn't even been sutured down yet. What if it got pulled out, or plugged? What about antibiotic coverage for what was hardly a sterile procedure? What about steroids or other treatment for brain swelling?

'Okay, okay,' she pleaded. 'Don't shoot her. Please. We're going. We're going.'

'I'll take care of her.'

Carl Gilbride spoke from the doorway, then stepped into the room, with Armand right behind him. His cheek was bandaged, and he looked disheveled in his bloodstained designer shirt and lab coat. But his eyes were clear, and the purpose in them unmistakable. For several seconds there was only silence.

'Thank you, Carl,' Jessie said softly, pushing herself off the bed to make room for him. 'Thank you.'

'Now!' Arlette barked. 'Let's go.' She turned to Armand. 'Let Dr. Gilbride do whatever he needs to here.'

'Jessie,' Gilbride said as she reached the door, 'what antibiotics do you want her on?'

Jessie turned back to him and, for the first time in longer than she could remember, liked what she saw of the man.

'You decide,' she said. 'I trust your judgment.'

# Chapter 34

The transport team consisted of Jessie and Emily, Grace and Derrick. Armand and Arlette were to remain on Surgical Seven. Another terrorist – the one who had held Emily captive in a room somewhere in the subbasement of the hospital – was not accounted for. Jessie strongly suspected he was either keeping an eye on Richard Marcus, or was outside, somewhere in the city positioning himself to detonate one or more of the vials of soman should anything go wrong.

Just having Emily there with her made the entire ordeal more bearable, although since her arrival back on Surgical Seven, there hadn't been one moment when the two of them could talk in private. Once they were in the OR, though, there would be a chance, thanks to the relative privacy of the space between the MRI tori.

Although ARTIE was scheduled to perform the entire operation, Malloche's head had been shaved as a precaution should Jessie have to go to a full craniotomy. He lay calmly on the stretcher, holding hands with Arlette. His headache had responded reasonably well to the narcotic injections, but he had needed to be kept almost constantly medicated throughout the night.

'You've done a good job holding everything together,' he said to his wife in French. 'I'm lucky to have you.'

'No,' she replied, 'we're all lucky to have you.'

Jessie refrained from letting them know her French was passable.

*Sweet monster love*, she thought. *Spare me!*

The elevator doors opened and Claude Malloche was wheeled inside.

'Grace, you have the gun?' he asked.

'Right here,' she replied, tapping the shoulder holster beneath her lab coat.

'Wait a minute,' Jessie said. 'If she's planning on coming into the operating room, everything metal must be left outside. The electromagnet would pull that gun right through someone's body.'

'Correction,' Malloche said. 'Everything *magnetic* must be left outside. Grace's little thirty-eight is a custom order cast especially for our visit here. Titanium, I think, and goodness knows what else, but nothing magnetic. And trust me, Grace knows how to use that pistol well. I forget, Grace, how many people have you sanctioned since you came to work with us?'

The slender American shrugged matter-of-factly.

'I don't know,' she said. 'Nineteen? Twenty? I don't keep count exactly. I just do what I'm told.'

'Please let that serve as a warning to you, Dr. Copeland. Do my operation well – no, do it perfectly – and get me back up here to recover. If there is anything that seems the least bit out of place or subversive of our goals, Grace, here, has instructions to shoot Mrs. DelGreco. We will then send Dr. Gilbride down to help you finish my case. Is that clear?'

'Clear.'

'Good.'

Jessie flashed a look of hatred down at Malloche, but his eyes had closed and his mellow half-smile suggested that he had allowed himself to yield to the euphoria of his pre-op medications.

'Dr. Copeland,' Arlette said, 'Derrick will be stationed outside the operating room. He is to be introduced to the others as being from hospital security, sent by Richard Marcus and his infection control team to ensure that no unauthorized personnel enter the operating room. Claude and I have reviewed this list you gave us of participants in his surgery. It will be Derrick's responsibility to see that nobody who is not on the list is allowed in the operating room.'

'I understand.'

'There is one name in the group that we are concerned about. Dr. Mark Naehring. Exactly who is he, and what will he be doing?'

It was not the actual question that caught Jessie off guard, so much as the timing. She wasn't at all certain Naehring would even show up in the OR, but she had decided it would be foolish to leave him off the list of participants that Malloche had demanded from her. As they were wheeling Malloche to the elevators, Jessie had allowed herself to believe that Naehring's name had simply slipped past them. She should have known better. Now, she wondered how much truth should be laced into her response. If Malloche or Arlette had looked up Naehring in the annotated directory of EMMC physicians, they would know something of the man. Any contradiction now between what Jessie told them and what they had learned would be a red flag, and would almost certainly put an end to her already shaky plan.

'Dr. Naehring is a psychopharmacologist,' she said carefully. 'I intend to do a great deal of surgery with your husband awake and responsive. Dr. Naehring is more experienced and expert at administering medications that allow patients to be maintained at that level than anyone in anesthesia, including Dr. Booker.'

Several frightening seconds passed during which Arlette assessed the information. Finally, she handed the list over to Derrick.

The elevator doors closed, and the five of them – Malloche, Grace, Jessie, Emily, and Derrick began the descent to the subbasement of the Surgical Tower. Ordinarily, before a difficult case, Jessie would have spent an hour, often more, in her office, poring over MRIs and neuroanatomy textbooks, setting up her plan for the surgery, and reviewing the anatomy she would encounter. Never before this moment had the elevator ride down to the OR doubled as her pre-op preparation.

Random snatches of thought passed through her mind like a meteor shower, making it difficult to concentrate on

ARTIE and on Claude Malloche's meningioma. This was hardly the state of mind she wanted to be in for a major case – much less one that could have such grave consequences. Throughout the operation, her ability to stay focused would determine the outcome as much as her surgical skill.

The elevator doors opened, depositing them just down the hall from the MRI-OR.

'I will be with you every inch of the way,' Grace said to Jessie as they pushed the stretcher toward the OR.

Jessie could see Michelle Booker waiting for them in the prep area, but there was no sign of Mark Naehring.

*Damn.*

It might well be academic now, Jessie realized, but Emily had no idea that Naehring had even been called in. She also reminded herself that at the moment, Michelle Booker might be sensing that this case was unusual, but she wouldn't have a clue as to why. It was going to be essential to find ways to communicate the situation to each woman without endangering anyone. Fortunately, they were among the sharpest people she knew.

What if the psychopharmacologist didn't show up? she asked herself now. Was there any way she could handle the drugs? He used some sort of mixture of three hypnotics – or was it four? Clearly, the answer to her question was a resounding no. If she tried using drugs to interrogate Claude Malloche and somehow screwed up, there was no doubt in her mind that a great many people would die.

Jessie introduced Grace to Michelle Booker as a biomechanics student from Chicago who had written her some time ago expressing an interest in ARTIE. Then, as instructed, she introduced Derrick to the console tech Holly as a hospital security officer, who was not going to allow anyone into the operating room other than those on the list she had provided for him. Neither of the lies would survive much conversation, but Holly and Michelle were usually all business anyhow, and the seriousness of the procedure was certain to keep them zeroed in on the patient.

The first real opportunity Jessie had to pass any information to Emily was in the scrub room. With her identity as a biomechanics student established, Grace had to remain several paces away from them. Jessie began her scrub by turning up the water full force so that it splashed noisily in the stainless steel sink. Emily quickly followed suit.

'I wish I knew how Sara was doing,' Jessie said, looking straight ahead as she spoke.

'Me, too. Jess, I know you're feeling guilty about not insisting on going in to see her last night, but you really had no choice. And you did a helluva job at getting that catheter in.'

'Thanks. I don't mind telling you now that I was scared stiff. Em, listen. I tried to get word to Alex last night to have Mark Naehring come down here.'

'The drug doc who called you the other day?'

'Exactly.'

'What for?'

'Come on, you two,' Grace called in over her shoulder. 'You said four minutes.'

'To use his stuff on Malloche so I can question him about the soman,' Jessie said. 'Naehring may not show up at all, but if he does, just follow my lead and do what you can to help me replace you with him.'

'Does Michelle know what's going on?'

'Not yet. You'll have to help me out there, too.'

'Keep Grace with you outside the OR for a few seconds, and I'll see if I can at least tell Michelle that there's some weird stuff going on around this case and she should be on her toes.'

'Just be careful. The microphones are on. Everything you say will be broadcast out here.'

Emily shook the excess water from her hands. 'Okay, it's show time,' she said. 'Give me a minute or so in there to get gowned, then you can make a grand entrance like Gilbride always does.'

'I don't know if I can pull it off without the scepter, crown, and cape.'

Thirty seconds of stalling was the best Jessie could do before Grace ordered her into the OR. Skip Porter, masked, gloved, and gowned, was just finishing preparations on ARTIE. Outside the window, she could see the console tech and radiologist Hans Pfeffer, preparing their equipment and checking communication with the computer lab upstairs. Behind them, standing almost at attention, was Derrick. He was posing as a security guard but he was inside the area where only scrubs and lab coats were allowed. His loose white coat, buttoned once in the front, completely hid the deadly machine gun that was slung over his shoulder. It was just past six-thirty. By eleven – noon at the latest – the resection of Claude Malloche's tumor would be over.

*What then?* Jessie asked herself. *What then?*

She accepted a towel from the scrub nurse and thanked him for coming in.

'No problem,' he said. 'Why the big deal about this case?'

'Eastman Tolliver is the administrator of a fund that is about to give the hospital several million dollars in research money.'

'That's why Richard Marcus is so anxious to get his operation done?'

'Exactly.'

'Well, I'm sorry I made a big deal about coming in, but I've got two little kids, and this virus thing really has me spooked.'

'I understand. Believe me, I don't want to die any more than you do. Trust me that it's safe. There have been no new deaths on Surgical Seven, and Mr. Tolliver's been kept well away from the floor since the outbreak.'

Jessie slid her arms into the sterile gown he opened for her and then thrust her hands down into her gloves.

*Spooked by the virus thing,* she was thinking. *Nice going, Claude. You don't miss a trick, do you.*

'Emily, I'm all set,' Michelle Booker called out. 'He's under and intubated. I'm going to slide him through.'

Jessie stood back and watched as the padded platform

bearing Malloche was eased along its track through the opening in the magnet to her right.

'Ready . . . and . . . stop,' Emily said when his head was positioned in the two-foot separation between the massive tori – the tightly contained universe where, for the next five hours or so, she and Jessie would work.

Emily began by prepping the area around Malloche's nose, and another at the hairline. The second site was for backup in case ARTIE could not be inserted through the right nostril as planned. Jessie remained outside the magnet. It was time to get Michelle Booker into the act.

'Michelle,' she said, 'there's a possibility that Dr. Naehring may be coming down to assist with part of this case.'

The anesthesiologist looked up quickly.

*Stay cool*, Jessie's eyes begged. *Stay cool.*

*What on earth are you talking about, woman?* From above the top of her mask, Booker's wise, dark eyes asked the question.

'Mark Naehring,' she said matter-of-factly. 'I admire his work.'

*Tell me more.*

'When we get to doing the functional MRI, he'll take over for you. But he'll be working across from me at the table, where Emily is now.'

'That's an interesting approach. I've never done a case like this with him before.'

*Are you crazy?*

'I hope he gets here. If, by any chance, he doesn't make it down, would you be able to handle the meds the way he did at grand rounds?'

Michelle made the faintest gesture toward Grace. *Does she have something to do with this craziness?*

Jessie nodded. Beneath her mask, she was smiling. Michelle Booker had no idea just what the ship was or where it was headed, but she was on board.

'I suppose I could try some of my own combinations,' Michelle said, 'but Naehring's the pro.'

'If we have to do it that way, I'll send Emily over to you for a quick in-service on monitoring the anesthesia equipment, and you'll get gloved and gowned and work with me.'

*I sure hope you know what you're doing,* Michelle's eyes were saying now. 'Hey, no problem,' she said. 'I like to teach.'

Jessie moved into her spot across from Emily, and together they draped Malloche's head and fixed his skull to the titanium immobilization frame. Grace was now screened from them by Jessie's back, although she was just a few feet away. She would have been able to observe more and hear more by standing on a riser, but Jessie had thought to nudge the two risers they had out of sight under an equipment table. Now she switched off her microphone and motioned to Emily to do the same.

'We can't keep these off for too long or Derrick will get suspicious,' she whispered. 'You keep yours turned off. We'll just use mine.' She switched her microphone on again. 'Okay, everyone, on your toes because we're ready to roll. Jared?'

'Ready,' the scrub nurse said.

'Sylvia?'

'All set,' replied the circulator.

'Skip?'

'All systems are go.'

'Hans?'

'We are ready.'

'Holly?'

'No problems.'

'Well, okay. Holly, how about popping in that Bob Marley CD?'

'You got it,' Holly said. 'It *is* a reggae kind of morning at that.'

'Come on, robot,' Jessie cooed. 'Please don't fail me now. Skip, we're going in.'

Jessie made a half-inch hole through the back wall of Malloche's nostril, cauterized the bleeding, and guided ARTIE through the opening and into the cranial cavity.

'Hans, are you ready to show me some views of this tumor?'

'It's on the screen right now. Quite an impressive lesion. Manipulate the orientation with your foot control as you wish.'

The views were perfect. And, as Pfeffer had observed, the tumor was extensive. Thanks to the transnasal entry, ARTIE was already just a centimeter and a half from it. A standard, non-robot approach would have presented a hideous technical problem, and would have undoubtedly destroyed some – maybe a good deal – of the uninvolved brain tissue. Once again, Malloche had justified his reputation for genius. There was no way Sylvan Mays could have promised a total excision with no residual neurologic deficits. Malloche must have gotten him to admit that before he killed him. With ARTIE, there was a very good chance.

The guidance system for the tiny robot was as smooth and responsive as Jessie could ever remember. Still, she held back, progressing much slower than she needed to, stalling in hopes that Mark Naehring might still show up. But with each passing minute, that hope diminished. Maybe Tamika had never gotten that final message through before the laptop was destroyed. Maybe Naehring couldn't be located. Whatever the reason, Jessie knew she was going to have to find another way, or else give up on her plan and simply pray that Malloche would recover from his surgery intact and head home, sparing the hospital and the city.

'Skip, ARTIE's working beautifully,' she said as she manipulated the unit until it was positioned at the very edge of the meningioma.

'I did some tinkerin',' the scientist said. 'Besides, ARTIE likes you. It always performs well for people it likes.'

Just then, through the intercom, Jessie heard an exchange of voices. 'Naehring. I'm Dr. Mark Naehring. I'm here to –'

'I know why you're here,' Derrick said. 'Go on in.'

Jessie rose on tiptoe to see over Emily. Naehring, who looked taller than she remembered, went directly to the scrub nurse's area, opened a Ziploc plastic bag, and dropped several vials out.

'They're sterile,' he said.

'Do you want gloves and a gown?' the nurse asked.

'Yes.'

There was something about Naehring's voice . . .

Jessie was straining to get a better look, when the man, now in his surgical gown, turned toward her.

*Alex!*

# Chapter 35

Jessie continued her ultrasound dissection and aspiration of Claude Malloche's tumor as Alex took Emily's place at the table.

'I'm glad you could make it, Dr. Naehring,' Jessie said, her eyes asking a dozen questions at once.

'Mark'll do fine,' Alex replied.

'Okay, Mark. I'm glad you could make it. Holly, is everything okay out there?'

Jessie used the question to be certain Alex knew they were being monitored.

"Everything's fine," the tech said. 'Why?'

'The MRI image seems a little grainy, that's all.'

'I'll check on it.'

Jessie switched off the microphone.

'The microphone's off,' she whispered, still working ARTIE through Malloche's tumor. 'But I can't keep it that way for long. The woman behind me is one of them.'

'I know.'

Jessie turned the microphone back on, straightened up, and worked some of the stiffness from her neck. In addition to the tightness in her muscles, she felt her touch on ARTIE's controls was getting a bit heavy. And although the Marley album might be making it easier for them to talk, it was also beginning to grate on her.

*Easy,* she warned herself. *Relax, stay focused. No screwups.*

'Holly, we're getting down to the nitty-gritty here,' she said. 'How about switching to *Rhapsody in Blue?*'

'*Rhapsody in Blue* coming up.'

Jessie waited for the music change, then switched off the

mike again. 'Now, what on earth are you doing?'

'Naehring's at a conference in Maui. It took most of the night for us to track him down. Once I learned what he did, I realized how brilliant your idea was.'

'What good does that do?'

'He told me where to find his potion and how to use it.'

'Over the phone?!'

'I've – um – had a little training in the area.'

Out of the corner of her eye, Jessie became aware of Grace, who had shifted over a few inches.

'Michelle,' she called out, switching the sound back on, 'everything looks great. Any problems?'

'None. I'm here elucidating some of the finer points of anesthesia to Nurse DelGreco.'

*Finer points of anesthesia. Hardly likely,* Jessie thought. *The notion made no more sense than her elucidating some of the finer points of neurosurgery.* Michelle was telling her that Emily had found some way to communicate more of the situation to her without calling attention to them. *Excellent.*

'Well, Mark,' Jessie said, 'the dissection is going fine so far. Hans, can you put up the pre-op screen? . . . Great. Mark, the yellow is his meningioma before we began. Back to the current screen now, Hans. . . . And this is what's left of the tumor as of this moment.'

'Nice job,' Alex said. 'Very nice. This is one lucky guy.'

He patted Malloche on the head as if he were a puppy. Jessie's eyes flashed a warning and directed him up to the overhead camera that was monitoring the operative field for Derrick and the others.

'Michelle,' she said, 'maybe seven more minutes and we're going to wake him up.'

'We're ready, Doc. This Gershwin's great. I never remember you playing it before.'

Mike off.

'Grace, the woman behind me, and Derrick, the guy outside, are both armed,' Jessie murmured. 'Malloche had a nonmagnetic gun made for her.'

'Well, isn't he something,' Alex replied. 'Tamika went

off-line. Is she okay?'

'For now. They smashed her computer, though.'

Mike on.

Jessie continued to guide ARTIE flawlessly, liquefying Malloche's tumor with ultrasound, then aspirating the melted cells and debris through the robot's suction port. The heavy core of the tumor – 60, maybe even 70 percent of it – was gone. They were in uncharted waters now. Gilbride's success with Marci Sheprow's uncomplicated, superficial tumor notwithstanding, they were clearly beyond where Jessie had taken ARTIE on the cadaver of Pete Roslanski, or where Carl had come apart in the ill-fated operation on Rolf Hermann. The complexity of the dissection ARTIE was accomplishing here was justification for the hundreds of hours she had spent at the drawing board and in the lab. If only the patient were someone she wanted to cure.

'Well, gang,' she said, 'it's time to get ready for the hard part. Michelle, please go ahead and start waking Mr. Tolliver up. We've got this thing about seventy percent gone. The next thirty will take us a while. Mark, let's take our time.'

Mike off.

'You sure about this?' she asked.

'Of course not. But Naehring spent almost an hour on the phone with me. The stuff I'll be using came from his office. It's all mixed – four drugs in just the right proportion.'

'What are they?'

'Scopolamine, *Pentothal*, I think. . . . I can't remember the other two. Jessie, I've been screwing up right and left ever since I learned about Gilbride using this robot, here. I'm not going to mess this up.'

'Good luck, Alex.'

Mike on.

'Michelle,' Alex said, 'if it's all right with you, I'd like to handle the meds myself, from right here.'

'There's an IV port under the drape just next to your right hand, Doctor,' the anesthesiologist replied. 'It's sterile. If there's anything I can do, just say the word.'

Jessie took a step back – out from between the tori – and turned to Grace.

'Things are going very well so far,' she said.

'I can tell,' Grace said. 'That's good. That's very good.'

Jessie stepped forward, once again positioning herself to block the young killer from Malloche and Alex.

'Doctor Naehring, he's all yours,' she said. 'For the time being, ARTIE and I will be dissecting around the left motor cortex. I need the patient to keep working his right hand and foot. Michelle, you can see his feet, yes?'

'They're right here.'

'Perfect. Mark, would you prefer music or none?'

'Music, most definitely. What you have on is fine. I want him wide awake, Michelle. Then I'll bring him back down again myself.'

Jessie's eyes smiled across at him. Claude Malloche, mythologized as the Mist, killer of so many, wide awake with his head screwed to an immobilization frame, a half-inch tube up his nose, through his skull, and into his brain. Not the full payback Alex wanted, but certainly a sweet, sweet ante.

'Mr. Tolliver,' Jessie said, 'it's Dr. Copeland. Can you hear me?'

'I can,' Malloche rasped.

'The operation is about three-quarters done, and everything is going perfectly.'

'Good.'

'As I told you, we've got you immobilized so you can't move your head. But you can move your hands and feet. Shake your right hand for me, please. . . . Good, good. Now your left . . . excellent. Your right foot?'

'These little piggies went to market,' Michelle called out.

'Now your left foot.'

'These little piggies had roast beef.'

'Terrific. Now, the tube you feel in your nose is ARTIE, the tiny robot. Do you understand?'

'Yes.'

'You may feel some movement or vibration as I guide

ARTIE further into the tumor. We're going to medicate you a bit more so that we can keep working without causing you too much discomfort. You'll hear commands from me or from Dr. Mark Naehring, who's right there on the other side of you. Just do whatever it is we ask. Some commands will be given in a loud voice, some will be softer. Sometimes we'll ask you over and over to do the same thing. That's how I'll be able to monitor things if I'm working close to a vital area.'

'Understand,' Malloche said.

'Good. You're doing great, Mr. Tolliver. Just great. Ready, Mark?'

'Ready. Could I have five ccs of the mixture in vial number one, please?'

'Five ccs,' the scrub nurse said, passing the syringe over.

'Half a cc, then wait one minute,' Alex said. 'Mr. Tolliver, lift your right hand. Good. Do it again. Once more.' He bent down closer to Malloche's ear and nodded for Jessie to cut the mike. 'What's your name?' he whispered harshly. '. . . *Your name!*'

'Claude . . . Paul . . . Malloche.'

Jessie glanced behind her to see if Grace had heard. She was nodding her head to the Gershwin piece.

'Move your right foot,' Jessie ordered after keying the mike again.

'Okay,' Michelle called out.

Jessie cut the mike and nodded to Alex. He tested the dose level with several inane questions about Malloche's birthplace and parents. On the fourth go-round with the mike off, he was ready.

'Soman,' he said. 'Do you know what I'm talking about, Claude?'

'I . . . do.'

'How many vials are there hidden in Boston?'

'Three . . . four . . .'

'Which? Three or four?'

'Three . . . four.'

Jessie raised her hand for Alex to stop and once again checked on Grace.

'We're still doing terrific,' Jessie said over her shoulder.

'Keep it up,' Grace replied.

*You bet! You bet we will!*

'Take your time, Mark,' Jessie said.

She continued her dissection and nodded that the mike was off once more.

'Where are the vials of soman, Claude?' Alex asked. 'Where are they?'

'Quincy. . . Market . . . rotunda . . .'

One.

'Go on. Where else?' Alex injected more hypnotic. 'Claude?'

Malloche looked to be unconscious.

*Too much!* Jessie's eyes cried out. *You gave him too much!*

'Government . . . Center . . . green . . . subway. . . ,' Malloche murmured suddenly.

Two.

Jessie turned the mike on and held a conversation with Hans Pfeffer that must have struck the radiologist as strange for its vapidness. Anything to keep the rhythm going and Grace and Derrick distracted. The dissection was more than 80 percent complete now. Only fragments of the tumor remained to be melted. It appeared Malloche was going to get his cure.

Just then Alex did, in fact, inject too much hypnotic. Malloche's breathing slowed and he slipped into unconsciousness. Jessie feared she might have to stop the operation to try to put a breathing tube in him. But just as she was about to make a move, Malloche coughed and muttered something unintelligible. A minute later, he had rasped out the third location – Filene's Basement.

'That may be it,' Alex said as Jessie flipped the mike back on.

She held up three fingers on one hand and four on the other.

*Which is it?* her eyes asked.

Alex shrugged and shook his head.

Frightened of having questioned Malloche too often,

Jessie took him through some unnecessary maneuvers with his feet.

'Right foot up . . . now down . . . now left . . . now down.'

Finally, it was time. Alex got another 5 cc of hypnotic and injected some.

'Claude, the last vial. Quincy Market, Government Center subway, Filene's, and . . . and where?'

'Don't know. . . ,' Malloche responded dreamily

'Is there another vial of soman?'

Jessie anxiously put a finger to her lips and motioned for Alex to lower his voice. Again, through the corner of her eye, she sensed Grace shifting to get a better angle. Clearly they were running out of time.

'Don't know . . . ,' Malloche said again. 'Don't know . . . don't know . . .'

'He seems confused,' Jessie whispered. 'Maybe if there was a fourth vial, it was the one here in the lab. We've got to stop.'

'Naehring said to give him one shot of two ccs at the end. Supposedly, once I do that, he won't remember any of this.'

'Just don't kill him.'

Jessie turned the microphone on once more and again issued some orders to Malloche until it was clear he was unable to respond anymore. Across the room, over Alex's shoulder, she could see Derrick. He had moved to one end of the console and was leaning forward, peering intently through the observation window. He was suspicious. She felt certain of it. Thank goodness they had ended the interrogation.

'Well, Mark,' she said, 'that was a terrific job. Michelle, Emily, we're almost ninety percent done. We could stop here, and I doubt the tumor would have enough blood supply left to survive. But I want this to be perfect, so we're going to keep working. Michelle, if you can keep him on the way to never-never land, we should be able to wrap this up in forty-five minutes or so. Em, do you want to come back and replace this genius, here?'

'Your wish is my command.'

'Thank you, Dr. Naehring.'

'I look forward to working with you again, Dr. Copeland,' Alex said.

As he turned to move past Emily, Jessie saw her suddenly thrust a piece of paper into his hand. He reacted to the surprise not at all. Instead, without even the slightest hesitation, he slipped the paper beneath his surgical gown and deposited it into his scrub pants pocket. Then he removed his gown and gloves and dropped them where the circulating nurse indicated.

Jessie held her breath as he approached the OR door. Half a minute more. No more than thirty seconds and he would be on his way out of the hospital with more information than she had even dared to hope for. As he opened the door, he checked back over his shoulder at her. The triumphant spark in his eyes was unmistakable.

Just then, through the observation window, Jessie saw Derrick stride up to Alex.

'You, Doctor,' he ordered, 'pull down your mask.'

# Chapter 36

Kill or be killed. When Alex arrived at the operating room, he had been approached and asked his identity by Malloche's man Derrick, who introduced himself as a security guard assigned to monitor this section of the hospital. Now, as the man strode up and confronted him, Alex sensed that this was it. One of them was going to die.

'You, Doctor,' Derrick demanded, 'pull down your mask.'

His knee-length lab coat barely concealed the weapon that was slung over his right shoulder – a semiautomatic of some sort, Alex guessed. He probably had a pistol concealed somewhere as well. He was about Alex's height, but much broader across the shoulders and ten or fifteen years younger. The hardness in his pale eyes said that he would kill without hesitation.

Slowly, Alex untied the upper strings of his cloth mask and let it flop over onto his chest. Derrick studied his face. Then Alex saw recognition spark in the man's eyes.

'I believe I have seen you before, Doctor,' Derrick said, easing his right hand inside his lab coat toward his low back. 'Where could that have been?'

*Kill or be killed.*

Derrick was reaching for a handgun. Alex was certain of that. He also knew that surprise, his only advantage, was fading fast, and would be completely gone in another second or so. He viciously brought his foot up between Derrick's legs, catching him firmly in the groin. The killer's knees buckled, but he stayed on his feet and reacted with the quickness of a professional, spinning away from the looping right hook Alex threw at his chin.

The console tech shrieked as Derrick pulled the pistol from his waistband and fired. But Alex was already sprinting away through the anesthesia prep area, staying low and weaving from side to side like a running back. A bullet pinged off the cement column by his ear. A second grazed his scalp. Over his years in the CIA, he had been shot at several times, but never at this close range, and never without a weapon with which to defend himself. The only choice he had right now was to run – try to put some distance between himself and the younger, stronger man who was intent on killing him.

He pulled several rolling carts into the path behind him as he reached one of the many tunnels connecting the various EMMC buildings. This tunnel, to the main hospital, was too long and too straight for him to chance making it to the end. Instead, Alex bolted one flight up a staircase and cut to his right. He was in the basement corridor of the Kellogg Building – the largest building in the hospital. The brightly lit hallway was almost deserted. But again, it was long and straight. Alex charged across the polished tile and dove through a doorway and into the computer lab. Alex knew that at best, he had bought himself a few seconds. Even if Derrick hadn't actually seen the computer lab door close behind him, he would know that Alex couldn't possibly have made it down the hall. Alex hit the light switches as he passed, throwing this end of the lab into relative darkness.

'Hey,' an accented voice called, 'what are you doing?'

'Shhhh.'

Alex raced toward the voice and found a bookish, rail-thin young man, interpreting the MRI data and monitoring the progress of the case he had just left in the MRI-OR.

'What the – ?'

'Get down and stay flat,' Alex ordered, shoving the man face first to the floor just as a prolonged burst of machine-gun fire shattered the computers and video screens over their heads.

*An Uzi*, he guessed from the sound.

He forged ahead on his knees, casting about for a

weapon – any kind of weapon. There was nothing – nothing except the computers themselves. He crawled around the corner of a row of instruments and screens just in time to see the edge of Derrick's lab coat as he crept around to where the computer geek lay.

'Please. Please don't hurt me!' the man begged.

Instantly, there was a brief burst of gunfire, an unearthly cry, then silence. Alex cringed and angrily clenched his fists, but he kept crawling. Derrick was exactly opposite him now, separated by the bank of workstations and instruments. Alex slid himself up and placed his hands on either side of a seventeen-inch video monitor screen. Slowly, noiselessly, he lifted the heavy screen off its base. Then, certain the soft scraping sound beyond the workstations localized Derrick, he stood up quickly, raising the monitor at arm's length over his head. The killer whirled, but not in time. Alex hurled the monitor down on him, striking him in the forehead. The picture tube shattered with the sound of a shell burst. Derrick cried out as he was knocked backward, but he was firing even before he hit the floor. Alex, up on the counter, preparing to leap at him, was hit in the shoulder and grazed alongside his chin. The shots spun him around and hurled him into the instruments across the aisle. He fell heavily, blood instantly staining the sleeve of his scrub shirt.

Forcing himself not to panic, Alex righted himself. Derrick had absorbed his best shot, and it hadn't been enough. The man was hurt, though – he had to be. From the other side of the workstations came the angry bellow of a wounded animal and another wild burst of gunfire, most of which ripped through the wooden shelves and snapped into the ceiling. Malloche's man was still on the floor, Alex reasoned, firing upward. But any moment he would be back on his feet. At that point, if Alex wasn't out the door, he was dead.

He crawled to the door and pulled it open. Light from the corridor flooded the darkened area of the lab. Instantly, a volley of shots slammed off the wall above his head.

Alex plunged out into the eerily deserted corridor,

scrambled to his feet, and bolted to his right, toward the pathology department, twenty yards away.

'Whoever he is,' Grace whispered to Jessie, 'he's a dead man.'

Jessie could only look across at Emily and shake her head. Their counterattack against Malloche and his people had gone so well. Then, in seconds, everything had come apart. She felt ill, and very frightened for Alex.

'Jessie, what on earth is going on here?' Hans Pfeffer asked. 'Who were those men?'

'Hans, I'll have to explain it all to you later. For now, it would probably be best for us just to get through this case. I have very little left to do.'

Jessie guided ARTIE into the last remaining portion of Malloche's tumor. The dissection – clean and complete with virtually no damage to intervening vital neurologic structures – was exceeding anything she could have done by hand. Now, though, she was working with far less composure and concentration than she had been, coupled with an overwhelming sense of foreboding.

'How much longer?' Grace asked, no longer bothering to lower her voice or even pretend to be a graduate student.

'Ten, fifteen minutes,' Jessie replied.

'I don't see any more tumor.'

'Well, there's just a tiny bit right at the tip of where the robot is now. It's yellow on the screen.'

'I'm still not sure I see it.'

'I don't care whether you do or not. It's there.'

At that moment, the feed from the computer lab to the OR viewing screens went dark. Pfeffer tried calling his associate for an explanation. There was no answer. Bewildered and angry, he raced upstairs to the lab. A few minutes later, he was back, pale, and shaken to the point where he was barely able to speak.

'Jessie,' he called into the OR, 'Eli Rogoff is . . . is dead. He's been shot . . . many times. There's blood all over. . . . My . . . my lab has been destroyed.'

Jessie whirled and confronted Grace, but the young killer could only shrug and shake her head.

'Well, your friend has really messed things up for us,' Jessie said. 'As far as I'm concerned, this is it for this case.'

'But you said you weren't done. Will this hurt Claude?'

'I don't know. We may not know for years. What little tumor remains may not have enough blood supply to regrow. Or it might. It doesn't matter now. We can't get at whatever is left, and that's that. Even if I did a craniotomy and open procedure, I doubt I'd be able to find it.'

'I'm going to call the police,' Pfeffer said.

'Hans, just wait a little while! Let me finish this case and get this man out of here, or a great many people could be killed. I'll explain to you and everyone else after I've gotten ARTIE out of his head.'

'And just how are you going to do that without an MRI,' Pfeffer cried shrilly, 'put your foot on his face and pull?'

'Emily and I will just have to back it out.'

'Do it now,' Grace said. 'I want to get Claude back upstairs as quickly as possible.'

'Who in the hell is she?' Pfeffer demanded.

'Hans, please,' Jessie begged. 'Em, you take over the controls. I'm going to put some gentle tension on ARTIE's cord. We'll bring him out together. Each time I say *now*, hit straight back reverse for like two seconds, then stop. With any luck and the right touch, I think I might be able to guide it back along the track it made going in. If we can't do this, we may have to open him up and go in after it.'

'You'll do nothing of the sort until Arlette approves it,' Grace said.

'Oh, just shut the fuck up!' Jessie snapped.

The glass doors to the pathology unit were closed, and behind them all was dark. There were stretches of yellow plastic ribbon across the entry, and above them a DANGER KEEP OUT sign, along with a red skull symbolizing lethal biologic activity. Alex charged toward the door, expecting to hear the staccato volley of shots at the instant a cluster

291

of bullets slammed into his back. The shots came just as he reached the doors, but miraculously, none of them hit home. Instead, the heavy glass door to his right suddenly spiderwebbed from top to bottom. Without breaking stride, he lowered his uninjured shoulder and rammed into it. The weakened glass shattered inward. As Alex barreled through the opening, he stumbled to one knee and rolled, sending a dagger thrust of pain from the gunshot wound up into his neck. Then he struggled to his feet and pounded on, deeper and deeper into the windowless darkness of the pathology department, away from the glow of the corridor lights.

Ahead of him, just to the left, was another door marked with plastic yellow ribbons and a warning sign. Through the dimming light, he could still make out the gold-leaf lettering on the glass half of the door: MICROBIOLOGY. Over his shoulder he could see Derrick nearing the shattered main door. He had, at best, a few seconds. Sensing what awaited him inside, Alex raced over to the microbiology door, carefully turned the knob, slipped in under the warning ribbon, and closed the door behind him.

The stench of death in the room was overpowering. Crouching low, he retied his surgical mask over his mouth and nose, making breathing a bit easier, and perhaps giving him the first tiny advantage over his pursuer since they left the OR. Remaining in a crouch, he duck-walked away from the door, then suddenly hit against a body and fell over it. His eyes had adjusted enough to see the face of a woman awash in drying vomit. Her mouth was agape and her eyes open. He shuddered and scrambled off her, then backed farther into the lab.

Six years ago, he and a badly wounded friend had spent the night huddled on the brink of a shallow, open death pit in Angola just a foot or so above at least a hundred decaying corpses. If that was the most sickening, repugnant situation in which he had ever found himself, this place was a close second.

Derrick's silhouette appeared at the door. Alex got up on his knees and ran his hands along the countertop, feeling for something that he could use as a weapon. He tripped over a second body, lost his balance, and inadvertently set his hand down on the face of a third. As he quickly moved his hand away, it hit against a small cardboard box. *Stick matches!*

He crawled with the matches to the end of the lab, where the fourth body lay spread-eagled amid shards of glass from equipment that the man's death throes had swept off the countertop. Cautiously, Alex raised his head above the counter and peered across at the door. Derrick's silhouette was gone, although certainly not for long. Assuming he was outside the microbiology lab when Malloche released the soman, and that he didn't see Alex enter the room, it would be the last place he would want to search. His eyes still fixed on the door, Alex struck one of the matches and cupped it in his hand.

The corpse next to him was a grotesque shade of violet. Its wide-open mouth held a pool of vomit. Alex gasped for a breath and shook out the match. Then he checked the door once more. Nothing yet. He tried another match. This time, his eyes were drawn immediately to the one intact piece of glassware on the floor, an opaque, glass-stoppered bottle, nestled in the crook of the corpse's rigid right arm. 'Hydrochloric Acid-1 m,' the label read.

*Now we're talking,* Alex thought, shaking out the match.

He had no idea what the '1 m' signified, but if it meant strong, he had his weapon. Another check of the door, and he lit a third match. Then he carefully removed the top from the nearly filled bottle and poured some of the contents on the chest of the corpse. Instantly, amid a swirl of smoke and even more stench, the concentrated acid ate through the dead man's shirt and into his skin.

*Bingo!*

Now, all he had to do was get close.

He dropped down once more and worked his way through the debris toward the door. He was on the other side of the central lab bench from where he came in. It had been three minutes, maybe even four. Had the killer given up and left?

At that precise moment, Derrick's silhouette reappeared at the glass. The door slowly opened, and he stepped inside the room. From where he was crouching, Alex could just make out the man's form as he looked about, no doubt trying to adjust to the heavy, fetid air. Then he turned to the wall by the door. *The lights!* His first move was going to be to turn on the lights. Alex pressed against some cabinets and steeled himself as he heard the switches being thrown.

Nothing.

*Of course.* At Malloche's orders, Richard Marcus had sealed off the area, and had probably done everything he could to delay intervention by investigators from state or federal agencies. It appeared as if no one had been in the lab since the disaster, so the lights had to have been shut off at the fuse box – probably for the whole pathology unit – to discourage anyone who might have made it past security. Another break. Alex inched his way along the base of the lab bench. Then he stopped and slowly set aside the stopper from the bottle of concentrated acid.

Derrick, wounded from the monitor screen, irritated by losing his quarry, and now distressed at having to be in the center of such an unpleasant stench, had to be off balance, as ripe for taking as he ever would be. The muted sound of his footsteps said that he was just on the other side of the lab bench now – not five feet away.

Alex held his breath and could hear Derrick's panting, possibly as he tried hyperventilating through his shirt.

*Are you feeling ill, bastard? Close to puking? Well, with any luck you're going to feel a hell of a lot worse in just another few seconds.*

Alex shifted his weight for better leverage, grasped the bottle tightly, and tried to imagine how Derrick was positioned – where he was facing. Slowly . . . slowly, he began to straighten up. Derrick was just three feet away, facing toward the far wall, searching for him in the carnage he and his employer had created. Alex raised the bottle over his head. Then, barely audibly, he cleared his throat. As Derrick swung around, Alex whipped his arm down, sending a full splash of the acid directly into the man's eyes. In the same motion, he ducked back behind the counter for safety. Piteous screaming erupted instantly from the terrorist, who managed to fire a short burst before his weapon clattered to the floor.

Alex shook his hand against the intense burning where several drops of the acid had hit him. He stayed low until the uncontrolled wailing had given way to whimpering. Then he rounded the lab bench and struck a match. The killer's eyes, brows, and much of his nose were already eaten away. Smoke was still rising from his flesh. His moans were unintelligible.

The semiautomatic was, in fact, an Uzi. Alex cradled the gun and headed for the door. Then he turned back.

'My brother's name was Andy Bishop,' he said.

And he emptied a burst from the Uzi into Derrick's skull.

# Chapter 37

'Atta girl, Jess,' Emily whispered as Jessie turned back to the table. 'I've been itching to tell her to fuck off, too.'

Cursing at Grace had been a great release for Jessie, but otherwise didn't seem to have had much effect, except to shock the scrub nurse, Jared, into dropping a hemostat.

'Em,' she said, 'I don't think Alex could have gotten away from that guy. I just can't believe this is happening. What do we do now?'

'First we finish,' Emily said. 'Then we worry.'

Jessie nodded across at her friend. The right advice at the right time, as always. First things first. When in doubt, just do what you can do. Simple wisdom until you try and give it to yourself.

'Thanks, pal,' she said. 'You're the ultimate friend in need.'

*Friend in need.* For almost the first time since the surgery on Malloche had begun, Jessie's focus shifted to Sara. The diagnosis of acute hydrocephalus and the treatment she had begun with the twist drill were right; she felt certain of that. But had she been in time? It was possible that at this moment Sara was already dead. Sara and Alex. Was there any way she could just wake up from this day and discover it had never happened?

Jessie looked down at the monster, sleeping so peacefully, secure in the knowledge that he had covered all the bases. For Claude Malloche, it was all about manipulation – his surgeon would perform a perfect operation because she wanted to keep her patients alive. Richard Marcus would lie and cover up murder to protect masses of people outside the hospital. If Sara Devereau died, so what? To Malloche she was worth keeping alive only so long as she added to their leverage. Jessie made a claw of her hand and, shielded from Grace, set it down over Malloche's face.

'I want to kill him, Em,' she whispered fiercely. 'For as long as I can remember, I've gotten guilt pangs from just swatting a mosquito. But right here, right now, I want to dig my fingers into his eyes, and rip his evil face right off.'

'You were thinking about Sara?'

'How did –?' Jessie laughed ruefully. 'Yeah,' she said. 'I was.'

'You did everything you could up there. I pray she's okay. But either way, you did everything you could. Just hang in there, Jess. What goes around comes around. Our turn will come.'

Emily's words unlocked the dam of Jessie's emotions. Tears of sadness, anger, and intense strain began to blur her vision. Ignoring her sterile field, she reached up a gloved hand, lifted her glasses, and wiped her eyes dry on the sleeve of her surgical gown.

'What's going on there?' Grace demanded, moving in close.

'Oh, nothing,' Jessie replied. 'We're just getting ready to bring our little friend ARTIE the robot back from Brainland. You're absolutely right, Em,' she added without bothering to lower her voice. 'What goes around comes around. Let's do it. I'm putting just a little bit of tension on the cord. Please put all six pods in reverse for a short burst right . . . now. Good. I got about an eighth of an inch back. And . . . again.'

The extraction of the tiny robot took most of twenty minutes, during which Jessie's voice and the soft gurgle of flowing oxygen were the only sounds to penetrate the tension and fear in the OR. The final move in the recovery was simply a gentle, blind tug. ARTIE, bloodied but intact, popped out through Malloche's nostril, still firmly connected to its polystyrene umbilical cord.

'Yes!' Jessie said softly 'Welcome back, little fella. You were immense.' She sutured the insertion hole closed, then called out, 'Michelle, *we . . . are . . . finished.* Could you wake up our patient, please?'

'One awake patient comin' up,' the anesthesiologist said.

Jessie packed Malloche's nose with gauze, then stripped off her gloves and stepped back from the table. She could tell that Grace had a grip on the pistol that was tucked into the waistband beneath her scrub shirt. It might be possible to overpower the woman and then try to make some sort of deal with Arlette – a trade involving Grace and Malloche for the hostages on Surgical Seven. But there were too many ifs and too many potential casualties to chance it. And if Grace was as competent as Malloche had boasted she was, disarming her might be extremely costly.

*No,* Jessie decided. For the moment, this one was simply going to have to play itself out.

'Now, what about my explanation?' Pfeffer demanded petulantly. 'My lab tech is dead up there.'

'*I'll* give you the explanation,' Grace said.

She marched quickly out of the operating room and straight over to where Pfeffer was standing beside the console. Then she pulled the snub-nosed revolver from beneath her shirt and jammed the barrel up under his chin.

'What –?'

'Not another sound from any of you, or I'll blow this man's brains out,' she said. 'And after I've done that, then I'll move over and do her.'

She motioned toward Holly, the console tech. Then, without moving her gun from beneath the radiologist's jaw, Grace picked up a phone, tucked it between her chin and shoulder, and called up to Surgical Seven.

'Arlette, the operation's over,' she said. 'Everything went well in that regard. The tumor has been removed and Claude is waking up. But there has been some trouble. I need Armand down here right away. . . . Derrick? He's – um – he's not here. He fired at a man who was down here, and then chased him. It's been about an hour since he left. But the other man wasn't armed. I think it's just taken Derrick a while to catch up with him. Now, please, send

298

Armand down. I'll explain everything that happened when we get back upstairs.'

There was nothing Jessie could think of to do at this point but cooperate and wait. It *had* been an hour since Derrick took off after Alex, and now she knew that Malloche's right-hand man hadn't returned to Surgical Seven either. He was heavily armed and wasn't that far behind his unarmed prey when he took off. Could Alex's hatred and determination possibly have been enough to overcome such odds?

One thing was certain. If Derrick didn't return with Alex or an account of his death, there was going to be hell to pay on Surgical Seven.

Alex smashed the window to the chemistry lab and found a flashlight and a first aid kit. He used gauze pads and tape from the kit to stem the bleeding from his shoulder, and ointment to ease the burning on his hand and arm. The concentrated acid that had splashed on him had left a dozen or more deep sores along his right forearm and across his hand. Finally, covering Derrick's Uzi with a towel, but keeping it at the ready, he left the hospital by a staircase in the back of the pathology department. In five years, he hadn't so much as bruised Malloche or his tightly knit, suicidally loyal organization. Now, at last, he had done some damage.

*This is just the beginning, Claude*, he was thinking. *Just the beginning.*

After the death-cave horror of the micro lab and the darkness of the pathology department, the bright noontime sunshine hit him like a slap. It took time to get his bearings. He was on a largely deserted street, behind the main building of the hospital. The van, with Stan Moyer and Vicki Holcroft, was a block and a half to his left. They had stayed up with him all night, chasing down first Mark Naehring in Hawaii, then the hypnotic truth concoction in his office. Now, with more than four hours gone since he left for the OR, he felt certain they were beginning to get antsy.

Alex carefully made his way out to the street. He had no doubt that once Malloche and his wife realized their man wasn't coming back, there would be trouble for Jessie and the others. Having reduced the opposition on Surgical Seven by 20 percent – 40 with Malloche now out of commission – he even gave thought to putting a force together, heading up to the floor, and attempting to end matters then and there. But according to what he had learned from Jessie, it was a good bet the neurosurgical unit was sealed off with Malloche's notorious thoroughness and skill.

There would doubtless be reprisals for his showing up in the OR as he did, and also for Derrick. As long as Malloche needed medical care, it seemed likely that Jessie was reasonably safe. But it was also clear that as long as one of Malloche's crew was roaming about with the trigger to three or four vials of soman, the people of Boston weren't. As things stood, an assault of any kind just didn't make sense – at least not yet. But whether they stormed Surgical Seven or found another way, one thing was sure – Derrick was not the last of the body count.

Stan and Vicki were struggling to come up with a Plan B when Alex knocked twice, then once on the rear door of the van. He fell as much as climbed inside, and lay on the floor for a while. He was mentally and physically exhausted, and much more battered than even he had appreciated. Vicki redressed his wounds from an elaborate first aid kit, as he filled in the two FBI agents on the events in the OR, and later, in the microbiology lab.

'Remind me not to get on your bad side,' Moyer said when he had finished. 'Hydrochloric acid. Nasty. Tasteful, but extremely nasty.'

'It wasn't Derrick's best day,' Alex replied.

'So,' Vicki asked, 'where do we go from here?'

'You know Boston better than I do. What do you think of the three places Malloche gave to us?'

Holcroft and Moyer decided with their eyes who should respond. Vicki won.

'The way I see it, they may have made a big mistake.'

'Tell me.'

'Assuming the information you got from Malloche is the truth, all three places they chose to hide the soman can be sealed off from the public and searched. The search crew is standing by.'

'How many?' Alex asked.

'As many as we can get. The number's probably growing by the minute.'

'But they're going to need time and some sort of serious exposure suits,' Moyer added. 'And if Malloche's man on the outside realizes what we're doing, and there is a fourth or even a fifth vial of the gas, all hell's gonna break loose.'

'Wait, tell me again,' Alex said. 'All three locations – the rotunda at Quincy Market, the Green Line at Government Center, and Filene's Basement, are normally locked for the night?'

'I'm not sure what time,' Vicki answered, 'but yes. Probably by one A.M. they'll all three be closed off. Filene's a lot earlier.'

'The break we have is that Malloche doesn't have a clue that we know anything.'

'What about the people who were with you in the OR?' Moyer asked.

'Jessie's the only one who knows why I was there. I don't think they'd hurt her.'

'The question may not be whether or not they hurt *her*. The question may be how well she can stand up to watching someone *else* get hurt.'

Alex was silent. Of course they wouldn't touch Jessie. With Malloche just recovering from surgery, they couldn't afford to – and they wouldn't have to. They could get at her through Emily, or Sara, or little Tamika, or any of the others she cared so deeply about. And if she broke before the soman locations could be sealed off, the vials could easily be moved to new locations . . . or even detonated.

It was all up to Jessie. Somehow, regardless of the pain Malloche's people inflicted on her patients, she had to keep herself from giving them any information until they were no longer suspicious that she had caved in too easily.

Then, smoothly and convincingly, she had to come up with some believable explanation for who Dr. Mark Naehring was, and what he was doing in the operating room – some explanation other than the truth.

*Too much*, Alex thought. It was too much to ask of anyone.

'We've got to assume Jessie will eventually tell them what Malloche disclosed to us,' he said.

'Would she do that?'

'It depends on how they try to break her down. They'll probably go after her patients. I don't know how she's going to respond, but we 've got to assume the worst.'

'If we seal off those places now, we'll be tipping our hand just as surely as if she *did* tell them everything.'

'What time is it?' Alex asked.

'One,' Vicki said. 'A little after.'

'Do you think we could get teams mobilized at all three places by midnight with the suits – or at least with gas masks?'

'Assuming the Boston police continue to cooperate, and I have no reason to think they won't.'

'Everything's got to look perfectly ordinary until the teams are inside the gates. I want them brought in gradually from directions where Malloche's man out there wouldn't notice. Damn! I wish we had some clue as to what he looked like.'

As Alex was speaking, he almost inadvertently slipped his hand into the rear pocket of his scrub pants. The folded paper Emily had given to him in the OR was still there. The sheet was an anesthesia record. At the top of the page, in pencil, was a decently done three-inch sketch of a man's face. Below the picture, Emily had printed:

**white male, 6'2", slim, 160–170, short light-brown hair, blue eyes, nose looks like it was broken and poorly set, name may be Stefan**

Alex studied the page, then handed it over to Moyer. Emily had done the drawing in the OR while she was pretending to work with the anesthesiologist. If she had been caught by either Grace or Derrick, it would have gone very poorly for her.

'Jessie's nurse risked dying for this,' he said. 'It's got to be Malloche's man on the outside. It gives me an idea.'

'I think we're already right with you on this one,' Holcroft said.

# Chapter 38

They were herded at gunpoint up to Surgical Seven in two groups. First, Grace took the console tech Holly, radiologist Hans Pfeffer, Skip Porter, the scrub and circulating nurses, and Emily. After the elevator was brought back down, Jessie and Michelle Booker made the trip with Malloche, on a gurney, and Armand. The young killer seemed high-strung and edgy; and never lowered his pistol.

'How is my patient in seven thirty-seven doing?' Jessie asked him as they approached the elevator.

Armand looked at her blankly and motioned her with his gun barrel to move ahead.

'Jesus,' Jessie exclaimed. 'I just saved your boss's life. The least you can do is answer my question. Do you understand me?'

'He speaks English,' Malloche said hoarsely, but with surprising force and clarity. 'He just doesn't like to.'

Since waking up from anesthesia, his responses had been groggy and monosyllabic. Clearly his condition was rapidly improving. He rattled at Armand in French and got a terse reply.

'Armand says your patient is alive,' Malloche reported. 'But he cannot vouch for her condition. The fact that I am this awake and alert and we have yet to return to the floor suggests that things have gone well for me, yes?'

'I suppose you could conclude that,' Jessie said. 'Believe it or not, I told you just a few minutes ago that the operation was a complete success. It may be a while before information hits your memory bank and gets deposited. You were actually awake quite a bit during your surgery.'

Then, heart hammering, she added, 'Do you remember anything of that?'

'Remember anything? Not really. I remember getting wheeled onto an elevator and heading down the corridor to the operating room. Then the next thing I remember, I am being wheeled back.'

Jessie silently sighed her relief. It appeared that neither Malloche nor Grace had any idea who Dr. Mark Naehring was, why he was in the operating room, or, in Grace's case, why Derrick confronted, then chased him. Jessie suspected that soon, though, very soon, they were going to be looking to her for answers. And whatever those answers were, they had better have the ring of truth.

Michelle Booker had been silently watching and listening. Jessie reached over and squeezed her hand.

'Hang in there, Michelle,' she said. 'I'll explain everything to you when I can.'

'You mean when we allow you to,' Malloche corrected.

'You just treat this woman well,' Booker said boldly. 'She just performed an operation on you that maybe no neurosurgeon anyplace could have done better.'

'I was counting on that.'

Arlette was there when the elevator arrived. She took her husband's hand and kissed him on the lips. Then she looked up at Jessie.

'He looks quite good. I understand the surgery went well.'

'As of this moment, it has. But post-op, much can happen. My patient Sara Devereau is a perfect example. How is she doing?'

'What do we do for my husband now?' Arlette responded, pointedly ignoring the question.

The battle of wills between the two of them had begun anew. After nearly seven hours in the operating room, Jessie was in no mood to back down.

'I asked you a simple question,' she said.

'And I –'

'Tell her, Arlette,' Malloche said with a weak wave. 'Tell her what she wants to know.'

'Very well. Dr. Gilbride has been in with your patient since you left. She is awake and seems to be responding to commands, and the doctor seems quite pleased with himself.'

'Oh, thank God! I want to see her.'

'My husband . . . ,' Arlette said stonily.

'Okay. The surgery was, I would have to say, an unqualified success. We were able to remove about ninety-five percent of the tumor.'

'You left some in?'

Jessie hesitated, wondering what the immediate fallout would be of explaining that the reason she couldn't get all the growth out was that Arlette's man Derrick had murdered the computer expert and destroyed his equipment. She decided now was not the time.

'The little I left in will probably never cause a problem. In fact, the blood supply to that fragment may have been disrupted enough to kill what cells remain.'

'Go on. What can we expect now?'

'Well, seizures may be a problem. We've medicated him for that with a drug he has taken before. My nurse practitioner, the one your people kidnapped, should stay with him continuously for a while to administer medications and monitor his vital signs. Infection is always a concern post-op. There is also the chance of a pressure buildup like the one that happened to my patient.'

'That could happen this soon?'

'Oh, yes, or up to several days after surgery. There's no way to predict whether this particular complication is going to happen, or when. Now, may I go in and see Sara Devereau?'

'First, get Claude settled in with his nurse. Then you may go and check on the Devereau woman. After that, Doctor, you and I have some very serious matters to discuss.'

'What matters?' Malloche asked dreamily.

Arlette kissed him on the forehead and spoke reassuringly to him in German. Apparently satisfied with whatever she said, Claude smiled feebly and closed his eyes, obviously exhausted.

Under Arlette's watchful gaze, Jessie and Booker wheeled Malloche into the deserted ICU. Then, while he was being transferred to a bed and hooked up to a monitor, Arlette and Grace huddled in the hallway. Jessie had no doubt whatsoever about the subject of their conversation. She was running out of time to prepare some believable explanation.

A fairly extensive neurologic exam on Malloche verified what Jessie already suspected – that ARTIE had excised nearly all of a very extensive, hard-to-reach meningioma without causing any gross neurologic damage. Sadly, ironically, she acknowledged that the tiny robot and the MRI guidance system may have come of age working within the skull of a demon. She was just finishing when Emily came in.

'Sara's wide awake,' she said excitedly.

'Talking?'

'She's not ready for the debating society, but she's certainly making her needs understood. You're on a helluva roll today, Jess.'

'Carl's still there with her?'

'A man on a mission.'

'Maybe someone should have smashed him across the face with a gun a long time ago.'

'Amen to that,' Emily said.

Jessie went over Malloche's up-to-the-minute condition and medications.

'Between you, me, Michelle, and the nurses, we should be able to provide him with continuous coverage.'

Arlette and Grace reentered the room. Neither looked too pleased. Until that moment, Michelle Booker had remained silent. But now her exasperation broke through.

'Would somebody please tell me what in the hell is going on?' she pleaded. 'I went off coverage half an hour ago, and my kids are expecting me home. I need to get out of here.'

'I don't believe that's going to happen,' Jessie said.

She received an assenting nod from Arlette and gave a capsule summary of their predicament. Michelle's expression – increasingly astonished and fearful – suggested that the reality of the situation on Surgical Seven was far more bizarre and dangerous than whatever her imagination had conjured up.

A muttered 'Dear God' was all she could manage when Jessie had finished.

Arlette motioned the two of them out into the hall, then down to the small conference room. She was wearing her machine gun over her shoulder and had a thick-barreled pistol stuck in her belt. For the first time Jessie could remember, the woman wore no makeup. Her porcelain skin was unlined, but her lips looked bloodless, and her eyes had an unsettling hollowness about them.

*Exhaustion? Tension? Anger?* Jessie wondered. All three, perhaps. It certainly seemed as if the strain of running such a show by herself was beginning to take its toll.

'Dr. Booker,' Arlette asked when they reached the conference room, 'do you have any knowledge of what transpired downstairs in the operating room?'

'Nothing other than what I saw,' Booker replied.

'Well, I'd like you to tell me exactly what that was. But first, Dr. Copeland, why don't you go on down the hall and see how your patient is doing. I'll send for you when I'm ready. It won't be long.'

Jessie knew that Arlette would have Booker go through the surgery on her husband step by step until she reached the part when Mark Naehring entered the OR. Then the questions would become more and more detailed until Arlette had a crystal-clear image of what the anesthesiologist had seen. And later, the details of Booker's story would be used to check off on Jessie's account.

*Just don't lie, Michelle,* Jessie begged silently. *Don't take any chances with this woman. Tell her what you saw.*

'I'll be down the hall,' she said, her eyes urging Booker to be strong.

With Armand in tow, Jessie hurried to Sara's room. Her friend and patient was indeed awake and alert, sitting up and sipping some juice. The shunt Jessie had placed through the twist-drill hole had been carefully sutured down and hooked up to a drainage system. Carl Gilbride was adjusting the valve that controlled the flow rate.

'Hey,' Jessie said, 'an island of sanity in the sea of madness. How're you doing, Sar?'

'Nah . . . so bad. Tube . . . inma . . . head.'

'I know. I know.' Jessie hugged her. 'Don't worry about it. If the tube needs to stay in to keep the pressure down, we'll hide it beneath your skin. Understand?'

'Yes.'

'The drainage was dropping off, so I repositioned the tube,' Gilbride said, sounding to Jessie like a four-year-old announcing he had picked up all his toys.

'You did great, Carl,' Jessie replied. 'She would have never made it without you.'

'How'd the case go?'

'ARTIE did well. Malloche is awake with no apparent residual neurologic problems.'

'Does that mean we're going to make it out of this?'

'You're asking the wrong person, Carl,' she said. She lowered her voice, making it difficult, if not impossible, for Armand to hear. 'Something happened during the operation that Arlette isn't too pleased about. One of their people – the big guy with the blond crew cut – took off after someone and hasn't returned.'

'Took off after who?'

'I don't know. I'll speak to you about it all later. Meanwhile, please just keep on doing what you can for Sara. How's everyone else on the floor?'

'I . . . um . . . haven't been around to see them. It seemed like this is what you wanted me to do.'

With the power to dictate all the rules in effect stripped from him, Gilbride seemed almost helpless.

'It was, Carl,' she said.

'Dr. Copeland?'

Arlette Malloche stood by the doorway. Red smudges of anger colored her cheeks.

'Yes?'

'Come with me now.'

'I'd like to make rounds on the other patients.'

Arlette grabbed the pistol in her belt, but didn't pull it out.

'Now!' she demanded.

Jessie took a calming breath. This was the moment she had been dreading since she realized that Derrick hadn't returned to the floor. She had never been much of an actress or much of a liar. But she knew she was going to have to be both now. She had to believe that Alex had somehow managed to get away from Derrick; he would need time to locate the soman vials and disarm them. The moment that Arlette suspected they had learned the locations, it seemed certain one or more of the setups would be detonated. No matter what pressure Arlette brought to bear, that was the one piece of information that had to be kept from her.

'Hang in there, Sar,' Jessie said. 'You, too, Carl. Keep up the great work.'

Arlette motioned her to the conference room and into a chair, and closed the door.

'I assume you know what I wish to learn about,' she said.

'The man who came into the OR.'

'Precisely. I warn you in advance, Doctor, that I have a version of this story from your anesthesiologist friend. If your account differs in the slightest from hers, I'm going to let you watch while I kill her.'

Jessie sucked in a jet of air, then moistened her lips.

*This had better be damn good, Copeland,* she was thinking. She had come up with the rough outline of a story that would jibe with anything Booker might have told Arlette. But there would hbe a major problem if Arlette went to Gilbride for confirmation. Somehow, he had to be kept out of the loop. Just as Jessie was preparing to ramble through the version she had created, something Alex had said about Gilbride gave her the answer she needed.

'I don't know as much as you might think,' she began.

'I don't believe that.'

'Well, you've got to. I don't want anyone to get hurt.'

310

'Go on.'

'The whole thing was set up some time ago by that woman Lisa from the FBI – the one that your husband shot. I don't know how, but somehow they knew Claude was in the States looking for a neurosurgeon. Eastern Mass Medical Center was just one of the hospitals they targeted. I don't know how many others there were. Lisa was the agent assigned here, and she was around almost all the time. She was certain Rolf Hermann was Claude, but she didn't trust Dr. Gilbride enough to tell him that. She said they had done some research on Carl, and felt there was a good possibility he had been paid off by you. So she spoke exclusively with me. When it was clear Hermann was going to die, she had people from the FBI lined up to storm the floor and capture you and the Count's so-called children.'

'But then your Dr. Gilbride made a mess of things by losing his temper at the agent and forcing her to identify herself before she wanted to.'

'Exactly. She had given me a number to call if there was trouble, but I never had a chance to use it until Dave Scolari, the man in seven-seventeen with the broken neck, had his seizure. During the commotion, I took a chance and slipped into the conference room to use the only phone you had left hooked up. The conversation with the FBI people who answered only lasted maybe a minute before I had to hang up. I was told to prepare the way for one of their people to come into the operating room. I said whoever it was should use the name Dr. Mark Naehring.'

Arlette motioned for Jessie to stop so that she could mentally pick through the story for inconsistencies.

'All right,' she said finally, 'what happened next?'

Jessie released the death grip she had on the arm of her chair. She was improvising – flying almost blind. But so far at least, her account seemed to be holding up.

'I made up the story that Dr. Naehring might be coming into the OR to help me with part of the case. He's a psychopharmacologist – someone who works with the sort of medications we use when patients are kept awake during brain surgery – so I thought if you checked up on

311

him, his helping me would make some sense, at least as long as you didn't try to call him.'

'That was very clever. Go on.'

'The night before the operation, I made it a point to say something to Dr. Booker about it when she was doing your husband's pre-op physical.'

'I remember.'

'I wasn't sure anyone was going to show up, but right in the middle of the case, someone from the FBI did. We were able to speak to one another by turning off our microphones and whispering. Because of the way the MRI magnets are set up, both Grace and Derrick were shielded by our backs.'

'What did this agent want?'

'He wanted to kill your husband, and then kill both of your people, and then go up to Surgical Seven and kill you.'

'And –'

'I had to tell him about the soman – that it was out there in the city someplace, and that you would have it released in a crowded area if anything happened to Claude. I also told him I had seen the way it killed the microbiology people.'

'That was good. What did he do then?'

Jessie regripped the chair. This chapter, the most far-fetched of the fish tale, had to be totally believable – and diverting.

'He said he had a tiny transmitter in the locker room that he wanted me to insert into your husband's head.'

'My, my,' she said.

'I told him the transmitter couldn't be brought into the MRI room because of the magnets. They would destroy it and it might damage the machine. He argued with me that there must be a way to do it, but I assured him there wasn't.'

'Then he left?'

'He did. He asked me how many people were being held on Surgical Seven and if anyone had been harmed. He said the FBI would work something out, but that no one would be placed in any more danger than they were in right now. Then he left. A few seconds later, I heard Derrick demand that he pull down his mask. Next thing I heard was shooting. I saw them take off, so I just finished the operation.'

For a full minute, Arlette studied her face, probing. Jessie forced herself to maintain eye contact.

'You're certain they know about the soman,' Arlette said finally.

'I . . . I'm sorry. I couldn't think of anything else to tell them but the truth.'

'You did right. I want them to know. In fact, I'm thinking about giving them a demonstration.'

'No! . . . I mean, please don't. As long as it's only a threat, I think the FBI will keep their distance. Once the gas is used, I think they'll just do whatever is necessary to get at you. Ask your husband if you don't believe me. There's no need for a demonstration.'

'We'll see,' Arlette said.

But Jessie could tell she understood the point. Once again, her hands stopped compressing the oak armrests.

'Could I please go and check on the other patients now?' she asked.

Arlette brought her hand across and rested it on the gun.

'I don't believe you,' she said.

A knot formed and tightened in Jessie's gut.

'Well, everything I said is just the way it happened.'

'We shall see.'

*Please. Please don't hurt anyone.*

'That woman Grace brought up from the operating room is an X-ray technician, is she not?' Arlette asked.

'She is,' Jessie replied, suddenly terrified for Holly. 'Why?'

'I'm going to send her off the floor with Grace to bring back a portable X-ray machine.'

'For what?'

'I want a picture done of Claude's head, that's what. You knew that one of the first things I'd think of was that the FBI man wanted you to insert a tracer into Claude's head. That's just the sort of thing they do. So you thought that by telling me they had asked you to do it, I'd believe that you hadn't. Well, I think you underestimate me. You did it, didn't you?'

The knot loosened. Jessie actually had to keep her lips pressed tightly together to prevent a smile. She had almost rejected using the idea of the implanted transmitter because it sounded so far-out.

'Believe me,' she said with genuine conviction, 'I did nothing but remove his tumor.'

'We'll see. I think between Grace, Claude, and me, we should be able to spot the device on an X ray. As things stand, I owe you some distress for calling the FBI the way you did. But you did a good job in the operating room, so I'm going to let that go as long as I don't find out you are lying.'

'I'm not,' Jessie said, perhaps too quickly.

Again, Arlette searched her face for signs of deceit.

'When do you think Claude will be ready to travel?' she asked.

'Do you mean travel without risk?'

'No. I mean the soonest he could travel at all. He won't have to sit up. We can keep him on a stretcher.'

'It's hard to say, because I've never done an operation with the robot before. I guess a day. Two or three would probably be better. As you saw with Sara Devereau, things can happen.'

'That's why you're coming with us.'

'What?'

'Armand will give you a large canvas bag. I want you to fill it with whatever medical supplies you are likely to need in any situation or emergency that might arise with my husband.'

'When are we leaving?'

'When we leave, you'll know,' Arlette said.

# Chapter 39

**Quincy Market Rotunda – RED TEAM**
**Green Line – Government Center – WHITE TEAM**
**Eilene's Basement – BLUE TEAM**
**??**

It was nearing ten in the evening. Alex was in the van, parked on Cambridge Street, just across from the entrance to the MBTA Government Center station. He was flipping through the pages in one of the three loose-leaf notebooks he, Stan Moyer, and Vicki Holcroft had put together. The notebooks contained as much information and as many maps as they could accumulate on each of the three soman locations Claude Malloche had disclosed. They also contained the list of team members assigned to find the vials of gas. The teams were a mix of FBI, local police, National Guard, and several Army specialists in biologic and toxic warfare flown in from D.C.

Moyer was coordinating the Red Team, assigned to the center rotunda in the tourist mecca Quincy Market. Less than a mile away, Holcroft was organizing her Blue Team people in Filene's Basement at busy Downtown Crossing. And in between them, Alex had taken responsibility for the largest team, with the daunting task of sweeping the sprawling Government Center T station.

The plan was straightforward enough, but did require the quiet cooperation of people in charge of each location. The teams would infiltrate their targets before they closed and hide out in various positions. Then, an hour or so after closing, they would seal off every window and systematically search until the gas had been found. Filene's had closed at eight-thirty; and there, the search was already under way.

The cavernous Government Center station would be the toughest nut. The plan was to have it first be inspected and cleared out by transit security people. Then, at 2 A.M., Alex's White Team would enter along the tracks through the tunnel from Haymarket station. The target would be divided into six-foot-square numbered grids and searched that way. A simple plan if ever there was one.

But there was one very major catch. Claude Malloche's drug-induced revelations had been fairly specific, but only up to a point.

*How many vials are hidden in Boston?*

*Three . . . four.*

Alex had mentally replayed the snippet of his conversation with the killer a hundred times.

*Three . . . four.*

What did that mean? Under heavy medication, Malloche had given out only three locations. Was there another? Malloche was a control freak. Would he ever allow a strategy that purposely deprived him of information? But on the other hand, he was also obsessive about detail – about having backup plans to his backup plans. Could he have covered himself for the possibility that either he or one of the others might be captured and tortured by having the location of a fourth vial withheld from him?

*Is there another vial of soman?*

*Don't know . . . don't know . . . don't know.*

In the end, Alex felt that they had no choice but to go with what they had. But the existence of a fourth vial could by no means be discounted. The key to dealing with that possibility was finding Stefan – Malloche's man on the outside. And the key to doing *that* was to have everything look exactly as he expected it to look until the very moment he pushed the button to release the gas.

Alex set the notebooks aside and swung around toward the aging police demolitions expert who was laboring at a small bench top beneath two powerful lights. The best of the best, he had asked the captain for. This rumpled senior citizen was the man they had sent. But Alex had already been with Harry Laughlin long enough today to know the captain hadn't let him down.

'How's it going back there?' he asked.

'Ten or fifteen minutes, boyo,' Laughlin said, with just a hint of a brogue. 'I should know the deepest mysteries of this beastie in that time.'

The beastie laid out before him was the detonation system that had been used to kill the four microbiology technicians. To obtain it had meant Alex had to return to the cave of death. Under the cover of evening darkness, he had slipped back into the hospital through the door in the rear of the pathology department. Laughlin, well into his sixties, had listened to Alex's description of what the lab would be like and, without batting an eye, had still insisted on going in with him.

'Once you've seen two buddies blown to bits tryin' to defuse a canister,' he said, 'nothin' affects you that much. I'm with you all the way.'

'Tell me that afterward,' Alex had replied.

They donned paper surgical masks, then Alex pulled away the yellow plastic tape and eased open the door to the lab. The wall of stench hit them like a blast furnace, with the pungent smell of chemically burned flesh even more repugnant than the other odors.

'Still with me?' he asked.

'When did I ever say that?'

The bodies, including Derrick's, were just as he had left them. But under the glare of their high-beam flashlights, the scene – the oddly positioned corpses, the rigor mortis, the blood, the vomit – looked even more eerie and repulsive. It took nearly half an hour, but they found the detonator still taped underneath an incubator stand – a neat package of circuits about five inches square. They carefully untaped it and set it in a plastic sack, along with shards of glass and what appeared to be a metal casing of some sort. Then, close to being overwhelmed by the hellish scene, they left.

317

'Nice place you took me to, there,' Laughlin said as they headed back to the van.

'If we can't find and deactivate those other packages, Harry, we may get to see the scene again, only on a much grander scale.'

Now, Alex made his way back to where Laughlin was working.

'Okay,' the policeman said, 'here's the pitch. A small charge is detonated by radio and blows a glass vial to bits. If the gas works the way you say it does, the circuitry and explosive in the three locations may be the same as here, but the gas containers must be larger – probably much larger. I would guess the total size of the package may be a foot or so long, and maybe half that wide and deep.'

'Can you disable the system?'

'I believe I can, yes.'

'And then put it back together again so it looks the same but just doesn't work?'

'With the gas?'

Alex thought about their need to draw Malloche's man as close as possible to the vials so that one of their observers might get a fix on him.

'I'll decide about that when we find one,' he said.

At three-thirty in the morning, the Blue Team scored. The twenty members of Vicki Holcroft's unit had drifted into the department store throughout the early evening, and had hidden on the upper floors until closing time. Then, after an hour's wait, they had assembled in the basement and set up their grids. The key to completing their search was Harry Laughlin's suggestion that the gas would not have been placed beneath clothes or inside of a cabinet where its diffusion would be restricted. Eliminating all cabinets, at least for the first pass through, made the search of the vast store basement at least manageable.

The deadly black glass cylinder, with its attached detonating device, was in plain sight, yet essentially invisible to any casual passerby. It was screwed in place beneath the customer side of a counter, not far from the escalator bringing shoppers up to the store from the Downtown Crossing MBTA station. The cylinder was shielded in front by a black metal plate drilled throughout with minute holes to allow diffusion of the poison.

Alex got word of the find at Filene's as his White Team of forty were halfway through a grid-by-grid search of the Government Center Green Line station. He had assumed that the gas would be placed in a spot likely to be densely populated, and so had the search begin with the central area of the terminal, and slowly fan out toward the more remote stretches of track. So far, nothing.

Reluctant to be seen entering the department store at this hour, Alex had the MBTA supervisor accompany him and Harry Laughlin down into Park Street station, then through the Red Line tunnel to Downtown Crossing, and up the dormant escalator to Filene's. Most of the Blue Team was sent back through the tunnels to join the White Team at Government Center. It was well after four and the station was due to be opened at five. A delay much later than six would certainly risk creating suspicion.

Alex donned a sealed antiexposure suit and ordered the transit authority supervisor, Vicki, and the two agents who would be left with her to try and spot Stefan, to wait for them at the base of the escalator. Laughlin set up a pair of powerful lights and lay down on the floor with his tools close at hand. He had refused the suit.

'The glass in them things fogs up too much for this kind of work,' he explained. 'Besides, after what I went through to get that beastie from the hospital, if I blow this one, I'd be too embarrassed to want to live.'

'Obviously, you didn't get a close enough look at those stiffs in the lab,' Alex replied. 'I'm not afraid of biting the big one with a bullet or a blast, but I can't stand the thought of puking to death.'

With Alex assisting, Laughlin took fifteen minutes to isolate the wire he wanted to cut.

'This cylinder's a big one,' Laughlin said, 'maybe ten times the content of the one that went off in the hospital.

319

With any air movement at all, my guess is there's enough to reach every cranny of this place.'

'At the moment, the only cranny I'm concerned about is this one.'

'You want me to leave everything here except this connection, right?'

'Yeah. If he comes by and checks, I want it all to look normal. Then, if he tries to detonate the thing, he won't know whether the screwup is in the circuitry or the transmitter. Something he'll do at that point will call attention to himself. I'm sure of it.'

'Actually, we can do better than that,' Laughlin said. 'Looking at the components of this receiver, I'm making an educated guess that the transmitter that will set it off is working somewhere on the VHF band. Once I get this thing deactivated, I have a scanner that should be able to isolate the frequency. Then all we have to do is give monitors to your people who are here, and they should know the instant someone tries to blow this thing.'

'That's perfect. Will it be the same for all three setups?'

'Most likely, but we'll check just to be sure. First, though, we've got to neuter this beastie. Okay, then, here goes. Just like in the movies.'

The click of the wire cutter was like a gunshot.

'Nothing,' Alex said after finally exhaling.

'That's the idea, bucko. In my job, nothing is *very good*.'

At that moment, Alex's cell phone went off. The Red Team had located the soman package bolted beneath a stool in the rotunda of the Quincy Market food court.

The unknown killer virus at Eastern Mass Medical Center remained headline news – especially now that a team from the MRI operating room had been placed on isolation precautions. Sitting at Sara's bedside, Jessie had watched the bogus story unfold on the first news program of the morning, complete with clips of Michelle Booker's businessman husband complaining that, although he had been assured by hospital administrators that his wife was all right, he had not heard a word from her since she left for the hospital twenty-four hours ago.

Now, in the supply room, Jessie systematically loaded the black nylon gym bag with first aid supplies and life-saving equipment, recording the items on a pad so that nothing would be overlooked. Next, she would raid the med room and stock up on all manner of drugs. The charade on Surgical Seven was wearing thin to the outside world. Arlette knew that as well as she did. It was only a matter of time before antiterrorist rescue teams came calling. Arlette planned to be gone when they did.

*Tracheotomy kit . . . laryngoscope . . . breathing bag . . . endotracheal tubes . . . hydrocephalus drainage system . . . urinary catheters . . . IV infusion sets . . . twist drill . . . blood pressure cuff . . . scalpel . . . sutures . . .*

Arlette, Grace, and Malloche had studied the portable X ray of Claude's head. For the moment at least, Arlette seemed to believe Jessie's tall tale about Mark Naehring. It was almost six in the morning. Malloche had been sleeping most of the time since his surgery, but he was always easy to arouse, and appeared to be doing remarkably well. Still, moving him at this point carried some danger. Jessie knew that Arlette was weighing her options, just as Jessie was weighing the merits of encouraging them to leave, versus stalling to give Alex more time. Leaving might well remove the patients and staff from harm's way. Stalling for time might save lives on the outside, especially if Arlette planned to use the chaos of a massive toxic gas exposure to divert attention from the hospital.

If only there was a way to get word from Alex about the results of his search. But she knew there wasn't.

Jessie was in the med room, loading a box with anti-biotics, anti-seizure meds, injectable steroids, anti-coagulants, and tranquilizers, when she made the decision to do whatever she could to maintain the status quo by keeping the Malloches from leaving. She had seen firsthand the horrors of soman, and she trusted that Alex wouldn't risk the carnage that would result from an assault on Surgical Seven. The longer she could stall their departure, the more chance he had of finding the three vials. All she needed was a plan.

Jessie looked down at the drug in her hand and realized the answer, the plan, was that close. Injectable diazepam – Valium. She filled several 5-cc syringes and carefully wrapped the empty vials in paper towels before throwing them into the trash.

*You don't know' it, Claude,* she was thinking, *but you're about to take a little turn for the worse.*

Six forty-five. A mechanical breakdown in the Government Center station had forced a two-hour delay. At least, that was the story the media had been fed. Dozens of buses had been rolled into service to bypass the station. The Blue Line, which also used Government Center, was being delayed as well.

Alex knew that the massive interruption was a potential red flag. But it was early, and Malloche's man, assuming he was even awake yet, had three locations to keep track of – at least three. With the addition of the Red Team, the force searching the station was now almost eighty – an irony that was hardly lost on Alex. For five years he had toiled alone and in obscurity, tilting at a deadly windmill that some in power denied even existed. Now, here he was, commanding a small army.

After Harry Laughlin had disarmed the detonator in Quincy Market, Stan Moyer and two other agents had been outfitted as maintenance men, given copies of the sketch and description of Stefan as well as monitors set to the detonator's frequency, and left inside the building.

Two of the locations were now secured and under observation. The third had proven to be incredibly difficult. Alex stood beside Laughlin, halfway up one of the staircases in the Government Center station, overseeing the search. The demolitions expert had to be near retirement age, if not past it, yet he looked as fresh after nearly twenty-four tension-filled hours on the job as he had when they started.

'What are you going to do if we can't find it?' he asked.

Alex shrugged. 'What do you do when you can't find a bomb?'

'It depends on how much we believe the tip we got.'

'I believe this one hundred percent.'

'Then we keep looking.'

'We've gone over every inch of this place, Harry. Most of it twice.'

'No, we haven't.'

'What do you mean?'

'We haven't gone over the inch that includes the device. We need to try and think about what we're doing wrong.'

For several minutes the two of them stood there, elbow to elbow, watching, thinking. Then Harry began nodding as if he had just realized something.

'What? What?' Alex asked.

'Look at them all down there.'

'Yeah?'

'What do you see?'

'I see a huge number of men and women searching – some of them hunched over, some on their hands and knees.'

'Where *aren't* they searching, bucko?'

'I don't understand.'

'For hours we've been looking down – under benches, behind trash cans, alongside the tracks, in alcoves. That's where the other two cylinders were – down. But –'

'Hey, everyone!' Alex called out without waiting for Laughlin to finish. 'I want all the spotlights and all your eyes focused up along the I-beams and across the ceiling. Start from your original grids. Those of you who don't have a grid, just pair up with someone and work the same area. Remember, what we're looking for is probably encased in black. It's not going to be easy to spot.'

'I admire a man who can make a decision,' Laughlin said.

Fifteen silent minutes passed. . . .

'We have about another half an hour, Harry,' Alex said as they continued surveying the deeply shadowed areas overhead. 'Then we're going to have to open those gates up there and let the passengers in. If there's a fourth location, sealing this one off much longer is going to be like asking them to set that one off. These people aren't stupid.'

'Neither are we, boyo,' Harry said suddenly, pointing upward and outward. 'Neither are we.'

Alex followed his line of sight for about fifty or sixty feet to the place where one of the dozens of support beams met the ceiling. There, virtually blending into the shadows, was the barely visible outline of a rectangular casing.

'Does the Boston Police Department appreciate how good you are?' Alex asked as they raced to the base of the beam.

'I think they might,' Laughlin said. 'I applied for retirement three years ago and haven't heard a word from them yet.'

It took twenty minutes on a ladder before Harry announced that the package had been neutralized.

'Well, bucko,' the policeman said after he had climbed down and most of the troops had been dispatched back through the tunnel to the Haymarket station, 'that's three out of three. Are you going to go after the hostages?'

'Not yet, Harry. If I was certain it was three out of three and not three out of four I might try and think of some way. But as long as Malloche doesn't know how much we know, I think the hostages are reasonably safe. We've got to see if we can flush out this Stefan.'

He gestured to the six undercover police who were now positioned around the area, waiting for the morning crush.

'I think I'll hang around until you do,' Laughlin said.

'Hey, that's not necessary.'

'Hell, this is all a movie, right? I want to see how it comes out.'

# Chapter 40

It had been nearly ten years since Jessie had adjusted the green felt doctoral cape over her shoulders and strode up onto the stage to accept the parchment that would forever make her a doctor of medicine. Over those years, over those countless hours in the hospital and the operating room, she had never knowingly done anything to injure a patient . . . until now. Throughout the day, every hour or two, she had been injecting Claude Malloche with Valium or with Haldol, another major tranquilizer – the former into his IV line, and the Haldol into a muscle. The combination of the drugs had resulted in a somnolence bordering on coma. Malloche could still be aroused, but only with a great deal of stimulation, and then only for a matter of seconds. The trick was to maintain him in that state without causing a life-threatening depression in his ability to breathe.

If Arlette had been planning to leave EMMC – and it certainly seemed as if she was – her husband's turn for the worse had delayed their departure. Throughout the day, she had maintained a nervous vigil near Claude's bed, leaving only to pace the hallways like a cat, checking in on the hostages and her people. At noon, Gilbride's post-op patient, Lena Levin, was found dead in bed from her infection. Arlette's only reaction was to have the door to her room closed. Otherwise, the hours crept on monotonously and without incident. Now, it was nearly seven.

Jessie knew she was flirting with disaster. Claude was breathing, but not deeply enough to keep his lungs fully expanded. Mucus was starting to pool in his alveolar sacs, and pneumonia was probably already beginning. He had been an operative marvel. Now, his surgeon was celebrating her success by slowly killing him. And if he died, there was no way any of them would survive Arlette Malloche's fury.

'What do you think?'

Arlette's question startled Jessie, who was wondering what was going on with Alex, assuming he and Derrick hadn't killed each other, and how he planned to approach rescuing forty-five hostages on a floor mined with explosives and controlled by three well-armed professionals.

'I don't know for sure,' she lied. 'I think it must be brain swelling.'

'You're treating him for that?'

'I am.'

'Can he travel?'

'I don't see how.'

'Well, he's going to have to, and soon.'

'Then it's on your head, whatever happens.'

Arlette grabbed Jessie by the shirt and shoved her roughly against the wall with surprising strength.

'No, it will be on your head! Believe me, it will.'

She stalked out of the room.

A few seconds after that, her husband stopped breathing.

'Jesus, Em,' Jessie whispered, her heart pounding. 'Quick, give me the Ambu bag. Michelle, there's a black gym bag in the med room filled with equipment and drugs. Bring back whatever equipment you need to intubate him, please.'

'Here's the breathing bag,' Em said.

Her expression left no doubt that she understood the gravity of the situation.

'Suction up, please.'

Malloche's complexion was already beginning to darken. His oximeter reading on the monitor screen began to edge downward. His pulse immediately jumped from eighty to a hundred as his body commenced the frantic

326

search for more oxygen. Jessie deep-suctioned his throat, pulled his chin up to straighten his airway, and with one hand tightened the triangular rubber seal over his nose and mouth. Then, with the other, she began rhythmic compressions of the breathing bag, monitoring that air was getting in by the rise and fall of his chest.

'What else can I do?' Em asked.

'What's your connection with the Almighty?'

'Decent enough.'

'Talk to her, then.'

At that instant, Malloche took a breath. Jessie suctioned him again. This time, he gagged and managed another, gurgling inhalation. Then another. Michelle Booker hurried in with the equipment to intubate. When she saw the improved situation, she stopped and sighed audibly.

'Ka-ching!' she said. 'The bullet is dodged.'

'Not by much,' Jessie replied.

She knew she had to stop. If Alex hadn't figured things out by now, he wasn't going to. She had to back off on the meds and let Malloche wake up.

'Exactly what is going on here?'

Arlette approached the bed and gestured at all the emergency equipment.

'He had a momentary slowdown in his breathing,' Jessie said. 'He's doing better now.'

Arlette stroked his hair and moved the plastic oxygen mask aside to kiss his still-violet lips.

'He had better be,' she said. She turned to Grace, who was standing by the doorway. 'Call the chopper in,' she ordered. 'We're moving in an hour.'

As Grace hurried off, Arlette stepped back and leveled her machine gun at Jessie and the others. Then she opened her cell phone and made a call. She spoke rapidly in French, but Jessie picked up the name *Stefan* and the phrase *il est le temps*: it is time.

'No,' Jessie pleaded. 'Please don't.'

'Shut up!' Arlette snapped. 'You just take care of my husband, and you may keep a lot of people you care about from getting hurt.'

She disdainfully jabbed the barrel of her gun at Jessie, then hurried from the room.

'She's going to do it,' Jessie said. 'She's going to have the gas released to create enough chaos for them to escape by helicopter.'

Emily put her arm around Jessie's shoulder.

'There's nothing you can do about it, Jess, except to pray that your friend Alex made it out of the hospital, and that he's been able to find where the gas was hidden. And also pray this guy keeps breathing.'

In fact, not only was Malloche breathing more comfortably, but he had started to move his head and arms. Michelle listened to his lungs, gestured up at the improving oximeter reading, and made a thumbs-up sign.

'Jessie, that woman doesn't seem disposed to shooting anyone right now. But I'm upset she's going to take you when she goes.'

'If she does, she does,' Jessie said. 'As long as Claude needs me, I'm safe enough. Once it's obvious he's recovered, I'm banking on them making me an honorary member of the gang.'

'That certainly would be quite a tribute.'

'I just wish I could have convinced them not to set off that gas. I watched what it does, and it's a horrible way to die.'

'It was their plan the whole time. Malloche wasn't going to be talked out of it.'

'I guess.'

Helpless, the three of them worked on their patient, reversing the effects of nearly twelve hours of sedation.

'Do you think the police'll try and storm Surgical Seven?' Emily asked.

'I think the moment that gas goes off, they'll seal up this place and start negotiating with the Malloches for our release and the location of the other tanks of gas.'

On the bed between them, Claude coughed, moistened his lips with his tongue, and began to blink.

'He's back,' Michelle said.

'I liked it better when there was only one Malloche to

worry about,' Emily added.

'Maybe being deeply stoned has been an epiphany for him,' Jessie whispered, 'like Mr. Scrooge. He'll wake up ready to devote his life to the lepers of the world. Here, help me pull him up in bed.'

Before anyone could move, Arlette burst into the room, breathless and agitated, her pistol in her hand. Behind her, machine gun ready, was Armand. She crossed to her husband.

'Claude? It's Arlette,' she said in German. 'Can you hear me?'

Claude groaned, then nodded. Her eyes flashing, Arlette whirled to face Jessie.

'You two, come with me,' she said, motioning first at Jessie, then at Michelle. 'You stay here with Armand and take care of my husband,' she said to Emily.

She directed them down the hallway to the area by the nurses' station. Then suddenly, fiercely, she jammed the muzzle of her gun against Michelle's temple and forced her to her knees.

'You have ten seconds, Dr. Copeland, to tell me what went on in the operating room, and what they know.'

'I don't –'

'Nine.'

'Please.'

'Eight.'

'Stop! Stop! Okay.'

Jessie looked around. They were at the exact spot where Lisa Brandon had been killed. At least a dozen patients and staff were watching, transfixed. Tamika Bing, with whom Michelle Booker had spent a good deal of time over the thirty hours since Malloche's surgery, was looking on in mute, wide-eyed terror.

'Quickly,' Arlette demanded. 'And no more lies. If you hesitate, if I even *think* you are lying, I will blow her brains out and start on someone else.'

'Okay. Okay.' Jessie was shaking. 'The FBI agent used a drug of some sort – a truth drug. He asked about the gas.'

'And what did he learn?'

Arlette jammed the pistol in so hard that Michelle cried out.

'He . . . he learned there were three locations – Quincy Market, Filene's, and the subway at Government Center.'

'Only three?'

Jessie felt herself go cold at the question.

'Only those three.'

Arlette lowered the pistol.

'My husband is a genius,' she said to no one in particular.

She dialed Stefan again on her cell phone. Jessie could pick out very little of her French this time, but she knew the essence of what Arlette was saying. There was a fourth soman site – a location that had been kept from Claude at his request – and she wanted the gas released.

'I saved your husband's life,' Jessie said. 'Please don't do this. You don't need to kill all those people to get away.'

Arlette put the phone away and again brought her gun up to Michelle's head.

'You lied to me, Dr. Copeland. That cannot go unpunished.'

'Please, you said you wouldn't hurt her.'

'You are right, I did.'

In one rattlesnake-quick motion, Arlette swung the pistol away from Michelle, pointed it into Dave Scolari's room, and fired. The big linebacker, propped up in his bed, never even had the chance to move. The bullet hole materialized just above the bridge of his nose and just below the steel halo frame that had been immobilizing his neck. The impact drove his upper body back several inches. His pillow instantly became spattered with blood. Then, with wide-eyed disbelief frozen on his face, Scolari toppled off the bed and fell heavily, face first, to the floor.

# Chapter 41

Alex was in Government Center station when the radio call came in from Stan Moyer at Quincy Market.

'Bishop, my monitor just started beeping! He's here someplace and he's tried to set the shit off! I have two people outside and me inside. We've all got the description you gave us and that little sketch. No sighting yet.'

'Are you watching the package closely?'

'I'm staring at the seat it's under right now. A teenage girl is perched on it.'

'Let's hope she doesn't knock it over. You and your people keep looking. I'll alert Vicki that our man's probably on the move.'

Alex radioed Filene's.

'Vicki, he just tried and failed at Quincy Market, but no one spotted him. I think he'll write off the first failure as some sort of mechanical glitch, and go for one of the other two. That means there's a fifty-fifty chance between your spot and mine, but we're closer, right?'

'Much closer. Right across the street, really.'

'Okay, make that seventy-thirty. Keep your eyes on the prize, though. It's possible this man isn't even the one we're looking for, but he's the only one we've got any description of.'

Alex slipped the radio into his belt. He had been going nonstop for more than thirty-six hours, but he was still riding on adrenaline rapids. He flashed on Jessie. She, too, had gone a day and a half now with virtually no sleep.

*Hang in there, Jessie*, he urged. *It's almost over.*

He turned to Laughlin.

'He's coming here, Harry, I'm sure of it. The bastard's

beginning to panic, and he's coming down here. Tell me again what you think the range of that transmitter is?'

'There's no way to say for sure, but it's got to be far enough away so he can escape before any gas reaches him. I would guess he's got to have a clear line of sight, though. So what – thirty yards? Forty at the outside.'

Alex scanned the station. It was rush hour. There were probably two hundred students, shoppers, and commuters on their way home. Overhead, unseen in the shadow of the support beam, was enough poison gas to kill almost every one of them. And somewhere, approaching the area, was a man determined to release it. Alex made visual contact with two of the four men scanning the station, and pointed to his eyes. *Stay sharp!*

'Harry, how long would it take him to get from Quincy Market to here?'

'Five minutes. Not much more.'

'Perfect. That gives me time.'

'For what?'

'For this.'

'A candy bar?'

'Not just a candy bar, an Almond Joy. I do them instead of cigarettes. Want one?'

Laughlin looked at him queerly, then said, 'Well, yes, boyo. As a matter of fact, I do.'

'Okay. But first you've got to let me show you the right way to eat it.'

After the lesson, the two men ate in silence, waiting, watching. They had just finished when Alex's monitor began beeping. He could tell by the reaction of his men that theirs had gone off as well. He searched the crowd. Nothing. Then the stairs. A train came roaring into the station at the instant he spotted Stefan. The killer, if in fact it was he, stood out because he was motionless halfway down a flight of stairs on the opposite side of the tracks, maybe fifty yards away. It looked as if he was holding the transmitter or a cell phone. Alex slipped his radio from his belt.

'Leaning against the railing on the stairs across the track

from where I am!' he said. 'Move slowly. We don't want him to bolt.'

But the man had probably reported the failure of his transmitter to Claude or Arlette and was already starting back up the stairs.

'Harry, help me. He's just reached the top of those stairs. There's got to be a fourth vial, and I think Malloche has just told him to go set it off.'

'He has a lot of options in this area. We've got to pick him up before he leaves the station, or else risk losing him. Don't wait for me. I can still run, but I was no track star even when I was young. Go! I'll follow.'

Amid screams, Alex leaped down onto the tracks and pulled himself up the other side. Then he charged up the stairs, scanning everywhere for a tall, brown-haired man in a tan jacket. At the last possible moment, he spotted him, moving quickly against the crowd up another staircase to the street. Alex shoved his way up through the dense crowd of commuters, knocking many of them off balance. Curses were still echoing up the stairwell when he slammed through the exit door onto the street. Stefan was at least fifty yards ahead of him now, on the other side of a busy street, jogging slowly to the left.

Sprinting between cars, Alex narrowly avoided being hit by one and rolled across the hood of another. The curses from the subway were replaced by the blasts of auto horns. By the time Alex reached the sidewalk, badly in need of some extra air, the killer had disappeared up a steep hill to the right. BEACON STREET, the sign read.

'Go up Beacon!' Harry shouted from across the street. 'He's headed for the State House – the capitol building!'

Pounding up the hill was agonizing on Alex's knees. A stiletto-like pain had developed under his ribs. Not far ahead, Stefan was running now, probably alerted by the blaring horns. But still, the gap between them was narrowing.

Ahead and to the right, early-evening sunlight glinted off the golden dome of the State House. Harry was right. Malloche's man had hidden the fourth canister of gas somewhere in the capitol! Defying the pain, Alex was sprinting now, fighting to keep his head up. A few yards ahead of him, Stefan was approaching a chanting crowd at the base of the capitol steps, many carrying pickets that urged the defeat of capital punishment. Near them, an equally large and noisy group was chanting in favor of it. The TV network vans were there, too.

As he reached the edge of the crowd, Stefan glanced back over his shoulder, tripped, and fell to one knee. He was stumbling to his feet when Alex launched himself in a flying tackle. The two of them hit the sidewalk heavily, already flailing at each other. Alex's fist connected firmly with the side of the killer's face – a blow that would have dazed most men. Nothing. Stefan was young, incredibly wiry, and strong in the way of men who worked at it. He landed one jackhammer punch to Alex's cheek, then another to his mouth. Alex was driven backward and down. His head struck the pavement, and for an instant, his consciousness vanished. He came to spitting blood from a cracked lip, blinking through waves of unfocused color, and expecting to be shot. Instead, he felt a hand on his shoulder and heard Harry Laughlin's voice.

'You okay?'

Alex rose shakily to one knee. 'Where is he?' he asked.

'He charged off through the crowd.'

'See what you can do to empty the building out. I'll go after him.'

'You sure you can?'

'Just get going!'

Harry took off as someone came over and helped Alex to his feet. Battling a wave of nausea, he pushed his way through the pickets, catching enough snatches of conversation to realize that a vote on the death penalty must be imminent. Stefan was nowhere in sight, but there was only one place he could have gone. Begging his legs to cooperate, Alex pounded up the several dozen granite steps to the main entrance – single doors on each side of the stairs. Just as he reached them, he was driven back by a frightened mob of reporters, legislators, and lobbyists trying to escape an apparent bomb threat. Harry!

Alex forced his way through to the central rotunda beneath the dome – stolid and elegant with flags, statues, and marble. No Stefan. He approached a cameraman, who was moving slower than the rest and was actually photographing the panicked crowd.

'Where are they taking the vote?' he asked breathlessly.

The man gave him a queer look, but then shrugged and pointed up the grand, curving staircase.

'House chambers,' he said. 'One flight up.'

Working off a new jet of adrenaline, Alex bolted up the stairs. Two guards, one an armed state policeman and the other a blue-uniformed court officer, lay on the floor by the open doors to the chamber, both wounded by gunshots. Inside, he could hear Harry Laughlin shouting that he was Boston police, that there was a bomb, and that people should leave immediately. The legislators were already clawing at one another to get out.

The wounded state cop groaned and looked up at him. Alex pulled his gun and motioned with his other hand for the man to stay calm.

'Alex Bishop. I'm CIA,' he said. 'Tall man, tan jacket? Quickly!'

Feebly, the policeman pointed up toward the fourth floor.

'Gallery,' he managed to say.

'Help these two men!' Alex barked at the legislators. 'Get them away from here!'

Then, he raced up the stairs toward the gallery. Another court officer lay slumped like a rag doll by the open door to the gallery. He had been shot through the mouth. Inside, people were frantically climbing over the seats to get up to the doorways. Some were screaming. From below, he could hear Harry bellowing at the legislators to calm down but clear out. Gun drawn, Alex pushed through the doorway just as Stefan reached the gallery railing.

'Hold it, Stefan!' he shouted. 'Hold it right there!'

Stefan froze.

Beyond and below him, Alex could see Harry, now near the front of the chamber, frantically trying to keep a large number of legislators from trampling their fallen comrades. All around Alex, observers in the gallery had responded to his gun by ducking beneath their seats. Slowly, the tall killer turned toward him. His silenced pistol was dangling loosely in his left hand. In his right, he held a transmitter.

'Don't move,' Alex ordered. 'Now, drop the gun. Drop it!'

Stefan grinned at him in a most uncomfortable way and then released his grip and let the gun clatter to the floor.

'Now that!' Alex demanded, approaching carefully. 'Set it down.'

The man's grin broadened and he shook his head. Then he whirled toward the speaker's podium. Alex fired three times, catching him in the head, neck, and back. But he knew it was too late. Stefan lurched forward and toppled over the balcony at the moment the large voting tote board to the right of the podium exploded. A rapidly expanding cloud of death billowed out.

'Get out! Harry, get out of there!' Alex yelled.

But his voice was lost in the screams from below, as the deadly gas began to take its toll. For a moment, he couldn't locate Laughlin. Then he spotted the aging policeman lying facedown in one of the aisles, being stumbled over by those escaping . . . and those dying.

# Chapter 42

The scene in the chambers below Alex was from hell. The billowing gray-black cloud of death had already reached the third or fourth row of seats. Several legislators – those closest to the epicenter of the blast – were already down. Others – perhaps twelve or fifteen of them – were lurching about in a violent, ungainly death dance, shrieking, vomiting, and collapsing. Still others were clustered at the doors directly beneath Alex, shoving and tearing at one another in their efforts to escape.

It was clear that the number of dead and dying would have been much higher had not Harry Laughlin raced to the front of the hall with his warning and the order to clear the place out. Now, the man who had just saved hundreds of lives by his skill in demolitions, and dozens more by his actions here, lay facedown and motionless, midway up the center aisle, two or three rows from the leading edge of the smoke and gas.

There was no possibility of making it down the stairs and through the crowd in time. Instead, Alex grabbed the gallery railing just above the center aisle, took as deep a breath as he could, and dropped. Two of the representatives charging toward the door inadvertently broke his fall. Screaming at him and flailing at his face with their fists, they fought to their feet and battled on, pushing and hammering at those in front of them. Alex fended off their blows as best he could, then, still holding his breath, he crawled toward where Harry lay. A woman, staggering and vomiting, stumbled over him and fell. Another collapsed a few feet away. The cloud of smoke and soman enveloped Harry at the moment Alex, now on his feet, grabbed him by the neck of his jacket and one arm, and began dragging him toward the exit. He closed his eyes tightly against the possibility the gas could be absorbed through that route, and pulled with all his strength. Harry was deadweight. Ignoring pain in his shoulder and head, Alex hauled him up the aisle. The crush at the door was nearly gone now, but there were still several people blocking the way. The smoke had diffused so that it was impossible to tell how close the soman was. Alex kept his lips pressed tightly together. In just a few more seconds, though, he was going to have to inhale. He staggered and fell to one knee. His chest felt as if it were about to explode. Suddenly, one of the escaping legislators reached down and grabbed Harry's other arm. Together, they dragged him through the door, and then slammed it closed behind them just as air burst from Alex's lungs.

'Thank you,' he gasped, as they continued hauling Harry's inert body toward the stairs.

The man, in his sixties like Laughlin, simply nodded.

'He saved us all,' he said.

'Get the rescue squad up here!' Alex bellowed down the stairway. 'Rescue squad!'

He rolled Laughlin to his back, preparing to begin mouth-to-mouth. The policeman's complexion was ruddy, not the violet Alex expected. His eyes were closed tightly, and his cheeks were puffed out like a squirrel's in autumn. Alex squeezed the tense skin, forcing a jet of air out between Laughlin's lips. It was only then that he realized the man had been holding his breath.

'Harry!' he shouted. 'For crying out loud, Harry, open your eyes and breathe.'

Laughlin's lids fluttered open, and he took a breath just as a rescue squad arrived with oxygen.

'I hear you, boyo,' he said weakly. 'Am I dead?'

Alex motioned the rescue people to get some oxygen on him and take over.

'I don't think so, Harry,' he said. 'I can't believe you held your breath so long.'

'Boy Scouts . . . I was the underwater champion.'

Harry closed his eyes again as the oxygen began to flow.

Alex patted the policeman on the shoulder and then headed down the stairs, anxious to get out of the way and to begin formulating some sort of plan to infiltrate Surgical Seven. He was on the capitol steps, watching the onslaught of police cruisers and rescue vehicles, when his radio sounded.

'Alex, it's Vicki. What happened?'

'He set off the gas in the State House. Thanks to Harry Laughlin, we got nearly everyone out in time, but about fifteen or so are down.'

'Well, something's happening at the hospital. Ryder, the man we left in the van, radioed a few seconds ago that a helicopter has come up from the south and has just landed on the roof of the Surgical Tower.'

'They're moving! How soon can we get a team onto the roof?'

'That depends on what they've done with explosives and what they've done to the elevators. I don't believe we'll be nearly on time to keep that chopper from taking off. Twenty minutes, maybe? I can't say for sure with all that's going to happen where you are.'

'Then I need a helicopter. Where can we get one?'

'The state police handle that. Let me make a call.'

'Hurry. If they take off, we've got problems. Whatever happens, no one should shoot the thing down. They'll have hostages.'

For an anxious two minutes, all Alex could do was pace and call out to the police and rescue people that they were dealing with a highly toxic gas, but that it had a relatively short time of potency. The first of the casualties was being hauled out when Vicki called.

'The State Police Air Wing is on the way,' she said.

'From where?'

'Norwood. Ten or twelve miles south and west of you. Go across the street to the open, flat part of Boston Common. They'll be there in ten minutes or less.'

'Less would be good.'

'They know that. These guys are the best, Alex. If anyone can pull this off, they can.'

'Did you tell them I want the thing forced down, but not shot down?'

'Yes. Apparently they're bringing someone who can help do that.'

'Keep in close touch with Ryder and get some other observers in the area of the hospital as well, if you can. If they take off, we've got to know exactly when and in what direction.'

'Roger that. Now get over to the Common. The area you want is down the hill and over to your right. I'll try and get over there to meet you. Stan's on his way to the hospital.'

Alex charged down the steps and across Beacon Street, pushing his way through the mob of protesters and legislators that was being herded in the same direction. There were already half a dozen cruisers and ambulances fighting for space on the sidewalk and street, and more strobes and sirens approaching from every direction – just the pandemonium Malloche had counted on.

Although night was settling in, the Common was still busy with couples, tourists, businesspeople, and groups of kids strolling the crisscrossing, tree-lined walkways. Many of them were now racing past Alex toward the commotion at the State House. He hurried past a tall monument and loped down a gentle slope to the broad, open field. Five minutes passed.

'Alex!'

Vicki Holcroft ran across to him, accompanied by a uniformed policeman.

'Ryder just called. They're lifting off right now,' she said, panting. 'Ryder says he knows helicopters. He thinks they're flying a Bell Jet Ranger. The State Air Wing should be here any minute.'

'Keep him on. We need to know what direction they go in.'

'I have two more men in the area watching,' she said.

A minute or so later, the thumping of its rotor announced the arrival of the state police chopper. Vicki circled a flashlight over her head. The aircraft swooped in through the evening gloom, over the buildings from the southwest, stopped almost directly overhead, and sank neatly to the turf. Vicki held her radio tightly against her ear.

'Northeast,' she said. 'It looks like they're headed toward the ocean.'

'You coming?' Alex asked.

'No. Less weight, more speed.'

'Thanks.'

Alex ducked down, sprinted to the open door, and was pulled inside by a man in short-sleeved fatigues, wearing a state police baseball cap.

'Agent Bishop, I'm Trooper Ken Barnes from STOP,' he said as they lifted off. 'Special Tactical Operations.'

'Rick Randall,' the pilot called out. 'And this geeky-looking guy next to me is Dom Gareffa. You can call him Giraffe. We would have been here a few minutes sooner, but from what I was told, I thought we'd need someone from STOP – that's Ken, there.'

'Boys' night out,' Barnes said with just the touch of a twang. 'I love it.'

'Well, as of two minutes and twenty seconds ago, they're airborne,' Alex said. 'Possibly headed northeast from Eastern Mass Medical Center.'

'Got it,' Randall said as they lifted off and banked sharply to the right. 'Keep talking.'

'It's a terrorist, his wife, and maybe some killers from his organization. He also almost certainly has a female neurosurgeon from the hospital along with them.'

'Any idea what they're flying?'

'The police spotter who's been watching the hospital thinks it's a Bell Jet Ranger.'

'That would be good news. The BJR is fine to look at, but she's slow. This Aerospatiale of ours can fly circles around any Ranger ever made, especially with them carrying a load of people.'

'Provided we can find them. Will they be on radar?'

'Not if they fly map-of-the-earth low and keep their transponder off, they won't.'

Alex looked out into the deepening blackness. Ahead of them, sky and ocean were almost one.

'Then how?' he asked.

Rick Randall turned around.

'We have our ways,' he said. He patted the control panel lovingly. 'FLIR. Forward Looking Infrared Radar.'

'Heat?'

'Exactly. Any engine for several miles, we'll know about. Right now we are moving at a hundred and forty-five knots. The Bell maxes out at one thirty, but with a full load she'll be going a hell of a lot slower than that. We'll assume your information is right, and keep on sweeping low and to the northeast.'

'Unless they're going to land on a boat, I would bet they swing more to the north,' Alex said.

'Maine?'

'Maybe.'

'You got it.'

The powerful airship nosed a few degrees west.

'These people are from Europe,' Alex said. 'How do you suppose they got a helicopter like that?'

'Probably corporate transport,' Randall replied. 'They could have bribed a corporate pilot to borrow the company's Ranger for a fun run. Everyone has his price.'

'If that's so, that's good news.'

'Why?'

'The terrorists are fanatically loyal to their boss, Claude Malloche. One of them just died so that he could make this escape. I doubt that any corporate jock would have that kind of zeal. If we can put some pressure on them, I'm willing to bet he'll fold.'

'You want this guy Malloche bad, eh?'

'I've been after him for five years,' Alex said. 'He's responsible for about five hundred deaths over his career. One of them was my brother. So yeah, I want him real bad. I have no desire to die bringing him down, though . . . unless that's what it takes.'

'Then let's hope it doesn't come to that,' Randall said. 'And remind me to stay on your good side.'

'Rick?' Gareffa said. 'Check it out.'

'Bishop, come see,' Randall called back. 'This dot right here. Altitude three hundred and fifty feet, moving to the northwest at a hundred and ten knots. Range almost five miles. Do we go after him?'

Alex barely hesitated. The sky they had to search was already vast, and getting bigger. And now, night had fallen completely.

'We do,' he said.

'Okay. Trooper Ken, you may want to get your toys ready.'

'You don't have to ask twice,' Barnes said.

He unwrapped a machine gun for himself and one for Alex.

'MP5s,' he said. 'Heckler and Koch from Germany. Best weapons makers in the world. You ever fire one?'

'As a matter of fact, they're sort of standard with the agency. I never set the world on end with my shooting, but I know the gun.'

'Good enough. We'll only use you if we have to.'

'Two and a half miles and closing,' Randall said.

'Can you raise them on the radio?' Alex asked.

'We can try, but I wouldn't recommend it until we're looking up their bunghole.'

'I agree. I'm really worried about the doctor they have with them. We've got to find a way to force them down without having them land in pieces.'

'Enter Heckler and Koch,' Barnes said.

'You know how to miss with that thing?'

'It goes against my grain, but I can try.'

'One mile,' Randall called back. 'Half a mile,' he announced a minute later. 'Let's hope it's them. They've sure not behaving like they know we're here. I'm going to wait until we have a visual, and then call them up. If it's not them, we may have shot our wad.'

They were over sparsely populated land now, knifing along at 145 knots. Another minute and they made visual contact. The totally dark shape was silhouetted against the blue-black sky and blotted out lights on the ground as it passed over them.

'Looks like a Ranger,' Gareffa said. 'No running lights, no cabin lights. That's got to be a good sign that it's them.'

Less than a hundred yards separated them now. Randall made several attempts to raise them by radio.

'Another good sign,' he said. 'I think we got 'em.'

'Not until we have them on the ground in one piece,' Alex said. 'We may be in for a firefight then. Is it worth alerting the Maine state police?'

'Can do.'

'I can't imagine they'd be interested in waltzin' with these MP5s,' Barnes said.

'Don't kid yourself. They may be better armed than we are.'

They were no more than twenty or thirty yards away now – behind the Ranger and just to the right.

'Giraffe, let's put a spot on them,' Randall ordered.

The spot hit the passenger-side window. Randall had been dead-on about the pilot and helicopter being bought. The chopper had the name and logo of Saito Industries painted on the side. He made yet another attempt to hail the pilot by radio. Less than twenty feet separated the two choppers now, as they careened through the night sky at 125 knots. Randall was handling the Aerospatiale with the deftness of a symphony conductor, inching slowly ahead of the Ranger. Alex strained to see inside as they passed. There was a woman in the forward passenger seat. Grace!

'The woman in the seat right here is one of them,' he said. 'I think she has a gun on the pilot.'

Ken Barnes settled in with his submachine gun.

'I can miss in front of them or I can miss through her head,' he said.

'No!' Alex said. 'I know you're good, but I don't want anything happening to that pilot. Let's send them a message.'

He could see both Grace and the pilot now, but none of those in the rear of the aircraft. She definitely was holding a gun.

'Anytime, trooper,' Randall said.

'How about now?'

The submachine gun rattled off a five-second burst. Reflexively, the Ranger veered off to the left.

'Put her down right now!' Randall demanded over the hailing frequency.

Then he nudged the Aero next to the Ranger's new position and repeated the order over a loudspeaker that had enough volume to awaken half the state. Barnes punctuated the order with another five-second barrage. Alex could see that there was discord in the Ranger's cabin. The pilot was shaking his head. Grace was waving her gun at him.

'We can't keep doing this indefinitely,' Randall said. 'I trust myself to be able to fly this close, but I don't trust him. Can you put a few rounds through the windshield without doing any other damage?'

'Probably not,' Barnes said. 'But I can certainly plant a few around the door.'

'Just stay away from the passenger and the pilot,' Alex insisted.

Barnes was more than up to the task. The H & K rattled off another burst. Sparks flared from just above the door, and the Ranger lurched to the left. For the Saito Industries pilot, the shots were clearly the last straw. The Ranger slowed, then began to descend.

'Way to go,' Alex said.

'Get your weapon ready, friend,' Barnes said. 'Rick, Giraffe, there's an MP5 for each of you back here.'

'Their leader just had a brain tumor removed,' Alex said. 'I don't think he'll be in any condition to mix it up or run. Just the same, keep some distance away and let me and Barnes here jump out. Don't follow us until you're absolutely certain they're not going to take off again.'

The Ranger touched down in a hay field. Randall brought the Aero in about twenty yards away and kept the spotlight drilled on the corporate chopper's side door. Alex and Barnes dove out, rolled, and came up low, sprinting across the grass. They split up as they reached the tail of the Ranger and flattened out on the ground on either side. The rotors slowed, then stopped. As soon as they had, Randall and Gareffa raced across and dove into place, one beside each of them.

'Come out with your hands high!' Alex called out. 'Quickly now.'

His heart seemed close to pumping right through his chest. Five years and it was about to end – this time for real.

'Get ready,' he said to Randall. 'They may come out trying to use the neurosurgeon as a shield.'

'What do you want to do then?'

'Remember what I said about my being willing to die if necessary to get Malloche?'

'Yeah.'

'Well, that goes double for saving the doctor. Hurry up!' he yelled at the helicopter. 'One at a time.'

The Ranger's door opened. The pilot quickly jumped down, his hands in the air. Then Grace appeared and meekly tossed her gun out before stepping onto the grass.

'Stay over there, Barnes,' Alex called out, rising to his feet.

He readied the MP5 and approached the chopper. The Malloches and Jessie were still inside.

*If you hurt her, you bastards . . .*

Alex was several feet away when Carl Gilbride appeared at the doorway, looking dazed. He reached a hand out for help, but Alex motioned him down. Another shadow, another person silhouetted in the cabin doorway. Emily DelGreco.

'Emily, where is she?' Alex asked. 'Where's Malloche?'

'They're not here,' she said grimly. 'I'm afraid we're it.'

# Chapter 43

Unnoticed in the panic and pandemonium that had gripped the city, an ambulance pulled up to the deserted bay behind the closed emergency ward of the Eastern Mass Medical Center and waited. Minutes later, Armand, Jessie, and Arlette Malloche emerged, wheeling Claude on a stretcher. With the help of the driver, a muscular Arab who was clearly another member of Malloche's gang, the stretcher was hoisted into the back of the ambulance and secured. Armand then climbed onto the passenger seat, and the large van eased away from the hospital.

Jessie set her bag of instruments and pharmaceuticals aside and sank onto the padded bench next to the stretcher. The Malloches hadn't said as much, but she could tell from snatches of conversation and the sounds of sirens audible even seven stories up, that they had ordered soman to be set off someplace in the city. And now, God only knew how many people were being sacrificed on the altar of their escape.

For an hour, Jessie had watched Armand, Grace, and Arlette gathering their weapons and packing their things. She knew they would be going momentarily, and she knew they would be taking her with them. Armand left the floor briefly and returned with the sort of stretcher used by ambulances and life-flight helicopters. Jessie made a final check of the supplies she had gathered and stopped to say good-bye to Sara and Tamika. Then, to her surprise and bewilderment, Carl and Emily were led off before she was, directed by Grace at gunpoint into the elevator.

'Where are they being taken?' Jessie had asked.

'Away,' was Arlette's annoyed reply. 'Now, let's get

Claude onto this stretcher. We have to get going.'

Cardboard had been taped over the windows in the back of the ambulance, hut Jessie could still monitor their progress through the windshield. As they were pulling away from the hospital, she heard the distinctive thrum of a helicopter, lifting off from directly overhead.

'Very clever,' she said sardonically.

'Actually, it is,' Arlette said. 'Don't you think so, dear?'

Claude, still somewhat groggy from what remained of the sedatives Jessie had been giving him, nodded and smiled.

'I do, my love,' he replied. 'I do, indeed.'

'The day we decided on your hospital,' Arlette boasted, 'we borrowed this ambulance and arranged for that helicopter and pilot up there, without even knowing we were going to have to use them. Now, I wouldn't just call that clever. I'd call it brilliant.'

'Brilliant,' Malloche echoed.

Arlette seemed displeased that Jessie hadn't commented on their genius.

'Maybe you should be doing something besides scowling, Doctor,' she said. 'Check my husband's blood pressure.'

'Whatever,' Jessie replied, rummaging through the nylon gym bag for her stethoscope and BP cuff.

'You'd best continue to do your job enthusiastically and well,' Arlette said. 'Your nurse friend is being brought along to ensure your cooperation. And Dr. Gilbride's presence up above us should assure you that once we all meet up again, you are no longer indispensable.'

'In that case, why don't you just let me out right here. I'll call a cab.'

Jessie peered ahead through the windshield. Half an hour ago, they had crossed the Tobin Bridge, cruising north. In another fifteen or twenty minutes they would be entering New Hampshire. Then what? Maine? Maybe even Canada. Arlette was right. Their preparations for the contingencies surrounding her husband's surgery *had* been brilliant. And now, it actually seemed they were going to make it.

Aside from Arlette's steely anger at the betrayal in the OR, there had been few threats directed toward Jessie. Still, she sensed that no matter how good a job she had done and would do in treating Claude Malloche, there was a very good chance that neither she nor her two colleagues in the helicopter would be allowed to remain alive. They were the only ones who would know where the killers had gone after leaving Boston.

Jessie was fearful for the others on Surgical Seven who knew what Malloche and his wife looked like, particularly Michelle Booker and the team from the OR. From the moment Arlette ordered her away to the ambulance, she had been terrified that they would set the timers on the explosives and kill everyone remaining on the floor. Now, she asked once more if that had been their plan, and once more Arlette gave her reassurance that the telephones had all been removed, the elevator disabled, and the doors rigged to detonate if they were opened, but that no timers had been set to destroy the neurosurgical floor and its patients.

'You had better be telling me the truth,' Jessie said.

Arlette looked at her dispassionately

'I will say this one more time. You are no longer indispensable to us. I would suggest you take care how you speak to me.'

The smugness in the woman's expression and words, the unbridled arrogance, had Jessie on the brink of lunging at her to gouge away her eyes. If Armand turned and shot her to death, so what? She was as good as dead anyway. At least by maiming Arlette, she would be hurting both of the Malloches before she died.

*Hurting both of the Malloches . . .*

The words resonated in Jessie's head.

*Hurting both of the Malloches . . .*

For a time, the notion swirled about without focus. But there was something there . . . something. Suddenly, Jessie knew. There was a chance, the smallest chance, for her to take control – to put her captors to the ultimate test. The plan was shaky, but it was still a plan. It required careful movement on her part, plus an unerring insight into Claude and Arlette. Which of them was the crueler? Which the more devoted to the other? Which the less likely to sit by and watch the other die? And to succeed, the plan required two other elements as well – the absolute devotion to the Malloches of both Armand and the driver, and an inordinate amount of luck.

They had just passed the sign welcoming them to New Hampshire when Jessie put her plan in motion. She knelt beside the stretcher and, under Arlette's watchful eye, examined Claude carefully. Then she went back and reexamined his eyes with her ophthalmoscope.

'Any headache at all?' she asked.

'Not really,' he replied. 'Why?'

'Squeeze my hand, please. . . . Now with your other hand. Spread your fingers and don't let me push them together. Harder. Is that the hardest you can push against me?'

'Yes.'

'Is something wrong?' Arlette asked.

'I don't think so. I don't know.'

'What are you talking about? He seems fine to me.'

'Mr. Malloche, repeat this phrase after me: Methodist Episcopal.'

'Methodist Episcopal,' Claude said, with the tiniest hitch.

Jessie shook her head just enough for the gesture to be noticed. Saying the two words, used by many physicians as part of their neurologic exam, was awkward enough to have tested even Demosthenes.

'There are some neurologic signs that haven't been present before,' she said. 'Very soft signs – a slight thickness in his speech as you just heard, a slight weakness in his right hand but I think both signs are real.'

'What does that mean?' Arlette asked.

'Maybe the early signs of a buildup in intracranial pressure.'

'Like the Devereau woman?'

'Yes, exactly.'

'What do you want to do about it?'

'I'm going to increase the steroids he's been getting, and add another medicine to reduce swelling.'

'Do whatever you have to.'

Jessie drew up some steroid and injected it into Claude's IV line. Then she drew up a second medicine and left the syringe just on the surface of her supplies, close at hand.

*Claude or Arlette?*

Another twenty minutes passed. They had traversed the narrow southeast corner of New Hampshire, entered Maine, and then left the highway. Nightfall was complete now. They were rolling along darkened country roads and through small villages. Jessie sensed the driver had taken the route before – probably on a practice run. As best as she could figure, they were still headed north, maybe northwest. Claude had drifted off to sleep. Arlette seemed heavy-lidded, but she remained vigilant, her stubby machine gun in her lap, her finger on the trigger.

'Where are we headed?' Jessie asked, loudly enough to wake Claude up.

'To a quiet place where my husband can finish his recovery. I don't believe we'll be on the road too much longer.'

Jessie knew she had to act soon. Once Carl, Emily, and the others met up with them, the chance would be gone. She was willing to risk her own life, but there was no way she could stand firm while someone threatened to kill her closest friend. And under pressure, there was every reason to believe Carl would crack. It had to be now. First, though, she had a decision to make.

*Claude or Arlette?*

She examined Claude once more and asked him all the same questions as before, ensuring that he was awake and alert. Then she motioned Arlette over. The decision had been made. She was the indispensable one. She was the one to fear.

'I think the swelling may still be increasing,' Jessie lied. 'Look. Look at what happens to the corner of his mouth when he shows his teeth.'

As Arlette moved forward, Jessie leaned back and slipped her fingers around the loaded syringe. She had chosen an exposed spot just at the base of the woman's neck.

'I don't see –'

Arlette Malloche never finished her sentence. In one motion, Jessie straightened up, drove the needle to the hilt into the trapezius muscle, and depressed the plunger. Arlette cried out and whirled, her gun leveled at Jessie's face.

'Kill me and you're dead,' Jessie said quickly. 'Claude, I've just injected your wife with a lethal dose of a medicine called Anectine. It's just like curare. In a minute or so, every muscle in her body will be paralyzed. She will be unable to breathe. But until the very moment she asphyxiates to death, she will be wide awake and aware of everything. Tell them to stop the ambulance. I can save her, but I won't unless you do as I say.'

'Don't believe her!' Arlette cried.

But her gun hand had already begun to shake. Claude forced himself up onto one elbow.

'Four minutes,' Jessie said. 'If I don't get a breathing tube in her within four minutes, her brain will be irreparably damaged. After that, you would not want her to be saved.'

Jessie made a theatrical point of looking at her watch. Claude Malloche's eyes met his wife's, and in that moment, Jessie knew she had chosen her victim well. Whether or not Arlette would have reacted as her husband was about to, she would never know. But Jessie had her doubts. Arlette, stunned and undergoing massive chemical change in her muscles, could no longer hold the gun up at all, and in fact, was having difficulty holding herself up as well. Still, she would not ask for help.

'Stop the ambulance immediately, Faoud!' Claude barked.

Without a word, the driver pulled over. Jessie took two rolls of adhesive tape from her bag and had Claude order the two men out of the cab and onto their faces on the ground. Faoud quickly did as he was ordered. Armand hesitated.

'A minute's gone,' Jessie said.

She gestured at Arlette, who was bracing herself on the seat but was no longer capable of speaking.

'You'll regret this,' the Mist growled. 'Armand, just do as she says or Arlette will die. We will get our chance. I promise you that.'

Slowly, shielded from Armand's line of sight by Malloche's stretcher, Jessie slid her hand over and wrapped it around Arlette's gun, adjusting her finger onto the trigger.

'Armand!' Malloche snapped. 'Quickly! Do as she says.'

Twisted around in his seat, the thin, ferret-eyed man looked at Jessie with hatred. But he didn't move.

'Armand!' Malloche barked again.

Jessie could see the indecision on the young killer's face. The muscles by his jaws twitched. His lips tightened. *Prison!* Jessie could almost hear the thought in his mind. She tightened her grip on the gun.

Suddenly Armand's pistol was up and firing. Jessie dove to the floor, knocking Arlette over as two shots ricocheted off the rear door. Then she shot back, a prolonged burst of machine gun fire up under the stretcher into the back of Armand's seat. The killer screamed once as he was slammed backward into the dashboard. Behind Jessie, the rear doors were thrown open. But before Faoud could even get a shot off, Jessie ripped him across the chest with another volley. Blood erupted from half a dozen wounds. The heavyset man spun around nearly full circle, and dropped to the ground.

Jessie, who had never handled anything more lethal than an air rifle, was astonished at how easy it had been to kill with a weapon built for that purpose. Her heart was pounding, but she was surprised at how little shock or remorse she was feeling. She took some time to catch her breath, and assured herself that both of the killers were dead. Then she set the machine gun aside and quickly taped Malloche's wrists and ankles to the stretcher.

'Help her,' Malloche said hoarsely, gesturing to his wife, who was now on her back on the ambulance floor, totally awake, but unable to breathe, staring wide-eyed at the ceiling, her paralyzed limbs in an odd, awkward position.

*No tube!* Jessie's mind screamed. *Just lie there! For Lisa and Scolari, and those people in the lab, and all the others you have killed, just lie there and die!*

'I wish I could do what I want to, Arlette,' she said as she taped the woman's ankles together, then her wrists. 'I really do.'

She retrieved the laryngoscope, endotracheal tube, and Ambu breathing bag from her kit. Then she pulled Arlette until her head hung backward out the rear door of the ambulance – a position that straightened her trachea. Finally, she hunched down beside where Faoud lay to get a good view along the lighted arm of the laryngoscope into Arlette's throat. The breathing tube slipped easily between the woman's vocal cords. Jessie inflated the balloon around it to seal it in place.

Finally, she dragged Arlette back into the van next to her husband and began ventilating her with the black latex bag. In just a few minutes, she would be breathing on her own. Even then, Jessie had no intention of removing the thick tube. It would be a perverse pleasure leaving it in Arlette's throat, but a pleasure nonetheless.

As expected, in five minutes or so, Arlette Malloche was breathing on her own, shaking her head against the profound discomfort of the tube, and piercing Jessie with a look so intense that it was unsettling even though the woman's wrists and ankles were tightly bound. Jessie responded with a bland grin and a thumbs-up sign.

Thanks to a med school rotation riding on the ambulances, she had little trouble working the radio. In just seconds, the C-Med operator had patched her through to the Maine State Police.

'We've got an awful lot of people looking for you,' the officer said. 'One in particular. Wait a minute.'

There was some static, then Alex's voice.

'Jessie?'

'Alex, where are you?'

'In the sky, headed your way.'

'They've got Emily.'

'Not anymore, they don't. She's okay. So is Gilbride. The pilot of the helicopter told us where they were headed in Maine, so we've been looking for you along the way. Where's Malloche?'

'Right here, Alex. He and Arlette are right here, but they can't come to the phone.'

'How did – ?'

'I'll tell you when I see you. Can you find me?'

'We think so. Listen, turn on the headlights and every other light and flasher you can find. It shouldn't be long.'

'Were many people killed by the soman?'

'It was bad, but it could have been much worse. Hang on, we'll be there soon. I'll tell you about it then.'

'It's almost over, Alex.'

Jessie switched on the ambulance lights and flashers. Then she checked on her prisoners and walked across the road to a small field. The night air was chilly and sweet. Overhead, the pitch black rural Maine sky was radiant with stars. Exhausted and drained, she sank onto the cool unmown grass and waited.

Ten silent minutes later, she realized that one of the thousands of stars was growing larger and moving steadily in her direction.

# Author's Note

While a flexible robot such as ARTIE remains a thing of our future, many of the neurosurgical innovations described in this novel, including intraoperative MRI, are available today. The remarkable evolution of computer technology that has revolutionized much of our world over the last three decades has advanced our surgical capabilities beyond what even the visionaries of medicine could have predicted. High-speed graphic computers are radically changing the face of surgery and information exchange. Virtual reality, the assembly of realistic realms within the computer environment, now enables a surgeon to see and experience in advance the intricate, physiological relationships and anatomical problems he or she will encounter during an operation.

Minimally invasive surgery using thin, flexible endoscopes is being applied to more and more clinical disorders, and the use of lasers and precisely guided radiation as alternatives to the scalpel is growing daily. Telesurgery, with the surgeon operating through robotic hands that may be hundreds of miles away, is being pioneered by the United States military. In the not-too-distant future, a surgeon may be able to perform simultaneous operations on patients in locations across the globe from one another, or even in outer space.

In fact, ARTIE's day may not be that far off. Currently, the use of robotic arms for performing tumor biopsies and placing counter-stimulating electrodes in the brains of epileptics is nearly routine. And one team of neurosurgeons is experimenting with a small, intraoperative robot that is steered through the brain to its target using strong magnetic fields.

Michael Palmer, M.D.

# References

Grimson, W. E. L., Kikinis, R., Jolesz, F. A., Black, P. M. 'Image-guided surgery.' *Scientific American*, June 1999; pp. 62–69.

MIT Medical Vision Group. http://www.ai.mit.edu/projects/medicalvision/surgery/surgical_navigation.html.

Textbook on computer workstation-guided neurosurgery. Alexander, E., III, and Maciunas, R. J. *Advanced Neurosurgical Navigation*. Stuttgart, New York: Thieme Medical Publishers, Inc., 1999. (See http://www.thieme.com/onGJHFFAEHKIEFM/display/5 90.)

# SIDE
# EFFECTS

*Michael Palmer*

arrow books

# Acknowledgment

A novel is hardly the sole endeavor many believe. I am both grateful and fortunate to have had Jeanne Bernkopf, my editor, and Linda Grey, editorial director at Bantam, in my writing life.

# PROLOGUE

# Mecklenburg, Germany
## August 1944

Willi Becker leaned against the coarse wood siding of the officers' club and squinted up at the late afternoon sun, a pale disk rendered nearly impotent by the dust from a hundred allied bombings of industrial targets surrounding the Ravensbrück concentration camp for women. He closed his eyes and for an instant thought he heard the drone of enemy planes somewhere to the south.

"Not a moment too soon, Dr. Becker," he muttered. "You will be leaving this hellhole not a moment too soon." He checked the chronometer his brother, Edwin, had sent him from "a grateful patient" in the Dachau camp. Nearly fifteen-thirty. After months of the most meticulous preparations there were now only hours to go. He felt an electric excitement.

Across the dirt courtyard, clusters of prisoners, their shaved heads glistening, worked on bomb shelters, while their SS guards jockeyed for bits of shade beneath the overhangs of barracks. Becker recognized two of the women: a tall, awkward teenager named Eva and a feckless Russian who had encouraged him to call her Bunny. They were but two of the three dozen or so subjects whose examinations he was forced to omit in the interest of escape.

3

For a minute, Becker battled the urge to call the two scarecrow women over and tell them that fate had denied them their parts in the magnificent work that scholars and generations to come would hail as the start of the Beckerian population control. Beckerian. The word, though he spoke it daily, still had a thrilling ring. Newtonian physics, Shakespearean drama, Malthusian philosophy; upon so very few had human history bestowed such honor. In time, Becker was certain, this immortality would be his. After all, he was still six weeks shy of his thirtieth birthday, yet already acknowledged for his brilliance in the field of reproductive physiology.

Adjusting the collar on the gray-green SS uniform he was wearing for the last time, the tall, classically Nordic physician crossed the courtyard and headed toward the research buildings on the north edge of camp.

The Ravensbrück medical staff, once numbering more than fifty, had dwindled to a dozen. Himmler, bending to the cry for physicians in military hospitals, had suspended the experiments in gas gangrene and bone grafting, as well as those on battlefield cauterization of wounds using coals and acid. The doctors responsible for those programs had been transferred. Only the sterilization units remained, three of them in all, each devoted to the problem of eliminating the ability to procreate without impairing the ability to perform slave labor. Becker strode past the empty laboratories—another sign of the inevitable—and turned onto "Grünestrasse," the tarmac track on which the officials and research facilities of his Green Unit were located. To the east, he could see the camouflage-painted chimney tops of the crematorium. A gentle west wind was bearing the fetid smoke and ash away from the camp. Becker smiled thinly and nodded. The Mecklenburger Bucht, fifty kilometers of capricious Baltic Sea between Rostock and the Danish island fishing village of Gedser, would be calm. One less variable to be concerned about.

Becker was mentally working through the other incalculables when he glanced through the windows of his office. Dr. Franz Müller, his back turned, was inspecting the volumes in Becker's library. Becker tensed. A visit from Müller, the head of the Blue Unit and director of reproductive studies, was not unusual, but the man was considerate to a fault and almost always called ahead.

Was Müller's visit on this of all days a coincidence? Becker paused by the doorway to his office and prepared for the cerebral swordplay at which the older man was such a master. He congratulated himself for holding back the documentation, however scant, of Blue Unit's deception. Müller's blade might be as quick as his own, but his own had poison on its tip. Müller, he felt certain, was a sham.

The Blue Unit work concerning the effect of ovarian irradiation on fertility looked promising on paper. However, Becker had good reason to believe that not one prisoner had actually been treated with radiation. The data were being falsified by Müller and his cohort, Josef Rendl. Whether they had gone so far as to assist prisoners in escaping, Becker was unsure, but he suspected as much. His proof, though skimpy, would have been enough to discredit, if not destroy, both men. However, their destruction had never meant as much to him as their control.

In an effort to gain some tiny advantage, Becker opened the outside door silently and tiptoed up the three stairs to his office door. Not a sound. Not even the creak of a floorboard.

Becker opened the door quickly. Müller as perched on the corner of his desk, looking directly at him. "Ah, Willi, my friend. Please excuse the brazenness of my intrusion. I was just passing by and remembered your mentioning that Fruhopf's *Reproductive Physiology* was among your holdings." First exchange to the master.

"It is good to see you, Franz. My library and laboratory are always yours, as I have told you many times." A perfunctory handshake, and Becker moved to his seat behind the desk. "Did you find it?"

"Pardon?"

"The Fruhopf. Did you find it?"

"Oh. Yes. Yes, I have it right here."

"Fine. Keep it as long as you wish."

"Thank you." Müller made no move to leave. Instead, he lowered himself into the chair opposite Becker and began packing his pipe from a worn leather pouch.

Not even the formality of a request to stay. Becker's wariness grew. Hidden by the desk, his long, manicured fingers undulated nervously. "Sweet?" he asked, sliding a dish of mints across the desktop. It was Müller's show, and Müller could make the initial move.

"Thank you, no." Müller grinned and patted his belly. "You heard about Paris?"

Becker nodded. "No surprise. Except perhaps for the speed with which Patton did the job."

"I agree. The man is a devil." Müller ran his fingers through his thick, muddy blond hair. He was Becker's equal in height, perhaps an inch or so more, but he was built like a Kodiak bear. "And in the east the Russians come and come. We wipe out a division and two more take its place. I hear they are nearing the oil field at Ploesti."

"They are a barbarous people. For decades all they have done is rut about and multiply. What our armies cannot do to them, their own expanding population will eventually accomplish."

"Ah, yes," Müller said. "The theories of your sainted Thomas Malthus. Keep our panzers in abeyance, and let our enemies procreate themselves into submission."

Becker felt his hackles rise. Cynicism was the finest honed of Müller's strokes. An irritated, angry opponent left openings, made mistakes. Calm down, he urged himself. Calm down and wait until the man declares himself. Could he know about the escape? The mere thought made the Green Unit leader queasy. "Now, Franz," he said evenly, "you know how much I enjoy discussing philosophy with you, especially Malthusian philosophy, but right now we have a war to win, yes?"

Müller's eyes narrowed. "*Quatsch*," he said.

"What?"

"I said *Quatsch*, Willi. Absolute nonsense. First of all, we are not going to win any war. You know that as well as I do. Secondly, I do not believe you care. One way or the other."

Becker stiffened. The bastard had found out. Somehow he had found out. He shifted his right hand slightly on his knee and gauged the distance to the Walther revolver in his top left drawer. "How can you impugn me in this way?"

Müller smiled and sank back in his chair. "You misunderstand me, Willi. What I am saying is a compliment to you as a scientist and philosopher. *Surtout le travaille*. Above all the work. Is that not how you feel? On second thought, I will have that sweet, if you please."

Becker slid the dish across. Here he was, bewildered, apprehensive, and totally off balance, and still with no idea of the reason for Müller's visit. Inwardly, and grudgingly, he smiled. The man was slick. A total bastard, but a slick one. "I believe in my research, if that is what you mean."

"Precisely."

"And *your* research, Franz, how does *it* go?" Time for a counterthrust.

"It goes and it stops and it goes again. You know how that is."

Sure, sure, but mostly it doesn't exist, Becker wanted to say. Instead, he nodded his agreement.

"Willi, my friend, I fear the war will be over anytime now. Weeks, days, hours; no one seems to know. I have no notion of what will happen to us—to those in our laboratory—after that. Perhaps our research will be made public, perhaps not. I feel it is crucial for each unit, Blue, Green, and Brown, to know exactly the nature and status of the work being done by the others. That way, we can be as well prepared as possible for whatever the future brings." Becker's eyes widened. "I have decided to start with your Green Unit," Müller went on. "A meeting has been scheduled for twenty-one hundred hours this evening in the Blue Unit conference room. Please be prepared to present your research in detail at that time."

"What?"

"And Willi, I would like time to study your data before then. Please have them on my desk by nineteen hundred hours." Müller's eyes were flint.

Becker felt numb. His data, including the synthesis and biological properties of Estronate 250, were sealed in a dozen notebooks, hidden in the hull of a certain Rostock fishing boat. His mind raced. "My . . . my work is very fragmented, Franz. I . . . I shall need at least a day, perhaps two, to organize my data." This can't be happening, he thought. Nineteen hundred hours is too early. Even twenty-one hundred hours is too soon. "Let me show you what I have," Becker said, reaching toward the drawer with the Walther.

At that instant, Dr. Josef Rendl stepped inside the office doorway. Rendl's aide, a behemoth whom Becker knew only as Stossel, remained just outside in the hall. They had been somewhere out there all the time. Becker felt sure of it. Rendl, a former pediatrician, was a short, doughy man with a pasty complexion and a high-pitched laugh, both of which Becker found disgusting. Becker's information had it that Rendl's mother was a Jew, a fact that had been carefully concealed. For a frozen second, two, Becker sized up the situation. Müller was but two meters away, Rendl three, and the animal, Stossel, perhaps five. No real chance for three kills, even with surprise on his side, which, it seemed now, might not be the case. The battle would have to be verbal . . . at least for the moment.

Becker nodded at the newcomer. "Welcome, Josef. My, my. The entire Blue Unit brain trust. What a pleasant honor."

"Willi." Rendl smiled and returned the gesture. "Leutnant Stossel and I were just passing by and noticed the two of you in here. What do you think of the meetings? A good idea to present our work to one another, no?"

You smarmy son of a Jew whore, Becker thought. "Yes. Yes. An excellent idea," he said.

"And you will honor us by presenting the Green Unit biochemical studies tonight?" Rendl, though an oberst, exactly the same rank as Willi, often spoke with Müller's authority dusting his words.

Becker, fighting to maintain composure, sucked in an extra measure of air. "Tonight would be acceptable." Both of the other men nodded. "But," he added, "tomorrow evening would be much better." Because, he smiled to himself, I intend to be a thousand kilometers away from here by then.

"Oh?" Franz Müller propped his chin on one hand.

"Yes. I have a few final chemical tests to run on Estronate Two-fifty. Some loose ends in the initial set of experiments." As Becker scrambled through the words, searching for some kind of purchase, an idea began to take hold. "There's an extraction with ether that I was unable to complete because my supply ran out. Late yesterday, several five-gallon tins arrived. You signed for them yourself." Müller nodded. Becker's words became more confident. "Well, if you would give me tonight to complete this phase of my work, I shall gladly present what I have tomorrow. You must remember that what I have is not much. Estronate Two-fifty is far more theory than fact. A promising set of notions, with only the roughest of preliminary work on humans."

Müller pushed himself straighter in his chair and leveled his gaze across the desk. "Actually, Willi, I do not believe that what you say is true." The words, a sledge-hammer, were delivered with silky calm.

"Wh . . . . what are you talking about?" The question in Becker's mind was no longer whether Müller knew anything, but how much. His trump card—Blue Unit's falsified data—would have to be played. The only issue now was timing.

"What I am talking about is information that your work on Estronate Two-fifty is rather advanced."

"That's nonsense," Becker shot back.

"Further, that you are lacking only stability studies and the elimination of a troublesome side effect—some sort of bleeding tendency, is it?—before more extensive clinical testing can be done. Why, Willi, are you keeping this information from us? You have here, perhaps, the most awesome discovery—even the most awesome weapon—of our time, yet you claim to know nothing."

"Ridiculous."

"No, Willi. Not ridiculous. Information straight from a source in your laboratory. Now either we receive a full disclosure of the exact status of your work, or I shall see to it that Mengele or even Himmler receives the information we have."

"Your accusations are preposterous."

"We shall judge that after you have presented your work. Tonight, then?"

"No. Not tonight." It was time. "My work is not ready for presentation." Becker paused theatrically, drumming his fingertips on the desktop and then stroking them bowlike across one another. "Is yours?"

"What?"

Becker sensed, more than saw, Müller stiffen. "Your work. The Blue Unit radiation studies. You see, the two of you are not the only ones with—what was the word you used?—ah, yes, sources, that was it. Sources."

Rendl and Müller exchanged the fraction of a glance. The gesture was enough to dispel any doubt as to the validity of Becker's information.

"Willi, Willi," Müller said, shaking his head. "You try my patience. I shall give you until tomorrow night. Meanwhile, we shall organize our data and present them at the same time."

"Excellent," Becker said, reveling in being on the offensive at last. "And, please, do try to have some of your human subjects available for examination. It would lend so much to the understanding of your work." This time, Müller and Rendl shared a more pronounced look.

"You don't really care, Willi, do you?" Müller said suddenly.

"I . . . I'm afraid I don't know what you mean, Franz."

"You see only yourself. Your place in history. The here and now mean nothing to you. Germany, the Reich, the Jews, the Americans, the prisoners, your colleagues— all are the same to you. All are nothing."

"You have your mistresses, and I have mine," Becker said simply. "Is immortality so homely that I should throw her out of my bed? You are right, Franz. I do not concern myself with petty day-to-day issues. I have already reached planes of theory and research that few have ever even dreamed of. Should I worry about the price of eggs, or whether the Führer's hemorrhoids are inflamed, or whether the prisoners here at Ravensbrück are pathetic inside the wire or without, on top of the dirt or beneath it?"

"Willi, Willi, Willi." Müller's voice and eyes held pity rather than reproach.

Becker looked over at Rendl, and there, too, saw condescension, not ire. Don't you dare pity me, he wanted to scream. Revere me. The children of your children will prosper because of me. The *lebensraum* for which so many have fought and died will be attained not with bullets, but with my equations, my solution. Mine!

Müller broke the silence. "We are all with the same laboratory. We all stand to lose much if we fall into disfavor— either now with the Reich or soon with the Allies. I expect a full disclosure of your work with Estronate Two-fifty, Dr. Becker."

Becker nodded his acquiescence and silently prayed that his portrayal of a beaten man would be convincing.

Minutes later, the three men from the Blue Unit were gone. Becker closed his eyes and massaged the tightness at the base of his neck. Then he poured three fingers of Polish vodka from a bottle Edwin had sent him, and drank it in a single draught. The encounter with Müller and Rendl, triumphant though it had been, had left him drained. He fingered his chronometer. Was there time for a nap? No, he decided. No sleeping until this filthy camp with its petty people and skeleton prisoners was a thing of the past.

He walked briskly from his office to the low, frame, barracklike building that housed the Green Unit's bio-chemical research section. With glances to either side, he backed through the rear door and locked it from the inside. The wooden shutters were closed and latched, creating a darkness inside that was tangible.

The flashlight was by the door—where he had hung it that morning. Using the hooded beam, Becker counted the slate squares making up the top of his long central workbench. Reaching beneath the fifth one, he pulled. The cabinet supporting the slate slid out from the others. Beneath it, hidden from even a detailed search, was the circular mouth of a tunnel.

"And the rockets red glare, the bombs bursting in air. . . ." Alfi Runstedt sang the words as he dug, although he had no idea of their meaning. The song, he knew, was the American anthem, and this day, at least, that was all that mattered. As a child in Leipzig, he had spent hours beside his family's new Victrola memorizing selections from a thick album of anthems of the world. Even then, the American "Star Spangled Banner" had been his favorite.

Now, he would have the chance to see the country itself and, even more wonderful, to become an American.

"Oh say does that star spangled ba-a-ner-er ye-et wa-ave. . . ." With one syllable, he rammed the spade into the sandy soil. With the next, he threw the dirt up to the side of the grave. The trench, three feet deep, was better than half done. Lying on the grass to Alfi's left, two meters from him, were the corpses of the peasant woman and her son, which would be laid inside as soon as the proper depth was reached. Alfi Runstedt paid them no mind.

He was stripped to his ample waist. Dirt, mingling with sweat, was turning his arms and walrus torso into a quagmire. The thick, red hair on his chest was plastered into what looked like a fecal mat. His SS uniform pants were soaked and filthy. ". . . and the home of the brave. O-oh say can you see. . . ."

"Alfi, take a break if you need one. We cannot make any moves until dark. I told you that." From his perch atop a large boulder, Willi Becker gazed down into the narrow crypt.

Alfi stopped his digging and dragged a muddy wrist across his muddy forehead. "It is nothing, Herr Oberst. Believe me, nothing. I would dig a thousand such holes in the ground for the honor you have done me and the reward you have promised. Tell me, do you know if many American women are thin like Betty Grable? One of the men in the barracks at Friedrichshafen had her picture by his cot."

"I don't know, Alfi." Becker laughed. "Soon, you shall be able to see for yourself. If we meet the boat in Denmark and if my cousin has made all the arrangements, we should be in North America with valid papers within a few weeks."

"Big ifs, yes?"

"Not so big. The biggest if anyplace is money, and hopefully we have enough of that. We'll need some luck, but our chances of making it out undetected seem rather good."

"And you do not think me a traitor or a coward for wanting to leave with you?"

"Am I?"

"You are different, Herr Oberst. You have research to complete. Important research. I am just a junior officer in an army that is losing a war."

"Ah, but you are also my aide. My *invaluable* aide. Was it not you who informed me of the old system of drainage pipes running beneath Ravensbrück?"

"Well, it was just my fortune to have worked with the sanitation department when I was younger and—"

"And was it not you who chose to keep that information our little secret and to help me with the connecting tunnel?"

" Well, I guess—"

"So don't say you are not deserving, Unteroffizier Runstedt. Don't ever say that."

"Thank you, Oberst. Thank you." And at that moment, Alfred Runstedt, the man who had overseen or assisted in the extermination of several thousand Ravensbrück prisoners, the man who had, not an hour before, calmly strangled to death a woman, her young son, her husband, and her father, wept with joy.

Hollywood, New York, baseball, Chicago—now just words, they would soon be his life. Since the June invasion at Normandy, and even more frequently since the abortive July attempt to assassinate the Führer at Rastenburg, in eastern Prussia, he had been forced to endure the recurrent nightmare of his own capture and death. In one version of the dream, it was execution by hanging; in another, by firing squad. In still another, ghostly prisoners, totally naked, beat him to death with sticks.

Soon, the nightmares would stop.

The grave was nearly deep enough. The wooded grove which was serving as an impromptu cemetery accepted the evening more quickly than did the adjacent field and was nearly dark when Becker pushed himself off the rock. "So, just a few more spadefuls, is it?" he said.

"I think so," Alfi answered. He had donned a windbreaker against the chill of dusk. His uniform shirt, hanging on a branch, would be kept clean for a final display.

"Cigar?"

"Thank you, Herr Oberst." Alfi paused to light the narrow cheroot, one of a seemingly endless supply possessed by Becker.

"I think you are deep enough now," Becker said after a half dozen more passes. "Let me give you a hand."

Alfi scrambled from the grave. One with the arms, and one with the legs, the two men unceremoniously tossed the bodies of the woman and the boy into the pit. Alfi replaced the dirt with the spade. Becker helped, using his foot.

"Forgive me if I am out of line, Herr Oberst," Alfi said as he shoveled, "but is there any possibility of notifying my sister at the munitions plant in Schwartzheide that, contrary to the reports she will receive, I am alive and well?"

Becker chuckled and shook his head. "Alfi, Alfi. I have explained to you the need for secrecy. Why do you think I waited until only a few hours ago to tell you of my escape plan? I, myself, have been measuring every word for weeks, afraid I might give it away. For now, and for the foreseeable future both of us must remain among the lamentable casualties of the war. Even my brother, Edwin, at the camp in Dachau will not know."

"I understand," Alfi said, realizing that he did not—at least not totally.

"By the morning, you and I shall be both free and dead." Becker stamped on the topsoil of the grave and began throwing handfuls of dusty sand and pine needles over the fresh dirt.

The idea of using the bodies of the farmer and his son-in-law was sheer genius, Becker acknowledged. Originally, he had planned to have the two farmers supply him with transportation to Rostock. Their lorry would now run just as well with him at the wheel. The other refinements in his original plan were dazzling. When all was said and done, Müller and Rendl would be left to face the music with little or no suspicion that he was still alive.

". . . and the home of the brave." Becker joined the startled Runstedt in the final line.

Both Runstedt and Becker groaned repeatedly with the effort of dragging first one body and then another through the sewage pipe to the false cabinet in the biochemical research building. Intermixed with the sounds of their effort were the scratching and scraping of countless rats, scurrying about in the pitch darkness.

The young farmer was, in height and frame, a virtual twin of Becker's. The older man, like Runstedt, was heavy, but taller than Runstedt by several centimeters.

"Don't worry about the difference in your heights, Alfi," Becker had reassured him. "By the time the explosion and fire are through with these bodies, no one will want to get any closer to them than it takes to remove our watches, rings, identification medallions, and wallets."

With Becker pushing from below, Runstedt hauled the corpses through the base of the cabinet and stretched them out on the wooden floor.

"Perfect, perfect," Becker said, scrambling through the hole. "We are right on time."

"Oberst," Alfi said, "I have one question, if I may."

"Of course."

"How will we keep the tunnel from being discovered after the fire and explosion?"

"Hah! An excellent point," Becker exclaimed. "One, I might add, that I am not at all surprised to have you make. I have kept the steel plate you removed to make the opening in the pipe. It fits perfectly, and stays in place with several small hooks I have welded on. With ashes and debris piled on top, I doubt the pipe will ever be discovered."

"Brilliant. Herr Oberst, you are a truly brilliant man."

"Thank you, Unteroffizier. And now, we must check. Have you said anything to anyone which might suggest you are planning to leave tonight?"

"No, sir."

"Good. And have you told the men in your barrack that you will be working late in the laboratory with me?"

"Yes, Oberst."

"Wonderful. We are ready to arrange the ether, to set the charge and the timer, and to exchange clothes with our friends here."

"Then it is off to hot dogs and Betty Grable," Alfi said.

"Hot dogs and Betty Grable," Becker echoed. "But first a toast to our success thus far. Amaretto?"

"Cheroots! Amaretto! My God, Oberst, how do you keep coming up with these things?" Alfi took the proffered glass, inhaled the wonderful almond scent, and then drained the liqueur in a gulp. The cyanide, its deadly aroma and taste masked, took just seconds to work.

Becker was removing his uniform and jewelry as Runstedt, writhing and vomiting on the floor, breathed his last.

With some effort, Becker dressed the young farmer in his own uniform, adding a ring, billfold, identification necklace, and, finally, Edwin's watch, an elegant piece which many in the camp associated with him.

Next, he stepped back and, with the use of the hooded flashlight, surveyed the scene. Everything, everyone had to be perfectly placed.

He undressed the farmer who was to have served as Alfi's double, tossed the clothes to one side, and then dumped the naked body down the tunnel. "Now, Alfi, my most loyal of servants, we must find a place for you." He shone the torch on the contorted, violet face by his feet.

In minutes the arrangement was complete. The young farmer's body lay in the center of the laboratory, his face resting beside a laboratory timer and a five-gallon tin of ether. Several other tins were spaced throughout the dry, wooden building. Alfi's body lay near the door, as far from the explosive vapors as possible. It would be the validity of Runstedt's face which would assure acceptance of Becker's own demise.

The simple elegance of the whole plan was as pleasing as a major research success, and Becker felt ballooned with pride as he made a final survey of the scene.

He checked the small ignition charge and set the timer for ten minutes.

Willi Becker was grinning as he dropped into the tunnel and pulled the workbench cabinet back in place. He sealed the drainage pipe opening, and without a glance at the farmer's body, crawled toward the exit beyond the camp's electrified fence.

He was behind the wheel of the lorry, a quarter mile from the camp, when the peaceful night sky turned red-gold. Seconds later, he heard the muffled series of explosions.

"Good-bye, Josef Rendl," he said. "I shall enjoy reading in *The New York Times* of your trial and execution. And as for you, Dr. Müller, it is game and match between us, eh? A shame you shall never know who really won. Perhaps someday, if you survive, I will send you a postcard."

His wife and son were waiting for him in Rostock. As Becker bounced down the road, he began humming the "Star Spangled Banner."

# THE PRESENT

# 1

## Sunday 9 December

The morning was typical of December in Massachusetts. A brushed aluminum sky blended into three-day-old snow covering the cornfields along Route 127. Dulled by streaks of road salt, Jared Samuels's red MGTD roadster still sparkled like a flare against the landscape.

From the passenger seat, Kate Bennett watched her husband negotiate the country road using only the thumb and first two fingers of his left hand. His dark brown eyes, though fixed on the road, were relaxed, and he seemed to be singing to himself. Kate laughed.

"Hey, Doc," Jared asked glancing over, "just what are you laughing at?"

"You."

"Well, that's a relief. For a moment there I thought you were laughing at *me*. . . . Tell me what I was doing that was so funny, I might want to write it down."

"Not funny," Kate said. "Just nice. It makes me happy to see you happy. There's a peacefulness in you that I haven't seen since the campaign began."

"Then you should have turned on the bedroom light last night at, oh, eleven-thirty, was it?"

"You didn't just pass out after?"

"Nope. Five minutes of absolute Nirvana . . . then I

21

passed out." He flashed the smile that had always been reserved for her alone.

"I love you, you know," Kate said.

Jared looked at her again. It had been a while since either of them had said the words outside the bedroom. "Even though I'm not going to be the Honorable Congressman from the Sixth District?"

"Especially because you're not going to be the Honorable Congressman from the Sixth District." She checked the time. "Jared, it's only nine-thirty. Do you think we could stop at the lake for a bit? We haven't in such a long time. I brought a bag of bread just in case."

Jared slowed. "Only if you promise not to poach when goddamn Carlisle starts hitting to my backhand."

"Once. I stole a ball from you once in almost two years of playing together, and you never let me forget it."

"No poaching?"

Was he being serious? It bothered her that after almost five years of marriage she couldn't always tell. "No poaching," she vowed finally, wary of making a response that would chip the mood of the morning. Lately, it seemed, their upbeat moods were becoming less frequent and more fragile.

"The ducks bless you," Jared said in a tone which did nothing to resolve her uncertainty.

The lake, more a large pond, was a mile off 127 in the general direction of the Oceanside Racquet Club. It was surrounded by dense thickets of pine and scrub oak, separated by the backyards of a dozen or so houses—upper-class dwellings in most communities, but only average in the North Shore village of Beverly Farms. At the far end of the ice cover, hockey sticks in hand, a trio of boys chased a puck up and down a makeshift rink, their bright mufflers and caps phosphorescing against the pearl-gray morning. Nearer the road, a spillway kept the surface from freezing. Bobbing on the half-moon it created were a score of ducks. Several more rested on the surrounding ice.

The couple stood motionless by their car, transfixed by the scene.

"Currier and Ives," Kate said wistfully.

"Bonnie and Clyde," Jared responded in the same tone.

"You're so romantic, Counselor." Kate managed a two-second glare of reproach before she smiled. Jared's often black sense of humor was hit or miss—"kamikaze humor," she had labeled it. "Come on, let's duck," she called.

Her runner's legs, objects of the fantasies of more than a few of her fellow physicians at Metropolitan Hospital of Boston, brought her easily down the snowy embankment, her auburn hair bouncing on the hood of her parka.

As she approached the water, a huge gander, honking arrogantly, advanced to get his due. Kate eyed the bird and then threw a handful of bread over his head to a milling group of smaller mallards and wood ducks. A moment later, from atop the bank, Jared scaled an entire roll precisely at the feet of the gander, who snatched it up and swaggered away.

Kate turned to him, hands on hips. "Are you trying to undermine my authority?"

"Always side with the overdog. That's my motto," he said brightly. "I even voted for Mattingly in the Sixth Congressional race. I mean who would want to waste his vote on a sure loser like the other guy?"

"A two-point defeat when you started out twenty-two behind? Some loser. Slide on down here, big boy, and I'll give you our traditional Sunday morning kiss."

"We have a traditional Sunday morning kiss?"

"Not yet."

Jared surveyed the embankment and then chose a safer, albeit much longer, route than Kate had taken.

She stifled a smile. *Never lift up your left foot until your right one's firmly planted* was a favorite saying of Jared's father, and here was the scion—the disciple—embracing the philosophy in its most literal sense. Someday,

Jared, she thought, you are going to lift up both of your feet at the same time and discover you can fly.

His kiss was firm and deep, his tongue caressing the roof of her mouth, the insides of her cheeks. Kate responded in kind, sliding both her hands to his buttocks and holding him tightly.

"You kiss good, Doc," he said. "I mean *good.*"

"Do you think the ducks would mind if we started making dirty snow angels?" she whispered, warming his ear with her lips.

"No, but I think the Carlisles would." Jared pulled free. "We've got to get going. I wonder why they keep inviting us to play with them when we haven't beaten them once in two years."

"They just love a challenge, I guess." Kate shrugged, tossed out the remaining bread, and followed him along the safe route to the road.

"Did someone call this morning?" he asked over his shoulder.

"Pardon?"

"While I was in the shower." Jared turned to her as he reached the MG and leaned against the perfectly maintained canvas top. "I thought I heard the phone ring."

"Oh, you did." A nugget of tension materialized beneath her breastbone. Jared hadn't missed hearing the phone after all. "It . . . it was nothing, really. Just Dr. Willoughby." Kate slid into the passenger seat. She had wanted to choose carefully the moment to discuss the pathology chief's call.

"How is Yoda?" he asked, settling behind the wheel.

"He's fine. I wish you wouldn't call him that, Jared. He's been very good to me, and it sounds so demeaning."

"It's not demeaning. Honestly." He turned the key and the engine rumbled to life. "Why, without Yoda, Luke Skywalker would never have survived the first *Star Wars* sequel. What else could I possibly call someone who's three feet tall, bald with bushy eyebrows, and lives in a swamp? Anyway, what did he want?"

Kate felt the nugget expand, and fought the sensation. "He just needed to discuss some twists and turns in the politics at the hospital," she said evenly. "I'll tell you about them later. How about we use the little time we have to plan some kind of strategic ambush for the Carlisles?"

"Don't poach. That's all the strategy we need. Now what was so important to ol' Yoda at eight-thirty on a Sunday morning?"

Although the words were spoken lightly, Kate noted that he had not yet put the car into gear. From the beginning of their relationship, he had been somehow threatened both by her career and by her unique friendship with her aging department head. It was nothing he had ever said, but the threat was there. She was certain of it. "Later?" She tried one last time.

Jared switched off the ignition.

The mood of the morning shattered like dropped crystal. Kate forced her eyes to make and maintain contact with his. "He said that tomorrow morning he was going to send letters to the medical school and to Norton Reese announcing his retirement in June or as soon as a successor can be chosen as chief of the department."

"And . . . ?"

"And I think you know already what comes next." Deep inside her, Kate felt sparks of anger begin to replace the tension. This exchange, her news, her chance to become at thirty-five the youngest department chief, to say nothing of the only woman department chief, at Metro—they should have been embraced by the marriage with the same joy as Jared's election to Congress would have been.

"Try me," Jared said, gazing off across the lake.

Kate sighed. "He wants my permission to submit my name to the faculty search committee as his personal recommendation."

"And you thanked him very much, but begged off because you and your husband agreed two years ago to start your family when the election was over, and you simply couldn't take on the responsibility and time demands of a department chairmanship—especially of a moneyless, understaffed, political football of a department like the one Yoda is scurrying away from now—right?"

"Wrong!" The snap in her voice was reflex. She cursed herself for losing control so easily, and took several seconds to calm down before continuing. "I told him I would think about it and talk it over with my husband and some of my friends at the hospital. I told him either to leave my name off his letter or wait a week before sending it."

"Have you thought what the job would take out of you? I mean Yoda's had two coronaries in the last few years, and he is certainly a lot more low key than you are."

"Dammit, Jared. Stop calling him that. And they weren't coronaries. Only angina."

"All right, angina."

"Do you suppose we could talk this over after we play? You're the one who was so worried about being late."

Jared glanced at his watch and then restarted the engine. He turned to her. There was composure in the lines of his face, but an intensity—perhaps even a fear—in his eyes. It was the same look Kate had seen in them when, before the election, he spoke of losing as "not the end of the world."

"Sure," he said. "Just answer me that one question. Do you really have a sense of what it would be like for you—for us—if you took over that department?"

"I . . . I know it wouldn't be easy. But that's not what you're really asking, is it?"

Jared shook his head and stared down at his clenched hands.

Kate knew very well what he was asking. He was thirty-nine years old and an only child. His first marriage had ended in nightmarish fashion, with his wife running off to California with their baby daughter. Even Jared's father, senior partner of one of Boston's most prestigious law firms, with all the king's horses and all the king's men at his disposal, couldn't find them. Jared wanted children. For himself and for his father he wanted them. The agreement to wait until after the election was out of deference to the pressures of a political campaign and the newness of their marriage. Now neither was a factor. Oh, yes, she knew very well what he was asking.

"The answer is," she said finally, "that if I accepted the nomination and got the appointment I would need some time to do the job right. But that is the grossest kind of projection at this point. Norton Reese has hardly been my biggest supporter since I exposed the way he was using money budgeted for the forensic pathology unit to finance new cardiac surgery equipment. I think he would cut off an arm before he would have me as a department chief in a hospital he administrated."

"How much time?" Jared's voice was chilly.

"Please, honey. I'm begging you. Let's do this when we can sit down in our own living room and discuss all the possibilities."

"How much?"

"I . . . I don't know. A year? Two?"

Jared snapped the stick shift into first gear, sending a spray of ice and snow into the air before the rear tires gained purchase. "To be continued," he said, as much to himself as to her.

"Fine," she said. Numbly, she sank back in her seat and stared unseeing out the window. Her thoughts drifted for a time and then began to focus on a face. Kate closed her eyes and tried to will the thoughts, the face, away. In moments, though, she could see Art's eyes, glazed and bloodshot; see them as clearly as she had that afternoon a dozen years before when he had raped her. She could smell the whiskey on his breath and feel the weight of his fullback's body on top of hers. Though bundled in a down parka and a warm-up suit, she began to shiver.

Jared turned onto the narrow access drive to the club. To Kate's right, the metallic surface of the Atlantic glinted

through a leafless hardwood forest. She took no notice of
it.

*Please Art, don't,* her mind begged. *You're hurting
me. Please let me up. All I did was take the test. I didn't
say I was going to apply.*

"Look, there are the Carlisles up ahead of us. I guess
we're not late after all."

Jared's voice broke through the nightmare. Damp-
ened by a cold sweat, she pushed herself upright. The
assault had taken place the day after the second anniversary of her previous marriage, and only an hour after her
husband, a failure first in a pro football tryout, then in
graduate school, and finally in business, had learned that
she had taken the Medical College Admission Test, and
worse, that she had scored in the top five percent. His
need to control her, never pleasant, had turned ugly. By
the evening of that day she had moved out.

"Jared," she pleaded quietly, "we'll talk. Okay?"

"Yeah, sure," he answered. "We'll talk."


The ball rainbowed off Jared's racquet with deceptive
speed. A perfect topspin lob.

From her spot by the net, Kate watched Jim and
Patsy Carlisle skid to simultaneous stops and, amidst flailing arms, legs, and racquets, dash backward toward the
baseline.

The shot bounced six inches inside the line and then
accelerated toward the screen, the Carlisles in frantic
pursuit.

"You fox," Kate whispered as Jared moved forward
for the killing shot they both knew would not be necessary.
"That was absolutely beautiful."

"Just keep looking sort of bland. Like we don't even
know we're about to beat them for the first time ever."

Across the net, Patsy Carlisle made a fruitless lunge
that sent her tumbling into the indoor court's green nylon
backdrop.

Kate watched the minidrama of the woman, still seated

on the court, glaring at her husband as he stalked away from her without even the offer of a hand up. Husbands and wives mixed doubles, she thought: games within games within games. "Three match points," she said. "Maybe we should squabble more often before we play." A look at Jared's eyes told her she should have let the matter lie. "Finish 'em with the ol' high hard one," she urged as he walked back to the service line. Her enthusiasm, she knew, now sounded forced—an attempt at some kind of expiation.

Jared nodded at her and winked.

Kate crouched by the net. Eighteen feet in front of her, Jim Carlisle shifted the weight of his compact, perfectly conditioned body from one foot to another. A successful real estate developer, a yachtsman, and club champion several years running, he had never been one to take any kind of loss lightly. "You know," he had said to her on the only attempt he had ever made to start an affair between them, "there are those like you-know-who, who are content to tiptoe along in Daddy's footsteps, and those who just grab life by the throat and do it. I'm a doer."

The reference to Jared, even though prodded forth by far too many martinis, had left an aftertaste of anger that Kate knew would never totally disappear. When Carlisle sent the Samuels for Congress Committee a check for five hundred dollars, she had almost sent it back with a note telling him to go grab somebody's life by the throat. Instead, out of deference to her husband, she had invited the Carlisles over for dinner. Her hypocrisy, however honorable its purpose, continued to rankle her from time to time, especially when Carlisle, wearing his smugness like aftershave, was about to inflict yet another defeat on team Samuels/Bennett.

At last she was beating the man. Not even a disagreement with her husband could dull the luster of the moment.

Through the mirror of Jim Carlisle's stages of readiness to return serve, Kate pictured Jared's movements behind her. Feet planted: Jared had settled in at the line. Hunching over, knees bent: Jared was tapping ball against racquet, gaining his rhythm. Just before Carlisle began the quick bouncing which would signal the toss, she heard Jared's voice. "The ol' high hard one," he said.

Kate tensed, awaiting the familiar, sharp *pok* of Jared's serve and Carlisle's almost simultaneous move to return. Instead, she heard virtually nothing, and watched in horror as Carlisle, with the glee of a tomcat discovering a wounded sparrow, advanced to pounce on a woefully soft hit. The serve was deliberate—vintage Jared Samuels; his way of announcing that by no means had he forgotten their argument.

"Jared, you bastard," Kate screamed just as Carlisle exploded a shot straight at her chest from less than a dozen feet away.

An instant after the ball left Carlisle's racquet, it was on Kate's, then ricocheting into a totally unguarded corner of the court. The shot was absolute reflex, absolute luck, but perfect all the same.

"Match," Kate said simply. She shook hands with each of their opponents, giving Jim's hand an extra pump. Then, without a backward glance, she walked off the court to the locker room.

The Oceanside Racquet Club, three quarters of an acre of corrugated aluminum box, squatted gracelessly on a small rise above the Atlantic. "Facing Wimbledon," was the way the club's overstuffed director liked to describe it.

Keeping her hair dry and moving quickly enough to ensure that Jared would have to work to catch up with her, Kate showered and left the building. The rules of *their* game demanded a reaction of some sort for his behavior, and she had decided on taking the MG, perhaps stopping a mile or so down the road. As she crossed the half-filled parking lot, she began searching the pockets of her parka for her keys. Almost immediately, she remembered seeing them on the kitchen table.

"Damn!" The feeling was so familiar. She had, in the past, slept through several exams, required police assistance to locate her car in an airport parking garage, and forgotten where she had put the engagement ring Art had given her. Although she had come to accept the trait as a usually harmless annoyance, there was a time when visions of clamps left in abdomens concerned her enough to influence her decision to go into pathology rather than clinical medicine. This day, she felt no compassion whatsoever toward her shortcoming.

Testily, she strode past their car and down the road. The move was a bluff. Jared would know that as well as she. It was an eight-mile walk to their home, and the temperature was near freezing. Still, some show of indignation was called for. But not this, she realized quickly. At the moment she accepted the absurdity of her gesture and decided to turn back, she heard the distinctive rev of the MG behind her. There could be no retreat now.

It was a game between them, but not a game. Their scenarios were often carefully staged, but they were life all the same; actions and reactions, spontaneous or not, that provided the dynamics unique to their relationship. There had been no such dynamics in her first marriage. Put simply, Arthur Everett decreed and his dutiful wife Kathryn acquiesced. For two destructive years it had been that way. Her childhood programming offered no alternatives, and she had been too frightened, too insecure, to question. Even now there were times, though gradually fewer and farther between, when dreams of the farmhouse and the children, the well-stocked, sunlit kitchen and the pipe smoke wafting out from the study, dominated her thoughts. They were, she knew, nothing more than the vestiges—the reincarnations—of that childhood programming.

Unfortunately, much of Jared's programming was continually being reinforced, thanks largely to a father who remained convinced that God's plan for women was quite different from His plan for men.

"You have a wonderful behind, do you know that?" Jared's voice startled her. He was driving alongside her, studying her anatomy through a pair of binoculars.

"Yes, I know that." She stiffened enough to be sure

he could notice and walked on. Please don't get hurt, she thought. Put those silly binoculars down and watch where you're going.

"And your face. Have I told you lately about your face?"

"No, but go ahead if you must."

"It is the blue ribbon, gold medal, face-of-the-decade face, that's what."

"You tried to get me killed in there." Kate slowed, but did not stop.

"It was childish."

"And . . . ?"

"And it was dumb."

"And . . . ?"

"And it didn't work."

"Jared!"

"And I'm sorry. I really am. The devil made me do it, but I went and let 'im."

He opened the door. She stopped, hesitated the obligatory few seconds, and got in. The scenario was over. Through it, a dram of purulence had been drained from their marriage before it could fester. Energy no longer enmeshed in their anger would now be rechanneled, perhaps to a joint attack today on the pile of unsplit wood in the yard and later to a battle with the *Times* crossword puzzle. As likely as not, before the afternoon was through, they would make love.

Eyes closed, Kate settled back in her seat, savoring what she had just heard. *I'm sorry.* He had actually said it.

*Apologizing has been bred out of Samuels men* was yet another teaching from the philosophy of J. Winfield Samuels. Kate had suffered the pain of that one on more than one occasion. She thought about Jared's vehement reaction to the possibility of her taking over the chairmanship of her department. The morning, she had decided, had been a draw: Dad 1. Wife 1.

"Now, Dr. Engleson, you may proceed with your report."

Tom Engleson's groan was not as inaudible as he would have liked. "Your patient is still bleeding, sir. That's my report." During his year and a half of residency on the Ashburton Service at Metropolitan Hospital of Boston, Engleson had had enough dealings with D. K. Bartholomew to know that he would be lucky to escape with anything less than a fifteen-minute conversation.

Dr. Donald K. Bartholomew held the receiver in his left hand, adjusted the notepad in front of him, and straightened his posture. "And what is her blood count?"

"Twenty-five. Her crit is down to twenty-five from twenty-eight." Engleson pictured the numbers being shakily reproduced in black felt tip. "She has had a total of five units transfused in the last twenty-four hours, two of whole blood, one of packed cells, and two of fresh frozen plasma." He closed his eyes and awaited the inevitable string of questions. For a few seconds there was silence.

"How many fresh frozen did you say?"

"Two. The hematology people have been to see her again. Her blood is just not clotting normally." He had decided to keep the complicated explanation for Beverly Vitale's bleeding problem out of the conversation if at all possible. A single request from Bartholomew for specifics, and the phone call could drag on for another half hour. In fact, there was no good explanation even available. The hematologists knew *what*—two of the woman's key clotting factors were at critically low levels—but not *why*. It was a problem the surgeon should have at least identified before performing her D and C.

"Have they further tests to run?"

"No, sir. Not today, anyhow." Getting D. K. Bartholomew to come into the hospital on a Sunday morning was like getting a cat to hop into the tub. "They suggested loading her up with fresh clotting factors and perhaps doing another D and C. They're afraid she might bleed out otherwise."

"How long will it take to give her the factors?"

"We've already started, sir."

There was another pause. "Well, then," Bartholomew said at last, "I guess the patient and I have a date in the operating room."

"Would you like me to assist?" Engleson closed his eyes and prayed for an affirmative response.

"For a D and C? No, thank you, Doctor. It is a one-man procedure, and I am one man. I shall be in by twelve o'clock. Please put the OR team on notice."

"Fine," Engleson said wearily. He had already scheduled Beverly Vitale for the operating room. He hung up and checked the wall clock over the door of the cluttered resident's office. Only eight minutes. "A record," he announced sardonically to the empty room. "I may have just set a record."

Moments later, he called the operating suite. "Denise, it's Tom Engleson. You know the D and C I scheduled for Dr. Bartholomew? . . . Vitale. That's right. Well, I was wondering if you could switch it to the observation OR. I want to watch. . . . I know you're not supposed to use that room on a weekend. That's why I'm asking in such a groveling tone of voice. . . . Bartholomew doesn't want anyone assisting him, but he can't keep me from watching through the overhead. . . . I owe you one, Denise. Thanks."

Looking down from behind the thick glass observation window into the operating room, Tom Engleson exchanged worried looks with the scrub nurse assisting Dr. Donald K. Bartholomew. The dilatation of Beverly Vitale's cervix and subsequent curettage—scraping—of the inner surface of her uterus was not going well. She had gone to the emergency ward three days before because of vaginal bleeding that started with her period but would not let up. For several years, she had been receiving routine gynecologic care through the Omnicenter—the outpatient facility of the Ashburton Women's Health Service of Metropolitan Hospital. As her Omnicenter physician, D. K. Bartholomew had been called in immediately.

In his admission physical, Bartholomew had noted a number of bruises on the woman's arms and legs, but elected nevertheless to proceed with a D and C—commonly done for excessive bleeding. He did not order blood clotting studies until after his patient's bleeding worsened postoperatively. Now, with the woman loaded with fresh clotting factors, Bartholomew was repeating the curettage.

Beverly Vitale, a thin, delicate young cellist with straight jet hair and fine, artist's hands lay supine on the operating table with her eyes taped shut and her head turned ninety degrees to one side. A polystyrene tube placed through her mouth into her trachea connected her with the anesthesia machine. Her legs, draped in sterile sheets, were held aloft by cloth stirrups hooked beneath each heel. Overhead, in the observation gallery Tom Engleson watched and waited. He was dressed in standard operating room whites, with hair and shoe covers, but no mask.

As he watched the level of suctioned blood rise in the vacuum bottle on the wall, Engleson wondered if D. K. Bartholomew was considering removing the woman's uterus altogether. He cursed himself for not throwing protocol to the winds and inviting himself into the OR.

The prospect of the old surgeon moving ahead with a hysterectomy brought a ball of anger to the resident's throat. Much of his reaction, he knew, had to do with Beverly Vitale. Though he had only spoken with her a few times, Engleson had begun fantasizing about her and had become determined to see her when she was released from the hospital. Now his thoughts added, *if* she was released from the hospital. He glanced again at the vacuum bottle and then at Bartholomew. There was a flicker of confusion and uncertainty in the man's eyes.

"Her pressure is dropping a bit."

Engleson heard the anesthesiologist's voice crackle

through a barely functional speaker on the wall behind him. "Young lady, get me the freshest unit of blood we have, and see if the blood bank can send us up ten units of platelets."

"Yes, sir," the nurse said. "Dr. Bartholomew, blood loss so far is four hundred and fifty cc's."

Bartholomew did not respond immediately. He stood motionless, staring at the steady flow of crimson from Beverly Vitale's cervix.

"Let's try some pitocin. Maybe her uterus will clamp down," he said finally.

"Dr. Bartholomew," the anesthesiologist said, an even tenseness in his voice, "you've already ordered pitocin. She's been getting it. Maximum doses."

Engleson strained to see the older surgeon's face. If he rushed into the OR and the man did not need assistance, a formal complaint was sure to. . . . Before he could complete the thought, the bellboy hanging from his waistband emitted the abrasive tone signaling a transmission. "Dr. Engleson, call two eight three *stat*. Dr. Engleson, two eight three *stat*, please."

An anxious check of the scene below, and the resident rushed to the nearest phone. It was a rule of the Ashburton Service that all *stat* pages were to be answered within sixty seconds. Telephones had even been installed in the residents' bathrooms for such purposes.

The call concerned a postop patient whose temperature had risen to 103; not a life-or-death situation. By the time Engleson had listened to the nurse's report, given orders for evaluating the patient's fever and returned to the observation window, Bartholomew had begun swabbing antiseptic over Beverly Vitale's lower abdomen.

Engleson switched on the microphone by his right hand. "What's going on?" he asked. Below, no one reacted to his voice. "Can you hear me?" Again no response. Through the door to the scrub area, Engleson saw Carol Nixon, a surgical intern rotating through the Ashburton Service, beginning to scrub. Apparently Bartholomew had called her in to assist, perhaps when Engleson could not be found.

"Over my dead body," Engleson said as he raced down the hall to the stairs. "No way do you open that woman up without my being there." In less than a minute, he had joined Nixon in the scrub room.

"The nurses said Stone Hands was trying to find you," the woman said. "I was just finishing up a case down the hall when Denise grabbed me. Do I have to stay?"

"You might want to learn from the master in there," Engleson responded acidly, cleaning his fingernails with an orange stick. The intern smiled, nodded a thanks-but-no-thanks, and left him to finish his scrub.

"Order a peach and you get a pear," was Bartholomew's comment on the change in assistants. He laughed merrily at his own humor and seemed not to notice the absence of response from around the room.

With Engleson handling sponges and hemostats, Bartholomew used an electric scalpel to make an incision from just below Beverly Vitale's navel to her pubis. The scalpel, buzzing and crackling like hot bacon grease, simultaneously sliced through the skin and cauterized bleeding vessels. Next, with the voltage turned up, he cut through a thin layer of saffron-colored fat to her peritoneum, the opaque membrane covering her abdominal cavity. A few snips with a Metzenbaum scissors, and the peritoneum parted, exposing her bowel, her bladder, and beneath those, her uterus.

In a perfunctory manner, too perfunctory for Engleson's taste, the older surgeon explored the abdominal cavity with one hand. "Everything seems in order," he announced to the room. "I think we can proceed with a hysterectomy."

"No!" Engleson said sharply. The room froze. "I mean, don't you think we should at least consider the possibility of ligating her hypogastric artery?" He wanted to add his feelings about rushing ahead with a hysterectomy in a thirty-year-old woman with no children, but held back.

Also unsaid, at least for the moment, was that the hypogastric ligation, while not always successful in stopping hemorrhaging, was certainly accepted practice in a case like this. Bartholomew was still guided by the old school—the school that removed a uterus with the dispatch of a dermatologist removing a wart.

D. K. Bartholomew's pale blue eyes came up slowly and locked on Engleson's. For five seconds, ten, an eerie silence held, impinged upon only by the wheeze of air into the vacuum apparatus. The tall resident held his ground, but he also held his breath. An outburst by the older surgeon now, and there would be a confrontation that could further jeopardize the life of Beverly Vitale. Then, moment by moment, Engleson saw the blaze in Bartholomew's eyes fade.

"Thank you for the suggestion, doctor," the surgeon said distantly. "I think perhaps we should give it a try."

The relieved sighs from those in the room were muffled by their masks.

"You or me?" Engleson asked.

"It . . . it's been a while since I did this procedure," Bartholomew understated.

"Don't worry, we'll do it together."

In minutes, the ligation was complete. Almost instantly, the bleeding from within the woman's uterus began to lessen.

"While we're waiting to see if this works," Engleson said, "would you mind if I got a better look at her tubes and ovaries?"

Bartholomew shrugged and shook his head.

Engleson probed along the fallopian tubes, first to one ovary and then to the other. They did not feel at all right. Carefully, he withdrew the left ovary through the incision. It was half normal size, mottled gray, and quite firm. This time, it was his eyes that flashed. *You said everything was in order.* Bartholomew sagged. There was a bewildered, vacant air about him, as if he had opened his eyes before a mirror and seen a painful truth.

The woman's right ovary was identical to her left.

"I don't think I've ever seen anything quite like this," Engleson said. "Have you?"

"No, well, not exactly."

"Pardon?"

"I said *I* hadn't either." There was an uncertainty, a hesitation, in the older man's words. He reached over and touched the ovary.

"You sure?" Engleson prodded.

"I . . . I may have felt one once. I'm trying to remember. Do you suggest a biopsy?" Engleson nodded. "A wedge section?" Another nod. The man's confidence was obviously shaken.

By the time the wedge biopsy was taken, the bleeding had slowed dramatically. As Engleson prepared to close the abdominal incision over the uterus he had just preserved, he sensed the irony of what was happening tighten in his gut. The uterus was saved, true. A fine piece of surgery. But if the pathology in Beverly Vitale's ovaries was as extensive as it appeared, the woman would never bear children anyhow.

"Denise," he said, "could you find out who's on for surgical path this month; both the resident and the staff person, okay?"

"Right away."

Engleson glanced at the peaceful face and tousled hair of the young cellist. Some women try for years to get pregnant, never knowing whether they can or not, he thought. At least you'll know. Glumly, he began to close.

Twenty minutes later, the two surgeons shuffled into the doctor's locker room.

"Dr. Bartholomew, have you been able to remember where you might have encountered ovarian pathology like this woman's?"

"Oh, yes, well, no. I . . . what I mean is I don't think I've ever seen anything like them."

"You look as if you want to say something more."

"I may have felt something like them once. That's all."

"When? On whom?" There was some excitement in Engleson's voice.

D. K. Bartholomew, MD, Fellow of the American College of Surgeons and Diplomate of the American College of Obstetrics and Gynecology, shook his head. "I . . . I'm afraid I don't remember," he said.

"What are you talking about?"

"It was surgery for something else. Maybe removal of a fibroid tumor. The ovaries felt like this woman's did today, but there was no one around to consult, and I think I had another case or two left to do and . . ."

"So you just ignored them and closed?"

"I felt they were probably a normal variant."

"Yeah, sure. Did you mention them on your operative note?"

"I . . . I don't remember. It might have been years ago."

The wall telephone began ringing. "Dr. Bartholomew," Engleson said, allowing the jangle to continue, "I don't think you should operate anymore." With that he turned and snatched up the receiver.

"Dr. Engleson, it's Denise. I called pathology."

"Yes?"

"I couldn't find out who the resident is on surgicals, but the staff person is Dr. Bennett."

"Good."

"Excuse me?"

"I just said that's good. Thanks, Denise."

"Thank you for what you did in there, Doctor. You made my day."

Kate's back was arched over the pillows beneath her hips as Jared knelt between her legs and used her buttocks to pull himself farther inside her. Again and again he sent jets of pleasure and pain deep into her gut and up into her throat. Her climax grew like the sound of an oncoming train—first a tingle, a vibration, next a hum, then a roar. With Jared helping, her body came off the pillows until only her heels and the back of her head were touching the carpet. Her muscles tightened on him and seemed to draw him in even deeper. He dug his fingers into the small of her back and cried out in a soft, child's voice. Then he came, his erection pulsing in counterpoint to her own contractions.

"I love you," he whispered. "Oh, Katey, I love you so much." Gently, he worked his arms around her waist, and guided her onto her side, trying to stay within her as long as possible. For half an hour they lay on the soft living room carpet, their lover's sweat drying in the warmth from the nearby wood stove. From the kitchen, the aroma of percolating coffee, forgotten for over an hour, worked its way into the sweetness of the birch fire.

A cashmere blanket, one of the plethora of wedding gifts from Jared's father, lay beside them. Kate pulled it over her sleeping husband and then slipped carefully from underneath. For a time, she knelt there studying the face of the man who had, five years before, arranged to have himself and a dozen roses wheeled under a sheet into her autopsy suite in order to convince her to reconsider a rebuffed dinner invitation. Five years. Years filled with so much change—so much growth for both of them. She had been a nervous, overworked junior faculty member then, and he had been the hotshot young attorney assigned by Minton/Samuels to handle beleaguered Metropolitan Hospital. The memory of him in those days—so eager and intense—brought a faint smile.

Kate reached out and touched the fine creases that had, overnight it seemed, materialized at the corners of her husband's eyes.

"A year, Jared?" she asked silently. "Would a year make all that much difference? You understand your own needs so well. Can you understand mine?"

Almost instantly another, far more disturbing question arose in her thoughts. Did she, in fact, understand them herself?

Silently, she rose and walked to the picture window overlooking their wooded backyard. Superimposed on the smooth waves of drifted snow was the reflection of her naked body, kept thin and toned by constant dieting and almost obsessive exercise. On an impulse, she turned sideways and forced her abdomen out as far as it would go. Six months, she guessed, maybe seven. Not too bad looking for an old pregnant lady.

Fifteen minutes later, when the phone rang, Kate was ricocheting around the kitchen preparing brunch. The edge of her terry-cloth robe narrowly missed toppling a pan of sweet sausages as she leapt for the receiver, answering it before the first ring ended. Nevertheless, through the door to the living room, she saw Jared stir from the fetal tuck in which he had been sleeping and begin to stretch.

"Hello," she answered, mentally discarding the exotic plans she had made for awakening her husband.

"Dr. Bennett, it's Tom Engleson. I'm a senior resident on the Ashburton Service at Metro. Do you remember me?"

"Of course, Tom. You saw me at the Omnicenter once. Saved my life when Dr. Zimmermann was away."

"I did?" There was a hint of embarrassment in his voice. "What was the matter?"

"Well, actually, I just needed a refill of my birth control pills. But I remember you just the same. What can I do for you?" Her mental picture of Engleson was of a loose, gangly man, thirty or thirty-one, with angular features and a youthful face, slightly aged by a Teddy Roosevelt moustache.

"Please forgive me for phoning you at home on Sunday."

"Nonsense."

"Thank you. The reason I'm calling is to get your advice on handling a surgical specimen. It's one you'll be seeing tomorrow: a wedge section of a patient's left ovary, taken during a hypogastric artery ligation for menorrhagia."

"How old a woman?" Reflexively, Kate took up a pen to begin scratching data on the back of an envelope. So doing, she noticed that Jared was now huddled by the wood stove with Roscoe, their four-year-old almost-terrier and the marriage's declared neutral love object.

"Thirty," Engleson answered. "No deliveries, no pregnancies, and in fact, no ovaries."

"What?"

"Oh, they're there. But they're unlike any ovaries I've ever seen before. Dr. Bartholomew was with me—the woman is his patient—and he has never seen pathology like this either."

Kate pulled a high stool from beneath the counter and wrapped one foot around its leg. "Explain," she said.

"Well, whatever this is is uniform and symmetrical. We took a slice from the left ovary, but it could just as well have been the right. Shrunken, the consistency of . . . of a squash ball—sort of hard but rubbery. The surface is pockmarked, dimpled."

"What color?" Kate had written down almost every word.

"Gray. Grayish brown, maybe."

"Interesting," she said.

"Does what I've described ring any bells?"

"No. At least not right off. However, there are a number of possibilities. Any idea as to why this woman was having menorrhagia?"

"Two reasons. One is a platelet count of just forty-five thousand, and the other is a fibrinogen level that is fifteen percent of normal."

"An autoimmune phenomenon?" Kate searched her thoughts for a single disease entity characterized by the two blood abnormalities. An autoimmune phenomenon, the body making antibodies against certain of its own tissues, seemed likely.

"So far, that's number one on the list," Engleson said. "The hematology people have started her on steroids."

"Was she on any medications?"

"Hey, Kate." It was Jared calling from the living room. "Do you smell something burning?"

"Nothing but vitamins," Engleson answered.

Kate did not respond. Receiver tucked under her ear, she was at the oven, pulling out a tray of four blackened lumps that had once been shirred eggs—Jared's favorite.

"Shit," she said.

"What?" Both Jared and Tom Engleson said the word simultaneously.

"Oh, sorry. I wasn't talking to you." A miniature cumulonimbus cloud puffed from the oven. "Jared, it's all right," she called out, this time covering the mouthpiece. "It's just . . . our meal. That's all."

"Dr. Bennett, if you'd rather I called back . . ."

"No, Tom, no. Listen, there's a histology technician on call. The lab tech on duty knows who it is. Have whoever it is come in and begin running the specimen through the Technichron. That way it will be ready for examination tomorrow rather than Tuesday. Better still, ask them to come into the lab and call me at home. I'll give the instructions myself. Okay?"

"Sure. Thanks."

"No problem," she said, staring at the lumps. "I'll speak to you later."

"Shirred eggs?" Jared, wrapped in the cashmere blanket, leaned against the doorway. Roscoe peered at her from between his knees.

Kate nodded sheepishly. "I sort of smelled the smoke, but my one-track brain was focused on what this resident from the hospital was saying, and somehow, it dismissed the smoke as coming from the wood stove. I . . . I never was too great at doing more than one thing at once."

"Too bad you couldn't have chosen to let the resident burn to a crisp and save the eggs," he said.

"Next time."

"Good. Any possibilities for replacements?"

"Howard Johnson's?"

"Thanks, but I'll take my chances with some coffee and whatever's in that frying pan. You sure that wasn't Yoda on the phone?"

"Jared . . ."

He held up his hands against her ire. "Just checking, just checking," he said. "Come on, Roscoe. Let's go set the table."

Kate noted the absence of an apology, but decided that two in one day was too much to ask. More difficult to accept, however, was Jared's apparent lack of interest in what the call was about. It was as if by not talking about her career, her life outside of their marriage, he was somehow diminishing its importance. In public, he took special pride in her professionalism and her degree. Privately, he accepted it as long as it didn't burn his eggs. Almost against her will, she felt frustration begin to dilute the warmth and closeness generated by their lovemaking. She walked to where her clothes were piled in the living room and dressed, silently vowing to do whatever she could to avoid another blowup that day.

Minutes later, the crunch of tires on their gravel driveway heralded a test of her resolve. Roscoe heard the arrival first and bounded from his place by the stove to the front door. Jared, now in denims and a flannel work shirt, followed.

"Hey, Kate, it's Sandy," he called out, opening the inside door.

"Sandy?" Dick Sandler, Jared's roommate at Dartmouth, had been best man at their wedding. A TWA pilot, he lived on the South Shore and hadn't been in touch with them for several months. "Is Ellen with him?"

"No. He's alone." Jared opened the storm door. "Hey,

flyboy," he called in a thick Spanish accent, "welcome. I have just what you want, señor: a seexteen-year-old American virgin. Only feefty pesetas."

Sandler, a rugged Marlon Brando type, exchanged bear hugs with Jared and platonic kisses with Kate, and then scanned what there was of their brunch. "What, no bloodies?"

Kate winced before images of the two men, emboldened by a few "bloodies," exchanging off-color jokes she seldom thought were funny and singing "I Wanna Go Back to Dartmouth, to Dartmouth on the Hill." Invariably, she would end up having to decide whether to leave the house, try to shut them off, or join in. When Ellen Sandler was around, no such problem existed. A woman a few years older than Kate, and Sandy's wife since his graduation, Ellen was as charming, interesting, and full of life as anyone Kate had ever known. She was a hostess with poise and grace, the mother of three delightful girls, and even a modestly successful businesswoman, having developed an interior design consulting firm that she had run alone for several years from their home and more recently from a small studio cum office in town.

Sandy, with his flamboyance, his stature as a 747 captain, and his versatile wit, was the magnet that drew many fascinating and accomplished people into the Sandlers' social circle. Ellen, Kate believed, was the glue that kept them there.

"So, Sandy," she said, dropping a celery stick into his drink and sliding it across the table, "what brings you north of Boston? How are Ellen and the girls?" It was at that moment that she first appreciated the sadness in his eyes.

"I . . . well actually, I was just driving around and decided to cruise up here. Sort of a whim. I . . . I needed to talk to Jared . . . and to you."

"You and Ellen?" Jared's sense of his friend told him immediately what to ask.

"I . . . I'm leaving her. Moving out." Sandler stared uncomfortably into the center of his drink.

At his words, Kate felt a dreadful sinking in her gut. Ellen had stated on many occasions and in many ways the uncompromising love she bore for the man. How long had they been married, now? Eighteen years? Nineteen, maybe?

"Holy shit," Jared whispered, setting a hand on Sandler's forearm. "What's happened?"

"Nothing. I mean nothing dramatic. Somewhere along the way, we just lost one another."

"Sandy, people who have been married for almost twenty years don't just lose one another," Kate said. "Now what has happened?" There was an irritability in her voice which surprised her. Jared's expression suggested that he, too, was startled by her tone.

Sandler shrugged. "Well, between running the house and entertaining and taking the girls to one lesson or another and scouts and committees at our club and that business of hers, Ellen simply ran out of energy for me. In some areas, meals and such, she still goes through the motions, but without much spark."

"How is Ellen handling all this?" Kate asked, checking Jared's face for a sign that she might be interloping with too many questions. The message she received was noncommittal.

"She doesn't know yet."

"What?" Her exclamation this time drew a *be careful* glare.

"I just decided yesterday. But I've been thinking about it for weeks. Longer. I was hoping you two might have some suggestions as to how I should go about breaking the news to her."

"Have you been to a counsellor or a shrink or something?" Jared asked the question.

"It's too late."

"What do you mean? You just said Ellen doesn't even know what you're planning to do." Jared sounded baffled.

Across the table, Kate closed her eyes. She knew the explanation.

"There's someone else," Sandler said self-consciously. "A flight attendant. I . . . we've been seeing one another for some time."

For Kate the words were like needle stabs. Jared was pressing to get a commitment from her to alter her life along pathways Ellen Sandler could negotiate blindfolded. Yet here was Sandy, like Jared in so many ways, rejecting the woman for not devoting enough energy to him. The image of Ellen sitting there while he announced his intentions made her first queasy and then frightened. The fear, as happened more often than not, mutated into anger before it could be expressed.

"Ellen doesn't deserve this," she said, backing away from the table. " 'We just lost one another.' Sandy, don't you think that's sort of a sleazy explanation for what's really going on? How old is this woman?"

"Twenty-six. But I don't see what her . . ."

"I know you don't see. You don't see a lot of things."

Jared stood up. "Now just one second, Kate."

"And you don't see a lot of things either, dammit." There were tears streaming down her face. "You two boys work out how you're gonna break the news to Ellen that she did everything she goddamn well could in life—more than both of you put together, probably—but that it just wasn't enough. She's fired. Dismissed. Not flashy enough. Not showy enough. Her services are no longer required. Excuse me, I'm going to the bathroom to get sick. Then I'm going to my hospital. People there are grateful and appreciative for the things I do well. I like that. It helps me to get up in the morning."

Fists clenched, she turned and raced from the room. Roscoe, who had settled himself under the table, padded to the center of the room and after a brief glance at the men, followed.

Ginger Rittenhouse, a first-grade teacher, had just finished her run by the ice-covered Charles River when she began to die. Like the random victim of a crazed sniper, she did not hear the sound or see the muzzle flash of the weapon that killed her. In fact, the weapon was nothing more malevolent than the corner of her bureau drawer; the shot, an accidental bump less than twenty-four hours before to a spot just above her right ear.

"That's one incredible lump!" her new roommate had exclaimed, forcing an icepack against the golfball-sized knot. The woman, a licensed practical nurse, had commented on the large bruise just below her right knee as well. Ginger was too self-conscious to mention the other, similar bruises on her lower back, buttocks, and upper arm.

Her death began with a tic—an annoying electric sensation deep behind her right eye. The wall of her right middle cerebral artery was stretching. Bruised by the shock from the bureau drawer, the vessel, narrow as a piece of twine, had developed a tiny defect along the inner lining. The platelets and fibrinogen necessary to patch the defect were present, but in insufficient amounts to do the job. Blood had begun to work its way between the layers of the vessel wall.

Squinting against the pain, she sat on a bench and looked across the river at the General Electric building in Cambridge. The outline of the building seemed blurred. From the rent in her right middle cerebral artery, blood had begun to ooze, a microdrop at a time, into the space between her skull and brain. Nerve fibers, exquisitely sensitive, detected the intrusion and began screaming their message of warning. Ginger, mindless of the huge lump over her ear, placed her hands on either side of her head and tried to squeeze the pain into submission.

Powered by the beating of her own heart, the bleeding increased. Her thoughts became disconnected snatches. The low skyline of Cambridge began to fade. Behind her, runners jogged by. A pair of lovers passed close enough to read the dial on her watch. Ginger, now paralyzed by pain that was far more than pain, was beyond calling for help.

Suddenly, a brilliant white light replaced the agony. The heat from the light bathed the inside of her eyes. Her random thoughts coalesced about woods and a stream. It was the Dingle, the secret hiding place of her childhood. She knew every tree, every rock. Home and safe at last, Ginger Rittenhouse surrendered to the light, and gently toppled forward onto the sooty snow.

# 2

## Monday 10 December

First there was the intense, yellow-white light—the sunlight of another world. Then, subtly, colors began to appear: reds and pinks, purples and blues. Kate felt herself drifting downward, Alice drawn by her own curiosity over the edge and down the rabbit's hole. How many times had she focused her microscope in on a slide? Tens of thousands, perhaps even hundreds of thousands. Still, every journey through the yellow-white light began with the same sense of anticipation as had her first.

The colors darkened and coalesced into a mosaic of cells; the cells of Beverly Vitale's left ovary, chemically fixed to prevent decay, then embedded in a block of paraffin, cut thin as a slick of oil, and finally stained with dyes specific for coloring one or another structure within the cell. Pink for the cytoplasm; mottled violet for the nuclei; red for the cell walls.

With a deep breath calculated at once to relax herself and to heighten her concentration, she focused the lenses and her thoughts on the cells, now magnified a thousand times. Her efforts were less successful than usual. Thoughts of Sandy and Ellen, of Jared and the discussion they had had following her return from the hospital the previous night, continued to intrude.

She had come home late, almost eleven, after meet-

51

ing with Tom Engleson, interviewing Beverly Vitale, examining the frozen section of her ovary, and finally spending an hour in the hospital library. Her expectations had been to find the former roommates in the den, comatose or nearly so, with the essence of a half a case of Lowenbräu permeating the room. Instead, she had found only a somber and perfectly sober Jared.

"Hi," he said simply.

"Hi, yourself." She kissed him on the forehead and then settled onto the ottoman by his chair. "When did Sandy leave?"

"A couple of hours ago. Did you get done whatever it is you wanted to?"

Kate nodded. His expression was as flat and as drained as his words. No surprise, she realized. First his wife stalks out of the house with no real explanation; then he has to listen to the agonies of the breakup of his best friend's marriage. "I . . . I guess I owe you an apology for the way I acted earlier. Some sort of explanation."

Jared shrugged. "I'll take the apology. The explanation's optional."

"I'm sorry for leaving the way I did."

"I'm sorry you left the way you did, too. I could have used some help—at least some moral support."

"Sorry again." The three feet separating them might as well have been a canyon. "Anything decided?"

"He went home to tell Ellen and to move out, I guess. It got awful quiet here after you left. Neither of us was able to open up very well. We each seemed to be wrapped up in our own bundle of problems."

"Three I'm sorries. That's my limit." She unsnapped her barrette, shook her hair free, and combed it out with her fingers. The gesture was natural enough, but at some level she knew she had done it because it was one Jared liked. "After what happened this morning—in the car, I mean—I couldn't listen to Sandy just brush off Ellen and their marriage the way he did. I mean, here I am, scrambling to do a decent job with my career and to be a reasonably satisfying friend and wife to you, and there's Ellen able to do both of those so easily and raise three beautiful, talented children to boot, and . . ."

"It's not right what you're doing, Kate."

"What's that?"

"You're comparing your insides to Ellen's outsides, that's what. She looks good. I'll give you that. But don't go and cast Sandy as the heavy just because he's the one moving out. There are things that are missing from that relationship. Maybe things too big to overcome. What's that got to do with our discussion this morning, anyway?"

"Jared, you know perfectly well what it has to do. Having children is a major responsibility. As it is, I feel like a one-armed juggler half the time. Our lives, our jobs, the things we do on our own and together . . . Toss in a baby at this point, and what guarantee is there I won't start dropping things?"

"What do you want me to say? I'm almost forty years old. I'm married. I want to have children. My wife said she wanted to have children, too. Now, all of a sudden, having children is a threat to our marriage."

"Christ, Jared, that's not what I mean . . . and you know it. I didn't say I won't have children. I didn't say it's a threat to our marriage. All I'm trying to say is there's a lot to think about—especially with the opportunities that have arisen at the hospital. It's not the idea I'm having trouble with so much as the timing. A mistake here and it's a bitter, unfulfilled woman, or a neurotic, insecure kid, or . . . or a twenty-six-year-old stewardess. Can you understand that?"

"I understand that somewhere inside you there are some issues you're not facing up to. Issues surrounding me or having children or both."

"And you've got it all together, right?" Kate struggled to stop the tears that seemed to be welling from deep within her chest.

"I know what I want."

"Well, I don't. Okay? And I'm the one who's going to have to pass up a chairmanship and go through a pregnancy and change my life so that I don't make the same horrible mistakes with our child that my mother made with us. I . . . Jared, I'm frightened." It was, she realized, the first time she had truly recognized it.

"Hi, Frightened. I'm Perplexed. How do you do?"

"You know, you could use a little better sense of timing yourself."

"Okay, folks, here we go. It's time once again to play let's-jump-all-over-everything-Jared-says. Well, please, before you get rolling, count me out. I'm going to bed."

"I'll be in in a while."

"Don't wake me."

The section from Beverly Vitale's left ovary was unlike any pathology Kate had ever encountered. The stroma—cells providing support and, according to theory, critical feminizing hormones—were perfectly normal in appearance. But the follicles—the pockets of nutrient cells surrounding the ova—were selectively and completely destroyed, replaced by the spindle-shaped, deep pink cells of sclerosis—scarring. Assuming the pattern held true throughout both ovaries—and there was no reason to assume otherwise—Beverly Vitale's reproductive potential was as close to zero as estimate would allow.

For nearly an hour, Kate sat there, scanning section after section, taking notes on a yellow legal pad. Why couldn't Jared understand what it all really meant to her? Why couldn't he see what a godsend medicine had been to a life marked by aimlessness and a self-doubt bordering on self-loathing.

"My God, woman, if I didn't know better, I'd swear you were a model the Zeiss Company had hired to plug their latest line of microscopes."

"Aha," Kate said melodramatically, her eyes still fixed

on the microscope, "a closet male chauvinist pig. I expected as much all along, Dr. Willoughby." She swung around and, as always, felt a warm jet of affection at the sight of her department head. In his early sixties, Stan Willoughby was egg bald save for a pure white monk's fringe. The pencil-thin moustache partially obscured by his bulbous nose was a similar shade. His eyes sparkled from beneath brows resembling end-stage dandelions. In all, Jared's likening him to the wise imp Yoda was, though inappropriate, not inaccurate.

Willoughby packed his pipe and straddled the stool across the table from Kate. "The young lady on Ashburton Five?" he asked. Kate nodded. "This a good time for me to take a look-see?"

Although Willoughby's primary area of interest was histochemistry, thirty-five years of experience had made him an expert in almost every phase of pathology. Every phase, that is, except how to administer a department. Willoughby was simply too passive, too nice for the dog-maim-dog world of hospital politics, especially the free-for-all for an adequate portion of a limited pool of funds.

"Stan, I swear I've never seen, or even heard of, anything like this."

The chief peered into the student eyepieces on the teaching microscope—a setup enabling two people to view the same specimen at the same time. "All right if I focus?" Kate nodded. Ritualistically, he went from low power magnification to intermediate, to high, and finally to thousand-fold oil-immersion, punctuating each maneuver with a "hmm" or an "uh huh." Through the other set of oculars, Kate followed.

They looked so innocent, those cells, so deceptively innocent, detached from their source and set out for viewing. They were in one sense a work of art, a delicate, geometrically perfect montage that was the antithesis of the huge, cluttered metal sculptures Kate had built and displayed during her troubled Mount Holyoke years. The irony in that thought was immense. Form follows function. The essential law of structural design. Yet here were cells perfect in form, produced by a biologic cataclysm tantamount to a volcano. A virus? A toxin? An antibody suddenly transformed? The art of pathology demanded that the cells and tissues, though fixed and stained, never be viewed as static.

"Did you send sections over to the electron microscopy unit?" Willoughby asked.

"Not yet, but I will."

"And the young woman is bleeding as well?"

"Platelets thirty thousand. Fibrinogen fifteen percent of normal."

"Ouch!"

"Yes, ouch. I spoke with her at some length last night. No significant family history, no serious diseases, nonsmoker, social drinker, no meds. . . ."

"None?"

"Vitamins and iron, but that's all. No operations except an abortion at the Omnicenter about five years ago." The two continued to study the cells as they talked. "She's a cellist with the Pops."

"Travel history?"

"Europe, China, Japan. None to third world spots. I told her how envious I was of people who could play music, and she just smiled this wistful smile and said that every time she picked up her cello, she felt as rich and fulfilled as she could ever want to feel. I only talked to her for half an hour or so, Stan, but I came away feeling like we were . . . I don't know, like we were friends." *Spend a day here sometime, Jared. Come to work with me and see what I do, how I do it.* "The hematology people are talking autoimmune phenomenon. They think the ovarian problem is long-standing, a coincidental finding at this point."

"Never postulate two diseases when one will explain things." Willoughby restated the maxim he had long since engrained upon her. "I suppose they're pouring in steroids."

"Stan, she's in trouble. Real trouble."

"Ah, yes. Forgive me. Sometimes I forget that there's more to this medicine business than just making a correct diagnosis. Thanks for not letting me get away with that kind of talk. Well, Doctor, I think you may really have something here. I have never encountered anything quite like it either."

"Neither had Dr. Bartholomew."

"That fossil? He probably has trouble recognizing his own shoes in the morning. Talk about a menace. All by himself he's an epidemic."

"No comment."

"Good. I have enough comments for both of us. Listen, Kate. Do you mind if I try a couple of my new silver stains on this material? The technique seems perfect for this type of pathology."

"I was about to ask if you would."

Willoughby engaged the intercom on the speaker-phone system—one of the few innovations he had managed to bring into the department. "Sheila, is that you?"

"No, Doctor Willoughby, it's Jane Fonda. Of course it's me. You buzzed my office."

"Could you come into Dr. Bennett's office, please?" There was no response. "Sheila, are you still there?"

"It's not what it sounds like, Dr. Willoughby," she said finally.

"Not what *what* sounds like?"

"Sheila," Kate cut in firmly, "it's me. We're calling because we have a specimen we'd like to try the silver stain on."

For a few moments there was silence. "I . . . I'll be over shortly," the technician said.

Willoughby turned to Kate, his thick brows presaging his question. "Now what was that little ditty all about?"

"Nothing, really."

"Nothing? Kate, that woman has worked for me for fifteen years. Maybe more. She's cynical, impertinent, abrasive, aggressive, and at times as bossy as my wife, but she's also the best and brightest technician I've ever known. If there's trouble between the two of you, perhaps I'd best know about it. Is it that study of the department I commissioned you and your computer friend, Sebastian, to do?"

"It's nothing, Stan. I mean it. Like most people who are very good at what they do, Sheila has a lot of pride. Especially when it comes to her boss of fifteen years. I know it's not my place to decide, but if it's okay, I'd like the chance to work through our differences without involving you. Okay?"

Willoughby hesitated and then shrugged and nodded.

"Thanks," she said. "If I were ever to take over the chairmanship of the department, I'd like to know I had a solid relationship with my chief technician—especially if she were someone as invaluable as Sheila Pierce."

"Invaluable is right. I keep giving her raises and bonuses even though she puts a knot in my ninny just about every time she opens her mouth. Say, did I hear you just give me the green light to submit your name to Reese?"

"I said 'if' and you know it."

Willoughby grinned mischievously. "Your voice said 'if,' but your eyes . . ."

"You rang?" Sheila Pierce saved Kate from a response. Fortyish, with a trim, efficient attractiveness, she had, Kate knew, earned both bachelor's and master's degrees while working in the department. By the time Kate had begun her residence, the one-time laboratory assistant had become chief pathology technician.

"Ah, Sheila," Willoughby said. "Come in."

"Hi, Sheila." Kate hoped there was enough reassurance in her expression and her voice to keep the woman from any further outburst, at least until they had a chance to talk privately.

Their eyes locked for a fraction of a second; then, mercifully, Sheila returned the greeting. The problem between them had, as Stan Willoughby suspected, arisen during Kate's computer-aided study of the pathology department's budget and expenditures, specifically in regard to a six hundred and fifty dollar payment for an educational meeting in Miami that Sheila could not document ever having attended. Kate had decided to drop the matter without involving the department chief, but the technician was clearly unconvinced that she had done so.

"How's my new batch of silver stain coming?" Willoughby asked.

"It's much, much thicker than the old stuff," Sheila said, settling on a high stool, equidistant from the two physicians. "Fourteen hours may be too long to heat it."

"I seem to recall your warning me about that when I suggested fourteen hours in the first place. Is it a total loss?"

"Well, actually I split about half of it off and cooked that part for only seven hours."

"And . . . ?"

"And it looks fine . . . perfect, even."

Willoughby's sigh of relief was pronounced. "Do you know how much that stain costs to make? How much you just saved me by . . . ?"

"Of course I know. Who do you think ordered the material in the first place, the Ghost of Christmas Past?"

Willoughby shot Kate a what-did-I-tell-you glance; then he picked up the slides and paraffin blocks containing tissue from Beverly Vitale's ovary. "Dr. Bennett has an interesting problem here that I think might be well suited to my silver stain. Do you think you could make some sections and try it out?"

"Your command is my command," Pierce said, bowing. "Give me an hour, and your stain will be ready." She turned to Kate. "Dr. Bennett, I think you should have a little review session with our chief here on the basics of hypertension. On his desk, right next to his blood pressure pills, is a half-eaten bag of Doritos. Bye, now."

\*     \*     \*

Sheila Pierce dropped off the paraffin block in histology and then returned to her office. On her desk was the stain Willoughby had referred to as "his." Pierce laughed disdainfully. If it weren't for her, the stain that was soon to be known by his name would be little more than an expensive beaker of shit. There they sat, she thought, Willoughby and that goddamn Bennett, sharing their little physician jokes and performing their physician mental masturbations and issuing orders to a woman with an IQ—a proven IQ—higher than either of theirs could possibly be. One-fifty. That's what her mother said. Genius level. One hundred and fucking fifty. So where was the MD degree that would have put her where she deserved to be?

Pierce glared at the small framed photo of her parents, carefully placed to one side of her desk. Then her expression softened. It wasn't their fault, being poor. Just their fate. They didn't want the stroke or the cancer that had forced their daughter to shelve her dreams and begin a life of taking orders from privileged brats who, more often than not, couldn't come close to her intellectual capacity. One hundred and fifty. What was Kate Bennett? One-ten? One-twenty tops. Yet there she was with the degree and the power and the future.

*Listen, Sheila, you're terrific at your job. I don't see that there's anything to gain by bringing this up to Dr. Willoughby, or even by making you reimburse the department. But never again, okay?*

"Patronizing bitch."

"Who's a bitch?"

Startled, Sheila whirled. Norton Reese stood propped against the doorjamb, eyeing her curiously.

"Jesus, you scared me."

"Who's a bitch?" Reese checked the corridor in both directions then stepped inside and closed the door behind him.

"Bennett, that's who."

"Ah, yes. What's our little Rebecca of Sunnybrook Farm up to now?"

"Oh, nothing new. It's that damn American Society meeting."

"Miami?"

"Yes. The time you assured me there was no way anyone would ever find out I didn't go."

"She is a resourceful cunt," Reese mumbled. "I'll say that for her."

"What?"

"Didn't she say she was going to do her Girl Scout good deed for the month and let the whole matter drop?"

"That's what she said, but she and Dr. Willoughby are like that." Sheila held up crossed fingers. "Either she's already told him or she's going to hold the thing over my head forever. Either way . . ." She shook her head angrily.

"Easy, baby, easy," Reese said, crossing to her and slipping his hands beneath her lab coat.

Sheila grimaced, but allowed herself to be embraced. Balding, moderately overweight, and wedded to three-piece suits, Reese had never held sex appeal for her in any visceral sense. Still, he was the administrator of the entire hospital complex, and time and experience had taught her that true sex appeal was based not so much on what a man could do *to* her as *for* her.

"You have the most beautiful tits of any woman I've ever known," Reese whispered. "Baby, do you know how long it's been?"

She blocked his move toward her breasts with an out-stretched hand. "It's not *my* fault, Norty. I'm divorced. You're the one with all the family commitments. Remember?"

Reese gauged the determination in her eyes and decided against another advance. "So," he said, settling into the chair by her desk, "Wonder Woman has been at it again, huh? Well, believe it or not, she's the reason—one of the reasons—I came down here."

"Oh?"

"Maybe you'd better sit down." Reese motioned her to her chair and then waited until she had complied. "Did you know that old Willoughby has decided to resign?"

"No. No, I didn't, actually." She felt some hurt that Reese had been told of the decision before she was.

"He's giving health as a reason, but I think the old goat just can't cut it anymore. Never could, really."

Sheila shot him a look warning against any further deprecation of the man she had worked under for fifteen years. "That's too bad," she murmured.

"Yeah? Well, baby, hang onto your seat. You don't know what bad is. For his successor, your Willoughby wants to recommend one K. Bennett, MD."

Sheila fought a sudden urge to be sick. For years she had, in effect, run the pathology department, using Willoughby for little more than his signature on purchase orders and personnel decisions. With Bennett as chief, she would be lucky to keep her job, much less her power and influence. "You said *wants* to recommend," she managed.

"Bennett refuses to give him the go-ahead until she's talked it over with her husband."

She picked a tiny Smurf doctor doll off her desk and absently twisted its arm. "How do you feel about it?" she asked.

"After what she did last year, writing what amounted to a letter of complaint about me to the board? How do you *think* I feel?"

"So?" The blue rubber arm snapped off in Sheila's hand.

"I won't have that woman heading a department in my hospital, and that's that."

"What can you do?"

The forcefulness in Reese's voice softened. "There, at least for the moment, is the rub. I've started talking to some of the members of the board of trustees and some of the department heads. It turns out that as things stand, she would have no trouble getting approval. It seems only a few beside me—" he smiled conspiratorially, "and now you—know what an incredible pain in the ass she is."

Sheila flipped the arm and then the body of the doll into the trash. "So we both know," she said.

"Baby, I need something on her. Anything that I can use to influence some people. The prospect of dealing with Bennett's crusades month after month is more than I can take. Keep your eyes and ears open. Dig around. There's got to be something."

"If I do find something," Sheila said, "I'll expect you to be grateful."

"I'll be very grateful."

"Good," Sheila said sweetly. "Then we shall see what we shall see." She rose and kissed him on the forehead, her breasts inches from his eyes. "Very grateful," she whispered. "Now don't you forget that." She backed away at the moment Reese reached for her. "Next time, Norty. Right now I've got work to do."

The Braxton Building was more impressive as an address than it was as a structure. At one time, the twenty-eight story granite obelisk had been the centerpiece of Boston's downtown financial district. Now, surrounded by high-rise glass and steel, the building seemed somehow ill at ease. No uninformed passerby could possibly have predicted from the building's exterior the opulence of the lobby and office suites within, especially the grandeur of the twenty-eighth floor, most elegant of the three floors occupied by the law firm of Minton/Samuels.

J. Winfield Samuels selected a Havana-made panatella from a crystal humidor and offered it to his son. Jared, seated to one side of the huge, inlaid Louis Quatorze desk, groaned. "Dad, it's not even eleven o'clock. Didn't Dr. What's-his-face limit the number you're supposed to smoke in a day?"

"I pay Shrigley to fix me up so I can do whatever the hell I want to do, not to tell me how many cigars I can smoke." He snipped the tip with a bone-handled trimmer and lit it from the smokestack of a sterling silver replica of the QE II. "I swear, if Castro had found a way to keep these little beauties from making it to the States, I would have found a way to cancel the bastard's ticket years ago. Think of it. We'd probably have world peace by now because of a cigar." He took a long, loving draw, blew half of it out, inhaled the rest, and gazed out the floor-to-ceiling window at the harbor and the airport beyond.

Jared sipped at his mug of coffee and risked a glance at his watch. Win Samuels had summoned him and Win Samuels would tell him why when Win Samuels was good and ready to do so. That was the way it had always been between them and, for all Jared knew, that was the way Jared Winfield Samuels, Sr. had related to Win. The notion left a bitter aftertaste. Beyond his grandfather, the family had been traced through a dozen or more generations, three centuries, and three continents. Not that he really cared about such things. His years of rebellion in Vermont had certainly demonstrated that. But now, with the possibility that he represented the end of the line he was . . . more aware.

"So, how's Kate?" The older Samuels was still looking out the window when he spoke.

"She's okay. A little harried at work, but okay." It was unwise, Jared had learned over the years, to offer his father any more information than asked for. At seventy, the man was still as sharp as anyone in the game. What he wanted to know, he would ask.

"And how are the negotiations coming with the union people at Granfield?"

"Fine. Almost over, I think. We're meeting with them this afternoon. If that idiot shop steward can understand the pension package we've put together, the whole mess should get resolved with no more work stoppage."

"I knew you could do it. I told Toby Granfield you could do it."

"Well, like I said, it's not over yet."

"But it will be." The words were an order, not a question.

"Yes," Jared said. "It will be."

"Excellent, excellent. How about a little vacation for you and Kate when everything is signed and sealed. Goodness knows you deserve it. Those union thugs are slow, but they're tough. Bert Hodges says his place in Aruba is available the week after next. Suppose we book it for you."

"I don't . . . what I mean is I'll have to talk with Kate. She's got quite a bit going on at the hospital."

"I know." Win Samuels swung around slowly to face his son. At six feet, he was nearly as tall as Jared and no more than five pounds heavier. His rimless spectacles and discreetly darkened hair neutralized the aging effects of deep crow's feet and a slightly sallow complexion.

"What?"

"I said that I knew she was having a busy time of it at the hospital." Samuels paused, perhaps for dramatic effect. "Norton Reese called me this morning."

"Oh?" The statement was upsetting. For five years, Jared had handled all of Boston Metro's legal affairs. There was no reason for Norton Reese to be dealing directly with his father, even allowing that the two of them had known each other for years.

"He tells me the head of pathology is retiring." Jared nodded that the information was not news. "He also said that this head pathologist, Willoughby, wants Kate to take over for him."

"She mentioned that to me," Jared understated.

"Did she now? Good. I'm glad you two communicate about such minor goings on." The facetiousness in Samuels's voice was hardly subtle.

Kate's independence had been a source of discussion between them on more than one occasion. Somewhere in the drawer of that Louis Quatorze desk was a computer printout showing that while he had received forty-nine percent of the total vote cast in the congressional race, he had garnered only forty-two percent of the women's vote. To Win Samuels, the numbers meant that if Mrs. Jared Samuels had been out stumping for her husband instead of mucking about elbow deep in a bunch of cadavers, Jared would be packing to leave for Washington. Self-serving, contrary, disloyal, thoughtless—the adjectives had, from time to time, flown hot and heavy from the old man, though never in Kate's presence. Toward her, he had always been as cordial and charming as could be.

"Look, Dad," Jared said, "I've still got some preparation to do for that session at Granfield. Do you think . . ."

"Donna," Samuels said through the intercom, "could you bring in another tea for me and another coffee for my son, please?"

Jared sank back in his seat and stared helplessly at the far wall, a wall covered with photographs of politicians, athletes and other celebrities, arm in arm or hand in hand with his father. A few of them were similar shots featuring his grandfather, and one of them was an eight by ten of Jared and the President, taken at a three-minute meeting arranged by his father for just that purpose.

With a discreet knock, Samuels's sensuous receptionist entered and set their beverages and a basket of croissants on a mahogany stand near the desk. Her smile in response to Jared's "Thank you" was vacant—a subtle message that her allegiance was to the man on the power side of the Louis Quatorze.

"So," Samuels said, settling down with a mug of tea in one hand and his Havana in the other, "what do you think of this business at Metro?"

"I haven't given it much thought," Jared lied. "As far as I know, nothing formal has been done yet."

"Well, I'd suggest you start thinking about it."

"What?"

"Norton Reese doesn't want Kate to have that position and, frankly, neither do I. He thinks she's too young and too inexperienced. He tells me that if she gets the appointment, which incidentally is doubtful anyhow, she'll run herself ragged, burn out, and finally get chewed to ribbons by the politicians and the other department heads. According to him, Kate just doesn't understand the way the game is played—that there are some toes that are simply not to be stepped on."

"Like his," Jared snapped.

"Jared, you told me the two of you were planning on starting your family. Does Kate think she can do that and run a department, too? What about her obligation to you and your career? It's bad enough she's married to you and doesn't even have your name. Christ, her looks alone would be worth thousands of votes to you if she'd just plunk her face in front of a camera a few times. Add a little baby to that, and I swear you could make a run for the Senate and win."

"Kate's business is Kate's business," Jared said with neither enthusiasm nor conviction.

"Take her to the Caribbean. Have a talk with her," Samuels reasoned calmly. "Help her see that marriage is a series of . . . compromises. Give and take."

"Okay, I'll try."

"Good. Kate should see where her obligations and her loyalties lie. Ross Mattingly may be on a downhill slide, but he still managed to hang on and win the election. Don't think he's going to roll over and play dead next time. The fewer liabilities we have the better. And frankly, the way things stand, Kate is a minus. Have I made my thoughts clear?"

"Clear." Jared felt totally depleted.

"Fine. Let me know when the Granfield business is done, and also let me know the date you two decide on, so I can tell Bert Hodges." With a nod, Winfield Samuels signaled the meeting over.

◆

In his sea-green scrub suit and knee-length white coat, Tom Engleson might have been the earnest young resident on a daytime soap opera, loving his way through the nurses one moment, stamping out disease the next. But his eyes gave him away. Kate saw the immense fatigue in them the moment she entered the resident's office on the fourth floor of the building renovated by the Ashburton Foundation and renamed in memory of Sylvia Ashburton. It was a fatigue that went deeper than the circles of gray enveloping them, deeper than the fine streaks of red throughout their sclerae.

"Been to sleep at all?" Kate asked, glancing at the clock as she set two tinfoil pans of salad on the coffee table. It was twenty minutes of two.

Engleson merely shook his head and began to work off the plastic cover of his salad with a dexterity that was obviously far from what it had been when he had started his shift thirty and a half hours before. Studying the man's face, Kate wondered how residency programs could justify the ridiculous hours they required, especially of surgical trainees. It was as if one generation of doctors was saying to the next, "We had to do it this way and we came out all right, didn't we?" Meanwhile, year after year, a cardiogram was misread here, an operation fumbled there; never a rash of problems, just isolated incidents at one hospital then another, one program then another—incidents of no lasting consequence, except, of course, to the patients and families involved.

"I hope you like blue cheese," Kate said. "Gianetti's has great vinaigrette, too. I just guessed."

"It's fine, perfect, Dr. Samuels," Engleson said between bites. "I've missed a meal or two since this Vitale thing started yesterday morning."

"Eat away. You can have some of mine if you want. I'm not too hungry. And it's 'Kate.' We pathologists have a little trouble with formality."

Engleson, his mouth engaged with another forkful of salad, nodded his acknowledgment.

"Sorry I missed you when I was here last evening. The nurse said you were in the delivery room."

"A set of twins."

"How's Beverly Vitale?"

"Her blood count's down this morning. Twenty-five. She's due for a recheck in an hour or two. Any further drop, and we'll give her more blood."

"Her GI tract?" Kate asked, speculating on the site of blood loss.

"Probably. There's been some blood in every stool we've checked. She's on steroids, you know."

"I do know. Withhold steroids, and her antibodies run wild, destroying her own clotting factors; use them, and she risks developing bleeding ulcers. It's one of those situations that makes me grateful I decided on pathology. Stan Willoughby and I reviewed the ovary sections this morning. His impression is that the findings are unique. He's doing some special stains now and has sent slides to a colleague of his at Johns Hopkins, whom he says is as good as anyone in the business at diagnosing ovarian disorders. He also is calling around town to see if anything like this has turned up in another department."

"Etiology?"

"No clues, Tom. Virus, toxin, med reaction. All of the above, none of the above, A and B but not C. She told you she wasn't on any meds, right?"

"None except vitamins. The multivitamin plus iron we dispense through the Omnicenter."

"Well I'm living proof those don't cause any problems. I've taken them for a couple of years. Make frail pathologist strong like bull." Kate flexed her biceps.

"Make pathologist excellent teacher, too."

"Why, thank you." Kate's green eyes sparkled. "Thank you very much, Tom." For a moment, she saw him blush. "How about we go say hello to Beverly. I'd like to make extra sure about one or two aspects of her history. Here, you can stick this salad in that refrigerator for later."

"Provided the bacteria who call that icebox home don't eat it first," Tom said.

The two were heading down the hall toward the stairway when the overhead page snapped to life. "Code ninety-nine, Ashburton five-oh-two; code ninety-nine, Ashburton five-oh-two."

"Oh, Jesus." Tom was already racing toward the exit as he spoke. Kate was slower to react. She was almost to the stairway door before she realized that Ashburton 502 was Beverly Vitale's room.

It had been a year, perhaps two, since Kate had last observed a cardiac arrest and resuscitation attempt. She was certified in advanced cardiac life support, but training and testing then had been on Resusci-Annie, a mannequin. Her practical experience had ended years ago, along with her internship. At the moment, however, none of those considerations mattered. What mattered was the life of a young woman who loved to make music. With an athlete's quickness, Kate bolted after Tom Engleson up the stairs from Ashburton Four to Ashburton Five.

There were more than enough participants in the code. Residents, nurses, medical students, and technicians filled room 502 and overflowed into the hall. Kate worked her way to a spot by the door, from which she watched the nightmare of Beverly Vitale's final minutes of life.

It was a gastric hemorrhage, almost certainly from an ulcer eroding into an artery. The woman's relentless exsanguination was being complicated by the aspiration of vomited blood. Cloaked in abysmal helplessness, Kate witnessed Tom Engleson, desperation etched on his face, issuing orders in a deceptively composed tone; the organized chaos of the white-clad code team, pumping, injecting, monitoring, reporting, respirating, suctioning; and through the milling bodies, the expressionless, blood-smeared face of Beverly Vitale.

For nearly an hour the struggle continued, though

there was never a pulse or even an encouraging electrocardiographic pattern. In the end, there was nothing but another lesson in the relative impotence of people and medicine when matched against the capriciousness of illness and death. Tom Engleson, his eyes dark and sunken, shook his head in utter futility.

"It's over," he said softly. "Thank you all. It's over."

# 3

## Tuesday 11 December

Simultaneously with hearing the report from the WEEI traffic helicopter of a monumental backup stemming from the Mystic/Tobin Bridge, Kate became part of it. Commuting to the city from the North Shore was an experience that she suspected ranked in pleasantness somewhere between an IRS audit and root canal work. Although Tuesday was normally a low-volume day, this morning she had encountered rain, sleet, snow, and even a bizarre stretch of sunlight during her thirty-mile drive, far too much weather for even Boston drivers to attack. With a groan, she resigned herself to being half an hour late, perhaps more, for the appointment Stan Willoughby had arranged for her at White Memorial Hospital.

The pathology chief's call had punctuated another confusing, bittersweet morning with Jared. It seemed as if the intensity and caring in their relationship was waxing and waning not only from day to day but from hour to hour or even from minute to minute. In one sentence the man was Jared Samuels, the funny, sensitive, often ingenuous fellow she had married and still loved deeply; in the next he was calculating and distant, a miniature of his father, intransigent on points they should have been working through as husband and wife. At last, after an awkward hour of lighting brush fires of dissension and then scurry-

72

ing to stamp them out, Jared had suggested a week or ten days together in Aruba, away from the pressures and demands of their careers.

"What do you say, Boots?" he had asked, calling on the pet name she favored most of the four or five he used. "Aruba you all over." The expression in his eyes—urgency? fear?—belied his levity.

"Aruba you too, Jared," she had said finally.

"Then we go?"

"If Stan can give me the time off, and if you can stand the thought of trying to hang onto a woman swathed in Coppertone, we go."

At that moment, Jared looked reborn.

"Grumper-to-grumper, stall-and-crawl traffic headed in a snail trail toward the bridge, thanks to a fender bender in the left-hand lane." The Eye-in-the-Sky was sparing none of his clichés in describing the mess on Route 1 south. Kate inched her Volvo between cars, but gained little ground. Finally, resigned to the situation, she settled back, turned up the volume on the all-news station, and concentrated on ignoring the would-be Lothario who was winking and waving at her from the Trans-Am in the next lane.

The news, like Stan Willoughby's call, dealt with the sudden death of Red Sox hero Bobby Geary, a homegrown boy who had played his sandlot ball in South Boston, not a mile from the luxurious condominium where he was found by his mother following an apparent heart attack. Stan's name was mentioned several times as the medical examiner assigned to autopsy the man who had given away thousands of free tickets and had added an entire floor to Children's and Infants' Hospital in the name of "the kids of Boston."

"Kate," Willoughby had begun, "I hope I'm not interrupting anything."

"No, no. Just getting ready for work," she had said, smiling at Jared, who was nude by the bathroom door dancing a coarse hula and beckoning her to the shower with a long-handled scrub brush.

"Well, I don't want you to come to work."

"What?"

"I want you to go to White Memorial. You have an appointment in the pathology department there at eight-thirty. Leon Olesky will be waiting for you. Do you know him?"

"Only by name."

"Well, I called around town trying to see if anyone had seen a case similar to our Miss Vitale's. Initially there was nothing, but late last night Leon called me at home. From what he described, the two cases—his and ours—sound identical. I told him you'd be over to study his material."

"How old was the woman?" Kate had asked excitedly.

"I don't remember what he said. Twenty-eight, I think."

"Cause of death?"

"Ah ha! I thought you'd never ask. Cerebral hemorrhage, secondary to minor head trauma."

"Platelets? Fibrinogen?" Her hand was white around the receiver.

"Leon didn't know. The case was handled by one of his underlings. He said he'd try to find out by the time you got there."

"Can't you come?"

"Hell, no. Haven't you heard the news about Bobby Geary?"

"The ball player?"

"Heart attack late last night. Found dead in bed. I'm posting him at ten-thirty. In fact, I'd like you back here before I finish, just in case I need your help."

"You've got it. You know, you are a pretty terrific chief, Stanley. Are you sure you want to retire?"

"Yesterday, if I could arrange it, Katey-girl. You hurry on back to Metro after you see Olesky, now. No telling what this shriveled brain of mine might miss."

White Memorial Hospital, an architectural polyglot of more than a score of buildings, was the flagship of the fleet of Harvard Medical School affiliated hospitals. Overlooking the Charles River near the North End, WMH had more research facilities, professors, grants, and administrative expertise than any hospital in the area, if not the world. Metropolitan Hospital had once held sway, reportedly supplying ninety percent of all the professors of medicine at all the medical schools in the country, but that time had long since been buried beneath an avalanche of incompetent administrators, unfavorable publicity, and corrupt city politicians. Although Metro had made a resurgence of sorts under the guidance of Norton Reese, there was little likelihood of its ever recapturing the prestige, endowments, and fierce patient loyalty of the glory days, when at least one man was known to have had "Take Me To Metro" tattooed across his chest.

It had been some time since Kate had had reason to visit the pathology unit at White Memorial, and she was uncomfortably impressed with the improvements and expansion that had occurred. Equipment her department congratulated itself on acquiring, this unit possessed in duplicate or triplicate. Corridors and offices were brightly lit, with plants, paintings, and other touches that made the work environment less tedious and oppressive. Almost subconsciously, Kate found herself making mental lists of things she would press to accomplish as chief of pathology at Metro.

Leon Olesky, a mild, Lincolnesque man, brushed off her apologies for her tardiness and after exchanging compliments about Stan Willoughby, left her alone in his office with the material from the autopsy of Ginger Rittenhouse. On a pink piece of paper by his elegant microscope were the data on the woman's blood studies. Only two of many parameters measured were abnormal: fibrinogen and platelets. The levels of each were depressed enough to have been life threatening. Her hands trembling with anticipation, Kate took the first of the ovarian sections and slid it onto the stage of the microscope. A moment to flex tension from the muscles in her neck, and she leaned forward to begin another journey through the yellow-white light.

Forty-five minutes later, the one had become three. Leon Olesky hunched over one set of oculars of the teaching microscope, controlling the focus with his right hand and moving the slide with his left. Across from him, in the seat Kate had occupied, was Tom Engleson.

"You know," Olesky said, "if Stan hadn't called me about your case, the findings on our young woman would have slipped right past us. I mentioned the matter last night at our weekly department conference, but no one responded. An hour later, Dr. Hickman came to my office. Young Bruce is, perhaps, the brightest of our residents, but at times, I'm afraid, a bit too quick for his own good."

Kate sighed. Olesky's observations described many of the so-called hotshot residents she had worked with over the years. "I'll take methodical over genius any day of the week," she said.

"Both is best," Olesky responded, "but that's a rare combination, indeed. I might mention, though, that it is a combination your mentor feels he is lucky to have found in you."

"Methodical, yes," Kate allowed, "but I've yet to receive a single membership application from Mensa."

"She's only the best in the hospital," Tom interjected somewhat impetuously.

"Finish telling us about your resident." Kate withheld reaction to Engleson's enthusiasm, sensing that what she felt was, in equal parts, flattered and embarrassed.

"Well, it seems our Dr. Hickman was uncertain about the pathology he was seeing in this woman's ovaries. However, rather than think that the finding might be unique, he assumed, although he won't say so in as many words, that the condition was one he should have known about, and hence one he would look foolish asking for help with. Since the cause of death was unrelated to the ovaries, he chose to describe his findings in the autopsy report and leave it at that."

"No harm done," Kate said.

"Quite the contrary, in fact. This event may be the pinprick Hickman's ego needs so he can reach his full potential as a physician. It will make even more of an impression if, as Dr. Willoughby and now yours truly, suspect, this pathology turns out to be one never before described."

Kate and Tom exchanged excited glances. "How would you explain its showing up in two woman in the same city at about the same time?" she asked.

The professor's eyes, dark and deeply serious, met first Engleson's and then Kate's. "Considering the outcome of the illness in both individuals, I would suggest that we work diligently to find an answer to that question. At the moment, I have none."

"There must be a connection," Engleson said.

"I hope there is, young man." Olesky rose from his stool. "And I hope the two of you will be able to find it. I have a class to teach right now at the medical school. This evening, I leave for meetings in San Diego, and from there, I go to the wedding of my son in New Mexico. My office and our department are at your disposal."

"Thank you," they said.

Olesky replaced his lab coat with a well-worn mackintosh. He shook hands first with Engleson and then with Kate. A final check of his desk and he shambled from the office.

Kate waited for the door to click shut. "I'm glad you were able to get here so quickly," she said. "Did you have any trouble getting the records people to let you take Beverly's chart out of the hospital?"

"None. I just followed Engleson's first law of chutzpah. The more one looks like he should be doing what he's doing, the less anyone realizes that he shouldn't. I'll have to admit that the crooks with moving vans and uniforms who pick entire houses clean thought of the law before I did, but I was the first one I know to put it in words. Are you okay? I went to find you after the code was over yesterday, but you were gone. Before I could call, I was rushed to the OR to do an emergency C-section."

"I was okay." She paused. "Actually, I wasn't. It hurt like hell to see her lying there like that. I can't remember the last time I felt so helpless." At the thought, the mention of the word, Arthur Everett's grotesque face flashed in her mind, his reddened eyes bulging with the effort of forcing himself inside her. Yes, I do, she thought. I do remember when. "How about you?" she asked.

Engleson shrugged. "I think I'm still numb. It's like I'm afraid that if I let down and acknowledge my feelings about her and what happened, I'll never set foot in a hospital again."

Kate nodded her understanding. "You know, Tom, contrary to popular belief, being human doesn't disqualify you from being a doctor. Are you married?" Engleson shook his head. "I think it's hard to face some of the things we have to face and then have no one to talk them out with, to cry on, if necessary, when we get home." She thought about the difficult morning with Jared and smiled inwardly at the irony of her words. "Had you known Beverly outside the hospital?"

"No. I met her when she came into Metro. But I thought about trying to start up a relationship as soon as she . . ." His voice grew husky. He cleared his throat.

"I understand," Kate said. "Look, maybe we can talk about our work and our lives in medicine some day soon. Right now, we've got to start looking for some common threads between these women. I'm due back at Metro in," she checked her watch, "—shoot, I've only got about twenty minutes."

Tom was thumbing through the thin sheaf of papers dealing with Ginger Rittenhouse. "It shouldn't take long to check. They have next to no information here. Ginger

Louise Rittenhouse, twenty-eight, elementary school teacher, lived and worked in Cambridge, but she was running along the Boston side of the river when she collapsed. Apparently she lived long enough to get an emergency CAT scan, but not long enough to get to the OR."

"Married?" Kate asked.

"No. Single. That's the second time you've asked that question about someone in the last two minutes." He narrowed one eye and fingered his moustache. "You have, perhaps, a marriage fixation?"

Kate smiled. "Let's leave my fixations out of this. At least for the time being, okay? What about family? Place of birth? Next of kin? Did they document any prior medical history?"

"Hey, slow down. We obstetricians are hardly famous for our swift reading ability. No known medical history. Next of kin is a brother in Seattle. Here's his address. You know, world's greatest hospital or not, they take a pretty skimpy history."

"It doesn't look like they had time for much more," Kate said solemnly. There had to be a connection, she was thinking. The two cases were at once too remarkable and too similar. Somewhere, the lives of a teacher from Cambridge and a cellist from a suburb on the far side of Boston had crossed.

"Wait," Engleson said. "She had a roommate. It says here on the accident floor sheet. Sandra Tucker. That must be how they found out about her family."

Kate again checked her watch. "Tom, I've got to go. I promised Dr. Willoughby I'd help out with the post on Bobby Geary. Do you think you could try and get a hold of this Sandra Tucker? See if our woman has seen a doctor recently or had a blood test. Don't teachers need yearly physicals or something?"

"Not the ones I had. I think their average age was deceased."

"Are you going to call from here?" Engleson thought

for a moment and then nodded. "Fine, give me a ring when you get back to Metro. And Tom? Thanks for the compliment you paid me before." She reached out and shook his hand, firmly and in a businesslike manner. Then she left.

With the pistol-shot crack of bat against ball, thirty thousand heads snapped in horror toward the fence in right center field.

"Jesus, Katey, it's gone," was all Jared could say.

The ball, a white star, arced into the blue-black summer night sky. On the base paths, four runners dashed around toward home. There were two out in the inning, the ninth inning. The scoreboard at the base of the left-field wall in Fenway Park said that the Red Sox were ahead of the Yankees by three runs, but that lead, it appeared, had only seconds more to be.

Kate, enthralled by the lights and the colors and the precision of her first live baseball game, stood frozen with the rest, her eyes fixed on the ball, now in a lazy descent toward a spot beyond the fence. Then into the corner of her field of vision he came, running with an antelope grace that made his movements seem almost slow motion. He left the ground an improbable distance from the fence, his gloved left hand reaching, it seemed, beyond its limits, up to the top of the barrier and over it. For an instant, ball and glove disappeared beyond the fence. In the next instant, they were together, clutched to the chest of Bobby Geary as he tumbled down onto the dirt warning track to the roar of thirty thousand voices. It was a moment Kate would remember for the rest of her life.

This, too, was such a moment.

The body that had once held the spirit and abilities of Bobby Geary lay on the steel table before her, stripped of the indefinable force that had allowed it to sense and react so remarkably. To one side, in a shallow metal pan, was the athlete's heart, carefully sliced along several planes to expose the muscle of the two ventricles—the pumping chambers—and the three main coronary arteries—left, right, and circumflex. Images of that night at Fenway more than four years ago intruded on Kate's objectivity and brought with them a wistfulness that she knew had no place in this facet of her work.

"Nothing in the heart at all?" she asked for the second time.

Stan Willoughby, leprechaunish in green scrubs and a black rubber apron, shook his head. "Must a' bin somethin' he et," he said, by way of admitting that, anatomically at least, he had uncovered no explanation for the pulmonary edema, fluid that had filled Bobby Geary's lungs and, essentially, drowned him from within.

Kate, clad identically to her chief, examined the heart under a high-intensity light. "Teenage heart in a thirty-six-year-old man. I remember reading somewhere that he intended to keep playing until he was fifty. This heart says he might have made it."

"This edema says 'no way,' " Willoughby corrected. "I'm inclined to think dysrhythmia and cardiac arrest on that basis. Preliminary blood tests are all normal, so I think it possible we may never know the specific cause." There was disappointment in his voice.

"Sometimes we just don't," Kate said. The words were Willoughby's, a lesson he had repeated many times to her over the years.

Willoughby glared at her for a moment; then he laughed out loud. "You are a saucy pup, flipping my words back at me like that. Suppose you tell me what to say to the police lieutenant drinking coffee and dropping donut crumbs right now in my office, or to the gaggle of reporters in the lobby waiting for the ultimate word. Ladies and gentlemen, the ultimate word from the crack pathology department you help support with your taxes is that we are absolutely certain we have no idea why Bobby Geary went into a pulmonary edema and died."

Kate did not answer. She had grabbed a magnifying

glass and was intently examining Geary's feet, especially between his toes and along the inside of his ankles. "Stan, look," she said. "All along here. Tiny puncture marks, almost invisible. There must be a dozen of them. No, wait, there are more."

Willoughby adjusted the light and took the magnifier from her. "Holy potato," he said softly. "Bobby Geary an addict?" He stepped back from the table and looked at Kate, who could only shrug. "If he was, he was a bloomin' artist with a needle."

"A twenty-seven or twenty-nine gauge would make punctures about that size."

"And a narcotics or amphetamine overdose would explain the pulmonary edema." Kate nodded. "Holy potato," Willoughby said again. "If it's true, there must be evidence somewhere in his house."

"Unless it happened with other people around and they brought him home and put him to bed. Why don't we send some blood for a drug screen and do levels on any substance we pick up?"

Willoughby glanced around the autopsy suite. The single technician on duty was too far away to have heard any of their conversation. "What do you say we label the tube 'Smith' or 'Schultz' or something. I'm no sports fan, but I know enough to see what's at stake here. The man was a hero."

"What about the policeman?"

"His name's Detective Finn, and he *is* a fan. I think he'd prefer some kind of story about a heart attack, even if the blood test is positive."

"Schultz sounds like as good a name as any," Kate said. "Are these the tubes? Good. I'll have new labels made up."

"I'll send Finn over to the boy's place, and then I'll tell the newsnoses they will just have to wait until the microscopics are processed. Now, when can you give me a report on the goings on at the WMH?"

"Well, beyond what I've already told you, there's not

much to report. We've got some sort of ovarian microsclerosis in two women with profound deficiencies of both platelets and fibrinogen. At this point, we have no connections between the two, nothing even to tell us for sure that the ovarian and blood problems are related."

"So what's next?"

"Next? Well, Tom Engleson, the resident who was involved with Beverly Vitale, is trying to get some information from the roommate of the WMH woman."

"And thou?"

Kate held her hands to either side, palms up. "No plan. I'm on surgicals this month, so I've got a few of those to read along with a frozen or two from the OR. After that I thought I'd talk to my friend Marco Sebastian and see if that computer of his can locate data on a woman named Ginger Rittenhouse."

"Sounds good," Willoughby said. "Keep me posted." He seemed reluctant to leave.

"Is there anything else?" Kate asked finally.

"Well, actually there is one small matter."

"All right, let me have it." Kate knew what was coming.

"I . . . um . . . have a meeting scheduled with Norton Reese this afternoon. Several members of the search committee are supposed to be there and well . . . I sort of wondered if you'd had time to . . ." Willoughby allowed the rest of the thought to remain unspoken.

Kate's eyes narrowed. He had promised her a week, and it had been only a few days. She wasn't at all ready to answer. There were other factors to consider besides merely "want to" or "don't want to." Willoughby had to understand that. "I've decided that if you really think I can do it, and you can get all those who have to agree to do so, then I'll take the position," she heard her voice say.

The girl's name was Robyn Smithers. She was a high school junior, assigned by Roxbury Vocational to spend four hours each week working as an extern in the pathology department of Metropolitan Hospital. Her role was simply defined: do what she was told, and ask questions only when it was absolutely clear that she was interrupting no one. She was one of twelve such students negotiated for by Norton Reese and paid for by the Boston School Department. That these students learned little except how to run errands was of no concern to Reese, who had already purchased a new word processor for his office with the receipts from having them.

Robyn had made several passes by Sheila Pierce's open door before she stopped and knocked.

"Yes, Robyn, what can I do for you?"

"Miss Pierce, I'm sorry for botherin' you. Really I am."

"It's fine, Robyn. I was beginning to wonder what you were up to walking back and forth out there."

"Well, ma'am, it's this blood. Doctor Bennett, you know, the lady doctor?"

"Yes, I know. What about her?"

"Well, Dr. Bennett gave me this here blood to take to . . ." she consulted a scrap of paper, "Special Chemistries, only I can't find where that is. I'm sorry to bother you while you're working and all."

"Nonsense, child. Here, let me see what you've got."

Casually, Sheila glanced at the pale blue requisition form. The patient's name, John Schultz, meant nothing to her. That in itself was unusual. She made it her business to know the names of all those being autopsied in her department. However, she acknowledged, occasionally one was scheduled without her being notified. In the space marked "Patient's Hospital Number" the department's billing number was written. The request was for a screen for drugs of abuse. Penned along the margin of the requisition was the order, "STAT: Phone results to Dr. K. Bennett ASAP."

"Curiouser and curiouser," Sheila muttered.

"Pardon, ma'am?"

"Oh, nothing, dear. Listen, you've been turning the wrong way at that corridor back there. Come, I'll show you." She handed back the vials and the requisition and then guided the girl to the door of her office. "There," she said sweetly. "Just turn right there and go all the way down until you see a cloudy-glass door like mine with Special Chemistries written on it. Okay?"

"Yes. Thank you, ma'am." Robyn Smithers raced down the corridor.

"Glad to help . . . you dumb little shit."

Sheila listened until she heard the door to Special Chemistries open and close; then she went to her phone and dialed the cubicle of Marvin Grimes. Grimes was the department's deiner, the preparer of bodies for autopsy. It was a position he had held for as long as anyone could remember.

"Marvin," Sheila asked, "could you tell me the names of the cases we autopsied today?"

"Jes' two, Ms. Pierce. The old lady Partridge 'n' the ball player."

"No one named Schultz?" Sheila pictured the bottle of Wild Irish Rose Grimes kept in the lower right-hand drawer of his desk; she wondered if by the end of the day the old man would even remember talking to her.

"No siree. No Schultz today."

"Yesterday?"

"Wait, now. Let me check. Nope, only McDonald, Lacey, Briggs, and Ca . . . Capez . . . Capezio. No one named . . . what did you say the name was?"

"Never mind, Marvin. Don't worry about it."

As she replaced the receiver, Sheila tried to estimate the time it would take the technicians in Special Chemistries to complete a stat screen for drugs of abuse.

"Curiouser and curiouser and curiouser," she said.

The dozen or so buildings at Metropolitan Hospital were connected by a series of tunnels, so tortuous and poorly lit that the hospital had recommended that its employees avoid them if walking alone. Several assaults and the crash of a laundry train into a patient's stretcher only enhanced the grisly reputation of the tunnel, as did the now classic Harvard Medical School senior show, *Rats*. Kate, unmindful of the legends and tales, had used the tunnels freely since her medical student days, and except for once coming upon the hours-old corpse of a drunk, nestled peacefully in a small concrete alcove by his half-empty bottle of Thunderbird, she had encountered little to add to the lore. The single greatest threat she faced each time she traveled underground from one building to another was that of getting lost by forgetting a twist or a turn or by missing the crack shaped like Italy that signaled to her the turnoff to the administration building. At various times over the years, she had headed for the surgical building and ended up in the massive boiler room, or headed for a conference in the amphitheater, only to dead end at the huge steam pressers of the laundry building.

Concentrating on not overlooking the landmarks and grime-dimmed signs, Kate made her way through the beige-painted maze toward the computer suite and Marco Sebastian. Nurses in twos and threes passed by in each direction, heralding the approach of the three o'clock change in shift. Kate wondered how many thousands of nurses had over the years walked these tunnels on the way to their charges. The Metro tradition: nurses, professors of surgery, medical school deans, country practitioners, even Nobel laureates. Now, in her own way and through her own abilities, she was becoming part of that tradition. Jared had to know how important that was to her. She had shared with him the ugly secrets of her prior marriage and stifling, often futile life. Surely he knew what all this meant.

In typically efficient Metro fashion, the computer facilities were situated on the top floor of the pediatrics building, as far as possible from the administrative offices that used them the most. Kate paused by the elevator and thought about tackling the six flights of stairs instead. The day, not yet nearly over, had her feeling at once exhausted and exhilarated. Three difficult surgical cases had followed the Geary autopsy. Just as she was completing the last of them, a Special Chemistries technician had dropped off the results of Geary's blood test. The amphetamine level in his body was enormous, quite enough to have thrown him into pulmonary edema. Before she could call Stan Willoughby with the results, she was summoned to his office. The meeting there, with Willoughby and the detective, Martin Finn, had been brief. Evidence found on a careful search of Bobby Geary's condominium had yielded strong evidence that the man was a heavy amphetamine user. It was information known only to the three of them. Finn was adamant—barring any findings suggesting that Geary's death was not an accidental overdose, there seemed little to be gained and much to be lost by making the revelation public. The official story would be of a heart attack, secondary to an anomaly of one coronary artery.

The elevator arrived at the moment Kate had decided on the stairs. She changed her mind in time to slip between the closing doors. Marco Sebastian, expansive in his white lab coat and as jovial as ever, met her with a bear hug. She had been a favorite of his since their first meeting, nearly seven years before. In fact, he and his wife had once made a concerted effort to fix her up with his brother-in-law, a caterer from East Boston. After a rapid-fire series of questions to bring himself up to date on Jared, the job, Willoughby, and the results of their collaborative study, the engineer led her into his office and sat her down next to him, facing the terminal display screen on his desk.

"Now then, Dr. Bennett," he said in a voice with the deep smoothness of an operatic baritone, "what tidbits can I resurrect for you this time from the depths of our electronic jungle? Do you wish the hat size of our first chief of medicine? We have it. The number of syringes syringed in the last calendar year? Can do. The number of warts on the derriere of our esteemed administrator? You have merely to ask."

"Actually, Marco, I wasn't after anything nearly so exotic. Just a name."

"The first baby born here was . . ." He punched a set of keys and then another. ". . . Jessica Peerless, February eighteenth, eighteen forty-three."

"Marco, that wasn't the name I had in mind."

"How about the two hundredth appendectomy?"

"Nope."

"The twenty-eight past directors of nursing?"

"Uh-uh. I'm sorry, Marco."

"All this data, and nobody wants any of it." The man was genuinely crestfallen. "I keep telling our beloved administrator that we are being underused, but I don't think he has the imagination to know what questions to ask. Periodically, I send him tables showing that the cafeteria is overspending on pasta or that ten percent of our patients have ninety percent of our serious diseases, just to pique his interest, remind him that we're still here."

"My name?"

"Oh, yes. I'm sorry. It's been a little slow here. I guess you can tell that."

"It's Rittenhouse, Ginger Rittenhouse. Here's her address, birthplace, and birthdate. That's all I have. I need to know if she's ever been a patient of this hospital, in or out."

"Keep your eyes on the screen," Sebastian said dramatically. Thirty seconds later, he shook his head. "*Nada*. A Shirley Rittenhouse in nineteen fifty-six, but no others."

"Are you sure?"

Sebastian gave her a look that might have been anticipated from a judge who had been asked, "Do you really think your decision is fair?"

"Sorry," she said.

"Of course, she still could have been a patient of the Omnicenter."

Kate stiffened. "What do you mean?"

"Well, the Omnicenter is sort of a separate entity from the rest of Metro. This system here handles records and billing for the Ashburton inpatient service, but the Omnicenter is totally self-contained. Has been since the day they put the units in—what is it?—nine, ten years ago."

"Isn't that strange?"

"Strange is normal around this place," Sebastian said.

"Can't you even plug this system into the one over there?"

"Nope. Don't know the access codes. Carl Horner, the engineer who runs the electronics there, plays things pretty close to the vest. You know Horner?"

"No, I don't think so." Kate tried to remember if, during any of her visits to the Omnicenter as a patient, she had even seen the man. "Why do you suppose they're so secretive?"

"Not secretive so much as careful. I play around with numbers here; Horner and the Omnicenter people live and die by them. Every bit of that place is computerized: records, appointments, billing, even the prescriptions."

"I know. I go there for my own care."

"Then you can imagine what would happen if even a small fly got dropped into their ointment. Horner is a genius, let me tell you, but he is a bit eccentric. He was writing advanced programs when the rest of us were still trying to spell IBM. From what I've heard, complete independence from the rest of the system is one of the conditions he insisted upon before taking the Omnicenter job in the first place."

"So how do I find out if Ginger Rittenhouse has ever been a patient there? It's important, Marco. Maybe very important."

"Well, Paleolithic as it may sound, we call and ask."

"The phone?"

Marco Sebastian shrugged sheepishly and nodded.

*   *   *

DEAD END. Alone in her office, Kate doodled the words on a yellow legal pad, first in block print, then in script, and finally in a variety of calligraphies, learned through one of several "self-enrichment" courses she had taken during her two years with Art. According to Carl Horner, Marco Sebastian's counterpart at the Omnicenter, Ginger Rittenhouse had never been a patient there. Tom Engleson had succeeded in contacting the woman's roommate, but her acquaintance and living arrangement with Ginger were recent ones. Aside from a prior address, Engleson had gleaned no new information. Connections thus far between the woman and Beverly Vitale: zero.

Outside, the daylong dusting of snow had given way to thick, wet flakes that were beginning to cover. The homeward commute was going to be a bear. Kate tried to ignore the prospect and reflect instead on what her next move might be in evaluating the microsclerosis cases—perhaps an attempt to find a friend or family member who knew Ginger Rittenhouse better than her new roommate. She might present the two women's pathologies at a regional conference of some sort, hoping to luck into yet a third case. She looked at the uncompleted work on her desk. Face it, she realized, with the amount of spare time she had to run around playing epidemiologist, the mystery of the ovarian microsclerosis seemed destined to remain just that.

For a time, her dread of the drive home did battle with the need to get there in order to grocery shop and set out some sort of dinner for the two of them. Originally, they had tried to eschew traditional roles in setting up and maintaining their household, but both rapidly realized that their traditional upbringings made that arrangement impractical if not impossible. The shopping and food preparation had reverted to her, the maintenance of their physical plant to Jared. Day-to-day finances, they agreed, were beyond either of their abilities and therefore to be shared. Again she checked out the window. Then after a final hesitation, a final thought about calling home and leaving a message on their machine that she was going to work late, she pushed herself away from the desk.

As she stood up, she decided: if it was going to be dinner, then dammit, it was going to be a special dinner. In medical school and residency, she had always been able to find an extra gear, a reserve jet of energy, when she needed it. Perhaps tonight her marriage could use a romantic, gourmet dinner more than it could her moaning about the exhausting day she had endured. Spinach salad, shrimp curry, candles, Grgich Hills Chardonnay, maybe even a chocolate soufflé. She ticked off a mental shopping list as she slipped a few scientific reprints into her briefcase, bundled herself against the rush-hour snow, and hurried from her office, pleased to sense the beginnings of a surge. It was good to know she still had one.

In the quiet of his windowless office, Carl Horner spoke through his fingertips to the information storage and retrieval system in the next room. He had implicit faith in his machines, in their perfection. If there was a problem, as it now seemed there was, the source, he felt certain, was human—either himself or someone at the company. Again and again his fingers asked. Again and again the answers were the same. Finally, he turned from his console to one of two black phones on his desk. A series of seven numbers opened a connection in Buffalo, New York; four numbers more activated the line to a "dead box" in Atlanta; and a final three completed an untraceable connection to Darlington, Kentucky.

Cyrus Redding answered on the first ring.

"Carl?"

"Orange red, Cyrus." Had the colors been reversed, Redding would have been warned either that someone was monitoring Horner's call or that the possibility of a tap existed.

"I can talk," Redding said.

"Cyrus, a woman named Kate Bennett, a pathologist

at Metro, just called asking for information on two women who died from the same unusual bleeding disorder."

"Patients of ours?"

"That is affirmative, although Dr. Bennett is only aware that one of them is. Both women had autopsies that showed, in addition to the blood problems, a rare condition of their ovaries."

"Have you asked the Monkeys about them?"

"Affirmative. The Monkeys say there is no connection here."

"Does that make sense to you, Carl?"

"Negative."

"Keep looking into matters. I want a sheet about this Doctor Bennett."

"I'll learn what I can and teletype it tomorrow."

"Tonight."

"Tonight, then."

"Be well, old friend."

"And you, Cyrus. You'll hear from me later."

# 4

## Wednesday 12 December

"Coronary Strikes Out Bobby." Kate cringed at the *Boston Herald* headline on her office desk. The story was one of the rare events that managed to make the front page in both that paper and the *Boston Globe*. Though the *Globe*'s treatment was more detailed, the lead and side articles said essentially the same thing in the two papers. Bobby Geary, beloved son of Albert and Maureen Geary, son of the city itself, had been taken without warning by a clot as thin as the stitching on a baseball. The stories, many of them by sportswriters, were the heart-rending stuff of which Pulitzers are made, the only problem being that they weren't true.

The storm, which had begun the evening before, had dumped a quick eight inches of snow on the city before skulking off over the North Atlantic. However, neither the columns of journalistic half-truths nor the painful drive into the city could dampen the warmth left by the talking and the sharing that had followed the candlelight meal Kate had prepared for her husband. For the first time in years, Jared had talked about his disastrous first marriage and the daughter he would, in all likelihood, never see again. "Gone to find something better" was all the note from his wife had said. The trail of the woman and her daughter had grown cold in New York and finally vanished in a morass of evanescent religious cults throughout southern and central California. "Gone to find something better."

Jared had cried as he spoke of the Vermont years, of his need then to break clear of his father's expectations and build a life for himself. Kate had dried his tears with her lips and listened to the confusion and pain of a marriage that was far more an act of rebellion than one of love.

Kate was finishing the last of the *Globe* stories when, with a soft knock, a ponderous woman entered carrying a paper bag. The woman's overcoat was unbuttoned, exposing a nurse's uniform, pin, and name tag. Kate read the name as the woman spoke it.

"Dr. Bennett, I'm Sandra Tucker. Ginger Rittenhouse was my roommate."

"Of course. Please sit down. Coffee?"

"No, thank you. I'm doing private-duty work, and I'm expected at my patient's house in Weston in half an hour. Dr. Engleson said that if I remembered anything or found anything that might help you understand Ginger's death I could bring it to you."

"Yes, that's true. I'm sorry about Ginger."

"Did you know her?"

"No. No, I didn't."

"We had shared the house only for a few months."

"I know."

"A week after she moved in, Ginger baked a cake and cooked up a lasagna for my birthday."

"That was very nice," Kate said, wishing she had thought twice about engaging the woman in small talk. There was a sad aura about her—a loneliness that made Kate suspect she would talk on indefinitely if given the chance, patient or no patient.

"We went to the movies together twice, and to the Pops, but we were only just getting to be friends and . . ."

"It's good of you to come all the way down here in the snow," Kate said in as gentle an interruption as she could manage.

"Oh, well, it's the least I could do. Ginger was a very nice person. Very quiet and very nice. She was thinking about trying for the marathon next spring."

"What do you have in the bag? Is that something of hers?" A frontal assault seemed the only way.

"Bag? Oh, yes. I'm sorry. Dr. Engleson, what a nice man he is, asked me to go through her things looking for medicines or letters or doctors' appointments or anything that might give you a clue about why she . . . why she . . ."

"I know it was a hard thing for you to do, Miss Tucker, and I'm grateful for any help."

"It's Mrs. Tucker. I'm divorced."

Kate nodded. "The bag?"

"My God, I apologize again." She passed her parcel across the desk. "Sometimes I talk too much, I'm afraid."

"Sometimes I do, too." Kate's voice trailed away as she stared at the contents of the bag.

"I found them in the top of Ginger's bureau. It's the strangest way to package pills I've ever seen. On that one sheet are nearly two months worth of them, packaged individually and labeled by day and date when to take each one. Looks sort of like it was put together by a computer."

"It was," Kate said, her thoughts swirling.

"Pardon?"

"I said it *was* put together by a computer." Her eyes came up slowly and turned toward the window. Across the street, its glass and steel facade jewellike, was the pride of Metropolitan Hospital of Boston. "The pharmacy-dispensing computer of the Omnicenter. The Omnicenter where Ginger Rittenhouse never went."

"I don't understand."

Kate rose. "Mrs. Tucker, you've been a tremendous help. I'll call if we need any further information or if we learn something that might help explain your friend's death. If you'll excuse me, there are some phone calls I must make."

The woman took Kate's hand. "Think nothing of it," she said. "Oh, I felt uncomfortable at first, rifling through her drawers, but then I said to myself, 'If you're not going to do it, then . . .'"

"Mrs. Tucker, thank you very much." One hand still locked in Sandra Tucker's, Kate used her other to take the woman by the elbow and guide her out the door.

The tablets were a medium-strength estrogen-progesterone combination, a generic birth control pill. Kate wondered if Ginger Rittenhouse had been too shy to mention to her roommate that she took them. Computer printed along the top margin of the sheet were Ginger's name, the date six weeks before when the prescription had been filled, and instructions to take one tablet daily. Also printed was advice on what to do if one dose was missed, as well as if two doses were missed. Common side effects were listed, with an asterisk beside those that should be reported immediately to Ginger's Omnicenter physician. Perforations, vertical and horizontal, enabled the patient to tear off as many pills as might be needed for time away. The setup, like everything at the Omnicenter, was slick— thoughtfully designed, considerate, and practical—further showing why there was a long list of women from every economic level waiting to become patients of the facility.

Kate ran through half a dozen possible explanations of why she had been told Ginger Rittenhouse was not a patient at the Omnicenter; then she accepted that there was only one way to find out. She answered, "Doctor Bennett," when the Omnicenter operator asked who was calling, emphasizing ever so slightly her title. Immediately, she was patched through to Dr. William Zimmermann, the director.

"Kate, this is a coincidence. I was just about to call you. How are you?" It was typical of the man, a dynamo sometimes called Rocket Bill, to forgo the redundancy of saying hello.

"I'm fine, Bill, thanks. What do you mean 'coincidence'?"

"Well, I've got a note here from our statistician, Carl Horner, along with a file on someone named Rittenhouse. Carl says he originally sent word to you that we had no such patient."

"That's right."

"Well, we do. Apparently there was a coding mistake or spelling mistake or something."

"Did he tell you why I wanted to know?"

"Only that this woman had died."

"That's right. Does your Carl Horner make mistakes often?" The idea of an error didn't jibe with Marco Sebastian's description of the man.

"Once every century or so as far as I can tell. I've been here four years now, and this is the first time I've encountered any screwup by his machines. Do you want me to send this chart over to you?"

"Can I pick it up in person, Bill? There are some other things I want to talk with you about."

"One o'clock okay with you?"

"Fine. And Bill, could you order a printout of the record of a Beverly Vitale."

"The woman who bled out on the inpatient service?"

"Yes."

"I've already reviewed it. A copy's right here on my desk."

"Excellent. One last thing."

"Yes?"

"I'd like to meet Carl Horner. Is that possible?"

"Old Carl's a bit cantankerous, but I suspect it would be okay."

"One o'clock, then?"

"One o'clock."

Ellen Sandler clutched her housecoat about her and sat on the edge of her bed staring blankly at a disheveled blackbird foraging for a bit of food on the frozen snow beyond her window. She was expected at the office in less than an hour. The house was woefully low on staples. Betsy's math teacher had set up a noontime conference to investigate her falling interest and grade in the subject. Eve needed help shopping for a dress for her piano recital. Darcy had come home an hour after weekday curfew, her clothes tinged with a musty odor that Ellen suspected was marijuana. So much to do. So much had changed, yet so little.

The silence in the house was stifling. Gradually, she focused on a few ongoing sounds: the hum of the refrigerator, the drone of the blower on the heating and air conditioning system Sandy had installed to celebrate their last anniversary, the sigh that was her own breathing.

"Get up," she told herself. "Goddamn it, get up and do what you have to do." Still, she did not move. The hurt, the oppressive, constricting ache in her chest seemed to make movement impossible. It wasn't the loneliness that pained so, although certainly that was torture. It wasn't the empty bed or the silent telephone or the lifeless eyes that stared at her from the mirror. It wasn't even the other woman, whoever she was. It was the lies—the dozens upon dozens of lies from the one person in the world she needed to trust. It was the realization that while the anguish and hurt of the broken marriage might, in time, subside, the inability to trust would likely remain part of her forever.

"Get up, dammit. Get up, get dressed, and get going."

With what seemed a major effort, she broke through the inertia of her spirit and the aching stiffness in her limbs, and stood up. The room, the house, the job, the girls—so much had changed, yet so little. She walked to the closet, wondering if perhaps something silkier and more feminine than what she usually wore to the office would buoy her. The burgundy dress she had bought for London caught her eye. Two men had made advances toward her the first day she wore it, and there had been any number of compliments on it since.

As she crossed the room, Ellen felt the morning

discomforts in her joints diminish—all, that is, except a throbbing in her left thigh that seemed to worsen with each step. She slipped off her housecoat, hung it up, and pulled her flannel nightgown off over her head. Covering much of the front of her thigh was the largest bruise she had ever seen. Gingerly, she explored it with her fingers. It was somewhat tender, but not unbearably so. She did not know how she had gotten it. She had sustained no injury that she could remember. It must, she decided, have been the way she slept on it.

She selected a blue, thin wool jumpsuit in place of the dress, which, it seemed, might not cover the bruise in every situation. She dressed, still unable to take her eyes off the grotesque discoloration. Her legs had always been one of her best features. Even after three children, she took pride that there were only a few threadlike veins visible behind her knees. Now this. For a moment, she thought about calling Kate for advice on whether or not to have a doctor check things out, but she decided that a bruise was a bruise. Besides, she had simply too much else to do.

A bit of makeup and some work on her hair, and Ellen felt as ready as she ever would to tackle the day. The face in her mirror, thin and fine featured, would probably turn some heads, but the eyes were still lifeless.

She was leaving the room when she noticed the note tacked to the doorjamb. Each day it happened like this, and each day it was like seeing the note for the first time, despite the fact that she had tacked it there more than a year before.

"Take Vit," was all it said.

Ellen went to the medicine cabinet, took the sheet of multivitamins plus iron from the shelf, punched one out, and swallowed it without water. Half consciously, she noticed that there was only a four-week supply remaining, and she made a mental note to set up an appointment with her physician at the Omnicenter.

Although she was limping slightly as she left the

house, Ellen found the tightness in her thigh bearable. In fact, compared to the other agonies in her life at the moment, the sensation was almost pleasant.

The sign, a discreet bronze plate by the electronically controlled glass doors, said, "Metropolitan Hospital of Boston; Ashburton Women's Health Omnicenter, 1975." Kate had been one of the first patients to enroll and had never regretted her decision. Gynecological care, hardly a pleasant experience, had become at least tolerable for her, as it had for the several thousand other women who were accepted before a waiting list was introduced. The inscription above the receptionist's desk said it all. "Complete Patient Care with Complete Caring Patience."

Kate stopped at the small coatroom to one side of the brightly lit foyer, and checked her parka with a blue-smocked volunteer. She could have used the tunnel from the main hospital, but she had been drawn outdoors by the prospect of a few minutes of fresh air and a fluffy western omelet sandwich, *spécialité de la maison* at Maury's Diner.

The receptionist signaled Kate's arrival by telephone and then directed her to Dr. Zimmermann's office on the third floor. The directions were not necessary. Zimmermann had been Kate's Omnicenter physician for four years, since the accidental drowning death of Dr. Harold French, his predecessor and the first head of the Omnicenter. Although she saw Zimmermann infrequently—three times a year was mandatory for women on birth control pills— Kate had developed a comfortable patient-physician relationship with him, as well as an embryonic friendship.

He was waiting by his office door as she stepped from the elevator. Even after four years, the sight of the man triggered the same impressions as had their first meeting. He was dashing. Corny as the word was, Kate could think of no better one to describe him. In his late thirties or early forties Zimmermann had a classic, chiseled handsomeness, along with an urbanity and ease of motion that Kate had originally felt might be a liability to a physician in his medical specialty. Time and the man had proven her concerns groundless. He was polite and totally professional. In a hospital rife with rumors, few had ever been circulated regarding him. Those that had gone around dealt with the usual speculations about an attractive man of his age who was not married. Active on hospital and civic committees, giving of his time to his patients and of his knowledge to his students, William Zimmermann's was a star justifiably on the rise.

"Dr. Kate." Zimmermann took both her hands in his and pumped them warmly. "Come in, come in. I have fresh coffee and . . . Have you had lunch? I could send out for something."

"I stopped at Maury's on the way over. I'm sorry for being so thoughtless. I should have brought *you* something."

"Nonsense. I only asked about lunch for your benefit. I have been skipping the meal altogether—part of a weight loss bet with my secretary."

Even if the bet were concocted on the spot, and considering the man's trim frame that was quite possible, his words were the perfect breeze to dispel Kate's embarrassment.

Zimmermann's office was the den of a scholar. Texts and bound journals filled three walls of floor-to-ceiling bookcases, and opened or marked volumes covered much of a reading table at one end of the room. On the wall behind his desk, framed photographs of European castles were interspersed with elegantly matted sayings, quotations, and homilies. "The downfall of any magician is belief in his own magic." "There are two tragedies in life: One is not to get your heart's desire; the other is to get it." And of course, "The Omnicenter: Complete patient care with complete caring patience." There were several others, most of which Kate had heard or read before. One, however, she could not recall having seen. Done in black Benedictine calligraphy, with a wonderfully ornate arabesque border, it said, "Monkey Work for the Monkeys."

Zimmermann followed her line of sight to the saying. "A gift from Carl," he explained. "His belief is that the energy of physicians and nurses should be directed as much as possible to areas utilizing their five senses and those properties unique to human beings—empathy, caring, and intuitiveness. The mechanics of our job, the paperwork, setting up of appointments, filling of prescriptions, and such, he calls 'monkey work.' His machines can do those jobs faster and more accurately than any of us ever could, and it seems Carl teaches them more almost every day."

"So," said Kate, "he's named his computers . . . the Monkeys." Zimmermann said the last two words in unison with her. Kate sensed a letup in the uneasiness she had developed toward Carl Horner and began looking forward to meeting the man.

"Now," Zimmermann asked, "can you brief me on what you have found in these two patients of ours? I have reviewed their records and found little that might be of help to you."

In the concise, stylized method of case presentation ingrained in physicians from their earliest days in medical school, Kate gave a one-minute capsule of each woman's history, physical exam, laboratory data, and hospital course. "I've brought sections from the ovaries of both patients. I think there's a decent microscope in the lab downstairs," she concluded.

Zimmermann whistled softly. "And the only link to this point is that both were patients here?" Kate nodded. "Well, I can't add much. Miss Rittenhouse had been an Omnicenter patient since nineteen seventy-nine. Nothing but routine checkups since then, except that she was within one missed appointment of being asked to go elsewhere for her gynecologic care. The contract we have our patients sign gives us that option."

"I know. I signed one," Kate said. The contract was another example of the patient-oriented philosophy of the

Omnicenter. Fees were on a yearly basis, adjusted to a patient's income. There was no profit to be made from insisting on compliance with periodic routine visits, yet insist they did. "What about Beverly Vitale?"

Zimmermann shrugged. "Six years a patient. Abortion here five years ago by suction. Had a diaphragm. Never on birth control pills or hormones of any kind. Always somewhat anemic, hematocrits in the thirty-four to thirty-six range."

"She was on iron."

"Yes. Dr. Bartholomew has had her on daily supplements since the day of her first exam."

"Who was Ginger Rittenhouse's doctor?" Kate was grasping for any connection, however remote.

"Actually, she was cared for by the residents, with the help of a faculty advisor. In this woman's case, it was me. However, there was never any need for me to be consulted. She became a patient just after I arrived. I saw her once, and she has had no trouble since." He grimaced at what he considered an inappropriate remark. "Excluding the obvious," he added.

DEAD END. Kate's mind's eye saw the words as she had written them. She glanced at her watch. There would be a surgical specimen processed as a frozen section in half an hour. Her reading would determine whether the patient underwent a limited or extensive procedure. Still, she felt reluctant to let go of the one common factor she had found. "I'm due back for a frozen in a short while, Bill. Do you think you could take me by to meet Carl Horner and his trained Monkeys?"

"Certainly," Zimmermann said. "He's expecting us. By the way, I understand congratulations are in order."

"For what?"

"Well, word has it that you are to be the next chief of pathology."

Kate laughed ruefully. "Welcome to the new game show, *I've Got No Secrets*. Actually, I don't even think my name has formally been presented for consideration yet, so you can hold the congratulations. Besides, with the financial mess the department is in, I'm not sure condolences wouldn't be a better response. You don't suppose that Ashburton Foundation of yours has a few extra hundred thousand lying around, do you?"

"I have no idea, Kate. Norton Reese handles that end of things. I am just one of the barge toters and bale lifters. You might talk to him, though. The foundation certainly has taken good care of us."

Kate stepped into the carpeted, brightly lit corridor. "I'll say they have," she said. The chance that Norton Reese would put himself out on behalf of her department was less than none.

"Monkey Work for the Monkeys." The message was displayed throughout Carl Horner's computer facility, which occupied an area at the rear of the first floor several times the size of Marco Sebastian's unit. Ensconced in the midst of millions of dollars in sophisticated electronics, Carl Horner looked to be something of an anachronism. Beneath his knee-length lab coat, he was wearing a plaid work shirt and a pair of farmer's overalls. His battered work boots might just as well have received their breaking in on a rock pile as in the climate-controlled, ultramodern suite.

Horner greeted Kate with an energetic handshake, though she could feel the bulbous changes of arthritis in every joint. Still the man, stoop shouldered and silver haired, had an ageless quality about him. It emanated, she decided, not only from his dress, but also from his eyes, which were a remarkably luminescent blue.

"Dr. Bennett, I owe you my deepest apology. The error regarding the Rittenhouse file was nothing more— nor less—than a spelling mistake on my part."

Kate smiled. "Apology accepted. Incident forgotten."

"Have you found the explanations you were looking for?"

"No. No, we haven't. Mr. Horner, could you show

me around a bit? I'm especially interested in how the machines work in the pharmacy."

"Carl," Zimmermann said, "if you and Dr. Bennett don't mind, I'm going to get back to work. Kate, I plan to review those slides later tonight and to do some reading. Together, I promise that we shall get to the bottom of all this. Meanwhile, enjoy your tour. We're certainly proud of Carl and his Monkeys."

Patiently, the old man took Kate through the filling of a prescription.

"These cards are preprinted with the patient's name and code number and included with the patient's chart when she has her appointment. The doctors tear 'em up if they're not needed. As you can see, there are twenty-five separate medications already listed here, along with the codes for dosage, amount, and instructions. The machines dispense only these medications, and then only in the form of a generic—as good as any brand-name pharmaceutical, but only a fraction of the cost. The machines automatically review the patient's record for allergies to the medication prescribed, as well as any interaction with medications she might already be taking." Horner's presentation had all the pride of a grandmother holding court at a bridge party. "If there's any problem at all, the prescription is not filled and the patient is referred to our pharmacist, who handles the matter personally."

"What if the physician wants to prescribe a medication other than the twenty-five on the card?" Kate asked.

"Our pharmacy is fully stocked. However, because of the Monkeys, we need only one pharmacist on duty, and he or she has more time to deal with problems such as drug interaction and side effects."

"Amazing," Kate said softly. "Have the Monkeys ever made an error?"

Horner's smile was for the first time somewhat patronizing. "Computers cannot make errors. There are programs backing up programs to guarantee that. Of course, human beings are a different story."

"So I've learned." Kate's cattiness was reflex. There was something about Horner's limitless confidence in the wires, chips, discs, and other paraphernalia surrounding them that she found disquieting. "Tell me, where do the generics come from that the machines dispense?"

"One of the drug houses. We hold a closed-bid auction each year, and the lowest bidder gets the contract."

"Which one has it now?" Horner's answer had been somewhat evasive, hardly in character with the man. She watched his eyes. Was there a flicker of heightened emotion in them? She couldn't tell.

"Now? Redding has it. Redding Pharmaceuticals."

"Ah, the best and the brightest." Kate was not being facetious. In an industry with a checkered past that included thalidomide and many other destroyers of human life, Redding stood alone in its reputation for product safety and the development of orphan drugs for conditions too rare for the drugs to be profitable. "Well, Mr. Horner, I thank you. Your Monkeys are truly incredible."

"My pleasure. If there's anything else I can do, let me know."

Kate turned to go, but then turned back. "Do you have a list of the companies that have held the contract in years past?"

"Since the Omnicenter opened?"

"Yes." For the second time, Kate sensed a change in the man's eyes.

"Well, it won't be much of a list. Redding's the only one."

"Eight auctions and eight Reddings, huh?"

"No bids have even been close to theirs."

"Well, thanks for your help."

"No problem."

Horner's parting handshake and smile seemed somehow more forced than had his greeting. Kate watched as he ambled off, feeling vaguely uneasy about the man, but uncertain why. She glanced at her watch. The frozen section was due in ten minutes, and the patient would be kept under anesthesia until her diagnosis was made. Aside from alerting Bill Zimmermann as to what was going on, her Omnicenter visit had accomplished essentially nothing. Still, the clinic remained the only factor common to two dead women. As she walked through the lobby to retrieve her coat, Kate ran through the possible routes by which the ovarian and blood disorders might have been acquired. Finally, with time running short, she stopped at the reception desk, and wrote a note to Zimmermann.

> Dear Bill—
> Thanks for the talk and the tour. No answers, but perhaps together we can find some. Meanwhile, I'm sending over some microbiology people to take cultures, viral and bacterial, if that's okay with you. They will also check on techniques of instrument sterilization—perhaps a toxin has been introduced that way.
> Let me know if you come up with anything. Also, check your calendar for a night you could come north and have dinner with my husband and me. I'd enjoy the chance to know you better.
> Kate

She sealed the note in an envelope and passed it over to the receptionist. "Could you see to it that Dr. Zimmermann gets this?" The woman smiled and nodded. Kate was halfway to the tunnel entrance when she stopped, hesitated, and then returned. She reclaimed the note, tore the envelope open, and added a PS.

> And Bill . . . could you please get me ten tablets of each of the medications dispensed by the Monkeys. Thanx.
> K.

◆

"Well, what do you say, Clyde. Can I count on you or not?"

Norton Reese set aside the paper clip he was mangling and stared across his desk at the chief of cardiac surgery. Clyde Breslow was the fourth department head he had met with that day. The previous three had made no promises to help block Kate Bennett's appointment, despite delicately presented guarantees that their departments would receive much-needed new equipment as soon as her nomination was defeated. In fact, two of the men, Milner in internal medicine and Hoyt, the pediatrician, had said in as many words that they were pleased with the prospect of having her on the executive committee. "Bright new blood," Milner had called her.

Breslow, Napoleonic in size and temper, watched Reese's discomfort with some amusement. "Now jes' what is it about that little lady that bothers you so, Norton?" he asked in a thick drawl that often disappeared when he was screaming at the nurses and throwing instruments about the operating room or screaming at the medical students and throwing instruments about the dog lab. "She refuse to spread those cute little buns of hers for ya or what?"

"The bitch made me look bad in front of the board of trustees, Clyde. You should remember that. It was your fucking operating microscope that caused all the trouble. I'll be damned if I'm going to have her on my executive committee."

"Whóa, there, Norton. *Your* executive committee? Now ain't you gettin' just the slightest bit possessive about a group you don't even have a vote in?"

"Look, Clyde, I've had a bad day. Do you back me on this and talk to the surgical boys or don't you?"

"Now that jes' depends, don't it?"

"The extra resident's slot? Clyde, I can't do it. I told you that."

"Then maybe you jes' better get used to seeing that pretty little face of Katey B.'s at the meetin's every other Tuesday."

Reese snapped a pencil in half. "All right. I'll try," he said, silently cursing Kate Bennett for putting him in a position to be manipulated by a man like Breslow.

"You do that. Know what I think, Norton? I think you're scared of that woman. That's what I think. A looker with smarts is more than you kin handle."

Without warning, Reese exploded. "Look, Clyde," he said, slamming his desk chair against the wall as he stood, "you have enough fucking trouble remembering that the heart is above the belly button without taking up playing amateur shrink. Now get the hell out of here and get me some support in this thing. I'll do what I can about your goddamn resident."

With a plastic smile, Clyde Breslow backed out of the office. Reese sank into his chair. Frightened of Kate Bennett? The hell he was. He just couldn't stand a snotty, do-gooder kid going around trying to act grown up. She ought to be home keeping house and screwing that lawyer husband of hers.

"Mr. Reese, there's a call for you on two." The secretary's voice startled him, and lunging for the intercom, he spilled the dregs of a cup of coffee on his desk.

"Dammit, Betty, I told you no calls."

"I know you did, sir. I'm sorry. It's Mr. Horner from the Omnicenter. He says it's very important."

Reese sighed. "All right. Tell him to call me on three seven four four." He blotted up the coffee and waited for his private line to ring. It was unusual for Carl Horner to call at all. Omnicenter business was usually handled by Arlen Paquette, Redding's director of product safety. In the few moments before 3744 rang, he speculated on the nature of a problem that might be of such concern that Horner would call. None of his speculations prepared him for the reality.

"Mr. Reese," Horner said, "I'm calling on behalf of a mutual friend of ours." Cyrus Redding's name was one Horner would never say over the phone, but Reese had no doubt whom he meant.

"How is our friend?"

"A bit upset, Mr. Reese. One of your staff physicians has been nosing about the Omnicenter, asking questions about our pharmacy and requesting Dr. Zimmermann to send her samples of the medications we dispense."

The word "her" brought Reese a bone-deep chill. "Who is it?" he asked, already knowing the answer.

"It's the pathologist, Dr. Bennett. She's investigating the deaths of two women who were patients of ours."

"Damn her," Reese said too softly to be heard. "Horner, are you . . . I mean, is the Omnicenter responsible for the deaths?"

"That appears to be negative."

"What do you mean appears to be? Do you know what's at stake? Paquette promised me nothing like this would happen." Reese began feeling a tightness in his chest and dropped a nitroglycerine tablet under his tongue, vowing that if this discomfort was the start of the big one, his last act on earth would be to shoot Kate Bennett between the eyes.

"Our friend says for you to remain cool and not to worry. However, he would like you to find some effective way of . . . diverting Dr. Bennett's interest away from the Omnicenter until we can fix up a few things and do a little more investigating into the two deaths in question."

"What am I supposed to do?"

"That, Mr. Reese, I do not know. Our friend suggests firing the woman."

"I can't do that. I don't hire and fire doctors, for Christ's sake."

"Our friend would like something done as soon as possible. He has asked me to remind you that certain contracts are up for renewal in less than a month."

"Fuck him."

"Pardon?"

"I said, all right. I'll think of something." Suddenly, he brightened. "In fact," he said, reaching into his desk drawer, "I think I already have."

"Fine," Carl Horner said. "All of us involved appreciate your efforts. I'm sure our friend will be extremely beholden when you succeed."

Reese noted the use of 'when' instead of 'if,' but it no longer mattered. "I'll be in touch," he said. Replacing the receiver, he extracted a folder marked "Schultz/Geary." Inside were a number of newspaper articles; the official autopsy report, signed by Stanley Willoughby and Kathryn Bennett, MDs; and an explanatory note from Sheila Pierce. Also in the folder were a number of laboratory tests on a man named John Schultz—a patient who, as far as he or Sheila could tell, never existed in Metropolitan Hospital. While the chances of some kind of coverup weren't a hundred percent, they certainly seemed close to that.

Sheila, he thought as he readied a piece of paper in his typewriter, if this works out, I'm going to see to it that you get at least an extra night or two each month. "To Charles C. Estep, Editor, *The Boston Globe*." Reese whispered the words as he typed them. He paused and checked the hour. By the time he was done with a rough draft, the pathology unit would be empty. A sheet of Kate Bennett's stationery and a sample of her signature would then be all he needed to solve any number of problems. The woman would be out of his hair, perhaps permanently, and Cryus Redding would be—how had Horner put it?—extremely beholden.

"Dear Mr. Estep . . ."

As Norton Reese typed, he began humming "There Is Nothing Like a Dame."

# 5

## Thursday 13 December

"Do you think God is a man or a woman, Daddy?"

Suzy Paquette sat cross-legged on the passenger seat of her father's new Mercedes 450 SL, parked by the pump at Bowen's Texaco.

Behind the wheel, Arlen Paquette watched the mid-morning traffic glide by along Main Street, his thoughts neither on the traffic nor on the question he had just been asked.

"Well, Daddy?"

"Well what, sugar?" The attendant rapped twice on the trunk that he was done. "Company account, Harley," Paquette called out as he pulled away.

"Which is it, man or woman?"

"Which is what, darlin'?"

"God! Daddy, you're not even listening to me at all." She was seven years old with sorrel hair pulled back in two ponytails and a China doll face that was, at that moment, trying to pout.

Paquette swung into a space in front of Darlington Army/Navy and stopped. Never totally calm, he was, he knew, unusually tense and distracted this morning. Still, it was Second Thursday and that gave him the right to be inattentive or cross, as he had been earlier with his wife. He turned to his daughter. She had mastered the expression she wanted and now sat pressed against the car door displaying it, her arms folded tightly across her chest. In that instant, Paquette knew that she was the most beautiful child on earth. He reached across and took her in his arms. The girl stiffened momentarily, then relaxed and returned the embrace.

"I'm sorry, sugar," Paquette said. "I wasn't listening. I'm sorry and I love you and I think God is a woman if you're a woman and a man to someone who's a man and probably a puppy dog to the puppy dogs."

"I love you too, Daddy. And I still don't know why I should have to pray to Our Father when God might be Our Mother."

"You know, you're right. I think that from now on we should say . . . 'Our Buddy who art in Heaven.'"

"Oh, Daddy."

Paquette checked the time. "Listen, sugar, my meeting is in half an hour. I've got to get going. You be brave, now."

She flashed a heart-melting smile. "I don't have to be brave, Daddy. It's only a cleaning."

"Well then, you be . . . clean. Mommy will be by in just a little while. You wait if she's not here by the time you're done." He watched as she ran up the stairs next to the Army/Navy and waited until she waved to him from behind the picture window painted *Dr. Richard Philips*, DDS. Then he eased the Mercedes away from the curb, and headed toward the south end of town and his eleven o'clock Second Thursday meeting with Cyrus Redding, president and chairman of the board of perhaps the largest pharmaceutical house in the world. The meeting would start at exactly eleven and end at precisely ten minutes to noon. For seven years, as long as Paquette had been with the company, it had been like that, and like that it would remain as long as Cyrus Redding was alive and in charge. Nine o'clock, labor relations; ten o'clock, public relations; eleven, product safety; an hour and ten minutes for lunch, then research and development, sales and production, and finally from three to three-fifty, legislative liaison: department heads meeting with Cyrus Redding, one on one, the second Thursday of each month. The times and the order of Second Thursday were immutable. Vacations were to be worked around the day, illnesses to be treated and tolerated unless hospitalization was necessary. Even then, on more than one occasion, Redding had moved the meeting to a hospital room. Second Thursday: raises, new projects, criticisms, termination—all, whenever possible, on that day.

The factory covered most of a thirty-acre site bordered to the south and west by pine-covered hills and to the east by Pinkham's Creek. Double fences, nine feet high with barbed wire outcroppings at the top, encircled the entire facility. The inner of the two barriers was electrified—stunning voltage during the day, lethal voltage at night and on weekends. The only approach, paralleling the new railbed from the north, was tree lined and immaculately maintained. Two hundred yards from the outer fence, a V in the roadway directed employees and shippers to the right and all others to the left. A rainbow sign, spanning the approach at that point announced:

**REDDING PHARMACEUTICALS, INCORPORATED**
**DARLINGTON, KENTUCKY**
***1899***
***"The Most Good for the Most People at the Least Cost"***

Paquette bore to the right beneath the sign and stopped by a brightly painted guardhouse, the first of a series of security measures. He found himself wondering, as he did on almost every Second Thursday, if knowing what he knew now, he would have left his university research position in Connecticut to become director of product safety. The question was a purely hypothetical one. He had taken the job. He had agreed to play Cyrus Redding's game by Cyrus Redding's rules. Now, like it or not, he was Cyrus Redding's man. Of course an annual salary that, with benefits, exceeded four hundred thousand dollars went far toward easing pangs of conscience. Suzy was the youngest of three children, all of whom would one day be in college at the same time. He stopped at the final pass gate, handed the trunk key to the guard, and drummed nervously on the wheel while the man completed his inspection. It hardly paid to be late for a Second Thursday appointment.

◆

Over the hundred and eighty years since Gault Darling led a band of renegades, moonshiners, and other social outcasts to a verdant spot in the foothills of the Cumberlands, and then killed two men for the right to have the new town named after himself, Darlington, Kentucky, had undergone any number of near deaths and subsequent resurgences. Disease, soldiers, Cherokees, floods, fires, and even a tornado had at one time or another brought the town to its knees. Always, though, a vestige survived, and always Darlington regrew.

In 1858, the Lexington-Knoxville Railway passed close enough to Darlington to send off a spur, the primary purpose of which was the transport of coal from the rich Juniper mines. By the end of the century, however, output from the Junipers had fallen to a trickle, and the railbed was left to rot. Darlington was once again in danger of becoming a ghost town. Shops closed. The schoolhouse and Baptist church burned down and were not rebuilt. Town government dwindled and then disappeared. In the end, where once there had been well over a thousand, only a handful remained. Fortunately for the town, one of those was Elton Darling, self-proclaimed descendant of Gault.

In 1897, Darling engineered a massive hoax utilizing three pouches of low-grade gold ore, two confederates, and a remarkable ability to seem totally inebriated when stone sober. Rumors of the "Darlington Lode" spread quickly through cities from Chicago to Atlanta, and Darlington acquired an instant citizenry, many of whom stayed on, either out of love for the beauty of the area or out of lack of resources to move elsewhere.

Having single-handedly repopulated his town, Elton Darling set about giving it an industry, making use of the area's only readily available resource, the sulfur-rich water of Pinkham's Creek, a tributary of the Cumberland River. In less than a year, with some food coloring, smoky-glassed bottles, an attractive label, and an aggressive sales force, the vile water of Pinkham's Creek, uninhabitable by even the hardiest fish, had become Darling's Astounding Rejuvenator and Purgator, an elixir alleged effective against conditions ranging from dropsy to baldness.

Over the years before his death in 1939, Elton Darling made such changes in his product as the market and times demanded. He also made a modest fortune. By the time his son, Tyrone, took control of the family enterprises, the rejuvenator had been replaced by a variety of vitamin and mineral supplements, and Darlington Pharmaceuticals was being traded, though lightly, on the American Stock Exchange.

Far from being the visionary and businessman his father was, Tyrone Darling spent much of his time, and most of his money, on a string of unsuccessful thoroughbreds and a succession of city women, each of whom was more adept at consuming money than he was at making it. Darling's solution to his diminishing cash reserves was simple: issue more stock and sell off some of his own. In the fall of 1947, at the annual Darlington stockholders meeting, the ax fell. Intermediaries for a man spoken of only as Mr. Redding produced proof of ownership of more than fifty-three percent of Darlington Pharmaceuticals and in a matter of less than a day, took over the company on behalf of Mr. Cyrus Redding of New York, New York. Stripped of influence, as well as of a source of income, Darling tried to negotiate. To the best of anyone's knowledge, he had not succeeded even in meeting with the man who had replaced him when, on the following

New Year's Eve, he and a woman named Densmore were shot to death by the woman's husband.

Thus it was that the fortunes of Darlington, Kentucky became tied to a reclusive genius named Cyrus Redding and to the pharmaceutical house that now bore his name. In the years to follow, there were a number of minor successes: Terranyd, a concentrated tetracycline; Rebac, an over-the-counter antacid; and several cold preparations. Redding Pharmaceuticals doubled in size, and the population of Darlington grew proportionally. Then, in the early 1960s, Redding obtained exclusive U.S. patents to several successful European products, including the tranquilizer that was, following a blitzkrieg promotional campaign, to become one of the most prescribed pharmaceuticals in the world. A year after release of the drug, Darlington was selected an All-American City, and shortly after that, the Darlington Dukes minor league baseball franchise was established.

Marilyn Wyman sipped at a cup of tea and risked a minute glance at her gold Rolex. Ten minutes to go and another Second Thursday would be over for Redding's director of public relations. From across his enormous desk, Cyrus Redding appraised her through his Coke-bottle spectacles.

"There are exactly eight minutes and thirty seconds to go, Marilyn," he said. "Does that help?"

"I'm sorry, sir." Wyman, in her midfifties, had been with the company longer than had any other department head. Still, no one had ever heard her refer to her employer as anything other than Mr. Redding or, to his face, sir. She had close-cut gray-brown hair and a sophisticated sensuality that she used with consummate skill in dealing with media representatives of both sexes.

"We have one final piece of business. No small piece, either. It's Arthgard."

"I thought it had been taken off the market."

"In England it has, but not yet here. It has been only eight weeks since we released it and already it is in the top forty in volume and the top twenty-five in actual dollar return."

"That's a shame. The feedback I've gotten from pharmacists and patients has been excellent, too. Still, the British have proven it responsible for how many deaths so far, sixty?"

"Eighty-five, actually."

"Eighty-five." Reflexively, Wyman shuddered. Arthgard had been released to the American market almost immediately after the patent had been acquired by Redding. Though she had no way of knowing how it had been accomplished, the FDA-required testing periods, both laboratory and clinical, seemed to have been circumvented. It was not her place to ask about such things. Testing was the province of Arlen Paquette, and the exchange of information between department heads was not only frowned upon by Redding but, in most cases, forbidden. "Well, we still have Lapsol and Carmalon," she said. "The figures I looked at yesterday showed them both in the top ten of antiarthritic preparations. I'll write a press release announcing the suspension of our Arthgard production and then see what I can do to remind the public about both of those other products."

"You will do no such thing, Marilyn."

"Pardon?"

Redding pulled a computer printout from a file on his desk. "Do you have any idea how many millions it cost us to buy the Arthgard patent, test the product, go into production, advertise, get samples out to physicians, and finally distribute the product to pharmacies and hospitals? Correction, Miss Wyman. Not how many millions—how many tens of millions?" Marilyn Wyman shook her head. Redding continued. "The projections I have here say that, at our present rate of increase in sales, the product would have to stay on the market for another ten weeks just for us to break even. That is where you will be concentrating your efforts."

"But. . . ." Redding's icy look made it clear that there was to be no dialogue on the matter. She stared down at the toes of her two-hundred-dollar Ferragamo pumps. "Yes, sir."

"I've got some preliminary data from that survey firm you contracted with showing that less than forty percent of physicians and less than ten percent of consumers are even aware of what's going on in England. I want those numbers to stay in that ball park for the next ten weeks."

"But. . . ."

"Dammit, I am not looking for buts. I am looking for ten weeks of sales so that we can get our ass out of this product without having it burned off. Our legislative liaison will do his job with the FDA. Now if you want to give me 'buts,' I'll find a PR person who does her job. And need I remind you that her first job will be to do something creative with that M. Wyman file I have locked away?"

Wyman bit at her lower lip and nodded. It had been several years since Redding had mentioned the collection of photographs, telephone conversations, and recordings from the company hotel suite she had vacationed in at Acapulco. Beneath her expertly applied makeup, she was ashen.

Redding, seeing the capitulation in her eyes, softened. "Marilyn, listen. You do your part. I promise that if there's any trouble on this side of the Atlantic with Arthgard, we'll pull it immediately. Okay? Good. Now tell me, how's that little buggy of yours riding?"

"The Alpha? Fine, thank you. Needs a tune-up. That's all."

"Well, don't bother. Just bring it over to Buddy Michaels at Darlington Sport. He's got a spanking new Lotus just arrived and itching for you to show it the beauty of the Kentucky countryside." He checked the slim digital timepiece built into his desk. "Eight minutes of eleven.

It's been a good meeting, Marilyn. As usual, you're doing an excellent job. Why don't you stop by next week and give me a progress report. I also want to hear how that new Lotus of yours handles the downgrade on the back side of Black Mountain." With a smile, a nod, and the smallest gesture of one hand, Marilyn Wyman was dismissed.

Arlen Paquette was drinking coffee in the sumptuous sitting room outside of Redding's office when Wyman emerged. Though they had worked for the same company for years, they seldom met in situations other than Second Thursday. Still, the greeting between them was warm, both sensing that in another place and at another time, they might well have become friends.

At precisely eleven o'clock, Marilyn Wyman exited through the door to the reception area and Paquette crossed to Redding's door, knocked once, and entered. Hour three of Second Thursday had begun.

Redding greeted Paquette with a handshake across his desk. On occasion, usually when their agenda was small, the man would guide his motorized wheelchair to a spot by the coffee table at one end of his huge office and motion Paquette to the maroon Chesterfield sofa opposite him. This day, however, there was no such gesture.

"I've sent for lunch, Arlen. We may run over."

Paquette tensed. In seven years, his eleven o'clock visit had never run over. "I'm all yours," he said, realizing, as he was sure the old man across from him did, that the words were more than a polite figure of speech.

"Have you any problem areas you wish to discuss with me before we start?"

Paquette shook his head. He knew Cyrus Redding abhorred what he called "surprises." If Paquette encountered major problems in the course of his work, a call and immediate discussion with Redding were in order.

"Fine," Redding said, adjusting his tie and then combing his gray crew cut back with his fingers. "I have two situations that we must ponder together. The first concerns Arthgard. Do you have your file handy?"

"I have my files on everything that is current," Paquette said, rummaging through his large, well-worn briefcase.

"Is our testing on Arthgard current?" Redding's tone suggested that he would consider an affirmative response a "surprise."

"Yes and no, sir. The formal testing was completed several months ago. You have my report."

"Yes, I remember."

"However," Paquette continued, "I began reading about the problems in the UK, and decided to continue dispensing the drug to some of the test subjects at the Women's Health Center in Denver."

"Excellent thinking, Arlen. Excellent. Have there been any side effects so far?"

"Minor ones only. Breast engorgement and pain, stomach upsets, diarrhea, hair loss in half a dozen, loss of libido, rashes, and palpitations. Nothing serious or life threatening."

Serious or life threatening. Even after seven years, Paquette's inner feelings were belied by the callousness of his words. Still, he was Redding's man, and Redding was concerned only with those side effects that would be severe enough, consistently enough to cause trouble for the company. Only those were deemed reason to delay or cancel the quick release of a new product into the marketplace. In a business where a week often translated into millions of dollars, and a jump on the competition into tens of millions, Redding had set his priorities.

"How many subjects were involved in the Arthgard testing?"

"Counting those at the Denver facility and at the Omnicenter, in Boston, there were almost a thousand." He checked his notes. "Nine hundred and seventy."

"And no one from the Omnicenter is receiving Arthgard right now?"

"The testing there was stopped months ago. There

were too many other products that we had to work into the system."

Paquette knew that the Arthgard recall in Great Britain was going to prove a fiasco, if not a disaster, for Redding Pharmaceuticals, a company that had not suffered a product recall or even an FDA probe since the man in the wheelchair had taken over. Testing of pharmaceuticals in Europe seldom met FDA standards. Still, the UK had a decent safety record, and the Boston and Denver testing facilities served as a double check on all foreign-developed products, as well as on drugs invented in Redding Labs. Problems inherent in various products—at least by Cyrus Redding's definition of problems—had always been identified before any major commitment by the company was undertaken . . . always, until now.

"Tell me, Arlen," Redding said, drawing a cup of coffee from a spigot built into his desk and lacing it with a splash from a small decanter, "what do you think happened? How did this get past us?"

Paquette searched for any tension, any note of condemnation in the man's words. There was none that he could tell. "Well," he said, "basically, it boils down to a matter of numbers." He paused, deciding how scientific to make his explanation. He knew nothing of Cyrus Redding's background, but he was certain from past discussions that there was science in it somewhere. Straightforward and not condescending—that was how he would play it. "The Arthgard side effect—the cardiac toxicity that is being blamed for the deaths in England—seems to be part allergy and part dose related."

"In other words," Redding said, "first the patient has to be sensitive to the drug and then he has to get enough of it."

"Exactly. And statistically, that combination doesn't come up too often. Arthgard has been so effective, though, and so well marketed, that literally millions of prescriptions have been written in the six years since it was first released in the United Kingdom. A death here, a death there. Weeks or months and miles in between. No way to connect them to the drug. Finally, a number of problems show up at just about the same time in just about the same place, and one doc in one hospital in one town in the corner of Sussex puts it all together. A little publicity, and suddenly reports begin pouring in from all over the British world."

"Do you have any idea how many hundreds of thousands of arthritis patients have had their suffering relieved by Arthgard?"

"I can guess. And I understand what you're saying. Risk-benefit ratio. That's all people in our industry, or any health provider for that matter, have to go by."

"I've decided to keep Arthgard on the American market for ten more weeks." Redding dropped the bomb quietly and simply; then he sat back and watched Paquette's reaction. Noticeably, at least, there was none.

"Fine," Paquette said. "Would you like me to continue the Denver testing? We have about an eighteen-month head start on the overall marketplace."

"By all means, Arlen."

Paquette nodded, scratched a note on the Arthgard file, and slid it back in his briefcase, struggling to maintain his composure. There was little to be gained by revealing his true feelings about what Redding was doing, and much—oh, so much—to lose. His involvement in the testing centers alone—involvement of which Redding possessed detailed documentation—was enough to send him to prison. In fact, he suspected that Redding could claim no knowledge of either facility and make that claim stick. Even if no confrontation occurred, the chances were that he would be fired or demoted . . . or worse. Several years before, a department head had been openly critical of Redding and his methods, to the point of discussing his feelings with the editor of the Darlington *Clarion Journal*. Not a week later, the man, a superb horseman, had his neck broken in a riding accident and died within hours of reaching Darlington Regional Hospital.

"Have you the product test reports for this month?"

"Yes, sir. I took them off the computer yesterday evening."

Paquette was rummaging through his briefcase for the progress reports on the fourteen medications currently being investigated when he heard the soft hum of Redding's wheelchair.

"Just leave the reports on my desk, Arlen," Redding said, gliding to the center of the room. "I'll review them later. Could you bring my coffee over to the table, please? I want to apprise you of a potential problem at the Omnicenter, and I could use a break from talking across this desk."

Paquette did as he was asked, keeping his eyes averted from Redding as much as possible, lest the man, a warlock when it came to reading the thoughts of others, realized how distasteful the Arthgard decision was to him. On the day of their first interview, over eight years ago, he had sensed that uncanny ability in the aging invalid. It was as if all the power that would have gone into locomotion had simply been transferred to another function.

"Arlen, the Omnicenter was already operational when you joined us, yes?"

"Sort of, sir." Paquette settled into the Chesterfield and took a long draught of the coffee he had surreptitiously augmented with cognac while Redding was motoring across the room. "The computers were in, our people were in place, and the finances had been worked out, but no formal testing programs had been started."

"Yes, of course. I remember now. You should go easy on that cognac so early in the day, my friend. It's terrible on the digestion. In the course of your dealings in Boston, did you by chance run into a woman pathologist named Bennett, first name Kathryn, or Kate?"

Paquette shook his head. He had set his coffee aside, no longer finding reassurance in the warm, velvety swallows. "Reese keeps me away from as many people as possible." He smiled and whispered, "I think he's ashamed of me."

Redding enjoyed the humor. "Such a reaction would be typical of the man, wouldn't it. He lacks the highly advanced abilities to appreciate and respect. With him, a person is to be either controlled or feared—none of the subtleties in between."

"Exactly." Paquette was impressed, but not surprised, by the insight. As far as he knew, Redding had had but one direct contact with the Metropolitan Hospital administrator, but for the Warlock, one was usually enough. "What about this Dr. Bennett?"

"She has begun investigating the Omnicenter in connection with two unusual deaths she has autopsied. The women in question had similar blood and reproductive organ disease, and both were Omnicenter patients."

"So are a fair percentage of all the women in Boston," Paquette said. "Have you talked to our people?"

"Carl called me. Both women have participated at various times in our work, but never with the same product. The Omnicenter connection appears to be a red herring."

"Unfortunately, we have other herrings in that building which are not so red."

"That is precisely my concern," Redding said, "and now yours. I have sent instructions to Reese that he is to find a way to divert young Dr. Bennett's interest away from our facility. He seems to think he can do so. However, I have had my sources do some checking on this woman, and I tell you, Norton Reese is no match for her, intellectually or in strength of character."

"He would be the last to admit that."

"I agree." Redding opened a manila folder he had apparently placed on the coffee table prior to Paquette's arrival. "Here are copies for you of all the information we have obtained thus far on the woman. I want you to go to Boston and keep tabs on things. Do not show yourself in any way without checking with me first. Meet with our Omnicenter people only if absolutely necessary."

"Yes, sir."

"There is a small item in that report which may be of

some help to us. Bennett's father-in-law heads the law firm that handles the Metropolitan Hospital account, as well as some of the Northeast business of the Tiny Tummies line of breakfast cereals. Although the connection is not generally known, Tiny Foods is a subsidiary of ours. The man's name is Winfield Samuels. From all I can tell, he's a businessman."

Paquette nodded. Coming from Cyrus Redding, the appellation "businessman" was the highest praise. It meant the man was, like Redding himself, a pragmatist who would not allow emotions to cloud his handling of an issue. "Do you have any idea of what Reese has in mind to deal with the doctor?"

"No, except that Carl Horner says he seems quite sure of himself."

"If that's the case," Paquette said, "I should be back in just a few days."

Redding smiled benignly. "I told you how I perceive the Bennett-Reese matchup, Arlen," he said. "I've had reservations made for you at the Ritz. Open-ended reservations."

◆

## METRO DOC LABELS BOBBY JUNKIE.

The layout editor of the *Herald* had, it seemed, dusted off type that had not been used since D-Day. The paper lay on the living room floor, along with the *Globe* and Roscoe, who was keeping an equal distance between himself and both his masters. It was still afternoon, but the mood and the dense overcast outside made the hour feel much later.

The calls had begun at two that morning and had continued until Jared unplugged their phones at four-thirty. Letters, typed on Kathryn Bennett's stationery and signed by her, had been dropped off at both Boston dailies and all three major television stations sometime during the previous night. The gist of the letters was that, driven by conscience and a sense of duty to the people of Boston, Kate had decided to tell the truth about Bobby Geary. Stan Willoughby, who was mentioned in the letter, and Norton Reese, as Metro administrator, were called immediately by reporters. The pathology chief, not as sharp as he might have been had he not been woken from a sound sleep, confirmed the story, adding that Kate was an honest and highly competent pathologist whom, he was sure, had good reason for doing what she had done. It was not until an hour after speaking with the first newsman that he thought to call her. By then, Kate's line was so busy that it took him almost another hour to get through. Meanwhile, Norton Reese, aided by Marco Sebastian and an emergency session with the hospital computers, had confirmed that there was, in fact, no patient named John Schultz ever treated or tested at Metropolitan Hospital. Reese was careful to add that he knew absolutely nothing of the allegations lodged by Dr. Bennett, whom he described as a brilliant woman with a tendency at times to rebel against traditional modes of conduct. Questioned for details, he refused further comment.

The house was like a mausoleum. Both Kate and Jared had attempted to go to work for business as usual, but both had been forced by harassing reporters to return home. Over the hours that followed, they sat, drapes closed, ignoring the periodic ring of the front doorbell. The telephones remained disconnected. There was a silence between them chilly enough to offset even the warmth from the wood stove.

"Jared, do you want a cup of coffee?"

"Thanks, but no. Three in an hour and a half is a little over my limit." He leaned forward from his easy chair and plucked the *Herald* from beside Roscoe's nose. Beneath the headline were insert photos of Bobby Geary's parents, along with a quotation from each about Kate, neither the least bit complimentary. "Goddamn tabloid really knows how to slobber it on," he said, unable to mask the irritation in his voice.

"Honey, you do believe what I said about not knowing anything about those letters, don't you?"

"Of course I believe you. Why would you think otherwise?"

"No reason, I guess." The anger she had felt earlier in the day had been greatly muted by frustration and the growing realization that beyond a simple denial and the call for a handwriting analysis of her signature, she had absolutely no cards to play. Even the signature was of doubtful assistance to her claims of innocence. No one had yet come forward with the original letter, and on the photostat she had seen, the signature appeared quite accurate.

"Why would somebody do this? Why?" Jared seemed to be talking as much to himself as to her, but it was clear that in his mind, confusion and doubt remained. "You say that Yoda and this Detective Finn were the only two besides you who knew about the amphetamines?"

"I said as far as I knew they were. Reese has it in for me, and he has his finger in just about every pie in Metro. He could have found out somehow, and. . . ." She shrugged and shook her head. "I don't think much of the man, but I can't imagine him doing a thing like this."

"You know, Kate, you could have told me you were going to fake Geary's autopsy report. I mean, I am your husband."

Kate glared at him. "Jared, the three of us decided that nobody else should know. Call Mrs. Willoughby or Mrs. Finn and ask if their husbands told them. Do you share all the inner secrets of your work with me?"

"You never ask."

"Give me a break, will you? Listen, I know you're upset. You are a public figure, and directly or indirectly, you're getting negative press. But don't go blaming me, Jared. I didn't do anything."

Jared rose, shuffled to the stove, and began stoking embers that were already burning quite nicely. "I spoke with my father this morning," he said over his shoulder.

"My God, Winfield must be absolutely fried over all this. Do you think it would help matters if I called him?"

"He thinks you should call a press conference and admit that you sent the letters."

"What?"

"It's his feeling that as things stand, it looks like you performed an act of conscience, and then *I* talked you out of owning up to it."

"So my father-in-law wants me to lie in public to keep his protegé from losing any votes."

Jared slammed the poker against the stove door. "Dammit, you already did lie. That's what caused all this trouble in the first place."

Kate felt herself about to cry. "I did what I thought was the kindest and fairest thing I could do for that boy and his family."

"Well, now you're going to have to think about what's kind and fair to *this* boy and *his* family."

"So you think that's what I should do, too?"

A loud pounding on the front door precluded Jared's response.

"Police. Open up."

Kate opened the door a slit and peered out, expecting to see another overly resourceful reporter. Instead, she saw Detective Lieutenant Martin Finn. Any lingering doubt they might have had about whether or not the policeman was responsible for the letters evaporated with the man's first words.

"You really fucked me, Dr. Bennett. Do you know that?"

"I'm sorry, but I didn't send those letters," she said with exaggerated calm. "Would you like to sit down? Can I get you some coffee?"

Finn ignored her questions, and instead, remained in the center of the room, pacing out a miniature circle on the rug. "I went along with this because I'm Irish and a fan, and look what it gets me. I was up for a promotion. Maybe captain. Now, thanks to you and your fucking grandstand play, I'm going to be lucky I don't get busted to dogcatcher."

"Went along with it?" Kate was incredulous. "Lieutenant Finn, it was your suggestion in the first place. For the kids of Boston. Don't you remember saying all that?" Her voice cracked. The day had been punishing enough without this.

Suddenly, Jared pushed past her and confronted the man. Though he was taller than Finn, the policeman was far stockier. "Finn, if you've said what you came to say, I want you and your foul mouth out of here. If not, say it. Then leave."

"I'll leave when I'm fucking ready."

"Get out."

Jared stepped forward, his fists clenched in front of him. It was only then that Kate sensed how heavily Finn had been drinking. She moved toward them, but not quickly enough. With no warning or windup, Finn sank a vicious uppercut into Jared's solar plexus. A guttural grunt accompanied the explosion of air from his lungs, as he doubled over and dropped to his knees.

Kate knelt beside her husband. "You damn animal," she screamed at Finn.

"I wish it had been you, lady," Finn said as he turned and walked clumsily from the house. The antique vase Kate threw shattered against the door as it closed behind him.

Jared remained doubled over, but his breathing was deepening. "You okay?" she said softly.

"Never laid a glove on me," he responded with no little effort. "Could you bring over the wastebasket, please? Just in case."

"You poor darling. Can I do anything else? Get you anything?"

Slowly, Jared sat back and straightened up. His eyes were glazed. "Just remind me again what I told that minister."

"For better or for worse. That's what you told him.

Jared, I don't want to sound corny, but that was a pretty wonderful thing you did standing up to that animal."

"For better or for worse? You sure that was it?"

"Uh-huh."

"Katey, I don't know how to tell you this, but in some perverse way getting hit the way I just did felt good."

"I don't understand."

"Right before Finn came in I was ready to tell you that I agreed with my father in thinking everything would be simpler and look better for all of us if you would just admit to writing the letter. Then that asshole started in. All of a sudden, I realized how wrong I was . . . and I'm sorry. I couldn't stand hearing him talk to you that way. Katey, please just try to remember that there's a lot going on that's confusing to me. Sometimes I feel that living with you is like trying to ride a cyclone. Sometimes I feel like a slab of luncheon meat between one slice of Winfield and one slice of Kate. Sometimes I . . ." He whirled to the wastebasket and threw up.

Sheila Pierce stared past Norton Reese's sweat-dampened pate at the stucco ceiling of their room in the Mid City Motel and reminded herself to continue the groans that the man found so exciting.

Careful not to disrupt his rhythm, she reached up and reassured herself that her new diamond studs hadn't come dislodged.

"Oh, baby," she murmured. "Oh, baby, you're so good. So good."

She wished she could have seen Kate Bennett's face when the reporters started calling. Reese was hardly a Valentino for her, but she had to give credit where credit was due, and Reese deserved what she was giving him for what he had given Bennett.

"Oh, baby, come to me. Come to me," she moaned.

It had been a thrill just to watch: Kathryn Bennett, MD, Miss Perfect, confused and irritable, suddenly not in control of every little thing. How good at last to be the one pulling the strings. Too bad there was no way for Bennett ever to know.

"Don't stop, Norty. Oh, yes, baby, yes. Don't stop."

# 6

## Friday 14 December

Compared with the conference rooms of other departments in Metropolitan Hospital of Boston, the one belonging to the pathology unit was spartan. French Impressionist prints mounted on poster board hung on stark, beige walls. Below them, metal, government-surplus bookcases were half filled with worn, dog-eared texts and journals. The meager decor, plus a large, gouged oak table and two dozen variegated folding chairs did little to obscure the fact that prior to a modest departmentwide renovation in 1965, the room had been the hospital morgue. Some among the twenty-nine assembled for the hastily called meeting still sensed the auras of the thousands of bodies that had temporarily rested there.

Kate, Stan Willoughby seated to her right, stood at one end of the table and surveyed the room. There were six pathologists besides the two of them, some residents, and a number of lab technicians. It bothered her terribly to think that one—or more—of them might be capable of an act as malicious as the Bobby Geary letter. Those in the room were, in a sense, her family—people she spent as many waking hours with each week as she did with her husband. It had always been her way to deal with them in a straightforward manner, respectfully, and with no hidden agendas. There were only two characteristics that they knew she would not tolerate—laziness and dishonesty. However, to the best of her knowledge, none in the room could be accused of either.

The closest had been the business of Sheila Pierce's claiming she had misplaced the required vouchers and certification for her Miami trip, and even then, Kate had no proof of her suspicions. Besides, the matter had been settled between them with little disagreement.

John Gilson, the unit's electron microscopist; Liu Huang, a meticulous pathologist, whom Kate tutored in English; Marvin Grimes, the always pleasantly inebriated deiner; Sheila, herself, so very bright, so dedicated to the department; momentarily, Kate's eyes met each of theirs.

"I want to thank you all for taking the time out of your schedules to hear me out," she began. "I know the last day and a half have been . . . how should I say, a bit disrupted around here." There was a murmur of laughter at the understatement. "Well, I'm here to tell you that compared to what you all have been through, my life has been absolutely nuked. At three o'clock this morning, my husband and I caught a reporter trying to sneak out of our bedroom in time to make the morning edition. He had disguised himself as our antique brass coatrack." Laughter this time was more spontaneous and animated. Kate smiled thinly. "Norton Reese has set up a news conference for me in about an hour. He wants me to state my position on the Bobby Geary business once and for all. Well, before I tell those vultures, I wanted to tell you.

"What the press has been saying about Bobby Geary is true. From all we were able to tell at post, he had been a longtime user of intravenous amphetamines. How he could do what he did to his body and still play ball the way he did is a mystery to me, but the chronic scarring we found along certain veins makes the truth clear. Sad for Bobby's family, sad for the baseball fans and the kids, and, I'm sure, a nightmare for Bobby. The decision to withhold our findings from the press was as much mine as Dr. Willoughby's or Detective Finn's." A jet of acid singed her throat at the mention of the man. "I have trouble with deceit in any form, but every sense I have of what is decent says that our decision was the right one. Now someone is doing his best to make me pay for that decision. I did not write the letter, and I have no idea who did, why they did it, how they got the information on Bobby Geary's post, or how they obtained my stationery. The possibility exists that it was someone from this department. I very much hope not—all of you are very important to me. I feel like we're a team, and that helps me show up every day ready to try and practice decent pathology in this dinosaur of a hospital.

"But what's done is done. I've agonized as much as I'm going to, and after the little Q-and-A session in Reese's office, I intend to begin stuffing this whole business into the barrel I use to dispose of the garbage in my life. If any of you have any questions, I'll be happy to answer them as best I can."

Stan Willoughby rose and put his arm around her shoulders. "No questions from me, Kate. Just a statement for everybody. I have submitted this woman's name to the search committee as my personal recommendation to succeed me as department chief. It's possible this whole business is someone's way of trying to sabotage that appointment. I want you all to know that I am more committed than ever to seeing that she gets it."

For a moment there was silence. Then diminutive Liu Huang stood and began applauding. Another joined in and then another. Soon all but one were demonstrating their support.

"We're behind you, Doc," a technician called out.

The reaction was as enthusiastic and sustained as it was spontaneous. In the back of the room, the lone holdout smiled around clenched teeth and then stiffly joined in the applause.

"That was pretty special, wasn't it," Willoughby said to Kate as the room emptied out. "Little Looie Huang standing there in his formal, inscrutable way, leading the cheers. I just love 'im. Are you all right?"

"If you mean am I about to come apart and start bawling like a baby, the answer is yes."

"So bawl," Willoughby said, taking her by the arm as they followed the last of the meeting-goers from the room.

"You know, Stan. I don't understand it. I don't think I ever will."

"What's that?" Willoughby bent over the bubbler he had tried for years to get replaced, and sucked vigorously for a sip of tepid water.

"People, I guess." She shrugged. "You know, you wake up in the morning, you get dressed, you march off for another encounter in the battle of life—all you want to do is grow a little, try your best, and grab some little morsel of peace and contentment along the way. No big deal. Every day you do that, and every day you think that everyone else is doing the same thing, trying for that same smidgen of happiness. It makes so much sense that way."

"Ah, yes, my child, but therein lies the rub. You see, what makes sense and what is are seldom the same thing. The stew you propose cooking up would taste just fine, but it's a bit short on the condiments of reality—greed, envy, bigotry, insecurity, to say nothing of that ol' standby, just plain craziness. No matter who you are, no matter how hard you try to tend your own little garden, no matter how kind you try to be to your fellow man, there's always gonna be someone, somewhere tryin' to stick it to you. You can count on it."

"Terrific."

"It all boils down to priorities."

"What do you mean?"

"Well, I know I have the reputation around here for being too passive. My door is always open. Bring in your troubles and problems whenever you want . . . as long as you bring in the solutions to them at the same time. I wasn't always like that, Kate. There was a time when I would have gone to the mat with the toughest of them.

And I did. Many times in the early days before you came on board. Then I started getting the pains beneath the ol' sternum, and I started visiting all those eager young cardiologists. Gradually, my priorities began to shift away from playing with the stick-it-to-you fanatics. I went back to basics. My wife, my children, my grandchildren, my health—physical and mental. I couldn't see how a new microscope or an extra technician or a refurnished room could measure up against any of them."

"But Stan, your work is important. It's your job to fight for the department. Don't you agree?"

"Yes."

"Well then, how do you resolve that fact with what you just said?"

Stanley Willoughby leaned over and kissed her gently on the forehead. "I can't, Kate. Don't you see? That's why I'm stepping down. See you at the conference." With a smile that held more wistfulness and sadness than mirth, he turned and entered the office that, if he had his way, Kate would occupy within a few months.

Kate's office, half the size of her chief's, was on a side corridor next to the autopsy suite. There was room only for a desk and chair, a file cabinet, a small microscope bench, and two high stools. On one of the stools sat Jared.

"Well, hi," she said, crossing to kiss him.

"Hi, yourself."

His response was chilly, perfunctory.

"How's your belly?"

"As long as I don't try to sit down, get up, or walk, it's only painful as hell," he said. "But not nearly as painful as this." He slid a handbill across to her. "Copies of this have been circulating all over South Boston and are beginning to work their way up into the city."

"Damn," she whispered, staring at the paper in disbelief. "Jared, I'm sorry. I really am." The flyer, printed on an orange stock bright enough to offend even the least political Irish Catholic, was headlined PARTNERS IN COMPASSION. Beneath the words were Kate and Jared arm in arm in a photograph she could not remember ever having posed for. It was labeled "Atty. J. Samuels and Dr. K. Bennett." At the bottom of the page was a photograph of Bobby Geary in the midst of his picture-perfect swing. It was captioned simply "Bobby, R.I.P."

"Finn?" she ventured.

"Maybe. Maybe not. He's hardly the only Irish Catholic around who'd like to firebomb us. The name Bobby Geary seems set to take its place right next to Chappaquiddick and Watergate in the list of political death knells. For all I know, Mattingly or his sleazy campaign manager decided to make sure I was no problem for them in the next election."

"I'm sorry."

"You already said that."

Kate sighed and sank down on her desk chair. "Jared, things aren't really going very well for me right now. Do you have to make them worse?"

"Things aren't going well for *you*? Is that all you can think of?"

"Please, honey. I've got this damn news conference in half an hour; I've got a biopsy due from the OR. Don't you remember saying yesterday how you were going to try to be more understanding?" She clenched her teeth against any further outburst.

"I remember getting laid out by a policeman I'd never seen before that moment. That's what I remember. My father tells me that Martin Finn is *numero uno* in power and influence in certain quarters of the BPD. With him for an enemy, it's possible that I might end up having my car towed while it's stopped for a red light."

Kate's eyes narrowed. Suddenly, Jared's appearance in her office made sense. Win Samuels. One of the man's countless sensors, scattered about the city and throughout the media, must have reported that his daughter-in-law was scheduled to meet the press. "Jared, did your father tell you to come here this morning to make sure I didn't disgrace anyone at the news conference?"

"We're just trying to avoid any more of this stuff." He held up the orange handbill.

Kate glared at her husband for a moment; then her expression softened. "You know, when you are yourself, you are the funniest, nicest, gentlest, handsomest man I have ever known. I swear you are. Given a build-it-myself husband erector set, I don't think I could have done any better. But when you start operating with that man in the Braxton Building, I swear. . . ."

"Look, let's leave my father out of this, shall we? I'm the one who's watching a political career go down the toilet, not him."

"I'm not so sure."

"What?"

"Nothing, Jared. Look, I've got some work to finish, and any moment I have to diagnose the biopsy of a woman's thyroid gland that one of the other pathologists is having trouble with. I can't talk about this any more right now."

"How about you just . . ."

His outburst was cut short by the arrival of a technician carrying a stainless steel specimen tray and cardboard slide holder, which she set on the microscope bench.

"Please tell Dr. Huang I'll call him in a few minutes with my diagnosis," Kate said.

Jared watched the young woman leave and then checked his watch.

"Look," he said coolly, "I've got to go. I have an appointment with Norton Reese in two minutes."

"What for?"

"Apparently he's been contacted by a lawyer friend of the Gearys. They're thinking of some kind of action against the hospital based on invasion of privacy."

"Jesus," Kate said, pressing her fingertips against the fatigue burning in her eyes.

Jared stood to go. "Don't forget about the Carlisles' cocktail party tonight." Kate groaned. "I guess you already have, huh?"

"I'm sorry. What time?"

"Seven-thirty."

"Okay, Jared, I. . . ."

"Yes?"

She shook her head. "Never mind." It wasn't, she decided, the moment to tell him that she felt she was losing her mind. Please hold me, Jared, she wanted to say. Come over here and hold me and tell me everything's going to be all right. Instead, she waved weakly and turned to the slide and tissue in the specimen dish.

Before Jared had crossed to the door, the telephone began ringing. Reflexively, he turned back.

"Hello? . . . Oh, hi," Kate said. "How're you holding up? . . . How long? . . . Have you tried pressure? . . . Ice? . . . Ellen, please. Just calm down and get a hold of yourself. Have you ever had any trouble like this before? . . . Any bruising you can't explain? . . . Your whole thigh? . . . Why didn't you call me? . . . Ellen, a few years ago, I helped get you accepted into the Omnicenter. Are you still going there? . . . All right. Now listen carefully. I want you to come up to the emergency ward here, but I don't want you to drive. Can you get someone to bring you? . . . Fine. Pack an overnight bag and ask your sister or someone to cover the girls, just in case. . . . Ellen, relax. Now I mean it. Coming apart will only make things worse. Besides, it raises havoc with your mascara. . . . That's better. Now, maintain pressure as best you can, and come on up here. I'll have the best people waiting to see you. You'll probably be home in a couple of hours. . . . Good. And Ellen, bring your medicines, too. . . . I know they're only vitamins. Bring them anyway."

"Ellen Sandler?" Jared asked as she hung up.

Kate nodded, her face ashen. "Her nose has been bleeding steadily for over two hours. Do you know where Sandy is, by any chance?"

"Europe, I think."

Kate stared down at the specimen tray and thought about the woman on the operating table, waiting word on whether the lump in her neck was cancerous or not.

Chances were that the initial biopsy had been done under local, so the woman would be fully awake, frightened. "Jared, there is something you can tell Norton Reese for me. Tell him that I won't be able to make his news conference. Tell him that I didn't do anything and didn't write anything, so I really don't have anything to say anyway."

"But . . ."

"Tell him that as my husband for almost five years, you know that whatever I say is the truth, and that if anyone wants to get at me, they'll have to go through you. Just like last evening. Okay?" She placed a slide under her microscope, and prepared for an encounter with the yellow-white light.

Jared moved to respond, but then stopped himself, walked to the door, and finally turned back. "I hope Ellen's all right," he said softly.

Kate looked up. Every muscle in her body seemed to have tensed at the prospect of what the blood studies on her friend might reveal. "So do I, Jared," she said. "So do I."

*Relax. Concentrate. Focus in. Center your mind. Center it.* It took a minute or two longer than usual, but in the end, the process worked. It always did. Extraneous thoughts and worries lifted from her like a fog until finally all that remained in her world were the cells.

Arlen Paquette sat by the window of his suite in the Ritz, watching the slow passage of pedestrians along the snow-covered walks of the Public Gardens. His schooling had been at Harvard and MIT, and no matter how long he lived in Kentucky, coming to Boston always felt like coming home. Watching the students and lovers, the vagrants and executives, Paquette found himself longing for the more sheltered, if much more improverished, life in a university. Over the seven years with Redding, he had gained much. The land, the house, the tennis court and pool, to say nothing of the opportunities for his children and lifetime security for himself and his wife. Only now was he beginning to appreciate fully the price he had paid. More and more, especially since the Arthgard recall, he avoided looking at himself in mirrors. More and more, as his self-respect dwindled, his effectiveness as a lover also declined. And now, a thousand miles from his exquisitely manicured lawn and the country club he was about to direct, two women had bled to death. As he looked out on the gray New England afternoon, Paquette prayed that the connection of the dead women to the Omnicenter was mere coincidence.

At precisely three o'clock, a messenger arrived with the large manila envelope he had been expecting. Paquette tipped the man and then spread the contents on the coffee table next to the dossier he had brought with him from Darlington. The thoroughness with which Cyrus Redding approached a potential adversary surprised him not in the least. The Warlock kept his edge, honed his remarkable intuitiveness, through facts—countless snatches of data that taken individually might seem irrelevant, but which, like single jigsaw-puzzle pieces, helped construct the truth; in this case, the truth that was Kathryn Bennett Samuels, MD.

Paquette found the volume of information amassed over just a few days both impressive and frightening. Biographical data, academic publications, medical history from a life insurance application, even grades and a year-book picture from Mount Holyoke. There were, in addition to the photostats and computer printouts, a dozen black-and-white photographs—five-by-seven blowups of shots obviously taken with a telephoto lens. Instinctively, the chemist glanced out the window of his eighth-floor suite, wondering if there were a spot from which someone might be taking photographs of him.

One at a time, Paquette studied the carefully labeled photographs. "K.B. and husband, Jared Samuels." "K.B. and pathologist Stanley Willoughby. (See p. 4B.)" "Samuels/Bennett residence, Salt Marsh Road, Essex." "K.B. jogging near home." The woman had a remarkable face, vibrant and expressive, with the well-defined features that translated into photogenicity. Her beauty was at once unobtrusive and unquestionable, and as he scanned the photos, Arlen Paquette felt the beginning pangs of loneliness for his wife.

"Pay special attention to Dr. Stein's report," Redding had instructed him. "The man has done this sort of thing for me before, on even shorter notice and with even less data than he has had to work with here. If you have questions, let me know and I'll have Stein get in touch with you."

The report was typed on stationery embossed "Stephen Stein, PhD; Clinical Psychologist." There was no address or telephone number. Paquette mixed himself a weak Dewar's and water and settled onto the brocaded sofa with the three, single-spaced pages.

Much of the report was a condensation of the data from the rest of the dossier. Paquette read through that portion, underlining the few facts he hadn't encountered before. Actually, he was familiar with Stein's work. Nearly seven years before, he had studied a similar document dealing with Norton Reese. He had wondered then, as he did again this day, if somewhere in the hundreds of manila folders locked in Cyrus Redding's files was one containing a Stein study of Arlen Paquette.

Two older brothers . . . high-school cheerleader . . . ribbon-winning equestrian . . . art department award for sculpture, Mt. Holyoke College . . . one piece, *Search #3*, still on display on campus grounds . . . fourteen-day hospitalization for depression, junior year. . . . Paquette added the information to what he already knew of the woman.

"In conclusion," Stein wrote, "it would appear that in Dr. Bennett we have a woman of some discipline and uncommon tenacity who would make a valuable ally or a dangerous foe under any circumstances. Her principles appear solidly grounded, and I would doubt seriously that she can be bought off a cause in which she believes.

Intellectually, I have no reason to believe her abilities have declined from the days when she scored very high marks in the Medical College Admission Test (see p. 1C) and National Medical Boards (also 1C). Her friends, as far as we have been able to determine, are loyal to her and trusting in her loyalty to them. (Statements summarized pp. 2C and 3C.)

"She does, however, have some problem areas that we shall continue to explore and that might yield avenues for controlling her actions. She likely has a deep-seated insecurity and confusion regarding her roles as a wife and a professional. A threat against her husband may prove more effective in directing her actions than a threat against herself. Faced with a challenge, it is likely that she would fight rather than back away or seek assistance.

"The possibility of influence through blackmail (areas for this being investigated) or extortion seems remote at this time.

"Follow-up report in one week or as significant information is obtained.

"Estimate of potential for control on Redding index is two or three."

Paquette set the report aside and tried to remember what Norton Reese had been graded on Redding's scale. An eight? And what about himself?

"A ten," he muttered. "Move over Bo Derek. Here comes Arlen Paquette, an absolute ten." He poured a second drink, this one pure Dewar's, and buried it.

In minutes, the amber softness had calmed him enough for him to begin some assessment of the situation. Bennett had sent specialists to the Omnicenter to take cultures. No problem. If they were negative, as he suspected they would be, the clinic had gotten a free, comprehensive microbiology check. If they were positive, investigation would move away from the pharmacy anyhow. She had asked for, and received, samples of the pharmaceuticals dispensed by Horner's Monkeys. No problem. The samples would prove to be clean. Horner had seen to that.

Would she press her investigation further? Stein's report and what he knew of the woman said yes. However, that was before she had become mired down in the baseball player mess. The more he thought about the situation, the more convinced Paquette became that there was no avenue through which Kate Bennett could penetrate the secret of the Omnicenter, especially since all product testing had been suspended. Tenacity or no tenacity, the woman could not keep him away from home for more than a few days.

As he mixed another drink, Paquette realized that there was, in fact, a way. It was a twisting, rocky footpath rather than an avenue, but it was a way nonetheless. After a moment of hesitation, he placed a call to the 202 area.

"Good afternoon. Ashburton Foundation."

"Estelle?"

"Yes."

"It's Dr. Thompson."

"Oh. Hi, Doctor. Long time no hear."

"Only a week, Estelle. Everything okay?"

"Fine."

"Any calls?"

"Just this one. I almost jumped out of my skin when the phone rang. I mean days of doing nothing but my nails, I . . ."

"Any mail?"

"Just the two pieces from Denver I forwarded to you a while ago."

"I got them. Listen, if any calls come in, I don't want you to wait until I check in. Call me through the numbers on the sheet in the desk. The message will get to me, and I'll call you immediately."

"Okay, but . . ."

"Thank you, Estelle. Have a good day."

"Good-bye, Dr. Thompson."

◆

To Kate Bennett the scene in Room 6 of the Metropolitan Hospital emergency ward was surreal. Off to one side, two earnest hematology fellows were making blood smears and chatting in inappropriately loud tones. To the other side, Tom Engleson leaned against the wall in grim silence, flanked by a nurse and a junior resident. Kate stood alone by the doorway, alternating her gaze from the crimson-spattered suction bottle on the wall to the activity beneath the bright overhead light in the center of the room.

Pete Colangelo, chief of otorhinolaryngology, hunched in front of Ellen Sandler, peering through the center hole of his head mirror at a hyperilluminated spot far within her left nostril.

"It's high. Oh, yes, it's high," he murmured to himself as he strove to cauterize the hemorrhaging vessel that because of its location, was dripping blood out of Ellen's nose and down the back of her throat.

Kate looked at her friend's sheet-covered legs and thought about the bruise, the enormous bruise, which had been a harbinger of troubles to come. *Don't let it be serious. Please, if you are anything like a God, please don't let her tests come back abnormal.*

In the special operating chair, Ellen sat motionless as marble, but her hands, Kate observed, were whitened from her grip on the armrest. *Please . . .*

"Could you check her pressure?" Colangelo asked. He was a thin, minute man, but his hands were remarkable, especially in the fine, plastic work from which surgical legends were born. Kate was grateful beyond words that she had found him available. Still, she knew that the real danger lay not so much in what was happening as in why. Gruesome images of Beverly Vitale and Ginger Rittenhouse churned in her thoughts. At that moment, in the hematology lab, machines and technicians were measuring the clotting factors in a woman who was no more than a name and hospital number to them. *Please . . .*

Colangelo's assistant reported Ellen's pressure at one-forty over sixty. No danger there. The jets of blood into the suction bottle seemed to be lessening, and for the first time Kate sensed a slight letup in the tension around the room.

"Come to papa," Colangelo cooed to the bleeding arteriole. "That's the little fellow. Come to papa, now."

"What do you think?"

Kate spun to her left.

Tom Engleson had moved next to her. "Sorry," he whispered. "I didn't mean to startle you." The concern she was feeling was mirrored in his face. His brown eyes, dulled somewhat by the continued pressures of his job, were nonetheless wonderfully expressive.

"I think Pete is winning," she said, "if that's what you're asking."

"It isn't."

"In that case, I don't have an answer. At least not yet. Not until the hematology report comes back." She continued speaking, but turned her gaze back to the center of the room. "If her counts are normal, and you have the time, we can celebrate. I'll buy you a coffee. If they're low, I'd like to—wait, make that need to—talk with you anyhow. Besides Stan Willoughby, you are the only one who knows as much as I do, and I think these past two days Stan has been battered enough by his association with me."

"I'm free for the rest of the day," Tom said. "If you like, maybe we could have dinner together." The moment the words were out, he regretted saying them. Impetuous, inappropriate, tactless, dumb.

Kate responded with a fractional look—far too little for him to get a fix on. "I think Pete's done it," she said, making no reference to his invitation.

Moments later, Colangelo confirmed her impression. "We've got it, Mrs. Sandler. You just stay relaxed the way you have been, and we should be in good shape. You are a wonderful patient, believe me you are. I love caring for people who help me to do my best work." He took a step back and waited, the reflected light from his head mirror illuminating the blood-smeared lower half of Ellen's face. Then he turned to Kate, his lips parted in a hopeful half-smile.

"Good job, Pete," she whispered. "Damn good."

Colangelo nodded and then turned back to his patient. "Mrs. Sandler, I think it best for you to stay overnight here. There are some lab studies that haven't come back yet, and I would also like to be sure that vessel stays cauterized."

"No," Ellen said. "I mean, I can't. I mean I don't want to if I don't have to. Kate, tell Dr. Colangelo all the things I have to do, and how responsible I am, and how I'll do exactly what he tells me to do if I can go home. Please, Kate. No offense, but I hate hospitals. Hate them. I almost had Betsy in a roadside park because I wanted to wait until the last minute."

Kate crossed to her friend and wiped the dried blood from her face with damp gauze. "Let's see," she said finally. "As I see it, you want me to arbitrate a disagreement in medical philosophy between the chief of ENT surgery, who also happens to be a professor at Harvard, and the chief of E. Sandler Interior Designs, Inc. . . ."

"Kate, please."

Ellen's grip on Kate's hand and the quaver in her voice reflected a fear far more primal than Kate had realized. Kate turned to the surgeon. "Pete?"

Colangelo shrugged. "I get paid to do surgery and give advice," he said. "If you're asking me whether I think admission is one hundred percent necessary, the answer is no. However, as I said, I get paid to give advice, and observation in the hospital is my advice."

Before Kate could respond, a white-coated technician from the hematology service entered and handed her three lab slips, two pink and one pale green. She studied the numbers and felt a grinding fear and anger rise in her throat. "Lady," she said, struggling to mask the tension in her voice, "I'm going to cast in with Dr. Colangelo. I think you ought to stay."

Ellen's grip tightened. "Kate, what do the tests show? Is it bad?"

"No, El. A couple of the numbers are off a bit and should be rechecked, but it's not bad or dangerous at this point." Silently, she prayed that her judgment of the woman's strength was correct, and that she had done the right thing in not lying. Ellen studied her eyes.

"Not bad or dangerous *at this point,* but it could be. Is that what you're saying?" Kate hesitated and then nodded. Ellen sighed. "Then I guess I stay," she said.

"You shouldn't be here long, and you'll have the very best people taking care of you. I'll help you make arrangements for the girls, and I'll also let them know what's going on."

"Thank you."

"I know it sounds foolish to say don't worry, but try your best not to. We'll keep an eye on your nose and recheck the blood tests in the morning. Most likely you'll be home by the end of the weekend." Kate fought to maintain an even eye contact, but somewhere inside she knew that her friend didn't believe the hopeful statement any more than she did.


"It's the Omnicenter. Somehow I just know it is."

Kate grimaced at the coffee she had just brewed, and lightened it with half-and-half ferreted out from among the chemicals in her office refrigerator.

"The Omnicenter is just that pile of glass and stone across the street. Every one of these reports is negative. Bacteriology, chemistry, epidemiology. All negative. Where's the connection?" Tom Engleson flipped through a sheaf of reports from the studies Kate had ordered. There was nothing in any of them so far to implicate the outpatient center.

"I don't know," Kate responded, settling in across the work bench from him. He was dressed in jeans and a bulky, ivory fisherman's sweater. It was the first time she had seen the man wearing anything but resident's whites.

The change was a positive one. The marvelous Irish knit added a rugged edge to his asthenic good looks. "I think it's a virus or some sort of toxin . . . or a contaminant in the pharmacy. Whatever it is is in there." She jabbed a thumb in the general direction of the Omnicenter.

"The pharmacy? These reports say that the analyses of Ginger Rittenhouse's medications and of the ones Zimmermann sent you were all perfectly normal. Not a bad apple in the bunch."

"I know."

"So . . .?"

"So, I don't know. Look, my friend has whatever this thing is that has killed two women. Platelets seventy thousand, fibrinogen seventy-five percent of normal. You saw the report. Not as bad as either of the other two, at least not yet, but sure headed in the wrong direction." Her words came faster and her voice grew more strident. "I don't really need you to come down here and point out the obvious. For that I can go get Gus from the newsstand outside. I need some thoughts on what *might* be the explanation, not on what *can't* be." Suddenly she stopped. "Jesus, I'm sorry, Tom. I really am. Between political nonsense here at the hospital, the mess with Bobby Geary and his damn amphetamine addiction, two young women dying like ours did, the everyday tensions of just trying to do this job right, and now Ellen, I'm feeling like someone has plunked me inside a blender and thrown the switch. You don't deserve this."

"It's okay. I'm sorry for not being more helpful." He was unable to completely expunge the hurt from his voice, and Kate reminded herself that while the five or so years difference in their ages meant little in most areas, hypersensitivity might not be one of them. "If you think it's the pharmacy," he said, "maybe you should call the FDA."

"One jot of evidence, and I would. I'm the one who talked her into going to the Omnicenter in the first place." Absently, she slipped her hands into her lab coat pockets. In the right one, folded back and again on itself, was the cardboard and plastic card containing what remained of Ellen's Omnicenter vitamins plus iron. She set them on the bench. "No luck finding any of Beverly Vitale's vitamins?" she asked.

"None."

Kate crossed to her desk, returned with a medication card similar to Ellen's, and slapped it down next to the other. "I think we should try one last time with our friends at the toxicology lab and their magic spectrophotometer. Ellen's vitamins and these. If the reports come back negative, I shall put all my suspicions in the witch-hunt file and turn my attention to other pursuits—like trying to regain some of the respect that was snatched away in the Bobby Geary disaster."

"Don't worry," Tom said, "you still have respect, admiration, and caring in a lot of places . . . especially right here." He tapped himself on the breastbone with one finger.

"Thank you for saying that."

"Whose pills are those other ones?" he asked.

"Huh?"

"The other card of pills, whose are they?"

"Oh. They're mine."

# 7

## Friday 14 December

There was an air of excitement and anticipation throughout the usually staid medical suite of Vernon Drexler, MD. The matronly receptionist bustled about the empty waiting room, straightening the magazines and taking pains to see that the six-month-old issue of *Practical Medical Science* with Drexler's picture on the cover was displayed prominently enough to be impossible for Cyrus Redding to miss, even if he were ushered directly into the doctor's office.

In the small laboratory, the young technician replaced the spool of paper in the cardiograph machine and realigned the tubes, needle, and plastic sleeve she would use to draw blood from the arm of the man Drexler had described as one of the most influential if not one of the wealthiest in the country.

Behind her desk, Lurleen Fiske, the intense, severe office manager, phoned the last of their patients and rescheduled him for another day. She had been with Drexler in 1967, when Cyrus Redding had made his first trip up from Kentucky. *Nineteen sixty-seven*. Fiske smiled wistfully. Their office in the Back Bay section of Boston had been little more than two large closets then, one for the doctor and one for herself. Now, Drexler owned the entire building.

It was twelve-thirty. Redding's private 727 had probably touched down at Logan already. In precisely an hour, the woman knew, his limousine would glide to a stop in front of their brownstone. Redding, on foot if he could manage it, in his wheelchair if he could not, would be helped up the walk and before entering the building, would squint up at their office window, smile, and wave. His aide, for the last five or six years a silent, hard-looking man named Nunes, would be carrying a leather tote bag containing Redding's medicines and, invariably, a special, personal gift for each of those working in the office. On Redding's last visit, nearly a year before, his gift to her had been the diamond pendant—almost half a carat—now resting proudly on her chest. Of course, she realized, this day could prove an exception. Some sort of pressing situation had arisen requiring Redding to fly to Boston. He had called the office late on the previous afternoon inquiring as to whether, as long as he had to be in the city, he might be able to work in his annual checkup.

"Mrs. Fiske," Drexler called from his office, "I can't remember. Did you say Dr. Ferguson would be coming in with Mr. Redding, or did you say he wouldn't be?"

"I said 'might,' Doctor. Mr. Redding wasn't sure." The woman smiled lovingly and shook her head. Vernon Drexler may have been a renowned endocrinologist, and a leading expert on the neuromuscular disease myasthenia gravis, but for matters other than medicine, his mind was a sieve. She and his wife had spent many amusing evenings over the years imagining the Keystone Comedy that would result were they not available to orchestrate his movements from appointment to appointment, lecture to lecture.

The thought of Dr. Ferguson sent the office manager hurrying to the small, fire-resistant room housing their medical records; she returned to her desk with the man's file. John Ferguson, MD, afflicted, as was Cyrus Redding, with myasthenia, was a close friend of the tycoon. The two men usually arranged to have their checkups on the same day, and then for an hour or so they would meet with Dr. Drexler. Lurleen Fiske suspected, though Drexler had never made her party to their business, that the two men were in some way supporting his myasthenia research laboratory at the medical school.

"Mrs. Fiske," Drexler called out again, "perhaps you'd better get Dr. Ferguson's chart just in case."

"Yes, Doctor, I'll get it right away," she said, already flipping through the lengthy record to ensure that the laboratory reports and notes from his last visit were in place. Drexler was nervous. She could tell from his voice. He was conducting himself with proper decorum and professional detachment, but she could tell nonetheless. Once, years before, he had been ferried by helicopter to Onassis's yacht for a consultation on the man's already lost battle against myasthenia. That morning, he had calmly bid the office staff good day and then had strode out minus his medical bag, journal articles, and sport coat.

Redding's limousine, slowed by the snow-covered streets, arrived five minutes late. Lurleen Fiske joined the two other employees at the window. Across the room, Drexler, a tall, gaunt man in his midfifties, watched his staff pridefully.

"Look, look. There he is," the receptionist twittered.

"Is he walking?" Drexler wanted to see for himself, but was reluctant to disrupt the ritual that had developed over the years.

Lurleen Fiske craned her neck. "His wheelchair is out," she said, "but yes . . . yes, he's taking a few steps on his own. Another year, Dr. Drexler. You've done it again." There was no mistaking the reverence in her voice.

In spite of himself, Drexler, too, was impressed. In sixty-seven he had predicted three years for Redding, four at the most. Now, after more than fifteen, the man was as strong as he had been at the start, if not stronger. *You've done it again*. Mrs. Fiske's praise echoed painfully in his thoughts. Myasthenia gravis, a progressive deterioration of the neuromuscular system. Cause: unknown. Prognosis:

progressive weakness—especially with exertion—fatigue, difficulty in chewing, difficulty in breathing, and eventually, death from infection or respiratory failure. Treatment: stopgap even at its most sophisticated. Yet here were two men, Redding and John Ferguson, who had, in essence, arrested or at least markedly slowed the progress of their disease. And they had performed the minor miracles on their own. Though his staff thought otherwise, and neither patient would ever suggest so, they had received only peripheral, supportive help from him. They were certainly a pair of triumphs, but triumphs that continually underscored the futility of his own life's work.

From the hallway, Drexler heard the elevator clank open. For years, his two prize patients had been treating themselves with upwards of a dozen medications at once, most of them still untested outside the laboratory. For years he had dedicated his work to trying to ascertain which drug or combination of drugs was responsible for their remarkable results. The answer would likely provide a breakthrough of historic proportions. Perhaps this would be his year.

Redding, seated in an unmotorized wheelchair, waved his aide on ahead and then wheeled himself to the doorway. Using the man's arm for some support, he pulled himself upright and took several rickety steps into the office.

"Thank you for seeing me on such short notice, Vernon," he said, extending his hand to give Drexler's a single, vigorous pump. "Mr. Nunes?" The aide, a sullen, swarthy man with the physique of an Olympic oarsman, slid the wheelchair into place for Redding to sit back down. Across the waiting room, Lurleen Fiske and the two other women beamed like proud grandmothers.

"You look wonderful, Cyrus," Drexler said. "Absolutely wonderful. Come on into my office."

"In a moment. First, I should like to wish your staff an early Merry Christmas. Mr. Nunes?"

The expressionless Nunes produced three gifts of varying sizes from the leather bag slung over his shoulder, and

Redding presented them, one at a time, to the women, who shook his hand self-consciously. Lurleen Fiske squeezed his shoulders and kissed him on the cheek.

"My limousine will go for Dr. Ferguson," Redding said, as he was wheeled into Drexler's office. "He will be here to share notes with the two of us, but not to be examined. He would rather keep the appointment he has for next month, if that is agreeable to you."

"Fine, fine," Drexler said.

The two men, Ferguson and Redding, had met perhaps a dozen years before in his waiting room and had developed an instant rapport. By their next appointment, Redding had asked that a half day be set aside for just the two of them. The request, supported as it was by the promise of substantial research funds, was, of course, granted.

Redding's bodyguard wheeled him into Drexler's office, set the bag of medications on the desk, and left to accompany the limousine to John Ferguson's house. Carefully, Redding arranged the vials and plastic containers on the blotter before Drexler. There were, all told, thirteen different preparations.

"Well, Doctor," he said, "here they are. Most of them you already know we have been taking. A couple of them you don't."

"Dr. Ferguson continues to follow exactly the same regimen as you?"

"As far as I know."

The endocrinologist made notes concerning each medication. There were two highly experimental drugs—still far from human testing—that he himself had only learned of in the past six or seven months. He bit back the urge, once again, to warn against the dangers of taking pharmaceuticals before they could be properly investigated, and simply recorded the chemical names and dosages. Somehow, the two men were screening the drugs for side effects. They had let him know that much and no more. As far as Vernon Drexler, MD, was concerned, with a goodly proportion of his own research at stake, there was no point in pushing the matter.

"This one?" Drexler held up a half-filled bottle of clear, powder-filled gelatin capsules.

"From Podgorny, at the Institute for Metabolic Research, in Leningrad," Redding said simply. "He believes the theory behind the compound to be quite sound."

"Amazing," Drexler muttered. "Absolutely amazing." Rudy Podgorny was a giant in the field, but so inaccessible that it had been two years since he had met with him face to face. Redding's resourcefulness, the power of his money, was mind-boggling. "Well," he said when he had finished his tabulations, "these two preparations have finally had clinical evaluations. Both of them have been shown to be without significant effect. We can discuss my thoughts when Dr. Ferguson arrives, but I feel the data now are strong enough to recommend stopping them."

Redding fingered the bottles. "One of these was your baby, yes?"

The physician shrugged helplessly and nodded. "Yes," he said, "I am afraid I have hitched my wagon to a falling star." He failed in his attempt to keep an optimistic tone in his voice. Four years of work had, in essence, gone down the drain.

"Then you must strike out in other directions, eh?"

*Just tell me*, Drexler thought, *tell me how in the hell you know the medications you are taking won't just kill you on the spot?*

"Yes," he said, through a tight smile, "I suppose I must."

The sleek, stretch limousine moved like a serpent through the light midafternoon traffic on the Southeast Expressway. In the front seat, Redding's portly driver chattered at the taciturn Nunes, whose contribution to the conversation was an occasional nod or monosyllable. In the rear, seated across from one another, surrounded on all sides by smoked glass, Redding and John Ferguson sipped brandy and reviewed the session they had just completed with Vernon Drexler.

"I am sorry things have not been going well with you, John," Redding said. "Perhaps we should have stayed and let Drexler examine you."

"Nonsense. I have an appointment next month, and that will be quite time enough."

"Yes, I suppose so." There was little question in Redding's mind that Ferguson, perhaps eight years his senior, was failing. The man, never robust, had lost strength and weight. He could shuffle only a few dozen steps without exhaustion. His face was drawn and sallow, dominated by a mouth of full, perfect teeth that gave his every expression a cadaverous cast. Only his eyes, sparkling from within deep hollows like chips of aquamarine, reflected the immense drive and intellectual power that had marked the man's life.

Their collaboration, for that is what it quickly became, had begun on the day of their first meeting in Drexler's office. Ferguson, though still ambulatory with a cane, had the more advanced disease of the two. He was employed at the time as medical director of a state hospital outside of the city and was already taking two experimental drugs after testing them for a time on the patients of his facility.

Within a year, Redding had begun locating new preparations, while Ferguson expanded his testing program to include them. Quickly, though, both men came to appreciate the need for a larger number of test subjects than could be supplied by Ferguson's hospital. Establishment of the Total Care Women's Health Center in Denver and, soon after, the Omnicenter in Boston, was the upshot of that need. Vernon Drexler continued as their physician, monitoring their progress and watching over their general states of health.

Redding's driver, still prattling cheerfully at Nunes, swung onto 95 North. Although they would eventually end up at John Ferguson's Newton home, his only other instruction had been for a steady one-hour drive.

"John," Redding said, setting his half-filled snifter in its holder on the bar, "how long has it been since you were at the Omnicenter?"

Ferguson laughed ruefully. "How long since I've been anyplace would be a better question. Two years, perhaps. Maybe longer. It's just too difficult for me to get around."

"I understand."

"I take it from our conversation yesterday evening that there's been some kind of problem. Zimmermann?"

This time it was Redding who laughed. "No, no," he said. "From all I can tell, Zimmermann was the perfect choice for the job. You were absolutely right in recommending him. A harmless fop with the intelligence to implement and monitor our testing program without getting in the way. No, not Zimmermann."

"Well, then?"

"Actually, there may not even be a problem. When you were working with Dr. French to set up the Omnicenter, did you ever run into a Dr. Kathryn Bennett?" Ferguson thought for a moment and then shook his head. "I suspected you wouldn't have," Redding said.

It took only a few minutes for Redding to review the events leading to Kate Bennett's inspection of the Omnicenter.

Ferguson listened with the dispassion of a scientist, his silence punctuated only by occasional gestures that he was following the account.

"Carl Horner assures me," Redding concluded, "that none of the pharmaceuticals we are studying could have been responsible for the problems young Dr. Bennett is investigating."

"But you are not so sure."

"John, you've worked with Carl. You know that being wrong is not something he does very often. The man's mind is as much a computer as any of his machines."

"But you think two such distinctive cases, and now possibly a third, are too many to explain by coincidence?"

Redding stared out the window; he removed his glasses

and cleaned them with a towel from the bar. "To tell you the truth, John, I don't know what to think. The facts say one thing, my instincts another. You know the Omnicenter better than I do. Could anyone be fooling around with some drug or other kind of agent behind our backs?"

"I hope not."

"John, mull over what I've told you. See if you can come up with any theories that might explain why all three women with this bleeding problem, and two of them with the same ovary problem, were all patients of the Omnicenter." He flipped the intercom switch. "Mr. Crosscup, you may drive us to Dr. Ferguson's house," he said.

"I will think it over," Ferguson said, "but my impression is that this once at least, your instincts should yield to the facts."

"A week."

"Excuse me?"

"A week, John," Redding said. "I should like to hear something from you about this matter in a week."

Ferguson probed the younger man's eyes. "You seem to be implying that I am holding something back."

"I imply nothing of the kind." He smiled enigmatically. "I am only asking for your help."

The limousine pulled into the snow-banked drive of John Ferguson's house, a trim white colonial on perhaps an acre of land. Redding engaged the intercom. "Mr. Nunes," he said, "our business has been concluded. Kindly assist our guest to his home."

The men shook hands and Redding watched as Nunes aided an obviously exhausted John Ferguson up the walk to the front door. The old man was many things, Redding acknowledged, a brilliant physician and administrator, an exceptional judge of human nature and predictor of human behavior, a gifted philosopher. What he was not, Redding had known since the early days of their association, was John Ferguson. Redding's investigators had been able to learn that much, but no more. There had been a John

Ferguson with an educational background identical to this man's, but that John Ferguson had died in the bombing of a field hospital in Bataan. Originally, Redding's instincts had argued against a confrontation with his new associate over what, exactly, the man was hiding from. That decision had proved prudent—at least until now.

Ferguson bid a final good-bye with a weak wave and entered his home.

Behind the smoked glass of the limousine, Cyrus Redding was placing a phone call through the mobile operator. "Dr. Stein, please," Redding said. "Hello, Doctor, this is your friend from Darlington. The man, John Ferguson, of whom I spoke last night: I should like the reinvestigation and close observation instituted at once. Keep me informed personally of your progress. He seems to have materialized shortly after World War Two, so perhaps that is a period to reinvestigate first. Thank you."

All right, my friend, he thought. For fifteen years, I have allowed you your deception. Let us hope that courtesy was not misplaced.

Kate Bennett set her dictaphone headpiece in its cradle and stared across the street at the darkened Omnicenter. Reflections from the headlights of passing cars sparkling off its six-foot windows lent an eerie animation to the structure, which stood out against its dark brick surroundings like a spaceship. Kate knew it was her never-timid imagination at work, knew it was the phone call she was expecting, but she still could not rationalize away her sense of the building as something ominous, something virulent.

The message had been on her desk when she returned from the Friday meeting of the hospital Infection Control Committee, which she had chaired for almost a year.

"Ian Toole at State Toxicology Lab called," the department secretary's note said. "One spec you sent normal, one spec contaminated. Please await phone call with details between six and seven tonight."

Contaminated.

"It's you. I know it is." Her mind spoke the words to the gleaming five stories. "Something inside you, inside your precious Monkeys, has gone haywire. Something inside you is killing people, and you don't even know it."

The ringing of the telephone startled her. "Kate Bennett," she answered excitedly.

"Kate Bennett's husband," Jared said flatly.

"Oh, hi. You surprised me. I was expecting a call from Ian Toole in the toxicology lab and . . . never mind that. Where are you? Is everything all right?"

"At home, where you're supposed to be, and no."

Kate glanced at the clock on her desk and groaned. "Oh, damn. Jared, I forgot about the Carlisles. I'm sorry."

"Apology not accepted," he said with no hint of humor.

Kate sank in her chair, resigned to the outburst she knew was about to ensue, and knowing that it was justified. "I'm sorry anyhow," she said softly.

"You're always sorry, aren't you?" Jared said. "You're so wrapped up in Kate's job and Kate's world and Kate's problems that you seem to forget that there are any other jobs or worlds or problems around. My father and several big-money people are going to be at that party tonight. What kind of an impression is it going to make when I show up without my wife?"

"Jared, you don't understand. Something is going on here. People are dying."

"People like Bobby Geary?"

Kate glanced at the clock. It was five minutes to seven. "Look," she said, "I'm waiting for a call that could help solve this mystery. I can call you back or I can get home as soon as possible, change, and make it over to the Carlisles by eight-thirty or nine."

"Don't bother."

"Jared, what do you want me to do?"

Jared's sigh was audible over the phone. "I want you

to do whatever it is you feel you have to do," he said. "I'll go to the Carlisles and make do. We can talk later tonight or tomorrow. Okay?"

"All right," she said, taken somewhat aback by his reasonableness.

"How's Ellen?"

"Pardon?" It was one minute to seven.

"Ellen. You remember, our friend Ellen. How is she?"

"She's in the hospital, Jared. Listen, I really am sorry, and I really am in the middle, or at least on the fringes of something strange. Ellen's life may be at stake in what I'm doing."

"Sounds pretty melodramatic to me," Jared said, "but then again, I'm just a poor ol' country lawyer. We'll talk later."

"Thank you, Jared. I love you."

"See you later, Kate."

Ian Toole's call came at precisely seven-fifteen.

"These are some little pills you sent me here, Dr. Bennett," he said. "My assistant, Millicent, and I have been running them most of the afternoon, and we still don't have a final word for you."

"But you said Ellen's pills were contaminated."

"Ellen Sandler's? Hardly. I think your secretary mixed up my message. Probably went to the same school as ours."

"What do you mean?"

"Ellen Sandler's vitamins are a pretty run-of-the-mill, low-potency preparation. B complex, a little C, a little iron, a splash of zinc. It's yours that are weird."

"Mine?" Kate's throat grew dry and tight.

"Uh-huh. You're not only taking the same vitamins as Ellen Sandler, but you're also taking a fairly sizable jolt every day of some kind of anthranilic acid."

"Anthranilic acid?"

"Millicent and I are trying to work out the side chains, but that's the basic molecule."

Kate felt sick. "Mr. Toole, what is it?"

"I'm a chemist, not a doctor, but as far as I've been able to determine, you're taking a painkiller of some sort. Nonnarcotic. Some kind of nonsteroidal anti-inflammatory drug. The basic molecule is listed in our manuals, but I don't think we're going to find the exact side chains. Whatever it is, it's not a commercially available drug in this country. If it were, we'd have it in the book. I'll check out the European manuals as soon as we know the full structure."

"Let me know?" Kate had written out the word "anthranilic" and begun a calligraphic version.

"Of course. Probably won't be until next week, though. I had to promise Millicent a bottle of wine to get her to put off her date with her boyfriend even this long."

"Mr. Toole, is it dangerous?"

"What?"

"Anthranilic acid."

"Like I said, I'm not a doctor. It's not poisonous, if that's what you mean, but it's not vitamins either. Any drug can do you dirt if you're unusually sensitive or allergic to it."

"Thanks," Kate said numbly. "And thanks to Millicent, too."

"No problem," Ian Toole said.

It was a hot, sultry day at Fenway Park when Kate, seated in a box next to Jared, began to bleed to death. Silently, painlessly, thick drops of crimson fell from her nose, landing like tiny artillery bursts on the surface of the beer she was holding, turning the gold to pink.

She squeezed her nose with a napkin, but almost instantly tasted the sticky sweetness flowing down the back of her throat. Jared, unaware of what was happening, sipped at his beer, his attention riveted on the field. Help me. Please, Jared, help me, I'm dying. The words were in her mind, but somehow inaccessible to her voice. Help me, please. Suddenly she felt a warm moistness inside her jeans, and knew that she was bleeding there as well. Help me.

In the box to her right, Winfield Samuels looked her way, smiled emptily as if she weren't even there, and then turned back to the field and genteelly applauded a good play by the shortstop.

The players and the grass, the spectators and the huge green left-field wall—all had a reddish cast. Kate rubbed a hand across one eye and realized she was also bleeding from there.

Giddy with fear, she stood and turned to run. Sitting in the row behind her chatting amiably and smiling as blandly as Jared's father had, were Norton Reese and a man with the overalls and gray hair of Carl Horner but the grotesque face of a monkey.

"I see you're bleeding to death," Reese said pleasantly. "I'm so sorry. Carl, aren't you sorry?"

Jared, please help me. Help me. Help me.

The words faded like an echo into eternity. Kate became aware of a gentle hand on her shoulder.

"Dr. Bennett, are you all right?"

Kate lifted her head and blearily met the eyes of night watchman Walter MacFarlane. She was at a table, alone in the hospital library, surrounded by dozens of books and journals dealing with bleeding disorders, ovarian disease, and pharmacology.

"Oh, yes, Walter," she said, "I'm fine, thank you. Really." Her blouse was uncomfortably damp, and the taste in her mouth most unpleasant.

"Just checking," the man said. "It's getting pretty late. Or should I say early." He tapped a finger on the face of his large gold pocket watch and held it around for her to see.

Twenty after two.

Kate smiled weakly and began gathering her notes together.

"I'll see you to your car if you want, Doctor."

"Thanks, Walter, I'll meet you by the main entrance in five minutes."

She watched as the man shuffled from the library. Then she discarded the notion of calling Jared, knowing that she would just be adding insult to injury by waking him up, and finished packing her briefcase. As she neared the doorway, she glanced out the window. Across the street, the winter night reflected obscenely in its dark glass, stood the Omnicenter.

# 8

## Sunday 16 December

The night was heavy and raw. Crunching through slush that had begun to gel and shielding her face from blowgun darts of sleet, Kate crossed Commercial Street and plowed along Hanover into the North End. Traffic and the weather had made her twenty minutes late, but Bill Zimmermann was not the irritable, impatient type, and she anticipated a quick absolution. Demarsco's, the restaurant they had agreed upon, was a small, family-owned operation where parking was as difficult to find as an unexceptional item on the menu.

Initially, when Kate had called and asked to meet with him, Zimmermann had proposed his office at the Omnicenter. It was, perhaps, among the last structures on earth she felt like entering on that night. Unfortunately if there were a list of such things, Demarsco's, his other suggestion, might also have been on it. Demarsco's was one of her and Jared's favorite spots.

And now Jared was gone.

"A sort of separation, but not a separation," he had called it in the note she had found waiting for her at three o'clock on Saturday morning. He had taken some things and gone to his father's, where he would stay until leaving for business in San Diego on Monday.

"A sort of separation, but not a separation."

There was no lengthy explanation. No apology. Not even any anger. But the hurt and confusion were there in every word. It was as if he had just discovered that his wife was having an affair—an up-and-down, intense, emotionally draining affair—not with another man, but with her job, her career. "Space for both of us to sort out the tensions and pressures on our lives without adding new ones," he had written. "Space for each of us to take a hard look at our priorities."

Kate wondered if, standing in the center of his fine, paneled study, his elegant mistress awaiting him on his black satin sheets, Winfield Samuels, Jr., had raised a glass to toast his victory over Kate and the return of his son and to plan how to make a temporary situation permanent. It was a distressing picture and probably not that far from reality.

However, as distressing to her as the image of a gloating Win Samuels, was the realization that her incongruous emotion, at least at that moment and over the hour or so that followed before sleep took her, was relief. Relief at being spared a confrontation. Relief at being alone to think.

Someone was trying to sabotage her reputation and perhaps her career. Her close friend was lying in a hospital bed bleeding from a disorder that had killed at least two other women—a disorder that had no definite cause, let alone a cure. And now, there was the discovery that she herself had been exposed to contaminated vitamins, that her own body might be a time bomb, waiting to go off—perhaps to bleed, perhaps to die.

Priorities. Why couldn't Jared see their marriage as a blanket on which all the other priorities in their lives could be laid out and dealt with together? Why couldn't he see that their relationship needn't be an endless series of either-ors? Why couldn't he see that she could love him and still have a life of her own?

Demarsco's was on the first floor of a narrow brownstone. There were a dozen tables covered with red-and-white checkered tablecloths and adorned with candle-dripped Chianti bottles—a decor that might have been tacky, but in Demarsco's simply wasn't. Bill Zimmermann, seated at a small table to the rear, rose and waved as she entered. He wore a dark sport jacket over a gray turtleneck and looked to her like a mix of the best of Gary Cooper and Montgomery Clift. A maternal waitress, perhaps the matriarch of the Demarsco clan, took her coat and ushered her to Zimmermann with a look that said she approved of the woman for whom the tall dashing man at the rear table had been waiting.

"They have a wonderful soave," Kate answered, settling into her seat, "but you'll have to drink most of it. I haven't been getting much sleep lately, and when I'm tired, more than one glass of wine is usually enough to cross my eyes."

"I have no such problem, unfortunately," he said, nodding that the ample waitress could fill his earlier order. "Sometimes, I fear that my liver will desert me before my brain even knows I have been drinking. It is one of the curses of being European. I stopped by the hospital earlier to see your friend Mrs. Sandler."

"I know. I was with her just before I came here. She was grateful for your visit. Whatever you said had a markedly reassuring effect." Kate smiled inwardly, remembering the girlish exchange she and Ellen had had regarding the Omnicenter director's uncommon good looks and marital status.

"Maybe I could rent him for a night," Ellen had said, "just to parade past Sandy a time or two."

Zimmermann tapped his fingertips together. "The lab reports show very little change."

"I know," Kate said. "If anything, they're worse. Unless there are several days in a row of improvement, or at least stability, I don't think her hematologist will send her home." She felt a heaviness in her chest as her mind replayed the gruesome scene on Ashburton Five during Beverly Vitale's last minutes. Ellen's counts were not yet down to critical levels, but there were so many unknowns. A sudden, precipitous fall seemed quite possible. The stream of thoughts flowed into the question of whether with Ian Toole's findings, Kate herself should have some clotting measurements done. She discarded the notion almost as quickly as she recognized it.

"I hope as you do that there will be improvement," Zimmermann said. He paused and then scanned the menu. "What will it be for you?" he asked finally.

"I'm not too hungry. How about an antipasto, some garlic bread . . . and a side order of peace of mind?"

Zimmermann's blue-gray eyes, still fixed on the leather-enclosed menu, narrowed a fraction. "That bad?"

Kate chewed at her lower lip and nodded, suddenly very glad she had gone the route of calling him. If, as seemed possible, a confrontation with Redding Pharmaceuticals was to happen, it would be good to have an ally with Bill Zimmermann's composure and assuredness, especially considering the fragility of her own self-confidence.

"In that case, perhaps I had best eat light also." Zimmermann called the waitress over with a microscopic nod and ordered identical meals.

"I want to thank you for coming out on such a grisly night," Kate began. "There have been some new developments in my efforts to make sense out of the three bleeding cases, and I wanted to share them with you."

"Oh?" Zimmermann's expression grew more attentive.

"You know I've had sample after sample of medications from the Omnicenter analyzed at the State Toxicology Lab."

"Yes, of course. But I thought the results had all been unremarkable."

"They were . . . until late Friday afternoon. One of the vitamin samples I had analyzed contained a painkiller called anthranilic acid. The basic chemical structure of the drug is contained in several commercial products—Bymid, from Sampson Pharmaceuticals, and Levonide, from Freeman-Gannett, to name two. However, the form contaminating the vitamins is something new—at least in this country. Ian Toole at the state lab is going to check the European manuals and call me tomorrow."

"Is he sure of the results?"

"He seemed to be. I don't know the man personally, but he has a reputation for thoroughness."

"What do you think happened?"

"Contamination." Kate shrugged that there was no other explanation that made any sense. "Either at Redding Pharmaceuticals or perhaps at one of the suppliers of the vitamin components, although I would suspect that a company as large as Redding can do all the manufacturing themselves."

"Yes. I agree. Do you think this anthranilic acid has caused the bleeding disorders in our three women?"

"Bleeding *and* ovarian disorders," Kate added, "at least ovarian in two of the women. We don't know about Ellen. The answer to your question is I don't know and I certainly hope not."

"Why?"

"Because, Bill, the vitamins that were finally positive for something were mine. Ones you prescribed for me."

Zimmermann paled. The waitress arrived with their antipasto, but he did not so much as glance up at her. "Jesus," he said softly. It was the first time Kate had ever heard him use invective of any kind. "Are you sure this Toole couldn't have made a mistake? You said yourself there were any number of samples that were negative."

"Anything's possible," she said. "I suppose Ian Toole and his spectrophotometer are no more exempt from error than . . . Redding Pharmaceuticals."

"Do you have more of a sample? Can we have the findings rechecked at another lab?"

Kate shook her head. "It was an old prescription. There were only half a dozen left. I think he used them all."

Zimmermann tried picking at his meal but quickly gave up. "I don't mean to sound doubtful about what you are saying, Kate. But you see what's at stake here, don't you?"

"Of course I do. And I understand your skepticism. If I were in your position and the Omnicenter were my baby, I'd want to be sure, too. But Bill, the situation is desperate. Two women have died. My friend is lying up there bleeding, and I have been unknowingly taking a medication that was never prescribed for me. Someone in or around Redding's generic drug department has made an error, and I think we should file a report with the FDA as quickly as possible. I spoke to the head pharmacist at Metro about how one goes about reporting problems with a drug."

"Did you mention the Omnicenter specifically?" Zimmermann asked.

"I may be nervous and frightened about all this, Bill, but I'm neither dumb nor insensitive. No. Everything I asked him was hypothetical."

"Thank you."

"Nonsense. Grandstand plays aren't my style." She smiled. "Despite what the papers and all those angry Red Sox fans think. Any decisions concerning the Omnicenter we make together." Kate nibbled on the edge of a piece of garlic bread and suddenly realized that for the first time since returning home to Jared's note, she had an appetite. Perhaps, after the incredible frustrations of the week past, she was feeling the effects of finally doing something. She passed the basket across to Zimmermann. "Here," she offered, "have a piece of this before it gets cold."

Zimmermann accepted the offering, but deep concern continued to darken his face. "What did the pharmacist tell you?"

"There's an agency called the U.S. Pharmacopia, independent of both the FDA and the drug industry, but in close touch with both. They run a drug-problem reporting program. Fill out a form and send it to them, and they send a copy to the FDA and to the company involved."

"Do you know what happens then?"

"Not really. I assume an investigator from the FDA is assigned to look into matters."

"And the great bureaucratic dragon rears its ugly head."

"What?"

"Have you had many dealings with the FDA? Speed and efficiency are hardly their most important products. No one's fault, really. The FDA has some pretty sharp people—only not nearly enough of them."

"What else can we do?" Absently, Kate rolled a black olive off its lettuce hillock and ate it along with several thin strips of prosciutto. "I need help. As it is, I'm spending every spare moment in the library. I've even asked the National Institutes of Health library to run a computer cross on blood and ovarian disorders. They should be sending me a bibliography tomorrow. I've sent our slides to four other pathologists to see if anyone can make a connection. The FDA seems like the only remaining move."

"The FDA may be a necessary move, but it is hardly our only one. First of all I want to speak with Carl Horner and our pharmacist and see to it that the use of any Redding products by our facility will be suspended until we have some answers."

"Excellent. Will you have to bring in extra pharmacists?"

"Yes, but we've had contingency plans in place in case of some kind of computer failure since . . . well, since even before I took over as director. We'll manage as long as necessary."

"Let's hope it won't be too long," Kate said, again thinking of Beverly Vitale's lifeless, blood-smeared face.

"If we go right to the FDA it might be."

"Pardon?"

"Kate, I think our first move should be to contact Redding Pharmaceuticals directly. I think the company deserves that kind of consideration for the way they've stood up for orphan drugs and for all the other things they've done to help the medical community and society as a whole. Besides, in any contest between the bureau-cratic dragon and private industry, my money is on indus-try every time. I think it's only fair to the Omnicenter and our patients to get to the bottom of matters as quickly as possible."

Kate sipped pensively at her wine. "I see what you mean . . . sort of," she said. "Couldn't we do both? I mean contact Redding and notify the FDA?"

"We could, but then we lose our stick, our prod, if you will. The folks at Redding will probably bend over backward to avoid the black eye of an FDA probe. I know they will. I've had experience with other pharmaceutical houses—ones not as responsive and responsible as Redding. They would go to almost any length to identify and correct problems within their company without outside inter-vention."

"That makes sense, I guess," she said.

"You sound uncertain, Kate. Listen, whatever we do, we should do together. You said that yourself. I've given you reasons for my point of view, but I'm by no means inflexible." Zimmermann drained the last half of his glass and refilled it.

Kate hesitated and then said, "I have this thing about the pharmaceutical industry. It's a problem in trust. They spend millions and millions of dollars on giveaways to medical students and physicians. They support dozens upon dozens of throwaway journals and magazines with their ads. I get fifty publications a month I never ordered. And I don't even write prescriptions. I can imagine how many you get." Zimmermann nodded that he understood. "In addition, I have serious questions about their priorities— you know, who comes first in any conflict between profit and people."

"What do you mean?"

"Well, look at Valium. Roche introduces the drug and markets it well, and the public literally eats it up. It's a tranquilizer, a downer, yet in no time at all it becomes the most prescribed and taken drug in the country. Unfortunately, it turns out to be more addicting than most physicians appreciated at first, and lives begin to get ruined. Meanwhile, a dozen or so other drug houses put out a dozen or so versions of Valium, each with its own name and its own claim. Slower acting. Faster acting. Lasts all night. Removed more rapidly. Some busy physicians get so lost in the advertising and promises that they actually end up prescribing two of these variants to the same patient at the same time. Others think they're doing their patients a big favor by switching. Some favor."

"Pardon me for saying it, Kate, but you sound a little less than objective."

"I'm afraid you hear right," she said. "I had some emotional stresses back in college, and the old country doctor who served the school put me on Valium. It took a whole team of specialists to realize how much my life came to revolve around those little yellow discs. Finally, I had to be hospitalized and detoxed. So I just have this nagging feeling that the drug companies can't be trusted. That's all."

Zimmermann leaned back, rubbed his chin, and sighed. "I don't know what to say. If speed is essential in solving this problem, as we both think it is, then the route to go is the company. I'm sure of that." He paused. "Tell you what. Let's give them this coming week to straighten out matters to our satisfaction. If they haven't done so by Friday, we call in the FDA. Sound fair?"

Kate hesitated, but then nodded. "Yes," she said finally. "It sounds fair and it sounds right. Do you want to call them?"

Zimmermann shrugged. "Sure," he said, "I'll do it first thing tomorrow. They'll probably be contacting you by the end of the day."

"The sooner the better. Meanwhile, do you think you could talk to some of your Omnicenter patients and get me a list of women who would be willing to be contacted by me about having their medications analyzed?"

"I certainly can try."

"Excellent. It's about time things started moving in a positive direction. You know, there's not much good I can say about all that's been happening, except that I'm glad our relationship has moved out of the doctor-patient and doctor-doctor cubbyholes into the person-person. Right now I'm the one who needs the help, but please know that if it's ever you, you've got a friend you can count on."

Zimmermann smiled a Cary Grant smile. "That kind of friend is hard to come by," he said. "Thank you."

"Thank you. Except for Tom Engleson, I've felt pretty much alone in all this. Now we're a team." She motioned the waitress over.

"Coffee?" the woman asked.

"None for me, thanks. Bill?" Zimmermann shook his head. "In that case could I have the check, please?"

"Nonsense," Zimmermann said, "I won't . . ."—the reproving look in Kate's eyes stopped him in mid-sentence—". . . allow you to do this too many times without reciprocating."

Kate beamed at the man's insight. "Deal," she said, smiling broadly.

"Deal," Zimmermann echoed.

The two shook hands warmly and, after Kate had settled their bill, walked together into the winter night.

Numb with exhaustion, John Ferguson squinted at the luminescent green print on the screen of his word processor. His back ached from hunching over the keyboard for the better part of two full days. His hands, feeling the effects of his disease more acutely than at any time in months, groped for words one careful letter at a time. It had been an agonizing effort, condensing forty years of complex research into thirty pages or so of scholarly dissertation, but a sentence at a time, a word at a time, he was making progress.

To one side of his desk were a dozen internationally read medical journals. Ferguson had given thought to submitting his completed manuscript to all of them, but then had reconsidered. The honor of publishing his work would go only to *The New England Journal of Medicine*, most prestigious and widely read of them all.

*The New England Journal of Medicine.* Ferguson tapped out a recall code, and in seconds, the title page of his article was displayed on the screen.

### STUDIES IN ESTRONATE 250
A Synthetic Estrogen Congener and
Antifertility Hormone
John N. Ferguson, MD

It would almost certainly be the first time in the long, distinguished publication of the journal that an entire issue would be devoted to a single article. But they would agree to do that or find the historic studies and comment in *Lancet* or *The American Journal of Medicine*. Ferguson smiled. Once *The New England Journal's* editors had reviewed his data and his slides, he doubted there would be much resistance to honoring his request. For a time he studied the page. Then, electronically, he erased the name of the author. There might be trouble for him down the road for what he was about to do, but he suspected not. He was too old and too sick even for the fanatic Simon Weisenthal to bother with.

With a deliberateness that helped him savor the act, he typed Wilhelm W. Becker, MD, PhD where Ferguson's name had been. Perhaps, he thought with a smile, some sort of brief funeral was in order for Ferguson. He had, after all, died twice—once in Bataan, forty years ago, and a second time this night.

With the consummate discipline that had marked his life, Willi Becker cut short the pleasurable interlude and advanced the text to the spot at which he had left off. Because of a pathologist named Bennett, Cyrus Redding had picked up the scent of his work at the Omnicenter. Knowing the man as well as Becker did, he felt certain the tycoon would now track the matter relentlessly. There was still time to put the work on paper and mail it off, but no way of knowing how much. He had to push. He had to fight the fatigue and the aching in his muscles and push, at least for another hour or two. The onset of his scientific immortality was at hand.

Furtively, he glanced at the small bottle of amphetamines on the table. It had been only three hours. Much too soon, especially with the irregular heartbeats he had been having. Still, he needed to push. It would only be a few more days, perhaps less. Barely able to grip the top of the small vial, Becker set one of the black, coated tablets on his tongue, and swallowed it without water. In minutes, the warm rush would begin, and he would have the drive, however artificial and short lived, to overcome the inertia of his myasthenia.

"You really shouldn't take those, you know, father. Especially with your cardiac history."

Becker spun around to face his son, cursing the diminution in his hearing that enabled such surprises. "I take them because I need them," he said sharply. "What are you doing sneaking up on me like that? What do you think doorbells are for?"

"Such a greeting. And here I have driven out of my way to stop by and be certain you are all right."

Three blocks, Becker thought. Some hardship. "You startled me. That's all. I'm sorry for reacting the way I did."

"In that case, father, it is I who should be sorry."

Was there sarcasm in his son's voice? It bothered Becker that he had never been able to read the man. Theirs was a relationship based on filial obligation and respect, but little if any love. For the greater portion of his son's years, they had lived apart: Becker in a small cottage on the hospital grounds where he worked, and his wife and son in an apartment twenty miles away. It was as necessary an arrangement as it was painful. Becker and his wife had tried for years to make their son understand that.

There were those, they tried to explain, who would arrest Becker in a moment on a series of unjust charges, put him in prison, and possibly even put him to death. In the hysteria following the war, he had been marked simply because he was German, nothing more than that. For their own safety, it was necessary for the boy and his mother to keep their address and even their name separate from his. Although Becker would provide for them and would visit as much as he could, no one would ever know his true relationship to the woman, Anna Zimmermann, and the boy, William.

"So," Becker said. "Now that we have apologized profusely to one another, come in, sit down, pour yourself a drink."

William Zimmermann nodded his thanks, poured an inch of Wild Turkey into a heavy glass, and settled into an easy chair opposite his father.

"I see you've started putting your data together," he said. "Why now?"

"Well, I . . . no special reason, really. It would seem that the modifications I made have greatly, if not completely, eliminated the bleeding problems we were experiencing with the Estronate. So what else is there to wait for?"

"Which journal will you approach?"

"I think *The New England Journal of Medicine*. I plan to submit the data and discussion but to withhold several key steps in the synthesis until a commission of the journal's choosing can take charge of my formulas and decide how society can best benefit from them."

"Sounds fine to me," Zimmermann said. "With all that's been happening this last week, the sooner I see the last of Estronate Two-fifty, the better."

"Have any further bleeding cases turned up?"

Zimmermann shook his head. "Just the Sandler woman I told you about. The one who's the friend of Dr. Bennett's. She was treated over eighteen months ago, in the July/August group, the last group to receive the unmodified Estronate."

"How is she doing?"

"I think she is going to end up like the other two."

"Couldn't you find some way of suggesting that they try a course of massive doses of delta amino caproic acid and nicotinic acid on her?"

"Not without risking a lot of questions I'd rather not answer. I mean I am a gynecologist, not a hematologist. Besides, you told me that that therapy was only sixty percent effective in such advanced states."

Becker shrugged. "Sixty percent is sixty percent."

"And my career is my career. No, father, I have far too much to lose. I am afraid Mrs. Sandler will just have to make it on her own."

"Perhaps you are right," Becker said.

The men shook hands formally, and William Zimmermann let himself out. Twelve miles away, on the fourth floor of the Berenson Building of Metropolitan Hospital of Boston, in Room 421, Ellen Sandler's nose had again begun to bleed.

# 9

## Monday 17 December

"Now, Suzy, promise Daddy that you will mind what Mommy tells you and that you will never, never do that to the cat again. . . . Good. . . . I have to go now, sugar. You better get ready for your piano lesson. . . . I know what I said, but my work here isn't done yet, and I have to stay until it's finished. . . . I don't know. Two, maybe three more days. . . . Suzy, stop that. You're not a baby. I love you very much and I'll see you very soon. Now, tell Daddy you love him and go practice that new piece of yours. . . . Suzy? . . ."

"Damn." Arlen Paquette slammed the receiver down. He had protested to Redding the futility of remaining in Boston over the weekend, but the man had insisted he stay close to the situation and the Omnicenter. As usual, events had proven Redding right. Paquette stuffed some notes in his briefcase and pulled on his suitcoat. Right for Redding Pharmaceuticals, but not for Suzy Paquette, who was justifiably smarting over her father's absence from her school track meet earlier in the day. How could he explain to a seven-year-old that the very thing that was keeping him away from home was also the sole reason she could attend a school like Hightower Academy? He straightened his tie and combed his thinning hair with his fingers. How could he explain it to her when he was having trouble justifying it to himself? Still, for what he and his family were gaining from his association with Redding, the dues were not excessive. He glanced down at the photographs of Kate Bennett piled on the coffee table. At least, he thought, not yet.

The cab ride from the Ritz to Metropolitan Hospital took fifteen minutes. Paquette entered the main lobby through newly installed gliding electronic doors and headed directly for Norton Reese's office, half expecting to have the woman whose life and face he had studied in such detail stroll out from a side corridor and bump into him.

"Arlen, it's good to see you. You're looking well." Norton Reese maneuvered free of his desk chair and met Paquette halfway with an ill-defined handshake. Theirs was more an unspoken truce than a relationship, and no amount of time would compensate for the lack of trust and respect each bore the other. However, Paquette was the envoy of Cyrus Redding and the several millions of Redding dollars that had sparked Reese's rise to prominence. Although it was Reese's court, it was the younger man's ball.

"You're looking fit yourself, Norton," Paquette replied. "Our mutual friend sends his respects and regards."

"Did you tell him about our speed freak outfielder and the letters to the press and TV?"

"I did. I even sent a packet of the articles and editorials to him by messenger. He commends your ingenuity. So, incidentally, do I." Try as he might, he could put no emotion behind the compliment.

Still, Reese's moon face bunched in a grin. "It's been beautiful, Arlen," he gushed. "Just beautiful. I tell you, ever since that story broke, Kathryn Bennett, MD, has been racing all over trying to stick her fingers in the holes that are popping open in her reputation. By now I doubt if she would know whether she had lost a horse or found a rope."

"You did fine, Norton. Just fine. Only, for our purposes, not enough."

"What?" Reese began to shift uneasily. "A diversion. That's what Horner asked me for, and by God, that's what I laid on that woman. A goddamn avalanche of diversion."

"You did fine, Norton. I just told you that."

"Why, she's had so much negative publicity it's a wonder she hasn't quit or been fired by the medical school." Reese chattered on as if he hadn't heard a word. "In fact, I hear the Medical School Ethics Committee is planning some kind of an inquiry."

Paquette silenced him with raised hands. "Easy, Norton, please," he said evenly. "I'm going to say it one more time. What you did, the letter and all, was exactly what we asked of you. Our mutual friend is pleased. He asked that I convey to you the Ashburton Foundation's intention to endow the cardiac surgical residency you wrote him about."

"Well, then, why was what I did not enough?" Reese realized that in his haste to defend himself, he had forgotten to acknowledge Redding's generosity. Before he could remedy the oversight, Paquette spoke.

"I'll convey your thanks when I return to Darlington," he said, a note of irritation in his words. "Norton, do you know what has been going on here?"

"Not . . . not exactly," he said, nonplussed.

Paquette nodded indulgently. "Dr. Bennett, in her search to identify the cause of an unusual bleeding problem in several women, has zeroed in on the Omnicenter. Although the women were Omnicenter patients, we see no other connection among them."

"The . . . the work you're doing . . . I mean none of the women got . . ." After years of scrupulously avoiding the Omnicenter and the people involved in its operation, Reese was uncertain of how, even, to discuss the place.

Paquette spared him further stammering. "From time to time, each of the women was involved in the evaluation of one or more products," he said. "However, Carl Horner assures me that there have been no products common to the three of them. Whatever the cause of their problem, it is not the Omnicenter."

"That's a relief," Reese said.

"Not really," Paquette said, his expression belying his impatience. "You see, our Dr. Bennett has been most persistent, despite the pressures brought about by your letter."

"She's a royal pain in the ass. I'll grant you that," Reese interjected.

"She has tested several Omnicenter products at the State Toxicology Lab, charging the analyses, I might add, to your hospital."

"Damn her. She didn't find anything, did she? Horner assured me that there was nothing to worry about."

Paquette's patience continued to fray. "Of course she found something, Norton. That's why I'm here. She even had Dr. Zimmermann phone the company to tell us about it."

"Oh. Sorry."

"Our friend in Kentucky has asked that we step up our efforts to discredit Dr. Bennett and to add, what was the word you used? distraction? . . . no, diversion, that was it—diversion to her life. We have taken steps to obscure, if not neutralize, her findings to date, but there is evidence in dozens of medicine cabinets out there of what we have been doing. If Dr. Bennett is persistent enough, she will find it. I am completely convinced of that, and so is our friend. Dr. Bennett has given us one week to determine how a certain experimental painkiller came to be in a set of vitamins dispensed at the Omnicenter. If we do not furnish her with a satisfactory explanation by that time, she intends to file a report with the US Pharmacopeia and the FDA."

"Damn her," Norton Reese said again. "What are we going to do?"

"Not we, you. Dr. Bennett's credibility must be reduced to the point where no amount of evidence will be enough for authorities to take her word over ours. The letter you wrote was a start, but, as I said, not enough."

Once again, Reese began to feel ill at ease. Paquette was not making a request, he was giving an order—an order from the man who, Reese knew, could squash him with nothing more than the eraser on his pencil. He unbuttoned his vest against the uncomfortable moistness between the folds of his skin.

"Look," he pleaded, "I really don't know what I can do. I'll try, but I don't know. You've got to understand, Arlen; you've got to make him understand. Bennett works in my hospital, but she doesn't work for me." There was understanding in Paquette's face, but not sympathy. Reese continued his increasingly nervous rambling. "Besides, the woman's got friends around here. I don't know why, but she does. Even after that letter, she's got supporters. Shit, I'd kill to make sure she didn't. . . ." His voice trailed away. His eyes narrowed.

Paquette followed the man's train of thought. "The answer is no, Norton," he said. "Absolutely not. We wish her discredited, not eliminated, for God's sake. We want people to lose interest in her, not to canonize her. She has already involved Dr. Zimmermann, a chemist at the state lab, and a resident here named Engleson. There may be others, but as far as we can tell, the situation is not yet out of control. We are doing what we can do to ensure it remains that way. Dr. Bennett's father-in-law does some business with our company. I believe our friend has already called him and enlisted his aid. There are other steps being taken as well." He rose and reached across the desk to shake Reese's hand. "I know we can count on you. If you need advice or a sounding board, you can reach me at the Ritz."

"Thank you," Reese said numbly. His bulk seemed melted into his chair.

Paquette walked slowly to the door, then turned. "Our friend has suggested Thursday as a time by which he wants something to have been done."

"Thursday?" Reese croaked.

Paquette nodded, smiled blankly, and was gone.

Half an hour later, his shirt changed and his composure nearly regained, Reese sat opposite Sheila Pierce, straightening one paper clip after another and thinking much more than he wanted to at that particular moment of the chief technician's breasts.

"How're things going down there in pathology?" he asked, wondering if she would take off her lab coat and then reminding himself to concentrate on business. The woman was going to require delicate handling if she was going to put her neck on the line to save his ass.

"You mean with Bennett?" Sheila shrugged. "She's getting some letters and a few crank phone calls every day, but otherwise things seem pretty much back to normal. It's been . . . amusing."

"Well," Reese said, "I know for a fact that the Bobby Geary business is hardly a dead issue."

"Oh?"

"I've heard the matter's going to the Medical School Ethics Committee."

"Good," Sheila said. "That will serve her right, going to the newspapers about that poor boy the way she did." They laughed. "Do you think," she went on, "that it will be enough to keep her from becoming chief of our department?"

Inwardly, Reese smiled. The question was just the opening he needed. "Doubtful," he said grimly. "Very doubtful."

"Too bad."

"You don't know the half of it."

"What do you mean?"

"Well . . ." He tapped a pencil eraser on his desk. He closed his eyes and massaged the bridge of his nose. He chewed at his lower lip. "I got a call this morning from Dr. Willoughby. He requested a meeting with the finance and budget committee of the board, at which time he and

Kate Bennett are going to present the results of a computer study she's just completed. They plan to ask for six months worth of emergency funding until a sweeping departmental reorganization can be completed."

Sheila Pierce paled. "Sweeping departmental reorganization?"

"That's what the man said."

"Did he say anything about . . . you know."

Reese sighed. "As a matter of fact, baby, he did. He said that by the time of the meeting next week, Bennett will have presented him with a complete list of lost revenues, including the misappropriation of funds by several department members."

"But she promised."

"I guess a few brownie points with the boss and the board of trustees outweigh her promise to a plain old technician."

"*Chief* technician," she corrected. "Damn her. Did it seem as if she had already said something about me to Willoughby?"

The bait taken, Reese set the hook. "Definitely not. I probed as much as I could about you without making Willoughby suspicious. She hasn't told him anything specific . . . yet."

"Norty, we've got to stop her. I can't afford to lose my job. Dammit, I've been here longer than she has. Much longer." Her hands were clenched white, her jaw set in anger and frustration.

"Well," Reese said with exaggerated reason, "we've got two days, three at the most. Any ideas?"

"Ideas?"

"I don't work with the woman, baby, you do. Doesn't she ever fuck up? Blow a case? Christ, the rest of the MD's in this place do it all the time."

"She's a pathologist, Norty. Her cases are all dead to begin with. There's nothing for her to blow except . . ." She stopped in midsentence and pulled a typed sheet from her lab coat pocket.

"What is it?"

"It's the surgical path schedule for tomorrow. Bennett and Dr. Huang are doing frozen sections this month." She scanned the entries.

"Well?"

Sheila hesitated, uncertainty darkening her eyes. "Are you sure she's going to report me to Willoughby?"

"Baby, all I can say is that Dr. Willoughby asked me for a copy of the union contract, expressly for the part dealing with justifiable causes for termination."

"She has no right to do that to me after she promised not to."

"You know about people with MD degrees, Sheila. They think they're better and smarter than the rest of us. They think they can just walk all over people." Sheila's eyes told him that the battle—this phase of it at any rate—was won.

"We'll see who's smarter," she muttered, tapping the schedule thoughtfully. "Maybe it's time Bennett found out that there are a few people with brains around who couldn't go to medical school."

"Make it good, baby," Reese urged, "because if she's in, you're out."

"No way," she said. "There's no way I'm going to let that happen. Here, look at this."

"What?"

"Well, you can see it's a pretty busy schedule. There's a lung biopsy, a thyroid biopsy, a colon, and two breast biopsies. Bennett will be working almost all day in the small cryostat lab next to the operating rooms. Usually, she goes into the OR, picks up a specimen, freezes it in the cryostat, sections it, stains it, and reads it, all without leaving the surgical suite."

"And?"

"Well, there are a lot of ifs," Sheila said in an even, almost singsong voice. "But if we could disable the surgical cryostat and force Bennett to use the backup unit down in the histology lab, I might be able somehow to switch a specimen. All I would need is about three or four minutes."

"What would that do?"

Sheila smiled the smile of a child. "Well, with any luck, depending on the actual pathology, we can have the great Dr. Bennett read a benign condition as a malignancy. Then, when the whole specimen is taken and examined the next day, her mistake will become apparent."

"Would a pathologist make a mistake like that?" Reese asked.

Again Sheila smiled. "Only once," she said serenely. "Only once."

Louisburg Square, a score of tall, brick townhouses surrounding a raggedy, wrought-iron-fenced green on the west side of Beacon Hill, had been *the* address in Boston for generations. Levi Morton lived there after his four years as vice president under Benjamin Harrison. Jennie Lind was married there in 1852. Cabots and Saltonstalls, Lodges and Alcotts—all had drawn from and given to the mystique of Louisburg Square.

Kate had the cab drop her off at the foot of Mount Vernon Street; she used the steep two-block walk to Louisburg Square to stretch her legs and clear her thoughts of what had been a long and trying day at the hospital. Two committee meetings, several surgical specimens, and a lecture at the medical school, combined with half a dozen malicious phone calls and an equal number of hate letters, all relating to her callous treatment of Bobby Geary and his family.

Ellen's nose had begun bleeding again—just a slow trickle from one nostril, but enough to require Pete Colangelo to recauterize it. Her clotting parameters were continuing to take a significant drop each day, and the unencouraging news was beginning to take a toll on her spirit. Late that afternoon, the National Institutes of Health library computer search had arrived. There were many articles listed in the bibliography dealing with sclerosing diseases of the ovaries, and a goodly number on clotting disorders similar to the Boston cases. There were none, however, describing their coexistence in a single patient. Expecting little, Kate had begun the tedious process of locating each article, photocopying it, and finally studying it. The project would take days to complete, if not longer, but there was a chance at least that something, anything, might turn up that could help Ellen.

At the turnoff from Mount Vernon Street, Kate propped herself against a gaslight lamp post and through the mist of her own breath, reflected on the marvelous Christmas card that was Louisburg Square. Single, orange-bulbed candles glowed from nearly every townhouse window. Tasteful wreaths marked each door. Christmas trees had been carefully placed to augment the scene without intruding on it.

Having, season after season, observed the stolid elegance of Louisburg Square, Kate had no difficulty understanding why, shortly after the death of his agrarian wife, Winfield Samuels had sold their gentleman's farm and stables in Sudbury and had bought there. The two—the address and the man—were made for one another. Somewhat reluctantly, she mounted the granite steps of her father-in-law's home, eschewed the enormous brass knocker, and pressed the bell.

In seconds, the door was opened by a trim, extremely attractive brunette, no more than two or three years Kate's senior. Dressed in a gold blouse and dark straight skirt, she looked every bit the part of the executive secretary, which, in fact, she had at one time been.

"Kate, welcome," she said warmly. "Come in. Let me take your coat."

"I've got it, thanks. You look terrific, Jocelyn. Is that a new hairstyle?"

"A few months old. Thanks for noticing. You're looking well yourself."

Kate wondered if perhaps she and Jocelyn Trent could

collaborate on a chapter for Amy Vanderbilt or Emily Post: "Proper Conversation Between a Daughter-in-law and her Father-in-law's Mistress When the Father-in-law in Question Refuses to Acknowledge the Woman as Anything Other Than a Housekeeper."

"Mr. Samuels will be down in a few minutes," Jocelyn said. "There's a nice fire going in the study. He'll meet you there. Dinner will be in half an hour. Can I fix you a drink?"

Mr. Samuels. The inappropriate formality made Kate queasy. At seven o'clock, the woman would serve to Mr. Samuels and his guest the gourmet dinner she had prepared; then she would go and eat in the kitchen. At eleven or twelve o'clock, after the house was quiet and dark, she would slip into his room and stay as long as she was asked, always careful to return to her own quarters before any houseguest awoke. Mr. Samuels, indeed.

"Sure," said Kate, following the woman to the study. "Better make it something stiff. As you can tell from your houseguest the last few days, things have not been going too well in my world."

Jocelyn smiled understandingly. "For what it's worth," she said, "I don't think Jared is very pleased with the arrangement either."

"I appreciate hearing that, Jocelyn. Thank you. I'll tell you, on any given Sunday in any given ballpark, marriage can trounce any team in the league." When she could detach the woman from her position, Kate liked her very much and enjoyed the occasional one-to-one conversations they were able to share.

"I know," Jocelyn said. "I tried it once, myself. For me it was all of the responsibility, none of the pleasure."

The words were said lightly, but Kate heard in them perhaps an explanation of sorts, a plea for understanding and acceptance. Better to be owned than to be used.

Kate took the bourbon and water and watched as Jocelyn Trent returned to the kitchen. The woman had, she knew, a wardrobe several times the size of her own, a remarkable silver fox coat, and a stylish Alfa coupé. If this be slavery, she thought with a smile, then give me slavery.

It was, as promised, several minutes before Winfield Samuels made his entrance. Kate waited by the deep, well-used fireplace, rearranging the fringe on the Persian rug with the toe of her shoe and trying to avoid eye contact with any of the big-game heads mounted on the wall. Samuels had sent Jared away on business—purposely, he made it sound—so that he and Kate could spend some time alone together talking over "issues of mutual concern." Before her marriage, they had met on several occasions for such talks, but since, their time together had always included Jared. Samuels had given no hint over the phone as to what the "issues" this time might be, but the separation—causes and cures—was sure to be high on the list. Kate was reading a citation of commendation and gratitude from the governor when the recipient entered the room.

"Kate, welcome," Win Samuels said. "I'm so glad you could make it on such short notice." They embraced with hands on shoulders and exchanged air kisses. "Sit down, please. We have," he consulted his watch, "twenty-three minutes before dinner."

Twenty-three minutes. Kate had to hand it to the man. Dinner at seven did not mean dinner at seven-oh-three. It was expected that the stunning cook cum housekeeper cum mistress would be right on time. "Thank you," she said. "It's good to see you again. You look great." The compliment was not exaggeration. In his twill smoking jacket and white silk scarf, Samuels looked like most men nearing seventy could only dream of looking.

"Rejuvenate that drink?" Samuels asked, motioning her to one of a pair of matched leather easy chairs by the hearth.

"Only if you're prepared to resuscitate me."

Samuels laughed and drew himself a bourbon and soda. "You're quite a woman, Kate," he said, settling in across from her. "Jared is lucky to have nabbed you."

"Actually, I did most of the nabbing."

"This . . . this little disagreement you two are having. It will blow over before you know it. Probably has already."

"The empty half of my bed wouldn't attest to that," Kate said.

Samuels slid a cigar from a humidor by his chair, considered it for a moment, and then returned it. "Bad for the taste buds this close to dinner, particularly with Jocelyn's duck à l'orange on the menu."

"She's a very nice woman," Kate ventured.

Samuels nodded. "Does a good job around here," he said in an absurdly businesslike tone. "Damn good job." He paused. "I'm a direct man, Kate. Some people say too direct, but I don't give a tinker's damn about them. Suppose I get right to the business at hand."

"You mean this wasn't just a social invitation?"

Samuels was leaping to equivocate when he saw the smile in her eyes and at the corners of her mouth. "Do you zing Jared like this, too?" he asked. Kate smiled proudly and nodded.

They laughed, but Kate felt no letup in the tension between them.

"Kate," he continued, "I've accomplished the things I've accomplished, gained the things I've gained, because I was brought up to believe that we are never given a wish or a dream without also being given the wherewithal to make that dream, that wish, a reality. Do you share that belief?"

Kate shrugged. "I believe there are times when it's okay to wish and try and fail."

"Perhaps," he said thoughtfully. "Perhaps there are. Anyhow, at this stage in my life, I have two overriding dreams. Both of them involve my son and, therefore, by extension, you."

"Go on."

"Kate, I want a grandchild, hopefully more than one, and I want my son to serve in the United States Congress.

Those are my dreams, and I am willing to do anything within my power to help them come to pass."

"Why?" Kate asked.

"Why?"

"Yes. I understand the grandchild wish. Continuation of the family, stability for Jared's home life, new blood and new energy, that sort of thing, but why the other one?"

"Because I feel Jared would be a credit to himself, to the state, and to the country."

"So do I."

"And I think it would be a fulfilling experience for him."

"Perhaps."

Samuels hesitated before adding, "And, finally, it is a goal I held for myself and never could achieve. Do you think me horrid for wanting my son to have what I could not?"

"No," Kate responded. "Provided it is something Jared wants, too, for reasons independent of yours."

"The time in life when a father no longer knows what is best for his son is certainly moot, isn't it?"

"Win, what you want for Jared, what you want for me, too, will always matter. But the hardest part about loving someone is letting him figure out what's best for himself, especially when you already know—or at least think you know."

"And you think I'm forcing my will on Jared?"

"You have a tremendous amount of influence on him," she replied. "I don't think I'm giving away any great secrets by saying that."

Samuels nodded thoughtfully. "Kate," he said finally, "humor this old man and let me change the subject a bit, okay?"

*Old man.* Give me a break, counselor, she wanted to snap. Instead she sat forward, smiled, and simply said, "Sure."

"Why do you want to be the chief of pathology at Metro?"

Kate met his gaze levelly and said silent thanks for the hours she had spent answering that question for herself. "Because it would be a fascinating experience. Because I think I could do a credible job. Because my work—and my department—mean a great deal to me. Because I feel a person either grows or dies."

"Jared tells me you feel accepting the position will delay your being able to start your family for at least two years."

"Actually, I said one or two years, but two seems a reasonable guess."

Samuels rose slowly and walked to the window and then back to the fire. If he was preparing to say something dramatic, she acknowledged, he was doing a laudable job of setting it up.

"Kate," he said, still staring at the fire, "when I phoned, I invited you to stay the night if you could. Are you going to be able to do that?"

"I had planned on it, yes." Actually, the invitation had been worded in a way that would have made it nearly impossible for her to refuse.

"Good. I'd like to take you for a ride after dinner. A ride and a visit. I . . . I know I sound mysterious, but for the moment you'll have to indulge me. This is something I never thought I would be doing."

There was a huskiness, an emotion to the man's voice that Kate had never heard before. Was he near crying? For half a minute there was silence, save for the low hiss of the fire. But when her father-in-law turned to her, his composure had returned.

"Kate," he said, as if the moment by the fire had never happened, "do you think that you are ready to handle the responsibilities of a whole department?"

She thought for a moment. "This may sound funny, but in a way it doesn't matter what I think. You see, Dr. Willoughby, the only person who knows both me and the job, thinks I can handle it. It's like becoming a doctor—or, for that matter, a lawyer. You only decide you *want* to do it. They—the bar or the medical examiners—decide whether or not you can and should. From then on, your only obligation is to do your best." She paused. "Does that sound smug?"

"Not really."

"I hope not, Win. Because actually I'm scared stiff about a lot of things. I'm frightened of taking the job and I'm frightened of not taking it. I'm frightened of having children and I'm frightened of not having them. And most of all, I am frightened of having to face the dilemma of either losing my husband or losing myself."

"There *are* other possibilities," Samuels said.

"I know that, but I'm not sure Jared does, and to be perfectly honest, until this moment, I wasn't sure you did, either."

"There are *always* other possibilities," he said with a tone that suggested he had voiced that belief before. "Kate, you know hospital politics are no different from any other kind of politics. There's power involved and there's money involved, and that means there are things like this hand-bill involved."

He took the garish orange flyer from his desk drawer and held it up for her to see. Kate shuddered at the sight of it. "Do you think that brilliant effort was aimed at me or at Jared?" she asked.

"The truth is it makes no difference. Politics is politics. The minute you start playing the game you have enemies. If they happen to be better at the game than you are, you get buried. It's that simple." He held up the flyer again. "My sense of this whole business—assuming, of course, that you didn't send Bobby Geary's autopsy report to the papers—is that someone is determined to keep you from becoming head of your department. If they have any kind of power, or access to power, your department could suffer dearly."

"My department?"

"Certainly. Your people end up overworked because of staffing cutbacks and outmoded equipment. Turnover is high, morale low. Quality of work drops. Sooner or later there's a mistake. You may be the best pathologist in the world, Kate, and the best-intentioned administrator, but unless you play the politics game and get past the competition to people like the Ashburton Foundation, you will end up an unhappy, harried, unfulfilled failure. And take it from me, winning that game means plenty of sacrifice. It means that if you know the competition is getting up at six, you damn well better be up at five-thirty."

"I appreciate your thoughts," she said. "I really do. All I can say is that the final decision hasn't been made yet, and that I was hoping to work the whole thing out with Jared."

"But you have okayed submission of your name."

"Yes," she said, averting her gaze for the first time. "Yes, I have." Samuels turned and walked again toward the window. For a time, there was only the fire. "Say, Win," she said, hoping to lead them in other directions, "how much do you know about the Ashburton Foundation?"

He turned back to her. "I really don't know anything. In the early days of their involvement here, my firm handled some of their correspondence with the hospital. But I haven't dealt with them in years. Why?"

"Just some research I've been doing at work. Nothing, really. Do you by any chance have their address?"

"I don't know," Samuels said, somewhat distractedly. "In the Rolodex over there on my desk, perhaps. I really don't know. Kate, you know it is my way to reason, not to beg. But for the sake of my son and myself, if not for yourself, I'm begging you to put the chairmanship on the back burner and devote yourself for a few years to your family and to helping Jared get his foot in the political door."

At that instant, a chime sounded from the kitchen. Kate glanced instinctively at her watch, but she knew that it was exactly seven o'clock. She rose. "When is Jared due back?" she asked.

"Wednesday or Thursday, I suspect."

"Win, I have no response to what you just asked. You know that, don't you?"

"Perhaps before too much longer you might. Let us eat. After our meal, there is a trip we must take."

With a faint smile, Samuels nodded Kate toward the dining room and then took her elbow and guided her through the door.

The IV nurse, a square-shouldered woman overweight by at least thirty pounds, rubbed alcohol on the back of Ellen Sandler's left hand, slapped the area a dozen times, and then swabbed it again.

"Now, Ellen," she said in the patronizing, demeaning tone Ellen had come to label *hospitalese,* "you've got to relax. Your veins are in spasm. If you don't relax, it will take all night for me to get this IV in."

*Relax?* Ellen glared at the woman, who was hunched over her hand. *Can't you tell I'm frightened? Can't you see I'm scared out of my wits by all that's happening to me? Take a minute, just a minute, and talk to me. Ask me, and I'll try to explain. I'll tell you how it feels to be seven years old and to learn that your father, who entered the hospital for a "little operation," has been taken to a funeral home in a long box with handles. Relax? Why not ask me to float off this bed? Or better still, just demand that I make the blood in my body start clotting, so you'll be spared the inconvenience of having to plunge that needle into the back of my hand. Relax?* "I . . . I'm trying," she said meekly.

"Good. Now you're going to feel a little stick."

Ellen grabbed the bedrail with her free hand as electric pain from the "little stick" shot up her arm.

"Got it," the nurse said excitedly. "Now don't move. Don't move until I get it taped down, okay? You know," she continued as she taped the plastic catheter in place, "you've got the toughest veins I've seen in a long time."

Ellen didn't answer. Instead, she stared at the ceiling,

tasting the salt of the tears running over her cheeks and into the corners of her mouth, and wondering where it was all going to end. Apparently, blood had begun appearing in her bowel movements. The intravenous line was, according to the resident who announced she was going to have it, merely a precaution. He had neglected to tell her what it was a precaution against.

"Okay, Ellen, we're all set," the nurse announced, stepping back to admire her handiwork. "Just don't use that hand too much. All right?"

Ellen pushed the tears off her cheeks with the back of her right hand. "Sure," she said.

The woman managed an uncomfortable smile and backed from the room.

*It isn't fair.* With no little disgust, Ellen examined the IV dripping saline into her hand. Then she shut off the overhead light and lay in the semidarkness, listening to the sighs of her own breathing and the still alien sounds of the hospital at night. *It isn't fair.* Over and over her mind repeated the impotent protest until she was forced to laugh at it in spite of herself.

Betsy, Eve, Darcy, Sandy, the business, her health. Why had she never appreciated how fragile it all was? Had she taken too much for granted? asked too few questions? Dammit, there were no answers, anyhow. What else could she do? What else could anyone do? Here she was, almost forty, lying in a hospital bed, possibly bleeding to death, with no real sense of why she had been alive, let alone why she should have been singled out to die. It just wasn't fair.

A soft tap from the doorway intruded on her painful reverie. Standing there, silhouetted by the light from the hall, was Sandy. He was holding his uniform hat in one hand and a huge bouquet in the other.

"Permission to come aboard," he said.

Ellen could feel, more than see or hear, his discomfiture. "Come on in," she said.

"Want the light on?"

"I don't think so. On second thought, I'd like to see the flowers."

Sandy flipped on the light and brought them to her. Then he bent over and kissed her on the forehead. Ellen stiffened for an instant and then relaxed to his gentle hug.

"How're you doing?" he asked.

"On which level?"

"Any."

"The flowers are beautiful. Thank you. If you set them over by the sink, I'll have the nurse get a vase for them later on."

"Not so great, huh." He did as she asked with the bouquet, then pulled a green vinyl chair to the bedside and sat down.

Ellen switched off the overhead light. "You look nice in your uniform. Have you been home yet?"

"Just long enough to drop off my things and look in on the girls."

"How do they seem to you?"

"Concerned, confused, a little frightened maybe, but they're okay. I think it helped when your sister brought them up to see you yesterday. I've moved back into the house until you're better."

"You may be there a long time."

"That bad?"

"Kate says no, but her eyes, and now this"—she held up her left hand—"say something else."

"But they don't really know, do they?"

"No. No, I guess not."

"Well, then, you just gotta hang in there a day or an hour or if necessary a minute at a time and believe that everything's going to be all right. I've taken an LOA from the air line to be with the girls, so you don't have anything to worry about on that account. I'll see to it that they get up here every day."

"Thanks. I . . . I'm grateful you're here."

"Nonsense. We've been through a lot these nineteen years. We'll make it through this."

Softly, Ellen began to cry. "Sandy, I feel like such a . . . a clod, an oaf. I know it's dumb, but that's how I feel. Not angry, not even sick, just helpless and clumsy."

"Well, you're neither, and no one knows that better than I do. Hey, that's the second time you've yawned since I got here. Are you tired, or just bored?"

She smiled weakly. "Not bored. A little tired, I guess. It turns out that lying in bed all day doing nothing is exhausting."

"Then how about you don't pay any attention to me and just go to sleep. If it's okay with you, I'll sit here for a while."

"Thanks, Sandy."

"It's going to be okay, you know."

"I know."

He took her hand. "Kate's watching out for you, right?"

"She's in twice a day, and she's doing everything she can to find out why I'm bleeding." Her voice drifted off. Her eyes closed. "Don't be afraid."

"I'm not," he said. "I'm not afraid. . . .It's going to be okay.

The ride in Win Samuels's gray Seville took most of an hour along a network of dark country roads heading south and east from the city. They rode largely in silence, Samuels seeming to need total concentration to negotiate the narrow turns, and Kate staring out her window at dark pastures and even darker woods, at times wondering about the purpose of their journey and at times allowing disconnected thoughts to career through her mind. Jared . . . Stan Willoughby . . . Bobby Geary . . . Roscoe . . . Ellen . . . Tom . . . even Rosa Beekes, her elementary school principal—each made an appearance and then quickly faded and was replaced by the image of another.

"We're here," Samuels said at last, turning onto a gravel drive.

"Stonefield School." Kate read the name from a discreet sign illuminated only by the headlights of their car. "What town is this?"

"No town, really. We're either in southernmost Massachusetts or northwestern Rhode Island, depending on whose survey you use. The school has been here for nearly fifty years, but it was rebuilt about twenty-five years ago, primarily with money from a fund my firm established."

The school was a low, plain brick structure with a small, well-kept lawn and a fenced-in play area to one side. To the other side, a wing of unadorned red brick stretched towards the woods. They entered the sparsely furnished lobby and were immediately met by a stout, matronly woman wearing a navy skirt, dull cardigan, and an excessive number of gold bracelets and rings.

"Mr. Samuels," she said, "it's good to see you again. Thank you for calling ahead." She turned to Kate. "Dr. Bennett, I'm Sally Bicknell, supervisor for the evening shift. Welcome to Stonefield."

"Thank you," Kate said uncertainly. "I'm not exactly sure where I am or why we're here, but thank you, anyway."

Sally Bicknell smiled knowingly, took Kate by the arm, and led her down the hall to a large, blue velvet curtain. "This is our playroom," she said, drawing the curtain with some flair to reveal the smoky glass of a one-way mirror. The room beyond was large, well lit, and carpeted. There were two tumbling mats, a number of inflatable vinyl punching dummies, and a stack of large building blocks. To one corner, her back toward them, a chunky girl with close-cropped sandy hair hunched over a row of large cloth dolls.

"She's never in bed much before two or three in the morning," Sally Bicknell explained.

"Kate," Samuels said. "I brought you here because I thought that seeing this might help you understand some of my urgency as regards your moving forward with starting your family. Mrs. Bicknell."

The evening shift supervisor rapped loudly on the glass three times, then three times again. The girl in the playroom cocked her head to one side and then slowly turned around.

"Kate, meet your sister-in-law, Lindsey."

The girl was, physically, a monster. Her eyes were lowset and narrow, her facial features thick and coarse, with heavy lips and twisted yellow teeth. What little there was of her neck forced her head to the right at an unnatural angle. Her barrel chest merged with her abdomen, and her legs were piteously bowed.

"That can't be," Kate said softly, her attention transfixed by the grotesquery. "Jared's sister Lindsey . . ."

"Died when she was a child," Samuels finished the sentence for her. "I'm afraid his mother and I chose not to tell him the truth. It seemed like the best idea at the time, considering that we were assured Lindsey would live only a few years. She has Hunter's Syndrome. You are familiar with that, yes?" Kate nodded. "Severe mental retardation and any number of other defects. Her mother, my wife, was nearly forty when she gave birth."

Kate continued staring through the glass as the gargoylelike child—no, woman, for she had to be in her thirties—lumbered aimlessly about the playroom. Reflected in the window, Kate saw the faces of Sally Bicknell and her father-in-law, watching for her reaction. You are the monster, Win Samuels, not that poor thing, her thoughts screamed. What do you think I am, a piece worker in a factory? Did you think this . . . this demonstration would frighten me? Do you think I know nothing of amniocentesis and prenatal diagnosis and counseling? Did you think I would just brush off the enormous lie you have been telling my husband for the past thirty years? Why? Why have you brought me here? Why haven't you included Jared?

"Take me home," she ordered softly. "Take me home now."

The antique clock on Win Samuels's huge desk said two-fifty. It had been nearly two hours since Kate had abandoned her efforts to sleep and wandered into the study searching for reading matter distracting enough to close her mind to the events of the evening. Something was wrong. Something did not sit right in the bizarre scenario to which her father-in-law had treated her. But what?

On the ride home from Stonefield, Samuels had quietly assailed her with statistics relating maternal age to infertility, fetal death, chromosome abnormalities, genetic mutation, spontaneous abortions, and mental retardation. He had, over many years apparently, done his homework well. The few arguments she had managed to give him on the accuracy of intrauterine diagnosis were countered with more facts and more statistics. Still, nothing the man said could dispel her gut feeling that something was not right. At one time during his presentation—for that is what it was—she came close to crying out that their whole discussion was quite possibly a futile exercise, because a production error at Redding Pharmaceuticals might have already cost her any chance of seeing her forties, let alone conceiving in them.

From the direction of Samuels's room on the second floor, she heard a door open and then close softly. Seconds later, the sound was repeated further down the hall. Jocelyn Trent had returned to her room.

The study, now divested of its fire, was chilly and damp. Kate shuddered and tightened the robe Jocelyn had given her. It was only around midnight in San Diego. Jared wouldn't mind a call, she thought, before realizing that she had forgotten to ask Win at which hotel he was staying. As she reached for a pad and pen to write herself a reminder, she noticed Samuels's Rolodex file. She spun it to "A." The man was right about having a card for the

Ashburton Foundation. On it were an address and a number that had been crossed out. A second, apparently newer, address and number were written in below.

Kate copied the new address and added a note to check in the morning on Jared's hotel. She glanced at the clock. Three-fifteen. How many surgicals were scheduled for the day? Five? Six? Too many. Desperate for sleep, she took her note and an anthology of Emily Dickinson and padded up two flights of stairs to her room.

Forty-five minutes of reading were necessary before Kate trusted the heaviness in her eyes and the impotence in her concentration enough to flip off the light. The realization that her drowsiness was continuing to deepen brought a relieved, contented smile. Then, in her final moments of consciousness, she sensed a troublesome notion. It appeared, then vanished, then appeared again like a faint neon sign. It was not the trip or the school or even the girl. No, it was the address—the address of the Ashburton Foundation; not the newer Washington, DC, address, but the one that was crossed out. With each flash, the neon grew dimmer, the thoughts less distinct. There was something, she thought at the moment of darkness, something special about Darlington, Kentucky. Something.

# 10

## Tuesday 18 December

Soundlessly, Kate unlocked the heavy oak door and slipped out of her father-in-law's home into the gray glare of morning. The deserted streets, sidewalks, and stone steps were covered with an immaculate dusting of white. Over the three days past, a blizzard had crushed the midwest and moved, unabated, into the mid-Atlantic states. Stepping gingerly down Beacon Hill toward Charles Street, Kate wondered if the feathery snow was, perhaps, the harbinger of that storm.

She had slept far too little. Her eyes were dry and irritated, her temples constricted by the ache of exhaustion—an ache she had not experienced so acutely since her days as a medical student and intern. She thought about the surgicals scheduled to begin at ten o'clock and run through most of the rest of the day. With tensions thrusting at her life from one direction after another like the spears in some medieval torture, she debated asking one of the others to take over for her. No way, she decided quickly. As it was, the members of her department were stretched beyond their limits. Stan Willoughby's repeated requests for an additional pathologist had been laughed at. No, she was expected to do her part, and she would find whatever concentration it took to do it right.

As she made her way toward the cab stand near

White Memorial, Kate began her morning ritual of mentally ticking off the events and responsibilities of her day. The cab was halfway to Metro when she ended the ritual, as she inevitably did, by scrambling through her purse for her daily calendar, certain that she had forgotten something crucial. Her schedule was abbreviated, due largely to a block of time marked simply "surgicals." Penciled in at the bottom was the one item she had forgotten, "Drinks with Tom." The three words triggered a surprising rush of feelings, beginning with the reflex notion to call and cancel, and ending with the sense of what her return home to an empty house would be like. Scattered in between were any number of images of the intense, gangly resident who had been her staunchest supporter during the difficult days that had followed the biopsy of Beverly Vitale. Tom Engleson was a man and a youth, enthusiastic at times even to exuberance, yet sensitive about people, about medicine, and especially about what her career involved and meant to her. The prospect of an hour or two together in the corner of some dark, leather and wood lounge might be just the carrot to get her through the day.

"Dammit, Jared," she muttered as the cab rolled to a stop in front of her hospital. "I need you."

She began her day as she had each of the last several working days, with a visit to Room 421 of the Berenson Building.

Ellen was lying on her back, staring at the wall. Her breakfast was untouched on the formica stand by her bed. Suspended from a ceiling hook, a plastic bag drained saline into her arm.

"Hi," Kate said.

"Hi, yourself." Ellen's eyes were shadowed. Her skin seemed lacking in color and turgor. Bruises, large and small, lined both arms. There was packing in one side of her nose.

Kate set the *Cosmopolitan* and morning *Globe* she had brought on the stand next to the breakfast tray.

"Something new's been added, huh?" She nodded toward the IV.

"Last night. A little while after you left."

Kate raised Ellen to a sitting position and then settled onto the bed by her knee. "They say why?"

"All they'll tell me is that it's a precautionary measure."

"Have you had some new bleeding?"

"In my bowel movements, and I guess in my urine, too." She took a glass of orange juice from her tray and sipped at it absently.

"That's probably why the IV," Kate said. "In case they have to inject any X-ray dye or give you any blood." *How much do you want to hear, El? Give me a sign. Do you want to know about sudden massive hemorrhage? About circulatory collapse sudden and severe enough to make emergency insertion of an intravenous line extremely difficult? Do you want to know about Beverly Vitale?*

"Listen, Kate. As long as you're on top of what's going on, I'm satisfied."

"Good." *Thank you, my friend. Thank you for making it a little easier.*

"Sandy's back. He flew in late last night and then moved into the house to look after the girls."

Kate motioned to a vase of flowers by the window. "From him?"

"Uh-huh."

"So?"

Ellen shrugged. "No significance. He's still on his way out, I think."

"I hope not."

"Am I?"

"Are you what?"

"On my way out."

"Jesus, Sandler, of course not."

Ellen took her hand. "Don't let me die, Katey, okay?"

"Count on it," Kate said, having to work to keep from breaking down in front of her friend. Silently, she vowed to place her efforts on Ellen's behalf ahead of every other task, every other pressure in her life. Somewhere, there was an answer, and somehow she would find it. "Listen, I've got to go and get ready for some biopsies. I'll check on your lab tests and speak with you later this afternoon. Okay?"

"Okay." The word was spiritless.

"Anything I can bring you?"

"A cure?"

Kate smiled weakly. "Coming right up," she said.

The flowers, in a metallic gray box with a red bow, were on her desk when Kate returned from the Berenson Building. First a huge bouquet for Ellen from Sandy and now flowers from Jared. The former Dartmouth roommates had come through in the clutch.

"I knew you guys must have learned something at that school besides how to tap a keg," she said, excitedly opening the box.

They were long-stem roses, eleven red and one yellow—the red for love and the yellow for friendship, she had once been told. She scurried about her office, opening and closing doors and drawers until she found a heavy, green-glass vase. It was not until the roses were arranged to her satisfaction and set on the corner of her desk that she remembered the card taped to the box. It would say something at once both witty and tender. That was Jared's style—his way.

"To a not so unexceptional pathologist, from a not so secret admirer. Tom."

Kate groaned and sank to her desk chair, feeling angry and a little foolish. Try as she might, she could not dispel the irrational reaction that Jared had somehow let her down.

*Call Tom.* She wrote the reminder on a scrap of paper and taped it in a high-visibility spot on the shade of her desk lamp. Still, she knew from experience that even a location only inches from her eyes gave her at best only a fifty-fifty chance of remembering. Perhaps now was the time to call. It was almost nine. If Tom wasn't in the OR, a page would reach him. Things were beginning to get out of hand, and at this point, meeting Tom for a drink hardly seemed fair.

Kate was reaching for the phone when it rang.

"Hello. Kate Bennett," she said.

"Dr. Bennett, how do you do? My name is Arlen Paquette, *Doctor* Arlen Paquette, if you count a PhD in chemistry. I'm the director of product safety for Redding Pharmaceuticals. If this is an inopportune time for you, please tell me. If it is not, I would like to speak with you for a few minutes about the report Dr. William Zimmermann phoned in to us yesterday."

"I have a few minutes," Kate said, retaping the Tom note to her lampshade.

"Fine. Thank you. Dr. Bennett, I spent a fair amount of time taking information from Dr. Zimmermann. However, since you seem to have done most of the legwork, as it were, I had hoped you might go over exactly what it was that led you to the conclusion there was a problem with one of our Redding generics."

"I'd be happy to, Dr. Paquette."

It was obvious from the few questions Paquette asked during her three-minute summary that Zimmermann's account to him had been a complete one and, further, that the director of product safety had studied the data well.

"So," the caller said when she had finished, "as I see it, your initial suspicions of trouble at the Omnicenter were based on a coincidence of symptoms in three patients of the thousands treated there. Correct?"

"Not exactly," Kate said, suddenly perturbed by the tone of the man's voice.

"Please," he said, "bear with me a moment longer. You then decided to focus your investigation on the pharmaceuticals provided for the Omnicenter by my company, and . . ."

"Dr. Paquette, I don't think it's at all fair to suggest that I jumped to the conclusion that the drugs were at fault. Even now I am not at all sure that is the case. However, of all the factors I checked—sterilization techniques, microbiology, and all others common to my three patients—the contaminated vitamins were the only finding out of the ordinary."

"Ah, yes," Paquette said. "The vitamins. Several dozen samples analyzed, yet only one containing a painkiller. Correct?"

"Dr. Paquette," Kate said somewhat angrily, "I have a busy schedule today, and I've told you about all there is to tell. You are sounding more and more like a lawyer and less and less like a man concerned with correcting a problem in his company's product. Now, I don't know whether Dr. Zimmermann told you or not, but I feel that the need to get to the bottom of all this is urgent, critical. A woman who happens to be a dear friend of mine is in the hospital right now, with her life quite possibly at stake, and for all I know, there may be others. I shall give you two more days to come up with a satisfactory explanation. If you don't have one, I am going to get the chemist from the state toxicology lab, and together we will march straight down to the FDA."

"By chemist, I assume you mean Mr. Ian Toole?"

"Yes, that's exactly who I mean."

"Well, Doctor, I'm a little confused. You see, I have in front of me a notarized letter, copies of which I have just put in the mail to you and Dr. Zimmermann. It is a letter from Mr. Ian Toole stating categorically that in none of his investigations on your behalf did he find *any* contamination in *any* product dispensed at the Omnicenter."

"What?" Kate's incredulity was almost instantly replaced by a numbing fear. "That's not true," she said weakly.

"Shall I read you the letter?"

"You bought him off."

"I beg your pardon."

"I gave you the courtesy of reporting this to your

company instead of going to the FDA, and you bought off my chemist."

"Dr. Bennett, I would caution you against carelessly tossing accusations about," Paquette said. "The statement in front of me is, as I have said, notarized."

"We'll see about that," she said with little force. The vitamins she had sent to Toole were all she had. In a corner of her mind, she wondered if Arlen Paquette knew that.

"I would like to confirm my company's sincere desire to correct any shortcomings in its products, and to thank you for allowing us to investigate the situation at your hospital." Paquette sounded as if he was reading the statement from a card.

"You may think this is the end of things, Dr. Paquette," Kate said, "but you don't know me. Please be prepared to hear from the FDA."

"We each must do what we must do, Doctor."

Kate had begun to seethe. "Furthermore, you had better hope that whatever you paid Ian Toole was enough, because that man is going to be made to visit a certain hospital bed to see first hand the woman he may be helping to kill." She slammed the receiver to its cradle.

Seated in his suite at the Ritz, Arlen Paquette hung up gently. He was shaking.

*You don't know me.*

Paquette snorted at the irony of Kate Bennett's words, splashed some scotch over two ice cubes, drank it before it had begun to chill, and then set the glass down on the photographs of the woman he had just helped nail to a cross of incompetence, mental imbalance, and dishonesty. Cyrus Redding had decreed that she be discredited, and discredited she would be. Kate Bennett had only herself and a few shaky allies. Cyrus Redding had an unlimited supply of Norton Reeses, Winfield Samuelses, Ian Tooles, and, yes, Arlen Paquettes.

He glanced down at the pad where he had written the words he had rehearsed and then used when talking to the woman, and he wondered if he could have come off so self-assured in a face-to-face confrontation. Doubtful, he acknowledged. Extremely doubtful. Their conversation had lasted just a few minutes, with all of the surprises coming from his end. Yet here he was, soaked with sweat and still trembling. He'd take a dozen in-person encounters with Norton Reese over the one phone call he had just finished. Water. That was it, he needed some water. No more goddamn scotch.

He snatched his empty glass from the coffee table. Beneath it was one of the five-by-seven blowups of Kate Bennett, this one of her bundled in a sweatsuit, scarf, and watch cap, jogging with her dog along a snowbanked road. Paquette turned and unsteadily made his way to the bathroom.

"You bastard," he said to the thin, drawn face staring at him from the mirror. "You weak little fucking bastard."

He hurled the glass with all his strength, shattering it and the mirror. Then he dropped to his knees amidst the shards and, clutching the ornate toilet, retched until he felt his insides were tearing in two.

"Don't you see, Bill? Someone at Redding Pharmaceuticals, maybe this . . . this Paquette, bought off Ian Toole. Damn, I knew I was right not to trust them. I knew it. I knew it." Kate, still breathless from her run across the snowy street and up three flights of stairs, screamed at herself to calm down.

William Zimmermann, as relaxed as Kate was intense, rose from behind his desk and crossed to the automatic coffee maker on a low table by his office door. His knee-length clinic coat was perfectly creased and spotless, his demeanor as immaculate as his dress. "How about a few deep breaths and a cup of coffee?"

"Coffee's about the last thing I need in my state,

thanks, but I will try the deep breaths. Vacation. Can you believe it? One day the man is at his little spectrophotometer running tests, and the next he's off on vacation and nobody knows when he'll be back. Now if that isn't a payoff, I don't know what is. Next thing you know, Ian Toole's name will be on a lab door somewhere in Redding Pharmaceuticals."

"The deep breaths?" Zimmermann asked, returning to his desk.

"Oh, yes. I'm sorry, Bill. But you don't blame me, do you?"

"No, I don't blame you." He paused, obviously searching for words. "Kate," he said finally, "I want to be as tactful as possible in what I have to ask, and if I'm not, please excuse me, but . . ."

"Go on."

"Well, since you brought the subject up at our dinner the other night, I feel I must ask. Just how badly do you have it in for the pharmaceutical industry?"

The question startled her. Then she understood. "What you're saying is that without Ian Toole, it becomes a matter of my word against theirs. Is that it?"

"If I'm out of line, Kate, I'm sorry. But remember, there is a lot at stake here—for me and my clinic, and as far as I know, this whole matter was between you and your Mr. Toole. I mean I called in the report because it was our facility, but the hard data are strictly . . ."

"Wait," Kate interrupted excitedly. "There is someone else. I just remembered."

"Who?"

"Her name's Millicent. She's Toole's assistant, and I remember him telling me she was put out about having to work late on the stuff I sent him."

"Do you have a last name?"

"No, but how many Millicents can there be at the State Toxicology Lab?" She was already reaching for the phone and her address book. "You don't know me, Dr.

Paquette," she murmured as she dialed. "Oh, no, you don't know me at all."

The call lasted less than a minute.

"Millicent Hall is no longer in the employ of the state lab," Kate said as she hung up, her expression and tone an equal mix of embarrassment, dejection, and anger. "They wouldn't give out any further information."

This time it was Zimmermann who took a deep breath. "First the baseball player and now this," he said. "You certainly aren't having a very easy time of it."

Kate's eyes narrowed. An emptiness began to build inside her. "You're having trouble believing me, aren't you?"

Zimmermann met her gaze and held it. "Kate, what I can say in all honesty is that at this moment I believe that you believe." He saw her about to protest, and held up his hands. "And at this moment," he added reassuringly, "that is enough. There is too much at stake for me to make any hasty moves. I shall await Redding's formal response to my report, meanwhile keeping our pharmacy on backup. No Redding generics until then. However, if there have been no further cases or further developments in, say, a week, I plan to reinstate our automated system."

"With Redding products?"

"We have a contract."

"But they . . ."

"Facts, Kate. We need substantiated facts."

Kate sighed and sank back in her seat, deflated. It was nearly ten and she had done nothing to prepare for the day's surgicals. "Have you started working on that list of patients who might be willing to allow me to have their medications analyzed?"

Zimmermann smiled patiently. "You can see how that might be a bit tricky to explain to a patient, can't you?" He handed her a brief list and five Omnicenter medication cards. "These belong to long-term patients of mine, who agreed to exchange them as part of what I said was a routine quality-control check."

"It is," Kate said. "Thanks, Bill. I know this isn't easy for you and I'm grateful."

"I'll try and get you some more today."

"Thanks. You're being more than fair. I know I'm right, and sooner or later I'm going to prove it." She stood to go.

"You know," Zimmermann said, "even if you find there was a manufacturing error at Redding, you have no way of tying it in with the cases you are following."

The faces of three women—two dead and one her friend—flashed in her thoughts. "I know," she said grimly. "But it's all I . . . it's all *we* have. Say, before I forget. Have you got the purchase invoices for the Redding generics that I asked you about?"

Zimmermann opened his file cabinet. "Carl Horner does the ordering. He gave me these and asked that I convey his desire to cooperate with you as fully as possible. He also asked that you return these as soon as you're done."

"Of course," Kate said, glancing at the pile of yellow invoice carbons. Redding Pharmaceuticals, Inc.; Darlington, Kentucky. The words sputtered and sparked in her mind. Then they exploded.

"Kate, are you all right?" Zimmermann asked.

"Huh? Oh, yes, I'm fine. Bill, something very strange is going on here. I mean *very strange*." Zimmermann looked at her quizzically. "I don't know how long ago they moved, but at one time, the Ashburton Foundation was located in Darlington, Kentucky."

"How do you know?"

"I found their old address in my father-in-law's Rolodex."

"So?"

Kate held up an invoice for him to see. "Darlington. That's where Redding Pharmaceuticals is headquartered."

For the first time, William Zimmermann seemed perturbed. "I still don't see what point you're trying to make."

Kate heard the irritation in the man's voice and, recalling his oblique reference to the Bobby Geary letter, cautioned herself to tread gently. Her supporters, even skeptical ones, were few and far between. "I . . . I guess I overreacted a little," she said with a sheepishness she was not really feeling. "Ellen's being in the middle of all this has me grasping at straws, I guess." She glanced at her watch. "Look, I've got to get over to the OR. Thanks for these. If I come up with any facts," she corrected herself with a raised finger, "make that substantiated facts, I'll give you a call."

"Fine," Zimmermann said. "Let me know if there's any further way I can help."

Kate hurried outside and across the street, mindless of the wind and snow. Ashburton and Redding—once both in Darlington, and now both at the Omnicenter. A coincidence? Not likely, she thought. No, not likely at all. The lobby clock read two minutes to ten as she sped toward the surgical suite and the small frozen-section lab. The room was dark. Taped to the door was a carefully printed note.

OR CRYOSTAT INOPERATIVE. BRING
BIOPSY SPECS
TO PATH DEPARTMENT CRYOSTAT FOR
PROCESSING

"Ten seconds to ignition. Nine. Eight. Seven. Six. Five. Four. Three. Two. One. Ignition." Tom Engleson struck the wooden match against the edge of an iron trivet and touched the brandy-soaked mound of French vanilla ice cream. "Voilà!" he cried.

"Bravo!" Kate cheered.

Tom filled two shallow dishes and set Kate's in front of her with a flourish.

The evening had been a low-key delight: drinks at the Hole in the Wall Pub, dinner at the Moon Villa, in

Chinatown, and finally dessert in Tom's apartment, twenty stories above Boston Harbor. She had forgotten to break their date, and for once her poor memory had proven an asset. Twenty minutes into their conversation at the Hole in the Wall, Kate had given up trying to sort out what she wanted from the evening and the man and had begun to relax and enjoy both. Still, she knew, thoughts of Jared were never far from the surface; nor were thoughts of Redding Pharmaceuticals and the Ashburton Foundation.

"Okay," Tom said as he poured two cups of coffee and settled into the chair next to her, "now that my brain is through crying for food and drink and such, it's ready to try again to understand. There is no Ashburton Foundation?"

"No, there's something *called* the Ashburton Foundation, but I'm not at all certain it's anything other than a laundry for money."

"Pharmaceutical company money."

"Right. I called the number I got from my father-in-law's Rolodex and got a receptionist of some sort. She referred every question, even what street they were located on in DC, to someone named Dr. Thompson, apparently the director of the so-called foundation."

"But Dr. Thompson was out of the office and never called you back."

"Exactly. I tried calling the receptionist again, and this time she said that Thompson was gone for the day and would contact me in the morning. It was weird, I tell you, weird. The woman, supposedly working for this big foundation, didn't have the vaguest idea of how to handle my call."

"Did you ask Reese about all this?"

"He was gone for the day by the time I called, but tomorrow after I see Ellen, I intend to camp out on his doorstep."

"But why? What does Redding Pharmaceuticals get out of funneling all this money into our hospital?"

Kate shrugged. "That, Thomas, is the sixty-four dollar question. At the moment, every shred of woman's intuition in my body is screaming that the tie-in has something to do with the contaminated vitamins our friend Dr. Paquette has gone to such lengths to cover up."

"Incredible."

"Incredible, maybe. Impossible?" She took a folded copy of an article from her purse and passed it over. "I came across this yesterday during one of my sessions in the library. It's part of a whole book about a drug called MER/29, originally developed and marketed by Merrell Pharmaceuticals."

"That's a big company," Tom said, flipping through the pages.

"Not as big as Redding, but big enough. This MER/29 was supposed to lower cholesterol and thereby prevent heart disease. Only trouble was that other companies were racing to complete work on other products designed to do the same thing. The good folks at Merrell estimated a potential yearly profit in the billions at just one twenty-cent capsule a day for each person over thirty-five. However, they also knew that the lion's share of that profit would go to the first company whose product could get cleared by the FDA and launched into the marketplace."

"I'm not going to want to hear the rest of this, am I," Tom said.

"Not if you have much trust in the pharmaceutical industry. Remember, the FDA doesn't evaluate products; the pharmaceutical companies do. The FDA only evaluates the evaluations. In its haste to get MER/29 into the bodies of the pharmaceutical-buying public, Merrell cut corner after corner in their laboratory and clinical testing. But since none of the shortcuts was evident in the massive reports they submitted to the FDA, in 1961, MER/29 was approved by the FDA and launched by Merrell. Two years later, almost by accident, the FDA discovered what the company had done and ordered the drug removed. By that time, a large number of people had gone blind or developed hideous, irreversible skin conditions or lost all their hair."

Tom whistled.

"Kids with no arms because their mothers took a sleeping pill called thalidomide. Kids with irreparably yellow teeth because tetracycline was rushed into the marketplace before all its side effects were known. The list goes on and on."

"You sound a little angry," Tom said, taking her hand and guiding her to the couch across the room.

"They paid off my chemist, Tom," she said. "They've made me look like a fool, or worse, a liar. You're damn right I'm angry." She sighed and leaned back, still holding his hand. "Forgive me for popping off like that, but I guess I needed to."

Tom slipped his free arm around her shoulders and drew her close. Together they sat, watching fat, wind-whipped flakes of snow tumble about over the harbor and melt against the huge picture window.

"Thank you," she whispered. "Thank you for understanding."

Again and again they kissed. First her blouse, then her bra, then Tom's shirt dropped to the carpet, as he bore her gently down on the couch. His lips, brushing across the hollow of her neck and over the rise of her breasts, felt wonderful. His hand, caressing the smooth inside of her thigh was warm and knowing and patient. She felt as excited, as frightened, as she had during her earliest teenage encounters. But even as she sensed her body respond to his hunger, even as her nipples grew hard against his darting tongue, she sensed her mind begin to pull back.

"Kate. Oh, Kate," Tom whispered, the words vibrating gently against the skin of her breast.

"Tom?" The word was a soft plea, almost a whimper.

"Hold me, Kate. Please don't stop."

She took his face in her hands. "Tom," she said huskily. "I . . . just can't."

Her emotions swirling like the snow on the interstate, Kate took most of an hour and a half to make the drive from Boston to Essex. Tom had been hurt and frustrated by her sudden change in attitude, but in the end he had done his best to understand and accept.

"I only hope Jared knows how goddamn lucky he is," he had snapped as she was dressing. Later, he had insisted on driving her back to Metro and her car, where they had shared a quasi-platonic good-bye kiss.

The phone was ringing as she opened the door from the garage to her house. Roscoe, who had spent most of the past two days at a sleepover with neighbors and their golden retriever, bounded down the hall, accepted a quick greeting, and then followed her to the den.

It was Jared. "Hi," he said. "I called the house at three A.M. and no one was home. Are you okay?"

"I'm fine, Jared. I spent the night at your father's. Didn't he tell you he had invited me?"

"No." There was no mistaking the curiosity in Jared's voice. "Did you get my letter?"

Kate thumbed through the pile of bills and throw-away journals she had carried in with her. Jared's letter was sandwiched between the magazines *Aches and Pains* and *Pathologist on the Go*.

"I just brought it in," she said. "If you want to wait, I'll read it right now."

"No need, Kate. I've got it memorized." Kate opened the letter and read along as he said the words. "It says 'I love you, I miss you, and I don't want to not live with you anymore. Jared.' "

Kate's heart was pounding so much she could barely respond. "I love you too, Jared. Very, very much. When are you coming home?"

"Day after tomorrow, unless you want me to hitch home now."

"Thursday's fine, honey. Just fine. I'll pick you up at the airport."

"Seven P.M. United."

"Perfect. I have a lot to tell you about. Maybe we'll

take a ride in the country. There's someone you should visit."

"Who?"

"You'll see. Let me leave it at that until Thursday. Okay?"

"Okay, but . . ."

"I love you."

"I love you, Boots. Sometimes I don't know who the heck you are or where Jared Samuels is on your list of priorities, but I love you and I want to ride it all out with you as long as I can hang on."

"We'll do just fine, honey. Everything is going to be all right."

As she hung up, Kate realized that for the first time in weeks she believed that.

# 11

## Wednesday 19 December

Arlen Paquette, stiff and sore from lack of sleep, cruised along the tree-lined drive toward Redding Pharmaceuticals. Paralleling the icy roadway were the vestiges of the first December snow in Darlington in eleven years. His homecoming the evening before had been a fiasco, marked by several fights with the children, too much to drink before, during, and after dinner, and finally, impotence and discord in bed—problems he and his wife had never encountered before.

He adjusted the rearview mirror to examine his face and plucked off the half dozen tissue-paper patches on the shaving nicks caused by his unsteady hand. Even without the patches he looked like hell. It was the job, the job he couldn't quit. Bribery, payoffs, deceptions, threats, ruined lives. Suddenly he was no longer a chemist. Suddenly he was no longer even an administrator. He was a lieutenant, a platoon leader in Cyrus Redding's army. It was an army of specialists, held together by coercion, blackmail, and enormous amounts of money—poised to strike at anything or anyone who threatened Cyrus Redding or the corporation he had built.

The guard greeted him warmly and performed a perfunctory search of the Mercedes. Paquette had once asked the man exactly what it was he was checking for. His polite, but quite disconcerting, reply was, "Anything Mr. Redding doesn't want to be there."

The executive offices, including Cyrus Redding's, were at the hub of the wagon wheel of six long, low structures that made up the manufacturing and packaging plants. Research and other laboratory facilities occupied an underground annex, joined to the main structure by tunnels, escalators, and moving walkways. Paquette parked in the space marked with his name, stopped at his office to leave his coat, and then headed directly for Redding's suite. He was ushered in immediately.

"Arlen, Arlen," Redding said warmly, "welcome home." He was in his wheelchair behind his desk and was dressed in the only outfit Paquette could remember him wearing at work, a lightweight blue-gray suit, white shirt, and string tie, fastened with a turquoise thunderbird ring.

"So," Redding said, when they had moved to the sitting area with coffee and a sugary pastry, "you look a bit drawn. This Boston business has not been so easy, has it?"

"You told me it might not be," Paquette said. "Do you remember when we decided to move the mailing address of the Ashburton Foundation?"

"Of course. A few months after you started working here. Six, no, seven years ago, right?" Paquette nodded. "It was an excellent suggestion and the first time I fully appreciated what a winning decision it was to hire you."

Paquette smiled a weak thank you. "Well," he said, "it was my feeling at that time that with the foundation registered as a tax-exempt philanthropic organization and located in DC, there was no way Redding Pharmaceuticals could ever be connected to it."

"And yet our tenacious friend Dr. Bennett has done so."

"Yes, although as I told you last night, I'm not certain she has put it all together."

"But she will," the Warlock said with certainty.

"She called twice yesterday trying to reach me—that is, trying to reach Dr. Thompson, the foundation director.

I couldn't even call her back for fear of having her recognize my voice."

"It was a wise decision not to."

"She's got to hear from someone today."

"She will," Redding said. He glanced at his watch. "At this moment, our persuasive legislative liaison, Charlie Wilson, is on his way to the foundation office to become Dr. James Thompson."

"Office?"

"Of course. We wouldn't want Dr. Bennett to try and locate the Ashburton Foundation only to find a desk, phone and secretary, would we?" Paquette shook his head. The man was absolutely incredible, and efficient in a way that he found quite frightening. "By eleven o'clock this morning, the office, its staff, photographic essays describing its good works, testimonial letters, and a decade or so of documented service will be in place, along with Charlie Wilson, who is, I think you'll agree, as smooth and self-confident as they come."

"Amazing," Paquette said.

"Are you feeling a bit more relaxed about things now?"

"Yes, Mr. Redding. Yes, I am."

"Good. You'll be pleased to know that the company will be taking care of that mirror at the Ritz."

Paquette froze. He had gone to great pains to pay for the damage himself and to insure that in no way would Redding find out about what had happened. Instability under fire was hardly the sort of trait the man rewarded in his platoon leaders. "I . . . I'm sorry about that, sir. I really am."

Redding gestured to the coffee table before them. Sealed under thick glass was the emblem of Redding Pharmaceuticals: a sky-blue background with white hands opening to release a pure, white dove. Below the dove was the name of the company; above it, in a rainbow arc, the motto: *The Greatest Good for the Most People at the Least Cost*. "Arlen, ever since the day I took over this company, I have tried to chart a course that would lead to exactly what this motto says. In this business—in any business—there are always choices to be made, always decisions that cannot be avoided. In the thirty-five years since I first came to Darlington, I've made more gut-wrenching decisions and smashed more glasses and more mirrors in anguish than I care to count. But always, when I needed direction, when I needed advice or council, it was right in front of me." He tapped the motto with his finger. "The legislators, state and federal, the competition, and especially the goddamn FDA are all doing their best to cloud the issue, but in the end it always boils down to this." Again, he tapped the glass.

If the pep talk was meant to buoy Paquette's flagging morale, it failed miserably. The greatest good for the most people at the highest profit was all he could think of. The shortcuts and the human testing, the clinics in Denver and Boston, the bribery and extortion involving FDA officials—all had been tolerable for him because all were abstractions. Kate Bennett was flesh and blood, a voice, a face, a reality; and worse than that, a reality he was growing to admire. Paquette snapped out of his reverie, wondering how long it had lasted. A second? A minute? Then he realized that Redding's eyes were fixed on him.

"I understand, sir," he said, clearing away the phlegm in his throat, "and I assure you, you have nothing to worry about." How did the man know about the stinking mirror? Spies in Boston? A bug in the room? Damn him, Paquette thought viciously. Damn him to hell.

"Fine, Arlen," Redding said. "Now, you have a flight back to Boston this afternoon?"

"Two o'clock."

"I suspect that our meddlesome pathologist is on the ropes. However, her father-in-law assures me that she is far from out on her feet. Her discovery regarding the Ashburton Foundation suggests that he is quite correct."

"I believe Norton Reese is arranging a surprise for her that may help," Paquette said, vividly recalling the glee in Reese's voice as he announced that something was set to fall heavily on Kate Bennett.

"Excellent," Redding said. "Her father-in-law has promised to do what he can to help us as well. One final thing."

"Yes?"

"Has anything further surfaced on the cause of the ovary and blood problems in those three women?" Paquette shook his head. "Strange," Redding said, more to himself than to the other man. "Very strange . . ." For several seconds, he remained lost in thought, his eyes closed, his head turning from side to side as if he were internally speedreading a page. "Well, Arlen," he said suddenly, opening his eyes, "thank you for the excellent job you are doing. I know at times your duties are not easy for you, but continue to carry them out the way you have, and your rewards will be great."

"Yes, sir," Paquette said. He sat for nearly half a minute before realizing that the Warlock had said all he was going to. Sheepishly, he rose and hurried from the room.

Cyrus Redding studied the man as he left. The Boston business seemed to be having some untoward effects on him, particularly in the area of his drinking. As he motored from the sitting area to his desk, Redding made a mental note to arrange a vacation of some sort for Paquette and his wife as soon as Boston was over. That done, he put the issue and the man out of his head. There was more important business needing attention.

Stephen Stein, the enigmatic, remarkably resourceful investigator, had made a discovery that he suspected would unlock the mystery of John Ferguson.

"Mr. Nunes," Redding said through the intercom of his desk, "would you bring that package to me now."

At the far end of the office, a perfectly camouflaged panel and one-way mirror slid open. The man Nunes emerged from the small; soundproof room from which he kept vigil, revolver at hand, whenever Redding was not alone in his office. The package, containing a book, several typewritten pages, and an explanatory letter from Stein, had arrived by messenger only minutes before Arlen Paquette.

"If you have errands to run, Mr. Nunes, this would be a good time. When you return in, say, an hour, we could well have a new slant on our friend, Dr. Ferguson." He smiled, nearly beside himself at the prospect. "I think this occasion might call for a pint of that mint chip ice cream I have forbidden you to let me talk you into buying."

The taciturn bodyguard nodded. "I can't let you talk me into it," he said, "but perhaps I could purchase some on my own."

Redding waited until his office door had clicked shut; then he locked it electronically and spread the contents of the package on his desk.

"My apologies," Stein wrote, "for missing this volume during the course of earlier efforts to tie our mysterious Dr. Ferguson's background in with the war. I borrowed it from the Holocaust Library at the university here with assurances of its return, along with some token of our gratitude. Its title, according to the German professor who did the enclosed translation for us, is *Doctors of the Reich; The Story of Hitler's Monster Kings*. The work is the product of painstaking research and countless interviews by a Jewish journalist named Sachs, himself a death camp survivor, and is believed by my source to be accurate within the limits of the author's prejudices. Only the chapters dealing with the experiments at the Ravensbrück concentration camp for women have been translated. The photographs on pages three sixty-seven and three sixty-eight will, I believe, be of special interest to you."

For most of the next hour, Cyrus Redding sat transfixed, moving only to turn the pages of the translation or to refer to specific photographs in the worn, yellowed text. John Ferguson was a physician and scientist named Dr. Wilhelm Becker. The photographs, though slightly blurred and taken nearly forty years before, left no doubt whatsoever.

"Amazing," Redding murmured as he read and re-read the biography of his associate. "Absolutely amazing."

There were two snapshots of Wilhelm Becker, one a full-face identification photo and one a group shot with other physicians at the Ravensbrück Camp. There was also a shot of what remained of the laboratory in which Becker was purported to have died, with the bodies of the man and his staff sergeant still curled amidst the debris on the floor. Redding withdrew a large, ivory-handled magnifying glass from his desk and for several minutes studied the detail of the scene. The body identified as Willi Becker was little more than an ill-defined, charred lump.

"Nicely done, my friend," Redding said softly. "Nicely done."

Familiar now with the man and with his spurious death, Redding turned to the page and a half dealing with Becker's research, specifically, with his research on a sub-stance called Estronate 250. Much of the information pre-sented was gleaned from transcripts of the war-crimes trial of a physician named Müller and another named Rendl, both of whom were sentenced to Nuremberg Prison in large measure because of their association with the suppos-edly late Wilhelm Becker. Redding found the men in the Ravensbrück group photo. Müller had served five years at hard labor before certain Ravensbrück survivors were able to document his acts of heroism on their behalf and get his sentence commuted. For Rendl, the revelations of his humanitarianism came too late. Three years after his incarceration, he hanged himself in his cell.

Redding read the Estronate material word by word, taking careful notes. By the time he had finished, he was absolutely certain that neither Wilhelm Becker nor the notebook containing his work on the hormone had per-ished in the Ravensbrück fire.

*A substance, harmless in every other way, that could render a woman sterile without her knowledge.* Redding was staggered by the potential of such a drug. China, India, the African nations, the Arabs. What would governments be willing to pay for a secret that might selectively thin their populations and thereby solve so many of their economic and political woes? What would certain governments pay for a weapon which, if delivered properly, could decimate their enemies in a single generation without the violent loss of one life?

Redding's thoughts were soaring through the possibilities of Estronate 250 when, with a soft knock, Nunes entered the office, set a package on the desk, and retired to his observation room. For another hour, Redding sat alone, savoring his mint chip ice cream and deciding how he might best break the news to Dr. John Ferguson that their fifteen-year-old collaboration was about to take on a new dimension.

"I love you, I miss you, and I don't want to not live with you anymore."

Kate read Jared's note again and then again, drawing strength and confidence from it each time. She had returned to her office following two distressing and frightening visits. One was to Ellen, who was, for the first time, receiving a transfusion of packed red blood cells. The second was to Norton Reese. If the connection between Metropolitan Hospital of Boston, the Ashburton Foundation, and Redding Pharmaceuticals was as intimate as Reese's clumsy evasions were leading her to believe, she would need all the strength and confidence she could muster. Thank you, Jared, she thought. Thank you for pulling me out from under the biggest pressure of all.

Her meeting with Reese had started off cordially enough. In fact, the man had seemed at times to be inappropriately jovial and at ease. Ever since their confrontation before the board of trustees over his diversion of budgeted pathology department funds to the cardiac surgical program, Reese had dealt with her with the gingerliness of an apprentice handling high explosives. Now, suddenly, he was all smiles. His congeniality lasted through several minutes of conversation about her department and Stan Willoughby's recommendation that she succeed him as chief, and ended abruptly with mention of the Ashburton Foundation. Whatever fortes the man might have, Kate mused at that moment, they certainly did not include poker faces. His eyes narrowed fractionally, but enough to deepen the fleshy crow's feet at their corners. His lips whitened, as did the tips of his fingers where they were touching one another.

"I'm afraid I'm not at liberty to open the Ashburton Foundation files to you," he had said, his eyes struggling to maintain contact with hers and failing. "However, I shall be happy to answer what questions I can."

"Okay," Kate said, shrugging. "My first question is why aren't you at liberty to open the Ashburton Foundation files to me?"

"It's . . . it's part of the agreement we signed when we accepted a grant from them." It was bizarre. In a very literal sense, the man was squirming in his seat.

"Well, suppose I wanted to apply for a grant for my department. How would I go about contacting them?"

"I'll have Gina give you the address on your way out. You can write them yourself."

"I already have a post office box number in Washington, DC. Is that it?"

"Yes. I mean, probably."

"Well, suppose I wanted to visit their offices in person. Could you ask Gina to give me a street address as well?"

Reese continued to fidget. "Look," he said, "I'll give you their mailing address and phone number. I'm sorry, but that's all I can do. Why do you want to know about the Ashburton Foundation anyway?" he managed.

"Mr. Reese," Kate said calmly, "If I answer that question, will you open their files to me?"

"Not without written permission from the Ashburton Foundation."

"Well then, it appears we've got a Mexican standoff, doesn't it? I'll tell you this much," her voice grew cold.

"Two women have died and a third may be dying. If I find out the Ashburton Foundation is connected in any way with what has happened to them, and you have kept significant information from me, I promise that I won't rest until everyone who matters knows what you have done. Is that clear?" Her uncharacteristic anger had, she knew, been prodded by the sight of Ellen Sandler mutely watching the plastic bag dripping blood into her arm and by the knowledge that this was, in all likelihood, just the first of many transfusions to come.

Reese checked his watch in a manner that was as inappropriate as it was unsubtle. It was as if he had left a message to be called at precisely nine-twelve and was wondering why the phone hadn't rung.

"Mr. Reese?"

The administrator shifted his gaze back to her. His face was pinched and gray with anger—no, she realized, it was something deeper than anger. Hatred? Did the poor man actually hate her?

"You really think you're something, don't you," he rasped in a strained, muddy voice.

"I beg your pardon?"

"Who made you the crusader? Do you think that just because you have an MD degree and all that old family money you can ride all over people?"

"What? Mr. Reese, I nev—"

"Well, let me tell you something. You don't intimidate me like you do some around here. No, sir, not one bit. So you just ride off on that high horse of yours and let me and the department heads—the *official* department heads—worry about grants and foundations and such."

Kate watched as the man sat there, panting from the exertion of his outburst. For five seconds, ten, her green eyes fixed on him. Then she rose from her chair and left, unwilling to dignify Reese's eruption with a response.

Now, alone in her office, Kate sat, trying to crystallize her thoughts and doodling a calligraphic montage of the words "Reese" and "Asshole." After finishing four versions

of each, she began adding "Ashburton" and "Paquette."
First there was the bribery of Ian Toole, an act which
seemed to her equivalent to shooting a chipmunk with an
elephant gun. She would have been quite satisfied with an
admission by Redding Pharmaceuticals that they had somehow allowed a batch of their generic vitamins to become
contaminated and would gladly recall and replace them.
Their illogically excessive response had to have been born
out of either arrogance or fear. But fear of what? "Omnicenter" made its first appearance in the montage.

The Ashburton Foundation had endowed an entire
ob-gyn department and subsidized a massive, modern
women's health center. Philanthropic acts? Perhaps, she
thought. But both of her calls to the foundation had gone
unanswered by Dr. Thompson, the director, and her efforts,
though modest, had failed to come up with an address for
the place. Then there was Reese's refusal to discuss the
organization that had been, at least in part, responsible for
the resurgence of his hospital. At that moment, almost
subconsciously, she began adding another name to the
paper. Again and again she wrote it, first in the calligraphic forms she knew, then in several she made up on
the spot. "Horner." Somehow the cantankerous, eccentric
computer genius was involved in what was going on. The
notion fit too well, made too much sense. But how? There
really was only one person who could help her find out.
Another minute of speculation, and she called William
Zimmermann.

Fifteen minutes later, she was on her way through
the tunnel to the Omnicenter when Tom Engleson entered from the cutoff to the surgical building.

"Hi," she said, searching his face for a clue as to how
he was handling the abortive end to their evening together.

"H'lo," his voice was flat.

She slowed, but continued walking. "Going to the
Omnicenter?"

Tom nodded. "I have a clinic in twenty minutes."

"You all right?"

"Yeah, sure. Great."

"Tom, I—"

"Look, Kate, it's my problem, not yours."

"Dr. Engleson, you weren't exactly alone on the couch last night," she whispered, glancing about to ensure that none of the tunnel traffic was too close. "I feel awful about giving out such mixed messages. But you are an incredibly comfortable and understanding man. With all the trouble at the hospital I'm afraid I just allowed myself to hide out in your arms. It was wrong and unfair—more so because I really care very much for you. I'm sorry, Tom."

They reached the stairwell leading up to the Omnicenter.

"Wait," Tom said. "Please." He guided her to a small alcove opposite the staircase.

"You know, considering the nature of the Metro grapevine, we'll probably be an item by . . ." Two nurses chattered past them and up the stairs. "Hell," she said, following them with her eyes, "we most likely are already."

"Do you really mean that, about caring for me?"

"Tom, I love my husband very much. We've had some trouble getting our lives back in sync since the election, but my feelings for him haven't changed. Still, you're very special to me. Believe me, if my home situation, my marriage, were any different, we would have been lovers last night."

"Yeah?" The muscles in his face relaxed, and some measure of energy returned to his voice.

"Yes," she said. Tom Engleson might have been nine years Jared's junior, but they still had much in common, including, it now appeared, the need for strong reassurance about such things.

"I said it last night, and I'll say it again. Jared is a very lucky man." Acceptance had replaced the strain in Tom's voice.

"I know," Kate said. "Tom, seriously, thank you for not making it any harder for me. Between the wretched business with Bobby Geary, the disappearance of my chemist, and some incredible crap from Norton Reese, I feel like I need all the friends—all the help—I can get." She glanced at her watch. "Say, do you have a few minutes?"

"Sure, why?"

"I'm going to see Bill Zimmermann to discuss the Ashburton Foundation. I'd love to have you come along if you can."

"Rocket Bill? I do have a little time if you think he wouldn't mind."

"Hardly," Kate said. "He knows how much help you've been to me through all this. Okay?"

During the four-flight climb, Tom reviewed for her the protocols for patient care in the Omnicenter. On arrival, both new and returning patients met with a specially trained female intake worker, who blackened in the appropriate spaces in a detailed computer-readable history sheet. Medications, menstrual history, new complaints, and side effects of any treatment were carefully recorded. The worker then slid the history sheet into a computer terminal on her desk, and in thirty seconds or less, instructions as to where the patient was to go next would appear on the screen along with, if necessary, what laboratory tests were to be ordered.

"Do you feel the system is a bit impersonal?" Kate asked.

"You're a patient here. Do you?"

"No, not really, I guess," she said. "I can remember when a visit to the gynecologist consisted of sitting for an hour in a ten-foot-square waiting room with a dozen other women, having my name called out, stripping in a tiny examining room, and finally having the doctor rush in, thumbing through my chart for my name, and then as often as not telling me to put my heels in the stirrups before he even asked why I was there."

"See," Tom laughed, "no system is perfect. But seriously, the one here is damn good. It frees me up to do a careful exam and to answer as many questions as my patients have."

The system might be great, Kate thought, but something, somewhere inside it, was rotten. Something was killing people.

Large, colored numbers marked each floor. The 3, filling half a wall at the third-floor landing, was an iridescent orange. Kate reached for the handle of the door to the corridor, but then stopped, turned to Tom, and kissed him gently on the cheek.

"Thank you for last night, my friend," she said.

Tom accepted the kiss and then squeezed her hand and smiled. "If you need anything at all, and I can do it or get it, you've got it," he said.

William Zimmermann greeted Kate warmly and Tom with some surprise. It was clear from his expression and manner that he was concerned about anything that might affect the reputation of the Omnicenter, including involvement of one of the Ashburton Service senior residents.

Kate sought immediately to reassure him. "Bill, as you know, Dr. Engleson's been an enormous help to me in sorting all this out. He knows, as do I, the importance of absolute discretion in discussing these matters with anyone."

"You've spoken to no one at all about this?" Zimmermann asked Tom.

"No, sir. Only K . . . only Dr. Bennett."

"Good. Well, sit down, sit down both of you."

"I'll try not to take up too much of your time," Kate began, "but I want to keep you abreast of what has been happening since we talked yesterday."

"You were concerned about the Ashburton Foundation."

"Exactly. You know how upset I was with Redding Pharmaceuticals after they bribed my chemist. Well—"

Zimmermann stopped her with a raised hand. "Kate, please," he said, with an edge of irritation she had never heard before. "I told you how I felt about the situation with the chemist. I believe that you believe, but no more than that." He turned to Tom. "Do you have any personal knowledge of this chemist, Toole?"

Tom thought for a moment and then shook his head. "No, not really."

"All right, then," Zimmermann said. "Substantiated facts."

Kate took a breath, nodded, and settled herself down by smoothing out a pleat in her charcoal gray skirt. "Sorry, Bill. Okay, here's a substantiated fact." She passed a telephone number across to him. "It's the number of the Ashburton Foundation in Washington, DC. At one time, maybe seven or eight years ago, the foundation was located in Darlington, Kentucky, the same town as Redding Pharmaceuticals. I tried calling them yesterday, several times, but all I got was a stammering receptionist who promised I would hear from a Dr. James Thompson, the director, as soon as he returned to the office. I never heard. Then this morning, I went to see Norton Reese and asked to see the Ashburton Foundation files. You would have thought I asked to read his diary. He refused and then exploded at me."

"Did he give any reason for refusing?" Tom asked.

Kate shook her head. "Not really. He seemed frightened of me. Scared stiff."

"Kate," Zimmermann asked, fingering the paper she had given him, "just what is it you're driving at?" The edge was still in his voice.

Even before she spoke, she sensed her theory would not sit well with the Omnicenter director. Still, there was no way to back off. "Well, I think Redding Pharmaceuticals may be investing money in hospitals—or at least this hospital—and using the Ashburton Foundation as some kind of front, sort of a middle man."

Zimmermann's pale eyes widened. "That's absurd," he said, "absolutely absurd. What would they have to gain?"

"I'm not certain. I have an idea, but I'm not certain. Furthermore, I think Norton Reese knows the truth."

"Well?"

Substantiated facts. Suddenly, Kate wished she had taken more time, prepared herself more thoughtfully. Then she remembered Ellen. Time was, she felt certain, running out for her friend. With that reality, nothing else really mattered. She girded herself for whatever Zimmermann's response was to be and pushed on.

"I don't think the anthranilic acid in my vitamins was an accidental contaminant," she said, forcing a levelness into her voice though she was shaking inside. "I think it was being tested on me, and probably on others as well; not tested to see whether or not it worked, because I didn't have any symptoms, but rather for adverse reactions, for side effects, if you will."

Zimmermann was incredulous. "Dr. Bennett, if such a thing were going on in the Omnicenter, in *my* facility, don't you think I would know about it?"

"Not really," Kate said. "It was starting to come together for me, but Tom's description of how the intake process works made it all fit. It's Carl Horner, downstairs. Horner and his Monkeys. You and the other docs here just go on prescribing his medications and then recording his data for him. There's no reason you have to know anything, as long as the computers know."

"And you think the Ashburton Foundation is bankrolling his work?" Kate nodded. "This is getting out of control." He turned to Tom. "Do you follow what she is saying?" Reluctantly, Tom nodded. "And do you believe it?"

"I . . . I don't know what to believe."

"Well, I think it's time I checked on some of these things for myself," Zimmermann said, snatching up the telephone and setting the Ashburton number on his desk. "Dr. William Zimmermann, access number three-oh-eight-three," he told the operator, as Kate looked on excitedly, "I'd like a Watts line, please."

Only a few more minutes, Kate told herself. Only a few more minutes, a few words from the confused, stammering receptionist, and Zimmermann would at least realize that something was not right at the Ashburton Foundation. For the moment, that would be enough. Measured against the fiascoes surrounding Bobby Geary and Ian Toole, the planting of even a small seed of doubt in the man's mind would be a major victory.

"Yes, good morning," she heard Zimmermann say. "I am Dr. William Zimmermann, from Boston. I should like to speak with the director. . . .Yes, exactly. Dr. Thompson." Kate turned to Tom and gave him a conspiratorial smile. Suddenly, she realized that Zimmermann was waving to get her attention and pointing to the extension phone on the conference table. She came on the line just as did Dr. James Thompson.

"This is Dr. Thompson," the man said.

"Dr. Thompson, I'm sorry to disturb you. My name is Zimmermann. I'm the director of the Omnicenter here in Boston."

"Oh, yes, Dr. Zimmermann, I know of you," Thompson said. "You took over for poor Dr. French, what was it, four years ago?"

"Five."

"Tragic accident, tragic, as I recall."

"Yes, he drowned," Zimmermann said, now looking directly at Kate, who was beginning to feel sick.

"What can I do for you, sir?" Thompson had a deep, genteel voice.

"I'm here with Dr. Kate Bennett, one of our physicians."

"Ah, yes. Her name is right in front of me here on my desk. Twice, in fact. She phoned here yesterday and was told I would return her call. However, my secretary had no way of knowing that my son, Craig, had fallen at school and broken his wrist and that I was going to be tied up in the emergency room for hours."

"He's all right, I hope?"

Thompson laughed. "Never better. That plaster makes him the center of attention. Now, what can I do for you and Dr. Bennett?"

"Nothing for me, actually, but Dr. Bennett has a question or two for you. One moment."

"Certainly."

Zimmerman, his expression saying, "Well, you asked for it, now here it is," motioned for her to go ahead.

Kate felt as if she were being bludgeoned. She had been sure, so sure, and now. . . . "Dr. Thompson," she managed, "my apologies for not being more patient." She glanced over at Tom, who shrugged helplessly. "I . . . I was calling to find out if there was any connection between the Ashburton Foundation and Redding Pharmaceuticals." There was no sense in trying anything other than a direct approach. She was beaten, humiliated again, and she knew it.

"Connection?"

"Yes, sir. Isn't it true that the foundation was once located in Darlington, Kentucky, the same town as Redding?"

"As a matter of fact, it was. John and Sylvia Ashburton, whose estate established the foundation, were from Lexington. Their son, John, Jr., ran one of their horse farms, Darlington Stables. For two years after his parents died, John stayed at the farm, tidying up affairs and setting up the mechanics of the foundation. I was hired in, let me see, seventy-nine, but by then, the center of operations had already been moved to Washington. I'm afraid that as far as Redding Pharmaceuticals goes, the geographical connection was pure coincidence."

"Thank you," Kate said meekly. "That certainly helps clear up my confusion." Another glance at Tom, and she grasped at one final straw. "Dr. Thompson, I was trying to find out the street address of your office, but there's no Ashburton Foundation listed in the DC directory."

"By design, Dr. Bennett, quite by design. You see, where there is grant money involved, there are bound to be, how should I say it, somewhat less than fully qualified applicants contacting us. We prefer to do our own preliminary research and then to encourage only appropriate institutions and agencies to apply. Our offices are at 238 K Street, Northwest, on the seventh floor. Please feel free to visit any time you are in Washington. Perhaps your pathology department would be interested in applying for a capital equipment grant."

"Perhaps," Kate said distractedly.

William Zimmermann had heard enough. "Dr. Thompson," he said, "I want to thank you for helping to clear up the confusion here, and also for the wonderful support your agency has given my Omnicenter."

"Our pleasure, sir," Dr. James Thompson said.

"Well?" Zimmermann asked after he had hung up.

"Something's not right," she said.

"What?"

"He mentioned my pathology department. How did he know I was a pathologist?"

"I told him you were at the very start of the call."

"I'm not trying to be difficult, Bill—really, I'm not— but you referred to me as a physician, not a pathologist. You remember, Tom, don't you?" A look at the uncertainty in Tom's eyes, and she began having doubts herself. "Well?"

"I . . . I'm not sure," was all the resident could say.

Kate stood to go. "Bill, I may seem pigheaded to you, or even confused, but I tell you, something still doesn't feel right to me. I just have a sense that Dr. Thompson knew exactly who I was and what I wanted before you ever called."

"You must admit, Kate," Zimmermann said clinically, "that when one looks first at the business with the baseball player, then at the conflict over whether or not a chemist actually performed tests he swears he never ran, and now at what seem to be groundless concerns on your part regarding the Ashburton Foundation and my long-standing computer engineer, it becomes somewhat difficult to get overly enthusiastic about your hunches and senses and theories. Now, if you've nothing further, I must get back to work."

"No," Kate said, smarting from the outburst by the usually cordial man. "Nothing, really, except the promise that no matter how long it takes, I will find out who, or what, is responsible for Ellen's bleeding disorder. Thanks for coming, Tom. I'm sorry it worked out this way." With a nod to both men, she left, fingers of self-doubt tightening their grip in her gut.

She bundled her clinic coat against the wind and snow and pushed head down out of the Omnicenter and onto the street. What if she were wrong, totally wrong about Redding and Horner, about the Omnicenter and Ellen's bleeding, about Reese? Perhaps, despite the critical situation in Berenson 421, despite the nagging fears about her own body, she should back off and let things simmer down. Perhaps she should listen to the advice of her father-in-law and reorder her priorities away from Metropolitan Hospital.

They were waiting for her in her office: Stan Willoughby, Liu Huang, and Rod Green, the flamboyant, black general surgeon who was, it was rumored, being groomed for a Harvard professorship.

"Kate," Willoughby said. "I was just writing you a note." He held the paper up for her to see.

Kate greeted the other two men and then turned back to Willoughby. He was tight. His stance and the strain in his smile said so. "Well?" she asked.

"Pardon?"

"The note, Stan. What would it have said?"

"Oh, I'm sorry. My mind is racing." He cleared his throat. "Kate, we need to talk with you."

"Well, sit down then, please." She felt her heart respond to her sudden apprehension. "A problem?"

Willoughby was totally ill at ease. "I . . . um . . . Kate, yesterday you did a frozen section of a needle biopsy on one of Dr. Green's patients."

"Yes, a breast. It was an intraductal adenocarcinoma. I reported the results to Dr. Green myself." Her pulse quickened another notch.

"Was there, um . . . any question in your mind of the—"

"What Dr. Willoughby is trying to say," Rod Green cut in, "is that I did a masectomy on a woman who, it appears, has benign breast disease." The man's dark eyes flashed.

"That's impossible." Kate looked first to Willoughby and then to Liu Huang for support, but saw only the tightlipped confirmation of the surgeon's allegation. "Liu?"

"I have examined specimen in great detail," the little man said carefully. "Track of biopsy needle enters benign adenoma. No cancer there or in any part of breast."

"Are . . . are you sure?" She could barely speak.

"Kate," Willoughby said, "I reviewed the slides myself. There's no cancer."

"But, there was. I swear there was."

"There was no cancer in my patient," Green said. "None." His fury at her was clearly under the most marginal control. "You have made a mistake. A terrible, terrible mistake."

Kate stared wide-eyed at the three men. It was a dream, a grotesque nightmare from which she would awake at any moment. Their stone faces blurred in and out of focus as her mind struggled to remember the cells. There were three breast biopsies, no, two, there were two. Green's patient was the first. The pathology was a bit tricky, but it was nothing she would ever miss in even one case out of a thousand, unless. . . .She remembered the fatigue and the strain of the previous morning, the stress of Jared's being away, the crank phone calls, and the disappearance of Ian Toole. No, her thoughts screamed, she couldn't have made such a mistake. It wasn't as if they were saying she had missed something, although even that kind of error would have been hard to believe, they were claiming she had read a condition that wasn't there. It was . . . impossible. There was just no other word.

"Did you check the slides from yesterday?" she managed. "The frozens?"

Willoughby nodded grimly. "Benign adenoma. The exact same pathology as in the main specimen." He handed her a plastic box of slides.

Green stood up, fists clenched. "I have heard enough. Dr. Bennett, thanks to you, a woman who came to me in trust has had her breast removed unnecessarily. When she sues, even though I will in all likelihood be one of the defendants, I shall also be her best witness." He started to leave and then turned back to her. "You know," he said, "that letter you sent to the papers about Bobby Geary was a pretty rotten thing to do." He slammed the door hard enough to shake the vase of roses on the corner of her desk.

Kate could barely hold the slide as she set it on the stage of her microscope. This time, the yellow-white light held no excitement, no adventure for her. She knew, even before she had completed focusing down, that the specimen was benign. It was that clear-cut. Her mistaking the pattern for a cancer would have been as likely as an Olympic diver springing off the wrong end of the board.

"Something's wrong," she said, her eye still fixed on the cells. The words reverberated in her mind. Something's wrong. She had said that to Bill Zimmermann not half an hour ago.

"Kate," Willoughby said gently, "I'm sorry."

Only after she looked up from the microscope did she realize she was crying. "Stan, I swear this is not the slide I read yesterday. It can't be." But even as she said the words, she admitted to herself that, as in the situation with Bobby Geary, her only defense was a protestation of innocence.

"You've been under a great deal of stress lately, Kate. Do you suppose that—"

"No!" She forced herself to lower her voice. "I remember the biopsy I saw yesterday. It was cancer. I didn't make a mistake."

"Look," Willoughby said, "I want you to take a few days off. Rest. After this coming weekend we can talk."

"But—"

"Kate, I'm taking you off the schedule for a while. Now I don't want you coming back into work until after we've had a chance to discuss things next week. Okay?" There was uncharacteristic firmness in the man's voice.

Meekly, she nodded. "Okay, but—"

"No buts. Kate, it's for your own good. I'll call you at home and check on how you're doing. Now off you go."

Kate watched her colleagues leave: Stan Willoughby, head down, shuffling a few feet ahead of Liu Huang, who turned for a moment and gave her a timid, but hopeful, thumbs-up sign. Then they were gone.

For a time she sat, uncertainly, isolation and self-doubt constricting every muscle in her body, making it difficult to move or even to breathe. With great effort, she pulled the telephone over and lifted the receiver. "I want to place a long-distance call, please," she heard her voice say. "It's personal, so charge it to my home phone. . . . I'm calling San Diego."

# 12

## Thursday 20 December

It had taken narcotic painkillers and amphetamines along with his usual pharmacopoeia, but in the end, Becker had prevailed. Now he ached for sleep. He could not remember his last meal. Catnaps at his desk, cool showers every six or seven hours, bars of chocolate, cups of thick coffee for four days, or was it five? These had been his only succor.

Still, he had endured. In the morning, a messenger would hand deliver his manuscript and box of slides to the editor in chief of *The New England Journal of Medicine*. The letter accompanying the manuscript would give the man ten days to agree to publish the Estronate studies in their entirety within four months and to oversee the appointment of an international commission to assume responsibility for the initiation of Beckerian population control.

The study was in a shambles, with reference books, scrap paper, coffee cups, discarded drafts, candy-bar wrappers, and dirty glasses covering the furniture and much of the floor. Like a prizefighter at the moment of triumph, Willi Becker, more skeleton than man, stood in the midst of the debris and pumped his fists in the air. After forty years and through hardship almost unimaginable, he had finished. Now there was only the matter of gaining acceptance.

It was ironic, he acknowledged, that decades of the most meticulous research had come down to a few frenetic days, but that was the way it had to be. With the pathologist Bennett snooping about the Omnicenter and Cyrus Redding's antennae up, time had become a luxury he could no longer afford.

*Studies in Estronate 250*. Becker cleared off his easy chair, settled down, and indulged in thoughts of the accolades, honors, and other tributes to his genius and dedication certain to result from the publication and implementation of his work. He was nearing receipt of a Nobel Prize when the phone began ringing. It took half a dozen rings to break through his reverie and another four to locate the phone beneath a pile of journals.

"Hello?"

"John? Redding here."

The voice brought a painful emptiness to Becker's chest. For several seconds, he could not speak.

"John?"

Becker cleared his throat. "Yes, yes, Cyrus. I'm here."

"Good. Fine. Well, I hope I'm not disturbing anything important for you."

"Not at all. I was just . . . doing a little reading before bed." Did his voice sound as strained, as strangled, as it felt? "What can I do for you?" Please, he thought, let it be some problem related to their myasthenia. Let it be anything but . . .

"Well, John, I wanted to speak with you a bit about that business at the Omnicenter." Becker's heart sank. "You know," Redding continued, "the situation with these women having severe scarring of their ovaries and then bleeding to death."

"Yes, what about it?"

"Have you learned anything new about the situation since we spoke last?"

"No. Not really." Becker sensed that he was being toyed with.

"Well, John, you know that the whole matter has

piqued my curiosity, as well as my concern for the safety of our testing programs. Too many coincidences. Too much smoke for there not to be a fire someplace."

"Perhaps," Becker said, hanging onto the thread of hope that the man, a master at such maneuvers, was shooting in the dark. For a time, there was silence from Redding's end. Becker shifted nervously in his chair. "Cyrus?" he asked finally.

"I'm here."

"Was there . . . anything else?"

"John, I won't bandy words with you. We've been through too much together, accomplished too many remarkable things for me to try and humiliate you by letting you trip over one after another of your own lies."

"I . . . I don't understand."

"Of course you understand, John." He paused. "I know who you are. That is the gist of what I am calling to say. I know about Wilhelm Becker, and even more importantly, I know about Estronate Two-fifty."

Becker glanced over at his manuscript, stacked neatly atop the printer of his word processor, and forced himself to calm down. There was little he could think of that Redding could do to hurt him at this stage of the game. Still, Cyrus Redding was Cyrus Redding, and no amount of caution was too much. *Stay calm but don't underestimate.* "Your resourcefulness is quite impressive," he said.

"John, tell me truly, it was Estronate Two-fifty that caused the problems at the Omnicenter, wasn't it?"

"It was."

"The hemorrhaging is an undesirable side effect?"

Becker was about to explain that the problem had been overcome and that his hormone was, to all intents, perfected. He stopped himself at the last moment. "Yes," he said. "A most unfortunate bug that I have not been able to get out of the system."

"You should have told me, John," Redding said. "You should have trusted me."

"What do you want?"

"John, come now. It is bad enough you didn't respect me enough to take me into your confidence. It is bad enough your uncondoned experiments have put my entire company in jeopardy. Do not try to demean my intelligence. I want to extend our partnership to include that remarkable hormone of yours. After all, it was tested at a facility that I fund."

"Work is not complete. There are problems. Serious problems."

"Then we shall overcome them. You know the potential of this Estronate of yours as well as I do. I am prepared to make you an on-the-spot offer of, say, half a million dollars now and a similar amount when your work is completed to the satisfaction of my biochemists. And of course, there would be a percentage of all sales."

*Sales.* Becker realized that his worst possible scenario was being enacted. Redding understood not only the chemical nature of Estronate, but also its limitless value to certain governments. How? How in hell's name had the man learned so much so quickly? "I . . . I was planning eventually on submitting my work for publication," he offered.

Redding laughed. "That would be bad business, John. Very bad business. The value of our product would surely plummet if its existence and unique properties became general knowledge. Suppose you oversee the scientific end and let me deal with the proprietary."

"If I refuse," Becker said, "will you kill me?"

Again Redding laughed. "Perhaps. Perhaps I will. However, there are those, I am sure, who would pay dearly for information on the physician whom the Ravensbrück prisoners called the Serpent."

For a time there was silence. "How did you learn of all this?" Becker asked finally.

"Why don't we save explanations, Dr. Becker, for a time after our new business arrangement has been consummated."

"I need time to think."

"Take it. Take as much as you need up to, say, twenty-four hours."

"The intrinsic problems of the hormone may be insurmountable."

"A chance I will take. You owe me this. For the troubles you have caused at our testing facility, you owe me. In fact, there is something else you owe me as well."

"Oh?"

"I wish to know the individual at the Omnicenter who has been helping you with your work."

Becker started to protest that there was no such person, but decided against testing the man's patience. In less than twelve hours a messenger would deliver the Estronate paper and slides to *The New England Journal of Medicine*, making the hormone, in essence, public domain. He had already decided that exposure of his true identity and the risk of spending what little was left of his life in prison was a small price to pay for immortality. "Forty-eight hours," he said.

Redding hesitated. "Very well, then," he said finally. "Forty-eight hours it will be. You have the number. I shall expect to hear from you within two days. The Estronate work and the name of your associate. Good-bye." He hung up.

"Good-bye," Becker said to the dial tone. As he drew the receiver from his ear, he heard a faint but definite click. The sound sent fear stabbing beneath his breastbone. Someone, almost certainly William, was on the downstairs extension. How long? How long had he been there?

In the cluttered semidarkness of his study, Willi Becker strained his compromised hearing. For a time, there was only silence. Perhaps, he thought, there hadn't been a click at all. Then he heard the unmistakable tread of footsteps on the stairs.

"William?" Again there was silence. "William?"

"Yes, Father, it is." Zimmermann appeared suddenly in the doorway and stood, arms folded, looking placidly across at him.

"You . . . ah . . . you surprised me. How long have you been in the house?"

"Long enough." Zimmermann strode to the bookcase and poured himself a drink. He was, as usual, immaculately dressed. Light from the gooseneck reading lamp sparked off the heavy diamond ring on the small finger of his left hand and highlighted the sheen on his black Italian-cut loafers.

"You were listening in on my conversation, weren't you?"

"Oh, perhaps." Zimmermann snapped a wooden swizzle stick in two and used one edge to clean beneath his nails.

"Listening was a rude thing to do."

"Me, rude? Why, Father . . ."

"Well, if you heard, you heard. It really makes no difference."

"Oh?"

"Just how long *were* you listening in?"

Zimmermann didn't answer. Instead, he walked to the printer, picked up the Estronate manuscript, and turned it from one side to the other, appraisingly. "A half million dollars and then some. It would seem there is some truth about good things coming in small packages."

"Give me that." Becker was too weak, too depleted by the drugs, even to rise.

Zimmermann ignored him. "Wilhelm W. Becker, MD, PhD," he read. "So that's who my father is."

"Please, William."

"How good it is to learn that the man John Ferguson, who so ignored and abused my mother all those years, was not my father. The Serpent of Ravensbrück. That's my real father."

"I never abused her. I did what I had to do."

"Father, please. She knew that you could have come home much more often and didn't. She knew about your women, your countless women. She knew that neither of us would ever mean anything to you compared to your precious research."

Becker stared at his son with wide, bloodshot eyes. "You hate me, don't you?" There was incredulity in his voice.

"Not really. The truth is, I don't feel much for you one way or the other."

"But I was behind you all the way. My money sent you through school. Your position at the Omnicenter, how do you think that came about? Do you think Harold French just happened to drown accidentally at the moment you were experienced enough to take over for him? It was me!" Becker's hoarse, muddy voice had become barely audible. "If you care so little about me, William, then why have you helped me in my work all these years? Why?"

Zimmermann gazed blandly at his father. "Because of your connections, of course. Your friend Redding triples what the hospital pays me. You suggested my name, and he arranged for me to get my professorship. I know he did."

"He got you the position on my say-so, and he can have it taken from you the same way."

"Can he, now." Zimmermann held up the Estronate manuscript. "You lied to him. You told him there were still flaws in the work. Why? Are you thinking that once he finds out you have sent this off for publication, he will just walk away and leave us alone? Do you think he won't find out who I am? What I have been helping you do behind his back? Do you?" He was screaming. "Well, I tell you right here and now, Father, this is mine. I have paid for it over the years with countless humiliations. Cyrus Redding will have his Estronate, and I shall have my proper legacy."

"No!" Even as he shouted the word, Willi Becker felt the tearing pain in his left chest. His heart, weakened by disease, and sorely compromised by amphetamines, pounded mercilessly and irregularly. "My oxygen," he rasped. "In the bedroom. Oxygen and nitroglycerine." The study was beginning a nauseating spin.

For the first time, William Zimmermann smiled. "I'm afraid I can't hear you, Father," he said, benevolently. "Could you please speak up a bit?"

"Will . . . iam . . . please . . ." Becker's final words were muffled by the gurgle of fluid bubbling up from his lungs, and vomitus welling from his stomach. He clawed impotently in the direction of his son and then toppled over onto the rug, his face awash in the products of his own death.

Stepping carefully around his father's corpse, Zimmermann slipped the Estronate paper into a large envelope; then he removed the disc from the word processor and dropped it in as well. Next he copied a number from the leather-bound address book buried under some papers on one corner of the desk. Finally, he stacked the three worn looseleaf notebooks containing the Estronate data and tucked them under his arm. He would phone Cyrus Redding from the extension downstairs.

The pharmaceutical magnate evinced little surprise at Zimmermann's call or at the rapid turn of events in Newton. Instead, he listened patiently to the details of Willi Becker's life as the man's son knew them.

"Dr. Zimmermann," he said finally, "let us stop here to be certain I fully understand. Your father, when he was supervising construction of the Omnicenter, secretly had a laboratory built for himself in the subbasement?"

"Correct," Zimmermann said. "On the blueprints it is drawn as some sort of dead storage area, I think."

"And the only way to get into the laboratory is through an electronic security system?"

"The lock is hidden and coded electronically. The door is concealed behind a set of shelves."

"Does anyone besides you have the combination?"

"No. At least not as far as I know."

"Remarkable. Dr. Zimmermann, your father was a most brilliant man."

"My father is dead," Zimmermann said coolly.

"Yes," Redding said. "Yes, he is. Tell me, this bleeding problem, it *has* been eliminated?"

"Father modified his synthesis over a year ago. It was taking from six to eighteen months after treatment for the bleeding problem to develop. The three patients you know about were all treated a year ago last July. There have, to our knowledge, been no new cases since. Keep in mind, too, that there weren't that many to begin with. And most of those were mild."

"Yes, I understand. It is remarkable to me that you were able to insert your testing program into Carl Horner's computer system without his ever knowing."

"As you said, Mr. Redding, my father was a brilliant man."

"Yes. Well, then, I suppose we two should explore the possibility of a new partnership."

"The terms you laid out for my father are quite acceptable to me. I have the manuscript and the notebooks. Since the work is already completed, I would be willing to turn them over to you, no further questions asked, for the amount you promised him."

"That is a lot of money, Doctor."

"The amazing thing is that until I overheard your conversation with my father, I had not fully appreciated the valuable potential of the hormone." Zimmermann could barely keep from laughing out loud at his good fortune.

"Are you a biochemist, Doctor?"

"No. Not really."

"In that case, I should like to reserve my final offer until my own biochemist has had the chance to review the material, to see the laboratory, and to take himself through the process of synthesizing the hormone."

"When?"

"Why not tomorrow? Dr. Paquette, whom you know, will meet you at your office at, say, seven o'clock tomorrow night. My man Nunes will accompany him and will have the authority and the money to consummate our agreement if Dr. Paquette is totally satisfied with what he sees."

"Sounds fine. I'll make certain the side door to the Omnicenter is left open."

"That won't be necessary, Dr. Zimmermann. Paquette has keys."

"All right, then, seven o'clock. . . . Was there something else?"

"As a matter of fact, Dr. Zimmermann, there is. It's this whole business with the Omnicenter and that pathologist."

"You mean Bennett?"

"She has proven a very resilient young woman. Do you believe she was convinced by her conversation with our man at the Ashburton Foundation?"

"No. Not completely. She said she was going to continue investigating. The woman currently hospitalized here with complications from Estronate treatment is a close friend of hers."

"I see. You know, Doctor, none of this would have happened if you and your father hadn't conducted your work so recklessly and independently." His voice had a chilling edge. "Don't you feel a responsibility to this company for what you have done?"

"Responsibility?"

"If we are to have a partnership, I should like to know that the millions I have spent on the Omnicenter will not be lost because we were unable to neutralize one woman."

"But she has been neutralized. A serious mistake on a pathology specimen. She's been put on leave by her department head. Isn't that enough to discredit her?"

"I am no longer speaking of discrediting her, my friend. I am speaking of stopping her. You heard my conversation with your father. You know the importance of keeping Estronate a secret. It has been bad enough that Dr. Bennett is threatening, by her doggedness, to bring the Omnicenter tumbling down about our ears. If she uncovers Estronate, we stand to lose much, much more."

"I'll see to it that won't happen."

"Excellent. But remember, I don't handle disappointment well. Until tomorrow, then, Doctor."

"Yes, tomorrow."

William Zimmermann made a final inspection of the house, taking pains to wipe off anything he had touched. The precaution was, in all likelihood, unnecessary. The houseboy was due in at eight in the morning, and the death he would discover upstairs would certainly appear due to natural causes.

As he slipped out the back door of his father's house, a fortune in notebooks and computer printouts under his arm, Zimmermann was thinking about Kate Bennett.

The nightmare was a juggernaut, more pervasive, more oppressive it seemed with each passing hour. Its setting had changed from the clutter of her office to the deep-piled, fire-warmed opulence of Win Samuels's study, but for Kate Bennett, the change meant only more confusion, more humiliation, more doubt.

*I know what it looks like. I know what it sounds like. But it isn't true. . . . I don't know who did it. . . . I don't know. . . . Dammit all, I just don't know.*

Jared's return earlier in the evening had started on a positive note—an emotional hug and their first kiss in nearly a week. For a time, as they weaved their way through the crowds to the baggage area, he seemed unable to keep his hands or his lips off her. It seemed he was reveling in the freedom of at last truly acknowledging his love for her. *I accept you, regardless of what you are involved in, regardless of what the impact might be on me. I accept you because I believe in you. I accept you because I love you.*

But as she shared her nightmare with him, she could feel him pulling back, sense his enthusiasm erode. It showed first in his eyes, then in his voice, and finally in his touch. He was trying, Kate knew, perhaps even trying his best. But she also knew that confusion and doubt were taking their toll. Why would a company as large as Redding Pharmaceuticals do the things of which she was accusing them? The Ashburton Foundation had an impeccable reputation. What evidence was there that they were frauds? Why would anyone do something as horrible as switching biopsies? How did they do it? Weren't there any records of the tests she had run at the state lab? How did the letter about Bobby Geary fit in with all this?

*I know what it looks like. I know what it sounds like. But it isn't true.*

With each *why*, with each *I don't know*, Kate felt Jared drifting further and further into her nightmare. By the time the subject of his father and sister came up, she was feeling isolated, as stifled as before, perhaps more so. They were nearly halfway home to Essex.

"That is absolutely incredible," Jared had said, swinging sharply into the breakdown lane and jamming to a stop. "I . . . I don't believe it." It was the first time since his return that he had said those words. "After all these years, why wouldn't he tell me my sister was alive?"

"I don't know." The phrase reverberated in her mind. "Perhaps he was trying to spare you the ugliness."

"That makes no sense. You say he took you to this institution to convince you to turn down the position at Metro and concentrate on having babies?"

"That's what he said."

Jared shook his head. "Let me be sure I have this straight. My father, who has never communicated all that well with my wife to begin with, sends me out of town so that he can take her to an institution in the middle of nowhere and introduce her to the sister he had led me to believe died thirty-odd years ago. Does that make sense to you?"

"Jared," she said, her voice beginning to quaver, "nothing has made sense to me for days. All I can do is tell the truth."

"Well, if that's the case," he said finally, "I think I'd like to find out first hand why my father has been holding out on me."

"Couldn't we at least wait until—"

"No! I can't think of a damn thing to do about Bobby Geary or the Omnicenter or the Ashburton Foundation or the runaway technician or the goddamn breast biopsies, but I sure as hell can do something about my father."

Without waiting for a reply, he had swung off and under the highway and had screeched back onto the south-bound lane, headed for Boston.

Now, in the uncomfortably warm study, Kate sat by a hundred-and-thirty-year-old leaded glass window, watching the fairyland Christmas lights of Louisburg Square and listening to her husband and her father-in-law argue over whether she was a liar, a woman in desperate need of professional help, or some combination of the two. Jared, in all fairness, was doing his best to give her the benefit of the doubt, but it had, purely and simply, come down to her word against his father's. When taken with the other issues, the other confusions she had regaled him with since his landing at Logan, it was not hard to understand why he was having difficulty taking her side.

"Once again, Jared," Win Samuels said with authoritative calm, "we dined together—Jocelyn's special duck. After dinner we talked. Then we went for a long drive in the country. I hadn't been out of the house all day and was getting a severe case of cabin fever. We did stop at the Stonefield School; I'm on the board of trustees there. But I assure you, Son, our visit was quite spur of the moment. We were only a few miles from the school when I remembered a set of papers in the back seat that I was planning on mailing off tomorrow to Gus Leggatt, the school administrator. While we were there, we did look in on some of the children. Largely because of our visit, on the way home I was able to share my fears with Kate about what happens to the rate of birth defects in children of older mothers. Kate explained the advances in amniocentesis to me; facts, I might add, that I found quite reassuring. I mentioned your sister, certainly, but I never implied she was alive. I'm sorry, Jared. And I am sorry for you, too, Kate." He looked at her levelly. "You've been under a great deal of pressure. Perhaps . . . a rest, some time off."

*Time off.* Kate sighed. Winfield had no way of knowing Stan Willoughby had already seen to that. She rose slowly, and crossed to Jared. "Stonefield School is listed in information," she said wearily. "Broderick, Massachusetts. If the snow doesn't get any worse, I can drive us there in forty-five minutes to an hour. That should settle this once and for all."

"Do you want to come with us, Dad?" Jared asked.

"There is no reason to go *anyplace*," Win Samuels said simply. "Kate, Jared's sister had severe birth defects and died exactly when he thinks she did, thirty years ago. Perhaps you had a dream of some sort. Strands of fantasy woven into reality. It happens, especially when one has been under an inordinate amount of stress such as you—"

"It is not stress! It is not stress, it is not a dream, it is not the desperate lie of a desperate woman, it is not . . . insanity." She confronted him, her eyes locked on his. Samuels held his ground, his face an expressionless mask. "It is the truth. The truth! I don't know why you are doing this, I don't know what you hope to accomplish. But I do know one thing. I'm not going to break. You manipulate the people in your life like they were pieces on some some enormous game board. Jocelyn to king's knight four, Jared to queen three. Not your turn? Well you'll just throw in a few thousand dollars and make it your turn."

Samuels moved to speak, but Kate stopped him with raised hands. "I'm not through. I want to tell you something, Win. You've underestimated me. Badly. I've made it through a childhood of total loneliness, an education of total aimlessness, and a marriage to an alcoholic madman who insisted on picking out my pantyhose for me. I've survived and grown in a profession where I am patronized, and discriminated against. I've dealt with men who couldn't bring their eyes, let along their minds, above my breasts. I've dealt with them and I've succeeded.

"It's been hard. At times, it's been downright horrible. But for the last five years, I've had a secret weapon. He's right there, Win. Right over there." She nodded toward Jared. "When I forget that I'm okay, he reminds me. When I have to face the Norton Reeses and the Arlen Paquettes and, yes, the Winfield Samuelses of this world, he gives me strength. I love him and I have faith in him. Sooner or later, he's going to see the way you toy with the lives of those around you. Sooner or later, you'll go to move him, and he won't be there."

"Are you done?" Samuels said.

"Yes, I'm done. And I don't want to hear any more from you unless it's an apology and the truth about the other night. How could you think I wouldn't tell Jared? How could you think I wouldn't remember where we went, what we did? Please, Jared, let's get going. It's late, and we have quite a drive ahead of us."

At that moment, there was a noise, the clearing of a throat, from the doorway. The three of them turned to the sound. Jocelyn Trent stood holding a silver tray with coffee and tea.

"How long have you been there?" Samuels demanded. The woman did not answer. "Well?"

She hesitated; then she set the tray on the nearest table and ran from the room.

"Stonefield School," Kate said. "See, I told you I could find it. Only two wrong turns." She swung into the driveway, past the small sign, and up to the front door. "This is almost the exact hour we were here the other night. With any luck, the nurse who was on duty then will be on again. Her name was Bicknell, Sally Bicknell; something like that. I'll recognize her. She wore about eighty gold bracelets and had rings on three or four fingers of each hand. What a character!"

Her chatter was, she knew, somewhat nervous. Jared

had said little during their drive. His pensiveness was certainly understandable, but she found herself wishing he could recapture at least some of the emotion he had shown at the airport. No matter, she consoled herself. Two minutes at Stonehill, and he would know that, in this arena, at least, she was telling the truth. How foolish of Win to think things would not develop the way they had. How unlike the man to miss predicting a person's actions as badly as he had missed hers.

The nurse, Bicknell, was working at her desk in a small office just off the lobby. Her hair was pulled back in a tight bun, and she was wearing only a single gold chain on one wrist. Hardly the flamboyant eccentric Kate had depicted. It was an observation, Kate noted uneasily, that was not overlooked by her husband.

"Are you sure it's the same woman?" he whispered, as they crossed the lobby.

"It's her. Hi, Miss Bicknell. Remember me?"

The woman took only a second. "Of course. You were with Mr. Samuels four—no, no,—three nights ago. Right?"

"Exactly. You have an excellent memory."

"An elephant," Sally Bicknell said, tapping one finger against her temple.

"This is my husband, Jared, Miss Bicknell. Mr. Samuels's son."

"Pleased to meet you." The woman took the hand Jared offered. "We don't get too many evening visitors here at Stonefield. In fact, we don't get too many visitors at other times, either." She looked around. "Sort of a forgotten land, I guess."

"Miss Bicknell, we came to see my husband's sister."

The woman's expression clouded. "I . . . I'm afraid I don't understand."

Kate felt an ugly apprehension set in. "Lindsey Samuels," she said, a note of irritation—or was it panic?—in her voice, "the girl we saw Monday night right over there." She pointed to the blue velvet curtain.

Sally Bicknell looked at her queerly and then ushered

them over and drew back the curtain. "Her?" The girl was there, lumbering about exactly as she had been before.

"Yes, exactly," Kate said. "That's her, Jared. That's Lindsey."

"I'm sorry, Mrs. Samuels, but you're mistaken. That girl's name is Rochelle Coombs. She is sixteen years old and has a genetic disease called Hunter's Syndrome."

Kate stopped herself at the last possible moment from calling the woman a liar. "Could I see her medical records, please?"

The nurse snapped the curtain shut. "Her medical records are confidential. But I assure you, her name is Rochelle Coombs, not—what did you say?"

"Lindsey," Jared said, "Lindsey Samuels." It was, Kate realized, the first time he had spoken since just after their arrival.

"It is not Lindsey Samuels." Sally Bicknell completed her sentence.

In that moment, Kate realized what had bothered her so about the girl the first time she had observed her. She was too young to have been Jared's sister. Far too young. Her thick features and other physical distortions added some years, but not twenty of them. The girl's grotesqueness had made her too uncomfortable to look very closely. Had Win Samuels counted on that? Silently, she cursed her own stupidity. Helpless and beaten, she could only shrug and shake her head.

"Will there be anything else?" Bicknell asked.

Kate looked over at Jared, who shook his head. "No," she said huskily. "We're . . . we're sorry for the intrusion."

"In that case," the woman said, "I have rounds to make." She turned and, without showing them out, walked away.

Kate felt far more ill than angry. As they approached the car, she handed Jared the keys. "You drive, please. I'm not up to it. Your father told me it was Lindsey, Jared. I swear he did. And that woman was right there when he said it."

There was, she realized, no sense in discussing the matter further. Win Samuels had set up a no-lose situation for himself. Either she would be impressed by his demonstration, in which case she might have agreed to back off at the hospital and, as he wished, turn her attention to domestic issues; or she would be angered enough to do exactly what she had done. His son, already in doubt about her, would be drawn further away from their marriage and toward a political future, unencumbered by a wife whose priorities and mental state were so disordered. All that for only the price of a tankful of gas and whatever it cost to buy off Sally Bicknell. Nice going, Win, she thought. Nice goddamn going. She sank into her seat and stared sightlessly into the night.

# 13

## Friday 21 December

"She's out, suspended, finished. I did it," Norton Reese boasted exultantly. "Yesterday afternoon. I tried to call you then, but there was no answer."

Still in his bed at the Ritz, Arlen Paquette squinted at his watch, trying to get the numbers in focus. Seven-thirty? Was that right? Was goddamn Reese waking him up at seven-thirty in the morning? He fumbled for the bedside lamp, wincing at the shellburst in his temples. Somewhere in the past four hours, he had passed from being drunk to being hung over. His mouth tasted like sewage, and his muscles felt as if he had lost a gang fight.

"Norton, just a second here while I wake up a little bit." He worked a cigarette from a wrinkled packet and lit it on the third try. Over the past week, his smoking had gone from his usual four or five cigarettes a day to three packs. For a moment, he eyed the half-empty quart of Dewar's on the bureau. "No, goddamn it," he muttered, "At least not yet." It took two hands to hold the phone steady against his ear. "Now, sir, just how did you go about accomplishing this remarkable feat of yours?"

Paquette listened to Reese's excited recap of the events leading to the unofficial suspension of Kate Bennett by her chief, Stan Willoughby. By the time the administrator had finished, Paquette had made his way across to the scotch and buried half a water glass full. The story was disgusting. A woman had lost her breast unnecessarily, and another had been professionally destroyed, and he, as much as the idiot on the other end of the phone, was responsible. As he listened to Reese's crowing, a resolve began to grow within him. He picked up a picture of Kate Bennett from the floor by his bed, wondering briefly how it had gotten there.

"Norton," he said cheerfully, "you've done one hell of a job there. Our friend's gonna be pleased when I tell him. Real pleased. Say, listen. Are you going to be at your office for a while . . . Good. I'd like to stop by and get some of the details in person. Probably be nine-thirty or so . . . Great. See you then."

He hung up and studied the picture in his hand. The scotch had stilled the shakes and begun to alleviate the pounding in his head. "I think you've taken enough shit from us, Dr. Bennett," he said. "It's time someone helped you fight back."

A glance at his watch, and he called Darlington. His wife answered on the second ring. "Honey, have the kids left for school yet? . . . Good. They're not going. I want you to pack them up and drive to your mother's house. . . . Honey, I know where your mother lives. If you step on it, you can be there by dinner time. There've been some problems here with old Cyrus, and I just want to be sure you and the kids are safe. . . . Maybe a few days, maybe a week. I don't know. Please, honey. Trust me on this one for a little while. I'll explain everything. And listen, I love you. I'm sorry about the other night and I love you. Not a word to anyone, now. Just get out and go to your mother's."

Paquette showered and then shaved, taking greater pains than usual not to nick himself. He dressed in a suit he had just bought, eschewing the vest in favor of a light brown cashmere sweater. Some Visine, another shot of scotch, some breath mints, and he was ready. On his way to the hospital, he would attend to one final item of business, stopping at an electronics store to purchase a miniature tape recorder.

"Okay, Doctor," he said to Kate's picture, "let's go get us some evidence." He glanced at the mirror. For the first time in nearly two weeks he liked what he saw.

*Nothing to do. Nowhere to go. No one to hold.* The thoughts, the futility, kept intruding on Kate's efforts to wring another hour, even another half hour, of sleep from the morning. They had spent the night—what was left of it after their return from Stonehill—in separate beds. Or perhaps Jared hadn't slept at all. She had offered him food, then company, and then sex, but his only request had been to be left alone. After an hour or so of staring at the darkened ceiling over their bed, she had tiptoed down the hall and peeked into the living room. He was right where she had left him, on the couch, chewing on his lower lip, and studying the creases in his palm. Her immediate impulse was to go to him, to beg him to believe her, to plead for his faith. The feeling disappeared as quickly as it had arisen. If their marriage had come down to begging, she was beaten. Aching with thoughts of what he was going through, at the choices he was trying to make, she had crept quietly back to bed, hoping that before long, she would feel him nudging his way under the covers.

*Nothing to do. Nowhere to go. No one to hold.* The ringing of the phone interrupted the litany. Kate glanced at the clock. Eight-thirty. Not too bad. The last time she had looked it was only six.

"Hello?"

"Kate?" It was Ellen.

"Hi. How're you feeling?"

"I got concerned when you didn't stop by this morning, and I called your office." Her voice was quite hoarse, her speech distorted. "When you didn't answer I rang the department secretary. Kate, what's the matter? Are you sick?"

"Hey, wait a minute, now. Let us not forget who is the patient here, and who is the doctor, okay?"

"Kate, be serious. She said she didn't know what day you'd be back. I . . . I got frightened. They're giving me more blood, and now I have a tube down my nose. I think the inside of my stomach has started bleeding."

"Shit," Kate said softly.

"What?"

"I said 'shit.' "

"Oh. Well, *are* you all right?"

Kate pulled a lie back at the last possible instant. "Actually, no," she said. "Physically I'm fine, but there's been trouble at work and here at home. I've been asked to take some time off while my department head sorts through some problems with a biopsy."

"Oh, Kate. And here I am all wrapped up in my own problems. I'm sorry. I know it sounds foolish coming from where I'm lying, but is there anything I can do?"

"No, El, just be strong and get well, that's all."

"Don't talk to *me*, Katey. Talk to these little platelets or whatever they're called. They're the ones who are screwing up. You said trouble at home, too. Jared?"

*Stop asking about me, dammit. You're bleeding to death!* "I'm afraid Jared's wife and his father in all their infinite wisdom have put him in a position where he's going to have to choose between them." At that moment, she began wondering where he was. Upstairs in the guestroom, perhaps? Maybe still on the couch. She listened for a telltale sound, but there was only heavy silence.

"You versus Win?" Ellen said. "No contest. Thank goodness. I thought it was something serious." Her cheer was undermined by the weakness in her voice.

"Listen, my friend," Kate said. "I'll see you later today. I may be shut out of the pathology department, but I'm not shut out of the library. There are two Australian journals I'm expecting in from the NIH. Together, we're going to beat this. I promise you."

"I believe you," Ellen said. "I really do. See you later, Doc."

Kate set the receiver down gently, then slipped into a blue flannel nightshirt, a gift from Jared, and walked to the living room. Roscoe, who had materialized from under the bed, padded along beside her. She glanced through the doorway and then systematically checked the rest of the house. She had, as she feared, read the silence well. Jared had left.

"Well, old shoe," she said, scratching her dog behind one ear, "it looks like you and me. How about a run together and then some shirred eggs for breakfast. Later, maybe we'll make love."

The letter, in Jared's careful printing, was on the kitchen table. He had taken their wedding picture from the mantel, and used it as a weight to keep the single sheet in place. Kate moved the photograph enough to read his words, but left it touching the page.

It sounds so easy, so obvious, that I'm not sure I even listened when the minister said the words. "For better or for worse." It all sounds so easy until one day you stop and ask yourself, For whose better? For whose worse? What do I do when her better seems like my worse? Dammit, Kate, I'm forty years old and I feel like such a child. Do you know that in all the time she was alive, I never once heard my mother say no to my father? Some role model, huh? Next came Lisa—bright, beautiful, and imbued with absolutely no ambition or direction. I thought she would make a perfect wife. She cooked the soup and pinched back the coleus, and I kept her pipe filled with good dope and decided when we could afford to do what, and that was that. I still don't know why she ran off the way she did, and if another Lisa had come along, I probably would have married her in a snap. But another Lisa didn't. You did.

Almost before I knew it, I had fallen in love with and married a woman who had as rich and interesting and complicated a life outside of our marriage as I did. Probably, more so. After first mother and then Lisa, it was like moving to a foreign country for me. New customs. New mores. What do you mean I was wrong to assume we'd have the same last name? What do you mean I was wrong to assume that you would be free to attend three rallies and a campaign dinner with me? What do you mean I should have asked first? What do you mean you've been involved in trouble at your job that might affect my career? I could go on all night listing my misguided assumptions in this marriage. It's as though I don't have the programming to adapt.

Well, I may not have the programming, but I do have the desire. It's taken most of the night sitting here to feel sure of that. If what you've said is all true, I want to do whatever I can to help straighten it out. If what you've told me is not true, then I also want to face that issue and my commitment to you, and we'll get whatever kind of help is necessary. If we don't make it, it won't be because I ran away.

I've gone to speak to my father and then, who knows, perhaps a chat with Norton Reese. Bear with me, Kate. It may say five years on the calendar, but this marriage business is still new stuff for me. I love you. I really do.

                                                        Jared

Kate reread the letter, laughing and crying at once. Jared's words, she knew, meant no more than a temporary reprieve, a respite from the nightmare. Still, he had given her the one thing she needed most next to answers: time. Time to work through the events that were steamrolling her life.

"We're going to find out, Rosc," she said grimly. "We're going to find out who, and we're going to find out why."

A sharp bark sounded from the living room, and Kate realized that she had been talking to herself. Through the doorway, she could see Roscoe prancing uncomfortably by the door to the rear deck.

"Oh, poor baby," she laughed. "I'm sorry." Focused on letting the dog out, she missed the slight movement outside the kitchen window and failed to sense the eyes watching her. She pulled open the slider, and Roscoe dashed out into a most incredible morning. The temperature, according to the thermometer by the door, was exactly freezing. Fat, lazy flakes, falling from a glaring, silver-white sky vanished into a ground fog that was as dense as any Kate could remember. Roscoe dashed across the deck, and completely disappeared into the shroud halfway down the steps to the yard.

Kate estimated the height of the fog at three or four feet. Much of it, she guessed, was arising off the surface of nearby Green Pond, a small lake that because of warm underground feeders, was always late to freeze and early to thaw. Winter fog was not uncommon on the North Shore, especially around Essex, but this was spectacular. It was a morning just begging to be run through.

She dressed and then stretched, sorting out the route they would run, mixing low spots and high hills and straight-aways along five miles of back roads. Wearing a gold watch cap and a high-visibility red sweatsuit, she trotted out the front door and whistled for Roscoe. He was almost at her side before she could see him.

"A fiver this morning, dog," she said, as they moved up the sloping driveway and out of the fog. "Think you're mutt enough to handle it?"

At the end of the drive, she turned right. Had she

mapped their route to the left, she might have wondered about the BMW, parked not particularly near anyone's house, and perhaps even noticed the blue Metropolitan Hospital parking sticker on the rear window.

It was near perfect air for running, cold and still. To either side of the narrow roadway, the fog covered the forest floor like cotton batting.

"Race pace, today, Rosc," she said. "Eight-minute miles or less. And I'm not waiting for you, so keep up." In reality, she knew Roscoe could maintain her pace all day, and still stop from time to time to sniff out a shrub or two. After a quarter of a mile, they left the pavement and turned onto a plowed dirt road meandering along an active stream named on the maps as Martha's Brook. Kate loved crossing the picturesque, low-walled fieldstone bridges that spanned the water; in part, she had chosen this route because of them.

By the end of the first mile, her thoughts had begun to separate themselves from the run. For the next two or three miles, she knew, her ideas would flow more freely, her imagination more clearly, than in any other situation. Following a kaleidoscope of notions, a kind of sorting-out process, her mind settled on the breast biopsy. Perhaps under the stress of exhaustion, Ellen's deteriorating condition, and the rest of the chaos in her life, she actually *had* made a mistake. For a time, the grisly thought held sway, bringing with it a most unpleasant tightness in her gut. Gradually, though, the truth reappeared, emerging like a phoenix from the ashes of her self-doubt. The cells she had read had been, she was certain, cancerous. But if they had been, then somewhere a switch had been made and later reversed. But how? who? The broken cryostat was, she decided, part of the puzzle. Sheila? Possible. But why? The images led into those of other tissues, other cells—the ovaries of Beverly Vitale and Ginger Rittenhouse. Ever since the discovery of anthranilic acid in her own vitamins, Kate had, several times a day, been checking herself for bruises and wondering if pockets of scar tissue in her ovaries had already made a mockery of their discussions about having children. She had to find out. The answer, almost certainly, lay in the Omnicenter, and more specifically, in the data banks of Carl Horner's Monkeys.

Kate was heading down a steep grade toward the first of the fieldstone overpasses when the blue BMW crested the hill behind her and accelerated. Immersed in the run and her thoughts, she lost several precious seconds after hearing the engine before she turned to it. The speeding automobile made a sharp, unmistakably deliberate swing to the right and headed straight for her. There was no time to think. There was only time to react. The waist-high wall of the bridge was only a few feet away. A single step, and she dove for the top of it. She was in midair when the BMW hit her just below her right knee. The impact spun her in a horizontal pinwheel. She struck the edge of the wall midthigh and then tumbled over it. As she fell, she heard the crunch of metal against stone and the agonizing cry of her dog.

The fall, twelve feet from the top of the wall, was over before she could make any physical adjustment whatsoever. She landed on her back in a drift of half-frozen snow; air exploded from her lungs, and a branch from a rotting log tore through her sweatshirt and her right side, just below her ribs. Desperately, she tried to draw in a breath. For five seconds, ten, nothing would move. Finally, she felt a whisper of air, first in the back of her throat and then in her chest. She tried to deepen her effort, but a searing pain from her side cut her short. She touched the pain and then checked the fingertips of her tan woolen gloves. They were soaked with blood.

Frantically, she tried to sort out what had happened. She had been hit. Roscoe had been hit, too. Possibly killed. It had not been an accident. Whoever was driving had tried to run them down. Gingerly, she tested her hands and then her legs. Her right leg throbbed, and her right foot, which was dangling in the icy water of the brook, seemed twisted at an odd angle. *Please, God, don't let it be broken*. There was pain, but, gratefully, there was full movement as well.

At that moment, overhead, a car door opened and closed. She turned toward the noise, but could see nothing. It took several seconds to realize why. She was quite literally buried in the fog. From somewhere above and to her left, a branch snapped; then another. The driver of the car was making his way down the steep embankment, more than likely to check the completeness of his work. Could he see where she was? Possibly not. The fog might well be concealing her, at least from farther away than ten feet or so. Carefully, she slipped off her gold cap and stuffed it into the snow. The burning rent in her side was making it hard to concentrate. Should she try crawling away beneath the fog? Would her battered legs even hold weight? Her back was hurting. Should she test it, roll to one side? Could she?

From farther to her left, she heard still another snap and then a soft splash and a groan. Her pursuer had stepped or slipped into the brook. It was definitely a man, or perhaps there were two. She thought about Roscoe. Was he still alive? Was he helpless? in pain? The images sickened her.

For a time, there was silence. Kate peered into the mist, but could see nothing. The pain in her legs, back, and side sent chilly tears down her cheeks. Then she heard it, a soft crunch, still downstream from where she was lying, but almost certainly moving in her direction. She swept her hand over the snow, searching for a rock or a stick of some sort. Her fingers touched and then curled about a dead branch, perhaps an inch and a half in diameter. She drew it toward her. Was it too long, too unwieldy, to use? She would get one swing, if that, and no more. Again, she jiggled the branch. It seemed unentangled, but she would not know for sure until she made her move.

Suddenly, she saw movement to her left, the legs and gloved hand of a man, not ten feet away. Dangling from his hand, swinging loosely back and forth, was a tire wrench.

Kate drew in a breath, held it, and tensed. At any moment she would be seen. The legs were just turning toward her when she lunged, rising painfully to her knees and swinging the branch in the same motion. Her weapon, three feet long with several protruding wooden spikes, came free of the snow and connected with the side of the man's knee. He dropped instantly to the water, as much from the surprise and location of the blow as from its force.

Ignoring the pain in her legs and side, Kate stood up, readying the branch for another swing. It was then she saw her attacker's face.

"Bill!" she cried, staring at the wild-eyed apparition. Her hesitation was costly. Zimmermann lashed out with his feet, sweeping her legs out from under her and sending her down heavily against the rocks and into the shallow, icy water. The wrench lay in the snow, just to his right. Zimmermann grabbed at it and still on his knees in the brook, swung wildly. Sparks showered from a small boulder, inches from Kate's hip. She rolled to her left as he swung again, the blow glancing off her thigh. Another spin and she was free of the water, scrambling for footing on the icy rocks and snow. Zimmermann, still clutching the wrench, crawled from the brook and dove at her ankles. He grabbed the leg of her sweatpants, but she was on her feet with enough leverage to jerk away. Before he could make another lunge, she was off, stumbling along the bank and then under the fieldstone bridge.

The ground fog, once her shield, was now her enemy. Again and again, she slipped on rocks she could not see and tripped over fallen logs. From the grunts and cries behind her, though, she could tell that Zimmermann was encountering similar difficulties. Still, the man was coming. She had been so stupid not to have considered that he might be involved in the evil at the Omnicenter, so foolish to think that he didn't know what was going on.

She glanced over her shoulder. Zimmermann, visible from the chest up, was bobbing along not thirty yards behind her. He was over six feet tall, and the deep snow was, she feared, more difficult for her to negotiate than it was for him. In addition, she was hobbled by the tightness and pain in her leg where the fender of Zimmermann's car had struck. She had only two advantages: her conditioning and her knowledge of the area. If the man caught up with her, she knew neither would matter. She risked another check behind her. He was closer, unquestionably closer. The snow was slowing her down too much. She cut to her left and into the brook. There, at least, Zimmermann's longer legs would be no advantage, possibly even a hindrance. The frigid, ankle-high water sloshed in her running shoes and bathed her lower legs in pain. Could she outrun or at least outlast him? It was possible, but one slip, one misplaced branch, and it would be over for her. She had to get back to the road. Either back to the road or . . . or hide.

She slowed, casting about for familiar landmarks. Somewhere nearby was a culvert, a steel tube, perhaps three feet across, running fifty or so feet through the high embankment on which the road had been built. If she could find it, and if it were not blocked, she could crawl inside, hoping that Zimmermann would not see her or, even if he did, would be too broad across the shoulders to follow.

She glanced downstream just as the man fell. In seconds, however, he was on his feet and, arms flailing for balance, was again beginning to close on her. If she was to do something, anything, it had to be soon. At that moment, she saw what she had been seeking. It was a huge old elm, sheared in two by lightning, its upper half forming a natural bridge across Martha's Brook. Fifty yards beyond it, if her memory hadn't failed her, the stream would bend sharply to the left, and just beyond the bend, at about knee level, would be the culvert that Roscoe had discovered two or three years before.

She ducked beneath the elm and ran low to the water, her eyes barely above the fog. At the bend, she dropped to all fours, and began crawling along the icy embankment. *Please, be there. Be there.* Frozen chunks of snow scraped her face, and rocks tore away the knees of her sweatpants. She felt a fullness in her throat and coughed, spattering the snow beneath her with blood, more than likely, she knew, from a punctured lung.

She crawled ahead, sliding one hand along the slope at the height where she remembered the culvert. Her hopes had begun to fade when she saw it. The diameter was even less than she had thought, nearer two feet than three, but it was still wide enough for her to fit. A fine trickle of water suggested that the small pond on the other side of the embankment was lower than her exit point. From somewhere in the fog, not far back, came a splash. Zimmermann was close. Kate ducked into the dank, rusty pipe; inches at a time, she began to pull herself toward the faint, silver-gray light at the other end.

The culvert, coarse and corroded, was painfully cold. With the exertion of her run now past, Kate was beginning to freeze. Her feet, especially her toes, throbbed, and the sound of her teeth chattering like castanets was resonating through the metal tube. Again she coughed. Again there was the spattering of blood. She was, perhaps, a third of the way along when she heard him, crunching about in the snow behind her. Fearing the noise her movement was making, she stopped, biting down on the collar of her sweatshirt to stop the chattering.

"Kate, I know you're hurt," he called out. "I want to help you. No more violence. We can work things out."

Did he know where she was? Dammit, why couldn't she stop shaking?

"Kate, you want to know about the drugs, about whether or not you are sterile, about how you can stop your friend's bleeding. I can answer all your questions. I can get you someplace warm."

Frightened of the bleeding in her chest and numb in those areas of her body that weren't in merciless pain, Kate found herself actually considering the man's offer. Warm. He had promised she would be warm. Warmth and answers. Maybe she *should* try and reason with him. She forced her mind to focus on the wrench and bit down on her sweatshirt all the harder.

"You know," Zimmermann called out, "even if you make it back, no one is going to believe your story. I have my whereabouts at this moment completely vouched for. You're crazy and a pathological liar. Everyone knows that. You're the talk of the hospital. Half the people think you're on drugs, and the other half think you're just plain sick. I'm the only person who can help you, Kate. I'm the only one who can save your friend. I'm the only one who can get you warm. Now come on over here, and let's talk."

Twenty feet away from where Zimmermann stood, Kate buried her face in the crook of her arm and struggled against the insanity that was telling her the man meant what he was saying about no violence.

"Suit yourself," she heard him say. "It's your funeral. Yours and your friend's."

Steaming coffee. Crackling, golden fire. Sunshine. White beach. Flannel. Down comforter. Fur slippers. Stifling her sobs in the sleeve of her sweatshirt, Kate fought the fear and the pain and the cold with images of anything that was warm. Cocoa. Wood stove. Jacuzzi. Tea. Quartz heater. Electric blanket. Soup. Behind her now, there was only silence. Had he left? She strained to hear the engine of his car. Had he found the culvert and crossed over the road to wait by the far end? Her legs and arms were leadened by the cold. Could she even make it out? *Damn him*, she thought, forcing herself ahead an inch. He knew how to save Ellen. *Damn him*. Another inch. He even knew whether she herself had been sterilized or not. *Damn him. Damn him. Damn him.* The silver-gray hole grew fainter. Her eyes closed. Her other senses clouded. Seconds later, what little consciousness remained slipped away.

◆

It was as if a decade had melted away. Jared faced his father as he had so many times during the confused years of Lisa and Vermont, struggling to remain reasonably calm and maintain eye contact.

"Kate is sick, son. Very sick," Samuels said. "I would suggest we make arrangements for her hospitalization as soon as possible, and as soon as that is done, you should begin to separate your career from her. She will bring you down. I promise you that. Martha Mitchell did it to her husband, and I assure you, Kate will do it to you—if she hasn't already. I've contacted Sol Creighton at Laurel Hill. He has a bed waiting for her, and he says we have grounds for commitment if necessary. With some time, and perhaps some medication, he assures me that even the worst sociopathic personality can be helped."

"Dad, stop using that word. You have no right to diagnose her."

"Jared, face the facts. Kate is a lovely woman. I care for her very much. But she is a liar, and quite possibly a liar who completely believes her own fabrications. I know she looks perfectly fine and sounds logical, but the hallmark of a sociopath is exactly that physical and verbal glibness. The only way to realize what one is dealing with is to catch her in lie after lie."

"But—"

"Do you really think someone other than Kate sent that letter to the papers about Bobby Geary?"

"I don't know."

"And the chemist, and the Ashburton Foundation, and the nurse at Stonefield. Do you think they were all lying?"

"I don't—"

"And what about the biopsy? You tell me everyone in Kate's department says she made a mistake. The truth is right there in the slides. Yet there is Kate, insisting she did nothing wrong."

Samuels withdrew a cigar from his humidor, tested

the aroma along its full length, and then clipped and lit it. He motioned for Jared to have one if he wished.

Jared glanced at his watch, made an expression of distaste, and shook his head. "Christ, Dad, it's only eight-thirty in the morning."

Samuels shrugged. "It's my morning and it's my cigar."

Jared looked across the desk at his father, trim and confident, wearing the trappings of success and power as comfortably as he wore his slippers. Unable to speak, Jared stared down at the gilded feet of his father's desk, resting on the exquisite oriental carpet. A secret weapon, that's what Kate had called him. A source of strength for her. She had spoken the words to his father, but they were really meant for him. With tremendous effort, he brought his eyes up.

"I hear what you are saying, Dad. And I understand what you want."

"And?"

"I can't go along with it. Kate says she's innocent of any lying, and I believe her."

"You what?"

Jared felt himself wither before the man's glare. "I believe her. And I'm going to do what I can to help clear her." There was a strength in his words that surprised him. He stood up. "I'll tell you something else, Dad. If I find that she's telling the truth, you're going to have a hell of a lot of explaining to do."

Samuels rose, anger sparking from his eyes. "I seem to recall a conversation similar to this. We were in that matchbox office of yours in Vermont. I warned you not to marry that rootless hippie you were living with. I told you there was nothing to her. You stood before me then just as you are now and as much as threw me out of your office. Two years later your wife and daughter were gone, and you were crawling to me for help. Have you forgotten?"

"Dad, that was then. This is—"

"Have you forgotten?"

"No, I haven't."

"Have you forgotten the money and the time I spent trying to find that woman despite my own personal feelings about her?"

"Look, I don't want to fight."

"Get out," Samuels said evenly. "When you come to your senses, when you discover once again that I was right, call me."

"Dad, I—"

"I said get out." Samuels turned his back and stared out the window.

As Jared opened the door, he nearly collided with Jocelyn Trent, who was standing up and backing away at the same time. Quickly, he closed the door behind him.

"What were you doing there?" he asked.

"Jared, please, don't make me explain." She took him by the arm, led him to the hall closet, and began helping him on with his coat. "Meet me in ten minutes," she whispered in his ear. "The little variety store on the corner of Charles and Mount Vernon. I have something important for you, for Kate actually."

The study door opened just as she was letting Jared out. Winfield Samuels stood, arms folded tightly across his chest, and watched him go.

Even dressed down, in pants and a plain wool overcoat, Jocelyn Trent turned heads. Jared stood by the variety store and watched several drivers slow as they passed where she was waiting to cross Charles Street. He left the shelter of the recessed doorway and met her at the corner. Their relationship, while cordial, had never approached a friendship in any sense. His father had taken some pains to keep the interaction between them superficial, and neither had ever been inclined to push matters further.

"Thank you for meeting me like this," she said, guiding him back to the shadow of the doorway. "I don't have much time, so I'll say what I have to say and go."

"Fair enough."

"Jared, I'm leaving your father. I intend to tell him this afternoon."

"I'm sorry," he said. "I know how much he cares for you."

"Does he? I think you know as well as I do that caring isn't one of Win Samuels's strong suits. It's too bad, too, because strange as it might sound, I think I might actually love him."

"Then why—"

"Please, Jared. I really don't have much time, and what I'm doing is very hard for me. Just know that I have my reasons—for leaving him and for giving you this." She handed him a sealed envelope. "Kate's a wonderful woman. She doesn't deserve the treatment he's giving her. I've been completely loyal to your father. That is until now. I know how hard it is to stand up to him. Lord knows I've wanted to enough. I think you did the right thing back there."

"Jocelyn, do you know if my father is lying or not? It's very important."

She smiled. "I'm aware of how important it is. I was listening at the door, remember? The answer is that I don't know, at least not for sure. There's a phone number in that envelope, Jared. Go someplace quiet and dial it. If my suspicions about that number are correct, you should be able to decide for yourself which of the two, Kate or your father, is telling the truth."

"I don't understand," he said. "What is this number? Where did you get it?"

"Please, I don't want to say any more because there's a small chance I might be wrong. Let's just leave it that the number is one your father has called from time to time since I've known him. I handle all of the household bills, including the phone bill, so I know. A year or two ago I accidentally overheard part of a conversation he was having. Some of what I heard disturbed me, so I noted down the exact time of the call. That's how I learned this number. I don't want to say any more. Okay?"

"Okay, but—"

"I wish you well, Jared. Both of you. The things I overheard Kate say last night have really helped me make some decisions I should have made a long time ago. I hope that what I've done will help her." She took his hand, squeezed it for a moment, and was gone.

Jared watched her hurry up Mt. Vernon Street; then he tore open the plain envelope. The phone number, printed on a three-by-five card, was in the 213 area. Los Angeles.

He drove to his office, trying to imagine what the number might be. Once at his desk, he sat for nearly a minute staring at the card before he finally dialed.

A woman, clearly awakened by the call, answered on the third ring. "Hello?" she said.

Jared struggled for a breath and pressed the receiver so tightly against his ear that it hurt.

"Hello?" the woman said again. "Is anybody there?"

Even after so many years he knew. "Lisa?" He could barely say the word.

"Yes. Who is this? Who is this, please?"

Slowly, Jared set the receiver back in its cradle.

# 14

## Friday 21 December

It was pressure pain from the pipe more than cold that tugged Kate free of a sleep that was deeper than sleep. In the twilight moment before she was fully conscious, she imagined herself buried alive, the victim of some twisted, vicious kidnapper. In just a few hours she would suffocate or freeze to death. Jared had that little time to raise her ransom, and the only one he could turn to, she knew, was his father. The sound of Win Samuels's laughter echoed in her tomb, growing louder and louder until with a scream she came fully awake.

She was on her back. Her lips and cheeks were caked with dried and frozen blood. Dim light from the ends of the culvert barely defined the corroding metal, just a foot or so from her face. *Lie still*, she thought. *Just don't move. Sleep until Jared comes. Close your eyes again and sleep.* The thoughts were so comforting, so reassuring, that she had to struggle to remember that they were no more than the cold, lying to her, paralyzing her from within. For a time, all she could think about was sleep, sleep and Zimmermann's taunting warning that even if she survived, no one would believe her story. Sick, crazy, drugged up, that's what they all believed. It was hopeless for her. Zimmermann said it, and he was right. Over and over again, in a voice as soothing as a warm tub, the cold spoke to her of hopelessness and sleep.

Kate flexed her hands and her feet, struggling against the downy comfort of the lies and the inertia. *Remain still and you will die. Surrender to the cold and you will never see Jared again; never get the chance to tell him how much his letter and his decision mean to you.*

She tried pushing herself along with her feet, but could not bend her knees enough to get leverage. She had to see him. She had to tell him that she, too, was ready to make choices. Aroused by the aching in her legs and the far deeper pain in her side, she twisted and wriggled onto her belly. She had been wrong to allow Willoughby to nominate her without trying harder to see things from Jared's perspective. She had been wrong. Now she could only admit that and hope Jared believed it had been he, and not the devastating events, who had helped her see the true order of her priorities.

She was less than halfway from the far end of the pipe. The fog seemed to have lifted. She could now make out the silhouettes of trees against the white sky. A few more feet and there was enough light to read the numbers on her watch. Eleven fifteen. She had been entombed for over an hour. *Was Zimmermann still out there? Could he possibly have stayed around in the snow and the cold for over an hour?*

Driven by the need to see Jared again, to set matters straight, she worked herself arm over arm along the icy metal. A foot from the edge she stopped and listened. Beyond the soft wisp of her own breathing, there was nothing. Had an hour been long enough? Wouldn't Zimmermann have left, concerned about having his car attract attention? Finally, she abandoned her attempts at reasoning through the situation. If he was out there, waiting, there was little she would be able to do. If he wasn't, she would overcome whatever pain and cold she had to and make it home. There were amends to be made.

With a muted cry of pain, she curled her fingers around the edge of the culvert and pulled.

"We're sorry, but we are unavailable to take your call right now. Please wait for the tone, leave your name, number, and the time, and Kate or Jared will get back to you as soon as possible."

"Kate, it's just me again. Ignore the previous two messages. I'm not going to stay at the office, and I'm not going to speak with Reese. I'm coming home. Please don't go anywhere. Thanks. I love you."

Something was wrong. In almost five years of marriage, Jared had never felt so intense a connection to his wife. With that heightened sensitivity and three unanswered calls home had come a foreboding that weighed on his chest like an anvil. The feeling was irrational he told himself over and again, groundless and foolish. She was at a neighbor's or on a run. With his MG still in the office garage, where it had been all week, he had taken her Volvo; but still, there were plenty of places to which she could have walked.

He left the city and crossed the Mystic River Bridge, the rational part of him struggling to keep the Volvo under seventy. She was fine. There was some perfectly logical explanation why she hadn't answered his calls the past hour and a half. He just hadn't hit on it. Certainly, his concentration and powers of reason were not all they could be. It had been one hell of a morning.

The call to California, the sound of Lisa's voice, had left him at once elated and sickened. His father had lied. He had lied about Lisa and possibly about Stonefield as well. Jared cringed at the thought of how close he had come to siding with the man. Silently, he gave thanks that he had made his decision, set down on paper his commitment to Kate, before he had learned the truth about his father. The man had been paying Lisa off all those years. That conclusion was as inescapable as it was disgusting.

They were some pair, his ex-wife and Winfield. One totally vapid, one totally evil. Some goddamn pair.

Then there was Stacy. As he weaved along past Route 1's abysmal stretch of fast-food huts, factory outlets, budget motels, garish restaurants, and raunchy nightclubs, Jared ached with thoughts of her. What did she believe had become of her father? Would there ever be a way he could reenter her life without destroying whatever respect she had for her mother, possibly thereby destroying the girl herself? Kate would have a sense of what was right to do. Together they could decide. Damn, but he had come close, so close, to blowing it all.

The house was deserted. Kate's running gear was gone, and so was Roscoe. It had been several hours since his first call—far too long. He checked the area around the house and yard. Nothing. There were but two choices: wait some more or call the police. The heavy sense of apprehension, so ill-defined while he was in Boston, seemed more acute. There was no sense in waiting.

As he walked to the phone in the kitchen, he glanced out the front window. Three neighborhood children, all around eight, were trudging up the driveway pulling a sled. On the sled was a cardboard carton. The path to the front door, only as wide as a shovel, was too narrow for the sled. Two youngsters stayed behind, kneeling by the box, while the third ran up the walk. Jared met her at the door.

"Mr. Samuels, it's Roscoe," she panted. "We found him in the snow."

Jared, a dreadful emptiness in his gut, raced past the girl to the sled. Roscoe, packed in blankets, looked up and made a weak attempt to rise. His tail wagged free of the cover and slapped excitedly against the cardboard.

"His leg is broke," one of the other children, a boy, said simply.

Jared held the dog down and pulled back the blanket. Roscoe's right leg was fractured, the bone protruding from a gash just above the knee. "Come kids," he said, scooping up the box. "Come inside, please, and we'll take care of Rosc. Do you think you can take me to where you found him?"

"Yes, I know," the little girl said. "We have teacher's conference today, so no school. We were sledding down the hill to the bridge, and there he was, just lying in the snow. My mom gave us the blankets and the box."

"It looks like he's been hit by a car," Jared said. "Kids, this is important. Did any of you see Kate—you know, my wife?" The children shook their heads. He reached down and stroked the dog's forehead. Blood trickled from the corner of his mouth where his teeth had torn through. "Well, let's get some help for Roscoe; then we'll go back to the spot where you found him." He felt consumed by feelings of panic and dread, and struggled to keep a note of calm in his voice. Frightened, confused children would be no asset to him—or to Kate.

Minutes later three of them, Jared and two of the youngsters, were in the car. The third had been left behind to keep the dog still and await the arrival of the veterinarian.

"Okay, kids," Jared said, "you said you were sledding near a bridge. The stone bridge over the little stream?" Both nodded enthusiastically. "Good. I know just where that is."

The short drive over the narrow, snowy road seemed endless. Finally, Jared parked the Volvo at the top of the hill and then half ran, half slid to the indentation in the snow where the children assured him they had found Roscoe. He had thought to take his parka but had not changed his slacks or loafers, and the trek from the spot into the surrounding woods was both awkward and cold. The snow around him was, save for his own footprints, smooth and unbroken. After a scanning search, he made his way back to the road and started down the hill. At his request, the children followed, one on each side of the road, checking to be sure he had not missed anything.

At the stone bridge, he stopped. There was evidence of some sort of collision at the base of the wall. A piece of granite had been sheared off, and a gouge, perhaps two feet long, extended along the wall from that point. He searched the roadway and then looked over the wall. The snow on one side of the shallow brook seemed disrupted. In the very center of the area, he saw a flash of bright yellow, partially buried in the snow.

Ordering the children to remain where they were, he raced down the steep embankment to the water. It was Kate's cap, quite deliberately, it seemed, wedged into the snow. Then, only a few feet from the cap, he saw a swatch of another color. It was blood, almost certainly, dried blood smeared across a small stretch of packed snow. There had been some kind of struggle. The marks around him made that clear. Had Kate been dragged off somewhere? He looked for signs of that, but instead noticed footprints paralleling the stream just beyond the bridge. Slipping in and out of the water, he ran to the spot. There were, he was certain, two sets. He looked overhead. The children, following his progress, had crossed the road and were peering down at him from atop the wall. The girl, he knew, lived just past the end of the road, half a mile, perhaps a bit more, away.

"Crystal," he called out, "is your mommy still home?"

"Yes."

"Can you two make it back home to her?"

"Yes."

"Please do that, then. Tell her Kate is lost and may be hurt. Ask if she can drive out here and help look for her. Okay?"

"Okay."

"And Crystal, you all did a fine job bringing Roscoe in the way you did. Hurry on home, now."

Jared stayed where he was until the crunch of the children's boots had completely vanished. Then he closed his eyes and listened within the silence for a sound, any kind of sign. He heard nothing. Increasingly aware of the cold in his feet and legs, he stepped in the deep tracks, fearing the worst, and expecting, with each stride, to have his fears become reality. A hundred yards from the bridge, the tracks turned sharply to the left and vanished into the stream.

"Kate?" He called her name once and then again. His voice was instantly swallowed by the forest and the snow. "Kate, it's me. It's Jared." There was a heaviness, a fastness, to the place and a silence that was hypnotic. As he trudged along the side of the stream looking for renewed signs, he felt the silence deepen.

Then suddenly, he knew. He felt it as surely as he felt the cold. Kate was somewhere nearby. She was nearby, and she was still. He called to her every few feet, as he ducked under a huge fallen tree and followed the stream bed in a sharp bend to the left. Then he stopped. There was something different about this place. Far to his right, embedded in the steep slope that he guessed led up to the road, was a drainage pipe. At the base of the pipe were footprints.

"Kate?" He closed his eyes and almost immediately felt a strange sense of detachment. She was not far, and she was alive. He felt it clearly. It was as if their lives, their energies, were joined by a thin, silken strand of awareness.

"Jared?" It was a word, but not a word; a sound, but not a sound. His eyes still closed, he exhaled slowly and then listened. "Jared, help me." Her voice, it seemed, was more within him than without. He worked his way along the embankment, calling her name. Then he shouted it several times into the long, empty culvert. Finally, hoping for a better vantage point, he hauled himself up to the road.

She was there, face down, a third of the way down the slope on the far side, still clawing, though feebly, at the snow. Jared leapt over the edge, sliding and tumbling down to her. Gently, he turned her onto his lap. Her hair was matted and frozen, her face spattered with blood. Her warm-up suit, shredded in spots, was stiffened with ice. Her eyes were closed.

"Katey, it's me," he said. "I've got you. You're going to be all right."

He worked her hair free from where it had frozen to her face. Her breathing was shallow, each expiration accompanied by a soft whimper of pain.

"Honey, can you hear me?"

Her eyes opened and then slowly focused on his face. "Oh, Jared . . . please . . . Roscoe . . ."

He kissed her. "He's hurt, but he's okay. Dr. Finnerty's coming to get him. What about you? Have you broken anything?"

"Ribs," she managed in a voice that was half groan, half cough. "Lung . . . may . . . be . . . punctured."

"Jesus. Kate, I'm going to lift you up. I'll try not to hurt you, but we've got to get up to the road."

With strength enhanced by the urgency of the moment, he had no trouble lifting her. Negotiating the steep, icy slope, however, was another matter. Footing was treacherous, and every two or three baby steps upward, he was forced to set her down in order to regain purchase. Inches at a time, they moved ahead. When he finally heaved over the top of the slope onto the roadside, Jared fell to his knees, clutching her to his chest and gasping for air.

Helplessly, he sat there, warming her face with his breath and watching the minute but steady rise and fall of her chest. Then through the silence surrounding their breathing, he heard the soft hum of an approaching car. Moments later, a beige station wagon rounded the bend ahead of them. In the front seat were a woman and two very excited children.

"Way to go, Crystal," Jared whispered. He put his lips by Kate's ear. "Help is here, honey. Just hang in there. Help is here."

Her eyes opened momentarily. Her lips tightened in a grim attempt at a smile. "Zimmermann did this," she said.

◆

Jared paced from the small, well-appointed quiet room out to the hall and back. Mary T. Henderson Hospital was reputed to be among the best community hospitals in the state, but it was still a community hospital, only a fraction of the size of the Boston teaching facilities.

Nearly three hours had passed since the surgeon, Lee Jordan, had taken Kate into the operating room. Jordan was, according to the emergency room physician, the finest surgeon on the hospital staff. Jared had to laugh at his total surprise when the distinguished, gray-templed man his mind had projected as Lee Jordan turned out, in fact, to be a slender, extremely attractive woman in her midforties. Would he ever truly overcome all the years of programming?

Kate's wound was a bad one. The gash, Jordan had explained, required debridement in the operating room, and in all likelihood, an open-chest procedure would be needed to repair the laceration to her lung.

Jared had been allowed to see Kate briefly during the wait for the OR team to arrive, but there had been no real chance to discuss any details of William Zimmermann's attempt on her life. An officer from the Essex Police Department had come, taken what little information was available from him, and left with promises of state police involvement as soon as Kate could assist them with a statement. Meanwhile, it was doubtful that Jared's word would be enough to issue an arrest warrant.

Jared was studying the small plaque proclaiming that the quiet room was the gift of a couple named Berman when Lee Jordan emerged through the glass doors to the surgical suite. Her face, which had been fresh and alert on her arrival in the emergency ward four hours before, was gray and drawn, and for a moment, he feared the worst.

"Your wife's okay," Jordan said as soon as she was close enough to speak without raising her voice. She appraised him. "Are you?"

"I . . . yes, I'm okay." He braced himself against the

wall. "It's just that for a moment there I was frightened that . . ."

Jordan patted him on the shoulder. "You married one tough lady, my friend," she said. "There's frostbite on the tips of her toes, ears, and nose, but it looks like she came in from the cold in time to save everything. The tear in her lung wasn't too, too big. I sewed it up and then fixed that gash in her side. She's in for a few pretty achy days, but I hope nothing worse than that. You'll be able to see her in half an hour or so. I've asked the nurses to come and get you."

"Thank you. Thank you very much."

"I'm glad she's all right," Dr. Lee Jordan said.

It was after five by the time Jared arrived home. Medicated and obviously affected by her anesthesia, Kate had managed only to squeeze his hand and acknowledge that she knew he was in her hospital room. Even so, Dr. Jordan had warned him that she would, in all likelihood, remember nothing of the first five or six hours postop.

Roscoe was another story. As soon as Jared arrived at the veterinarian's, the dog was up and hopping about his cage, mindless of his plaster cast and showing no residual effects from the anesthesia that had allowed a metal plate to be screwed in place across the fracture in his leg. After seeing Kate with half a dozen tubes running into and out of her body, the sight of the battered and broken animal was the last straw. Zimmermann would pay. Whatever it took, Jared vowed, the man would pay dearly.

Exhausted from the day and, in fact, from almost thirty-six hours without sleep, Jared brought a bottle of Lowenbräu Dark to the bedroom, finished half of it in two long draughts, and then stripped to his underwear and stretched out on the bed. There was little sense, the nurses had told him, in returning to the hospital before morning. So be it. He would rest and read and say a dozen prayers of thanks for Kate's life and for Roscoe's, and for Jocelyn Trent, and for being allowed to learn the sad truth about his father before it was too late.

He had bunched up two pillows and was looking through the magazines on the bedside table when he noticed their telephone answering machine. It had been on since Kate left for her run, and there were a number of messages. The first three were from Jared himself, another was from Ellen, and still another was from one of the firm's VIP clients, who had apparently been assured that Winfield's son wouldn't mind in the least being called at home. The final message was for Kate from a man named Arlen Paquette.

"Kate Bennett, this is Arlen Paquette from Redding," the man said in a rushed, anxious tone. "I won't be alone for more than a few seconds. I have answers for you. Many answers. Come to the subbasement of the Omnicenter at precisely eight-thirty tonight. Bring help. There may be trouble. Please, trust me. I know what we've done to you, but please trust me. He's coming. I've got to go. Good-bye."

Jared raced for pen and paper; then he played the message over and wrote it down verbatim. Answers. At last someone was promising answers. He scrambled into a pair of jeans, a work shirt, and a sweater. It was already after seven. There would barely be time to get to Metro by eight-thirty, let alone to try and pick up police help on the way. He would have to hurry to the subbasement of the Omnicenter and rely on himself. *The Omnicenter*. He threw on his parka and rushed to Kate's Volvo. That was Zimmermann's place. The man would be there. He felt certain of it.

"I'm coming for you, you fucker," he panted as he skidded out of the drive and down Salt Marsh Road.

# 15

## Friday 21 December

Like so many works of greatness, the formulas derived by William Zimmermann's father were elegant in their simplicity. Even without Zimmermann's help in translating the explanatory notes from the German, Arlen Paquette suspected he would have been able to follow the steps involved in the synthesis of the hormone Estronate 250—especially in the subbasement Omnicenter laboratory, which was specifically equipped for the job.

The message to call Cyrus Redding had been waiting at the front desk when Paquette returned to the Ritz from surreptitiously recording a conversation with Norton Reese during which the gloating administrator had incriminated himself and a technician named Pierce a number of times. The compact recorder still hooked to his belt, Paquette had entered the elevator to his floor.

"I was beginning to think you had run away," a man's voice said from behind.

Startled, the chemist whirled. It was Redding's bodyguard, a wiry, seemingly emotionless man whom Paquette had never heard called any name other than Nunes.

"Why, hello," Paquette said, wishing he had stayed at the tavern on the way back for a third drink. "I just picked up a message from Mr. Redding, but it says to call him at the Darlington number. Is he—?"

"He's there," Nunes said, showing nothing to dispel Paquette's image of a gunman whose loyalty to the pharmaceutical magnate had no limits. "He's waiting for your call."

From that moment on, Paquette had barely been out of Nunes's sight.

Now, in the bright fluorescence of the subbasement laboratory, Paquette glanced first at Zimmermann and then at Nunes and prayed that the forty-five minutes until eight-thirty would pass without incident. A deal had been struck between Redding and Zimmermann—money in exchange for a set of formulas. Redding had let him in on that much. However, the presence of the taciturn thug suggested that Redding anticipated trouble, or perhaps he had no intention of honoring his end of the bargain—quite possibly both.

"Okay, that's seven minutes," Zimmermann said, seconds before the mechanical timer rang out. "There's a shortcut my father used at this juncture, but I never did completely understand it. Dr. Paquette, I suggest you just go on to the next page and continue the steps in order. He performed these next reactions over in that corner, and he checked the purity of the distillate with that spectrophotometer."

Paquette nodded and moved around the slate workbench to the area Zimmermann had indicated. The Omnicenter director was neither biochemist nor genius, but he had observed his father at work enough to be able to oversee each step of the synthesis. And oversee he had—each maneuver and each microdrop of the way.

The laboratory was quite remarkable. Hidden behind a virtually invisible, electronically controlled door, it had no less than three sophisticated spectrophotometers, each programmed to assess the consistency of the hormone at various stages of its synthesis and, through feedback mechanisms, to adjust automatically the chemical reaction where needed. It was a small area, perhaps fifteen feet by thirty, but its designer had paid meticulous attention to the maximum use of space.

"Did your father design all this?" Paquette asked.

"Be careful, Doctor, your reagent is beginning to overheat," Zimmermann said, ignoring the question as he had most others about his father. "Excuse me, but are you timing a reaction I don't know about?"

"No, why?"

"That's the third time you've looked at your watch in the past ten minutes."

"Oh, that." Paquette hoped his laugh did not sound too nervous. Out of the corner of his eye, he saw Nunes, seated on a tall stool at the end of the lab bench, adjust his position to hear better. "A habit dating back to high school, perhaps beyond, that's all."

He had made up his mind that there was no way he would complete the Estronate synthesis and turn the three notebooks over to Nunes. That act, he suspected, would be his last. He and Zimmermann were not scripted to leave the laboratory alive. The more the evening had worn on, the more certain he had become of that. He glanced at the metal hand plate to the right of the entrance. Though unmarked, it had to be the means of opening the door.

There were less than thirty minutes to go. If Kate Bennett had gotten his message, and if she had taken it seriously, she would be waiting, with help, in the storage area outside the laboratory.

Paquette's plan was simple. At eight thirty-five, allowing five minutes for any delay on Bennett's part, he would announce the need to use the men's room. They had passed one a floor above on their way in. With surprise on their side, whatever muscle Bennett had brought with her should have a decent chance at overpowering Nunes. If there was no one in the storage room when the door slid open, he would have to improvise. There was one thing of which he was sure: once outside the laboratory, he was not going back in. God, but he wished he had a drink.

Traffic into the city was inordinately light for a Friday evening, and it was clear to Jared that barring any monstrous delays, he would make it to Metro with time to spare. Still, he used his horn and high beams to clear his way down Route 1.

*Risks. Bring help. There may be trouble.* With each mile, Arlen Paquette's warning grew in his thoughts. He had made a mistake in not calling the Boston police before he left Essex. He could see that now. Still, what would he have said? How lengthy an explanation would have been required? His father, he knew, could pick up the phone and with no explanation whatsoever have half a dozen officers waiting for him at the front door to the Omnicenter. Answers. Paquette had promised answers. Perhaps for Kate's sake it was worth swallowing his pride and anger and calling Winfield. Then he realized that the issue went far deeper than pride and anger. The man could not be trusted. Not now, not ever again.

*Bring help.* Jared pulled off the highway and skidded to a stop by a bank of pay phones. It was seven forty-five. He was twenty minutes, twenty-five at the most, from the Omnicenter. There was still time to do something, but what? With no clear idea of what he was going to say, he called the Boston Police Department.

"I'd—ah—I'd like to speak to Detective Finn, please," he heard his own voice say. "Yes, that's right, Martin Finn. I'm sorry, I don't know what district. Four, maybe."

Finn. The thought, Jared saw now, had been in the back of his mind all along. Tough but fair: that's how his father had described the man. If that was the case, then it would take only the promise of some answers to get him to the Omnicenter.

Finn was not at his desk.

"Has he gone home for the night?" Jared asked of the officer who answered Finn's phone. "Well, does anyone know?" . . . "Samuels. Jared Samuels. I'm a lawyer.

Detective Finn knows me. What is your name?" . . .
"Well, please Sergeant, this is very urgent and there isn't
much time. Could you see if you could get a message to
Lieutenant Finn to meet me at eight-fifteen at the front
entrance to the Omnicenter at Metropolitan Hospital?" . . .
"That's right, in half an hour. And Sergeant, if you can't
locate him, could you or some other officer meet me
instead?" . . . "I don't know if it's a matter of life or death
or not. Listen, I don't have time to explain. Please, just
try."

Jared hurried back to the Volvo, wishing he had more
of an idea of who Arlen Paquette was or at least of what
was awaiting him at the Omnicenter. It was exactly eight
o'clock when he sped over the crest of a long upgrade and
saw, ahead and to his right, the glittering tiara of Boston at
night.

Perhaps it was the tension of the moment, perhaps
the six hours since his last drink; whatever the reason,
Arlen Paquette felt his hands beginning to shake and his
concentration beginning to waver. He pulled a gnarled
handkerchief from his back pocket and dabbed at the cold
sweat on his forehead and upper lip. It was only ten
minutes past the hour. The hormone synthesis, which had
proceeded flawlessly, was well over half completed.

"Are you all right?" Zimmermann asked.

"Fine, I'm fine," Paquette said, clutching a beaker of
ice water with two hands to keep its contents from slosh-
ing about. "I . . . I'd like to talk with Mr. Nunes for a
moment. Privately."

"Why?" Zimmermann asked with a defensiveness in
his voice. "There's no problem with the procedure up to
now. I assure you of that. You are doing an excellent job of
following my father's notes. Just keep going."

"It's not that. Listen, I'll be right back. Nunes," he
whispered, his back turned to Zimmermann, "I need a
drink."

"No booze until you finish this work. Mr. Redding's orders." As Nunes leaned forward to respond, the coat of his perfectly tailored suit fell away just enough for Paquette to see the holstered revolver beneath his left arm. Any doubt he harbored regarding his fate once the formulas were verified vanished.

"Nunes, have a heart."

The gunman's only response was an impatient nod in the direction of the incomplete experiment.

"Any problem?" Zimmermann called out.

"No problem," Nunes said as Paquette shuffled back. "Say, Dr. Zimmermann, where's the nearest john?"

Paquette slowed and listened. In less than twenty minutes he planned to ask the same question and wait for Nunes to open the door for him. Then an unexpected push from behind, and the man would be in the arms of the police. It was perfect, provided, of course, that Kate Bennett had gotten his message.

William Zimmermann pointed to the wall behind the gunman. "See that recessed handle in the wall right under that shelf? Just twist it and pull."

Nunes did as he was instructed, and a three-foot-wide block of shelves pulled away from the wall, revealing a fairly large bathroom and stall shower.

"Father had this obsession about hidden doorways and the like," Zimmermann said.

His next sentence, if there was to be one, was cut off by the beaker of ice water, which slipped from Paquette's hands and shattered on the tile floor.

Save for the security light in the front lobby, the Omnicenter was completely dark. Jared parked across the street and was beginning a walking inspection of the outside of the building when a blue and white patrol car pulled up. Martin Finn stepped out, looking in the gloom like a large block of granite with a homberg perched on top. Even at a distance, Jared could sense the man's impatience and irritation.

"I got your message," Finn said, with no more greeting than that. "What's going on?" Behind him, a uniformed officer remained at the wheel of the cruiser. The engine was still running.

"Thanks for coming so quickly," Jared said. "I . . . didn't know whom to call."

"Well?"

Jared checked the time. There were thirteen minutes. "My wife is in Henderson Hospital. Someone tried to run her down with a car earlier today while she was jogging." Finn said nothing. "She's had to have surgery, but she's going to be okay." Still nothing. "She couldn't speak much, but she said it was Dr. Zimmermann, the head of the Omnicenter, who tried to run her down and then chased her with a tire wrench."

"William Zimmermann?"

"Yes. Do you know him?"

Finn looked at him icily. "He delivered my daughter."

Inwardly, Jared groaned. "Well, he was involved in something illegal, possibly in connection with one of the big pharmaceutical houses. Kate discovered what was going on, so he tried to kill her."

"But he missed." There was neither warmth nor the slightest hint of belief in the man's voice.

"Yes, he missed." Jared swallowed back his mounting anger. There was far too much at stake and hardly time for an argument. "When I returned home from the hospital a short while ago, there was a message on our answering machine for Kate from a man named Arlen Paquette. I think he works for the drug house. He asked that she meet him here, in the subbasement of this building, and that she bring help. That's why I called you. I suspect that Zimmermann is in the middle of all this and that he's in there right now."

"In there?" Finn gestured at the darkened building.

"He said the *subbasement*."

"Mr. Samuels, Dr. Zimmermann's office is on the third floor. On the corner, right up there. I've been there several times. Now what on earth would he be doing in the subbasement?"

"I . . . I don't know." There were eleven minutes. "Look, Lieutenant, the man said exactly eight-thirty. There isn't much time."

"So you want me to go busting into a locked hospital building, looking to nail my wife's obstetrician, because you got some mysterious message on your telephone answering machine?"

"If the doors are all locked, we can get in through the tunnels. We don't have to break in. Dammit, Lieutenant, my wife was almost killed today. Do you think she's lying about the broken bones and the punctured lung?"

"No," Finn said. "Only about everything else. Mr. Samuels, I had a chance to do some checking up on your wife. She's in hot water with just about everyone in the city, it seems. Word has it she's just been fired for screwing up here at the hospital, too. Face it, counselor, you've got a sick woman on your hands. You need help, all right, but not the kind I can give."

"Then you won't come with me?" Jared could feel himself losing control.

"Mr. Samuels, because of your wife, I still have enough egg on my face to make a fucking omelet. I'll file a report if you want me to, and even get a warrant if you can give me some hard facts to justify that. But no commando stuff. Now if I were you, I'd just go on home and see about lining up some professional help for your woman."

Before he could even weigh the consequences, Jared hit the man—a roundhouse punch that landed squarely on the side of Finn's face and sent him spinning down into a pile of plowed snow. Instantly, the uniformed officer was out of the cruiser, his hand on the butt of his service revolver. Finn, a trickle of blood forming at the corner of his mouth, waved him off.

"No, Jackie," he said. "It's all right. The counselor,

here, felt he had a score to settle with me, and he just settled it." He pushed himself to his feet, still shaking off the effects of the blow. "Now, counselor, you just get the fuck out of my sight. If I hear of any trouble involving you tonight, I'm going to bust your ass from here to Toledo. Clear?"

Jared glared at the detective. "You're wrong, Finn. About my wife, about refusing to help me, about everything. You don't know how goddamn wrong you are."

He glanced at his watch, then turned and raced down the block toward the main entrance to the hospital and the stairway that would lead to the Omnicenter tunnel. There were less than five minutes left.

Visiting hours had ended. The hospital was quiet. Jared crossed the lobby as quickly as he dared without calling attention to himself and hurried down the nearest staircase. Although he used the dreary tunnels infrequently, he distinctly remembered seeing a sign indicating that the Omnicenter had been tacked onto the system. But where?

The tunnel was deserted, and it seemed even less well lighted than usual. A caravan of stretchers lined one wall, interspersed with empty, canvas industrial laundry hampers. On the wall opposite was a wooden sign with arrows indicating the direction to various buildings. The bottom three names, almost certainly including the Omnicenter, were obscured by a mixture of grime and graffiti. Kate had once told him that it took a special kind of character to love working at Metro, intimating that the spirit of the hospital staff and the loyalty of many of its patients were somehow bound to the physical shortcomings of the place. The concept, like so much else about his wife, was something Jared realized he would have to work a little harder at understanding.

His often far from dependable sense of direction urged him toward the right. There was no time to question the impulse. His footsteps echoing off the cement floor and walls, Jared raced that way, instinctively casting about for something he could use as a weapon, and at the same time, cursing his failure to obtain help.

His sense, this time at least, was on the mark. The spur leading to the Omnicenter was fifty yards away.

It was exactly eight-thirty. The darkened passageway was illuminated only by the dim glow from the main tunnel. Sprinting head down, Jared caught a glimpse of the metal security gate only an instant before he hit it. The gate, an expanded version of the sort used to child-proof stairways, was pulled across the tunnel and bolted to the opposite wall. Stunned, he dropped to one knee, pawing at the spot just above his right eye that had absorbed most of the impact. Then he sank to all fours. If timing was as critical as Arlen Paquette's message had made it sound, he was beaten. The gate, with no space below, and less than a foot on top, was solid.

Exhausted and exasperated, Jared hauled himself up, grabbed the metal slats, and like a caged animal, rattled them mercilessly. *I'm sorry, Katey*, was all he could think. *I'm sorry I fucked up everything so badly*.

"Just hold it right there, son, and turn around very slowly." Jared froze, his hands still tight around the gate. "I've got a gun pointed in your general direction, so don't you go getting too rattled or too adventurous."

Jared did as he was told. Thirty or forty feet away, silhouetted by the light from behind him, was a night watchman.

"Who are you? What are you doin' down here?" the man demanded.

"Please, you've got to help me!" Jared took a few steps forward.

"That'll be far enough. Now how can I go about helpin' you, young man, if I don't even know who in the hell you are?"

Jared forced himself to calm down. "My name is Samuels. My wife is a doctor on the staff here. Dr. Bennett. Dr. Kathryn Bennett. Do you know her?"

The night watchman lowered his revolver. "You the lawyer?"

"Yes. Yes, I am. Listen, you've got to help me." He approached the watchman, who this time made no attempt to stop him.

"Do I, now," the man said. His khaki uniform appeared a size, perhaps two, too big for him. A shock of gray hair protruded from beneath his cap. Even with the revolver, he was hardly a menacing figure.

"Please, Mister—"

"MacFarlane. Walter MacFarlane. Known your wife for years—even before you were married to her."

"Well, Mr. MacFarlane, my wife's in a hospital on the North Shore right now. Someone tried to run her down. We know who, but not why. A few hours ago, a man called and promised me answers if I would meet him in the Omnicenter subbasement right now."

"Subbasement?"

"Yes. He said to bring help because there might be trouble, but there just wasn't enough time for me to get any."

"You sure it's the subbasement? That's the level beneath this one. Ain't nothin' down there but a bunch of cartons and spare cylinders of oxygen."

"All I know is what he said. Please. It's already past time."

"That Kate has been gettin' herself into some kinds of trouble lately."

"I know. Please, Mr. Mac—"

"People talk and talk. You know how it is. Well I'll tell you something, mister. They have their thoughts and I have mine. Ten years I've walked that woman to her car when she stayed until late at night. Ten years. She's class, I tell you. Pure class."

"Then you'll help me?"

Walter MacFarlane sorted a key out from the huge ring on his belt and opened the security gate. "If it'll help straighten things out for Dr. Bennett, count me in," he said.

Arlen Paquette was terrified. There was no way out of the laboratory except past the killer, Nunes, and yet to stay, to complete the Estronate synthesis meant, he was convinced, to die. It was twenty-five minutes to nine. As yet there had not been even the faintest sound from beyond the electronically controlled door. Kate Bennett either had not received his message or had disregarded it. Either way, he was on his own.

Desperately, he tried to sort out the situation and his options. There was no way he could buy time by claiming the procedure was inaccurate. Zimmermann was watching his every step. Could he somehow enlist Zimmermann's help in overpowering Nunes? Doubtful. No, worse than doubtful: impossible. Nunes had already shown him the money, packed neatly in a briefcase that now rested on the benchtop. Zimmermann's expression had been that of a starving wolf discovering a trapped hare.

"Anything the matter?" Zimmermann asked, indicating that once again Paquette was dawdling.

"No!" Paquette snapped. "And I want you off my back. It's my responsibility to verify these formulas, and I'll take all the time I need to do the job right."

At the far end of the lab, Nunes adjusted his position to keep a better eye on the two of them. Suddenly he waved to get their attention and placed a silencing finger over his lips. With his other hand, he pointed to the door. Someone was outside. With the sure, fluid movements of a professional, he slid the revolver from its holster and flattened himself against the wall beside the door.

Paquette decided that he had but one option—and not a very appealing one. He had been a wrestler during his freshman and sophomore years in high school, but had never been that good and, in fact, had been grateful when a neck injury forced him to quit. Since that time, he had never had a fight in any physical sense with anyone. Nunes was taller than he by perhaps two inches and certainly more experienced, but he had surprise and desperation on his side.

Separated from the gunman by one of the spectrophotometers and a tangle of sophisticated glass distillation tubing, Paquette eased his way along the slate-topped work bench until he was no more than ten feet from him. For several seconds, all was quiet. Then he heard muffled voices, at least two of them, from the storage room beyond the door. He strained to pick up their conversation, but could make out only small snatches. Nunes, that much closer, was probably hearing more. Paquette wondered if those outside the door had mentioned his name. If so, and if Nunes had heard, it was the final nail in his coffin.

The voices grew less distinct. Had they just moved away, or were they leaving, Paquette wondered. Even if they were to discover the door—and that was most unlikely—there was no way they could locate and activate the coded electronic key.

Carefully, Paquette slid the final few feet to the end of the laboratory bench. Zimmermann was a good twenty-five feet away—far enough to keep him from interfering. Paquette gauged the distance and then focused on his two objectives: Nunes's gun and the electronic plate on the right side of the door. A single step, and he hurled himself at the man, grasping his gun arm at the wrist with both his hands and spinning against the metal plate.

The door slid open, and Paquette caught a glimpse of a uniformed man fumbling for the pistol holstered at his hip. There was a second figure behind the man, whom he recognized as Kate Bennett's husband. In that moment, Nunes freed his hand and whipped Paquette viciously across the face with the barrel of his revolver. Paquette dropped to his knees, clutching at the pain and at the blood spurting from his cheek and temple.

"All right, mister, drop it! Right now, right there!"

Walter MacFarlane stood in the doorway, his heavy

service revolver leveled at Nunes, whose own gun was a foot or so out of position. Nunes froze, his head turned, ever so slightly, toward the intruder.

From his position four feet behind and to the left of MacFarlane, Jared could see the gunman's expression clearly. He seemed placid, composed, and totally confident.

*Back up! Get away from him!* Before Jared could verbalize the warning, the gunman was in action. He flicked his revolver far enough away to draw MacFarlane's eyes and then lunged out of the watchman's line of fire and up beneath his arm. MacFarlane's revolver discharged with a sharp report.

The bullet splintered several glass beakers, ricocheted off a wall, and then impacted with a large can of ether on the shelf behind William Zimmermann. The can exploded, the blast shattering most of the glassware in the room. Jared watched in horror as Zimmermann's hair and the skin on the back of his scalp were instantly seared away, his clothes set ablaze.

"Help!" he shrieked, reeling away from the wall. "Oh, God, someone help me!"

He flailed impotently at the tongues of flame that were darting upward through the crotch of his trousers and igniting his shirt. His struggles sent a shelf of chemicals crashing to the floor. There was a second explosion. Zimmermann's right arm disappeared at the elbow. Still, he stayed on his feet, lurching in purposeless circles, staring at the bloody remains of his upper arm, and screaming again and again. A third blast, from just to his left, sent his body, now more corpse than man, hurtling across the slate tabletop, through what remained of the glassware.

Zimmermann's screeching ended abruptly as he toppled over the edge of the table and onto Arlen Paquette. The chemist, though shielded from the force of the explosion by the counter, was far too dazed from the blow he had absorbed to react.

MacFarlane and Nunes both went down before the blast of heat and flying glass. Jared, still outside the laboratory door, was knocked backward, but managed to keep his feet. He stumbled to the doorway, trying frantically to assess the situation.

Intensely colored flames were breaking out along the benchtops, filling the air with thick, fetid smoke. To his right, Walter MacFarlane and the gunman lay amidst shards of glass. The side of the watchman's face looked as if it had been mauled by a tiger. Both men were moving, though without much purpose. To his left there was also movement. The man he assumed was Arlen Paquette was trying, ineffectually, to extricate himself from beneath the charred body of William Zimmermann.

Crawling to avoid the billows of toxic smoke, Jared made his way to Zimmermann, grabbed the corpse by its belt and the front of its smoldering shirt and heaved it onto its back.

"Paquette?" Jared gasped. "Are you Paquette?"

The man nodded weakly and pawed at the blood—his and Zimmermann's—that was obscuring his vision. "Notebooks," he said. "Get the notebooks."

Jared batted at the few spots on Paquette's clothing that were still burning, pulled him to a sitting position, and leaned him against the wall. The fumes and smoke were worsening around them.

"I've got to get you out of here. Can you understand that?"

Paquette's head lolled back. "Notebooks," he said again.

Jared glanced about. On the floor beneath Zimmermann's heel was a black looseleaf notebook. He tucked the book under his arm and then began dragging Paquette toward the doorway. Several times, glass cut through Jared's pants and into his leg. Once he slipped, slicing a flap of skin off the edge of his hand. The wooden cabinets and shelves had begun to blaze, making the room unbearably hot.

Paquette was making the task of moving him from the

room harder by clawing at Jared, at one point getting his hand entangled in Jared's parka pocket.

"For Christ's sake, let go of me, Paquette," Jared shouted. "I'm trying to get you out of here. Can you understand that? I'm trying to get you out."

The smoke was blinding. His eyes tearing and nearly closed, Jared hunched low, breathed through his parka, and with great effort, pulled Paquette's arm over his shoulder, hauling the man to his feet. Together they staggered from the lab. Jared was about to set Paquette down against a wall in order to return for MacFarlane when he remembered the oxygen. There were thirty or forty large green cylinders bunched in the far corner of the storage area. They possessed, he suspected, enough explosive potential to level a good portion of the building.

"Paquette," he hollered, "I'm going to help you up the stairs. Then you've got to get down the tunnel and as far away from here as possible. Do you understand?" Paquette nodded. "Can you support any more of your own weight?"

"I can try." Paquette, his face a mask of blood, forced the words out between coughs.

One arduous step at a time, the two made their way up to the landing on the basement level. Acrid chemical smoke, which had largely filled the storage area below, drifted up the stairway around them.

"Okay, we're here," Jared said loudly. "I've got to go back down there. You head that way, through the tunnel. Understand? Good. Here, take your book with you and just keep going." He shoved the notebook into the man's hands.

At that instant, from below, there was a sharp explosion. Then another. Jared watched as Paquette lurched away from him and then pitched heavily to the floor, blood pouring from a wound on the side of his neck.

Jared dropped to one knee beside the man, surprised and confused by what was happening. "Paquette!"

"Notebook . . . Kate . . ." were all Paquette could

manage before a torrent of blood sealed his words and closed his eyes.

It was then Jared realized the man had been shot, that the explosions he had heard were from a gun, not from the lab. He turned at the moment Nunes fired at him from the base of the stairs. The bullet tore through his right thigh and caromed off the floor and wall behind him. The man, blackened by smoke and bleeding from cuts about his face, leveled the revolver for another shot.

Distracted by the burning pain in his leg, Jared barely reacted in time to drop out of the line of fire. Behind him and from the mouth of the tunnel, alarms had begun to wail. Below him, the man had started up the stairs through the billowing smoke.

*Notebook . . . Kate . . .* Jared plucked the black notebook from beside Arlen Paquette's body, tucked it under his arm like a football, and in a gait that was half hop and half sprint, raced down the tunnel toward the main hospital. Zimmermann, Paquette, and probably Walter MacFarlane as well: all dead, quite possibly because he had gone to the subbasement rendezvous without enough help. The distressing thought took his mind off the pain as he pushed on past the security gate. Paquette had promised answers for Kate, and now he was dead. Silently, Jared cursed himself.

A gunshot echoed through the tunnel. Hunching over to diminish himself as a target, Jared limped on, weaving from side to side across the tunnel, and wondering if the evasive maneuver was worth the ground he was losing. The main tunnel was less than thirty yards away. There would be people there—help—if only he could make it. Another shot rang out, louder than the last. The bullet, fired, Jared realized now, from MacFarlane's heavy service revolver, snapped through the sleeve of his parka and clattered off the cement floor. He stumbled, nearly falling, and slammed into the far wall of the main tunnel.

"Help," he screamed. "Somebody help!" The dim tunnel was deserted.

A moment later he was shot again, the bullet impacting just above his left buttock, spinning him a full three hundred and sixty degrees, and sending white pain lancing down his leg and up toward his shoulder blade. He tumbled to one knee, but just as quickly pulled himself up again, clutching the notebook to his chest and rolling along the wall of the tunnel. Somewhere in the distance he could hear another series of alarms, then sirens, and finally a muffled explosion.

He was, for the moment at least, out of the killer's line of fire, stumbling in the direction away from the main hospital and toward the boiler room and laundry. Despite the pain in his leg and back, he was determined that nothing short of a killing shot was going to bring him down. With Paquette and Zimmermann dead, the black notebook, whatever it was, might well represent Kate's only chance.

The gunman, crouching low and poised to fire, slid around the corner of the Omnicenter tunnel just as Jared reached the spur to the laundry. Jared sensed the man about to shoot, but there was no explosion, no noise. Or was there? As he pushed on into the darkened laundry, he could swear he had heard a sound of some sort. Then he understood. The killer *had* fired. MacFarlane's revolver was out of bullets, tapped dry. Now, even wounded, he had a chance.

The room he had entered was filled with dozens of rolling industrial hampers, some empty, some piled high with linen. Beyond the crowded hamper lot, Jared could just discern the outlines of rows of huge steam pressers. He gave momentary consideration to diving into one of the hampers, but rejected the notion, partly because of the helpless, passive situation in which he would be and partly because his pursuer had already turned into the tunnel and was making his way, though cautiously, toward the laundry.

Ignoring the pain in his back, Jared dropped to all fours and inched his way between two rows of hampers toward the enormous, cluttered hall housing the laundry itself. Pressers, washers, dryers, shelves and stacks of linens, more hampers—if he could make it, there would be dozens of places to hide . . . *if* he could make it.

There were twenty feet separating the last of the canvas hampers from the first of the steam pressers. Twenty open feet. He had to cross them unnoticed. Kneeling in the darkness, he listened. There was not a sound—not a breath, not the shuffle of a footstep, nothing. Where in hell was the man? Was the chance of catching a glimpse of him worth the risk of looking? The aching in his back was in crescendo, dulling his concentration and his judgment. Again he listened. Again there was nothing. Slowly, he brought his head up and turned.

The killer, moving with the control and feline calm of a professional, was less than five feet away, preparing to hammer him with the butt of MacFarlane's heavy revolver. Jared spun away, but still absorbed a glancing blow just above his left ear. Stunned, he stumbled backward, pulling first one, then another hamper between him and the man, who paused to pick up the notebook and set it on the corner of a hamper before matter-of-factly advancing on him again.

"It's no use, pal," he said, shoving the hampers aside as quickly as Jared could pull them in his way, "but go ahead and make it interesting if you want."

Jared, needing the hampers as much for support as for protection, knew the man was right. Wounded and without a weapon, Jared had no chance against him.

"Who are you?" he asked.

Nunes smiled and shrugged. "Just a man doing a job," he said.

"You work for Redding Pharmaceuticals, don't you."

"I think this little dance of ours has gone on long enough, pal. Don't you?"

In that instant, Jared thought about Kate and all she had been through; he thought about Paquette and the aging watchman, MacFarlane. If he was going to die, then, dammit, it wouldn't be while backing away. With no more plan in mind than that, he grabbed another hamper, feigned pulling it in front of him, and instead drove it forward as hard as he could, catching the surprised gunman just below the waist. Nunes lurched backward, colliding with another hamper and very nearly going down.

Jared moved as quickly as he could, but the advantage he had gained with surprise was lost in the breathtaking pain of trying to push off his left foot. The killer, his expression one of placid amusement, parried the lunge with one hand, and with the other, brought the barrel of the revolver slicing across Jared's head, opening a gash just above his temple. Jared staggered backward a step, then came on again, this time leading with a kick which connected, though not powerfully, with the man's groin.

Again Nunes lashed out with the gun, landing a solid blow to Jared's forearm and then another to the back of his neck. Jared dropped to one knee. As he did, Nunes stepped behind him and locked one arm expertly beneath his chin.

"Sorry, pal," he said, tightening his grip.

Jared flailed with his arms and shoulders and tried to stand, but the man's leverage was far too good. The pressure against his larynx was excruciating. His chest throbbed with the futile effort of trying to breathe. Blood pounded in his head and the killer's grunting breaths grew louder in his ear. Then the sound began to fade. Jared knew he was dying. Every ounce of his strength vanished, and he felt the warmth of his bladder letting go. *I'm sorry, Kate. I'm sorry.* The words tumbled over and over in his mind. *I'm sorry.*

Through closed eyes, he sensed, more than saw, a bright, blue-white light. From far, far away, he heard a muffled explosion. Then another.

Suddenly the pressure against his neck diminished. The killer's forearm shook uncontrollably and then slid away. Jared fell to one side, but looked up in time to see the man totter and then, in grotesque slow motion, topple over into a hamper.

Jared struggled to sort out what was happening. The first thing he saw clearly was that the overhead lights had been turned on; the second thing was the stubbled, slightly jowled face of Martin Finn.

"I was halfway back to the station when I decided there was no way you would have chanced popping me like you did unless the situation was really desperate," Finn said. "How bad are you hurt?"

Jared coughed twice and wasn't sure he was able to speak until he heard his own voice. "I've been shot twice," he rasped, "once just above my butt and once in my thigh. My legs are all cut up from broken glass. That lunatic beat the shit out of me with his gun."

"The emergency people are on their way," Finn said, kneeling down. "It may be a few minutes. As you might guess, there's a lot of commotion going on around here right now. Is Zimmermann dead?"

Jared nodded. Then he remembered MacFarlane. "Finn," he said urgently, "there's a man, MacFarlane, a night watchman. He was—"

"You mean him?" The detective motioned to his left.

Walter MacFarlane, one eye swollen shut and the side of his face a mass of dried and oozing blood, stood braced against a hamper.

"Thank God," Jared whispered.

"We would never have known what direction to go in without him," Finn explained.

At that moment a team of nurses and residents arrived with two stretchers. They helped MacFarlane onto one and then gingerly hoisted Jared onto the other.

"As soon as these people get you fixed up, Counselor, you're going to have a little explaining to do. You know that, don't you?"

"I know. I'll tell you as much as I can. And Finn . . . I appreciate your coming back."

"I think I might owe you an apology, but I'll save it until someone explains to me what the fuck has been going on around here."

"Okay," one of the residents announced. "We're all set."

"Wait. Please," Jared said. "Finn, there's a notebook around here somewhere. A black, looseleaf notebook."

The detective searched for a few moments and then brought it over. "Yours?" he asked.

"Actually, no." Jared tucked the notebook beneath his arm. Then he smiled. "It belongs to my wife."

# 16

## Saturday 22 December

"Mr. Samuels, I'm here to take you up to your room. Mr. Samuels?"

Jared's eyes opened from a dreamless sleep. He was on a litter, staring at the chipped, flaking ceiling of the emergency ward where a team of surgical residents had worked on his wounds. His last clear memory was of one of the doctors, a baby-faced woman with rheumy eyes behind horn-rimmed glasses, announcing that she was about to give him a "little something" so that his wounds could be explored, cleaned, and repaired.

"I'm Cary Dunleavy, one of the nurses from Berenson Six," the man's voice said from somewhere at the head of the litter.

Jared tried to crane his neck toward the nurse, but was prevented by a thick felt cervical collar and a broad leather restraining belt across his chest. He ached in a dozen different places, and he sensed that he was seeing little or nothing through his left eye.

Dunleavy took several seconds to appreciate his patient's predicament. Then he muttered an apology and moved to a spot by Jared's right hand. "Welcome to the land of the living," he said. His voice was kind, but his eyes were sunken and tired. "You've been out for quite a while. Apparently they overestimated how much analgesia to give you."

Jared brought his left hand up and gingerly touched the area about his left eye.

"It's swollen shut," the nurse announced. "You look like you've been kicked by a mule."

Jared felt his senses begin to focus, and he struggled to reconstruct the hazy events following the explosion in the Omnicenter. His first clear image was of William Zimmermann spinning wildly about, his clothes ablaze, the skin on one side of his face hideously scorched. That one was for you, Katey, he thought savagely. An I'm-sorry-for-not-believing-you present from your husband. "What time is it?" he asked.

"Almost four."

"In the morning?"

The nurse nodded. "According to the report I got from the ER nurses, you've been out for about three hours since they finished working on you. We've been too busy on the floor for anyone to come and get you until now. Sorry."

"I need to get out of here," Jared said, fumbling at the restraining strap with his left hand. His right hand, with an intravenous line taped in place, was secured to the railing of the litter.

"Hey, partner," the nurse said, setting a hand on his shoulder. "Easy does it."

"I've got to see my wife. I've—" Suddenly, he remembered the notebook. "My things. Where are my things?"

"We've got 'em, Mr. Samuels. They're put away safe awaiting the moment when we read a legitimate order from your doctor discharging you. Rounds are usually at seven. Until then, if you go, you go in a Johnny."

Jared glared at the man. *I'm a lawyer*, he wanted to shout. I can sue you and this whole hospital for violating my civil rights, and win. Instead, he assessed his situation. In just three hours or so his physicians would make rounds and he could explain to them his need to leave. Three hours. Almost certainly, Kate would be sleeping through them anyhow, under the effects of her anesthesia. He sank back on the litter. "You win," he said.

The nurse said silent thanks with a skyward look and started maneuvering the litter out of the small examining room.

"Just one thing," Jared said.

The man stopped short and again walked around to make eye contact. "I'll listen, but no promises." His tired voice was less good-natured than he intended.

"I had a notebook. A black, looseleaf notebook. It should be in with my things. Get me that, and I promise to be a model patient."

Cary Dunleavy hesitated, but then withdrew the notebook from the patient's belongings bag, which was stashed on the litter beneath Jared. "I'm taking you at your word, Mr. Samuels. Model patient. I'm nearing the end of a double. That's over sixteen straight hours of nursing on a floor that would fit right in at the Franklin Zoo. It's been one hell of a long night, and my usual overabundance of the milk of human kindness is just about dried up. So don't cross me."

Jared smiled, made a feeble peace sign with his bandaged left hand, and tucked the notebook between his arm and his side.

The exhausted nurse returned to the head of the litter and resumed the slow trek through the tunnels to the Berenson Building.

The doors to one of the Berenson elevators opened as they approached, and a patient was wheeled out by two nurses. Jared saw the two bags of blood draining into two separate IVs, and a woman's tousled black hair, but little else, as Cary Dunleavy stopped and spoke to the nurses.

"What gives?" Dunleavy asked.

"GI bleeding. Getting worse. She's going to the OR for gastroscopy. The team's already up there waiting."

"Good luck. Let me know how it goes."

"Will do," the nurse said. The stretchers glided past

one another. "Sorry for the delay, Mrs. Sandler," she continued. "We'll be there in just a minute or two."

*Mrs. Sandler.* Several seconds passed before the name registered for Jared. "Ellen!" he called out, struggling once again against the leather strap.

Dunleavy stopped. "Hey, what're you doing?"

Jared forced himself to calm down. Ellen was on her way to the operating room, hemorrhaging. The option of waiting for seven o'clock rounds no longer existed. Kate had to see the notebook as quickly as possible. Even if the odds were one in a million against finding an answer for Ellen, she had to see it.

"Dunleavy, I've got to talk to you," he said with exaggerated reason. "Please."

Wearily, the nurse again walked to where he could be seen.

"Dunleavy, you care. I can see it in your face. You're tired and wasted, but you still care."

"So?"

"That woman who just went past here on the litter is Ellen Sandler, a friend of my wife's and mine. Dunleavy, she's bleeding—maybe bleeding to death. There's a chance the answer to her bleeding problem may be in this notebook, but it's written half in German and half in English, and it's technical as hell."

"So?"

"My wife is Kate Bennett, a pathologist here. Do you know her?" Dunleavy's acknowledging expression suggested that he might actually know too much. "Well, she speaks some German, and she knows what's been going on with that woman who just passed us. I've got to get this to her. She's a patient at Henderson Hospital in Essex."

"Mr. Samuels, I can't—"

"Dunleavy, please. There's no time to fuck around. Undo this strap and help me get to a cab. I can move all my extremities, see? I'll be fine."

"I—"

"Dammit, man, look at me! That woman is dying and

we might be able to help her. Get me an against-medical-advice paper and I'll sign it. I'll sign whatever the hell you want. But, please, do it now!"

The nurse hesitated.

"That woman needs us, my friend," Jared said. "Right this minute she needs us both."

Dunleavy reached down and undid the restraint. "It's my ass unless you come back and talk to the nursing office. Probably my ass anyway."

"I'll speak to them. I promise. So will my wife."

Dunleavy's eyes narrowed. "Please, Mr. Samuels," he said. "Don't do me any favors."

Even through the analgesic mist of Demerol and the distracting pain in her chest, Kate Bennett could sense the change in her husband. Bandaged, bruised, and needing a crutch to navigate, he had made a wonderful theatrical entrance into her room, sweeping through the doorway past a protesting night supervisor and announcing loudly, "The fucker's dead, Katey. Dead. He won't ever hurt you again." Then he had crossed to the bed, kissed her on the lips, and firmly but politely dismissed the supervisor and the special duty nurse.

Now he sat on a low chair by her left hand, mindless of his own discomfort, watching intently as she opened the black notebook—the sole useful vestige of the fire, pain, and death in the Omnicenter. There was a strength about the man, an assuredness, she had never sensed before. *The fucker's dead, Katey. He won't ever hurt you again.*

The words on the first page landed like hammer blows. *Studies in Estronate 250, Volume III of III*. Kate's heart sank.

"Jared," she said, swallowing at the sandpaper in her mouth and painfully adjusting the plastic tube that was draining bloody fluid from her chest, "have you looked at this?"

"Just to flip through. Why? Too much German? We'll find someone to translate."

"No. Actually, there's not that much. . . . Honey, it says here volume three of three."

"What?" He shifted forward and read the page. "Damn. I never saw any other books. There might have been others, but there was so much smoke. Everything was happening so fast. . . . Paquette could have explained everything if he had made it."

Kate searched her husband's face as he spoke. It was not an excuse, not an apology, but a statement of fact. Paquette had held the key to a deadly mystery. But Paquette was dead. And Jared, battered, bruised, clearly in great pain, was alive. If she could unlock the answers, it would be because he had risked his life for her. "We'll do the best we can with what we have," Kate said, turning to the first page of what appeared to be a series of clinical tests on a substance called Estronate 250. "I'm still foggy as hell from the anesthetic and that last shot, so bear with me."

There were, all told, one hundred and twenty carefully numbered pages. Paquette, or whoever had conducted this research, had been meticulous and precise. Stability studies; dosage modification studies; administration experiments in milk, in water, in solid food; investigation of side effects. Kate plodded through thirty years of terse German and English explanations and lengthy lists of test subjects, first from the state mental hospital at Wickford and in more recent years, from the Omnicenter. *Thirty years*. Arlen Paquette had not sounded that old over the phone, but perhaps he had taken over the Estronate research from someone else.

Ten minutes passed; then twenty. Jared shifted anxiously in his seat, and stared outside at the sterile, gray dawn. "How long does a gastroscopy take?" he asked.

Kate, unwilling to break her fragile concentration, glanced over at him momentarily. "That depends on what they find, and on what they choose to do about it. Jared,

I'm close to figuring out some things. I need a few more minutes."

"You look pretty washed out. Stop if you need to."

"I'm okay."

"Here. Here's some water."

She took a sip and then moistened her cracked, bleeding lips; then she returned her attention to the notebook. Another ten minutes passed before she looked up. Despite the pain and the drugs, her eyes were sparkling.

"Jared," she said, "I think I understand. I think I know what Estronate Two-fifty is."

"Well?"

"This is amazing. Assuming he's the one who conducted this research—or at least completed it—the late Dr. Paquette was worth his weight in gold to Redding Pharmaceuticals. Estronate Two-fifty is an oral antifertility drug that causes irreversible sterilization. It can be given to a woman by pill or even secretly in a glass of milk."

"Irreversible?"

Kate nodded vigorously, wincing at the jab of pain from her side. "Exactly. Think of it. No more tubal ligations, fewer vasectomies, help for third-world countries battling overpopulation."

"Then the scarred ovaries weren't a mistake?"

"Hardly. If I'm right, the microsclerosis was the desired result, not a side effect."

"But what about the bleeding? What about Ellen?"

Kate motioned him to wait. She was scanning a column marked *Nebenwirkung*.

"Look, Jared," she said excitedly. "See this word? It means side effects. All these women were apparently given this Estronate and monitored for side effects. Jesus, they're crazy. Paquette, Zimmermann, Horner—all of them. Absolutely insane. They used hundreds of people as guinea pigs."

"E. Sandler," Jared said.

"What?"

"E. Sandler. There it is right at the bottom of the page."

Kate groaned. "I may be even worse off than I think I am. Twice over the page and I missed it completely. Bless you, Jared."

Ellen's name was next to last in a column of perhaps three dozen. Halfway down a similar list on the following page, Kate found the names B. Vitale and G. Rittenhouse. She pointed them out to Jared and then continued a careful line-by-line check of the rest of the column and yet another page of subjects.

"I thought those were all the bleeding problems you know about," he said.

"They are."

"Well, whose name are you looking for?"

She looked up and for a moment held his eyes with hers. "Mine," she said.

She checked the pages once and then again before she felt certain. "I'm not here, Jared. I may be in some notebook marked anthranilic acid, but I'm not here."

"Thank God," he whispered. "At least volume three's given us that much."

Kate did not respond. She was again immersed in the columns of data, turning from one page to another, and then back. From where he sat, Jared studied her face: the intensity in her eyes, the determination that had taken her through twelve years of the most demanding education and training. At that moment, more so than at any other time in their marriage, he felt pride in her—as a physician, as a person, as his wife.

"Jared," she said breathlessly, her attention still focused on the notebook, "I think you did it. I think it's here."

"Show me."

"See these two words: *Thrombocytopenie* and *Hypofibrinogenamie*? Well, they mean low platelets and low fibrinogen. Just what Ellen is bleeding from. There's a notation here referring to Omnicenter Study Four B. Modification of *Thrombocytopenie* and *Hypofibrinogenamie* Using a Combination of Nicotinic Acid and Delta Amino Caproic Acid."

"I've heard of nicotinic acid. Isn't that a vitamin?"

"Exactly—another name for niacin. The other is a variant of a drug called epsilon amino caproic acid, which is used to reverse certain bleeding disorders. See, look here. All together, seven women on these three pages developed problems with their blood. They were picked up early, on routine blood tests in the Omnicenter."

"But Ellen and the other two aren't listed as having problems with their blood. There's nothing written next to their names in the side effects column."

She nodded excitedly. "That's the point, Jared. That's the key. Ellen and the two women who died were never diagnosed. Maybe they just didn't have Omnicenter appointments at the right time."

"The others were treated?"

Kate nodded. "That's what this Study Four B is all about. They got high doses of nicotinic acid and the other drug, and all of them apparently recovered. Their follow-up blood counts are listed right here. I think you did it. I think this is the answer. I just hope it's not too late and that somebody at Metro can get hold of the delta form of this medication. If not, maybe they can try the epsilon."

Jared handed her the receiver of the bedside telephone. "Just tell me what to dial," he said.

Kate's hand was shaking visibly as she set the receiver down. "Ellen's still in the operating room. Nearly three hours now."

"Who was that you were talking to?"

"Tom Engleson. He's a resident on the Ashburton Service. In fact, he's the one who called— Never mind. That's not important. Anyhow, he's been up to the operating room several times to check how it's going. The gastroscopist has found a bleeding ulcer. They've tried a number of different tricks to get it to stop, but so far no dice. They've had to call in a surgical team."

"They're going to operate?"

Kate shook her head. "Not if they can't do something with her clotting disorder."

"And?"

"Tom's gone to round up the hematologist on call and the hospital pharmacist. I'm sure they can come up with the nicotinic acid. It's that delta version of the EACA I'm not sure of. Goddamn Redding Pharmaceuticals. I'm going to nail them, Jared. If it's the last thing I do, I'm going to nail them for what they've done."

"I know a pretty sharp lawyer who's anxious to help," he said.

"I'm afraid even you may not be that sharp, honey."

"What do you mean?"

"Well, we've got this notebook and your word that it belongs to Paquette, but beyond that all we have is me, and I'm afraid my word isn't worth too much right now."

"It will be when they see this."

"Maybe."

"Either way, we're going to try. I mean somebody's going to have to come up with a logical explanation for all this that doesn't involve Redding Pharmaceuticals, and I really don't think that's possible. Do you?"

"I hope not."

"How long do you think it will take before we hear from this resident—what's his name?"

Kate suddenly recalled a gentle, snowy evening high above Boston Harbor and felt herself blush. "Tom. Tom Engleson." Did her voice break as she said his name? "I don't know. It shouldn't be long." It had better not be, she thought.

They waited in silence. Finally, Jared adjusted his cervical collar and rubbed at his open eye with the back of his hand. "Kate, there's something else, something I have to tell you," he said. "It has a good deal to do with what you were saying before about your word not being worth too much."

She looked at him queerly.

He held her hand tightly in his. "Kate, yesterday morning I spoke to Lisa."

Kate sat in the still light of dawn, stroking Jared's forehead and feeling little joy in the realization that, in his eyes at least, she had been vindicated. Nearly fourteen years that he might have shared in some way with his daughter had been stolen. Fourteen years. His hatred of Win Samuels was almost palpable. To her, the man was pitiful—not worth hating.

She had tried her best to make Jared see that and to convince him that whatever the circumstances, no matter how much time had gone by, he had a right to be a father to his daughter. He had listened, but it was clear to her that his pain and anger were too acute for any rational planning. There would be time, she had said, as much to herself as to him. If nothing else, there would be time.

The telephone rang, startling Jared from a near sleep.

Kate had the receiver in her hand well before the first ring was complete. For several minutes, she listened, nodding understanding and speaking only as needed to encourage the caller to continue.

Jared searched her expression for a clue to Ellen's status, but saw only intense concentration.

Finally, she hung up and turned to him. "That was the hematologist," she said. "They've started her on the drugs."

"Both of them?"

Kate nodded. "Reluctantly. They wanted more of a biologic rationale than Tom was able to give them, but in the end, her condition had deteriorated so much that they abandoned the mental gymnastics. They have her on high doses of both."

"And?"

She shrugged. "And they'll let us know as soon as

there's any change . . . one way or the other. She's still in the OR."

"She's going to make it," Jared murmured, his head sinking again to the spot beside her hand.

Less than ten minutes later, the phone rang again.

"Yes?" Kate answered anxiously. Then, "Jared, it's for you. Someone named Dunleavy. Do you know who that is?"

Bewildered, Jared nodded and took the receiver. "Dunleavy? It's Jared Samuels."

"Mr. Samuels. I'm glad you made it all right."

"Are you in trouble for letting me go?"

"Nothing I can't handle. That's not why I'm calling."

Jared glanced at his watch. Seven-fifty. Dunleavy's sixteen-hour double shift had ended almost an hour before. "Go on."

"I'm at the nurses' station in the OR, Mr. Samuels. They've just started operating on Mrs. Sandler. I think they're going to try and oversew her bleeding ulcer."

Jared put his hand over the mouthpiece. "Kate, this is the nurse who took care of me at Metro. They're operating on Ellen." He released the mouthpiece. "Thank you, Cary. Thank you for staying and calling to tell me that."

"That's only one of the reasons I called. There are two others."

"Oh?"

"I wanted you and Dr. Bennett to know I'm going to stay on and special Mrs. Sandler after she gets out of surgery."

"But you've been up for—".

"Please. I was a corpsman in Nam. I know my limitations. I feel part of all this and . . . well, I just want to stay part of it for a while longer. I'll sign off if it gets too much for me."

"Thank you," Jared said, aware that the words were not adequate.

But Dunleavy had something more to say. "I . . . I also wanted to apologize for that last crack I made about your wife." He went on, "It was uncalled for, especially since I only know what I know second or third hand. I'm sorry."

"Apology accepted," Jared said. "For what it's worth, she didn't do any of the things people are saying she did, and no matter how long it takes, we're going to prove it."

"I hope you do," Cary Dunleavy said.

"That was a curious little exchange," Kate said after Jared had replaced the phone on the bedside table. "At least the half I got to hear."

Jared recounted his conversation with the nurse for her.

"They've gone ahead with the surgery. That's great," she said, deliberately ignoring the reference to her situation. "Ellen's bleeding must have slowed enough to chance it. . . ."

Her words trailed off and Jared knew that she was thinking about her own situation. "Katey," he said. "Listen to me. Zimmermann is dead and Ellen isn't and you're not, and I'm not. And as far as I'm concerned that's cause for celebration. And I meant what I said to Dunleavy. You are innocent—of everything. And we're going to prove it. Together." He leaned over and kissed her gently. Then he straightened and said, "Rest. I'll wait with you until we hear from Metro." Kate settled back on the pillow.

A moment later, as if on cue, the day supervisor and another nurse strode into the room.

"Dr. Bennett," the supervisor said, "Dr. Jordan is in the hospital. She'll be furious if she finds out we haven't even done morning signs on her prize patient, let alone any other nursing care."

"Don't mind me," Jared said. "Nurse away."

The supervisor eyed him sternly. "There are vending machines with coffee and danish just down the hall. Miss Austin will come and get you as soon as we're through."

Jared looked over at Kate, who nodded. "I'll send for you if they call," she said.

"Very well, coffee it is." He rose and swung his parka

over his shoulder with a flourish. As he did, something fell from one of its pockets and clattered to the floor by the supervisor's feet.

The woman knelt and came up holding a miniature tape cassette.

"Did that fall from my parka?" Jared asked, examining the cassette, which had no label.

"Absolutely," the supervisor said. "Isn't it yours?"

Jared looked over at Kate, the muscles in his face suddenly drawn and tense. "I've never seen that tape before." His mind was picturing smoke and flames and blood . . . and a hand desperately clawing at the pocket of his parka. "Kate, we've got to play this tape. Now." He turned to the nurses. "I'm sorry. Go do whatever else you need to do. Right now we've got to find a machine and play this."

The supervisor started to protest, but was stopped by the look in Jared's eyes. "I have a machine in my office that will hold that, if it's that important," she said.

Again, Jared saw the hand pulling at him, holding him back. *For Christ's sake, Paquette, let go of me. I'm trying to get you out of here. Let go!* "It just might be," he said. "It just might be."

"So, Norton, first that brilliant letter to the newspapers about the ballplayer and now this biopsy thing. We asked you for something creative to stop Bennett, and you certainly delivered."

The entire tape, a conversation between Arlen Paquette and Norton Reese, lasted less than fifteen minutes. Still, for the battered audience of two in room 201 of Henderson Hospital, it was more than enough.

*"It was my pleasure, Doctor. Really. The woman's been a thorn in my side from the day she first got here. She's as impudent as they come. A do-gooder, always on some goddamn crusade or other. Know what I mean?"*

For Kate and Jared, the excitement of Reese's disclosures was tempered by an eerie melancholy. Paquette's conscience had surfaced, but too late for him. The man whose smooth, easy voice was playing the Metro administrator like a master angler was dead—beaten, burned, and then most violently murdered.

"You know what amazes me, Norton? What amazes me is how quickly and completely you were able to eliminate her as a factor. We asked, you did. Simple as that. It was as if you were on top of her case all the time."

"In a manner of speaking I was. Actually, I was on top of her chief technician—in every sense of the word, if ya know what I mean."

"Sheila." Kate hissed the word. "You know, I tried to believe she was the one who had set me up, but I just couldn't."

"Easy, boots. If you squeeze my hand any tighter, it's going to fall off."

"Jared, a woman lost her breast. Her breast!"

"You must be some lover, sir, to command that kind of loyalty. Maybe you can give me a few pointers some time."

Maybe I can, Arlen. Actually, it wasn't that tough to get Sheila to switch biopsy specimens. She had a bone of her own to pick with our dear, lamented, soon-to-be-ex pathologist. I just sweetened the pot by letting her pick on my bone for a while beforehand.

Norton Reese's laughter reverberated through the silent hospital room, while Kate pantomimed her visceral reaction to the man.

"I wonder," Jared mused, "how the lovely Ms. Pierce is going to respond when a prosecutor from the DA's office plays this for her and asks for a statement. I bet she'll try to save herself by turning State's evidence."

"She can try anything she wants, but she's still going to lose her license. She'll never work in a hospital again."

"Well, you really stuck it to her, Norton. With that chemist from the state lab in our pocket, Bennett's father-in-law doing what he can to discredit her even more, and now this biopsy coup, I doubt she'll ever be in a position

*to cause us trouble at the Omnicenter again. Our friend is
going to be very impressed."*

*"And very grateful, I would hope."*

*"You can't even begin to imagine the things in store
for you because of what you've done, Nort. Good show.
That's all I can say. Damn good show."*

*"We aim to please."*

The tape ran through a few parting formalities before
going dead.

Jared snapped off the machine and sat, looking at his
wife in absolute wonder. "I would have broken," he said.

"Pardon?"

"If those things had come down on me like they did
on you, I would have cracked—killed someone, maybe
killed myself. I don't know what, but I know I would have
gone under. It makes me sick just to think of how isolated
you were, how totally alone."

"That's where you're wrong. You see, you may have
had doubts about me, and justifiably so, but I never had
doubts about you; so I wasn't really as alone as you might
think."

"Never?"

Kate took her husband's hand and smiled. "What's a
doubt or two between friends, anyway?" she asked.

# EPILOGUE

# Friday 9 August

Though it was barely eight-thirty in the morning, the humidity was close to saturation and the temperature was in the mideighties. August in DC. It might have been central Africa.

Silently, Kate and Jared crossed the mall toward the Hubert H. Humphrey building and what was likely to be the final session regarding her petition to the FDA for action against Redding Pharmaceuticals.

The hearings had been emotional, draining for all concerned. Terry Moreland, a law-school classmate whom Jared had recruited to represent them, had been doing superb work, overcoming one setback after another against a phalanx of opposition lawyers and a surprisingly unsympathetic three-man panel. One moment their charges against the pharmaceutical giant would seem as irrefutable as they were terrifying, and the next, the same allegations were made to sound vindictive, capricious, and unsubstantiated. Now the end of the hearings was at hand—all that remained were brief closing statements by each side, a recess, and finally a decision.

"Yo, Kate! Jared!" Stan Willoughby, mindless of the sultry morning, trotted toward them carrying his briefcase and wearing a tweed jacket that was precisely six months out of phase with the season. He had attended all the sessions and had testified at some length as to Kate's character and qualifications. "So, this is going to be it, yes?" he said, kissing Kate on the cheek and shaking Jared's hand warmly.

Over the months that had followed the arrest and resignation of Sheila Pierce and Norton Reese, the two men, Willoughby and Jared, had formed a friendship based on more than superficial mutual respect. In fact, it had been Jared who suggested a year or two of cochairpersons for the department of pathology, and who had then cooked the dinner over which Willoughby and Kate had come up with a working arrangement for dividing administrative responsibilities.

"We can't think of anything else that could go wrong—I mean go on—this morning," Jared said.

"You were more correct the first time," said Kate. "Most of this has been pretty brutal. First, all the threads connecting that animal Nunes to Redding Pharmaceuticals evaporate like morning dew. Then, suddenly, Carl Horner gets admitted to Darlington Hospital with chest pains and gets a medical dispensation not to testify. I don't know. I just don't know."

"We still have the notebook and the tape," Jared said.

Kate laughed sardonically. "The notebook, the tape, and—you neglect to add—a dozen earnest barristers asking over and over again where the name Cyrus Redding or Redding Pharmaceuticals is mentioned even once."

"Come, come, child," Willoughby chided. "Where's that Bennett spirit? We've made points. Plenty of them. Trust this old war horse. We may not have nailed them, but we've sure stuck 'em with a bunch of tacks."

"I hope you're right," she said, as they spotted Terry Moreland waiting for them by the steps to the Humphrey building.

The gray under Moreland's eyes and the tense set of his face spoke of the difficult week just past and of the ruling that was perhaps only an hour or two away.

"How're your vibes?" Kate asked after they had exchanged greetings and words of encouragement.

Moreland shook his head. "No way to tell," he said. "Emotionally, what with your testimony and Ellen's account of her ordeal, I think we've beaten the pants off them. Unfortunately, it doesn't seem as if we have a very emotionally oriented panel. When that fat one blew his nose in the middle of the most agonizing part of Ellen's testimony, I swear, I almost hauled off and popped him one. Watching the indifference creep across his face again and again, I couldn't help wondering if he hadn't already made up his mind."

"Or had it made up for him," Jared added.

"Absolutely," Moreland said as they pushed into the air-conditioned comfort of the office building and headed up to the second floor. "That sort of thing doesn't happen too often, I don't think, but it does happen. And all you have to do is look across the room to realize what we're up against. Hell, they could buy off St. Francis of Assisi with a fraction of what those legal fees alone come to."

The hearing room, modern in decor, stark in atmosphere, was largely empty, due in part to the surprisingly scant media coverage of the proceedings. Moreland had called the dearth of press a tribute to the power of Cyrus Redding and the skill of his PR people.

Redding's battery of lawyers was present, as were two stenographers and the counsel for the Bureau of Drugs. The seats for the three hearing officers, behind individual tables on a raised dais, were still empty.

Moreland and Stan Willoughby led the way into the chamber. Kate and Jared paused by the door. Through the windows to the north, they could see the American flag hanging limply over the Senate wing of the Capitol.

"I don't know which is scarier," Kate said, "the pharmaceutical industry controlling itself or the government doing it for them. I doubt Cyrus Redding's tactics would make it very far in the Soviet Union."

"I wouldn't bet on that, Dr. Bennett."

Startled, they turned. Cyrus Redding was less than five feet from them, wheeled in his chair by a blond buck who looked like a weightlifter. The words were the first they had heard the man say since the hearings had begun.

"I have many friends—and many business interests—in the USSR," he continued. "Believe me, businessmen are businessmen the world over."

"That's wonderfully reassuring," Kate said icily. "Perhaps I'd better submit an article to the Russian medical literature on the reversal of the bleeding complications of Estronate Two-fifty."

"I assure you, Doctor, that all I know of such matters you have taught me at these hearings. If you have a moment, I was wondering if I might speak with you."

Kate looked at Jared, who gestured that he would meet her inside and then entered the hall.

Redding motioned his young bodyguard to a bench by the far wall.

"I suspect our hearing to end this morning," he said.

"Perhaps."

"I just want you to know what high regard I have for you. You are a most remarkable, a most tenacious, young woman."

"Mr. Redding, I hope you don't expect a thank you. I appreciate compliments only from people I respect."

Redding smiled patiently. "You are still quite young and most certainly naive about certain facts."

"Such as?"

"Such as the *fact* that it costs an average of sixty million dollars just to get a new drug on the market; often quite a bit more."

"Not impressed. Mr. Redding, because of you and your policies, people have suffered and died unnecessarily. Doesn't that weigh on you?"

"Because of me and my policies, dozens of so-called orphan drugs have found their way to those who need them, usually without cost. Because of me and my policies millions have had the quality of their lives improved and countless more their lives saved altogether. The greatest good for the most people at the least cost."

"I guess if you didn't believe that, you'd have a tough time looking at yourself in the mirror. Maybe you do anyway. I mean, a person's denial mechanism can carry him only so far."

Redding's eyes flashed, but his demeanor remained calm. "Considering the hardship my late employee has put you through, I can understand your anger," he said. "However, soon this hearing will be over, and soon we both must go on with our lives. I would like very much to have you visit me in Darlington, so that we might discuss a mutually beneficial joint endeavor. You are a survivor, Dr. Bennett, a woman who knows better than to subvert her needs in response to petty pressures from others. That makes you a winner. And it makes me interested in doing business with you."

"Mr. Redding," she said incredulously, "you seem to be ignoring the fact that the reason we're here is so that I can put you *out* of business."

Redding's smile was painfully patronizing. "Here's my card. The number on it will always get through to me. If you succeed in putting Redding Pharmaceuticals out of business, you don't have to call."

Kate glared at him. He was too smug, too confident. Was Terry Moreland's fear about some sort of payoff justified? "We're going to win," she said, with too little conviction. She turned and, disregarding the proffered card, entered the hearing room.

"What did Dr. Strangelove want?" Jared asked as she slid in between him and Terry Moreland.

Kate shook her head disparagingly. "The man is absolutely certifiable," she said. "He told me how little understanding I had for the difficulty, trials, and tribulations of being a multimillion-dollar pharmaceutical industry tycoon, and then he offered me a job."

"A job?"

"A mutually beneficial endeavor, I think he called it."

"Lord."

At that moment, without ceremony, the door to the right of the dais opened, and the three hearing officers shuffled into their seats, their expressions suggesting that there were any number of places they would rather have been. Before he sat down, the overweight, disheveled chairman pulled a well-used handkerchief from his pocket and blew his bulbous nose.

Kate and Jared stood by the stairway, apart from the groups of lawyers, reporters, and others who filled the corridor outside the hearing room. The recess was into its second hour, and with each passing minute, the tension had grown.

If over the previous four days the Redding forces had held the upper hand, the brilliant summation and indictment by Terry Moreland had placed the final verdict very much in doubt.

Of all those in the hallway, only Cyrus Redding seemed totally composed and at ease.

"I have this ugly feeling he knows something we don't," Kate said, gesturing toward the man.

"I don't see how the panel can ignore the points Terry made in there, boots. He's even better now than he was in law school, and he was a miniature Clarence Darrow then. But I will admit that Strangelove over there looks pretty relaxed. Say, that reminds me. You never said what your response was to his offer of a job."

Kate smiled. "I thought you were never going to ask. The truth is, I told him I would be unsuitable for employment in his firm because the first thing I'd have to do is take maternity leave."

Jared stared at her. "Slide that past me one more time."

"I was saving the news until after the verdict, but what the heck. We're due in April. Jared, I'm very excited and very happy. . . . Honey, are you all right? You look a little pale."

"This is for real, right?"

Kate nodded. "You sure you're okay? I can see where going from having no children to having a fourteen-year-old daughter and a pregnant wife might be a bit, how should I say, trying."

Jared held her tightly. "I keep thinking I should say something witty, but all that wants to come out is thanks. Thank you for this and for helping me reconnect with Stacy."

"Thanks accepted, but I expect something witty from you as soon as the business in this chamber is over. And please, don't make it sound like I've done something altruistic. I'm as excited about Stacy's visit as you are."

Jared's daughter would be in Boston in just ten days. Her first trip east. It was a journey that would include visits to Cape Cod and Bunker Hill, to Gloucester and the swan boats and the Old North Church. But there would be no visit to Win Samuels. Not now, and if Jared had his way, not ever.

"Hey, you two, they're coming in," Terry Moreland called from the doorway.

"What's the worst thing the panel could do to Redding?" Kate asked, grateful that Jared had chosen not to distract his friend with the news of her pregnancy.

"I guess turning the case over to the Justice Department for further investigation and prosecution would be the biggest victory for us. A hedge might be the referral of the whole matter to administrative channels within the FDA, in order to gather more information prior to a follow-up hearing." They settled into their seats. "Either way," Moreland added, "we'll know in a minute."

Kate slid the black notebook off the table before them, and held it tightly in her lap.

"Ladies and gentleman," the chairman announced, shuffling through a sheaf of papers and then extracting one sheet to read, "this panel has reached a unanimous decision regarding the charges brought by Dr. Kathryn Bennett against Redding Pharmaceuticals, Incorporated, of

Darlington, Kentucky. It is our feeling that the late Dr. Arlen Paquette did, in fact, conduct illegal and dangerous human research on the synthetic hormone Estronate Two-fifty and that he may well have also experimented illegally with other unproven substances. However, all available evidence indicates that the man, though in the employ of Redding Pharmaceuticals, was acting on his own and for his own personal gain. There is insufficient evidence to demonstrate prior knowledge of Dr. Paquette's criminal activities by Mr. Cyrus Redding or any other director of Redding Pharmaceuticals.

"Therefore, it is our recommendation that no further action be taken on this matter, and that all charges against Redding Pharmaceuticals be considered dealt with in a fair and just manner. Thank you all for your cooperation."

Without another word, the panel rose and marched from the chamber.

Kate and the three men with her sat in stunned disbelief, while across the room, lawyers were congratulating one another boisterously.

"I don't believe it," she said. "Not a recommendation for further study, not a reprimand for hiring someone as unprincipled as Arlen Paquette, nothing."

She glanced to one side, and almost immediately her eyes locked with Cyrus Redding's. The man favored her with another of his patronizing grins, and a shrug that said, "You have to expect such things when you play hardball with the big boys, young lady."

Kate glared at him. The battle may be over, Cyrus, she was thinking, but not the war. Somewhere out there is a noose so tight that even you won't be able to wriggle free—and I'm going to find it. Reese, Horner, Sheila Pierce. Somewhere, somehow, someone's going to come forward with proof of what you've done.

Jared took her hand, and together, they walked from the hearing room. "I'm sorry," he said softly.

"Me, too. But mostly, Jared, I'm frightened."

"Frightened? I don't think they'd dare try and hurt you."

She laughed sardonically. "You heard the verdict in there. I'm sure they don't even think I'm worth bothering to hurt."

"Then what?"

"It's the damn drugs, Jared. Starting with Estronate. Think of how many human guinea pigs there are in this one notebook. We contacted as many of the women as we could find, but there are others we just couldn't locate—and, I'm sure, other drugs. How many women out there are just starting to bruise? How many people—men and women—are developing weird tumors from medications they are trusting to make them well or keep them healthy?"

Jared gestured helplessly. "Kate, there are injustices all around. You've done what you could do."

"It's not enough. Jared, these drugs are like time bombs—unpredictable little time bombs capable of exploding inside anyone. I've got to keep after Redding. I've got to find some way to turn some heads around here, and if not here, then publicly. Somewhere, there's got to be a way. There's—"

"What is it, Kate?"

"What about an ad?"

"An ad?"

"In *The Globe*, *The Herald*, all the Boston and suburban papers—a classified ad asking women to search through their medicine cabinets for Omnicenter medications we can analyze. Maybe that's where the rope is to hang that bastard and put the other companies on notice. Right in those medicine cabinets. If enough Redding products were found contaminating enough Omnicenter medications, even the FDA panel wouldn't be able to ignore the company's involvement. I'm going to do it, Jared. As soon as we get back to Boston, I'm going to do it. And if it doesn't work, I'll try something else."

She glanced back down the corridor just as Redding was wheeled into the elevator. That sound you keep hearing in your ears is my footsteps, Cyrus, she was thinking. You had better get used to it.